A FOREBODING OF WOE

A PRACTICAL GUIDE TO SORCERY
BOOK FOUR

AZALEA ELLIS

CONTENTS

JOIN THE INNER CIRCLE**

Become part of the Inner Circle.

Instantly receive a free excerpt from Siobhan's illustrated grimoire.

https://www.azaleaellis.com/newsletter

I will send you new release updates, exclusive content like pre-release or deleted scenes, as well as news about giveaways or contests I'm doing (signed paperbacks, posters, etc.) and other cool stuff I think you might enjoy. Sometimes I tell weird stories about my life.

Plus, you get discounts on all products sold through my online shop, many of which you can't get on other retailers.

Support me on Patreon

https://www.patreon.com/azaleaellis

Read along chapter by chapter as I write the next book in the series, with early access chapters not available elsewhere, plus exclusive short stories/bonus chapters, and other goodies like various illustrated excerpts from Siobhan's grimoire.

NOTE TO READERS

The world-building for this story is extensive and can be quite complicated. If you find yourself forgetting terminology or wanting a little more detail about a term, the end of this book holds a Glossary of Magical Terms.

Thank you for reading!

Azalea

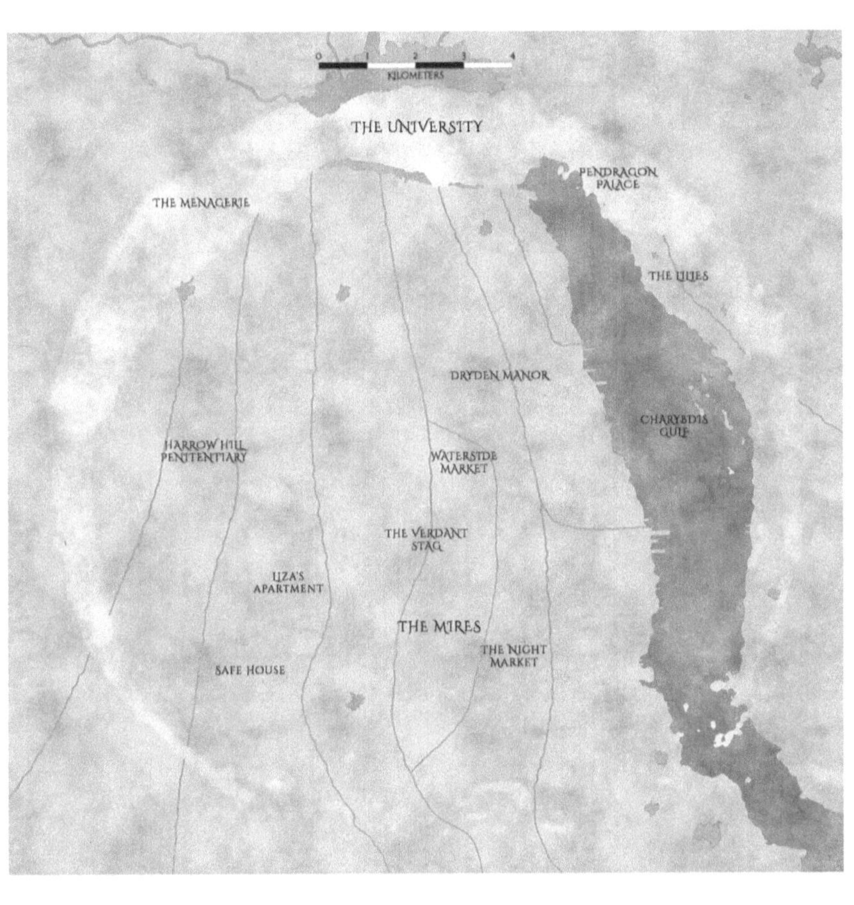

KILOMETERS
THE UNIVERSITY
THE MENAGERIE
PENDRAGON PALACE
THE LILIES
DRYDEN MANOR
CHARYBDIS GULF
HARROW HILL PENITENTIARY
WATERSIDE MARKET
THE VERDANT STAG
LIZA'S APARTMENT
THE MIRES
THE NIGHT MARKET
SAFE HOUSE

A PRACTICAL GUIDE TO SORCERY
RECAP

If you have not read the first three books in the Practical Guide to Sorcery series, spoilers lie ahead.

Previously, in *A Conjuring of Ravens*:

Siobhan Naught unwittingly becomes a wanted criminal when her father steals a mysterious book during their visit to the Thaumaturgic University. Her hopes of becoming a student dashed, she runs from the coppers with the book. Later, in danger from being caught by their ambush, she meets Oliver Dryden, who tries to help her escape.

When the coppers corner them, she accidentally activates a transformation amulet that had been hidden in the stolen book, turning herself into a young man who looks nothing like her original form. With this new body, she deceives the coppers and escapes arrest. To have a chance at entering the University under a new identity, she takes a huge loan—one thousand gold—from Oliver and Katerin at the Verdant Stag, the criminal organization they run.

Oliver helps her create a new identity for herself as Sebastien Siverling, but she makes a bad first impression on Damien Westbay and his group of Crown Family friends upon their first meeting.

When Siobhan learns the coppers caught her father Ennis, she and Oliver enlist the help of local illegal thaumaturge Liza, who helps Siobhan contact Ennis with a spelled raven messenger. To Siobhan's disappointment, Ennis has tried to sell her—and the stolen book—to the Gervin Family in marriage, in exchange for benefits for himself.

Much disillusioned, Siobhan studies for the University entrance exam and works for the Verdant Stag, who actually seem to serve and help the people within their community. When young Theo, Katerin's nephew, injures himself, Siobhan unthinkingly uses some harmless blood magic learned from her grandfather to heal the boy, earning both Katerin and Oliver's ire for the reckless use of illegal magic that could get her executed, and them implicated by association.

As Sebastien Siverling, she takes the University entrance exam, but her results are poorer than she hoped, and the panel of professors who administer the verbal portion of the exam plan to deny her entrance. In a fit of rage, she refuses to be dismissed, casting a hastily prepared spell to prove that she has the only thing that matters to a potential sorcerer—a strong Will.

Professor Thaddeus Lacer, a famous free-caster and Siobhan's childhood hero, takes an interest in her and overrides the panel of other professors, forcibly admitting Sebastien Siverling under special circumstances.

Sebastien falls into her University classes with glee, learning with feverish enthusiasm. She keeps to herself except for a budding new friendship with Anastasia Gervin, a Crown Family heiress, and Damien Westbay, who remembers their first meeting and finds Sebastien abrasive, nurturing the pseudo-rivalry between them. One of their student liaisons, Newton Moore, also extends an olive branch of friendship, believing her to—secretly—be a poor student just like him.

When she is not studying, Sebastien brews alchemical concoctions for the Verdant Stag to pay back the debt she owes them.

Oliver makes moves to expand the power of the Verdant Stags, but things backfire when the Morrows, a rival gang, attack one of his warehouses with the help of a mysterious sorceress. Oliver sets off Sebastien's alarms, waking her in the middle of the night to give emergency aid to his people.

Returning to her female form, Siobhan uses the minor spell exercises she's been practicing for Professor Lacer to sling balls of shattered glass at the Morrows. When the fighting is over, she tries to help the Verdant Stag warehouse workers, some of whom have been severely injured. Unable to do much, she patches up what she can before the coppers arrive.

Trying to give the others a better chance to escape, Siobhan uses a harmless esoteric spell that controls her shadow, molding it into a frightening creature of tattered darkness with a huge raven's beak. The coppers are successfully frightened, but one of them shoots a grasping spell at Siobhan, tripping her and cutting her hand.

She and Oliver escape to a safe house owned by one of Oliver's subjects, but the coppers found some of her blood left behind at the scene and use it to cast scrying magic on her. Siobhan's warding medallion, given by her grandfather, holds off the scrying attempt—at the cost of Siobhan's Conduit—and they go to Liza for a more permanent solution.

Liza creates a divination-diverting ward, anchored in five disks that she inserts underneath Siobhan's skin. The ward uses her blood for power, and can activate at low efficiency on its own or be further empowered by Siobhan's conscious efforts.

Thaddeus is called to the scene of the crime to consult on the investigation at Titus Westbay's request. Given the available evidence and witness accounts, they come to some erroneous conclusions. Siobhan Naught—codename Raven Queen—is a free-caster with some unknown, nefarious purpose that involves curses and blood magic.

She fascinates Thaddeus.

Siobhan, now without a Conduit, contacts Ennis in jail again, hoping to retrieve her mother's Conduit from him, but learns that he gave it to the Gervin Family as a bond for his word in the marriage agreement he gave on her behalf. Enraged and desperate, she spends most of her remaining funds to buy a dinky, overpriced replacement Conduit, then breaks down in tears.

But she isn't the same person who came to Gilbratha with Ennis those months ago. She's no longer under his—or anyone else's—control. She takes ownership of her life and her choices, pulls herself back together, and returns to the University.

In *A Binding of Blood*:

Sebastien does her best to keep her Will-strain concealed, but she remains concerned about future attacks from the Morrows. To better prepare, she experiments with ink-and-paper spell arrays with some success.

One day, while practicing slicing spells, Damien distracts her, causing her to accidentally injure him. She uses her flesh-mirroring spell to heal him, concealing the mechanics and the fact that it is technically blood magic. The effort re-strains her already fragile Will.

Feeling guilty and impressed, Damien resolves to befriend her.

Sebastien then begins to develop a sleep-proxy spell that will allow her to avoid her nightmares, as another sleeps on her behalf.

Professor Lacer sets up an in-class tournament for the sphere-spinning spell and becomes dissatisfied with her sandbagging against Damien, believing she does so to ingratiate herself with a powerful peer. Sebastien insists neither of them tell Professor Lacer the truth.

When the rogue magic sirens go off, the frightened students shelter in the library, and Sebastien discusses named Aberrants with Damien, asserting that they are more dangerous and less well-contained by the Red Guard than it might seem.

As classes continue, delving deeper into the details of both transmutation and transmogrification, Sebastien researches divination in the hopes of stealing or destroying the blood sample the coppers have been using to scry for her. When she manages to take advantage of a scrying attempt to trace her blood back to Eagle Tower on University grounds and only a short distance away, Damien stubbornly follows her.

Damien believes Sebastien is going on an "adventure," and is surprised and intrigued to learn he is spying on an attempt to find the Raven Queen, his imagination leading him to some dramatic conclusions.

Their student liaison, Tanya Canelo, interrupts the scrying attempt with an explosion just as Sebastien is becoming concerned. After talking about the situation with Oliver, Sebastien inducts Damien into a fake secret organization and together they hire their other student liaison, Newton, to help them keep tabs on Tanya.

While contemplating the foiled attempt on the Raven Queen, Thaddeus has an epiphany: When Sebastien refused to cast to her full ability, she had Will-strain. He interrogates Damien, who hints that Sebastien needs a better Conduit. Thaddeus wakes Sebastien in the middle of the night to lend her a Conduit and threaten her against similar recklessness.

After putting a tracker in Tanya's boot, Siobhan goes to a meeting with Lord Lynwood, leader of the Nightmare Pack gang, whom Oliver allied with. Lynwood and his prognos sister Gera give Siobhan a tribute of a black star sapphire, and request she help Millennium, Gera's cambion child who cannot sleep. As this happens to be Siobhan's area of expertise, she develops a spell to help the boy, leaving the Nightmare Pack leaders both fearful and in awe of her.

Later, following Tanya's suspicious activity, Siobhan discovers a secret organization of thaumaturges and joins. Her divination-diverting ward activates for the entrance interview, leaving the administrators convinced that she is the Raven Queen and frightened by her abilities.

Together with the Nightmare Pack, Oliver is planning an attack on the Morrows, who have become more aggressive toward people in the Verdant Stag's territory. He hires Siobhan as a healer's assistant for this.

In the meantime, Sebastien competes in the Practical Casting tournament and performs well, but sees the first classmate dead from Will-strain.

She knows they will not be the last.

The day of the battle arrives, and as Siobhan helps to heal the injured enforcers and civilians, Oliver attacks the Morrows' main warehouse and kills Lord Morrow, only to discover a storage room filled with beast cores and magical supplies all meant for the University.

Ana rushes home to comfort her little sister Natalia, who is being badly bullied by her adult cousin and uncles, as they hope to discredit Ana and her sister in their father's eyes, so that neither can become the Fourth Crown Family's heir.

Newton reveals that some of his family members were injured in the fighting and their house was lost. Desperate for coin to continue studying at the University, he accompanies Tanya to one of the secret meetings.

Siobhan is trailing them, keeping tabs on them with the tracker in Tanya's boot. Paranoid, Tanya realizes they are being followed and decides to attack.

Despite Newton's fear, the three of them are in a stand-off, but Tanya calls for backup from what few Morrows were not killed or captured in the earlier battle. When the Morrows come, they decide to capture all three of them, despite Tanya's protests, hoping to receive a ransom for them.

But when one of the Morrows sees Siobhan's face and recognizes her as the Raven Queen, fear causes them all to attack. In the confusion, Siobhan casts her shadow-familiar spell to draw attention and spell-fire away from herself.

Newton loses control of the spell he was casting and experiences a break event, turning into a string-based Aberrant. When the strings touch a human being, they unravel them alive.

Together with Tanya and the surviving Morrows, Siobhan works out how to pass somewhat safely through the strings and helps move them to safety.

But her bag is still with the Aberrant, and she decides to go back for it, as it could be used to find her, and she does not want to give up her place at the University to flee the law again. She manages to retrieve her bag and return to Sebastien's form, but the Red Guard has arrived and, when they notice strange divination readings, knock her unconscious.

Professor Lacer arrives to monitor her questioning and they are quickly joined by Gera, who misleads the investigation. As Professor Lacer takes Sebastien, cleared of suspicion, back to the University, she tells him her suspicions of Tanya and some of the other University faculty.

Not knowing Sebastien's fear of sleep, he then knocks her unconscious.

In *A Sacrifice of Light*:
Red Guard agents have captured and entombed two Aberrants for transport. One was once Newton.

Thaddeus Lacer investigates the coppers' investigation into the Raven Queen, and her father Ennis reveals that Siobhan's mother died after casting through her own flesh, and later their home village was destroyed by an Aberrant incident from which only Siobhan escaped. Ennis tracked her down and found her traumatized and in jail some months later, and took her on the road with him.

Siobhan takes some time to recover from the trauma of Newton's death, and back at school is subjected to Grandmaster Kiernan's probing questions about the Aberrant incident, which she refuses to answer. People everywhere, including the newspapers, are gossiping that Newton must have been doing morally bankrupt magics to corrupt his Will and become an Aberrant, which enrages Sebastien and her friends.

Meanwhile, Oliver runs into an incident of the coppers using excessive force on a civilian. Percy Irving, a teenager with unusually, ridiculously bad luck, accidentally takes a photograph of the incident. Upon learning that Percy also took a photograph of the Raven Queen but has been keeping it secret, Oliver decides to hire Percy to work for his new newspaper, *The People's Voice.*

Ana requests that Sebastien help her in a risky plan to frame and overthrow her uncles, who encourage abuse toward her and her little sister Natalia. Sebastien replies rudely, making Ana angry, but Ana comes back with an offer Sebastien cannot refuse. If she helps depose Ana's uncles, Ana will ensure the textile sub-commission that Oliver needs.

Sebastien negotiates with Oliver for payment and a stake in the textile company he will set up, and then she, Ana, and Damien begin Operation Defenestration.

They break into Malcolm Gervin's office and take photographs of his documents. (Sebastien secretly steals back her mother's heirloom ring that her father gave them as collateral for her hand in marriage.)

Then, they have Sebastien dress up in a costume of the Raven Queen to meet with the uncles and frame them for collusion with a criminal.

Siobhan discovers that the ring she retrieved actually has a thaumaturge-created diamond instead of a celerium gem, and concludes that Ennis must have switched them out and sold the celerium at some point. Enraged, she disowns and curses him.

As Sebastien learns new concepts in her classes and works on output detachment with Professor Lacer, Oliver pulls her into working as a healer's assistant to "seal the tongues" of the Morrows who they will be turning over to the coppers for sentencing and imprisonment.

However, Grandmaster Kiernan and the Architects of Khronos, who desperately want the stolen book that started everything, betray Oliver. They attack the prisoner convoys with several powerful thaumaturges, including an old man that casts an almost unfathomably powerful spell to trap everyone inside Knave Knoll and infect them with spores that affect their minds.

Siobhan and the enforcers work together to escape, and as she is trying to escape, the old man captures her satchel. She sets off the disintegration mine inside and kills him along with his companions.

Soon after, the friend trio confronts Malcolm Gervin to place the final nail in his coffin as he attempts to kill them to escape, and Ana plants a fake journal in his handwriting detailing his crimes and plans to kill her father, the head of their Crown Family.

While she's still unrecovered from these events, the coppers try one more scrying attempt on Siobhan, which is so powerful it forces her to leave the city. She's unable to cast her dreamless sleep spell that night, and has a nightmare of a twisted mirror locked away in her childhood house.

Finally gathering her courage, Sebastien visits Newton's family, only to find that they have had their memories and opinions modified—poorly—by the Red Guard. They, too, now believe that Newton was experimenting with unethical magic and deserved to turn into an Aberrant.

Sebastien goes to Professor lacer, and is horrified to learn that this is standard practice for the Red Guard.

To follow up that blow, Oliver lets slip the idea to create a scapegoat for the Raven Queen to divert attention and suspicion, leading her to suspect that he did the same to her. She considers all the evidence for and against this new theory, and vows to uncover the truth. Thaddeus Lacer contacts Oliver to pass along a request to meet the Raven Queen. He secretly stole her mother's heirloom ring and replaced it with a fake, and plans to give the original to her as tribute when they meet.

A Foreboding of Woe begins a couple of weeks after these events, after a short time-skip.

1

ALLIANCE AGAINST CURIOSITY

Thaddeus
Month 3, Day 19, Friday 10:00 p.m.

Thaddeus paused in his writing, his gaze drawn to the window by a flash of lightning. The following clap of thunder was so close and loud that his desk vibrated. When the noise eased back to the comparatively tame roar of the wind-driven rain against his cottage wall, he turned back to the nearly finished project laid out before him: a guide to translating one of the more common pre-Cataclysm languages. Such a comprehensive and coherent reference would have been invaluable to him some years ago, but as none existed, he had been forced to learn the hard way.

While writing the book, he had idly begun to consider how one might create a matrix of vocabulary and grammatical rules to inform an artifact that could do the translation automatically. Even if such a complex spell array would take months to develop, span an entire room, and be unfortunately clumsy without the help of a human operator's deeper understanding and intuition to draw from, it was an intriguing concept.

If he took the time to develop such a spell and then publish his work, it might bring him some extra coin...but little else. Unfortunately, there was no way for him to create a translator for a language he did not already know, so the time and effort involved would not help him further approach the true goal of all his research. A human, even a powerful thaumaturge such as himself, had a limited lifespan; he needed to spend his only nonrenewable resource—time—in the most efficient way possible.

As often happened, thoughts of his research led Thaddeus's mind to the Raven Queen. Just a couple days before, he had finally reached out to request a meeting through her associate, Lord Stag. He had hoped that she might contact him without the need for such, but as time passed Thaddeus had realized he must be more proactive if he wanted to move her little game of hints and intrigue toward something less nebulous. "She is stubborn," he murmured aloud. "Not one to concede first."

Thaddeus added the observation to his developing mental model of the powerful woman, and his thoughts turned toward her most recent exploit. He had suspected, from examining the function of the strange boon she had given his apprentice, that she may have been involved in the Haze War. The response of the protective effect to his various tests reminded him of some of the more innovative solutions the military researchers had come up with during that time, though obviously they had been expanded and improved upon.

The method she had used to kill the rogue Red Guard agent, who allied with the Architects of Khronos to attack the Stags, had provided further evidence toward this possibility, as well as a reminder of her cruelty and recklessness.

A trip to one of the Red Guard bases had been enough to get confirmation of the attacker's identity as a former member, as well as pick up some of the gossip from the emergency response squad that had first deployed to the location of the fighting when the gravity of the situation—and the type of spells being cast—became known. Observing from a roof with a good vantage point a few blocks away while they waited for backup, one of them had seen the Raven Queen kill the man. Unfortunately, even with a shaman to help solidify his memories, the details were unclear. The gang members had been throwing around battle philtres to cover their escape, clouding the view.

The rogue agent, an old man who'd gotten his hands on some dangerous items before deserting, had cast some sort of spell at those fleeing. The witness's sight of that part had been blocked by a building. The man pulled back an item, most likely a purse but possibly a suitcase, and a woman they strongly suspected to be the Raven Queen stepped around the corner in the opposite direction of those fleeing.

She stopped to look at the old sorcerer, and without any obvious motions, free-cast an unknown spell to kill not only him, but the half-dozen enemies surrounding him.

When the resulting turbulence had settled enough for the emergency response squad to see clearly again, the Raven Queen was gone, seemingly having made an appearance solely for that attack.

The three prognos Titus had called to the site, along with the Red Guard's reconnaissance and assessment team, had examined what killed the group of Architects and left behind such an alarming after-effect as thoroughly as possible before it faded. All agreed that it had been the same particular blend of disintegration magic that Lenore's army used in their mines during the Haze War, combined somehow with a space-bending spell to increase the sheer gruesomeness while also decreasing the chances that any standard shield could ward against the damage. There were several other twists of different types of magic that seemed random and had been hard to define, but which seemed to have increased the spectacle. They had all agreed that there was a strong flavor of darkness, along with some strange extracts of meaning related to sleep, the moon, and a few dozen other things, all too fleeting to be pinned down properly.

Thaddeus knew quite a few divination spells meant to check for anomalous effects, but the strange manifestation of magic, which was already fading by the time he arrived, was complex and delicate. He was not an expert in that particular field, and his efforts had yielded no additional insight. He had considered the possibility that the lingering remnants of magic contained a message meant to be deciphered, or some kind of hint, but if that was the case, he was not deft enough to grasp it.

Perhaps it was some reference to the Black Wastes, into which the expedition had traveled to find Myrddin's hermitage. It was said that the brillig had infected the land itself with their dangerous magic when humans were at war with them. Thaddeus had seen similar effects just a couple of times, when he caught a glimpse of the more restricted research in the Red Guard's black sites, but nothing quite like this.

Still, if the Raven Queen had been involved in the Haze War, she was likely not much younger than him, and could even be older. Thaddeus considered, for a moment, the possibility that the Raven Queen was older—and conceivably more powerful—than Thaddeus himself. Had they ever met? Perhaps he had unknowingly sparked her interest at some point then.

Of course, that evidence did not fit with the identity of Siobhan Naught, who had been born two decades after the war. But her sheer power also seemed impossible for a girl of only twenty.

Thaddeus's apprentice, a genius in his own right, was at that age and still far from becoming a free-caster, let alone reaching the power required to achieve some of the Raven Queen's more arrogant displays of prowess.

His thoughts were forcefully drawn back to reality as his faculty token alerted him to a security-related summons. He was to report to the deployment point at Eagle Tower. Outside his window, the storm raged on, rain lashing against the glass and the occasional branch of lightning spreading a purple-white glow over the city. With a deep sigh, hoping that he was not about to be urged to catch some students missing after curfew, Thaddeus donned his coat and left his neglected manuscript on his desk, nearly, and yet still not, finished.

With a simple twist of his Will, having long become instinctive, he cast a dome-shaped shield around himself to protect against the lashing wind and rain and strode off toward the west side of the grounds.

When Thaddeus arrived, he found Grandmaster Kiernan waiting for him, alone. His eyes narrowed. It seemed there was no widespread emergency; Kiernan had summoned Thaddeus specifically. "Why have you called for me?" he asked without preamble.

The stress Kiernan had recently been under manifested itself clearly in his too-tight neck muscles and the sagging skin under his eyes. Even bathed in the warm, recycled sunlight of the light crystals, his skin looked pale and sallow. Still, he smiled with joviality, clapping Thaddeus on the arm. "Thank you for coming, Professor Lacer."

Thaddeus resisted the urge to cast a shield between them to push away the man's hand. He did not appreciate it when others touched him without his explicit permission.

"I would like to speak with you about...a sensitive matter. One that could involve the security of our school and the safety of the students. My apologies for the method of contact. I would have sent you a paper bird, but the administration center is closed this late." He motioned for Thaddeus to walk with him and began making his way to the stairwell. "As you may know, the High Crown has been...*concerned*, one might even say paranoid, in the days following the terrorist attack by the Architects of Khronos. He has even gone so far as to question people tangentially or even completely unrelated to the events." Kiernan remained silent for a long few moments as they walked up the stairs, bypassing the door to the second floor.

Thaddeus did not enjoy conversational vagueness or the way the man skirted around the issue, but that did not mean he could not play with words as weapons and pregnant pauses as lures. "Yes. I heard he has shown an interest in your department, particularly," he said.

Kiernan threw Thaddeus a glance, gritting his teeth together with grim viciousness, the creak of bone on bone just loud enough to be audible.

The Crowns had allocated even more resources to investigating the terrorist attack than they had to the Raven Queen. Though not widely known, they had even collaborated with the Red Guard's investigation, providing additional manpower and what information they could.

Titus suspected that some faction of the University faculty, including Kiernan and some of those close to him, were either members of the Architects of Khronos or had been sponsoring them. There had simply been too many coincidences: rumors about the kind of magical components that were being smuggled into the city en masse, the convenient timing of the explosion at Eagle Tower, the University's handling of Newton Moore's break incident as well as Tanya Canelo's involvement with it, and the most recent attack on the Verdant Stag's various holdings, seemingly timed to coincide with the Architects' actions. But most importantly, the History Department was still determined to keep the contents of the archaeological haul to themselves. While legally they could do so, in practice it was a dangerous move.

Unlike normal civilians, the University faculty had all taken certain oaths and could not simply refuse to answer the coppers' questions. None of the faculty had been arrested yet, which would suggest their innocence, but Thaddeus knew just how little an oath could mean. Wards and divination against untruth, already fallible, could be overcome with the right knowledge and preparation.

Kiernan continued to lead Thaddeus up the stairs until they reached the top floor, then reached out and unlatched the hatch door to the roof. "Do you mind?" Kiernan asked. "It seems an appropriate place to speak, but I would rather not get drenched. These old bones might just fall ill!" He grinned again, but his gaze was flat and predatory.

Raising an eyebrow, Thaddeus cast his shield spell again, this time enveloping both of them within it, and led the way onto the roof. "A rather dramatic meeting place, no?" he asked, moving closer to the edge, which forced Kiernan to move with him to remain within the sphere of protection. "It must be a sensitive topic, indeed."

Kiernan didn't respond to the jab. "You are right that the coppers have shown a particular interest in my department. At first, I thought perhaps they were using the investigation as an excuse to apply pressure in the hopes of getting their hands on things they have no right to. But then, I considered another possibility. What if the investigators know something I don't?"

"Like what?" Thaddeus asked, playing along as he began to suspect, with some amusement, where this was going.

Kiernan didn't answer him directly. "I am aware you've been helping with the investigation into the Raven Queen, which is now somehow connected to these horrible terrorist attacks." For a moment, real anger slipped through his mask, directed out at the rain-obscured city to the south. "I am worried that there might be some danger to the school—to the students as well as the faculty under my command. As one of the leaders of the security committee, it is my duty to take measures to ensure student safety. Do you know anything that might be relevant to the situation? Why are the investigators showing such interest?" He turned to Thaddeus beseechingly, his expression surprisingly sincere.

If Thaddeus had any less control over his expressions, he might have let a carnivorous smile slip. "The Raven Queen is said to bear grudges," he said simply.

Kiernan did an admirable job of controlling his expression, but his fingers twitched.

Thaddeus continued, "There are some accounts that she fought against these terrorists, though the exact reason for her actions is debatable."

"Grudges," Kiernan repeated. His eyes narrowed slyly. "You've been working against her on this investigation for some time now, but as I understand it, the Raven Queen not only failed to harm your apprentice when they met but gave him a boon. What could be the reason for that?"

Thaddeus thought Kiernan might have intended it as some kind of vague threat, but the question only pushed control of the conversation directly into Thaddeus's hands. And how convenient, that Kiernan had something Thaddeus wanted. "Perhaps she understands my motivations," he said. After a moment to let those words hang in the air, he added, "I am an inquisitive creature."

This time, Kiernan couldn't control the widening of his eyes. "Oh?"

Thaddeus took a half-step closer so as to loom just slightly over the other man and continued, "Indeed. I act as a consultant because Titus Westbay is a friend, and because I find the subject of these investigations rather fascinating, but mostly because I enjoy being let in on details not available elsewhere. I find such edification rather...useful. As you may know, my vows to the Red Guard preclude me taking superseding vows of loyalty to the Crowns—which is why I am only an unofficial consultant."

Kiernan was not slow to understand Thaddeus's implication, judging by the suspicion and surprise warring for dominance on his face.

"In return for access to interesting information, I offer my own knowledge, whether that be my understanding of magic, simple observations about things I have seen, or deductions based on the evidence provided. Often, the obvious is sitting right under their nose, waiting for me to point it out. In truth, however, I have no particular investment in helping the coppers find the Raven Queen." It was both a threat of what he might tell and an offer of what he could do for Kiernan instead. The University might be an enemy to the Raven Queen just as the coppers were, but at this point Thaddeus found it unlikely that she could be in any true danger from either party, and thus had no compunction about giving his nominal aid.

Kiernan cleared his throat roughly. "What kind of information, exactly, do you find so interesting that it entices you to spend your precious time assisting them?"

"Well, you know my prior field of work. Quite fascinating. But there is a reason I took this liaison position at the University. Like you, I, too, have an interest in history. I am an expert in pre-Cataclysm society and languages, for instance, many of which have survived to this day only due to the strong protections keeping them isolated and preserved. As I understand it, your people have found decrypting the texts you retrieved quite stymieing. You asked why the Raven Queen has shown me no malice. Perhaps she is laying the foundation for a collaboration attempt. She may be experiencing similar difficulties with her stolen text and has realized that I could be a solution."

Kiernan took a step back, startling when he reached the edge of the protective shield, which Thaddeus had allowed to shrink in around them. Kiernan caught a splash of cold rain across his back.

But Thaddeus was not finished yet. "Even you will likely be forced to bring in outside experts soon if you cannot show progress, perhaps hired by the Crown Families. The potential significance of what you have found is simply too great to allow failure, no matter the technicalities of the law."

They both remained silent for a long few moments, the rain beating against Thaddeus's Will and running down the sides of the dome in distorting ripples.

Finally, Kiernan spoke. "It occurs to me that someone of your capabilities might find this decryption project quite intellectually stimulating."

"Yes."

"And as you've said, you cannot take vows to the Crowns."

Thaddeus remained silent.

"But would you be willing to take a non-disclosure vow?"

"I would," Thaddeus replied immediately. That did not mean, necessarily, that he would be willing to *keep* said vow.

Kiernan swallowed, looked at the ground for a moment, and then met Thaddeus's gaze again. He nodded sharply. "Very well. As we will be working so closely together, I hope that you will take the opportunity to sate my curiosity when applicable, as well. And if the Raven Queen does contact you... Perhaps she is *curious*, too." As if doubting that Thaddeus was clever enough to understand his meaning, Kiernan clarified, "She may be interested in a similar exchange of information. After all, we do still have the rest of Myrddin's research journals, and everything else left behind in his hermitage."

"Perhaps we will have a chance to find out," Thaddeus said, a twist of vicious amusement curling in his belly.

2

A CITY OF WHITE STONE

Sebastien
Month 3, Day 25, Thursday 9:00 a.m.

As the clear bell signifying the start of the test rang, Sebastien removed her blindfold, blinking as she adjusted to the sudden brightness. Beside her, Damien and Rhett did the same. They stood in a featureless room made of the same white stone that composed the white cliffs and the Flats. All three wore grey one-piece protective suits provided by the proctors, though their equipment beyond that varied.

The white stone formed the vague shape of a desk at the corner of the room, possibly useful as a shield against enemy spells, and an empty window hole let in light from the outside. Behind the three, the stone formed an open doorway into the rest of the building. The proctor who had led them up from the tunnels below was long gone.

In the far corner of the room, a small, dome-shaped silver mirror clung to the ceiling, watching. Sebastien met her own gaze for a moment, lifting her chin defiantly. "Let's get to work," she said, her voice tight. She crouched down, slinging off the backpack she'd traded some of her defense points for as she moved to the window hole.

Behind her, Damien moved toward the doorway, placing his back against the wall to peek safely around the corner as he pulled off his own backpack and retrieved the simple scanning artifact within. He had chosen to focus on reconnaissance.

Sebastien peeked out through the empty window. They were on the third floor, it seemed. The street below, along with the buildings directly across from her and in every direction she could see, were made of the same white stone. "Just like we thought, Damien. Urban warfare." She scanned for color or movement, either of which could indicate they were not alone. "Looks clear." The faculty had drawn the arena for their test—and the exhibition—up from the stone of the Flats over the course of the last week, with the huge circular wall that mimicked Gilbratha's own being the first feature.

Several upper-term students had tried to scale the wall using various methods to get an early glimpse of what lay on the other side, only to be caught and receive demerits for the attempted cheating.

Crouching down away from the window, she poured out the contents of her backpack. She had three metal disks to draw spell arrays on, two pieces of paper detailing the simplest spells that would interact with the sensors on their suits, and a handful of components, including a beast core. Each student had been allotted a certain number of points based on their performance in Fekten's Defense class thus far. Not unlike the University's contribution point scheme, these defense points could be used to buy supplies for the exam. This was quite necessary, as they were required to leave all of their personal belongings except for their Conduits in a secure locker.

As Damien worked with the scanning artifact, Rhett moved to the window, his white teeth standing out against the darkness of his skin as he searched the streets below. His faux battle wand tracked along with his eyes, its tip held steady in his skillful grip. "How long is this going to take you two?" A bandolier across his chest was filled with false-explosive clay shells, marking him clearly as the offensive-focused member of their team.

"A few minutes for me," Sebastien said, using a quick-drying paint stick to draw out the spell array for the faux battle spell that would trigger their protective suit's damage sensors without actually harming the person within. When it was ready, she could hold it up with the handles on either side and actively cast one of the same spells that were stored in Rhett's wand. Except *she* wouldn't run out of charges.

Damien glanced up from the scanning artifact, which looked like a round dinner platter with a handle on either side. "No enemy signals within range."

"Good," Sebastien said without looking away from her work. "I want you two to scope out the building and the surrounding area and report back to me."

Damien nodded immediately, but Rhett frowned. "Why are we following you?" he complained. "I have the highest grade in the class. Shouldn't I be the one in charge?"

Damien's smile held a hint of smugness. "Because Sebastien is the best strategist. Let's go together."

Sebastien nodded. "Watch each other's backs. The scanning artifact is useful, but you can't depend on it. Meet back here in five minutes."

Damien left the room with a serious glare, his head swiveling back and forth as he searched for anything relevant.

This gave Rhett no choice but to follow Damien, though Rhett's murmured complaints were audible. "How do you even know Sebastien's a good strategist? *I'm* a good strategist! I'm great at chess, and you know dueling takes a lot of tactics."

"Just trust me. Sebastien works well under pressure," Damien replied faintly. "Now hush! We're supposed to be stealthy."

As the paint of her spell array dried, the symbols and glyphs within the bounding Circle working together to define the Word that would help guide her magic, Sebastien placed the components. They, along with the power from her beast core, would form the Sacrifice. Each spell array disk had little domes that snapped into place to hold components safely in their spot on the spell array, but she made doubly sure the few components necessary would stick with a bit of quick-drying glue. All that was left was her Will, to be channeled on a moment's notice through the Conduit Professor Lacer had given her.

Each disk had only been meant for a single spell array, but when the front was finished, she turned them around and began to draw careful lines across the back with the thick white paint. There were no component capsules for the back sides, but where necessary, she carefully dabbed a bit of that same quick-drying glue and simply pressed the components into it to hold them safely in place. This was a little dangerous, as a sloppy thaumaturge could slip and accidentally spread their Will into the wrong spell array, but she had already proved through experience that she could manage something like this. To some, like the shield array, she added the instructions for output displacement along a single plane—an option she had asked for Professor Lacer's permission to use beforehand.

Sebastien finished barely in time for her two teammates to return, already slipping two of the metal disks into her backpack. Though she had a worse grade than either Rhett or Damien, with this she had managed to give herself as many options as both of them combined. She was their wildcard, their all-rounder utility member. "Report," she said, not missing Rhett's small eye-roll.

Damien immediately began to speak, standing tall with his chest puffed out. "We're in what seems to be a warehouse, but there's nothing strategic down below. Just some basic stone shapes of large equipment and some piles of wooden planks. There's roof access, though. From what we could see up there, we seem to be near the center of the city, and I'd estimate the outer wall is about eight hundred meters away. There are two towers flying the black nearby. None flying the red, which is good."

"That doesn't mean anything," Rhett said, shaking his head. "It's too early for the enemy to have made much progress, yet. One of our towers is about ten blocks away to the west, and the other eight blocks away, closer to the center. Some signs of fighting in the distance, but nothing closer than three blocks. I say we head out now, see if we can take out an enemy team or two and get some extra points before making it to the tower."

As first-term students, their main objective was simply to remain "alive," which meant ensuring that their suits didn't register enough damage to make the fabric turn stiff and lock them in place. That would net them the lowest grade. It would be higher if they could get to one of the towers flying the black ally banner. For extra points, they could complete various bonus objectives, such as assisting ally "troops" or working against the enemy in various ways.

"Planks, you say? Made of actual wood, not stone?" she asked.

"Yes," Damien confirmed. "I suspect they're meant to be supplies for us to set up makeshift barricades, but I didn't find any nails or other supplies."

She stood and swung her backpack over her shoulder, leading the way downstairs. She eyeballed the planks, then moved to the nearest window and measured the width of the street with her eyes. It was narrower than a real city, only about three meters across. She looked up speculatively at the edges of the rooftops.

The sounds of fighting came faintly from the east, toward the center of the urban arena.

"Enemy signals!" Damien whispered.

Instinctively, all three of them crouched down, out of sight.

They waited a few minutes for the signals to pass, and when Damien motioned they were clear, she peeked up just enough to see the red suits of the enemy forces turning the corner away from them a few buildings down the street.

"We should have attacked. We have the element of surprise and there were only two of them," Rhett muttered.

"Any extra points are a secondary objective. Our first priority is to get to one of the black towers safely." She moved over to the planks, choosing two that looked suitable for her budding idea. "Is the roof flat?"

"Yeah," Damien confirmed, watching her curiously but without doubt.

"Okay, I've got an idea. Damien, I need your help bringing two of the planks up to the roof. Rhett, you cover us. Don't draw unnecessary attention, but you have the okay to attack."

"Wait, what?" Rhett said, shooting her an incredulous look. "You want to fortify this place? This isn't a good strategic location. We're too far away from any tower."

"That's not what I'm thinking," Sebastien said, moving carefully up the stairs.

"Then what?" Rhett asked, trailing behind.

"We don't need to put ourselves in danger moving through the streets rife with fighting and scattered with enemies. If there's a suitable path, we can travel by rooftop instead."

Rhett eyed the planks dubiously. "That seems…dangerous."

This time, it was Damien who rolled his eyes. "What, you're fine to attack two enemies, but you're afraid of heights?"

Rhett glared back but didn't answer.

Yet another open doorway led them to the rooftop, from which the view of the miniature city was even more impressive. *'Is this how they raised the white cliffs in the first place? Did they just draw the stone up from the ground and mold it?'* she wondered.

A tall building blocked the path to the nearest tower, the one to the east, but in the opposite direction, there was a straight line of sight toward the one farther away. "Ten blocks," she murmured. She knew it would still be a dangerous journey, but it would likely be safer than scurrying through the streets. People often forget to look *up*.

With the planks side by side on the ground, she took out her remaining paint and drew out a wood-focused mending spell on the white stone beneath her feet. With the quick-drying glue as a component, she melded the two planks together, section by section, to create a wider surface. When she finished, she stepped back to admire her work. The bridge was crude, but it would get them across the gap between the rooftops. "It should hold," she said, looking at Rhett and Damien. "Let's get going."

Damien went first, his arms spread wide for balance as he moved with surprising speed. The combined planks didn't even wobble too badly. Once on the other side, he moved along the edge of the roof to scout out the surrounding streets, then waved for them to follow.

Sebastien went next, and Rhett followed behind her. Suspended above the unforgiving white stone of the street, the planks bending and bouncing back slightly with every step, the ground seemed twice as far away as it had before. She had to resist the urge to fall to her hands and knees and wrap her arms around the planks to keep from falling. Instead, she went to that cold, focused place in her mind, consciously directing every twitch of muscle and movement of her limbs. *'This is nothing,'* she reassured herself, though she was pretty sure her face was pale and her expression stiff enough to give her real feelings away.

They made it three blocks like that, traversing two flat roofs and inching along the circular edge of a domed roof. They passed several more small mirror domes, and in the distance, the dull roar of a cheering audience sounded, peaking at random moments when someone in the exam arena did something particularly impressive. When they found themselves above a fight in the street below, they paused. Three grey-suited allies—other first-term students—fought against three red-suited enemies. Each group seemed to have just the basic attacking and shielding spells, and both groups already had one member "dead," lying on the ground under the restriction of their body-suits.

The wind at this altitude wasn't to be stopped even by the walls of the miniature city, carrying the faint chalky smell of the white stone and the sounds of screaming and fighting from all around the arena.

Rhett beamed with excitement, pushing past Sebastien to get closer to the fighting. "Extra points!" he exclaimed to Damien. Without waiting for confirmation from either of them, he pointed his battle wand and loosed one of the offensive spells. A pale purple sphere containing the slightest crackle of electricity shot out, moving at a sedate three meters per second until it impacted the back of one of the attackers.

Damien dropped his scanning artifact to the roof as he hurriedly fumbled at the camouflaging bands strapped around his suit. As the spell shimmered to life, his suit and the area around him all turned an off-white that almost blended into the stone as he moved pointedly away from the enemy's return fire.

Sebastien cursed under her breath. She was on her own, struggling to control the plank and keep it out of sight as she pulled it back from the rooftop's edge. She knew if she lost her balance, she would plummet to the unforgiving stone below.

Luckily, Rhett fought with unexpected ferocity, taking down the second enemy in a matter of seconds without even coming close to being hit himself. He whooped, yelling, "Come on!" at his downed opponents.

The two remaining grey-suited students below stared up at them with wide eyes. "Thank you!" one of them yelled.

Rhett grinned back, bowing with a flourish.

Damien turned off the camouflage to save his second artifact's limited power, then moved to help Sebastien lay the planks over the next gap between buildings. "Come on!" Sebastien snapped at Rhett, who was communicating through charades with the students below. The extra points were, of course, useful, but she would have appreciated it if Rhett could have waited to coordinate with the rest of his team before attacking.

As the duo below watched Sebastien's trio traverse the roofway, the two survivors spoke quietly. With a quick farewell to the third member of their party, stuck unmoving on the ground, they hurried to follow along the street below. Just as Damien reached the next roof, one called, "We're coming up!" just loud enough to be heard without drawing undue attention.

Rhett moved quickly to the opposite side of the roof, and his excitement grew palpable.

Sebastien's eyes narrowed. "Do you see some—"

Out of nowhere, he stopped and tossed one of the clay faux-grenades—explosive potions—over the side of an intervening roof. The clay sphere landed and went off with a flash of light and a loud bang.

Sebastien flinched down automatically. "What are you doing!?"

He grinned at her, unrepentant. "I noticed an enemy-flagged supply stash about a block away. It was behind an old, rickety wooden barricade. More points!"

Sebastien gasped in shock at his recklessness, quickly ushering them forward and hurrying to place the planks down again. They needed to get away before anyone could spot them. "What were you thinking?" she demanded. "If we're spotted—"

Sebastien's scolding was cut off by the arrival of the two first-term students, one young man and one woman. The woman's eyes widened as she got a closer look at the three of them.

"You're that Sebastien guy," she said, her face breaking into a wide grin. "The one who saved those civilians by fighting an Aberrant!"

Her partner was less enamored but gave them all an excited grin. "Thanks again for the help. Would you like to team up? Safety in numbers, and all that. Not like you need it, but—"

Damien eyed them both warily before turning to Sebastien for confirmation. "What do you think?"

"Extra points for heroic actions," Rhett said. "That would be two allies rescued *and* escorted to safety. I say they join."

Sebastien hesitated, looking them over. The extra points could be useful, but she wasn't keen on taking responsibility for two more students. They didn't have any special equipment, and from the little she'd seen they weren't especially skilled.

The two of them smiled hopefully at her. "We won't be any trouble, I promise," the woman said.

"Alright," Sebastien agreed with a sigh. "You can join us, but you have to listen to my orders. Failure to do so, or reckless actions that endanger the rest of the group, will see you kicked out immediately." She gave Rhett a pointed look, which he ignored while grinning at her response.

The two were quick to agree, and with that the team of five started making their way across the rooftops again. Sebastien gave orders and kept them all organized as they scurried from building to building. Damien continued to scout the way, and several times they paused to hide from an enemy patrol passing below, despite Rhett's protests.

"Sure, we can take a few of them out, but what happens when one of them gets word back to the rest or alerts a more powerful enemy that we're a threat?" she argued back. "If we fail to make it safely to the tower, we don't just lose those additional points, Rhett. We fail the test entirely. That's not a risk I'm willing to take."

"Maybe you're less willing to take the necessary risks because you have less riding on this test. No matter how well you perform today, there's no chance you'll end up the best student of the term. But I could, with the right assessment today. I need these bonus objectives, Siverling," Rhett urged. "It's ridiculous to ignore enemies that we could defeat."

Luckily, both of her new charges were quiet and quick to obey her orders. When Rhett looked around for agreement with his argument, neither of them met his gaze. "We're already down one original teammate, and that will affect our grade," the young man explained. "I'd just rather get there safely. I can't afford to fail."

"I wouldn't mind taking on some extra enemies," Damien said, "but not while we're still so far from the tower. Maybe we can spend a few minutes patrolling around that area once we've dropped these guys off."

Rhett huffed but seemed to realize he was outnumbered. "There's a time limit too, you know."

A large group of enemies below forced them to take a detour, and a couple more precarious roofs with precipitous drops slowed them.

Crouching in the middle of a thankfully flat roof as she listened to sounds of the enemies below, Sebastien estimated that they were halfway to their destination. She didn't have her watch, but thought thirty minutes or so had passed. They were making good time.

"They're gathering on this location," Damien said.

"Do you think they know we're here?" the woman, whose name Sebastien had immediately forgotten after she introduced herself, asked.

Damien shook his head. "No. I think they're doing something else. Fighting, or setting up some strategic location. This building had no direct roof access, so they have no way to get to us even if they do realize."

"But how do we get across without them noticing us?"

"We wait till they're all inside," Damien answered, staring down at the scanning artifact. "Any moment now, we'll make a break for it."

Everyone froze as a loud banging echoed over the bare stone, followed by shouts and screams coming from the floor below.

Damien crept forward, his camouflage active, and Sebastien followed behind him.

A few meters below, a girl rushed out to the balcony. "It's too far! We can't jump," the girl called back to her companions inside the building. Her suit was slightly darker than Sebastien's own, indicating that she was a second or maybe third-term student.

"The barricade won't last long!" a man's throaty voice called back to her, his voice breaking with strain. "I don't think we can fight them all."

Damien and Sebastien shared a look, and when she did a quick sweep of her periphery for danger, she found the other two first-term students staring at her expectantly.

"How are we going to save them?" the young man asked.

"You could drop down there and surprise the enemy when they break down the barrier," the woman suggested.

"There are at least eight enemy signals," Damien said darkly. An explosion rumbled through the stone, much weakened from real battle magic but still powerful enough to cause several shouts of fear and dismay from the students below. "And...yep, those are more on the way," Damien added.

The five of them ducked down even further to make sure they weren't seen. The woman bit her thumbnail. "I don't think even Sebastien can take on that many."

"I can take them," Rhett offered, smiling at the woman reassuringly. "I'll jump down to the balcony, the rest of you can find a way down to the street, and then we'll do a pincer attack on the whole group of them. They're in the stairwell; there's nowhere to run."

Sebastien opened her mouth to say that they had neither the time nor the ability to save this group from so many enemies, but she stopped herself. "I... actually have an idea," she realized.

Reaching into her backpack, she pulled out a different spell array disk. "I can create handholds in the stone—a ladder of a sort—for them to climb up." She had loaded up the stone disintegration and gust spells on it, thinking that she might use it to blow a fine dust at the enemy that would irritate their lungs and eyes, or even, with enough dust, create cloud cover for her team.

With the addition of a couple glyphs to allow her to distance the output in the vertical direction, Sebastien began to cast. Sand trickled away from a section of the wall, leaving behind a divot a couple inches deep and a single hand's width across.

"I'll get them on board with the plan," Damien said. Turning his camouflage on once again, he swung himself over the edge of the roof and dropped down to the balcony as softly as possible.

"Take this!" Rhett said, pulling an artifact off of his bandolier and tossing it down to Damien. "One-time-use shield. If they break down the barricade, just shout and I'll be right behind you." Sebastien was thankful that at least he hadn't insisted on being the one to go down.

Gripping her Conduit tighter, she drew more power from the small, dull beast core, causing the sand to flow faster. With quick adjustments of her Will, she drew the distanced output up the side of the wall, step by step.

Whatever Damien said below, he managed to get the other students on board more quickly than she had expected. "Hurry," he urged, looking back over his shoulder, where another soft explosion rumbled out, shaking the stone beneath their feet.

The students wasted no time climbing up, squinting their eyes against the crumbled white stone that continued to fall from above as Sebastien created the last of the handholds.

As the first of them reached the top, she dropped the spell and reached out to help haul them up. She counted five new students, three men and two women. Flecks of white stone stuck to the sweat along their temples, which was already drying under the caress of the wind.

Below, Damien knelt to set up the shield artifact, then brought up the rear, scowling as some of the lingering dust kicked up by the students climbing above him got in his hair.

"Titan's balls," one of the young men murmured, staring at Sebastien. "Is he a free-caster already?"

"He's Thaddeus Lacer's apprentice," the first woman responded in a murmur.

"Quiet!" Sebastien bit out, scowling at the group as she gestured for one of the men to help her move the plank bridge to the far edge of the building.

Damien went first again, since he was the scout, but a couple of the new upper-term students paled at the sight of the precarious pathway. "No, I can't do that," one of the women whimpered. "Mr. Siverling, I can't. I'm afraid of heights." She looked down at the street below, then stepped back and squeezed her eyes shut, crouching as if she thought she might fall off the edge of the roof.

"I'm afraid of heights, too," one of the men said sheepishly.

Rhett reached out to take the woman's hands. "Don't worry, we'll definitely keep you safe." He turned to Sebastien. "Your plan isn't going to work anymore. I vote we stay and use our superior numbers to overwhelm the enemy. I'll stay on the roof with those who can't use the bridge, and the rest of you can find a way down, then circle around to meet up with us."

"Are you sure?" the woman asked, looking up at him with watery eyes.

"Just watch," he said, smirking. "If the others don't hurry, I'll have taken down all the enemies and snatched all the extra points for myself."

Sebastien's chest flared hot with outrage, but she tamped it down, keeping her face expressionless. "If you would like to stay behind and act as a sacrifice for the remainder of the group to get away, you may. But I will not be staying in this location for even more reinforcements to arrive. As soon as they catch wind of what we're doing, we're trapped up here. You realize that they don't actually have to stick around and fight us? They can retreat back down that stairwell at any time. They could pick us off easily as we try to cross the bridge, and climbing down the side of the building would be even stupider. We need to move quickly—" She cut herself off as explosions resounded through the streets from the direction of a red tower in the distance. Dust clouds rose, and screams of fear and anger cut through the wind.

It was a good reminder: arguing with Rhett was just wasting time.

She let her eyes rove over the others. "If you want to come with us, you had better move quickly. Otherwise, remain here," she said, her words clipped and her tone cold. "If you falter or make a mistake, you could very well fall to your deaths. I have no way to save you before you break yourselves across the ground like an egg. Don't slow the rest of us down." Turning, she hurried across the plank.

Those left behind hesitated, and Rhett gave her a long, dark glare as she reached the other side, but no one decided to remain behind, even the woman so afraid of heights.

Getting all ten students across still took an excruciating amount of time, and by the time they had done so, the enemy on the floor below had spotted them. A couple tried to follow using the handholds Sebastien had created. Her group quickly took out the first, sending him falling back to the balcony below, but the next red-suited enemy crawled up holding a shield above his head. He grinned triumphantly at them, then ducked down again, calling out to his comrades.

A couple moved to the nearest windows facing their direction and began to shoot up at them.

"Damien, find a roof with stairwell access," Sebastien ordered. "Move fast, and take the others. We'll hold up the rear." They had no choice but to stay and fight in the hopes of stopping, or at least delaying, the enemy from calling reinforcements. As such a large group, they could no longer move fast enough to effectively escape.

The largest advantage of her rooftop travel plan had been negated. Luckily, the spell-fire was enough incentive for several of the students to hurry along to escape with Damien, hesitation erased.

Rhett actually managed to hit one of the enemy's spells in mid-air. This feat detonated both spells close enough to the enemy to send the woman reeling back, her suit constricting around her and toppling her stiffly to the floor. Rhett tried to toss an explosive shell through the window as a follow-up, but his aim was off, and the clay sphere hit the wall and exploded harmlessly.

With her spell array disk, Sebastien managed to down another enemy, and one of the rescued men who had decided to stay behind with them got a lucky shot off at a red-suited woman hurrying out of the building at the ground floor. Soon after, the attacks stopped.

Rhett and the other man grinned with exhilaration, but Sebastien knew this was far from a victory. Her mouth was dry, and though the wind still carried a chill, the sun beat down on her back with enough strength to leave her armpits dripping with sweat.

Damien had led most of the students to an adjacent roof, though it was in the opposite direction of the nearest tower flying the black. As if he could feel her gaze, he pointed to the next roof and mouthed "stairs."

They hurried to follow, crouching low and staying silent. Even Rhett seemed a little disgruntled at the reduced speed of their crossing. After all, the longer it took them to reach the tower, the fewer points they would receive for that objective.

However, Sebastien was no longer worried about points. As long as they could make it without their suits recording any serious "injuries," they would easily pass the test. To the contrary, she was questioning her decision to save the extra students at all. Just because she had an idea of *how* to do it didn't necessarily mean she *should* have.

After all, their safety wasn't her priority. If she and Damien had partnered with anyone else but Rhett, maybe it wouldn't even have been an issue in the first place.

They had just made it to the stairwell when Damien reported an enemy presence below.

Silently, Sebastien signaled for the rest of the group to wait while she and Rhett moved closer to Damien so they could discuss the situation.

Without waiting for her to question him, Damien explained. "I caught a glimpse of red below, but no enemy signals are showing up on the scanner. They must have a cloaking device."

Rhett gazed out at the tower flying the black flag, only a couple hundred meters away. "Either we go down and fight or we try to make a break for it across the rooftops. Or maybe we could split up, with the more combat oriented of us going down and the rest moving as quickly as they can to safety."

Sebastien was surprised he suggested leaving those they had rescued to their own devices, but it wasn't a bad idea. Only, she didn't really like either option. She couldn't continue to inch across the gap between rooftops with the others, but going down the stairs and having to fight her way out also did not sound appealing. As her mind spun in search of a third route to safety, the flapping of wings drew her gaze to the side.

Cresting the edge of the roof was a young drake, flapping its wings frantically. Cousin to the dragon and as large as a house cat, the creature wore a bright red collar. '*An enemy familiar,*' Sebastien realized with horror.

The creature let out a loud screech half a second before Rhett's spell hit it in the mouth and sent it fleeing back toward the ground.

Around the corner only a couple blocks from them, a group of twelve red-suited enemies turned in their direction. The leader's arm rose, pointing right at them.

3

WALK THE PLANK

Sebastien
Month 3, Day 25, Thursday 9:35 a.m.

Sebastien took a deep breath and bellowed, "Down the stairwell! Get down to the ground floor!" loud enough for her voice to echo off the stone around them for several blocks.

Damien flinched, pressing one hand protectively over his ear as he stared at her incredulously.

She hurried to the center of the roof, crouched down, and waved frantically at the others to keep them from actually going down the stairs. Instead, she pointed at the building in the opposite direction from which the enemy reinforcements were coming. It didn't have direct roof access, but it had a balcony. "We're making a run for that balcony. We have to move faster than them, or they'll see us. We can only hope everyone else is too focused on catching us in the stairwell or ambushing us on the ground floor of this building to notice what we've done until it's too late."

With that, she sprinted across the roof with the plank bridge over her shoulder, maneuvering the opposite end over and down to the balcony across the narrow street as silently as possible. Two of the bigger men helped to hold down the end and keep it stable, and when Damien got across, he did the same on the other end.

"Remember, you can feel free to stay here and slow down the enemy," Sebastien said when several of her group members stared at the precariously placed bridge with hesitation. "We'll laud your heroic last stand to the examiners."

In the end, two of them did decide to stay behind. As Sebastien shuffled across the makeshift bridge, feeling bile rise in her throat, she couldn't blame them. But her grade in Fekten's class wasn't high enough that she could afford to fail the final exam and still pass. In the distance, the roar of the audience rose to a fever-pitch.

She caught a splinter in her palm from clutching the sides of the sloping planks too hard but ignored the pinch of pain in favor of maintaining her precarious stability.

As she reached the balcony, several hands reached out to steady her way down, but her pant leg caught on the white stone mimicking a decorative wrought-iron fence and tore loudly. Her suit shifted strangely as it registered the "injury," but thankfully didn't consider it debilitating enough to theoretically kill her. Still, it would lower her final score.

Grim-faced, Sebastien motioned her orders, and the others pulled the plank bridge into the room beyond the balcony to keep it hidden. She pulled the splinter out of her palm with her teeth, sucked the blood off of it, and then licked her palm a few times just to be sure. She spat out the splinter, examined it, and tucked it into her pocket. She would dispose of it safely later. One could never be too paranoid.

Without hesitation, they continued deeper into the building and down the stairwell, moving so fast that Damien barely had time to scout ahead. The ground floor was not as empty as they had hoped, and Sebastien's heart stilled for a moment, then crashed into her ribcage as it began to race.

But the people down below wore the black of upper-term allies, not red. They were picking up supplies from a black-flagged stash surrounded by a barrier of sandbags.

A woman raised a finger to her lips for silence, then waved them on. Her eyebrows rose as she watched all eight of them hurry to the nearest window and crouch down beside it.

"No enemies in sight," Damien reported. "The black tower is that way. Do we just make a run for it?"

Everyone turned to Sebastien.

"Yes," Sebastien agreed reluctantly. "Damien as scout, shielders and damage dealers pair up. I'll bring up the rear." Nominally, with her spell array disks, she was the wildcard, but if the worst came to pass, she could abandon the rest of the group and perhaps still make it to the tower.

Without argument, they exited silently through the nearest window. When Sebastien glanced back over her shoulder before following, the upper-term woman winked at her.

Soon after, the sounds of fighting erupted behind them. Sebastien didn't look back.

They made it almost all the way to their destination without serious incident, meeting a few more grey and black suited students along the way. They took down a pair of injured enemies who were trying to retreat from the black tower's territory. The sounds of fighting all around them grew louder, and they passed several sandbag barricades, some manned, some empty or collapsed.

Finally, they turned the corner toward the street that would lead them directly to the tower entrance. To their right, only a couple blocks away, the tower flew the black flag high above. At its base, students in dark grey and black manned sandbag barricades.

To their left, much closer, marched an entire unit of enemy troops, at least a couple dozen people, shielding spells up to protect them as they bludgeoned their way forward. *'So this is what the audience was making such a big fuss about,'* Sebastien realized.

The woman at the front of the enemy unit wore a dark red cloak and epaulets to signify her high ranking—and commensurate danger level. They were marching on the tower with the intent to bring it down. If they succeeded, it would fly the red flag, and those students charged with its protection would fail.

Their entire group caught sight of the advancing enemy at the same time, and as one, they made the same decision.

"Run!" Rhett yelled, shooting a futile offensive spell at the enemy.

Sebastien's group scattered across the narrow street, sprinting for all they were worth as their allies shot spells past them to try to cover their retreat.

Sebastien kept an eye on the enemy with her peripheral vision, her shielding spell array ready to activate at any moment. The harmless test spells moved slower than real battle spells, and if she reacted quickly enough, she could either dive out of the way or block them. With the wild way some of her allies were attacking, she might even need to shield against friendly fire. *'I'm only a first-term student. If I can just make it to the base, my part of the test will be over, no matter what happens next.'*

Damien turned around, looking for her, then slowed down enough to run beside her instead of sprinting ahead at the front of the group. "I've got your back, you've got mine," he said, only slightly out of breath.

Sebastien nodded curtly.

But of course, a unit meant to bring down a tower base was not short of spell power.

Sebastien saw the telltale foggy shimmer of a faux concussive blast spell roll out of the leader's battle wand, followed by two more to either side, perfectly placed so that there was no dodging all three.

The low-powered, small-area shielding spells that she and the other first-term students had would do nothing against it.

"Tuck and roll!" Sebastien snapped half a second before the magic reached them.

Wide-eyed, Damien copied her, throwing himself to the ground in a fetal position as the magic pushed at their heels.

The faux concussive blast spell was gentler than a real one, and moved slower, but in some ways it was more powerful. Instead of slamming them into the ground and leaving them fractured, bruised inside and out, it lifted them up and sent them flipping through the air.

Sebastien collided with Damien, and then the ground, and then they were rolling and tumbling together in a painful tangle of limbs. Something bashed into her hand and sent her Conduit flying. As they settled, she looked up dizzily toward the approaching enemy, cursing the rules that had forced her to leave her pocket watch and the chain that would have secured her Conduit behind.

Several of the enemy unit's people were laughing at them, and as they neared, they raised their wands again.

Sebastien still had the handle of the shielding spell array in one of her hands, and though her suit's sensors had registered more damage and had begun to restrict her movement, she was not entirely out of the test yet. She was still considered "alive."

A sparkle caught the corner of her eye, resting beside Damien's hip. His Conduit had fallen out of his pocket.

Sebastien raised the shielding spell array and her leg at the same time, confirmed that she had thought to add the basic output distancing symbols and that the beast core was still held securely in its place, and brought her calf down hard on top of Damien's Conduit. Her ripped pant leg provided the perfect patch of bare skin to access the celerium through, and the crystalline gem dug painfully into her calf.

She grinned ferally and cast the shield spell, just in time to block the offensive sphere of light heading toward her chest. "Damien, I need you to get up without moving me—carefully, and pick up my Conduit."

"What?" Damien asked, his voice low and horrified.

Several of the enemies showed their surprise at their offensive spells impacting harmlessly against her shield, which was only a foot across but flitted about like a hummingbird to position itself perfectly in front of each attack. A few hesitated, looking toward their leader for instruction, but others continued the assault.

Tangled together as she and Damien were, it didn't take much movement for Sebastien to position the shield's output between them and any spell that seemed like it might hit. "Hurry!" she snapped.

"How are you casting without your Conduit!?" he hissed, scrambling to pick it up from where it had rolled and almost catching a stray spell to the head. He moved so quickly he almost tripped before he could return and press it into her free hand. "Oh, by all the planes-damned idiotic things to do, Sebastien. Are you casting through your own flesh?" he wailed, his hands flapping about uselessly.

"Of course not!" she snapped.

Slowly, still holding the shielding spell between them and the enemy, she rose to her feet. "Pick up your Conduit from the ground, and get behind me." Any little advantage might help them make it to the tower unscathed.

She began to walk backward as quickly as her bruises and the restrictive suit would allow, blocking the increasingly frequent offensive spells and praying that the leader didn't send another concussive blast at her. Sebastien's mind spun through all the possible options, wondering if there was anything they could do to improve their chances.

At this point, they needed powerful backup, someone to come out from the tower and take the enemy's attention while they retreated.

But before she could retreat more than a few meters, Professor Fekten's voice resounded through the narrow streets, bouncing off the walls and almost screaming with tension. "Code red! Code red shutdown of area C! The exam is delayed!"

Sebastien dropped her shielding spell, looking around in confusion, relief, and a little bit of apprehension. Code red meant that there was significant danger to the students' wellbeing nearby and that they needed to retreat to safety.

She turned, hurrying faster toward the tower as her suit released all of its restrictions. There would be tunnels at its base to lead them out of the exam arena, the same way they'd been brought into it. And at the very least, she would feel safer sheltered behind the back of someone like Fekten than right out in the middle of the street.

Except...everyone around her was scrambling back. Those closest to the tower were heading toward it, but the enemy unit was retreating in the opposite direction. Several people wearing black and grey were running beside them. Even Damien had retreated away from her, his expression screwed up in gut-wrenching pain as he met her gaze.

Sebastien slowed, the weight of a horrible premonition settling on her shoulders.

Fekten had left the tower and was sprinting toward her.

She stilled, dropping the spell array disk and raising her hands in the air. After a moment of hesitation, she dropped her Conduit, too, lest someone think she planned to keep casting.

"Possible break event!" Fekten screamed, tossing a small golden sphere at her feet, where it sprouted legs that dug into the ground and then bloomed with a spherical shield spell.

The shield surrounded her, semi-opaque and somehow solid enough to drown out most of the screams coming from outside. Idly, Sebastien realized that she could feel the rumble of the audience's screams through the stone beneath her feet. This must have been the most exciting thing to happen all day.

His battle wand trained on her, Fekten stepped cautiously closer. "Get control of yourself, Siverling. Do *not* continue casting anything. If I catch even a hint—even a whiff—of magic coming off you, I'll knock you unconscious. If you resist, I'll do what needs to be done." His gaze was flinty, and his meaning was clear. If he felt he had to, he would kill her to protect the other students.

Sebastien swallowed hard, her throat suddenly bone dry. She kept her hands raised high and met his gaze as she nodded slowly and clearly. "I understand. But I think there's been a misunderstanding."

4

HARRY HAROLD HAD NO HANDS

Damien
Month 3, Day 25, Thursday 9:45 a.m.

As the shield went up around Sebastien, who stood with his hands raised while Professor Fekten threatened him, Damien's vision swam and his knees almost buckled. He was hyperventilating. Wrapping both his hands loosely over his mouth, he blinked rapidly as he tried to force himself to take slow, even breaths despite his lungs screaming that they lacked for air.

Why. Why? *Why?* This exam wasn't even important. It was just a *test!* Even if they hadn't made it to the tower, they still probably would have gotten some points for those they had helped to rescue. There was no need for Sebastien to risk his life for this.

"Get back, Westbay!" Fekten barked at him. "Back!"

Between one moment and the next, Damien had lost something so precious. He knew that the true gravity of the situation, the depth of the consequences, hadn't hit him yet. It had been like that when his mother died, too. It had taken weeks for him to truly accept the fact that she *no longer existed*, and even years later he still had moments of metaphorical vertigo when he remembered she was gone.

Sebastien was saying something, his voice scratchy with fear and muffled by the semi-opaque barrier, and Damien forced himself to focus.

"I realize it might have looked bad, but I didn't channel magic through my own body. I'm not in any danger of a break event. I don't even have Will-strain," Sebastien said.

Damien stared at his friend, who, for the first time since the exam started, actually looked apprehensive.

As if reading Damien's mind, Sebastien turned to meet his gaze and repeated, "I'm fine. This is a misunderstanding."

Damien's breathing began to slow, and he pulled his hands away from his open mouth, a string of saliva trailing between his palm and his lips. He had apparently started crying at some point. His face and hands were covered in tears, and salt was getting into his mouth. "A mis—misunderstanding?" Damien asked, his breath hitching. He didn't understand how that could be, but Sebastien's calmness was contagious.

Fekten wasn't listening, instead screaming back to the tower to evacuate the area and let them pass through.

Sebastien drew a deep breath and yelled through the barrier, causing Fekten to flinch and his hand to tighten around his battle wand. "I did not cast through my own flesh! Damien's Conduit fell out of his pocket, and I borrowed it."

Fekten's eyes narrowed. "I know what I saw, Siverling. You were casting with empty hands. I watched as Westbay returned your Conduit to you, and he didn't pick up his own off the ground until you were already standing."

"I was casting with my leg. My pant leg is torn, so I was able to press my skin against Damien's Conduit where it rested on the ground," Sebastien insisted, enunciating every syllable. He lifted his leg, displaying the long rip in the grey fabric that reached up to his knee. The pale skin of his leg was plainly visible, and though it was hard to see clearly through the barrier, it looked like there was a red mark where he might have pressed it against the faceted edges of Damien's Conduit.

It was a ridiculous, unbelievable explanation, but something inside of Damien still unclenched. "It—it's true," he croaked, drawing Fekten's attention. Damien swallowed to clear his throat and tried again, holding up his Conduit for Fekten to see. "It had fallen out of my pocket when we got hit by that soft concussive blast spell. I didn't see it until after Sebastien stood up. It makes sense that he would have been lying on it."

The area around them had already emptied of other students, but a few members of the faculty were slowly approaching, battle wands and other arti-facts out and ready.

Professor Fekten narrowed his eyes, and the tip of his wand remained unwaveringly focused on Sebastien. "You expect me to believe that you, in a moment of panic, learned to cast through your leg," he said, his tone completely deadpan.

Sebastien huffed. "Let me reiterate, I did not cast *through* my leg. I cast through Damien's Conduit. I just…gripped it with my leg. Skin contact is all you need, not actual fingers. It's not like this is the first time I've ever done such a thing. It might be slightly harder, but it's far from impossible. Please, be reasonable. There's no way I would have put all the students around me in such danger just to win a mock battle. Hells, I wouldn't put *myself* in such danger just for the results of a test. I'm not anywhere close to failing, and if I thought the Defense *elective* was going to be the thing to hold me back, I could simply drop it from my schedule this coming term."

Damien leaned over, pressing his hands to his knees and taking a couple more deep breaths. He wiped the snot and tears from his face with the rough grey fabric of his sleeve.

The other faculty members had arrived, and Fekten shared a look with a couple of them. "The boy claims he didn't cast through his flesh, but through a Conduit touching his leg," he explained, his skepticism clear.

"Is there any way to test it?" Sebastien asked. "I'm telling the truth, and I'm not experiencing any uncontrollable urges to cast through my flesh, but how am I supposed to prove that?"

"Put him under observation in one of the rogue magic shelters," suggested one of the professors. "Three days should be long enough to be sure."

"*Three days!?*" Sebastien echoed, outraged. "I'm slotted to be in the Practical Casting exhibition later today. I can't miss that."

At the reminder of who he was apprenticed to, several of the professors shared glances again.

"Have him examined by a healer and give a statement to one of our Masters of divination," someone else suggested.

Fekten agreed reluctantly, lowering his wand just slightly. "We'll do it in the shelter under the sim room." He reached into his pocket and fiddled with something, and the hazy barrier around Sebastien withdrew into the golden artifact at his feet. "I'm warning you, Siverling. If you're lying, casting through your own flesh again is likely to cause a break event, in which case I will do my absolute best to kill you before you can complete the transformation." He turned to Damien. "Didn't I tell you to step back, Westbay? It's not safe. You need to evacuate the area with the rest of the students."

Sebastien turned to Damien. "I need you to go get Professor Lacer. Tell him it's an emergency."

Fekten's wand rose again. "You have something to hide, boy?"

Sebastien's tone was cold as he stared Fekten down. "On the contrary. I simply don't feel safe being trapped underground with a professor who has repeatedly made it abundantly clear just how hair-trigger his murderous tendencies are. I can demonstrate to anyone who wishes how simple it is to cast basic spells with a Conduit touching my calf, or my shoulder, or even my ass. But I will do so under the supervision of my mentor. If you truly mean me no harm, that shouldn't be a problem. After all, he's trained to deal with much worse situations than an Apprentice-level Aberrant. His presence could only be a boon."

"I'll get him," Damien said. Not bothering to wait for Fekten's agreement, he turned to sprint ahead, toward the tower and the exit tunnels that would lead him to the edge of the Flats. He didn't stop until he found Professor Lacer, then explained the situation in as few words as possible so that his panting for breath would waste less time.

Professor Lacer rose from his seat at the Practical Casting exhibition's judges' table and strode off in the direction Damien had come from without even a farewell to the others or a second glance toward the student on stage. "Explain the situation *clearly*," he bit out as Damien hurried to keep up with the man's much longer stride.

Damien did his best to explain, trying to gauge from Professor Lacer's severe expression just how bad the situation was. "Did you know he could cast through other parts of his body? Is that part of the training you were giving him?" Damien asked, because there was no way he was going to ask if Professor Lacer believed Sebastien was telling the truth. He didn't even want to ask that question of himself.

"I did not know, but such a skill is not unheard of, if somewhat difficult to develop safely," Professor Lacer said, falling silent as they entered the heavy iron doors of the shelter.

The space beyond looked larger than Damien expected, but as he thought back to how packed together the students had been as they huddled in the shelter underneath the library, he realized that it probably only seemed larger because it was so empty.

Sebastien's shoulders visibly relaxed when the two of them arrived, but only for a moment before he drew them back and lifted his chin again with the imperiousness that came so naturally to him, staring Fekten down as if looking at some kind of unruly puppy.

Damien moved to stand supportively at Sebastien's side, despite the protests of the healer Fekten had retrieved, while Professor Lacer spoke to Fekten, who explained the situation much less charitably than Damien had.

Professor Lacer's expression didn't change at all throughout the entire thing. "My apprentice is very talented with these kinds of exercises."

Fekten stared at him for a moment, speechless.

"It's true," Damien piped up, smoothing his disheveled hair back when everyone turned to look at him. "Sebastien has already learned how to distance the output of his spells. I'm not sure if you were aware, but he's a genuine genius. Rather than doubting him and casting aspersions on his character, don't you think you should be giving him contribution points for his impressive feats?"

The edge of Professor Lacer's mouth quirked up for just a moment. "Indeed. Let us get this over with quickly, shall we? I have duties to attend to."

Fekten bristled, letting out an audible snort that reminded Damien of the rumble of a dragon's breath. The diviner and the healer both hesitated, looking at each other as if asking if this was normal, but when Professor Lacer waved his hand impatiently, they jumped into action.

Sebastien stepped into the spell array the diviner had drawn on the floor while Professor Lacer murmured with the woman, something Damien couldn't quite catch about a "boon," and "increasing the required power," that made the woman pale uncomfortably. Damien suspected it had something to do with whatever the Raven Queen had done to Sebastien that he wasn't able to talk about.

The woman cast the spell, and there were a few seconds where things felt strange, and Damien found himself looking away. As he examined the others, he was surprised to see both Fekten and the healer looking back at him.

Then Damien looked to Professor Lacer, who was staring into the center of the spell array with fascination. He followed the older man's gaze back to his friend, who shuddered uncomfortably, rolling his shoulders.

"I'm ready," Sebastien said.

There really wasn't much to say, and though Fekten and the diviner questioned him multiple times about the details and forced him to repeat things, that part finished quickly.

Professor Lacer shot Fekten a disdainfully raised eyebrow. "Why don't you demonstrate your capabilities for us, Mr. Siverling?" he asked.

With a sigh of relief, Sebastien acquiesced, pulling the Conduit Professor Lacer had lent him out of his pocket. Under the watchful eyes of all five of them, he pulled out a disk painted with a simple gust spell array from his backpack, which he was still wearing. He cast normally, first, holding the Conduit in a firm grip. Then he cast with the Conduit sitting on the back of his hand. Then, drawing a gasp from the healer, he held the Conduit in the crook of his elbow, between his bicep and his forearm, and cast the same gust spell just as easily as before.

Damien found himself grinning so wide his cheeks almost hurt, a heady cocktail of relief and pride urging him to gloat, to strut around making pointed comments in Fekten's general direction.

Then Sebastien sat on the ground, placed the Conduit between the skin of his calf and the floor, and cast again, looking at Fekten.

The healer cleared her throat. "No signs of elevated heart rate, dilation of the eyes, bodily convulsions, or trembling in the fingers. If he were experiencing the extreme sensation that accompanies channeling magic through one's own flesh, I would expect to see some sign of it."

"As you can see, my apprentice is simply talented," Professor Lacer said.

"Well," Fekten said with a harrumph. "You still acted recklessly, Siverling. We had to suspend the end of term exam for dozens of students. I must insist that you submit yourself to the infirmary for a more thorough battery of tests before participating in the next exhibition." He paused, then added, "At least this was a false alarm, but I cannot believe that those imbeciles acting as the enemy continued to attack you despite all the evidence of someone who was about to have a break event."

He made a few threats that Damien tuned out before stomping off, accompanied by the healer and the diviner, who bowed to Professor Lacer before leaving.

As soon as the three of them were alone, Damien couldn't hold it in any longer. "How long have you been able to control a Conduit through your leg!?"

Sebastien rolled his eyes. "I don't even know, Damien. As long as I remember, I suppose. Using a Conduit touching other parts of the body is actually not that difficult. I suspect that most people just have some mental block they never attempt to overcome. As Professor Lacer might say, they get into a rut. I had no idea it would be such a big deal."

"How could you not realize?" Damien asked. "Do you see people going around casting with their wrists, or their belly buttons?"

"Do you remember that children's rhyme about Harry Harold who had no hands? He wore jeweled shoes so he could cast through his feet."

Damien blinked twice. "Yes. I remember that nonsensical rhyme for children. I also remember other similar stories about children walking into a dragon's mouth and being transported to another world, then climbing out of the dragon's nose years later, unharmed. Or about a girl who could transform at will into a pegasus. Or the one about the one-inch boy who might come to live with you if you built an appropriately detailed miniature house for him and filled it with all of your baby teeth."

Sebastien crossed his arms. "Well, that's not the same thing at all."

"Yes, yes it is. For normal people, it is. Normal people cast magic through their hands, or maybe sometimes their foreheads." He turned to Professor Lacer for help, but the man was just watching them with something that might have been amusement. Damien threw up his hands with exasperation. "Let me be clear, the reason the coppers search peoples' crevices is not because they're afraid criminals will start channeling spells through the Conduit shoved up their assholes!"

Sebastien raised one eyebrow in challenge, an expression that was eerily reminiscent of Professor Lacer, and drawled, "I know I'm impressive, but I'm sure you could do it too with a little bit of practice, if you weren't so close-minded. Myrddin would never have been able to create Carnagore or sneak into the secret realm of the fey and marry their princess if he was so pessimistic."

Damien reached up to tug at his hair in frustration, but Sebastien laughed. Whatever tension had remained in the other young man's frame was gone as he grinned smugly at Damien. Damien squinted at him suspiciously, keeping the warm glow of relief that had bloomed in his chest from showing on his face. "You're poking fun at me."

Sebastien gave him a one-shouldered shrug, turning to walk toward the shelter's exit. "Only partially. Right?" he asked, turning to Professor Lacer.

The man hummed, looking Sebastien over speculatively. "I suppose you may be correct. I can cast with a Conduit touching other parts of my body, but I still find using my hands much easier. I cannot free-cast without them, and even some of the more difficult spells would be beyond me. I am surprised you managed to distance your spell's output under such restrictions. However, I did not start developing the ability until I was in my thirties. Perhaps if I had started younger, I would have progressed with similar ease."

Sebastien seemed surprised by this, and then thoughtful, his dark eyes staring into the distance as he frowned.

After they closed the shelter door behind them, Professor Lacer returned to his duties, but Damien insisted on accompanying Sebastien to the infirmary, where Ana and her little sister Nat were already waiting for them.

"We saw what happened on the big mirrors," Nat announced immediately, her eyes searching Sebastien's face with an endearingly sincere worry. "Are you alright? We tried to read people's lips when you were talking with Fekten, but I'm not very good at it yet, and it was hard to see you clearly inside of that bubble."

Damien flushed, realizing that his response—the tears and his complete loss of composure—had likely been shown in great detail, duplicated from the small mirrors in the arena onto the much larger ones erected for the audience to watch the most interesting events of the mock battle. The practical part of the Defensive Magic exam was automatically displayed as part of the exhibition, and one of the biggest lures of the entire event.

Sebastien reached out to take Nat's hand, squeezing it reassuringly and making the girl's cheeks flush pink. Once again, he quickly explained the misunderstanding that had caused so much pandemonium.

"Of course you would be able to do that. Doesn't anyone here know you're going to be a free-caster soon?" Nat asked, blowing out her cheeks with frustration.

Ana nodded sagely, the only sign of her own worry the wrinkled spots on her blouse where she must have clutched it in white-knuckled fear, which no amount of smoothing with her fingers could completely hide. "That is a good point, Nat. One that I think everyone should hear before too much undesirable gossip spreads. As they say, a lie can travel halfway around the world before the truth can get its boots on."

Nat pressed her lips together and patted the back of Sebastien's hand, which was still holding her own. "Don't worry. We'll make sure people don't think badly of you just because that idiot professor got so frightened."

"He's a respected man," Ana chided. "We can't call him an idiot. Just... overly anxious about the safety of his students. He fought through a lot of horrible battles. Perhaps there is some lingering trauma from the Haze War." She turned to Sebastien and gave him a brief, tight hug.

Damien smiled at her. "Thank you, Ana."

"Think nothing of it," she replied, taking out a small mirror from her pocket and checking her appearance, slipping on a sweet smile like a general arming himself for battle. When she finished, she passed the mirror down to Nat, who tried out several different expressions, muttering to herself as if she was rehearsing a speech.

Sebastien looked between the two young women with a bemused expression. "Yes... thank you."

Nat tossed a lock of hair over her shoulder nonchalantly, but she couldn't hide her excitement. "Think nothing of it. We're Gervins, you know. This is nothing we can't handle."

After they left to influence public opinion in Sebastien's favor, one of the healers took Sebastien into a private room for another checkup. Sufficiently alone but assured that plenty of healers would be around to help him if he needed it, Damien tried to cast the simplest spark-shooting spell on a piece of paper, with his Conduit held in the crook of his arm.

He did not find it nearly so effortless as Sebastien and Thaddeus Lacer had made it seem.

He felt barely any connection to the magical energy that should have been —*needed* to be—within his grasp. Frightened that he would lose control of the insignificant spell entirely, Damien released the energy, retracted his Will, and gripped his Conduit in his hand as he waited for his racing heartbeat to slow.

$$5$$

A TREE OF SAND AND LIGHT

Sᴇʙᴀsᴛɪᴇɴ
Month 3, Day 25, Thursday 2:00 p.m.

Aғᴛᴇʀ ʟᴇᴀᴠɪɴɢ the infirmary with a clean bill of health, Sebastien and Damien returned to the Flats to give their "after-action reports," which took a distressingly long time. She was sure most of the other students weren't treated like witnesses in an investigation, forced to repeat things and dig for details and motivations over and over again. The proctors taking her report kept making notes and stopping to murmur together, throwing her odd looks.

In the end, she insisted upon leaving in time to make it to her scheduled slot in the Practical Casting exhibition. Once again dressed in her own clothing, with the security of her holster and the black sapphire Conduit pressed against the skin of her back, she hurried across the grounds. As she strode with purpose, those in the crowds milling about made way for her. Sebastien ignored the various stages, food carts, and game stations to arrive at the stage that had been set aside for the Practical Casting students.

The performances were running behind schedule, so Sebastien took a seat in the small area at the front of the stands set aside for students like her, setting the box that contained her supplies by her feet. Several of the nearby students introduced themselves, while others whispered together, not even trying to hide the fact that they were talking about her.

Sebastien sighed, turned her attention toward the stage, and did her best to ignore them like the irritating flies they were. Small mirrors similar to those used in the Defense exam arena had been set up on stands, replicating the image reflected in them onto much larger mirrors that would allow even those at the back of the stage to see clearly, though they carried no sound.

A third-term student who had cast a fairly simple spell with only a single glyph stepped down, replaced by a fourth-term who quickly moved to set up their own performance. They then used a single spell array to create a fountain show from a shallow basin of water. It seemed the Practical Casting exhibitions at this point were nothing particularly impressive. She suspected the upper-term students had been scheduled for the day after, saving the best for last.

As another lackluster presentation followed, Sebastien's thoughts wandered to more impressive magics. Professor Lacer had done more ambitious spells with a casual wave of his hand. She could only imagine what he was capable of with transmogrification's higher-order connections. Had he ever traveled to one of the Elemental Planes, perhaps? She would love to experience such wonder.

Sebastien thought back to that strange twinkling meteor that the old man from the Architects of Khronos had cast above Knave Knoll. It, too, must have been some kind of transmogrification. She still hadn't figured out how it might work, or even why a spell would be designed like that. Perhaps a fourth-order association, the kind Professor Lacer had said was beyond the scope of their class?

The breeze blew her hair into her face, carrying the scent of sweet treats, fresh mud, and the budding greenness of spring, all riding over the ever-present salt of Charybdis Gulf. Sebastien tucked her pale hair behind her ears. Even her hair was an example of the kind of magic her fellow students could not hope to imitate. It had grown longer after all the time spent in this body. Perhaps it was time to cut it.

Shortly after the Knave Knoll attack, Sebastien had overheard a group of upper-term students gossiping. Apparently, one man had gone down to peek around the crime scene, making himself temporarily popular with all the classmates who were hungry for gossip. When she had inserted herself into the conversation, the man had been eager to tell her what he could.

"Well, I couldn't get close because the Red Guard are still swarming around the site. They have it cordoned off, and the coppers were stationed around the edge to keep people from slipping past. But I saw the crater! It was dozens of meters across. I can't even imagine the type of spell that could have caused such a thing." The man had continued on for a long while after that, sharing inane details and his own speculation while Sebastien tried to pretend like she was still interested. "Whoever those terrorists were, they must have been as dangerous as an Aberrant, don't you think? But if you're interested just because the Red Guard was there, I'll have to disappoint you, because I'm pretty sure no actual Aberrants made an appearance."

"What?"

"Oh, well, I heard you were interested in Aberrants, right?"

"Where did you hear that?" Sebastien had asked, frowning.

The man had raised his eyebrows, then gave her a commiserating smile. "Oh, you know, around. It's common knowledge that you fought one. I really admire your courage, but you shouldn't be so reckless. I'm sure Professor Lacer would be willing to recommend you to the Red Guard once you've gotten your certification and completed your apprenticeship. There are rumors he used to work for them." He'd laughed, then. "Well, you'd know that better than I, wouldn't you?"

Sebastien frowned, ignoring the latest student's presentation as she stared off into the distance. *'Even if it was a fourth order association, why would it create such a wasteful spell? Are there some rules or principles I'm unaware of? What is the point of creating a physical manifestation and destroying an entire building when it would seemingly have been simpler to just use some mass paralysis spell or send in some sedative?'* Perhaps the wards had been set up to block more common applications, and the Architects had needed to get creative to bypass them, she reasoned. Or maybe the thaumaturge she'd accidentally killed was just showing off.

"—erling. Mr. Siverling!"

Sebastien jerked to alertness, turning to the student aide calling her name in an annoyed tone.

The woman rapped her knuckles on her clipboard. "Are you prepared? Please take your place on the stage."

Sebastien stood and hurried to climb the stairs with her box of supplies. As a student at third term or below, she'd only been given ten minutes to display her skills, so she needed to set up quickly. As she crouched to draw out her spell array, a quick glance up revealed that the audience stands were packed much fuller than they had been when she arrived. Many of the seats were taken not by outside guests but by her fellow students, indicated by the wooden tokens they all wore.

She shot a quick look to the judge's table, where Professor Lacer sat. Now that her mind was not so occupied with the possibility of being blasted to smithereens by another of her professors, seeing him reminded her of Oliver's recent secret note. Again, it had been disguised as a promotional letter from a local tailor's shop, but the message inside implied that Thaddeus Lacer had requested to meet the Raven Queen. Oliver had sent a second note after that, asking to meet at her earliest convenience, but even if she hadn't been avoiding him, she'd had no free time during finals week.

As she crouched on the stage, staring up at Professor Lacer, she had a moment of vertigo. She didn't know what to do with that information. Not after the recent upheaval in her situation. Or at least her comprehension of the reality of her situation.

Professor Lacer gave her a small, almost imperceptible nod, jarring her attention back to the current moment. She focused her Will into the setup, every movement purposeful, chalk lines large enough to sprawl over almost the entire stage. Both a triangle and a pentagram went inside, for control over both energy and matter. Three glyphs—*"light," "shaping,"* and *"heat"*—went at equidistant points around the center. She finished by setting two clay pots in their smaller component Circles on either side, and one pot full of gravel at the front, nearest the stage and the judges. For this spell, she didn't even need a beast core. In fact, taking the power from elsewhere was part of the show.

Finally, she stood to the side of one of the largest spell arrays she had ever used, took a deep breath, and wrapped her fingers around her Conduit. She was ready.

Her Will contracted down, caught the light within the area bounded by the Circle, and channeled it into the lines of the spell array. Sebastien's heart beat firmly, a little too fast but without fear, and she couldn't help the smile that spread across her face as she pulled the darkness back to create a backdrop. She pulled heat from the area, reaching deeper and deeper into the pitch black shadows until the water particles in the air turned to ice.

As the breeze dragged at the area with ephemeral fingers, a white fog manifested from the shadows. Sebastien had practiced this several times and knew that the effect was quite dramatic. Ominous, even.

She held that steady for a few seconds before moving on to the second step. While maintaining the Sacrifice of light and heat, she pulled at the sticky, metallic sand in the leftmost component pot. The clumped chunks and tendrils moved through the air slowly, almost invisible against the darkness until she used some of the light she was siphoning off from the back half of the Circle to add a glow. As the glowing particles and tendrils arrived at the front, she compressed them into the shape of a single glowing seed.

Then she did the same for the other pot, pulling a dark amber, honey-like substance to the seed, where she integrated the two in marble-like patterns. It was a resin that she had mixed various incense oils into until she got just the right smell.

That was the final step. She closed her eyes and imagined the finished product, then opened them, a blazing determination in her chest, fueling her Will as she began to showcase her abilities in earnest. She pulled on the light and the heat and used its energy to fuel her control of the sand, the resin, and the ethereal glow all at once.

She had been practicing this in phases, first teaching herself to mold the sticky sand like a sculptor, then doing so while adding tiny sparkles and wisps of light, and then the addition of the backdrop of darkness to set it all off.

None of the pieces of this spell were so difficult by themselves, but doing them all at once was a strain on her multitasking abilities, and she felt likely to fumble the whole thing due to sheer complexity. One spell, multiple complex effects, but each of them based on simple principles. Most of which she had learned in Professor Lacer's class, or from the auxiliary exercises he had assigned: complex movement of an object, the particulate to stone spell, using light as both Sacrifice and output. If she hadn't been practicing with all the individual elements for so long, this likely would have been impossible, even with a complex spell array with dozens of glyphs and a fully written Word.

The glowing seed broke open, a delicate, hopeful leaf sprouting out from it even as roots dug downward into the gravel. She fed the living sculpture more metallic sand and amber resin, weaving them together as the seed sprouted into a sapling, sprouting branches and leaves as it shoved its way out and up from the dark ground. The tree grew bolder and more robust as it aged under her Will. As if speeding through days, weeks, and months, strands of resin and sand layered atop each other and reaching outward toward the sky.

As the tree grew larger, the strain on her Will increased, pushing at it from every direction as if the tree was trying to burrow out of her grasp like roots through an old cobblestone wall.

She had tried using a tree nut to add some transmogrification to the spell and thus make the shaping easier and more instinctive but found that it only made everything harder and left her struggling to weave all the pieces seamlessly together. Instead, she had to hold the evolving shape entirely in her mind, the evocative parts meant to stimulate emotion carefully planned and controlled.

The living sculpture reached the height of her hip. She had wanted to add sounds and maybe illusory birds in the tree's branches at this point, but that was still beyond her. Instead, for the final step, she molded the last of the resin into the shape of tiny fruit, then channeled heat into the tree, from root to crown. The resin layered throughout the tree began to smoke and glow a smoldering orange that would burn for a couple of hours, until it was all burnt away. The heat had the added effect of solidifying and hardening all of the sticky metallic sand firmly in place.

Breathing hard, she let the spell stay as it was for a moment. Then, slowly, the ethereal glow disappeared. The darkness that she had held toward the back of the Circle swept forward to make a complete dome once more, gobbling up the tree.

Two precise seconds of darkness passed, and then she dropped that as well, revealing the final result.

A miniature tree sat on the stage in its gravel-filled pot, only a few feet high but as gnarled and detailed-looking as she could make it. The resin ran through its bark in decorative, marble-like stripes and hung from the tips of its branches like teardrops. It fumed like dying lava, smoke from the carefully blended incense that she had mixed into it beforehand riding on the breeze in tendrils that looked surprisingly graceful.

Sebastien eyed the result with mixed feelings. It looked pretty enough, she supposed, but it was nothing special. She wasn't powerful enough yet to produce any truly impressive spectacles. She looked out at the audience, and then at the judges, trying to gauge their reaction. They were all still and silent, staring down at her. She had been worried that she was unable to make the tree any larger but hoped the image replicating mirrors would have mitigated that problem. Now, she was less sure.

She bowed to the audience. '*Maybe I should have chosen something besides a tree? Perhaps the audience would have appreciated something more dramatic, like a sculpture of a sky kraken. Using the animal from their crest would have even shown loyalty to the University. Why didn't I think of that beforehand?*' Trying to keep her disappointment from her face, Sebastien picked up the tree sculpture and turned to walk off the stage, leaving the two empty pots behind.

"Sebastien Siverling, first-term student and apprentice of Professor Thaddeus Lacer!" the student aide repeated somewhat belatedly.

Someone in the audience screamed with excitement, then started clapping wildly. Sebastien looked up in surprise.

Damien stood there grinning with all his might, surrounded by his group of Crown Family friends, all packed into the stands amongst their classmates. Others soon followed his example. The applause grew louder than she had expected, with several shrill voices screaming her name, some even stamping their feet when it seemed that their hands and mouths together couldn't create enough noise.

One girl actually *threw* a rose at her, and Sebastien had to duck to avoid being caught in the face by its thorny stem.

Wide-eyed, Sebastien hurried toward the judge's table, where several of them were whispering together, no doubt discussing her fate. She sat the tree down in its center, cleared her throat against the smoking incense, and said simply, "A gift. Thank you for the opportunity."

The bark and leaves glinted as the texture caught the light, and the resin within seemed to seethe with rage. She hoped that, seeing it up close, the detail she had put so much effort into might impress them a little, along with the smell. Pecanty loved it when his students talked about smell. There might be those among the judges just as obsessed with it as him.

As she turned to walk away, the audience was still clapping and yelling. Fighting down a blush, she bowed to them awkwardly again, then moved through the stands to join Damien and the others. She sat down and tried to drown out the noise, letting her mind relax after the arduous undertaking of her performance.

The judges conferred for a couple of minutes while the student aide helped ready the stage for the next exhibition. To her surprise, the one in the center stood up, holding a megaphone cone to his mouth. "To Sebastien Siverling, seventy contribution points for exceptional power, depth of range, and stability," he announced.

Officially, contribution points weren't finalized until the exhibitions had ended, after which they would be posted on the announcement board in the library and at the University entrance, as well as mentioned in most of the local newspapers. After all, there were a limited number of points to go around, and the most impressive exhibitions were saved until Friday. The judges only made immediate announcements of contribution points for those who made an extraordinary showing.

Damien screamed in Sebastien's ear, seemingly more excited about this than she was. "By all the greater hells! Sebastien, why didn't I know you were going to do something that amazing? You told me you were just going to display your grasp on the stuff we mastered in class!"

While those around her were jostling and cheering, she looked over to Professor Lacer, who gave her a smile and a single, slow nod.

"I'm an official apprentice, now," she murmured, laughing as she slumped back into her seat.

6

AUXILIARY EXERCISES
ASSESSMENT

Sebastien
Month 3, Day 26, Friday 9:00 a.m.

Friday was the last day of the exhibitions, but as first-term students, all their tests were already finished, and Sebastien and her growing group of friends could peruse the spectacle at their leisure. The University grounds were transformed, packed with stalls alongside all the cobblestone paths and temporary stages with amphitheatre-like grandstands for the audience.

Sebastien had been too caught up in the workload and stress that accompanied the end of term to really appreciate the sheer effort the University put into the exhibitions. They wanted to show, indisputably, why they were the most prestigious University in the known lands. The best of the best fought for a spot within its lauded grounds, and any employer or organization could be assured of a graduate's drive and skill.

There was nowhere else in the world like this.

At this point, all of the exhibitions were focused on upper-term students, some of whom already had their Master's certification and had stuck around on research-focused courses in the hopes of becoming Grandmasters.

Some students had recently patented artifacts, including one that could literally lift you out of bed and dress you for the day in under sixty seconds, including a necktie and accessories. A clockwork cat with sapphire gems for eyes seemed to track the movement of passersby, its ears swiveling and tail swishing. One student had hired a chef to show off his portable camping cook-set, which heated food without a fire, light, or smoke.

It made her jealous that she'd not had the space to fit artificery into her own schedule.

Damien bought the group little baggies of exotic nuts that had been tossed in a butter and brown sugar mix and then coated in a floury powder. Each bag was two silvers, an exorbitant price for such a small snack, but like the food at the Glasshopper, it was somehow worth it simply for the decadent experience.

After that, they watched five witches put on a spectacular mock battle. The men and women had familiars from each of the five elements, and their fight seemed more like a choreographed dance as they allowed themselves to be tossed high into the air and caught safely in the grip of the massive earth and water elementals. The show was very popular with the masses, and even though it had little real-world application, Sebastien could admit that it was impressive. Waverly, of course, loved it, and hung around after the show to try and talk with the witches, staring at their familiars with covetous, shiny eyes.

There was even a small mathematics exhibition where chalk-wielding students raced to solve complex equations on large blackboards. Even though Sebastien was watching them solve the equations step by step and the progression should have been clear, she still found herself with squinty eyes and a headache trying to comprehend what they were doing.

Damien coaxed her away with skewers of some flaky white fish that had been battered, fried, and then artfully drizzled with a tangy sweet sauce. Sebastien actually drooled while eating it, and had to wipe the edge of her mouth surreptitiously to make sure no one noticed.

Unfortunately, one girl on the edge of the path had apparently been watching her, and when their eyes met, she blushed, looked away, and then returned to staring at Sebastien. Then, she actually licked her lips with an exaggerated amount of wet, pink tongue, held one finger up in a shushing motion, and winked.

Sebastien turned her head away, her face blank as she died a little inside. *'Erase it. Erase it from your brain,'* she urged herself. *'Oh, look, there's so much magic to watch!'*

Despite her fascination pulling her in five different directions at once, she did her best to stay with the rest of the group. Their presence acted as a kind of shield against the rest of the crowd, and several times one of them had to step in to help guard one of the others from overeager strangers.

Rhett, hands deep in his pockets and the arms of his jacket tied around his neck, sidled closer to Sebastien as they watched a horticulture student's trained flowers open and close in waves along with the music the woman played for them. "I made things difficult during the Defense exam," he said.

Sebastien didn't reply, glancing briefly at him before refocusing on the performance.

"I'm not the best at teamwork sometimes. My mother says it's because I'm an only child." Rhett rocked back and forth on his heels, and then finally said, "I'm sorry."

Sebastien nodded. "We're all learning," she said, and knew by the somewhat hesitant smile Rhett gave her that he took it as forgiveness. She reminded herself that she was trying to be kinder and refrained from saying what she really wanted to. *'I can forgive, if the person is deserving. But I never forget. I won't give him a chance to repeat his mistake in any situation where the outcome is actually important.'*

Still, she knew how difficult it could be to admit you had been wrong, and there was something to respect in that.

After another snack of beautifully pleated steamed buns, each stuffed with a range of fillings from sweet to savory, their group shoved into the packed audience area of an illusion-play.

Cute stylized animals were the main characters, and the theme was all about friendship, forgiveness, and banding together to fight against a greater enemy—an Aberrant that threatened the continued existence of the animals' village.

Three students ran the entire thing, including not only the pristine illusion itself, complete with realistic shadows and complex facial expressions, but also a moving backdrop and spells to create sound effects and the animals' voices. The play even featured the occasional gust of wind carrying faint scents. The three casters synced their efforts seamlessly together, creating a thing of wonder.

Sebastien felt lucky to experience it, ignoring the contents of the play in favor of appreciating the sheer skill and polish it demonstrated. As they walked away, it left her somewhat dissatisfied with herself. *'I still have a long way to go before I can brag about having any real grasp on light or illusions.'*

Damien distracted her with a strange, cylindrical roll of colorful vegetables and rice wrapped tightly in a translucent dough. "You dip them in this brown sauce!" he explained excitedly, holding out a cup full of dark liquid for them to share. "They're from the East."

They were divine. *'I could really get used to being rich enough to eat like this all the time. How am I supposed to go back to cafeteria food?'* Suddenly, the complaints from her fellow students at the beginning of the term made more sense. *'What a wonderful incentive to earn and spend contribution points. Stick, meet carrot,'* she mused. She caught Damien watching her eat with an irritating, smug expression on his face but decided not to protest. After all, she was eating for free.

But the highlight of her day was the aspiring Grandmaster student who had announced that he would publicly open a portal to the Plane of Radiance.

Sebastien and Waverly were equally enthusiastic about dragging the others into the warded University classroom where the feat would be displayed, early enough that they were sure to get seats. This exhibition required them to sign a waiver acknowledging the risk to their safety, but at least their student tokens got them in for free.

The organizers were handing out large glasses covered with black cloth. When she looked closely, Sebastien could see the glyphs embroidered into the fabric and chiseled into the glass around the edges. The overwhelming, cleansing Radiance could blind one just as surely as staring into the sun, and the glasses were necessary to protect their eyes.

Sebastien chose a seat as close to the front as possible, giving her a good view of both the complex spell arrays, drawn onto the floor at the front of the classroom in polished stone and precious metals, and the rare components placed around the edges. The Word for the planar portal itself was ridiculously complex, and around that a secondary barrier spell had been drawn. Both required multiple large, gem-like beast cores for power.

The secondary barrier was manned by a professor—as a failsafe—while the would-be Grandmaster began to cast. The spell took almost twenty minutes to complete. When the shimmering sphere of the portal finally appeared like a bubble of light, Sebastien put on the cloth-covered goggles, watching wide-eyed as the shining bubble grew to the size of a person.

When the bottom of the sphere barely touched the center of the spell array, it stabilized. Here was an example of output detachment—or perhaps just distancing—at work, the center of the effect hanging in the air to allow a full sphere rather than a dome.

Beyond the edge of the portal, vague, bright outlines of what seemed to be a field of flowers swayed gently in an inaudible wind. In the distance, trees of light rose up with a strange, coherent symmetry that spoke to her of justice, hope, and an unflinching judgment of all that was less perfect.

A small form raced across the field, perhaps some rabbit-like creature, white on white. Before her eyes could parse what they were seeing, a streak descended from the sky like a lance, and burning gold splashed out from the small creature.

A feathered being looked up from its kill, seeming to meet her gaze all the way across the field and through the portal.

As she watched, the student caster climbed into a one-piece protective suit that covered him from head to toe, sealing together seamlessly like it was made of a thick liquid instead of fabric. He stepped forward with deliberate care and obvious apprehension, pierced the portal, and entered the Plane of Radiance. If he remained within the sphere, he should be safe enough.

Watching the feathered predator in the distance as it began to tear at its prey, he crouched down and dug up several of the flowers, placing them in sealed glass containers. After only a couple minutes, he stood and returned to the mundane plane, holding up the retrieved samples to resounding applause.

The portal closed with little fanfare, as if there had never been a doorway to another world just hanging right there, only a few dozen feet away.

Sebastien sat still as the rest of the audience filtered out of the large class-room, replaying the experience in her mind, her skin rough with goosebumps. She remembered Professor Lacer mentioning offhand that he'd once seen someone weaponize a planar portal, then shot upright like she'd been struck by lightning. "I—I have to go!" she told the others, already hurrying off at a pace that was only slightly below a run, stretching each stride as far as it would go.

'*I can't believe I forgot!*' Her mind raced, but quickly settled on a destination. She found Professor Lacer just as the Practical Casting exhibitions were ending. He was retying his hair with a leather cord at the base of his neck, the edges of his mouth turned down with fatigue. He'd trimmed his beard recently and scratched at it idly as she stopped in front of him.

"I'm ready to be assessed on the auxiliary exercises you assigned whenever you want," she said, breathing heavily. "If this is an inconvenient time, I'll be available during the Sowing Break. I'm staying in the dorms."

"I was wondering if you were conveniently forgetting about that in an attempt to avoid scrutiny," he drawled. "Mr. Westbay found me to complete this days ago."

Sebastien remained silent, without excuses.

Professor Lacer sighed good-naturedly, waving for her to accompany him. "Go retrieve the practice supplies and come to my office, then, lest you gain an unfair advantage from extra time to practice." The words were scathing, but his tone was mild.

Sebastien eyed him with puzzled amusement. '*Was that a joke?*' Once again, she turned and hurried off, this time to the dorms where the box of spell exer-cise instructions and supplies waited. Thinking back to the beginning of term when he had given her the assignments, she remembered planning to master them by mid-term to prove her dedication. That seemed a laughable goal now. Even after the entire term, she was still apprehensive about her results.

When she arrived at his office, a Henrik-Thompson testing artifact sat on Professor Lacer's desk. "We might as well keep abreast of your progress in the more conventional metric, as well," he said. "But start with the exercises."

She set up her small slate table as a casting surface, then began with the first auxiliary exercise from the beginning of term. The mirrored movement spell used two of the plain metal balls Lacer's students had practiced so much with, one following the motion of the other. She was able to replicate the simple back-and-forth movement of the first ball in reverse, angled, or even in a curved sweep. To show off a little, she finished by lifting the "mirrored" ball a few inches off the slate surface, something she hadn't practiced but which now came with surprising ease.

Then came the three-dimensional glass maze, which would rearrange itself and force her to start from the beginning any time the metal ball touched one of its walls. Here, too, the magic was malleable and acquiescent, her Will having little trouble accelerating and decelerating the ball on a moment's notice. When she had proved her capability with that, she redrew the simplistic spell array to demonstrate some more innovative solutions, such as creating a repelling force along the glass walls of the maze that made failure almost impossible.

Professor Lacer raised an eyebrow at this, but his reaction was inscrutable. She couldn't help but think that this must all seem so banal to him. She was akin to a toddler playing with wooden blocks while he built Titanic monuments.

Next, she displayed a less obvious spell, the air-compression exercise, which could be vaguely visible as a shimmer in the air.

Professor Lacer cast something with a wave of his hand, then stared more intently at the mirage in the center of her Circle.

'*A divination of some sort,*' she realized. Whatever it was, it only caught the barest edges of her divination-diverting ward and was easy enough to ignore.

She drew as much air as she could into a single point, then allowed it to explode outward with enough force to create a popping sound and blow her hair back from her face. Then she repeated the compression but released the air with gentle control. Then, rather than a uniform sphere, she pressed the air into simple shapes of increasing complexity.

Finally, she adjusted the spell array and created a more complex form, like a string of oddly shaped pearls formed in a loop. She took some time to concentrate, adjusting the details until everything was just right. Then, one after the other, she allowed the areas of compressed air to pop. Each let off a slightly different sound, and all together they formed an extremely rudimentary, frankly horrible-sounding tune made up of about six different notes.

Professor Lacer hummed ambivalently, and the sense of observation from his divination spell dropped.

Sebastien rolled her head from side to side to stretch her tense neck muscles, then rolled her jaw. She had been clenching it without realizing.

With a deep breath, she erased that spell array and drew out yet another, this time setting a small tea candle in the center and lighting it. She fed her Will gently into the spell array, trying to imagine the transition of wax into gases, heat, and light. Changing the color, brightness, and shape of the candle flame had been much more difficult before all the practice she did for the exhibition, but at this point it didn't give her much trouble.

It was the final exercise that made her most apprehensive.

She had taken a second autumn leaf transmogrification exercise so that Professor Lacer would teach her output detachment. To complement the in-class exercise, which used the idea of light stored in the leaf's creation, she had chosen something relatively simple—the darkness of a long winter night.

But as she brought down shadow to the center of the Circle, it was noticeably less stark than what she could have achieved using simple transmutation or even absorbing light as a Sacrifice. Without the glyph for *"light"* allowing her to affect that energy, trying to smother the area in darkness instead was so much more difficult than she could have expected.

Professor Lacer frowned, and this time there was no question about his verdict. "What is your intention?"

She explained the exercise she'd picked. "The spell instructions specifically say that the light doesn't disappear, but darkness descends, overpowering day."

His frown grew deeper. "Try again, but this time think about the retreat of the sun."

He asked her to change her focus thrice more, focusing on the connotation of the time just after sunset, a winter night with only stars, and even a night sky with the clouds blocking out the moon. His frown grew deeper with each attempt, and she thought her shadows might actually be growing *weaker*. Perhaps it was her lack of familiarity with these new twists on the concept.

She flushed, unable to meet his gaze. She forced herself not to hunch her shoulders or hang her head like a snail trying to retreat into its shell. "It doesn't really make sense to me," she admitted. "Darkness doesn't descend. It's just an absence of light. Shadow can't *overpower* light."

Professor Lacer sighed, moving away to lean against his desk. "This is not the first issue you've had with transmogrification, correct? I noticed your in-class exercise of a similar nature was weaker than your usual standard. And I believe you mentioned some struggles with Pecanty?"

"Yes..." she agreed in a small voice, placing her hands carefully on her knees. "I can create shadows or darkness a lot of other ways, but... Maybe I'm just not grasping the concept correctly?"

He nodded thoughtfully. "Not everyone has natural talent in this area. At least you did not attempt to cheat by using transmutation."

The words hit her like a blow, but she didn't flinch. Her heart had begun to crash against her ribcage from the inside, but her cheeks lacked the tingle of a blush. Professor Gnorrish had once shown how a strong grasp of transmutation principles could improve one's performance when creating the same effect with transmogrification. *'If I hadn't been researching light so deeply, would my attempts have been even more lackluster?'* Sebastien turned her head to meet Professor Lacer's steady gaze. "Is there anything I can do?"

"Let us try once more." He palmed his Conduit, weighing it for a moment before he closed his fingers around it. "Look at the leaf again. Trace its veins with your eyes. Remember its smell. You must know that this leaf came from a tree that witnessed the final winter of its world."

His Will began to swim through the air, coiling tighter and tighter, bringing with it a strange chill and changing the light, as if she were staring at the world from underwater, or perhaps during an eclipse. She shuddered but forced her focus onto the leaf and his words. No thaumaturge worth their salt would be distracted by the insignificant details of their environment while in the middle of casting. Her shadow was still more "shrouded twilight" than "inky midnight," but at least it had improved from her most recent attempt.

"On the shortest, coldest day of the year, the sun was like weak tea, barely breaking through the gloom. The world, like the tree that this leaf fell from, had gone into hibernation in an attempt to conserve energy until the sun grew strong and came close again."

A depressive bleakness settled against her skin, and when she breathed, it rode the air inside her and coated her lungs. She breathed out, trying to push that feeling into the shadow that came from this imaginary leaf from the end of the world.

"But instead," Professor Lacer said, his voice low and sinister, "the sun set, never to rise again. The long night went on and on, and the cold sank deeper and deeper, past the crust of the earth and into its warm core. It smothered the last warmth and light of the world like a baby strangled in its crib. And the tree sat there, this dead leaf abiding in the placid, frigid darkness."

Sebastien shivered at the imagery, her eyes stinging from the cold as she struggled to breathe in the syrup-like air, which pressed on her from the inside and out as if urging her to lie down and die. Her bones ached. Two tears spilled down her cheeks, and even she couldn't tell if it was a response to the cold or to the infectious emotion. The shadow at the center of the spell array was a godforsaken sooty grey, significantly better than before but still an obvious disappointment.

As Professor Lacer drew back whatever spell he had been casting, she released her own as well. "I have been practicing as much as I'm able," she said. "Though perhaps I haven't put in as many hours on this spell as some of the earlier ones, I'm really not sure why I'm having such trouble. Perhaps it's because my other spell with the same leaf was using such a completely opposing concept. I think I did a lot better with that one."

"I believe I understand what your problem is, but it is something that you must overcome on your own. You may not be naturally apt with transmogrification, but you are stubborn and resourceful. Try harder. Dig deeper. Dissect your failure." He looked at her, his gaze heavy and piercing.

"I will," she promised, her voice scratchy.

"Let us test your capacity," he said simply.

Sebastien's knuckles went bloodless-white as she squeezed her Conduit. She stood and moved over to his desk where the artifact sat. He handed her a beast core, and she held nothing back, sucking power from it like the hungry maw of a whirlpool and slamming it into the artifact as if her life depended on it.

She pushed until she had to close her eyes against the brightness of the light. Her ears rang with a high-pitched buzz. She breathed out and tasted blood, though she knew it was only an illusion from how hard her heart and lungs were working, as if she was pushing herself to the limit in a dead sprint for Fekten's class.

When she reached her breaking point, the arm of her clenched fist was trembling. She opened her eyes, staring into the light for a moment, and then released the spell even as she began to release her Conduit. She loosened one stiff finger at a time, until it dropped to hang helplessly from the chain that connected it to her pocket watch.

"Four hundred twelve thaums," he announced. "We will have to recalibrate the settings for a higher-term student next time, or you will blind us both."

Students who had never cast before entering the University could expect to end their first term with a capacity between eighty to one hundred sixty thaums, depending on how much time and effort they put in. Her head start had given her more than just the obvious advantage, as the Will advanced faster when the foundation it grew from was larger. Archmage Zard, who was over a hundred years old and whose capacity was estimated to be in the tens of thousands, could probably improve by a couple hundred thaums within half the time it had taken her. And at the age of eleven, it had taken her almost two weeks of strictly supervised, short practice sessions to improve by a single thaum.

For her to break four hundred thaums now was not unexpected, as she had been improving at a steady pace, but when she thought back to the beginning of term, it put her firmly in the middle range of a standard Apprentice who had just received their license. It also meant that she had more than *doubled* her capacity from the beginning of term. In only five months, she had achieved almost as much as in all the years since she began learning from Grandfather. Her progress had stagnated for much of that time, however, with not enough time spent practicing and no new magic to stretch her Will. *'It was the right decision to come here. Despite everything.'* When trying to do the math on the ratio of improvement, she realized that her birthday had passed, without her even realizing it, and she was now two decades old.

Professor Lacer moved around to the other side of his desk, reaching into one of the drawers and pulling out a parcel wrapped in brown paper and tied with twine. "I must commend your dedication. It is obvious from your rate of improvement."

Normally, praise from him would leave her feeling like she could float on air. It still did, to some extent, especially after the poor performance she'd shown just before, but the feeling was more relief than pride. She remembered the complete nonchalance of his expression after she told him what happened to the Moore family. '*Where does he draw the line?*' she couldn't help but wonder, some of that cold bleakness he had spread through the room earlier returning to her chest. '*If he would do that to them, just for being related to Newton, for loving him... What would it take for him to do something similar to me?*' Sure, she was his apprentice, but that could only hold so much weight.

She swallowed. '*I will have to observe him for much longer to understand him. To find out if, like Ennis, Thaddeus Lacer is the type to throw those closest to him to the wolves when it becomes convenient.*'

He held the parcel out to her. "For you."

Sebastien accepted it, her eyes widening with surprise. She could tell by the feel that it was a book.

Professor Lacer gave her a small, amused smile—as if they shared some joke. "As you have succeeded in becoming my official apprentice, you should read that and heed the advice within. I bought it specifically thinking of you."

Whatever doubts and suspicions she held were nothing in the face of his words, and she flushed. Bowing deeply to avoid his gaze, she tried to settle her expression. "Thank you."

"Alright, off with you then," he said, waving his hand in a shooing motion. "Don't do anything foolish with all this free time."

Sebastien exited the office and closed the door behind herself, then took almost a minute just to settle her rioting emotions. She was unused to feeling so many different things at once.

Realizing how embarrassing it would be if Professor Lacer exited his office and found her still outside, she hurried off. Outside, the sky was streaked with the orange and pink of an approaching sunset; the assessment had taken longer than she expected.

With careful movements and slightly trembling fingers, she unwrapped the book without tearing the plain brown paper. It was large but less than an inch thick, with glossy, colorful ink embossed on the front cover.

Sebastien read the title, then read it again. She blinked twice.

100 Clever Ways Thaumaturges Have Committed Suicide it read, and in smaller print down below, *How to Avoid Offing Yourself Through Sheer, Reckless Stupidity*.

"Heed the advice within," he had said, smiling as if they were both sharing a joke. "I bought it specifically thinking of you."

Sebastien let out a sharp, scoffing laugh that somehow ended up morphing into real mirth. "Okay," she muttered to herself, looking back over her shoulder in the direction of his office. "I can admit, it's a pretty appropriate gift."

7

MYSTERIES AND MISSIONS

Sebastien
    Month 3, Day 26, Friday 8:00 p.m.

Sebastien flipped through *100 Clever Ways Thaumaturges Have Committed Suicide* as she returned to the dorms, skimming the entries and the simultaneously fascinating and often horrifying illustrations that accompanied them. Some of those whose mistakes had been considered worthy entries into the book were turned into Aberrants. Others died in a more traditional manner. Just as Sebastien was beginning to get sucked into a gruesome account of an alchemist who had tried to Sacrifice a potion to empower another potion with its effects, she arrived at her group's dorm room and was distracted by the ant nest hubbub of the remaining students preparing to leave.

She found Ana at the far side of the room instructing some of her Family's servants, who had come to help her pack up and move her things. Unlike Sebastien, who didn't own more than would fit into the large trunk at the foot of her bed and the drawers of her bedside table, Ana's belongings had filled the empty space under her bed as well as some shelving that she'd set up along the wall of her cubicle.

Sebastien had packed up none of her own things, as she was one of the handful of students in their group who planned to stay at the University over the break. If they were assigned new quarters for the upcoming terms, she would simply move her things directly—while of course making sure to erase the traces of what modifications she'd made to her cubicle.

When Ana's things were all packed up and her servants were busy hauling them off, Sebastien sidled up to her, doing her best to act nonchalant.

Ana raised her eyebrows inquisitively, most likely seeing through to Sebastien's underlying tension.

"I'll walk you out," Sebastien offered.

Ana smiled with pleased surprise, linking their arms together and leading the way.

Since Sebastien could think of no natural way to segue into her question, she simply asked. "What happens to the students who've gone insane from Will-strain?"

Ana slowed, but did not stop. "They are treated in the infirmary by some of the best healers in the known lands. The University will do its best to fix them."

"And for those who cannot be fixed? Or those whose treatment will take months?"

Ana squeezed Sebastien's arm tighter. "They will be sent to the Retreat at Willowdale. It is a long-term treatment center where they will receive the care they need while being given time and every opportunity to heal. My Family makes a sizable contribution every year to cover the costs for those who have no family or estate to do so for them, and I know several of the other Crown Families do the same. Sometimes, if there is no one to pay and the damage is severe enough for one of the more secure wards, the University will cover the costs. I cannot say what's happened to them will be alright, but they will suffer as little as possible in their remaining time. Did you…know any of the students who succumbed?"

"I was just wondering," Sebastien said quietly. There had been several more incidents of Will-strain as the end of the term descended, some more severe than others, and even some during the exams and exhibitions. Students had died, too, though the faculty did their best not to make a production out of that fact.

'It would place a bit of a damper on the exhibitions, to be talking about all those who accidentally killed themselves trying to do something impressive.' Sebastien knew the University had wards, guards, and emergency response policies in place to deal with the issues that arose from such a thing. Perhaps they even had more subtle protections in place, but she couldn't help but think how dangerous it was to pack thousands upon thousands of desperate thaumaturges together.

Remembering the book Professor Lacer had gifted her, she postulated that things must have gone wrong quite a lot over the few hundred years of the University's existence, and it could only be luck that none of the mishaps had been so catastrophic as to wipe it off the map. Aberrants were rare, true, but over time even low probabilities meant only one thing. There was a chance that something irreparable could go wrong, and so, eventually, it must.

'*Hopefully I will be finished with my schooling and long gone by that point,*' Sebastien thought. She shuddered, immediately realizing that kind of thought for what it was: a glorious temptation for the forces of irony. At least she hadn't said it out loud.

Ana squeezed her arm again as they came to a stop at the top of the transport tube station, which bustled with people. "I don't know if it would make you feel better, but the Retreat at Willowdale does allow volunteers to come interact with and entertain the patients. When I was young, I went there with my caroling group."

A slow smile stretched across Sebastien's face. "That's a wonderful idea. Thank you, Ana." She leaned closer to bump their shoulders together.

A few meters away, two girls squealed, obviously watching them.

Ana and Sebastien turned a simultaneous wrathful glare at them, and Sebastien wasn't ashamed of the petty vindication she felt as the other two girls paled and looked away, not even daring to continue whispering to each other.

After extending an open invitation to visit the main Gervin manor over the break, Ana left.

When Sebastien returned to the dorms, she found Damien pacing in front of her cubicle, continuously smoothing his hair back even though not a strand was out of place. As soon as he saw her, he stomped up, grabbed her by the elbow, and dragged her out of the room. To her surprise, he marched them to the nearest bathroom, shoved an angled rubber stopper under the door to keep it shut, and then dragged her into the farthest stall.

"What's wrong?" she asked, alarm tightening her shoulders.

Damien's eyes were bloodshot and a little wild despite his otherwise impeccable attire. "Sebastien, I'm going to ask you something, and I need you to tell me the truth. Please."

"Okay...?"

"Promise me."

Sebastien swallowed her foreboding. "I will tell you the truth, or keep my silence. I swear it."

Damien grimaced, obviously not appreciating her caveat, but didn't argue. "Has Oliver Dryden ever made you uncomfortable, flirted with you, or attempted to get you to repay his help with sexual favors? Is he trying to coerce you into some sort of relationship?"

"What? No. What?" Sebastien had spoken before even considering her response, reeling from the completely unexpected line of questioning.

Damien stared at her searchingly. "Are you sure?"

For a moment, Sebastien considered the gifts Oliver had given her, the meals they had eaten together, and the conversations they'd had. But Oliver treated everyone like they were important and special. She had seen it, with his servants, random waiters, and even occasionally strangers he met on the street, regardless of gender or species. It was one of the ways he slowly and subtly gathered power. "I'm sure," she said firmly.

Damien turned to try and pace again, though the stall they were in constricted his movement to only a single stride. He muttered almost inaudibly under his breath, "...so oblivious, would he even notice?"

Sebastien reached out to stop Damien, grabbing him by the shoulder. "Yes, I think I would notice. Mr. Dryden and I do not have that kind of relationship."

"What kind of relationship *do* you have, then?"

That was the obvious next question, but it still took Sebastien aback.

"He paid for you to come to the University, didn't he? You have no family, you said as much. And you were poor." When Sebastien blinked at him, he scoffed impatiently. "Your clothes may be of good quality, and fashionable, but you only have a few sets. You couldn't even afford a proper Conduit! Who else here so meticulously cares for their things, to the point of casting a mending spell at the first sign of a loose thread, or keeps any leftover components when we are done casting in class? Of course I noticed, Sebastien."

As she wondered what explanation she could give that would fit the verifiable facts without being incriminating, she almost wished she'd gone along with Damien's suspicions. "Where is this coming from?" she asked quietly. "Something happened."

"Titus came—to pick me up, I thought—but actually to make some ridiculous accusations and warn me to be careful of you. He thinks you're using your charm to manipulate Dryden. But one of his coppers told me that she thought Dryden was trying to take advantage of you, maybe abuse you. Titus was investigating it." Damien tugged at his hair, mussing up the perfect style he'd been smoothing it into obsessively. "It's all so convoluted and absurd. Do you remember when you dressed up as a certain infamous woman so we could get photos of Ana's uncles trying to trade with her? Titus thinks we're in some sort of relationship because the hotel employee noticed that we only used one room and tried to blackmail him about announcing my secret relationship with you. And the copper told me she saw Dryden with a prostitute that looks like you—he has some sort of obsession, a fixation. Apparently Titus confronted him and he basically admitted it. You can be really oblivious, and maybe Dryden was trying to keep it a secret, but you shouldn't trust him so blindly, Sebastien."

Sebastien reeled from the deluge of information, trying to organize it all in her head. "Titus was investigating..." She left the '*me*' unsaid, suddenly nauseated. "Is there any particular reason that I shouldn't trust Mr. Dryden, except for this nonsensical belief that he has a...'fixation' on me?"

"Isn't that enough!? Why else do you think he would give you the coin needed to attend the University? I'm not stupid, Sebastien. I know how expensive it is. Did he give you your clothes, too? And he lets you stay at his home when you're not here. Don't you see that it's strange? Do you have some other explanation?"

She hesitated, trying to come up with something plausible that wouldn't contradict whatever Titus might have found. Could she say that she had agreed to work for Oliver after graduation, maybe? Or maybe it would be better to just go along with Damien's version of things. But he would still have questions about her backstory with Oliver.

She hesitated too long, and Damien was watching her face the whole time. His hands fell to his sides, some of the nervous energy leaving him. "What kind of favor did you have Ana do for Lord Dryden?"

Ice flowed through her veins and stiffened her muscles.

"Because you told me that—" He swallowed. "That our mutual secret, the leaders wanted us to do it for more than Ana's sake. And Ana mentioned offhand doing something for you that was really more for him." Damien lifted a hand to his mouth, fingers pressing delicately against his lips as he stared at the wall of the stall behind her, lost in realization. Then his gaze snapped back to hers. "Is he the leader?" he demanded. "Myrddin's balls, has he been the one giving the orders the whole time?"

"No!" Sebastien protested, shaking her head violently. "No," she repeated, putting her sincerity into her voice. Suddenly, she realized that Oliver, too, had one of the thirteen-pointed star coasters that she'd made for herself and Damien. *'Did he plan that, too? A token that would give him influence over one of the powerful Crown Family members, conveniently associated with the law enforcement that could give him so much trouble?'*

She shook her head again, casting off the errant thoughts. Oliver was also Lord Stag, who was closely connected to the Raven Queen. She could not afford to entangle Sebastien with him so intimately if she wanted to remain free of suspicion. Especially now that she had realized she could not trust him —that he might have something to do with the stolen book.

Oliver being the leader of her fake secret organization hit a little too close to the truth, and when things inevitably went south, as she was trying to remind herself would always happen at some point, she did not want Damien to draw the—correct—conclusions. She doubted his loyalty would extend that far.

"He is not the leader," she said. "He's not even a member."

Damien's eyes narrowed. "Is he...a provisional member?" His voice rose in pitch with delight. "Just like me? He doesn't even have access and just does what he's told?" Damien didn't wait for her confirmation, turning to pace again. He threw back his head and smothered a laugh with his hand. "Oh, that's better than I could have ever imagined."

Sebastien considered denying Damien's ridiculous mental leap, but then she would have to find some other way to explain the loan, their relationship, and the Gervin textile commission. This fit...and it would keep Damien's mouth shut. Ennis had mentioned once that people were more likely to believe an explanation that they had come up with themselves. She cleared her throat awkwardly, both relieved and strangely guilty. "Well, yes. But between you and me, Damien, I'm not sure he's going to be accepted as a full member. He's philanthropic, but not as reliable as he might seem. It might be better if he just continues to do his part separately from our own efforts."

Damien's eyes were wide and shiny, and he smothered another crowing laugh.

"Titus cannot know about this."

Damien nodded readily. "No one can know. Don't worry, none will hear a peep out of me. But why isn't Dryden reliable? Did he fail a mission?"

Sebastien raised an eyebrow and remained silent.

"Of course you won't tell me," Damien huffed. "It's confidential, yadda yadda."

"Do I need to worry about Titus digging into things he shouldn't?" she asked.

That sobered Damien somewhat. "I don't...think so? Mostly, he just seemed concerned that you were trying to use and manipulate me. I mean, he thought you were being so rude to me in the beginning so that I would notice and think about you. That way I would care more once you schemed your way to flipping our dynamic on its head and making us friends." He caught her incredulous expression and laughed. "I know, it's ridiculous! But he didn't mention any suspicious activity, not even the part of Operation Defenestration everyone knows about."

"But he dug into my background?"

"Yes... He said you were an orphan who experienced a lot of hardship and learned how to make hard choices and see the world differently because of it."

Well, that was at least partially false, but this whole situation was concerning. She needed to talk to Oliver. *'Was this what the note he sent a couple days ago asking to meet with me was about?'* He had people in Harrow Hill who might be able to warn them if Titus was getting too close to the truth, and he was the one who'd actually spoken to the man. As much as she'd wanted to avoid him until she'd learned more about whatever he had secretly stolen, it looked like she wouldn't be able to put it off any longer. She would have to bury her hurt and suspicion deep and hope he wasn't able to see through her.

She had been silent too long, and Damien asked, "Is that a problem? I know you don't like to talk about your past. He didn't tell me any details, Sebastien."

"It's fine," she said.

"I was going to invite you to spend the break with us, but I'm not so sure that's a good idea anymore."

She let out a humorless laugh. "I'll be staying here over the break. I already planned to do that, even before all this."

"I'm not sure how much use I can be, but if you need me to help throw him off the trail somehow, I'll do my best. And while we're speaking of it, are there any new missions from the higher-ups? What am I doing next?"

Sebastien's eyes flicked away as she tried to think. It was a little too much at once, and she hadn't considered what to do with Damien now that Operation Defenestration was over. She should have known he would be getting restless.

"There is something!" he stated triumphantly. "Just tell me. I might still be a provisional member, but I've proved I'm trustworthy, haven't I? I can be quite useful. Otherwise, I'll just spend the whole break practicing magic, studying, and dueling until I end up surpassing you. And then maybe Professor Lacer will decide to take a second apprentice…"

She was ignoring him by this point, because she'd had an epiphany. "There is a mission," she said, interrupting him. "But I was going to take it myself. It's a ton of work, and will take a very long time."

Damien crossed his arms and thrust his chest out in umbrage. "I can handle a real project."

"The mission is to compile all records of rogue magic incidents that have required the involvement of the Red Guard, within a twenty-kilometer radius of Gilbratha and the last thirty years. Include detailed information noting when the records of the situation before do not exactly match the follow-up report. Also, when someone who hasn't shown signs of 'corrupted Will' is suddenly revealed to have been secretly experimenting with things they shouldn't. And finally, take special note of when the details of any immoral experimentation are vague."

Damien's eyes widened. "Like Newton." It wasn't a question, and she didn't answer it, continuing on with her instructions.

"I imagine you'll be reading a lot of newspapers. Take note of when the explanations are worded the same or extremely similarly. Keep note of the authors of any relevant articles. Note how the Red Guard responded to each incident, and search for patterns." She lifted a finger, the idea for this mission solidifying in her mind as she spoke through it. "Those are the generalities, but as I said, this is a large project. It must be approached in steps. First, and perhaps most tedious, you simply need to make a thorough compilation of all records you can get access to. If you find anything interesting, don't start digging deeper. Just make a note of it for later perusal during the actual research and pattern-finding phases. I'm not sure how much of this kind of thing will be public record. If you can, you may need to use your connection to the coppers to get access to more complete records. Discreetly."

Damien remained silent for a few moments, and then said solemnly, "I accept."

But she was already worried, remembering what had happened to Newton. "This is dangerous, and not just as a hypothetical," she warned. "It might lead to serious consequences for you if the wrong person becomes suspicious. It is *not* safe," she reiterated.

"I understand."

She didn't think he did. How could he, when he didn't know what she knew about the Moore family? "If you dig deep into this, you will almost certainly learn things that are dangerous simply to know. And when I say that, I am not exaggerating. Even worse if you were to somehow let slip any information. Deadly dangerous, horrifyingly dangerous," Sebastien said, putting as much gravitas into her tone as possible as she reached out and squeezed his arm a little too tight. He needed to *understand.*

Damien had gone a little pale, but his jaw was firm. "I can guess at the kind of things I might uncover just from the mission parameters." He spoke in a low murmur, as if they might be overheard despite his earlier precautions. "Newton is the one that triggered the higher-ups' interest? Well, whatever there is to find out, I want to know, too. And if I complete this… It seems like a big enough mission to make me a full member."

He nodded to himself, turning away just in time to miss the dismay that Sebastien knew she hadn't been able to keep from her expression. "Be careful," she said as he opened the stall door.

She hung around awkwardly as he left, wondering if she could take back the mission as she listened to him complain about how someone should really invent luggage with little legs that would follow its owner so one didn't have to lug their belongings around personally. "Or at least *wheels,* damn it," he whined, huffing and puffing until Sebastien had mercy on him and took two of his stuffed-full bags into her own hands.

She watched him ride down the transparent tubes, then turned back to the darkened grounds. There was another thing that she needed to investigate. The first step was finding the few people who had survived the archaeological expedition into the Black Wastes. "The Retreat at Willowdale, hmm?" she murmured aloud.

8

ONE HUNDRED WAYS TO DIE

Sebastien
    Month 3, Day 27, Saturday 3:00 a.m.

Sebastien sat at the head of her dormitory bed, looking through the window. The University was quiet enough to hear the wind. She hadn't realized how much ambient noise thousands of students could add to a place, even at night when they were all supposed to be asleep.

It reminded her of traveling between distant cities with Ennis on roads protected only by man-sized ward stones and the occasional army patrol. When she woke in the dead of night, after the fire had gone out and the howls of wolves and magical beasts sounded too close, so many more stars were visible in the night sky, enough that she might have almost been able to navigate by starlight alone.

Sebastien picked up *100 Clever Ways Thaumaturges Have Committed Suicide* and settled in to pass the time with a few entries. The title was not entirely accurate. Sometimes, "clever" experiments didn't kill the caster but rather the subject of the spell or even completely unrelated innocents who happened to get too close. All told in an almost comically dry tone, about half of the entries within referenced something done during the era of the Blood Empire, notorious for its immoral exploration of magic's furthest reaches.

The other half were from random thaumaturges who thought they'd had an ingenious idea that would revolutionize the world. Many of these ideas were obviously foolish, but somewhat frighteningly, many others seemed almost reasonable. As the title said, "clever."

She picked up where she had left off, a story of an apprentice alchemist, who, dissatisfied with his lot in life, attempted to Sacrifice a potion to empower another potion, believing that, as they were the same type of potion and even brewed as part of the same batch, doing so would simply boost the effects.

'But what would be the point?' Sebastien wondered. *'If he wanted a stronger brew and could produce a minimum of two weaker potions in the same batch, he could have simply altered the alchemical process to make only one significantly stronger potion. Doing so by casting a spell would actually be less efficient, because some part of the original is always lost in Sacrifice. Well, perhaps this was only the initial test—a supposedly safe trial before he moved on to more daring experiments.'*

The apprentice alchemist's attempt led to his immediate death via magical explosion, but according to the book, his theory hadn't been completely wrong, only improperly executed. It was hypothetically possible to Sacrifice a potion to enhance another potion, but the process was complicated, delicate, and dangerous. The book didn't get too far into advanced theory, but apparently rituals involved in alchemy created a kind of self-referential weave of magic based on the components and process of combining them. The magic of the completed potion was not the same as the magic of the individual components beforehand.

Rather than simple addition—one potion plus one potion equals a super potion—it was like trying to combine the threads of two embroidered three-dimensional symbols after the fact. The practice was of little use other than bragging rights over one's theoretical understanding and fine control.

Next came the story of Severin Whilkes, a woman known for developing several modern cosmetic glamours, had decided to experiment with Sacrificing her own fat stores for power. She found initial success, but while demonstrating this feat to a group of her contemporaries, lost control. Rather than mercifully dying, her Will broke, and she became an Aberrant. Most of those in the audience were downed by the experience, but one woman's daughter, a girl of twelve who had not yet begun to practice magic, had fumbled out the battle wand from her mother's purse and used every single fireball spell stored within to kill the Aberrant.

In the process, six women were killed by the Aberrant, which was classified as a Fiend-type as its attack was touch-based and lacked any abstract effects. While using illusions to appear as a young, slender girl, it ate them from the inside, leaving empty bags of skin behind.

Afterward, the investigation used divination to reconstruct an image of the Aberrant from its charred remains. It was nothing more than a huge ball of layered, wrinkled, and sagging flesh peppered with random eyes, mouths, and noses.

'It would be like trying to cast through a Conduit that's been embedded inside your body—possible, but incredibly dangerous. Without the natural barrier of your skin, the only thing containing the magic would be your Will. Any tiny mistake and suddenly you're not just Sacrificing your fat stores but channeling through your own flesh.' This was not one of the particularly clever experiments.

The next entry was about a thaumaturge who lived during the Third Empire—under the reign of the infamous Blood Emperor. The man had attempted to develop a spell that could directly improve one's Will, under the theory that thaumaturges had a magical "core" that could be stimulated externally. After multiple failures that involved the death of his test subjects, he concluded that there was, in fact, no magical core, and no way to directly improve the Will. He tossed that idea aside and decided to develop a spell that would practice magic *for* the subject.

Sebastien didn't need to read the rest of the entry to know how badly this would go, but she continued on, grotesquely fascinated. After even more failures, and the threat of his research being defunded, the thaumaturge decided that the way to do this was to create a spell that could take over the subject entirely, affecting perfect mind, body, and emotional control, as all those were needed to effectively exert the Will.

After the death of even more subjects as he fine-tuned this delicate and powerful spell, he saw initial success, followed by the subjects repeatedly going insane and dying from Will-strain. In addition to the mental strain, exacerbated by whatever was left of the subjects' original personality fighting against the curse he'd forced on them, there was only so much effort a person could exert over a given period of time without hurting themselves.

His efforts, however, did lead to a wave of popularity among the wealthy and influential, who began cursing their "lazy" children with a much milder compulsion to make them more driven to practice. This was, of course, still accompanied by all the associated negative side effects, including debilitating Will-strain, and thankfully outlawed with the fall of the Third Empire and the rise of the Thirteen Crowns.

The next two entries were similar.

In the entry after that, several people over the course of history had tried to Sacrifice a spell array to improve another spell array. This was not simply difficult, like with potions, but impossible, and it invariably led to immediate loss of control of the spell, accompanied by severe backlash.

Spell arrays could, however, reference attached or embedded sub-arrays, often seen in artificery when complex instruction was required. Spell arrays could be incredibly complex and multi-layered, performing sub-functions that fed larger functions. But if you wanted to make your array itself more robust, there was only one way: use better conductive materials, the best being celerium.

The entry after that was worryingly reasonable. A man had the clever idea that Sacrificing things could be used as a direct form of attack.

Sebastien stopped reading, hoping to figure out the dangers on her own, admittedly as a way to soothe her worries that she might try something similarly unsafe without proper consideration. *'This would require one to either be a free-caster, or for the enemy to step into or be close to the spell array's Circle. It would require the caster to be close to or in sight of the enemy. With those restrictions, how would I attack someone else, and conversely defend against such an attack?'*

She wasn't a free-caster, so her enemy would need to be directly within her spell array, but she could lay a trap and lure them into it. The easiest thing to Sacrifice would be the heat within the Circle. She would have to channel that energy into the spell array, and then onto something else, even if that was only forcing the heat to radiate outward.

But her capacity was too low to absorb heat fast enough to cause more than a mild chill. If she could pull the heat directly from the enemy's body, that would be more effective. *'But what about the natural barrier of their skin? Would authority gained within the bounds of the spell array take precedence over that?'* She anticipated it would make things more difficult, at the very least. Against a being with a strong Will of their own, it might make more direct attacks nearly impossible.

If she had some of their blood, that could be bypassed, but then it seemed simpler just to curse them directly. Even Thaddeus Lacer couldn't do something edgy like Sacrificing the heart right out of his enemies' chests.

But above all, before Sebastien made any debilitating progress with such a method, the enemy was likely to just walk out of the Circle.

What if she could draw a spell array around a sleeping enemy? Though if she could do that, again it seemed better to subdue or kill them more directly.

'I could Sacrifice the oxygen in my enemy's lungs. The open pathway to the outside world should negate the skin's barrier, and everyone needs to breathe.' It could be done fast enough to cause confusion and disorientation. If she did that in conjunction with Sacrificing the light, someone might not be able to find their way out before they collapsed. The targeting would need to be precise, and her focus clear, but it seemed plausible.

'How would I defend against something like that?' Immediately, the answer came to her. Just as she had fought over the spell array to spin a metal ball around a circle in Professor Lacer's class, she could fight over control of a spell array surrounding her. She may not have drawn it, but who was to say it, and the area within it, didn't still belong to her? Even if her opponent was stronger, with the right application of surprise and intent, she might be able to make them lose control of the spell. In the worst case scenario, the extra stress

could even cause her opponent's Conduit to shatter. Most people did not carry a handy backup somewhere on their person—and even if they did, she had recently discovered that most people wouldn't have such an easy time using one.

Feeling that she understood the biggest dangers, Sebastien returned to *100 Clever Ways Thaumaturges Have Committed Suicide.*

The man who had inspired this entry hadn't settled for anything so mundane as her ideas. He had a much higher capacity than Sebastien, and thus greater options. He had designed a torture cage of sorts for his ex-wife, also a powerful thaumaturge in her own right. When she entered the bounds of his pre-drawn Circle, he immediately Sacrificed all the air around her, leaving her in a low-temperature, depressurized vacuum, just as Myrddin had postulated filled the space between planets and stars. The air that was Sacrificed powered the barrier, keeping her trapped inside.

Unlike the common misconception, without the conduction and convection of heat facilitated by the atmosphere, the only way to lose heat was through radiation, even at low temperatures. Thus, the man's wife did not immediately turn into a human-shaped icicle.

Sebastien knew this because, for some time as a child, she had dreamed of riding a sky kraken beyond the edge of the world, into space, and had spent a lot of time trying to find solutions for all the ways Grandfather warned she would die. She didn't remember that dream ending. Just, one day it was gone.

Sebastien shook her mind back to the present and the page in front of her.

The absence of pressure was a problem. The woman had tried to hold her breath as the air in her lungs expanded, and ended up rupturing the delicate tissue. The blood in her veins began to boil, essentially causing embolisms— blood vessels being blocked by gas bubbles in the bloodstream.

Without oxygen, her brain immediately began to shut down, and she would have passed out in less than half a minute and died in under two, except for the fact that she was as paranoid as her ex-husband was sadistic. She carried an expensive healing potion at all times, with the bottle's lid spelled with the same modified piercing spell Healer Nidson had used to get Humphries' adapting solution directly into the bloodstream.

Using the overpowered reparative effects, the woman bought herself time, which she used to bombard the spell's barrier with a battle wand while simultaneously wresting control of the spell array from her husband.

He couldn't withstand the dual-sided attack and lost control. The air rushing back in caused the woman more damage, but not enough to overcome the lingering effects of her healing potion.

In the end, she caught him, overpowered and beat him bloody, then dragged him literally kicking and screaming into the spell array he had meant for her. He died approximately two minutes later. There were illustrations to drive home the point.

His ex-wife was questioned and charged with excessive force when retaliating, but as she was now the lover of the town's most influential man, her actions were deemed self-defense and all charges were dropped.

Sebastien set the book down. Fascinating as it was, this was not helping to soothe her anxiety. *'Maybe, just maybe, sitting around in bed reading about everything that can go horribly wrong is making it worse.'*

The sun was not yet rising, but the University grounds were lit, and the streetlamps in the nice areas of town had been on all night. No carriages would be out at this early hour, but she was no stranger to walking, and she still had a key to Dryden Manor.

She arrived quite chilled, closing the front door stealthily behind her and tiptoeing through the dark house up to the guest room set aside as her own. A couple minutes of work got Myrddin's journal out from its hiding place within the stone floor, and she couldn't help but let out a breath of relief upon seeing it. Though she had no particular reason to believe Oliver would suddenly go after her book, or that he even knew where it was, her current lack of trust in him had left her paranoid.

It had been weeks since she received the decryption spells from the secret thaumaturge meetings, but she had been so busy she hadn't made much progress after that first night.

She tried the more standard divination spell first, while she was still mentally fresh. It required her to make an extremely fine alchemical powder, which she sprinkled over and around the book. When she finally cast the actual divination spell, the powder shifted and began to glow, highlighting areas of recent interaction and possible interest. As she had feared, it showed a few of her own fingerprints, as well as drawing attention to the otherwise invisible signs of tampering where she had cut away the binding to search for clues. Nothing seemed like an actual clue toward decrypting it, or any potential password.

She had expected as much and wasn't too disappointed.

The brute-force mathematical decryption came next, which still required a few more hours of work on her part to reduce the power requirements— which she achieved by extending the casting time—and to solidify the Word so that a layman such as herself could understand. In the end, she put an entire stack of notes within one of the component Circles because she couldn't actually fit everything within the spell array scratched onto the floor in chalk.

Finally, she spent the next three hours feeding the spell array a steady stream of energy from a grouped series of candles. Her beast core didn't have the power to last that long, and besides, she wanted to reserve it in case of some future emergency.

It was too much power, and too long spent concentrating, even for her. The book sat there innocently, the glyph on the front shifting as steadily as ever. Once it was clear she was not making any progress, and she could not safely continue, she dropped the spell. She had to close her eyes against a wave of dizziness and nausea as the room spun around her.

The sun was up now, and despite the early hour, she felt almost sick with sheer mental fatigue, as if her thoughts were unmoored.

When the dizziness passed, she stared impassively down at the mess of her latest attempt. It took a while to build up the energy, but eventually she roused herself to clean it all up and hide the book away again. She hesitated before sealing it beneath the floor. *'I cannot take it with me to the University, and I dare not leave it somewhere without wards better than I can cast... Perhaps Liza would be willing to keep it securely?'* Sebastien considered. But she hadn't forgotten Oliver's warning when he first introduced her to Liza. The woman was *trustworthy*, but not *honorable*. Even if she agreed to house something so potentially dangerous, could Sebastien trust her with the temptation?

In the end, she sealed the floor seamlessly over it once again.

As she exited her room and walked down the stairway into the entrance atrium, Oliver turned from the front doorway he had just been about to step through. His eyes widened with surprise.

Simultaneously, they said, "We need to talk."

9

A TROUBLESOME REVELATION

Sebastien
Month 3, Day 27, Saturday 7:30 a.m.

Oliver was in a hurry that morning, rushing off to a meeting with some new business contacts across the city, and so Sebastien joined him in his carriage.

She watched him carefully, trying to divine—metaphorically—his secrets, his thoughts, and his feelings.

As soon as they began rolling, the carriage wheels and horse's hooves clattering against the cobblestones, Oliver spoke. "Titus Westbay, the commander of the coppers, came to visit me."

Sebastien's stomach churned sourly, empty for long enough that it was trying to devour itself. "He paid Damien a visit, too," she said dryly. "Apparently, he made some very interesting accusations."

Oliver cringed and cursed. "By all the greater hells. I swear I did my best to dissuade him."

"What did he say to you?" she asked, keeping her tongue from tripping over itself with hard-won restraint. "Is my identity as Sebastien Siverling compromised?"

Oliver's foot bounced up and down. "No. I've thought a lot about this. My people did good work fabricating your information from the beginning, and from my conversation with Titus…if anything he's a little too convinced that you really are a Siverling."

"What does that mean?"

Oliver coughed with uncharacteristic awkwardness. "Well, it's somewhat convoluted..."

Sebastien had absolutely no patience for prevarication. "Tell me what you spoke of, from the beginning."

Oliver drew himself up, took an excessively deep breath, and spoke rapidly. "First, he accused me of paying your way through the University in exchange for sex. I denied it, but apparently one of his people saw us together on the first night we met, when I intimated that we had been so 'occupied' that we couldn't answer the door for the coppers searching for you. So he accused you of being a prostitute. I was able to convince him that it wasn't you, but ended up trapping myself and had to agree that I have an unfulfilled obsession with you, to the point that I'd hire a prostitute that looks similar."

Sebastien choked on her own saliva and sputtered, wide-eyed, but he continued with the explanation at breakneck speed, reaching into a drawer beneath the seat and taking out a canteen of water which he handed to her as he spoke.

"He asked about how we met, and I said you were an orphan I stumbled across while traveling and then decided to sponsor. But then Westbay started making strange, insinuating comments and giving me a history lesson. Apparently the Siverling name...isn't as innocuous as we thought. Various small clues point to the possibility that King Krell, who ruled before the Blood Emperor, had a daughter who married a Siverling and gave birth to a child who survived the culling. Thus, the Siverling line would be the last surviving blood of the Krell line, and some might say the rightful heir to Lenore."

Sebastien closed her eyes, her head reeling. "You're obsessed with me, and I'm the secret heir of some king from hundreds of years ago?"

"Well, not really an heir. Just the closest equivalent." Oliver raised his hands to stop her response, taking the opportunity for another deep breath. "This isn't as bad as you think! Lord Westbay doesn't actually care about any of that, and most other nobles wouldn't, either. The claim isn't nearly plausible enough to threaten the Thirteen Crowns. In fact, the whole conversation was more of a ploy to try and get a response out of me by insinuating a threat toward you."

Sebastien wondered how this blindsiding blow could get any heavier. "What threat, exactly?"

"Well, that you would be in danger for political reasons...and that you had contact with a Blight-type Aberrant as a child and could be a danger to those around you. I thought he was trying to blackmail you into being bait for the Raven Queen...but in the end, it turns out he was spouting nonsense just to get a rise out of me, to gauge how far I was willing to go for our relationship.

You see, for some reason, I believe he's under the impression that you're trying to seduce his little brother."

Sebastien, who had been trying to settle her scratchy throat with a drink of water, choked again, this time unable to keep herself from spraying it out in a fine mist over her lap. She doubled over coughing until her eyes ran with tears.

Oliver crouched over her with worry, slapping her back.

'If anything, he's just knocking the water back down into my lungs. Just like always, acting like he's helping but actually making it worse.' She waved him off, refocusing her mind on the most important aspect. When she could speak again, she rasped, "He thinks I was infected by a Blight-type?"

Oliver opened his mouth but didn't speak, instead tilting his head to the side.

"When, where, what effects?" she asked, staring at him without blinking despite her watering eyes.

"When you were a baby, the town near Vale that got encapsulated in a sundered zone. Spalding, I think he said? I don't know what the exact effects were, but you shouldn't worry about that accusation. There is no evidence, and even he doesn't actually believe it. He said as much himself."

Sebastien relaxed marginally. Such an infection would be a death sentence, and rightfully so. Luckily, she had no involvement with that incident. "There's no way the anomalous effect wouldn't have spread by now if that were true," she agreed. "Now let's go back to how the last name you chose for me is practically designed to draw attention and trouble from the most powerful people in the country. What a strange coincidence," she said flatly.

Oliver closed his eyes and grimaced. "It's my fault. I didn't pay enough attention when I was picking the name." He opened his eyes, fixing her with a pleading expression. "I thought it was old, vaguely high class, and there would be no living members to protest your existence. It's not like the Siverlings themselves ever had any noble claim, and even if they had, there's nothing beyond rumors that would suggest anyone actually did escape the culling. And even then, even if some remnant did remain, not any longer, after the incident in Spalding."

Sebastien stared at him, contemplating his earnest features. *'What would Oliver gain from me being mistaken for someone with an extremely vague claim to rule Lenore? I suppose, if I were to make a name for myself, with connections like Thaddeus Lacer and the high class students at the University, I might be of use to the kind of revolution he's planning. A "legitimate" icon to endorse his actions, to rally those who care about such things.'* Despite Oliver's denials, this seemed more likely than the alternative—that he had made such a coincidental mistake.

The manipulation, just another secret meant to control her, made her dizzyingly angry. But at the same time, it was almost a relief. Because this was a long-term plan, and it meant he had use for her that didn't require her current meager magical expertise or even the Raven Queen, both of which they had agreed would be best to distance her from.

Sebastien nodded slowly. "Okay."

"Really?" Oliver exhaled, falling back against the seat across from her. "I thought you would definitely be irate."

"Oh, I am," she said with a small quirk of her lips. "I think you'll agree that you owe me a rather large favor to make up for this?"

Oliver let out a breath in a soundless laugh. "Large? I don't think it's—" Seeing her expression, he cut off and nodded rapidly. "Large. Yes, a large favor. That's what I owe you."

Some of her anger seeped into her tone, deepening her voice and sharpening the edges of her words. "Please don't forget. I certainly won't." A large favor from a person like him could be useful, though she wasn't sure she could trust him to actually deliver on his promise. Asking him to take a blood print vow would likely make him suspicious, and she couldn't afford to do that until she knew the truth. Maybe not even then. She took a deep breath, rolling her shoulders back and letting her emotions settle deep inside with a tingle that raised the small hairs across her body.

Oliver shifted uncomfortably under her gaze.

"So Titus Westbay is suspicious of me and has been digging into my background and interrogating or threatening those close to me. Did he learn anything that we actually do need to be worried about? What if he goes searching for Sebastien Siverling's nonexistent childhood?"

Oliver nodded. "That is the point that's most concerning. When we spoke, there were no hints that he knew about either of our less-than-legal activities. Or at least not that our current identities had anything to do with those activities or the people behind them. I don't think he has anything on either of us. But if he were to really go digging, he might find that no one remembers Sebastien Siverling, talented orphan with the white-blonde hair. There's only so much that faked records can do."

"But there's nothing magic cannot do. Perhaps you could send someone to plant a few memories." It couldn't be harder than erasing memories, and she had seen the effects of that spell first-hand.

Oliver raised his eyebrows. "Is that actually possible? I don't think Liza can do that. It certainly would have come in handy a few times so far, if so. I have no contacts with such a skill. Perhaps more reasonably, we should come up with a believable story. We need to be proactive without being visibly *reactive*. Too much fuss could make us seem guilty, like ants scrambling around after their hill was kicked."

"A reason that I have no memorable ties to this world," she mused.

"Rather depressing, isn't it?"

"Not at all. My Will, it will tie me firmly to this world long after even memories have turned to dust."

Oliver was silent for a moment, then shook himself as if the chill air had seeped into his body. "That is quite bleak, even for you." He turned around and pounded a fist against the ceiling area behind the driver to signal the carriage to stop. "There's a meat pie stall that opens quite early," he explained. "You're beginning to look gaunt, Sebastien. Have you been eating enough?"

"Three meals a day at the University cafeteria," she replied succinctly.

"And is that enough for you? How much time do you spend casting compared to the other first-term students? And you're quite tall. Maybe still growing, even."

"I'm fine," she assured him, irritated by his badgering.

'Could I be still growing?' She had no idea about the biological age of Sebastien Siverling's body, but she knew that some men could have a final growth spurt as late as twenty or twenty-one.

Oliver looked pointedly down at her hands. "Your fingers are trembling, Sebastien. When was the last time you had a proper meal? And if I had to guess, you got at most a few hours' sleep last night. At worst, none at all. You realize that this, too, increases your need for sustenance?"

Her fingers were indeed trembling—faint tremors that she hadn't even noticed. *'Hunger, or withdrawal?'* she wondered. *'Surely enough time has passed that it shouldn't be withdrawal? I even took that detoxifying potion to deal with lingering side effects.'* But even as she thought that, she acknowledged how wonderful even a tiny speck of the beamshell tincture would feel at that particular moment. It would make everything so much easier, if she just had its lightning-bright energy crackling through her. *'But I don't need it,'* she told herself firmly. *'My Will is enough.'*

Still, as soon as she got the meat pie in her hands, the scent summoned cramps through her stomach and flooded her mouth with so much saliva she felt nauseated for a moment.

Oliver tossed a few extra coins to the stall owner as payment for the tins the pies were cooked in so that they didn't need to stay and eat.

Sebastien ate quickly, stuffing herself until her cheeks bulged out as Oliver spoke, mannerly enough not to speak with his own mouth full.

He explained his conversation with Titus in more detail, then moved on to solutions. Surprisingly, he had already come up with a feasible backstory for her. He'd had several days to worry and think about this already, after all. His version wasn't too different from her real history—sans Ennis—and had just enough detail to seem realistic while being vague enough to stay hard to verify. It only needed to be adjusted slightly for anything she might have mentioned about her life as Sebastien.

She shook her head quickly and swallowed. "I don't talk about my past, or my childhood. Anything that I've mentioned would be vague at best, and nothing should contradict." If someone was truly determined to find fault, even the best backstory wouldn't stop them. She finished her second pie and washed it down with more water from the canteen.

With a small smile, Oliver handed her his own second meat pie. "I already ate some toast before leaving," he said.

Sebastien was halfway through it before realizing that Oliver had lied. Sharon hadn't yet arrived at work when they had left, and Sebastien's room was close to the kitchen's ceiling. She thought she would have heard if Oliver were puttering around below her. Sebastien took another vicious bite, uncaring. This was the least he could do for her. "I think I should go on the offensive rather than let Titus continue whatever digging he's doing behind the curtains."

"What do you propose?"

"I'm going to request a meeting. It's a reasonable response from someone who finds out a person has been digging into their backstory and trying to malign their character with those close to them. It would probably be stranger if I just ignored it."

Oliver nodded thoughtfully. "It wouldn't fit your persona."

Sebastien snorted around the last bite of crispy crust.

"What about Thaddeus Lacer's request for an audience?" Oliver murmured. "Do you want me to turn him down, since the Raven Queen will be lying low?"

Sebastien stilled, swallowed, and slowly shook her head. "No. I'll handle it."

"What are you going to do?"

"I'm...not sure yet," she admitted. It was risky, but his request felt like an opportunity she couldn't afford to let go. At the worst, Lacer probably wouldn't turn her in. And if, somehow, things went well, he could be the kind of ally that even Oliver Dryden couldn't match. Really, the risk lay in her uncertainty about what he wanted from her.

But she had decided to stop allowing things to happen *to* her. In the same way she could preemptively prepare for disaster, Sebastien would aggressively confront both secrets and threats. For what felt like the first time in a long time, she would take control.

And once she had it, she would never let go.

10

FOR THE HIGH CROWN

SEBASTIEN
Month 3, Day 27, Saturday 8:15 a.m.

WHEN OLIVER ARRIVED at his destination, he offered to have the carriage drive Sebastien back, but she declined.

With the map of the city that she'd attempted to memorize, she was able to find the nearest post office, where they had letter-writing stations and would deliver one's post to anywhere in the country—for a fee. It was the kind of thing she couldn't have afforded before coming to Gilbratha. Not that she had anyone to write, anyway. She and Ennis had traveled so frequently, she had learned early on not to get too attached.

She could only rely on herself.

At the mail office, Sebastien wrote two letters on the nicest paper they had to offer. One to Titus Westbay, and one to the Retreat at Willowdale. To the treatment center, she introduced herself and tried to seem like a bleeding-heart type who cared deeply even for those she'd never met. She wanted to visit and spend time with the long-term patients, as she'd read in a recent study—which she cited—that normalizing their lifestyle and interactions with others could help to ease disturbed minds. She could read to them.

To Titus Westbay, she was more succinct.

Finally, she bought two of the most popular local papers and took them to a room at a cheap inn nearby. '*It's good to shake up my normal routine. Especially because now I know someone might be having me watched.*'

Within the privacy of the rented room, she put together a third message using letters cut from the newspapers, with the mending spell joining the letters to the page in a coherent, neat order, much better than trying to paste them on by hand. When she was finished, she folded the message inside a thick envelope and cast the shedding-disintegration spell on the whole thing so that it couldn't possibly be used against her.

The envelope was addressed, in big block letters from the newspapers' titles, "For the High Crown."

She considered using a messenger to deliver it, or even just sending it from the local mail office, but either would find such an envelope strange, and both would want to see her face, which could lead an investigator back to her. Either method seemed likely to get her reported by some suspicious do-gooder, but spending fifty gold on a Lino-Wharton raven messenger was too much. She might have more monetary leeway now, but throwing gold around with no assurance of a return on her investment would lead her right back into poverty.

Then she thought of simply delivering the message to Harrow Hill herself, perhaps taking advantage of a late-night shift change and affixing the envelope conspicuously near the entrance. She had been halfway through an elaborate plan to avoid being tracked by dogs or prognos after the fact, which would have required more research into anti-divination spells, some battle philtres, and a winding, two-hour walk through the nighttime city, when she realized there was a simpler solution.

All she needed was a trustworthy messenger to send it on her behalf. One who knew not to ask questions.

Normally, Sebastien would go to Oliver about such a thing, or even Katerin, but she didn't want him to know. He had been interested in facilitating her meeting with the Architects of Khronos, but that had been for his own gain. The High Crown was an enemy to Oliver in truth, and she doubted he would take kindly to any plans to negotiate with the man. Oliver had never wanted her to give up her copy of Myrddin's journal.

So Sebastien kept the letter to the High Crown and sent a runner to someone else—with a very different note. After taking the time to eat lunch, she found an artisan who could create something specific for her, in lieu of her destroyed seaweed paper tome. Back at the winding, narrow street of the Night Market, she bought another dowsing artifact and a used but high-end battle wand, since her last two had been confiscated by the coppers. With the license from Professor Lacer, it was no longer illegal for her to carry. All that plus a dramatic dress made of velvet that was only wearing thin in a few places cost her almost one hundred gold, with the battle wand being the most expensive. Now, she could afford such an expense. As long as Oliver's textile business continued, more would come at steady intervals. This was the kind of necessary purchase that could definitely save her life.

All the time, she watched for a tail, but couldn't quite relax even when she found none. Many of the things she had used to transform into Silvia weren't safe anymore, but the experience had taught her how useful some simple aids could be to disguise her identity—even in her original body—and so she picked up more makeup and a few cosmetic items.

Back in her cheap one-day room, she continued preparations. The new dress she dyed a deep scarlet that edged on black. When the sun had begun to slide over the horizon, she transformed into Siobhan and dressed herself as Silvia, with pastel-colored clothes and lips, a few carefully applied wrinkles around her eyes and mouth, and a sweet smile. She even lightened her hair to a softer brown. Examining herself in the mirror was like looking at yet another stranger. All her colors seemed to match each other in tone. *'If I were photographed, I would blend into a nondescript middle grey.'* Only her eyes stood out, but those would be hidden by the evening darkness.

She left openly, walking without haste with her senses tuned for any hint of pursuit. Halfway to her destination, she stopped at a different inn and changed into the Raven Queen's outfit: no wrinkles, hair a blue-black that shimmered like a raven's wing and sprouted feathers, the dark dress, and lips painted dark enough to match it, as if she had been feasting on the corpse of her prey. She tried a smile, and it looked sinister and savage. Her pitch-dark eyes fit so much better in this face. It all disappeared under the shadow of a cloak with a deep hood.

From there, she activated her new dowsing artifact to search for a piece of velvet from her dress and thus utilize the divination-diverting ward's side effects. This dowser was nicer than her last and had a few different power settings. The strongest would empty its charge faster but also do a better job of hiding her, should it become necessary.

Finally, with a deep breath, Siobhan crawled out of the window, having unfortunate flashbacks to her first day in Gilbratha. She had fallen backward off the wall of that rundown inn after sneakily retrieving her items from the room Ennis had rented, landing on her pack and knocking the wind from her lungs.

This time, at least, she made it to the ground safely. The night was chilly, but her purpose warmed her.

As she had promised in the note sent earlier by runner, she walked up to the front gate of Lord Lynwood's mansion, where a guard was stationed in front of the wrought iron metal.

The man didn't notice her until she was directly in front of him, only the bars between them. When he did, he reeled back in shock, but recovered with impressive alacrity. He bowed deeply to her, one hand pressed to his chest, where his heart must have been pounding. "Welcome, Queen of Ravens. We are honored that you grace us with your presence." Without even looking up, he fumbled with the gate's latch and pulled it open for her with a grating creak of unoiled hinges.

As Siobhan entered, he waved her toward the front door, peeking at the darkness under her hood despite his obvious inclination to look away. "I am Wilbur Johnson, my queen. I cannot tell you how overjoyed I am to meet you in person. I burn incense to you every evening, and write down all I remember of my dreams every morning. Each Sunday, I feed the ravens in the park. Fresh white bread, fruit, and raw meat."

They had reached the front door, so she stopped, turning to him with a raised brow that he couldn't see past her cloak. *'What in the greater hells is he talking about?'*

He opened the door for her, continuing to babble. "Yesterday, my efforts bore fruit. I was able to come awake while dreaming for the first time. I prayed for your guidance, but I woke too quickly."

"Come awake while dreaming?" she asked, stepping inside.

"Yes. I have been training. There is a dream-shaman in the neighborhood that preaches the methods."

Gera rounded the corner at a fast walk at that exact moment. Siobhan immediately felt the increased pressure on her ward, as she always did in the woman's presence.

The prognos woman's single large eye was tight with worry, despite its sightlessness, and she stopped a few feet from Siobhan and Wilbur, mimicking his earlier bow. "Mr. Johnson, did I not warn you about delaying our guest? Back to your station at once!"

The man hesitated, but Gera had already turned her attention to Siobhan, gesturing for her to lead the way down the hall. "Is the drawing room acceptable?"

Siobhan agreed wordlessly, somewhat reluctantly leaving this Wilbur and his talk of waking dreams behind to take the same path she remembered from her previous visit.

Unlike the last time, the drawing room was empty except for a couple of servants. Neither one would meet her eyes, both staring studiously at the floor.

"Lord Lynwood will not be joining us, I take it?" Siobhan asked.

Gera flinched. "My apologies. He is on a trip at the moment, and we were not able to retrieve him on such short notice. But your message did not specify that you required his attendance. I am happy to discuss whatever brings you here, my lady."

Nodding idly, Siobhan took a seat in one of the ornate, plush armchairs furthest from the fire and pulled back her hood to reveal her face. Gera offered her food and drink from prepared platters, or anything else that the servants might be able to retrieve for her, but Siobhan refused with a wave of her hand.

Gera hesitated, then sat across from her, her back straight and her hands primly cupping her knees. "I believe we are even," she said.

Siobhan tilted her head to the side in a silent question.

"I know that you saved my subordinate, just as I saved Sebastien Siverling."

Siobhan was careful to keep the confusion from showing on her face. She didn't remember saving anyone, but thought it probably wasn't a good idea to admit as much. Gera's subordinate had probably been saved coincidentally while there was a raven around or something. If Gera knew, then maybe Siobhan *would* owe her. "I agree," Siobhan said. "We are even."

Gera deflated an inch or so with obvious relief.

"I came to see if you would like to enter into another agreement. Well, two, actually. Each optional, one simpler than the other," Siobhan said.

Gera tensed again. "I am listening, my lady. Please, speak freely."

"Send your servants away. This is a sensitive matter, and I have come to doubt their ability to keep their tongues still." Gera grimaced and apologized but complied immediately, and Siobhan continued. "I have a letter that I need delivered, discreetly. To the High Crown."

Gera hesitated. "Is that…all? Does it need to be left on his pillow, or in his pocket, or in his daughter's crib or something?"

Siobhan forced down an incredulous laugh, responding in a serious tone. "No. I simply need him to read it."

Gera seemed more surprised than relieved. Was the woman actually disappointed? "I…can manage that."

"Good." Siobhan ran a forefinger delicately over the shell of her ear, drawing attention to the feathers sprouting seamlessly from her hair. "Secondly, I need a thaumaturge who is both powerful and discreet. This could be you personally, or someone trustworthy under your command. This person would cast a certain spell at a certain time. It will draw extreme attention to their location, and they will need to escape without being caught. If they are caught, they will likely be arrested and questioned in connection with my own actions. It is a dangerous task, but should be easy enough if the person is competent."

"What is the spell they would cast?"

Siobhan suspected Gera was coming up with some strange ideas. "It is a simple enough spell that I would teach them myself. It is not harmful to either the caster or those nearby. In fact, its purpose is specifically to draw a certain kind of attention."

Gera's blind gaze was strangely penetrating. "Drawing attention away from you?"

"Well, more or less. The caster would be placed at a remote location, with prepared escape routes, and if you wish, guards. It will draw the eyes of the entire city."

Gera nodded to herself. "I could do this. Would you owe me a debt?"

"Not an unspecified one. I have a particular boon in mind. In return for these two favors, I have a new spell that could benefit Millennium. You mentioned that his visions continue to grow stronger as he matures, and spells that once worked to allow him sleep become less useful. There may be a time when the current solution ceases to work. I am developing a spell that allows one to trade their sleep to another, without harm or consequence. It should entirely, and safely, eliminate Millennium's current problems, independent of the increasing strength of his visions. It could allow him to reach full maturity, no matter how many years that takes. By then, his mental and magical strength should have grown enough to handle the visions even during sleep."

Gera's eye had grown wider as Siobhan explained.

Siobhan paused, the flickering light of the fireplace warming one half of her face while the other sat in cool shadow. "Of course, if you do not want access to this spell, you need not accept."

Gera hesitated. "I am interested. But is it necessary for me to decide on the boon right away? It is possible that what you have already done for him will be enough."

Siobhan remained silent for a while too long, partially as a way to show her displeasure. Finally, when the air was as thick as honey and the fine hairs on Gera's arms had risen, she said, "I do not agree to owe unspecified favors. If you choose no particular boon, you may still do me a favor, but I would be the one to decide how to repay it. You may not enjoy the results."

"I will choose the sleep spell," Gera said quickly.

Siobhan smiled and roughly outlined the details of her plan, including the date.

None of it helped Gera to relax, but the woman seemed determined. "I will take on this task myself. I do not wish there to be any ambiguity."

Siobhan gave the barest of smiles. She stood, pulling out a piece of red wax from her pocket and using it to draw a spell array on the surface of the low table between them. "Are you familiar with summoning magic?"

"I dare not say I am."

"This spell is simple. Even a child could cast it, at low power." She explained it once and then had Gera repeat the instructions and intent to her, which the woman did with the same eager nervousness many students showed in front of Professor Lacer.

Siobhan, feeling that their business was settled, sat back. "How is Miles doing? I wondered if I might check up on him."

Before Gera could reply, a thump sounded from one of the cabinets on the far side of the room.

Both women startled, and Siobhan stood with her Conduit gripped firmly in one hand, and the other ready to retrieve her new battle wand from her boot, where she had tucked it before coming. It was charged with an impressive thirteen charges of the standard three offensive spells—stunners, concussive blasts, and slicing spells.

A small boy spilled out of the cabinet.

"Miles!?" Gera said, clutching her chest. She looked fearfully at Siobhan and then back to her son.

Siobhan relaxed, her lips twitching with amusement.

Millennium's skin shone faintly golden, subtle enough to be from the application of a shimmering lotion, but she knew it was a result of his fey heritage. His undertone was less sallow than the last time she'd seen him. His eyes were bright and alert, and even as she watched, a bright flush rose up from his neck and turned his whole face red.

He clasped his hands in front of him and looked down at the ground. "I apologize for my dishonorable actions." With a quick peek up at Siobhan, his flush grew redder, and he bowed even more deeply.

Siobhan's lips twitched harder, and she stopped trying to hold back her smile. "Rise. I am not angry over this little bit of mischief."

Gera was visibly doubtful, but perhaps she could sense Siobhan's amusement, because after a moment she released her grip on the cloth over her heart. She glared at her son, fear giving way to anger at his misbehavior. Still, she held herself back from scolding him.

Rising from his bow, Miles examined Siobhan's face, and his own broke into a wide smile. "I'm very glad to meet you again. I have been hoping you would visit!"

"If you plan to secretly gather information in the future," Siobhan said, "you might do better to use a stealth or reconnaissance spell than to hide in a cupboard."

"Is that an offer? Will you teach me a stealth spell?" he asked shyly, as eager as Theo often was but with an entirely different manner.

Siobhan calculated his age. Based on appearance, he might be ten or so, but prognos and cambions both matured more slowly than humans. And chronic lack of sleep could have stunted his growth. "Are you already learning magic?" she asked.

"I have been meditating to strengthen my mind and prepare my Will for casting. I started out with a candle flame as a focus, but I like using a wind reed much better." Struggling to meet her gaze from a combination of shyness and her ward, he held his arm out with a suave flourish that somehow reminded Siobhan of Lord Lynwood. "If I might invite you on a tour of my home? I would love to show you our interesting things and, um, get you caught up on what's transpired since your last visit."

Gera let out a strangled noise and gave a tiny shake of her head.

Miles glared at her, then immediately smiled at Siobhan, his expressions shifting like sand. "It's only proper to give guests a tour."

Siobhan wasn't sure whether Gera simply didn't want her spending time with her son or if the woman was hiding something she feared Miles might reveal. "It would be my pleasure," she said.

The boy shuffled over to her, then gestured for her to walk with him. "We'll go to my room first," he said in a soft voice. His room was on the second floor, with a balcony overlooking the inner courtyard and gardens.

Gera followed behind them but didn't enter or speak.

Miles introduced Siobhan to a few of his more interesting toys and belongings, including an hourglass of euphonic sand that made a pleasant tinkling as the grains fell against each other, and a vial of scent that smelt very pleasantly of ozone and sleep. He smiled proudly when she said so. "My uncle and I made it together. It took a long time to get just right."

Under his mattress, a huge spell array was carved into the floor. "That's what the Pack thaumaturges use to help me sleep. At first, it was a little creepy to have them standing over me every night, but I got used to it, and the scent helps me relax and feel safe. But it would be better if someone would sleep with me."

At the doorway, Gera raised her fingers delicately to her lips, frowning.

"Ah, I know just the thing for that," Siobhan said. "All you need is a leather flask filled with hot water and a pillow with the right shape."

Millennium's eyes widened with curiosity. "I only have rectangular pillows, though?"

"Well, you will need a few, then. Three at least. You can attach them together like this," she said, demonstrating the shape with the pillows on his bed. "Two for your back and legs, and one to wrap around you like an arm. You put the hot water flask inside the one at your back or feet, and go to sleep like you're being hugged."

"Whooah," Miles exclaimed, his eyes even wider. He turned to Gera. "Mother, I need you to get someone to make a hugging pillow for me as soon as possible."

She sighed. "I will set your nanny to the task."

Miles took Siobhan to the garden after that, where small paths were lined with soft-glowing lamps and servants watched them furtively from the back porch and through the mansion's windows. Gera trailed further behind, in sight but at the edge of hearing. Siobhan recognized several of the garden's plants as useful spell components, most mundane but a few magical, which required a permit. "This is my favorite place," Miles explained solemnly.

"Especially at night, when the city gets quieter. I can almost hear the heart-beat of Gilbratha itself, underneath all the clamor."

They sat on an ornately carved stone bench, both listening silently for minutes on end. The moon was almost exactly half full, and hung above the edge of the white cliffs, mostly obscured by clouds.

Finally, Miles murmured, "I can hear them gossiping about you, you know."

She hummed. "And what do they say?"

"Everyone has all these crazy ideas about you. Some of our people have been lighting incense to you on little altars. My nanny is one of them, even though I told her you can't hear her even if she calls your name three times in the dark. You can't, right?"

"I cannot," Siobhan agreed.

"And you can't curse people with nightmares of their greatest fear? They say you enter the dreams of those who offend you, and when you kill them there, their hearts stop in real life from fear. That's not true, right?"

"I have never killed someone like that," she agreed.

"But *could* you?"

Siobhan hesitated. She knew quite a lot about sleep and dream magic. She was sure she could put together a curse that caused someone to have night-mares if she really wanted. "I don't think they would die from fear unless their heart was already quite weak."

"My mother thinks you're dangerous. But I told her you're way nicer than people think. They're just scared because you like the dark and you look a little strange." He gestured to his ears, indicating the feathers. "My mother says you're a black hole of nothingness, like a scar walking through the world. She says I'm never to make any promises to you, or ask for any favors. I think she's worried if you like me too much, you'll steal me away to go live with you. Or maybe eat me."

Siobhan raised a wry eyebrow. "That does seem excessive."

"She's irrational. But she won't listen to me when I tell her you're not dangerous."

"I would not agree that I am harmless, but neither am I the hazard many people seem to think. And I do not eat little boys," she said with a small smile, poking him in the side.

He smiled brightly for a moment but quickly grew serious. "But being associated with you can still be dangerous, right?"

Siobhan was surprised. After a moment of hesitation, she said, "Yes, I suppose so."

"They may be lies, but ideas have power," Miles murmured.

She nodded slowly, standing from the bench to look up at the stars, visible through a gap in the clouds. "They do. And if you tell a lie enough times, it becomes the truth." She turned to wave at him, then reached into the expensive, enchanted replacement satchel she'd bought after losing her last one. She increased the power output of her dowsing artifact until the force was enough that she needed to actively empower her divination-diverting ward.

Miles's eyes tried to track her but quickly wandered away and did not return.

Siobhan walked further into the garden, reaching the shadows of the surrounding stone wall. When she was sure that she was unobserved, she walked back to the wrought-iron gate at the front. Wilbur the guard was still there, watching the street. She considered speaking up and startling him, but eyeing the space between the gate's bars, she had an idea.

Moving slowly, she put her head through first, and then angled the rest of her body sideways. It was a bit of a squeeze, but she slipped through easily enough, and her bag of supplies followed. She pressed a hand to her waist, feeling for her ribs. They didn't exactly stand out, ridge by ridge, but there was little padding over them. Perhaps Oliver had been right, and she had lost a little weight.

Still unobserved by the gate guard, she slunk away.

11

EXPERIMENTING ON HUMANS

Siobhan
Month 3, Day 28, Sunday 8:00 a.m.

Siobhan had taken the time to put on a full face of makeup, which she had learned from watching Ana create her own natural-seeming look in the morning. It was soft and feminine, much like Siobhan's dress, a bright pastel green with flowery lace and skirts with too much fabric. She had colored her hair a dark auburn, with the grey streaks looking like sun-kissed highlights instead. The larger prosthetic nose remained, holding up a pair of fake glasses —wire-framed, large, and round, making her look somewhat like an owl. Fake wrinkles framed her eyes, but she wished now that she had bought another set of colored contact lenses after all. This disguise was meant for the light of day and would bear more scrutiny.

Making a mental note to correct this oversight, she left the room she had rented in Gilbratha's largest hotel, leaving the building from a different entrance than she had entered from. With so much traffic and so many people visiting the city at this time of year, no one would be able to watch all the entrances or keep track of who should and shouldn't be there.

Siobhan took a carriage to a somewhat rundown business hotel, which had once been in Morrow territory and was now owned by the Verdant Stags. Liza was already waiting in a large conference room on the third floor, bossing around a few of the hotel employees. She looked quite frazzled from the effort of setting the room up for their experiments. The large meeting table had been pushed up against one wall, its spot replaced by empty floor space for the spell arrays and bird cages—still unoccupied at the moment.

The large table held some of the supplies they would be using, including a new, larger diagnostic artifact. Another smaller table against the shorter wall by the door held bowls and plates—for the food they would supply their test subjects as part of the enticement for joining.

Chairs were being laid out in rows on the far side of the room, along with a few cots for emergency use, and Liza was directing the workers about where to place various other items, including what looked to be school workbooks, puzzles, and dozens of paper-filled binders.

To Siobhan's surprise, several people sporting the dirty and ragged look of the homeless and destitute were milling about near the still unfilled food table, looking awkward and unsure. She and Liza had planned that actual testing wouldn't start until Wednesday or later. *'Why are these people here already?'*

Liza waved Siobhan over, eyeing the modified appearance. "Good work. Silvia, is it?" This was the first time Liza had seen Siobhan in this particular disguise, but they had discussed the plan beforehand.

Siobhan nodded, glancing questioningly toward the people milling about.

"I only put out word and a few fliers yesterday, but some of them are rather eager," Liza explained. "They found the address and caused a bit of a fuss with the hotel employees. When I arrived this morning, the hotel was trying to throw them out, causing an argument in the lobby."

"Too much attention," Siobhan said.

"Yes, so I brought them up. I thought, perhaps if we work quickly enough, we can get this small batch of test subjects started early. We'll have to provide their meal for the afternoon and evening, but I've already ordered a simple soup and some loaves of bread from the hotel kitchen. In the meantime, start conducting the intake interviews."

Siobhan had been initially skeptical of Liza's claim that they were ready to move on to human testing already. The book Professor Lacer had recommended to her about the proper way to run an experiment said that testing on animals should take months, or possibly years, and go through hundreds of test subjects, at minimum. They had completed dozens of tests, with Liza completing many of them on her own, but probably less than two hundred.

However, Siobhan wasn't prepared to wait for years. Everything had been going so well, with no cases of failure or unforeseen side effects. And so, she hadn't protested.

By the time a meal had been brought up and served, Siobhan had interviewed the first handful of volunteer test subjects, run them through the fancy diagnostic artifact, and recorded all their baseline information. During that same time, Liza had set up the spell array within a curtained-off section of the room and shooed all the nosy hotel employees out. "Don't want them stealing any of our secrets," she said, locking the door after them, though Siobhan knew that really, Liza didn't want to take the chance that any of them would find some aspect of the spell suspicious. Then she left and returned shortly afterward with a cage full of sedated, already enhanced ravens.

Some of their human test subjects were quite nervous. While they shied away from Liza with her barked orders and gimlet-eyed stare, most seemed more comfortable with Silvia, the pretty assistant with the fluffy dress and pink-painted lips.

A woman with a name tag reading "Jane" murmured surreptitiously, leaning into Siobhan. "Do you know about what magic spell she's going to be casting on us? Is it going to hurt? Or leave us with strange boils? I heard stories about one o' them alchemy stores making a new hand cream they wanted tested. It was supposed to make you as soft as a baby's bottom, but instead it made all the skin just peel right off, leavin' people raw and bloody."

Awkwardly, Siobhan smiled with her best expression of sympathy and patted Jane's hand. "It's nothing like that. This spell has been tested on animals already, and shown to be safe. You shouldn't feel any pain at all, and there will definitely be no scarring or…boils."

Another man, who had introduced himself as Kriffer, no last name, piped up with a wise tone. "I heard they're going to keep us awake until we start seeing hallucinations, like old Williams who's got the 'non-somnia.'"

"But we get a bed and three meals a day the whole time, until the hallucinations start? Plus three gold payment?" a third person asked. "That doesn't sound so bad. I'll take a long nap when it's finished and wake up with enough money to rent a bed in one of the boarding houses. It'll last me long enough to get a real job, maybe."

"But what if the hallucinations don't stop?" Jane asked anxiously. "I don't want to get non-somnia like old Williams."

Siobhan raised her hand to stop the conversation before it could devolve further. "I believe old Williams has *in*-somnia. And—"

Kriffer was shaking his head. "No, that can't be right. 'Cause 'somnia' means sleep, and 'non' means not. So non-somnia means 'not-sleeping.' In-somnia would mean 'inside-sleep,' which just doesn't make any sense. But even if you look at it sideways that would still mean he's always sleeping." He squinted at her as if he was skeptical that she was smart enough to understand him. "And old Williams *can't* sleep. Besides, have you ever even met him? How would you know?"

Siobhan blinked a couple times, took a deep breath to refute Kriffer no-last-name from his foundational misconception all the way up, and then let it out again with a big sigh. Arguing with someone like him was useless. "In any case," she said, "this spell doesn't forcefully keep you awake. It just keeps you so...*healed* that you don't get tired very quickly. When the test ends, you might be a little extra tired for a day or so, and then everything will go back to normal."

Jane seemed skeptical. "But you made us sign those papers saying we wouldn't try to sue you if something went wrong, and we can't talk about what happens here, even to the coppers."

"That does *not* mean we believe something will go wrong," Siobhan said firmly. Her smile was becoming more and more difficult to maintain, so she let it drop entirely. "It's just standard procedure. Besides, the contract also mentions that if something does go wrong, we'll pay your medical bills. That would include regrowing your skin, dealing with any boils, or teaching your brain how to sleep again."

That seemed to mollify the whole group.

"As long as it's our spell at fault," Siobhan continued, "Which you would have to prove."

Kriffer scowled, grumbling something about them being stingy, but the conversation seemed to have reassured the others. When she asked for a volunteer to go first, Kriffer eventually stepped forward. "Let's just get this over with."

Liza checked over the paperwork Siobhan had filled out for the man, then waved him over to the spell array. This one was significantly simpler than the one in her house, without as many sub-arrays, since most of the steps had already been completed.

The ravens, already boosted, were gathered in cages behind another curtain and inside the effects of an active healing spell. Only the binding of man and raven remained.

Kriffer stepped past the dividing line of the curtains and into the Circle of black salt gingerly, then sank down to sit cross-legged in the middle, on Liza's command.

"We don't want you getting startled or dizzy and falling over when this starts," Liza explained.

Kriffer swallowed hard, his eyes darting around as if expecting danger to rush in from some unexpected direction. When he was presented with the blindfold and waxen earplugs, his apprehension only grew, but Siobhan did her best to reassure him. "It's to keep our spell design from being leaked, just in case," she explained. "You might feel a pricking or poking sensation on your hand during the process, but don't worry, that's normal. When you feel a tap on your shoulder, that means we're done, and you just need to take a deep breath. And, if you can, think about gratefully accepting this healing."

The mandrake pot was in place, and when Kriffer was blindfolded and deaf, they placed the sedated sleeper raven, the preserved raven's egg, and the beast core that would power it all.

Together, Siobhan and Liza cooperated to cast the spell, their Wills swirling through the spell array, channeling thrumming power and plucking at the strings of reality.

Kriffer tensed up as Liza poked him with the needle to retrieve a tiny dot of blood, but relaxed with an expression of pleasant surprise at the ease and lack of pain when she moved on almost immediately.

Liza moved with dancer-like grace, dragging the incense made of elcan iris pollen and the mixed blood through the air, leaving behind trails of smoke in the shape of glyphs as she whispered the chant they had created to help solidify and anchor the Word that would guide its effect. Siobhan could only do her best to match her.

Even after the dozens of iterations on lesser creatures, which had allowed both Liza and Siobhan to become more familiar with the spell—and for the magic itself to grow marginally less wild—casting this spell on a human was much more difficult. Even Liza seemed to feel the strain, her curls springing up and frizzing out and her temples and upper lip beading with sweat. Her voice was tense with effort as they spoke the chant together, their voices little more than a murmur.

Luckily, it was over quickly, with Liza waving the last of the incense around Kriffer and the raven in a final circle. Siobhan tapped Kriffer on the shoulder and said, "Take a deep breath," though he shouldn't be able to hear her.

Both Kriffer and the raven complied, and it was done.

Kriffer's breath caught on his exhale, and he got halfway through a gasp before breaking into a coughing fit.

Siobhan and Liza both hurried forward anxiously. "What's wrong?" Siobhan snapped.

"He can't breathe!" Liza said. "I've got an airway-clearing philtre on the supply table."

Siobhan spun to retrieve the philtre as Liza tried to make Kriffer lie down. "I don't understand why this is happening. Some reaction to the smoke, maybe?"

Siobhan returned, dropping to her knees beside Kriffer and prying at the philtre's cork stopper, but stilled as Kriffer waved them off, his coughing devolving into deep laughter.

"I'm fine, I'm fine!" he called. He took a deep breath, then threw back his head to face the ceiling as a huge smile spread across. "I was just…surprised. Choked myself by accident. Is it okay for me to stand up now?"

Liza scowled at him, her fingers twitching as if she longed to strangle him. "As long as you are sure you're having no trouble breathing or other negative symptoms."

Kriffer literally hopped to his feet, taking some deep breaths and moving his limbs experimentally. "I feel really good, actually. Like…like I've got money in my pocket and a pretty girl on my arm, and we're off to see a street show. Like watching the sun rise from the roof of the tallest house in the neighborhood. You said this is a healing spell? Myrddin's balls, I must have been sick before or something, because I feel *great.*"

He started laughing, then took big, careful steps out of the Circle and threw back the curtain with a flourish before ripping off his blindfold and popping out the earplugs. "Nothing to be afraid of at all!" he called to the others. "No boils, no hallucinations, no missin' skin! It feels like the time my grandma took me to one of those fancy cafes for my twelfth birthday and I got a cup of coffee from fresh beans ground on the spot. Except better. Like kissin' a siren."

Jane harrumphed. "You've never kissed a siren!" she declared, but she stepped up to the curtain eagerly. "I'll go next."

When the spell took hold of her, she reacted more calmly than Kriffer. "It really is…quite nice. How long will it last?" she asked.

"Three days, maybe," Liza said. "That's part of what we're testing." Turning her back with a mischievous smile, she added, "Please let us know when the hallucinations start."

Siobhan glared at Liza, then had to spend the next few minutes reassuring Jane and the others that the taciturn older woman really had been just joking. But despite the annoyance, Siobhan doubted anything could have lowered her mood at that moment.

The spell had worked. These people were fine. Better than fine.

She resisted the almost overwhelming desire to stretch out her arms, throw back her head, and start laughing aloud from sheer joy.

The moment passed as Liza cast the spell on the third test subject, and then the fourth.

Siobhan's elation softened, and then sank into a relief so heavy and deep it pulled on her shoulders and made her want to cry. As long as everything went well, soon they would be able to cast it on her, too.

It had been so long, but finally, here was real hope, created with her own hands.

Liza and Siobhan took a second round of diagnostics after the whole group was bound to a sleeper raven. Though they requested that the test subjects stay in the hotel, it wasn't strictly required. However, Liza made sure to warn all of them very firmly to abstain from alcohol or any other mind-altering substances. "If you do partake in something you should not, tell us, so that we will know what might be the cause if something goes wrong," Liza said.

The group of test subjects seemed frightened enough by her insistence that

Siobhan doubted they would be willing to risk it. None of them were addicts who, given the opportunity, might not be able to help themselves.

As Siobhan helped Liza to put away the binding spell array, moving components back to the large conference table and clearing away the black salt, she considered what they had just done. Binding magic was mysterious, seeming to overcome some of the limitations that modern sorcery suffered. In essence, binding magic generated an ongoing exchange of some sort. Obviously, most binding magic worked off the principles of transmogrification, but unlike most transmogrification spells, which were actively cast and would cease to work when the Will and power were removed, binding magic was cast once and continued to work afterward.

It was almost as if the binding itself was some kind of tether that worked on the principles of transmutation.

'Is it like a slow-release artifact? Or, perhaps more accurately, like a potion?' she wondered. Potions, after all, used a ritual to create a structure of magic that was not bound within a spell array but absorbed and woven into the ingredients to create something wholly new and inherently magical in and of itself. It was not permanent, and over time, a potion's physical form would degrade and spoil as the magic dissipated.

'Binding magic probably works on a similarly complex theory that I only have the most basic grasp on.' Her classes hadn't covered it, and the research she did previously uncovered notably few texts that explored the subject on the University library's first floor.

Unlike potions, however, this binding could be broken. They had made sure to set a trigger for it to break when the rejuvenating spell on the sleeper raven ran out of power, but it could also be broken manually with a simple unbinding that thematically and practically negated the agreement allowing the initial binding.

To develop the sleep-proxy spell, Siobhan had relied quite a lot on copying structures and methods from other spells, and then even more on Liza's extensive expertise. She couldn't claim that she even came close to understanding how everything worked. And yet, somehow, it did.

As she sprayed a concoction that would make the honey and nightshade oil binding the black salt to the floor dissolve more easily, Siobhan asked, "Where did you learn magic, Liza? If that's not too invasive a question."

Liza hesitated, the small dustpan she was using to pour the black salt back into its jar pausing in mid-air. "I joined the army," she finally replied. "Of course, I knew a little before that. My mother made a living as an unlicensed diviner, when she wasn't working as a prostitute." She paused, as if waiting for Siobhan's reaction, but Siobhan remained silent.

Liza continued. "I was young when the Haze War started, and got myself a job in one of the army workshops. It was off the front lines, mass-producing artifacts for the soldiers. They promised to provide free education after we'd done our stint, and magical education for those who qualified. I qualified. They kept their promise, and after it was all over, they really did put me through the University."

"Oh!" Siobhan said. It was no wonder Liza was so knowledgeable and powerful.

"Only problem was, after I and the others gained our Mastery, they didn't want us to go free afterward. To be honest, I didn't particularly mind at that point. I got to work in experimental artifact development at first, but after a while I joined a small squad. We did interesting, worthwhile work, and got paid well for it." Liza smiled absently, rolling a couple grains of salt between her fingers. Soon, though, the smile drained away, leaving a sickening grimness behind. "Or so I thought. Eventually, I realized the truth, but it always seems to be too late by the time that happens, doesn't it? For me, much too late." She clenched her fist until her knuckles turned white, small muscles in her face twitching with rage.

Siobhan actually felt the urge to shrink back from the older woman, the chill across her skin telling her that Liza was dangerous and might strike out at any moment. Instead, Siobhan froze, hoping her lack of response would keep her from attracting Liza's attention.

After a few moments, Liza relaxed, releasing her breath and her clenched fist. "I apologize, child. Not all my memories from that time are bad, you know. Before the end..." She stood abruptly, putting the lid on the jar of salt. "Well, did Oliver ever tell you how we met? I was on assignment, up north in Osham, and I met this young boy with dark, curly locks and the brightest eyes you've ever seen. He was already a sweet-talker then, and he tried to convince me and my squad mates to let him and his sister ride along with us to the next city. He had it all planned out. The sister was significantly older, so he was going to pretend she was his mother. They were going to go in disguise and find work in the local lord's stables; their family had experience raising horses, you see?" She chuckled, but then sighed, shaking her head.

"Osham's regime had just changed, and he was worried about the yearly conscription, since his sister was a Null, and historically Osham has rather valued them for their particular characteristics. It's not like how they're treated here. Well, his father found out about the boy's plan and put a stop to it all. Perhaps the man wished he hadn't, later." She fell silent again for a few seconds. "Why does it seem like, if you keep going long enough, no story has a happy ending?"

Siobhan didn't know what to say to that. After thinking for a while, she suggested, "Who gets to choose that the unhappy part is the ending? If you keep on, maybe it's just another low moment along the way to triumph."

"Hah! If death is not an ending, what is, child?"

Siobhan could have argued that, viewing the metaphorical story from another perspective, things continued on as long as anyone was still alive. Everyone was the protagonist of their own story, after all. But it didn't feel true. *'Death would be an ending of the story for the person I care most about—myself. The only story that matters.'*

Clearing her throat to disperse the tension, Siobhan changed the subject. "I have five hundred gold. You said before that would be enough to hire you. If I can give you, in advance, both the time and the location where the coppers will be scrying for me, can you retrieve or destroy the sample they're using for the sympathetic connection?"

Liza stood and moved to the bound ravens, checking them over for signs of abnormality. "If you can do that much, it seems the job would be quite simple. Depending on the quality of their wards, of course." She stuck her finger between the slim metal bars, poking at one of the ravens that seemed sleepier than the rest.

"It should be whatever wards are around the divination room in Eagle Tower."

Liza's finger stopped wriggling, and she withdrew her hand, rising and turning to face Siobhan. "That makes things difficult. They have some experimental advancements, and without knowing their setup ahead of time—acquiring the blueprint and ward plans from whoever set them up—I would need to be quite close to brute-force my way past."

Siobhan nodded easily. "I already considered that after my last plan failed. They seem to have given up for the moment, but I'm sure they have other plans. I believe I can control the timing of their next scrying attempt. Then, all we need to do is make sure you're in place ahead of time. They'll come to you and get caught in an ambush."

"After everything that's happened, the coppers are on high alert. If someone catches sight of me, they might mistake me for the Raven Queen."

Siobhan blinked twice, stared into the distance, and then a wide smile spread across her face. "That's...a genius idea. It would fit perfectly! We'll have to get you a Raven Queen disguise."

Liza made a choked noise. "No, that's not what I meant."

Siobhan ignored that. "If all goes well, even if they do end up having some blood kept in reserve, they'll realize that there's no point in trying to use it, for scrying or anything else."

"And just how do you plan to manage that?" Liza asked acerbically.

"By doing something...big," Siobhan admitted. Even now, she was uncomfortable with her plan. But hiding away would only leave her vulnerable and easy to manipulate. Her ideas were a little reckless—and a little dangerous—but she was facing that head-on. Personally, she would be the one in the least danger. Once this was done, the Raven Queen really would be able to disappear back into the shadows for good. *'I suppose Ennis did teach me to gamble, in the end,'* she mused.

"They're practically setting me up to do something the day of Ennis Naught's sentencing, after all," she said. "But it won't be what they're expecting, and not focused where they're looking."

12

EVIDENCE AND EVENNESS

Sebastien
 Month 3, Day 29, Monday 9:00 a.m.

A mixture of euphoric eagerness and stomach-turning anxiety would have kept Sebastien awake, except for a careful dose of calming potion, taken once in the evening and again in the middle of the night when she woke to refresh her dreamless sleep spell. It might not have been as effective as something like an elixir of euphoria, but she liked to think she could learn from her mistakes. No more addictive substances. Especially when it seemed like she needed them just to function.

During breakfast, a paper bird messenger fluttered down next to her plate. She unfolded it to find a list of the classes available to second-term students, as well as a reminder to make her choices and submit payment as soon as possible. Sebastien frowned. *'Did they send these to all the students in Gilbratha? What a horrible waste of resources, just to show off. How much of my tuition payment goes toward things like this?'* They could have sent one of the student aides who was staying over the break out to deliver this message across the campus, and normal letters through the post office to those students who had gone home for a couple weeks of freedom.

In addition to the standard four core curriculum classes that everyone was required to take, there were an enticing number of electives, many of which had not been available to first-term students. Modern sorcery had several broad branches of magic which one could focus on to receive a Mastery, such as artificery, divination, alchemy, and even witchcraft. Those branches could be narrowed down further into sub-specializations, like warding, which was technically a branch of artificery but was very different from other sub-specializations, like enchantment or automation. From there, warding even had its own smaller branches of specific focus, including ward-breaking.

The class list reflected this, with several branching classes being offered from the introductory elective classes, which were either prerequisites or corequisites.

In addition, the University offered several other interesting electives, such as: Introduction to Esoteric Magics; Kitchen Magic for Chefs; Advanced Spell Array Theory and Design; Introduction to Healing Theory; An Exploration of Animism; The Magic of Fate: Blessings, Charms, and Benedictions; and even Zoology and Horticulture.

They also offered several math-based options, which would be required for some of the more advanced classes people could start to take in their fourth term. She knew what Statistics was, but what about Advanced and Esoteric Spatial Calculations? *'Perhaps you need that to learn space-bending magic,'* she postulated. But she had no idea what Physical Approximations in Mathematics could be, and Non-real Numbers and Their Application didn't even make any sense.

She selected Studies in Modern Magic, Natural Science, Sympathetic Science, and History of Magic, which she and every other student had to take for at least three terms and which still had the same professors. Then she added Elementary Practical Will-based Casting, which was only available to those who had passed the introductory class *as well as* received Professor Lacer's permission to advance. Students who had shown the proper dedication and improvement may have passed but not yet be considered ready for the next step. *'Maybe that's why Nunchkin had to repeat the first-term class three times.'* Each term, Professor Lacer changed the spells taught in class, so repeat students wouldn't be going over the exact same thing.

Sebastien hesitated over Defensive Magic. Professor Lacer only allowed her to take six classes, with her apprenticeship with him taking the place of the seventh. Which meant, if she wanted to explore something different, Defensive Magic was the only thing she could give up. But, considering the number of times that she'd been in an altercation over the past term, there was simply no replacement for the sheer increase in survivability that came with being fit and familiar with what to do when the spells started flying. No matter how enticing some of the other class options looked, taking Defensive Magic was a matter of disaster preparedness.

And so, she handed in a class list that looked almost exactly like the one for her previous term, and with an aching heart wrote out a cheque from her new account at one of the local banks. Three hundred gold, gone just like that.

'And…suddenly I don't have that five hundred gold I promised Liza,' she realized with a sinking feeling in her stomach. Adding up her account balance and the coin she had kept in readily accessible physical gold, she had a little over three hundred remaining. A small fortune, to be sure. Enough to support two people for a year, if they were more frugal than she had become. But not enough.

On the bright side, Oliver's textile business would pay her again in a few months. If she couldn't haggle Liza down, Sebastien could pay in installments, even if that meant doing more brewing for the Verdant Stag.

Perhaps whatever tribute Thaddeus Lacer had prepared for the Raven Queen would be valuable enough to cover the difference, but she wasn't ready to meet him yet. Not until she had improved her current precarious situation and ensured his intentions were wholly friendly.

A woman at the administration center fed Sebastien's class list into an artifact, which spat out a class schedule. She gave Sebastien a huge smile, then said, "Exam and exhibition results for first-term students are already up, Mr. Siverling. You might want to check them," and then winked with exaggerated care.

Perplexed, Sebastien walked to the announcement boards, which were covered in fresh paper and tiny print. First, she searched for her name under the exhibition results. To her surprise, in addition to the seventy points from Practical Casting, she had received fifty contribution points for the Defense exhibition. A short explanation mentioned only "great leadership and a display of exceptional magical prowess."

A tall, broad-shouldered form stepped up beside her, and Sebastien recognized Professor Lacer just fast enough to keep herself from jumping when he spoke. "Professor Boldon insisted that he be allowed to keep your smoking tree sculpture for himself. The scented smoke was a thoughtful touch. It probably accounted for at least ten of those contribution points." He turned to face her, his hands clasped behind his back. "Do you have plans for any particular purchase?"

Sebastien quickly calculated her total. "I wonder if two hundred eighty-seven points can be exchanged for anything interesting." She hadn't checked the items on display in the Great Hall lately, but she remembered, in addition to the physical items, they had a book listing many more rewards, like better meals in the cafeteria, private dorm rooms, and if she remembered correctly, temporary access to certain sections of the library's upper floors.

Professor Lacer's eyes flicked back to the board. "You received one hundred points from Grandmaster Kiernan, correct?" When she nodded, he said, "Then I must tell you that students who placed in the top ten percent of their term receive extra points. You should recalculate."

Sebastien's eyes widened, and she walked over to the adjacent rankings board. She had indeed scored in the top ten percent. Somehow, she'd even received a good grade in Defense, despite not actually finishing the practical portion of the exam due to Fekten's interference. Perhaps that had actually helped her—the proctors making up for Fekten's misunderstanding. It had been the class pulling down her average the most, and without its weight, she'd performed surprisingly well. A slow smile spread across her face. *'And to think, just five months ago I scored only green five-fifteen on the entrance exam's spectrum. That was barely passing, and if not for Professor Lacer, I wouldn't have made it through the oral exam.'*

"Next term, I will expect you to place in the top five percent," Professor Lacer said. "I am sure you are capable."

Her smile grew. "Of course." She turned to face him, mimicking his stance with her hands clasped behind her back. "Do you think three hundred eighty-seven points would be enough to purchase instructions to an esoteric spell?" Learning to distance the output of a simple spell had greatly increased her utility, but it would be even better if she had more options that didn't require her to make preparations like drawing out a spell array or brewing a concoction beforehand. Her makeshift paper tome had been useful, but even it couldn't compare to the ease of casting her shadow-familiar, or even Newton's calming spell.

He hummed, and she could tell from his expression that it was unlikely. Actionable records of esoteric spells were rare, since they were often passed down through oral tradition in families or from Master to Apprentice. She knew already that most of the ones the University had were held in the subterranean archives.

"How much would I need, do you think?" she asked, considering the feasibility of getting illegal access to a different part of the archives by bribing or manipulating one of the administration workers again. If she did that, she might even be able to snatch more than one spell. The only downside was the potential for punishment if she were caught.

Someone at the secret thaumaturge meetings might have an interesting esoteric spell, but she had decided to avoid those until things were safer. A few thaumaturges sneaking around the law surely couldn't match the selection of the world's greatest repository of information, anyway.

Professor Lacer thoughtfully rubbed his wild beard, which had grown longer than the close crop he usually kept it at. "Three hundred points just happens to be enough to buy an hour of my time, in which I could do you a small favor," he mused. "I would be willing to escort you to an area of the archives with safe esoteric spells, where you could peruse until you found one that met your interest. Of course, given your history of displaying a certain lack of judgment, I will have to approve your final choice."

There were faint signs of a smile at the edges of his lips, and Sebastien suspected he was at least bending, if not outright breaking the rules for her. Not that she would complain about such a thing. "Can we go now?" she asked, rocking back and forth on her feet eagerly.

He let out a single chuckle that immediately turned into a poker-faced cough, but spun on his heel so that his long coat flared out. As he walked away, he waved for her to follow without looking back.

She hurried behind him, mimicking his confident and aggressive stride and ignoring the curious looks of the administrative staff as they passed. None would dare to question Thaddeus Lacer.

Rather than one of the staircases to the upper floors, Professor Lacer led Sebastien to the reinforced door leading to the underground archives, where the truly interesting material was entombed.

As she followed silently behind him into the hallways carved from the stone of the white cliffs, she wondered what he might think of her recent actions and the admitted danger of her plan. *'But if I am going to be in danger either way, isn't it best to take action to try to change my circumstances?'* she reasoned. She was doing her best not to be reckless, to consider the variables and take safety precautions. And she had even considered the possibility of resolving the situation through social and political means, despite how foreign the idea felt. That was why she had reached out to the High Crown, though she hadn't forgotten all the reasons she had avoided doing so before. Even if it didn't work out, she needed to at least attempt to open up additional avenues by which she might resolve her problems. Perhaps Lord Pendragon, first and greatest of the Thirteen Crowns, would surprise her.

Yes, if her plan worked, it would change a lot for her and leave her with the agency to make choices instead of responding to emergencies, but it wouldn't completely resolve her situation with Oliver and the secrets he was keeping. Even the thought of him and his puppet strings caused anxiety and anger to rise in her chest.

She eyed the back of Professor Lacer's head, noting the few strands of grey peeking through his black hair. If anyone were to have useful advice that would cut to the heart of the matter, it would be Thaddeus Lacer, wouldn't it? He wouldn't spare her feelings.

Hesitantly, Sebastien spoke over the echo of their footsteps. "Professor Lacer," she began, "I have recently found myself in a difficult situation, and I would value your counsel."

He spared her a look over his shoulder. "Elaborate."

She took a moment to mull over her words. "I believe I may have been betrayed. Or, perhaps more accurately, manipulated?" She shook her head. "But I'm not sure. Perhaps I'm just blowing things out of proportion, seeing clues where there are only mundane coincidences. I know I need more evidence, but I'm not confident I can gather absolute proof of anything. And to be honest, I'm apprehensive about confronting this person directly."

He slowed, allowing her to walk by his side as he studied her face for a few seconds. "Without knowing the details of your conundrum, I cannot give you specific advice. But I can, perhaps, provide guidelines through which you can attack the issue yourself."

Professor Lacer was silent for a long few moments, reaching the end of the hallway and turning to the left. Finally, he spoke. "Many would advise you, if you value your relationship with this person, to simply confront them and communicate openly. But I have found this to be ineffective, unless you are in a clear position of advantage. Knowledge is power, and can be that advantage in mundane and life-altering conflicts alike."

Fekten had said something similar in one of his lectures. "The greatest weapon in the battle to live a long life is knowledge," she quoted in a murmur.

Professor Lacer quirked one eyebrow. "Indeed. Perhaps this is why the pursuit of truth is at the core of the Way. We have spoken about curiosity, the ability to relinquish ideas and beliefs, and the technique of twisting the knife of inquiry where it hurts worst. Your current issue moves further into the topic. I could say much about it, warnings and techniques and concepts, but I do not wish to overwhelm your fledgling steps along the path. Tell me, you already have a theory, correct? There must be evidence of some sort or you would not hold suspicions."

Sebastien hesitated half a second, then belatedly answered, "Yes."

"I have no need of the details." He waved his hand as if shooing away a fly. "However, if you suspect betrayal, you must require outside corroboration or contradiction. If your trust in this person was great enough—based on past evidence of their loyalty or honor—to believe their assurances, you would either not suspect them in the first place or would have confronted them immediately. That you are asking me suggests you believe they might lie to you. Correct?"

"Yes," she repeated, a little stronger.

"And yet, you have some doubt. You could be biased toward suspicion because of insecurities, misunderstanding of the evidence, or an incomplete understanding of the situation. You may not know all the ways in which our thought processes are geared toward failure and our minds can lead us astray, but you are at least aware of the fact that you are susceptible to error. This is good. In my opinion, the thing that separates sapience from sentience is the ability to think about thinking, to recognize that your brain is an artifact of sorts with built-in flaws that lead to incorrect perceptions and conceptions. But most importantly, having understood that we are flawed, and in which ways, we can consciously correct for errors."

He paused to look her over, searching her face for something mysterious.

She nodded eagerly at him, urging him with her expression both to continue walking and speaking.

He snorted but began to stride onward again. "You have a theory already, and this is not only incorrect, but it is also dangerous. It is common, and extremely easy, to come up with a theory and then work toward proving it."

"Rather than disproving it?" she asked. Gnorrish had talked about this. It was the duty of a natural scientist to try to disprove their hypotheses rather than prove them. Only in this way could they consistently progress past their ignorance.

But Professor Lacer's response surprised her. "No, that is not what I mean." He stopped in front of a door, motioning to it. "Provide all the evidence that texts on blood magic rest behind this door."

Sebastien blinked at him a couple times, then turned to the door. "Do they?"

"That is not what I said. I asked you to provide all the evidence toward that conclusion."

She remained silent for a few seconds. "It makes sense that the largest repository of written knowledge in Lenore, if not the entire known lands, would have information on blood magic." He nodded, so she continued. "This is a restricted section, where either powerful or dangerous knowledge is stored. From my somewhat limited knowledge and experience, these rooms beneath the library hold even more sensitive information than what is held on the upper floors. I have previously found hints at spells considered blood magic in another of these subterranean rooms. Also, you retrieved the Comprehensive Compendium of Components from a room somewhere down here, which could technically be considered a text on blood magic, as many of its entries cover the uses of totally illegal and unethical components. All in all, it seems more likely than not that at least one text beyond that door could be considered to hold information on blood magic."

"Now, provide all the evidence that no texts on blood magic rest behind the door."

She opened her mouth, then closed it again, her mind flipping uncomfortably. She believed her original argument more likely, but that didn't mean she couldn't argue in the other direction, even if it required some misdirection and even direct contradictions of what she'd just argued. "With the extreme aversion Lenore has shown to blood magic after the fall of the Third Empire, it's likely that most texts detailing their methods were destroyed, either out of aversion or out of fear that someone might find them and use them. While these rooms are restricted, they are far from inaccessible, as I have proved. Any truly dangerous information would likely be held in a more secure location. As a professor, you would not lead me to a room filled with dangerous and unethical information." She paused, eyes narrowed. "I think I see your point."

He hummed. "Indeed. You need not attempt to disprove all of your theories, but to evenly prove or disprove them. This may seem obvious, but I state it because emotion can lead one to weigh evidence unevenly. You have heard advice to attempt to disprove your theories because this is most likely to mitigate the failure of the average person's natural tendencies. A researcher attempting to prove a new theory of magic or natural science is likely emotionally biased in favor of their premise. Thus, the attempt to disprove it, as well as University's requirements for peer review and duplicable results, more often achieves unbiased truth. But you can also be biased toward disbelief. One who wishes to believe may ask, 'Does the evidence permit me to believe?' while one who wishes to disbelieve may ask, 'Does the evidence force me to believe?' If you know the destination you wish to reach, you have already arrived. Consciously remind yourself that, above all, you wish to know the truth of the matter, whether it will surprise you or make you feel stupid, or even make you wrong."

To her surprise, rather than opening the door, he turned and led her down the hallway again, to another stairwell leading down. *'Just how big are these subterranean archives?'* she wondered. Each of the doors was labeled with a short string of letters and numbers, but they didn't seem to follow an exact order. To the uninitiated, it would be very easy to get lost.

"In addition to searching only for the evidence that supports one's beliefs, a common error is to somehow find that *all* evidence proves your theory. For instance, it could be argued that a suspect acting guilty or secretive is evidence toward their crimes. But if they instead act unconcerned and unburdened, this could be evidence that they are attempting to manipulate opinion and are, in fact, guilty. Do you see the issue here?"

She nodded.

"Explain it."

"Opposite evidence should lead to opposite conclusions. If the suspect acting innocent is evidence toward their guilt, then acting guilty should actually be evidence toward their innocence. If either option leads to the same conclusion, then neither option is actually evidence, but rather an unrelated fact that is being inaccurately attributed as evidence."

He kept walking without turning to glance at her. "And if I suspect that my colleague has stolen my sandwich, but can find no evidence of food residue on their fingers or mouth, no witnesses of them near my food, no footprints that match theirs, and none of my divinations point toward them as the culprit... Is it reasonable to then assume that my colleague is simply extremely cunning and has cleverly avoided evidence of their deeds, having paid off all the eyewitnesses, destroyed all the crumbs, changed their shoes, and cast a preemptive anti-divination spell that I have never heard of before?"

"The lack of evidence…*is* evidence!" she said brightly. "Unless you have some other, really compelling reason to believe your colleague ate your sandwich, like the two of you are in a prank war of one-upmanship, then perhaps there is another explanation entirely. Maybe the simplest explanation is that you forgot your sandwich at home, or got distracted and misplaced it."

"You continue to satisfy expectations, Mr. Siverling." Professor Lacer stopped in front of a door that, to Sebastien, seemed no different than all the rest.

'Is that…a compliment?' It was such faint praise that, coming from anyone else, she would have labeled it an insult.

He waved his faculty token in front of a door and strode through as the wards lowered.

"Absence of evidence is evidence of absence. So, as you are investigating this betrayal, remember that your judgment is imperfect. Allow the evidence to change your mind in either direction, according to its weight, weak or strong. And it is best to be clear ahead of time about what direction any particular piece of evidence will sway your opinion."

He motioned for her to step past him. As she did, he created a bright light that hung in the air vaguely above her head and then crossed his arms.

This archive, like the other she had entered, was hewn roughly from the stone. The shelves were filled with a scattering of books, a disproportionately large number of scrolls, and even a few tablets and tapestries.

"As for how much proof one needs to be sure of something, that is a difficult question, because it is hard to properly quantify your own surety. However, it does do to be wary that we are prone to jumping to conclusions without sufficient evidence, and that in the face of evidence to the contrary, our levels of surety remain much higher than they should. Do not be so complacent as to believe that simply because you are more intelligent than the average person and also aware of this fallibility that you can easily escape it."

'If everyone followed these precepts, would the Raven Queen have gained her current notoriety?' Sebastien wondered, her eyes tracking over what must be hundreds and hundreds of esoteric spells. *'Would she even exist, or would she still be Siobhan Naught, desperate girl in over her head?'*

Professor Lacer gestured to the shelves with his chin. "Well, go on. You only have an hour."

13

NINE-LIGHT FILTERS

Sᴇʙᴀsᴛɪᴇɴ
Month 3, Day 29, Monday 10:00 a.m.

Sᴇʙᴀsᴛɪᴇɴ ᴀᴛᴛᴀᴄᴋᴇᴅ the archive like an extremely respectful hurricane, careful not to do any damage as she familiarized herself with its contents at top speed. She explored methodically, starting from the shelves on the far left of the room and moving right. Many were either copies of the originals or translations, complete with notes left by the translator in the margins, but at least half remained in their original language, and thus unintelligible to her.

Sebastien quickly found that everything was organized incomprehensibly. "All the different types of magic and thaumic requirements, from Apprentice to Grandmaster, are all jumbled together."

"Information on these spells is organized by location of use and time period, respectively," Professor Lacer explained, moving to sit at the room's only table. "This room is meant for historical and anthropological research, not to conveniently supply young thaumaturges with instructions to lost spells."

'*That…is going to make things harder.*' Sebastien sped up her search, quickly discarding any texts written in a different language, or that dealt with farming, community rituals, warding against pests and other common threats, or that did something so simple that the convenience of an esoteric spell didn't make much difference—like creating a candle-sized flame. She also discarded anything that was obviously beyond her thaumic requirements. Unlike with modern sorcery, which contained the written Word as a spell array, it wouldn't be so easy to adjust an esoteric spell to be less magically demanding in exchange for time and preparatory precision.

She set aside a few interesting options, like a spell that enhanced the five senses, and one that purported to turn the user's bones to steel over the course of seven years of repeated casting. One scroll described a spell that allowed the caster to turn the tip of their finger into a burning coal, useful for lighting fires…or burning symbols into things. She was a bit dubious about how literal such a thing might be, as charring off your fingertip in exchange for a spell that could let you draw out a single other spell array without writing implements seemed a costly exchange. Even worse, the scroll seemed shoddily translated. *'How horribly wrong could attempting to cast with mistranslated instructions go?'* she wondered ironically.

Still, with a peek at Professor Lacer, Sebastien read through the instructions twice, committing them to memory as best she could without seeming suspicious. There might be a time when she was willing to sacrifice a finger in exchange for her life or freedom.

As she went along, she found a spell that allowed the user to mold their own flesh, though it was unclear to what degree or whether this effect would be permanent or not. Another offered to open the third eye and allow the caster to take one step closer to the "perfection" of the prognos. Yet another claimed to give a self-blessing, but was so vague as to be suspicious. As far as Sebastien knew, "good luck" magic didn't actually exist, though a fraudster hag might tell you differently when trying to sell one of their charms or talismans.

Several more powerful texts contained intriguing attacks, like calling forth lightning or causing bone spikes to explode from the caster's fist after a hard enough impact—like a punch. Those, however, required a capacity well beyond hers, and were obviously incredibly dangerous as well.

No, she was looking for something more like her shadow-familiar. Something innocuous but with flexibility and wider utility.

A very interesting spell allowed the caster to step down into the earth as if descending into water, but the thin book it was written in mentioned a range of additional spells the caster would need to know to further mold the earth once submerged—to keep from suffocating or being crushed. Instructions for those additional spells were not given, and so the whole thing was useless. The capacity requirements weren't mentioned, but she probably didn't meet them anyway.

One spell supposedly allowed the caster to communicate with aquatic creatures, but not understand them in return. Another allowed the caster to leave an invisible mark on something that they would be able to find forever after, which seemed like an early foray into modern sympathetic divination. That one, she also read twice, as unlike the fingertip burning spell, it actually made sense and seemed fairly easy to cast, though with admittedly convoluted requirements that would take a long while to complete.

Professor Lacer was reading a yellow-paged book, the title of which was written in a looping script she couldn't read but vaguely recognized as originating from the tribes of the Tataroc Desert. Despite saying that he would check any spell she picked up for safety, he didn't seem concerned that she might be able to memorize more than one during her hour of access.

As she made her way through the shelves, time wore on and she became increasingly anxious. While the magical knowledge was fascinating, she didn't feel that she'd found the perfect option yet. *'If only I'd been able to research what was available ahead of time!'*

However, she eventually found one spell that stood out from the rest, two scrolls bound to each other—the original and the translation. Unlike most of the options contained in this room, this spell was based on what seemed to be fairly complex physical movements. A preface by the translator noted that it required abnormally high amounts of both physical and mental control, but there were no specific thaumic requirements. Even the weakest thaumaturge could cast it, hypothetically.

It drew Sebastien in with its frankly ridiculous benefits. The spell was called "nine-light filters" and allowed the caster to absorb sunlight to heal and repair not only the body but, more specifically, the mind. It sped up mental recovery, reduced the need for sleep, and improved mental strength, clarity, and defenses. Over the long term, it was supposedly able to reduce the chance of Will-strain.

'How is that even possible?' she wondered, a shiver of excitement coming from deep in her chest. *'Is it improving the framework of the Will itself? Increasing clarity and stability? Or somehow improving the robustness of the brain directly, like Liza and I do to the mice?'* However it worked, this discovery was extraordinary. Even a small decrease in the likelihood of a break event was incredibly valuable. And even if it didn't improve casting capacity, stabilizing the Will and increasing mental endurance was almost like a gift from the stars above. And beyond all of that, if she could combine this with the sleep-proxy spell, she might be able to go even longer without dreams.

'It must be incredibly difficult to cast. Or have a really slow return on investment.' There was no other way something like this wouldn't have spread among the more powerful thaumaturges, at least. But then again, maybe it had, and she'd just never learned of it. There was a reason the scroll was tucked away dozens of meters beneath the surface of one of the most protected places in the known lands, after all.

She unfurled the scroll further, reading through the dense text and examining the extensive diagrams of the human body in motion. There was even an audible component, though luckily, no actual words that she would have to struggle to pronounce in the original tongue of those who developed the spell. Her stomach sank as the scroll continued to unfurl, until the total length was taller than she stood. In total, it probably reached two or three times her height, each inch densely packed with information.

She checked her watch. Less than fifteen minutes remained in the hour Professor Lacer had allotted her. No matter how voracious her mind was, she couldn't memorize all the instructions—some of which were translated confusingly and would need thought to decipher—along with the diagrams and notations. It would take even longer to try and make a copy by hand.

Sebastien turned to Professor Lacer, hoping that he would once again provide a solution for her. "This is the one I want," she said. "But I'm going to need more time to study it. It's too complex to memorize. Maybe you could cast a duplicating spell to transfer the information to another scroll?" The delicate spellwork needed to preserve the integrity of text was beyond her, but she was sure he could manage it.

Professor Lacer waved her over and held out his hand for the scrolls.

Instead of the translation, he skimmed through the original with the same ease as someone reading in his native tongue, his eyebrows slowly rising. She did her best to subdue the urge to fidget impatiently, but by the time he had reached the end, the hour allotted to her had already passed.

Finally, Professor Lacer looked up, rolling the scroll back together. "An interesting choice. Difficult, to be sure, but if you can manage it, it could be useful to fortify yourself against memetic effects and compulsion-based magic. While you may not be in danger of such attacks, they are the kind of thing it is best to start preparing for well ahead of time, rather than attempting to undo only after it becomes relevant." He gave a single nod of approval, strangely heavy with meaning.

'He's hinting at whatever the Red Guard did to Newton's family,' she realized. 'He thinks I'm interested in the spell because of that.' Admittedly, she now found the spell even more tantalizing.

He thought for a moment, and then said, "This spell was developed by the gestura. Are you familiar with them?"

She had never met one, even in the University, which boasted of its diversity, but she had heard the stories. "They are thaumaturges who practice a different craft," she said. "They train from the age of three in monasteries, until they are able to control the elements through sympathetic connections to their movements. Some say their craft is halfway to free-casting, though much less versatile, as they can do nothing outside manipulating the elements."

"That manipulation of the elements has more utility than you might think. After all, consider all the applications water or stone have as components. But it is a fact that the gestura are dying out. Their craft takes too long to master, and is indeed less versatile. They made wonderful battle mages, but the world is moving on, and they cannot keep up."

He slapped the scroll gently against his palm, scrutinizing her. "Learning one simple spell from a new craft is very different from becoming a master of their methods. But even so, this will be difficult for you to learn. I know without even needing to watch you attempt it that you do not have the physical stamina or precise control to succeed."

She clenched her fists, hoping that he was not going to tell her to put the scrolls back and choose another.

"I will not be able to help you when you inevitably struggle. If you feel any doubt about your desire to dedicate yourself to such an endeavor, speak now."

"I am not afraid of hard work or learning new things. I will learn it," she promised him with dark intensity.

"Hmm," Lacer said noncommittally, then glanced at the contents of the translated version and immediately frowned. "Nine-Light Filters?" he muttered. "That is a very poor translation." He looked at her, back to the scroll, and then stood up decisively, his chair scraping against the rough stone of the floor. "Allowing the University archives to make do with such a sloppy translation is unacceptable. As the purported greatest institution of knowledge in the known lands, this is a source of shame. I will be checking this text out and re-translating it as a service to the institution." He tucked both scrolls into one of the wide inner pockets of his long coat. "You may come by my office to pick up a copy of my translation in three days," he added, as if the statement was unimportant and incidental.

She blinked a couple times, remembering the length of the scroll. If made into a book, it would probably contain at least a hundred pages of dense instruction. To translate something like that in three days, he would have to spend his time on little else. She swallowed hard past a sudden lump in her throat, looking away. Ennis would never have gone to such trouble for her. Not without expecting her to somehow repay him tenfold. No one since Grandfather had been willing.

But there was nothing Sebastien Siverling could do for Thaddeus Lacer, wealthy and powerful Grandmaster. And he must know that as well as her.

She blinked again, more rapidly, turning her eyes to the ceiling to nip any watering in the bud, and nodded jerkily. "Thank you."

He made no comment, turning to the door and waving over his shoulder for her to follow.

It was hard to reconcile this kind of decision with the callous way Professor Lacer had responded to notice of the Moore family's mental tampering. *'But people are nuanced,'* she reminded herself, *'and there's a lot I don't know about the hidden side of this world. A lot I don't know about him.'* It might not be safe to put her fate in his hands, her deepest vulnerabilities laid bare, but he was proving, again and again, that at least she could trust him with any possible responsibility a Master held to their Apprentice. She smiled wryly. "Best three hundred contribution points I'll ever spend."

He snorted but neither turned nor replied.

She redoubled her determination to learn the spell. She might not be able to repay him, but she would, at the very least, prove that his investment in her wasn't in vain.

Professor Lacer led her back to the library's ground floor, then waved her off with a reminder to stop by his office in three days.

Her strange but pleasant mood was somewhat ruined when she picked up a discarded copy of that morning's newspaper on one of the benches outside, left behind by some careless student. Stamped large and black at the top of *the Daily Sun's* front page were the words:

High Crown's Pledge of Justice!

Lord Pendragon Vows to Catch and Execute Raven Queen

Her message to the High Crown had outlined the method and timing of his response—a coded ad in one of Gilbratha's most popular newspapers, three days hence. The High Crown's response had come sooner than she had expected, but there was no need to agonize about the meaning: her tentative offer of negotiations toward some form of cooperation had been firmly rejected.

Rather than agreeing to any sort of meeting, he had called for her to turn herself in before the might of the law that she might be judged, for the Crowns—and especially Lord Pendragon, greatest of the Thirteen—did not submit to fear-mongering and would never let "evil" go unpunished.

Sebastien stared at the flimsy paper and the arrogant, unbending words spread across it. Her eyes unfocused until the letters looked like little more than squiggly black bugs ready to be crushed under her thumb. *'How strange and foolish it is, for him to respond like this,'* she thought. *'It must be impossible to keep an organization of any type running smoothly when pride becomes more important than effectiveness.'*

But perhaps there was something she was missing. Some plan that she didn't understand. She forced her jaw to unclench and read the article once more, searching for any clues in the message. In the end, she was forced to concede that it was merely a straightforward denial of her overture.

It was a shame, but it wasn't as if this left her any worse off than she had been before. After all, she was already putting her other idea into motion. This had always been Plan B.

14

SHIFTING TOPOGRAPHY

Sᴇʙᴀsᴛɪᴇɴ
Month 3, Day 29, Monday 11:15 a.m.

Sᴇʙᴀsᴛɪᴇɴ sᴇᴛ *The Daily Sun* back on the bench where she'd found it, then stood in thought under the tree sheltering the area as small flakes of snow started to fall, melting soon after they hit the ground. Perhaps in the city below, they would turn to sleet or rain before they made it all the way down. It was always colder at the altitude atop the white cliffs.

The downside to Plan A was that it required a lot of planning, preparation, help, and what she suspected was a deadline she didn't want to miss. The coppers hadn't tried scrying for her since their sudden attempt drove her out of Gilbratha during the night. But it was clear they hadn't given up, and she could think of no better time for whatever they were planning next than Ennis's sentencing at the end of Sowing Break.

So, with some precautions to make sure it wasn't traced back to her, Sebastien again slipped a note into Tanya Canelo's cubicle, requesting a meeting at a discreet location in a couple of days' time. Like Sebastien, the other woman was staying at the University over the break. The note had no signature, but Sebastien knew that Tanya would guess the sender correctly, and was equally sure that the woman would show up.

After that, Sebastien's mind automatically searched for the next urgent task and found…nothing. She was strangely free, with no classes, no homework, and not even any exercises for Professor Lacer. Sure, there was always

magic she could practice or study, but nothing with an urgently looming deadline that felt like a tidal wave about to crash down on her.

*'The most urgent problem is probably my shortage of coin. Liza is a black hole of
greed. What could she even be spending it all on? And after that, some research and
experimentation with the degradation of sympathetic links. And some curses.'* Plan
A might not require her to do much personally, but she still needed to
ensure that what she thought were clever ideas weren't likely to backfire.
Despite her issues with Oliver, the safest way for her to make a reasonable amount of coin in a short period was still selling alchemical concoctions to the Verdant Stag. And coincidentally, she now had time to work
on the improvement to the philtre of darkness that she'd come up with
before.

A cloud of darkness that only blinded the enemy could come in extremely
useful for her own plans. And if she could figure it out, she was sure Oliver
would pay a premium to get such an advantage over any potential enemies,
including the coppers.

And that was how Sebastien found herself back in the library once more,
this time surrounded by alchemical research.

Modifying alchemical concoctions wasn't as straightforward as tweaking
the spell arrays of modern sorcery. Alchemy was ritual magic, more like music
than a mathematical equation. Each of the preparatory steps changed the
whole in such a way that they couldn't be switched out for something
different without complex and possibly unforeseen consequences.

Sebastien knew there was some science to it all—whether to grind something into a powder, mince it, or tear off small chunks with your bare hands. It
mattered how many times you stirred, in what direction, at what speed, and
even the depth of your stirring implement within the cauldron. But she would
be the first to admit that the principles were so opaque and seemingly inconsistent that it would probably take her years of study to understand well
enough to create a theoretical concoction from scratch.

However, despite her lack of theoretical understanding, she had experience
brewing dozens of simple concoctions, many of which used whatever components could be found within the area they were traveling, at whatever time of
year they were passing through. She knew at least six different variations of a
fever-reducing potion, a handful of pain relievers, and a dozen different
concoctions to ward off different pests. Above all, she probably knew more
tinctures, potions, sachets, salves, and teas meant to affect dreams and sleep
than any alchemist in Lenore who didn't have the privilege of access to the
University's entire library.

Sebastien might not understand the rules for creating concoctions from
scratch, but she had a feel for how small changes required other adjustments
to balance the results. Even if she couldn't design the exact concoction she

wanted on paper, she could experiment until she found one that worked. *'Luckily, alchemy is less likely than a standard spell to fail horribly.'*

Sebastien frowned, remembering several times when, as a less experienced alchemist, her concoctions had failed. Sometimes simply by burning or turning into a questionable, foul sludge that no one with any sense of self-preservation would ingest. One memorable time, by erupting from her cauldron in a volcanic spew of foam.

'Well, at least not the kind of failure that's likely to kill the caster and everyone around them,' she amended. But then she remembered several horror stories about the effects of incorrectly brewed concoctions. Her grandfather had tucked her into bed with one such tale about a childhood rival of his. The young man had been working his way through a complicated brew that took six months to complete when a simple mistake caused the concoction to form arms and legs and crawl out of the cauldron three months in. Somehow, Grandfather's rival had accidentally added a branch taken from a dryad instead of mundane wood. The living potion had proceeded to eat his rival's legs and maim three other people before someone managed to neutralize it.

Sebastien was also pretty sure she had seen an illustration of an exploding cauldron leveling an entire building in the book Professor Lacer had given her.

'At least the type of concoction I want to brew…shouldn't be dangerous?' She cringed and rubbed her temples. *'I'll test it on mice first.'*

Sebastien had been studying for a few hours, making cryptic notes in her spider-scrawl handwriting, when one of the younger library administrators informed her that a letter had been delivered to her by runner. The young woman smiled prettily and handed the letter over, then tried to make some conversation about whatever Sebastien was studying, but Sebastien cut her off as soon as she saw the signature over the sealed mouth of the envelope. Titus Westbay had scrawled his name so that it would be difficult to sneakily open and read the contents without alerting someone—a cheaper, more convenient alternative to the formal wax seal.

Within was a simple agreement to meet if she was available immediately, at a location surprisingly far south, where the normal city began morphing into the more extreme poverty of the Mires.

Acid-sharp anxiety rushed through Sebastien's veins. She had discussed a reasonable backstory with Oliver, who assured her there would be some small amount of documentation in the records to corroborate her existence as Sebastien Siverling. It would be suspicious if someone without wealth, backing, or formal education like her were to have *too* many records, after all.

She had prepared as best she was able, but Oliver had warned her that Titus Westbay was a tricky conversationalist, and, perhaps because of his job, skilled at getting people to admit to things they wanted to keep hidden. And all evidence pointed to the fact that he had some kind of vendetta against her.

Deciding to meet with him, despite the short notice and her own reservations, she immediately packed up her things. As she rode the transport tubes and then a carriage, she couldn't help but run possible scenarios of their conversation through her head in endless permutations. Somehow, this was almost as nerve-wracking as going into battle.

Sebastien stepped out of the carriage into an area surrounded by dilapidated warehouses. *'Why does he want to meet here?'* she wondered. And then, more darkly, *'Perhaps it would be easier for him to make me "disappear" in a place like this.'*

Sebastien shook her head at her own nonsense and walked forward, looking for the elder Westbay brother. Soon enough, she saw people walking around with the standard metallic footsteps of the copper uniform. Ropes cordoned off access to a half-destroyed building, and while some milled around inside, others questioned the locals in the street.

One of the coppers, a short woman, noticed Sebastien and seemed to recognize her, waving her closer and hurrying inside. Soon after, the woman came back out with Titus Westbay in tow. She smiled brightly at Sebastien with a knowing, conspiratorial look that made Sebastien uncomfortable and had Westbay sighing with weariness.

Titus Westbay was taller than Damien, and despite the heavy workload his position must entail, the bags under his eyes were less obvious. However, he seemed to take similar care of his hair, which was perfectly styled without a strand out of place. Sebastien had met him before, after Newton's break event, but was understandably too distracted to take note of little details at the time.

The man looked Sebastien up and down, and then reached out to shake her hand with a firm grip that she matched. Neither of them smiled.

"Apologies for the location," Westbay said. "Some vigilante caused an incident. You requested a meeting, but I am too busy to set aside much time. Shall we walk while we talk?" He waved a hand past the crime scene and moved away before she could respond.

To Sebastien's surprise, instead of heading north, he walked further south. She followed, but neither spoke. She had been right that the snow would melt before reaching the ground here, but after mixing with the dirt and filth of the street, it had left a wet, unpleasantly sticky film over the ground.

The dead carcass of a dog lay in a corner, stripped down to the bones and tendons, but no flies buzzed around it, and no maggots crawled through what little wet flesh remained. A woman sat next to the carcass, idly squeezing at an inflamed abscess on her arm until it dribbled green pus.

This area was outside of Oliver's territory. Those that lived in the Mires under him were poor, to be sure, but he hired workers to keep the streets clean and the wells clear. Because of his loans, predatory though they might be, no one walked around with festering wounds or died of illnesses that a few gold could treat. In the height of the summer, things would look even worse here as the heat allowed things to fester, but within the reach of the Verdant Stag, conditions would probably only get better.

"The smell doesn't bother you?" Westbay asked, drawing Sebastien's attention back to him. He wasn't using a perfumed handkerchief to cover his mouth and nose or making an overt expression of disgust like she had expected.

"It does," she said. "But it won't go away just because I don't like it."

He nodded slowly, but there was something mean in his eyes when he said, "I thought you might feel some nostalgia. You grew up similar to this, correct?" He waved toward a couple children racing past them on the street, their knobby, scarred knees visible through holes in their pants.

Her heartbeat sped up, but she kept her face and tone controlled. "Not exactly like this, but if you mean poor, then yes." Did he think he would aggravate her into making a mistake? If this was one of the romance periodicals that some of the girls in her dorm liked to read, he would shortly be tossing a cheque for hundreds or even thousands of gold in her face and telling her to break off her friendship with Damien. Except the situation didn't quite fit, because usually the one tossing the cheque would be the noble mother, and that would make Sebastien the commoner girlfriend.

Again, Westbay spoke without preamble. "I assume Damien told you about our conversation?"

"And Oliver Dryden, too," Sebastien added dryly, a hint of a glare creeping into her expression as she stared at Westbay's profile.

"Well, I will not apologize for that. Have you come to plead your innocence to me?"

Sebastien's eyelids fluttered as rage flared up within her like a fire splashed with oil, but she did her best to press it back down into her stomach. "On the contrary. I wanted to meet you so I could impart some facts about myself and give you the castigation you are so clearly in need of."

Westbay stopped, turning to face her with a slow, dramatic spin on his heel. "You are here...to castigate me?" His hands were in his pockets, making his autumn-colored uniform coat flare out slightly.

"And provide you with the critical information that your shoddy investigation failed to reveal," she said, staring unblinkingly into his eyes. Her fingers were itching to grab her Conduit, but she restrained herself, keeping her hands still and clearly visible.

Westbay's lips quirked up in the same condescending sneer that Damien sometimes wore. "Oh? This seems like it will be interesting. Go ahead."

Oliver had explained that Titus Westbay was the type to keep pushing until he forced a response. Rather than trying to avoid digging into her weak points, it was better to give him that response from the beginning and steer their conversation in the direction most beneficial to her. If Westbay thought she was angry enough to lose control, it would seem more likely that she was being truthful. However, Oliver had also warned her not to overshare, as a story with unnecessary detail could hint at extra time spent coming up with the lie beforehand.

Truthfully, this kind of interaction was the area where Sebastien felt least skilled. But she had to get through it. Even if she couldn't hope to make Titus Westbay like or trust her, he at least needed to believe her relatively harmless.

"It is true that I grew up poor, and sometimes desperate, and that I experienced things that linger in my nightmares to this day. I was an orphan, and my uncle took me in when I was too young to remember. He fed and clothed me, kept my hair dyed brown, and taught me, though I don't know if we are biologically related or if he gave the title of "uncle" to himself out of kindness. I cannot ask him now because he is long dead." The man she was talking about had existed and had been known to feed the local urchins of Vale. He had been a mediocre thaumaturge, and Oliver assured her that he had died in a gruesome way that left little evidence of his life behind.

"If my uncle knew the history behind my name, that, too, is lost to me. However, as far as I'm concerned, I have no claim or connection to any throne, historical or current. And if I did, I would try to get rid of it," she added truthfully, grimacing at the thought. "Trying to rule must be ridiculously unpleasant and inconvenient. How is one supposed to wrangle all the idiots?"

She waved the thought aside and began to walk again, forcing Westbay to follow. "After the fire that killed my uncle, which I suspected was deliberately started by one of his rivals, I left Vale and spent a few years traveling from town to town, often under an assumed name. And at some point, I grew fed up with pretending to be someone else. I want my name and accomplishments to be remembered."

Sebastien stopped, buying two slightly withered apples from the basket of a woman kneeling on the sidewalk. The fruits were small, wrinkled, and ugly, but not rotten—the last remnants of the previous year's harvest. Sebastien bit into one and offered the other to Westbay, who declined with a dubious expression. With a shrug, she tucked the second apple into her pocket. "I've done a lot of research on you, too, you know."

"Oh?"

She took a second bite, and then a third, chewing for a long moment as she built up courage for what came next. "I learned about you from those you're closest to, and of course your background and circumstances are common knowledge. Anyone you pass on the street knows at least a few things about Titus Westbay. Hells, you've even been in the papers a few times. I didn't even need to meet you to know how contemptuous you are." She took a deep breath and spoke quickly. "You care more for politics and maneuvering for the favor of your father and the other Crowns than you do for justice. How many people have you unjustly arrested and imprisoned? You've slept with several of your servants and then fired them. I also heard you like quintessence of quicksilver a little too much, and maybe that's what's been—"

Westbay raised one hand to his forehead, and the other toward her, palm out. "Stop!" He took a deep breath and then lowered his hands "That's the most ridiculous drivel I've ever heard. Who are your sources?"

Taking another bite of apple, she crossed her arms and raised a stubborn eyebrow. "Do you deny it?"

"Yes!"

She scoffed, looking around. Almost everyone in the street was watching them surreptitiously. Her accusations hadn't been quiet.

Westbay stepped closer, lowering his voice. "Wherever you heard those things from—those close to me would never say such things! None of what you just accused me of is true. You cannot act as if you know everything about me simply—" He closed his mouth with a sharp click of teeth and stared at her for a couple of seconds. "Ah. I see I am making your point for you."

She smirked. "Haven't you learned at your age that rumors cannot be trusted?"

His eyebrows rose nearly to his hairline, and he reared back. "At my age? How old do you think I am?"

"Old enough to be treated like an adult and held accountable for your actions," she said softly.

He took a deep breath, smoothed his fingertips over his hair, and looked around for a moment while settling his emotions. "That's...fair."

Sebastien did her best to hide her relief, but braced for the counter-blow that must be coming.

"Those who know me would never believe such malicious gossip. I can admit, those who know you defend you with similar vehemence. Damien beseeched me to keep an open mind. But I hope you can see that you seem... quite suspicious?"

Her apple pit was down to some hard bits and a few seeds, which she tossed into the gutter along with the rest of the filth. "You may see my background as a disadvantage, but I view it differently. My past taught me to be who I am. It seems like you're worried that I want to attach to Damien like some sort of leech, but I..." She held out her empty hands, palms up. "I don't need anything that he can give me."

Westbay tilted his head a few degrees to the side.

"I look at the University students around me and I see naive, weak children. If I had never gone through hardships, I wouldn't be magically weak, but I might still be naive. I wouldn't have gained depth and the certainty that I can survive anything." Her words came slow and precise as she stared him in the eyes. "I might bend, but I will never break. All Damien has is money and influence."

Westbay snorted, holding a hand over his mouth as he looked up at the sky. He mouthed something to himself, then looked down at her again, his eyes suddenly narrowing.

His expressions were so mercurial that they left her suspicious. Some of them might not be real. Surely his emotions weren't shifting so quickly?

"Was the plan to go after the Gervin branch lines your idea?" he asked.

Sebastien blinked, thrown mentally off balance by the non-sequitur, but at least she could answer truthfully. "It wasn't. I did my best to mitigate the danger in the original plan and make sure we were prepared with options in case things went wrong. Mostly, they didn't, except for Malcolm Gervin becoming so violent. But I *know* they could have. Professor Lacer already gave me a dressing down for putting myself in danger, but…Ana was going to do something, with or without my help. She's very protective of her little sister, you know. Perhaps you can relate."

"What did they do to Nat?" Westbay asked, his fingers twitching at his side.

"Nothing punishable by the law, as far as I know. If you want details, you should ask those directly involved." Sebastien turned and began to walk again, her eyes roving the streets in an instinctual search for danger. Two wealthy men delving into the Mires without obvious protection were a temptation. Even just stripping them of their clothes could buy someone a few weeks of food. If these people knew who she and Westbay were, they would think twice, but she couldn't count on desperate people to be either knowledgeable or prudent. "I understand you don't like it when Damien is in danger, but there's no way he would have agreed not to be involved. And if you really wanted to do something about Ana's uncles…you should have gotten there first." She sneered, watching him from the corner of her eye. "I won't believe you if you tell me you never heard any rumors, that you had no inkling of crimes committed."

Westbay didn't flinch, the next question coming immediately. "You've admitted to visiting the Silk Door. Are you a patron…or an employee?"

Sebastien tripped over the edge of a tilted cobblestone and when she tried to catch her balance, instead slid across the wet film covering the road. If not for Westbay catching her by the arm, she would have fallen.

Her cheeks tingled with embarrassment. He peered at her suspiciously, and, more forcefully than she had intended, she spat out, "Neither! I have never sold my body for coin…or any other benefits!"

She looked around, again finding everyone watching them, and shook off his grip with a scowl. "Though would that be so horrible, if I had? Prostitution might be unpleasant and sometimes dangerous, but it's honest work. It's just another sign of the veil of nobility over your eyes that you think yourself fit to judge without the faintest hint of understanding."

She drew herself up until, despite their equal height, she could look down on him. "I don't have the free coin to patronize those who work at the Silk Door, either. I merely have friends who work there. If you find such associations distasteful...I don't care." She bit her tongue to keep herself from spewing even harsher words, reminding herself that her ire was meant to be at least partially an act. She couldn't let his probing accusations unsettle her.

Again, the next question came without hesitation, almost as if he had come up with it beforehand. "You may not have sold him your body, but can you really say that you're not aware of, and taking advantage of, Oliver's feelings for you? Or that you aren't attempting to seed an unhealthy attachment in Damien?"

"What?" She scowled with the darkness of an enraged thundercloud. "I'm not so alluring that anyone I interact with falls for my supposed charms. If anything, people find my personality abrasive and my honesty off-putting, and that's if they don't find my competence intimidating."

He actually rolled his eyes at her, muttering something she couldn't make out.

"I have little interest in a romantic relationship at all, and most especially not with Oliver Dryden. I don't believe he feels for me the way you're suggesting, and if he did..." She swallowed, her outrage dampened. "If he did, it would be in my own best interest to dissuade *his* interest with fervor."

Westbay's eyes narrowed and he leaned in as if magnetized by curiosity, but then his expression smoothed out again into perfectly mild interest.

"As for Damien, the fact that he didn't immediately abandon me during the Defense exhibition isn't an unhealthy attachment. It's evidence of a modicum of observational skills and a good helping of actual friendship. He hasn't had the kindness beaten out of him yet, though he does a good job of hiding it under his sneer." Almost immediately, Sebastien realized that there were other things beyond the Defense exhibition that might count as seeding unhealthy attachments. Such as inducting Damien into a fake secret organization. But she certainly wasn't going to bring that up.

"Why would it be best for you to avoid Oliver's interest?" Westbay asked, his voice mild in a way she suspected was deceptive. In fact, she was beginning to wonder how much of the conversation had been guided by the man despite her resolution to outwit him.

"He is...manipulative. If he was really attracted to me in that way, I would probably find circumstances around me twisting to make me dependent on him, and only him. He'd try to make himself the center of my world and make me think it was my idea," she said heavily.

"And he...hasn't been doing that?"

Sebastien clenched her jaw. "I hope you're not about to start jumping to conclusions that he's a criminal or something, just because I admitted he's not a perfect specimen of altruism."

Westbay let out a single, barking laugh that seemed to have been surprised out of him. "Damien mentioned that he wanted you to come stay with us over the break. What are your current—"

Something knocked into Sebastien from the side, and her first instinct was to protect her pocket from sticky fingers reaching where they shouldn't be, but as she flinched and turned, a spew of vomit arced from the mouth of the woman who had bumped into her.

The chunky brown and red liquid splashed against Sebastien's legs and splattered down to her boots, some of it catching around the top of her boot, where it would no doubt seep inside.

Sebastien and Titus Westbay both stared in open-mouthed shock as she was doused with an amazing amount of stomach acid and rancid, half-digested food of indistinguishable origin.

15

PROJECTILE VOMIT

Sebastien took a half-step back but reached out to steady the woman when she swayed and heaved again. The arm under her hand was distressingly thin, so little muscle or fat covering the bone that she could have easily wrapped her fingers all the way around with room to spare.

Sebastien's first thought was that Titus Westbay had arranged this for some impenetrable reason.

"Oh, no, no," the woman moaned, then heaved again.

The stench was nose-searing, but held none of the distinctive scent of alcohol. Other substances that might cause a backlash like this weren't so distinctive, but as the woman rose, Sebastien quickly cataloged that her nail beds were not flushed but blue with cold, and her eyes were slightly unfocused but not overly dilated. She wasn't a user of either of the common, cheap substances that caused nausea, and the vomit itself contained none of the foam that would have accompanied legal sources of ipecac syrup.

The woman drew her arm away, clasping her hands together in front of her chest. "Oh, my lord, I'm so sorry. Please forgive me." Her eyes struggled to focus, but as she looked at Sebastien she grew only more anxious. "Oh, your clothes, so fancy—are they ruined? Oh no, oh Myrddin no—I can't—"

Sebastien reached out and gripped the woman's cold hands within her own. They were so small. Sebastien adjusted her estimate of the woman's age.

She might even be younger than Sebastien, but the starvation drawing her skin tight around her skull, cracking her lips, and painting deep bruises beneath her eyes made her look older.

"Do not worry," Sebastien said. "This little bit of mess is nothing, I swear. I can clean it with a few quick spells, quick as you snap your fingers, and these clothes will be as good as new."

The girl cringed, her voice hoarse as she whispered, "I'm so sorry, Master Sorcerer. I beg your forgiveness." The fabric of her skirt trembled as her knees shook from weakness, fear, or a combination of both. If this situation had been set up, the girl was a wonderful actress. But in any case, the starvation was real.

Sebastien considered continuing to argue that she wasn't angry but changed her mind. "You shall have my forgiveness if you answer my questions truthfully and agree to a few demands."

The girl tensed up, silent, and Sebastien took the opportunity to turn her head to Westbay, who was watching the whole thing with his mouth hanging slightly open. "I believe I've said everything I needed. I know you're busy, so feel free to return to your investigation."

Then she turned back to the girl, who nodded reluctantly, no doubt assuming Sebastien was going to enact some sort of revenge on her. "Where's the nearest healer?" Sebastien asked the girl, who stammered out some vague directions and then offered to lead Sebastien there, as she didn't know the address. Sebastien agreed, as she'd never gotten around to memorizing the layout of the entire city, and the Mires were convoluted.

She kept the girl's arm tucked within the crook of her elbow for balance, and they walked slowly, because the girl was too weak for Sebastien's usual long-legged stride, with occasional pauses for the girl to heave out a little bile.

Instead of returning to work, Titus Westbay followed along silently behind them. This was irritating, but Sebastien couldn't be bothered to argue with him.

Sebastien continued asking questions of the girl, learning that her name was Betty and that she lived what Sebastien considered a pretty typical orphan waif life.

Betty had a residence, so technically wasn't homeless, but it was only a spot in the corner of a wooden shack that she shared with several strangers. For coin, she did odd jobs where she could find them. Betty didn't admit it, but it was likely that she stole or prostituted herself to make up the difference. But when winter hit, things got harder for everyone, and sometimes the weakest didn't make it.

Betty had last eaten that morning, but when questioned about the meal, grew reticent and could only say, "It was a kind of...pie thing. All chopped up and mixed together." Then, mournfully, "I can't believe I threw it up." Even the thought had the girl heaving again, the effort leaving her panting for breath and her face as pale as death.

Sebastien had fresh water for her to sip, and mint oil, which she dabbed on Betty's temple and chin, but nothing to truly control the nausea. Even a pain potion would come up again before it could do much good. When they arrived at the healer's, Sebastien turned back to Westbay. "Must you continue following me? If there is something further you wish to speak about, you may send me a letter, or even set up a meeting for a later date. As you can see, I am busy."

Westbay grinned at her, his hands tucked in his jacket pockets. "Oh, no. There is no way I'm missing this. Whatever this is."

Sebastien grimaced at him in disgust, turning away from him to push open the healer's doorway. "None of the rumors mentioned that you are a sadist who enjoys watching the suffering of ill children."

"What?"

The healer ambled out from a back room, his eyes sliding over Betty to focus on Sebastien, and then on Westbay who entered behind her. "I'm honored by your presence at my humble establishment. What can I do for you, my lord?" he asked, bowing subserviently, his eyes lingering on the vomit soaked into Sebastien's clothes and chilling her legs.

Sebastien scowled, putting a hand on Betty's arm to guide her to a seat. "She has food poisoning."

The girl's eyes widened, but she nodded, unable to speak past another dry heave that had green-tinted saliva pooling into the hand she cupped in front of her face.

Sebastien grimaced. Left unsaid was that Betty had probably taken a risk with that "pie thing" because she was literally starving to death and couldn't afford to be picky about what she ate. Without treatment, it could be enough to kill her, most likely through dehydration, but if not that, from the lingering weakness that would make it impossible to provide for herself without help.

Sebastien knew what it was like to be so incredibly hungry that normal reticence about what you would eat, or what you would *do* to be able to eat, fell away. For a time there, after Grandfather died and before Ennis found her, she, too, had eaten whatever she could. Food that was dirty, half-rotten, or meant for animals. She'd gotten sick a few times until her stomach adapted. Eventually, she'd become wiser about how to get what she needed, but that got her caught and put in jail for beating a wealthy, fat little boy to steal from him.

"She'll need a stomach soother, a pain reliever, a nourishing draught, and if you have one, a bed for the night. Check to see if she has a fever, as well." Sebastien was already counting out the coin for the potions. Licensed magical supplies were prohibitively expensive, but it wasn't as if Sebastien could bring the girl to a Verdant Stag apothecary with the Lord Commander of the coppers following her around.

She shot Westbay a peeved look as she almost emptied her coin purse. "Actually, since you are so starved for 'entertainment,' perhaps you should be the one paying for Betty's treatment."

Mouth opening and closing like a drowning fish, Westbay pointed to himself, and then Betty, and then back to himself. "Wait, you think I—but you—"

The sick, half-starved girl was looking around with wide eyes and stammering questions about what was going on that Sebastien ignored. Somehow, Betty seemed to have missed the fact that they were going to the healer's for her sake. She tried to get up, but a single sharp glance from Sebastien was enough to sit her back in the chair.

"And a thorough diagnostic, as well?" the healer asked obsequiously, his eyes on the gold in Sebastien's hand. "There's been obvious starvation, which could lead to damage in the digestive system that needs to be repaired." He flinched back from Sebastien's expression.

"How much?" she asked.

Before the man could answer, Westbay stepped forward. "Titus Westbay," he said, introducing himself perfunctorily, but he was staring at Sebastien with a considering expression. "Send the bill to me at the manor."

The healer basically tripped over himself to see to Betty, who tried to protest but was quickly silenced.

Sebastien remained for a few minutes after the first round of alchemical concoctions, sitting beside the thinly cushioned pallet that would be the patient's bed for the night and watching as the visible signs of Betty's nausea and pain eased.

The girl took Sebastien's hand in hers, pulling it into her lap. "Thank you so much, my lord. It's the greatest fortune of my life to have met someone as kind as you. Is there...any way I can repay you? Any way at all?" She bit her lip, her eyes seeming a little too large in the gaunt frame of her face.

"Westbay's the one who paid for you, so you owe me nothing. Don't even bother to worry about the coin. He has plenty." She looked to Westbay, still standing on the other side of the room, and narrowed her eyes speculatively. "So much so that he could easily afford to give you a few coin to get you through the next week or two. Right?"

Westbay's eyebrows rose, pinching together in a strange, confused mix of surprise, frustration, and suspicion. "Really, Mr. Siverling?"

"Siverling?" the girl repeated, obviously recognizing the name.

"Really," Sebastien repeated firmly. Again, it was Westbay's fault that she couldn't suggest the girl find temporary housing or even possibly a job in Verdant Stag territory.

Westbay's eyes flashed with a hint of something, and his lips stretched into a faint smirk. "Alright. You may come by Westbay Manor tomorrow evening and pick up a few coin, Miss. I'd love to hear your story." He stared challengingly at Sebastien, as if they were playing a game of chess and he had just trapped her king.

She peered at him with pity. Did he think she would be shocked just because he'd invited a commoner to his home? That didn't make him any less of an arrogant snob.

Perhaps he saw this judgment on her face, because his triumph slipped away and was replaced with surprise and confusion.

The girl tossed around more effusive thanks and attempted offers of repayment, but when the healer returned with his diagnostic artifact and the first nourishing draught, Sebastien took her leave.

Outside, she shivered as her wet clothing made itself known again. She looked left and right, noted the lack of carriages for hire, and spent a couple seconds searching her memory for the best path back toward the University that was likely to pass by a reasonably priced restaurant or food stall. Some place where the smell of vomit wouldn't inconvenience the other customers. Her stomach felt terribly, achingly empty, and she wanted to stuff herself until even the thought of more food made her ill.

"How did you know it was food poisoning?" Westbay asked, stepping up to the curb beside her.

"It was easy enough to rule out the other common causes of explosive vomit. I may not be an investigator, or Aberford Thorndyke, but I have eyes and a working brain."

She shivered again, then retrieved the folding slate table from her bag and drew a quick spell array to suck the liquid out of her clothes. With her Conduit in her free hand, she carefully ran the slate table over her lower half, letting the water coalesce in a small puddle around her feet while the cold air, chilled even further by the spell's use of heat energy, dispersed in the breeze. The spell was meant to combat the misery of traveling in the rain, not to actually clean anything, and left most of the vomit behind, only dried. This was a marked improvement, even if it pulled some of the disgusting paste deeper into Sebastien's boots and left her skin itchy.

Westbay had watched the whole thing as if she were some kind of fascinating anomaly, like a talking toad. Truly, he was beginning to irritate her more than Damien ever had. Sebastien walked forward, heading in the direction that would lead her into an area she knew better and could navigate more confidently.

Westbay walked beside her, matching her stride as if it were natural. "Betty was a very conveniently timed interruption. Don't you need to find some way to bathe and wash your clothing? Or change into something else? A spare copper uniform, perhaps?"

"Are you offering me a spare copper uniform?" she asked. Being able to impersonate a copper might be useful at some point. But, no doubt, she'd be expected to return the clothing. And go to one of the copper's substations to pick it up. "Never mind, I don't want it. Some vomit is not the end of the world. I can make it back to the University without fainting from the horror of it all."

"Are you truly trying to tell me this wasn't all a ploy to gain my interest and sympathy?"

Sebastien stopped, turning to stare at him. Her left eye twitched as she tried to keep her anger and disgust contained in her belly, but some of it boiled up. "You think far too highly of yourself." Before a full diatribe could slip out, she turned on her heel again and walked away, more quickly this time.

Westbay hurried to catch up. "Is that a no? I'd ask if you'd be willing to state that under a ward against untruth, but that boon from the Raven Queen is very convenient."

Sebastien drew in a sharp breath.

There was a pause, and then Westbay said, "I'm sorry. I shouldn't have brought up such a traumatic event. That was too far."

'So he doesn't actually suspect my connection with her?' "You said that...just to get a rise out of me?" she asked aloud.

"I apologize. Somehow, I do actually believe that the whole thing was unplanned. Do you do things like that often? Helping the destitute, I mean."

"Of course not. That was an exceptional incident."

"Why?"

Sebastien examined his expression, trying to gauge if that was a serious question. "Because without help, that girl had a good chance of dying. And I just happened to have the thing she needed—gold. I may occasionally be accused of being a miser, but even I can admit that a person's life is worth a little inconvenience on my part." The cost for Betty's treatment would have been covered in just one or two days of brewing potions for the Verdant Stags. "And in the end, I didn't even have to pay."

"Would you consider yourself a philanthropist, then? Like Mr. Dryden? Or, excuse me, Lord Dryden?"

Sebastien snorted. "To the contrary. But even I can't just ignore someone right in front of me." She shut her mouth and pressed her lips together. That had been a little too honest. The whole point of this meeting was to make herself seem less suspicious, after all.

But Westbay only said, "I think you might be surprised how easy many people would find it to practice deliberate blindness. May I ask, where is it that you are headed?"

"To a food stand."

"To buy the girl a meal?"

Sebastien side-eyed him. "To buy *myself* a meal."

"Would you be amenable to some company? My treat."

Sebastien stared at him suspiciously for a few long, silent seconds as they waited for a carriage to pass so they could cross the street. Something about this interaction was giving her déjà vu. Finally, she realized where the feeling was coming from. "You're just like Damien!" She narrowed her eyes. "Are you a masochist? The ruder someone is to you, the more you like them?"

Westbay choked and started coughing. "What? No! What do you mean?" He blinked. "Is Damien—" He closed his eyes, pressing a closed fist against his mouth as he cleared his throat. When he opened his eyes again, he seemed resolved to forget the short exchange had ever happened. "You may escape my company if you answer one more question."

Sebastien suspected this would be the question that counted. She steeled herself to not respond involuntarily.

"You once told Damien that free-casting runs in your family. How could that be, if you have no knowledge of them?"

"I...did?" Sebastien's eyes moved away from Westbay's as her thoughts raced. '*Is that true? How could I have let something like that slip?*' But she was quick enough to come up with a solution. She could only hope her acting was good enough to make it seem believable. "I don't remember saying that," she admitted. "But I can guess the context, and, um, the reason."

She blushed, a natural enough reaction because this kind of slip up really was terribly embarrassing. "I wasn't being entirely truthful with Damien. That free-caster wasn't my actual family." She cleared her throat, examining the cobblestones near the edge of the sidewalk. "So. When I was young, I collected newspaper clippings about Thaddeus Lacer. Orphaned children often like to make up stories about their parents. Pretend that they have family still alive out there and come up with reasons why they were abandoned or lost and will someday be reunited." This was all true enough, though didn't exactly apply to her.

Westbay lifted a hand to his mouth, probably concealing a smile. "Go on."

She forced herself to meet Westbay's gaze. "I used to pretend that Thaddeus Lacer was my father. So, maybe when Damien was bragging about his own family, I got irritated and said that."

Westbay's hand fell away, revealing that he was indeed sporting an enormous smile, as if he'd just discovered his biggest rival had a bout of diarrhea in front of the High Crown during court. "And *is* he? That would explain why he took you as his apprentice..." His voice turned into a mutter as he gripped his chin between thumb and forefinger, looking her over. "He would have had to mate with an albino to produce you. Or some magical accident during childhood? Perhaps his sperm are all damaged from repeated Aberrant exposure."

Sebastien held out both hands toward Westbay's face as if to thrust his ideas away with her palms. Surely he couldn't actually be considering that? "No! No. We are not biologically related in any way."

Westbay's sadistic grin suggested that he was only teasing her.

She balled her fists at her side. "Professor Lacer is my mentor only, and I would sincerely appreciate it if you never mentioned this to anyone else. I really do not need any more strange rumors circulating about me."

Westbay clasped his hands together. "Of course, I will keep this incredibly embarrassing secret for you. Did you know I am quite good friends with Thaddeus? It hurts me to keep things from him, but as long as I'm assured that Damien is safe in your company… Of course, if that ever changes…"

Sebastien rolled her eyes. "And *I* will take care not to mention this meeting of ours and the way you dredged up my traumatic memories to Damien, hm?"

Westbay's smile fell away. "Touché." He returned his hands to his pockets and, somewhat somberly, said, "Unless you are fearsomely good, I can see that you're not the person I thought. Thaddeus often warns about jumping to conclusions and has rebuked me for my tendency to conflate the most *interesting* theory with the most likely. I thought I had grown out of that, but it seems the rather unfortunate confluence of adventure and mystery around you skewed my thought processes. I…apologize."

Sebastien drew a deep breath and let it out, her skin cooling as the flush faded from her cheeks. "You did me no true harm, so I will forgive you. But if you find yourself in a position to keep others from digging into my past or personal life while looking for gossip and drama, I would appreciate it if you take action to stop it. I do not want to be defined by my past or my circumstances. If possible, I would wipe those things from my mind entirely. I do not want to deal with them being dredged up over and over." She blinked rapidly against the wind.

Westbay placed a hand on her shoulder, squeezing gently. "Would you like to come to the manor for dinner? I'm sure Damien would be overjoyed."

Sebastien sidestepped away from his grip. "Thank you, but no. I have studying to do."

Instead of becoming irritated or offended, Westbay seemed amused. "Ah, yes. Damien has told me how you are 'struggling' to catch up to the rest of the students. Well, perhaps some other time."

Sebastien answered him with a nod, but inwardly she resolved to avoid further interaction with Titus Westbay if at all possible.

16

SHELTERED UNDER WINGS OF MIDNIGHT

Siobhan
Month 3, Day 30, Tuesday 5:00 a.m.

Sebastien woke in a cold sweat and immediately reached for something in the drawer of her bedside table. Only when she didn't find it did she become fully alert and realize that she had been instinctively reaching for the beamshell tincture.

She snatched her hand back, clutching it to her chest and shuddering. '*I made a mistake. From the beginning, I shouldn't have…*'

Sebastien tried to get back to sleep, but after only a half hour it became apparent that rest was impossible. Instead, she got up and dressed in the dark, then headed down into the city. She found a safe place to transform into Siobhan—or more accurately, Silvia—and then went to the Verdant Stag.

Unnoticed, Siobhan made her way up to the apothecary, which stayed open all night for emergencies. It wasn't Katerin's assistant Alice at the counter but another young woman.

"The beamshell tincture," Siobhan said without preamble.

The young woman blinked at her sleepily. "Yes?"

"Don't sell it to me," Siobhan ordered.

"Uh…what?"

"Tell Alice. Don't sell it without a healer's orders, no matter who someone says they know or what reason they give. And especially not to me, okay?"

The young woman stared at Siobhan.

"Repeat what I just said back to me. What are you going to do, and what are you going to tell Alice?"

"I'm...not going to sell you any beamshell tincture?"

"Don't sell it to *anyone*! Not without a healer's order, which could be forged, so you should definitely contact the signing healer to confirm that they wrote it. Do you need to write this down in order to remember it?"

At Siobhan's rather forceful insistence, the young woman wrote down her words, and then Siobhan stormed back out into the dawn light. There might be other ways to get more beamshell tincture, but none as easy or safe as the Verdant Stag's apothecary.

Despite her complete lack of appetite, she stopped by a food stall on the way back to the University and ate until the trembling receded from her fingers.

At breakfast time the next day, Sebastien arrived at the Kaiseki Ryori, a fancy restaurant owned by the Nightmare Pack. A quick flash of one of the gold invitation cards Gera had given her got her silently escorted to a private room in the back. Gera had suggested it as a discreet location to hold meetings and had set this room aside for anyone who could produce one of the exclusive cards.

The restaurant charged exorbitant prices to serve various dishes from the East, many of which apparently contained raw meat. These "delicacies" had grown popular recently, and though the idea of eating raw flesh made her shudder, Sebastien felt that such boldness—edging on savagery—matched the Raven Queen's persona.

It was free, and worth it for the unpredictability alone. If someone were following Sebastien, they would have no chance to notice anything suspicious. None would speak of anything that happened in this room, which she had come into as Sebastien and would leave as Sebastien.

While waiting for the food to be delivered, Sebastien ignored the fancy tea in small ceramic cups that probably cost their weight in gold, instead taking the opportunity to make doubly sure there were no artifacts or spell arrays that would allow someone to spy on those within. After the food arrived, Sebastien informed the waitress that she and her soon-to-arrive guest were not to be disturbed in the name of service. Alone, she changed her form and apparel. Everything she needed to become the Raven Queen, except for her transformation amulet, was in a small briefcase.

When Tanya arrived, Siobhan was sitting on a cushioned mat in front of the low, heated table. Her divination ward was activated at a low strength courtesy of her dowsing artifact. Siobhan waved for Tanya to sit across from her, and the other woman complied, not even trying to meet Siobhan's gaze after an initial glance.

While Siobhan sat with her legs tucked to the side, Tanya kneeled and sat atop her calves, the tops of her feet pressed flat to the cushion below, her hands cupping her knees.

"Eat whatever you would like," Siobhan said, waving to the beautiful spread of food, laid out in an artistic smorgasbord of small dishes and bowls, some heated or chilled to preserve the temperature of their contents. Siobhan had sampled a few of the offerings herself while waiting for Tanya—out of hunger more than optimism—and had been pleasantly surprised.

When she heard of the Kaiseki Ryori's food, Siobhan had imagined biting into the flank of a raw, dead fish and ripping away the meat with her teeth. But the raw fish here had been exquisitely sliced, then marinated or seasoned, and paired with rice and various fresh vegetables in colorful bite-sized servings sprinkled with small flower petals.

Tanya's eyes swept over the various dishes, but she only took a few bites of decoratively sliced vegetables for her own plate. She ate a radish shaped like a flower, then forced herself to look at Siobhan across the table.

"I can tell you are apprehensive, so we might as well get down to business and relieve you of your suspense," Siobhan said, pausing to slide a wedge of raw, pink fish atop a bed of compressed rice into her mouth.

Tanya, watching with horrified fascination, nodded and let out a slow, tense breath.

"I have a mission for you, if you are willing. It is moderately dangerous, and you may refuse me, if you wish. I will not be angry or take any sort of retribution."

Tanya cleared her throat and shifted uncomfortably. Her legs were probably falling asleep from her kneeling stance. "Is this mission going to pit me against my employers? I don't want to make an enemy of them."

Siobhan took a sip of a savory, cloudy soup sprinkled with chive slices, savoring the rich warmth. "This mission has nothing to do with the Architects of Khronos."

Tanya frowned, tilting her head to the side. "I...think there must be some misunderstanding? I don't work for those terrorists. I'm employed as...well, basically an errand girl for some University faculty members who don't want to be seen doing their dirty work themselves."

Siobhan remained silent but raised an eyebrow pointedly.

Tanya's frown slipped away, along with all the color in her face. "Are you sure?" she asked, grasping Siobhan's implication with admirable speed.

"Quite sure," Siobhan said. "In fact, the Architects of Khronos were part of the attack on Knave Knoll, as well as the simultaneous attack on the Verdant Stag. They raided the Verdant Stag's vaults while the Stag forces were spread thin and occupied elsewhere. I think you can imagine what they were hoping to find."

"But…they sent me to warn you. Why would they do that if they were the ones attacking?"

"You were insurance. The Architects wanted plausible deniability in case their plan failed. With your warning, they could pretend that they were still allies of the Stags. And if you failed, or were killed in the fighting, they got rid of a liability and only lost a…what was it you called yourself? An errand girl. You didn't know the truth because Grandmaster Kiernan didn't trust you with it."

Siobhan's words left Tanya visibly reeling. "But that—this whole time?" she muttered to herself, staring at the table blankly. She looked up again, meeting Siobhan's gaze despite the pressure to look away. "What are they planning? Why do they want your book so much?"

"I believe they have grown tired of the restrictions the Crowns place upon them. The Crowns cannot allow anyone else to gain too much power, and those at the University would be in the perfect position to do so, if not for the Crowns' measures." Oliver had said as much, and, except for those involved, he was probably the most informed.

"What do you want from me, then?" Tanya asked, her clenched fists resting on her thighs.

"If you accept it, your task will be very simple. I want you to impersonate me." Siobhan allowed the edges of her lips to spread outward in a hungry smile. She took a bite of some meat that had been sliced into strips, doused in a dark red sauce, and then gathered in a ball that resembled yarn. Flavor exploded over her tongue, sweet and salty mixed together with the rich under-taste of rare steak.

Tanya swallowed visibly, staring at Siobhan's painted lips, then back to the meat dish, and then back to Siobhan's lips. "I don't understand," she said finally. "I don't think I have the skill to impersonate you properly. And for what purpose?"

"Do not worry, the task is not as difficult as you imagine. You would be provided with all the necessary supplies to approximate my appearance. Your goal would be to send a message to a specific place at a specific time, using a raven messenger that I would prepare for you. You would remain at a distance, and as long as you do not get yourself captured, no one will learn of your involvement. Your job is simply to be the raven's handler."

Tanya hesitated for a long while but, to her credit, didn't ask why Siobhan needed someone to impersonate her or why she couldn't do this herself. "I would be willing to work for you…if you can keep me safe."

It was an understandable request considering Tanya's position with the Architects. She was in danger from her employers' callousness as well as the justice of the Thirteen Crowns, were she to be caught. "I am not omniscient or all-powerful," Siobhan admitted. "I cannot protect you when I am not present, or from everything that might endanger you. It is even possible that a closer association with me will put you in further danger. I might be able to lower your risk, but I cannot promise to keep you safe."

Tanya gave a single nod that was more a bow of the head. "I understand. That is enough for me. Please, tell me the details of this mission, my queen."

"Eat while we speak," Siobhan said, motioning to the food once again. "I abhor waste." Tanya still hesitated, so Siobhan chose a piece of the thin-sliced fish over rice and placed it on the woman's plate. "Try this."

Tanya stared at it as if it were a piece of mud, but her lips wobbled in a tremulous smile, and she shoved the whole thing into her mouth. Her expression remained forcibly pleasant while she chewed, but she was unable to suppress a full-body shudder as she swallowed it all in a huge gulp. "Very… interesting, my queen. The chefs here are quite skilled."

Siobhan let out a low, throaty laugh.

Tanya startled, but then relaxed, her smile smoothing into something more genuine.

"Quite the diplomatic answer," Siobhan praised. "You do not have to eat the fish. Fill your belly with the dishes you find palatable, and I will explain your part in what is to come."

17

DECRYPTION CLUES

SEBASTIEN
Month 4, Day 1, Thursday 5:30 a.m.

SEBASTIEN WOKE early on Thursday morning, for once due to nothing more than her own irrepressible excitement. It had been three days since Professor Lacer took the esoteric spell for translation.

Unfortunately, it was so early that the sun had not yet risen, and Professor Lacer would not be in his office until after breakfast hours at the earliest. So Sebastien worked on her new application for the philtre of darkness. That project, along with helping Liza with the sleep-proxy experiments and brewing a few batches of important concoctions for the Verdant Stag, had taken up most of her free time this week.

After much frustration, she'd had to give up on her initial idea to allow selective vision through the dark clouds.

Creating a potion that could slightly increase the range of light that one's eyes could see was the obvious solution. One she had no doubt someone else had already come up with. All future philtres of darkness that she brewed would take this possibility into account and dampen or absorb the widest range of radiation she could manage.

Her next idea was to somehow link the philtre of darkness with a counter-potion, allowing only those with the counter-potion to see. This sounded great in theory, but she had no idea how to actually implement such a thing without completely changing the way the philtre of darkness worked. It would have to be more of an alchemical hex, if the effects were short-lived, or a curse, if they were not. In other words, she would need to turn the philtre into an air-borne poison that would cause blindness, with the counter-potion being an antidote.

This was a step further than she wanted to take things. Especially because she couldn't control the spread of a philtre once it was released, and might at some point need to use it in an area with civilians—innocents.

But Sebastien still felt that somehow linking the philtre of darkness to a counter was the right idea. She briefly wondered if perhaps she could create a concoction to impart some sort of echolocation sense, but discarded that option, as not only would an improved philtre's particles easily interfere with sound, she remembered Professor Gnorrish's warnings about the side effects of trying to give oneself extra senses.

And then the idea that had been taking root in little pieces of gathered information bloomed in her mind, like a lotus made of sunlight. *'I don't need to see through the darkness at all. I only need to know what's there. And humans already have a sixth sense. It's just that no one ever thinks about it. Proprioception.'* If she could adapt the group-proprioception potion she'd brewed for the Verdant Stags previously, she would be able to sense the cloud of darkness just as she could sense her own elbow or her big toe. If it worked the way she imagined, she could know everything within it by judging where it came into contact with something that stopped its spread.

'Testing is in order,' she decided. *'I'm going to need to buy up a big stock of magical cluster lichen.'* It would be best if she could keep it alive in seawater until she had need of it, but that would require both space and maintenance. Perhaps Liza could be convinced to lend out space in her apartments once more, after Sebastien had proof in the form of a viable concoction.

By the time Sebastien had finished noting down all of the ideas that came with her sudden epiphany, dawn was long gone and the breakfast hour had passed. "Surely Professor Lacer will be ready by now?" she murmured to herself, hurrying to put on her boots and scarf.

As she passed through the grounds, she noted a group of people standing around at the entrance, near the admissions center. One of them had hair pulled into a small bun at the nape of his neck and was attempting to grow a —patchy—beard. He even had a long coat. Just like Professor Lacer.

Sebastien lifted a hand to her mouth to cover her smile, and hurried on to his office.

Professor Lacer's voice was scratchy as he called for her to enter, and he seemed uncharacteristically enervated, his motions a little clumsier, his blinks a little slower.

"Are you ill?" she asked.

"Only tired. You may not be aware of this, but there is a second round of admissions, often called the 'off-term' round. We use it to fill in the gaps left by those who were expelled or dropped out during the past term. I have once again been pulled into helping with the process. There may be fewer people, but the restriction of completing the whole process within the two weeks of Sowing Break makes things rather taxing."

'Both Newton and Tanya must have been part of the off-term admissions, to be in their fourth term while I was starting my first,' she realized. *'What might have happened if Ennis and I had arrived to Gilbratha just one week later? I would have missed the standard admissions testing. Maybe I would be one of those students outside, hoping to squeeze into a spot opened through someone else's devastating failure.'*

"In addition to that," Professor Lacer said, "I have a new side project. I have begun attempts to decrypt the books brought back by the Black Wastes' archaeological expedition. Myrddin's journals. Until now, the History department has met only failure. They have grown desperate for results."

If they'd had as little success as her, they probably couldn't refuse arguably one of the most talented sorcerers on staff. As Professor Lacer had once mentioned, it required power to keep valuable things for oneself—even knowledge. *'But wait, Myrddin's* journals? *As in more than one?'* It shouldn't have been so surprising, but she'd always thought of her book as *the* book. Sure, the expedition may have recovered lots of historically relevant texts, but she'd thought of hers as special, written by Myrddin himself and encrypted to keep his most important secrets. But if Myrddin had written more…

Professor Lacer raised a palm toward her to cut off any questions. "I anticipated your interest in this topic, but I have given a non-disclosure vow about any information that I might uncover." He lowered his hand. "However…" He raised his eyebrows with subtle, secretive amusement. "The vow does not cover what methods of decryption I am attempting, nor my theories. If you would like to hear about my efforts…" he added.

"Yes!" Sebastien exclaimed, hurrying over to his desk and taking one of the chairs across from him. "You said there were multiple journals? How many? If you can talk about that, of course."

Professor Lacer hummed, looking unseeingly at the wall while his lips moved soundlessly, almost as if he were testing out the words before he said them. "Myrddin's hermitage was filled with quite a lot, but the most important items were four heavily encrypted journals that the historians believe contained his notes and theories on spell development. The Raven Queen has one. The University retains the remaining three. They're quite unlike any journals that I have seen before, and seem to be fully"—he frowned, his words coming slower and with some effort, perhaps due to dissuasion from his vow —"artifacts in their own right."

Sebastien thought of the ever-shifting glyph on the surface of the leather-bound book and the way none of the pages ever looked the same twice. Even the diagrams and illustrations shifted incomprehensibly. "So what are you doing to decrypt them?" she asked.

"I suspect the journals are not actually 'encrypted,' using the standard meaning of that word. I am not attempting to use logic or mathematics to reverse-engineer the original meaning. In fact, all such efforts to this point, using all variations of currently known ciphers, have been entirely unsuccessful, revealing no coherent patterns in the text, whether that be words, symbols, or even individual letters. One possible conclusion in such a case would be that Myrddin was a mathematician so skilled that even all advancements and discoveries made in the intervening one thousand years cannot match his innovations. So skilled that the University's considerable magical resources and the sheer weight of our combined computational power cannot brute force past his novel encryption scheme, given months of effort." Professor Lacer gave her a wry, pointed look that communicated exactly how little he thought of this theory.

"Another possibility is that anyone who comes into contact with the artifacts is placed under a confusion hex so that they see the contents but cannot parse or remember them. This would be quite clever, but hexes do not travel well through reproductive media. If, for instance, a camera obscura were used to take photographs of the pages, those photographs would not also contain the hex. Even if those who came into contact with the text were permanently cursed, you could bypass the curse by having that photograph developed by someone who'd never come into contact with the journals. Then, the photograph could be viewed from a distance, through a spyglass, by someone who had never even personally met those who had contact with the journals. No matter how robust, tenacious, or infectious the curse, that person would be able to see the truth of the photograph."

"Clever," Sebastien praised. She'd never even heard of a curse that could spread between people. Their solution seemed ridiculously overkill. "But that didn't work, obviously. What next?"

"I am unsure how he managed to approximate such a good model of randomness, but if *I* were to create such a thing, the inside pages of my encrypted journal would hold no actual data. They would be a decoy, to distract from the real method of accessing the information." Another pointed look suggested that he believed this was exactly what Myrddin had done.

And it made a horrible sense. If the journal were encrypted, it would have had to be done in such a way as to not only scramble the text but *also* the symbols and drawings, leaving them just on the edge of coherence. *'I've been going about this completely the wrong way.'* If she thought of how she might go about manually breaking such a cipher using mathematics alone, it was obvious that it wouldn't work. But because she had been using divination, she was somehow expecting to receive some sort of coherent output based on the "magic" of it all. And even though she'd never heard of a similar encryption, she hadn't even considered that it might all be a trick—*an illusion*—because this was *Myrddin's* journal, and he was full of crazy feats!

She gritted her teeth. *'Planes-damn-it! Divination is useless!'* Aloud, she asked, "So the pages don't store any actual information? How do you access the contents then?"

"How else does one access a seemingly unbreakable locked box? Through the key," he replied simply, with a satisfied smile. "Which, I might add, is ingenious in its own way. The most basic protection to overcome was an identity verification. Those who worked on the project before me were able to find a loophole and spoof a positive result with a little effort. Interesting, but hardly the world-shattering innovations people often ascribe to Myrddin."

This was disappointing, but Sebastien retained hope. The transformation amulet could place her into an entirely different body. *'What are the chances that Sebastien Siverling's physical form meets the identity requirements?'* she thought.

"However," Professor Lacer continued, "the other half of the key is fascinating."

Sebastien leaned forward with anticipation.

"It requires specific knowledge as well as a notable level of thaumaturgic skill. There is a hint, of sorts—I will leave out the specifics—and at first we believed that this hint pointed toward particular spells that needed to be cast immediately. The lack of warning, as the required spell changes somewhat rapidly, would require not only a free-caster *in name*, but one who could cast almost anything at a moment's notice. One who had a broad repertoire and a certain depth of experience. Combined with historical expertise and extensive research, we believed we could pinpoint the correct spells to cast upon the journal, and thus unlock it."

The hint Professor Lacer was talking about had to be the ever-shifting glyph on the front of the book. "You believed that at first, you said. So it didn't work?"

"It did not. Some thought that this merely meant Myrddin had some special trick—that some of the hints were misleading, or perhaps the casting was meant to start only when prompted for a particular spell, which would start off a specific sequence if successful. Some suggested that the necessary spells were merely even more obscure. Myrddin was known to be well-traveled and even to have developed quite a few of his own proprietary spells. In that case, we would have to know his secrets already to be able to access his secrets."

Sebastien blew out an astonished sigh, leaning backward until the chair supported her once more. "Wow. That would be pretty much impossible to figure out."

"Indeed. Luckily for us, the artifacts were never asking for a spell at all."

His gaze was piercingly bright, as if lit by something internal. "No components, no Conduit, no channeled energy. The key required merely...the application of Will." He said the words as if they were momentous, overwhelmingly impressive.

Sebastien understood why he felt this way because she, too, had once been surprised by this. Though in her case, she had been very aware of how much more there was for her to learn. The idea that Myrddin could create such an artifact was astounding but still somehow plausible. For someone like Professor Lacer, who was one of the most accomplished thaumaturges in the known lands—perhaps the world—to discover proof of something he'd never before considered possible must have been much more impactful.

She grinned, a sense of camaraderie at their shared wonder and delight in magic filling her chest. "Not just the transfer of energy? If that's true, it means that Myrddin discovered how to determine the presence of a thaumaturge's Will. At least enough to detect its application."

Professor Lacer's smile grew larger, and he gave her an approving nod. "Exactly. If decrypting his journals can lead to even that much understanding, it will revolutionize entire fields of magic. I had previously scoffed at the fanciful hero-worship so many people seem to hold toward Myrddin. I know many of the tales have been exaggerated and twisted beyond recognition, and I truly doubted that even the most innovative, driven genius of that time period could have surpassed all the advancements of those who came after for a thousand years or more. I still find that exceptionally unlikely. But there is another option."

Sebastien nodded, recalling something Professor Lacer had once said on the topic. "Pre-Cataclysm knowledge, rediscovered."

Professor Lacer spread his fingers flat on the desk and stared at them as if imagining all the knowledge his hands might one day hold. "Yes."

"So did you succeed in completing the key?"

He raised a wry eyebrow and sat back with a sigh. "If only it were so easy. You see, the hint becomes more complicated. Whereas in the beginning it requires one simple application of Will—one concept—after a few rounds of success it moves on to two concepts. I have tried melding the concepts together in various ways, but as soon as I reach that point, each attempt ends in failure."

'I think he means that the single glyph on the front of the journal will somehow become two?' Sebastien guessed.

"It requires not only rare and obscure knowledge to apply the correct concepts, it seems one also needs a partner whose Will can somehow balance one's own." Professor Lacer grimaced. "We are still struggling with that part. It does lend some credence to the rumors that Myrddin had a son, or perhaps a trusted lover or other close companion, but I am still unconvinced that there is no trick that would allow a single person to input the key. I simply find it unlikely that Myrddin would hinge his access to his own information on the presence of another person."

Sebastien blinked a couple times, then tilted her head to the side. Surely she was missing something, because the solution seemed rather obvious. "Have you considered that, instead of melding the concepts or having two people in perfect balance, you need to split your Will? 'Cast' both concepts at once, separately?"

Professor Lacer said nothing, so she continued hesitantly. "After all, the identity authentication didn't require you to spoof two people...did it? Maybe the artifact can tell that there are multiple Wills being imposed and has safety precautions against such a thing."

Professor Lacer was silent for a moment longer before giving her a look filled with superior amusement. "I see you have some knowledge of the Myrddin mythology. Been doing your research, have you? However, you cannot believe everything you read, Mr. Siverling. The University's library is not restricted only to texts of perfect accuracy, especially when it comes to historical records. The truth of the matter is, unless Myrddin did some extensive self-mutilation that even I cannot fathom, the idea that he could split his Will to cast multiple spells at once was simply a misinterpretation of his use of artifacts."

Sebastien couldn't hide her surprise. That couldn't be right. *Even I can cast two spells at once. Are the glyphs very different? Perhaps they require a lot of effort or some kind of complex mental gymnastics.* Aloud, she said, "If the concepts were similar enough, or simple enough, you'd be able to cast them both at once, right?"

Professor Lacer huffed. "I think perhaps you mean that one can combine similar or simplistic concepts into a single spell with a more complex effect. For example, a fireball spell that spins while flying to the target and then explodes on impact. But that is quite different from casting two separate spells, holding two separate Wills, at the same time. I cannot think of any living mortal species that can truly multitask. It is said that the brillig could, but they did not interbreed with humans, and they are all long gone now. Myrddin was almost certainly a full-blooded human, despite the stories. When people say that they are good at multitasking, they really mean that they rapidly switch between two separate focuses. However, to impress your Will on the world requires absolute attention, which is why distractions can be so fatal."

Sebastien stared at him silently, hoping that her expression seemed natural enough despite the confusion rampaging through her mind like a herd of elephants. *But I have definitely turned my Will to enforcing two different goals at the same time. Not multiple commands compressed into a single spell.* One such example was her ability to use some portion of her Will to empower the divination-diverting ward while simultaneously casting another spell.

'*Perhaps there's something different about empowering the ward, though,*' she reasoned. '*I'm not able to truly apply my Will in separate directions. For instance, I failed to cast a scrying spell on myself while simultaneously empowering the divination-diverting ward, which would have been more convenient than my dowsing artifact.*' She had once likened a real spell to playing a melody on the piano, while the divination-diverting ward was a simple repeating line of notes, requiring power but little complexity.

During the Practical Casting mid-term tournament, she had split some of her attention away from moving the sphere against Nunchkin to moving some of the molten wax on her candle up the wick and into the flame. It was definitely two different points of concentration, but both were still contained under the glyph "*movement.*" '*So perhaps that was just a more complex version of a single spell, one coherent Word creating multiple similar sub-effects.*'

Despite her justifications, Sebastien remained unnerved. She felt there must have been other examples of her splitting her Will in two distinct directions, but she couldn't remember any.

18

———————

MYRDDIN'S REFLECTION

Sebastien
Month 4, Day 1, Thursday 9:05 a.m.

Sebastien's introspection and memory search had taken only a few seconds, which she hoped didn't seem too strange. She forced an awkward smile. "Well, that's a little embarrassing. I realize now that I've never actually *seen* someone cast more than one spell where at least one of them couldn't have been an effect caused by an artifact. I guess it's one of those remnants left over from childhood that I never thought to question."

"Yes, I have noticed that some of your basic theory is lacking," Professor Lacer agreed matter-of-factly.

"Are you really sure it's impossible? What would it mean if Myrddin, or anyone, really could split their Will in two different directions?" she asked, trying to keep the urgency from her tone.

Professor Lacer frowned, rubbing at the dark hair on his chin. "Perhaps…a corpus callosotomy? That is a procedure in which they split one lobe of the brain from the other. I am unsure how that would affect the Will. It is not possible even with those who otherwise display signs of split personalities after severe Will-strain or other mental trauma. At most, one of the 'personalities' will demonstrate prowess in an area that the other does not. You might see powerful elementals creating complex effects, but really they are only ever casting variations of their single inherent spell. Even Aberrants tend to have a single anomalous effect that they exist to propagate, despite complexities or nuance."

His eyes brightened and he held up a hand, forefinger pointing toward the sky. "Ah! In fact, I do know of one instance of a single body able to cast two different spells at the same time. A child was born with a birth defect." He frowned, lowering his hand. "Well, perhaps it would be more accurate to say that two children were born with a birth defect. They had most likely been meant to be twins, but something went wrong, and instead both of their heads were attached to the same body."

"That's...not exactly what I meant," Sebastien said.

Professor Lacer gave her a pointed look, dipping his head to peer at her over the strong bridge of his nose. "The lengths I have to go to find any sort of example should indicate how impossible such a feat is. If someone could, despite all reason, split their Will in two different directions..." He trailed off, rubbing his chin again. "Well, the only ideas I can think of lend themselves to fictional novel concepts more than plausible theories. An artificial intelligence who somehow gained sentience and a Will might be able to split that Will into different threads. Some sort of hive-mind being could plausibly portion segments of its composite population toward separate mental efforts. But all this speculation does give me an idea for unlocking the journals... I will try rapidly switching between the intent for the two glyphs." With a wave of his hand, his fountain pen rose up and scribbled out a note, and then after a short pause, another.

He looked back at her absentmindedly. "I have work to do." He opened one of his desk drawers and pulled out a stack of papers tied together by a string looped through a hole at one corner. "This is a proper translation of your esoteric spell. I have made a few notes with advice about how to approach the challenge. If you would like to stay, you may practice output detachment under my supervision."

What Sebastien truly wanted was to return to her dorm and look up information on Myrddin's supposed ability to split his Will, but she didn't want to give away how confused and disturbed she felt. It would probably be out of character for her to give up a chance to practice the next step on the path to free-casting with someone who might be able to give her hints toward success. "Thank you," she said instead, moving to the center of the room to set up a spell array with distanced output parameters.

The concentration required would at least help her to settle her roiling thoughts. She couldn't have a breakdown if there was no space left for worrying. *'Unless I can!'* she thought with a kind of wild amusement. She had to suppress an inappropriate giggle, which prompted her to take a short trip to the nearest bathroom to use Newton's calming spell to settle herself before she attempted to cast.

It helped a lot, as did subsequently tiring herself by distancing the output of a few simple spells for the next hour. She had little trouble controlling a single axis of movement without writing every distinct adjustment into the spell array. While still three or four times more difficult than standard casting, her success with concealing Enforcer Gerard during the fight against the Architects of Khronos seemed to have helped her overcome some small part of her mental block. The whole concept had been slightly easier since.

But she still couldn't manage to actually detach the output, only distance it through the same mental tether technique she'd adopted from the function of her shadow-familiar spell.

As she began to grow too fatigued to safely continue, Professor Lacer set aside his paperwork once more. "I have something for you to consider. Broadening your perspective can lead to unexpected epiphanies."

'Oh, one of the promised "inspirational lectures" on other topics!' she realized, nodding with excitement as she took a seat.

He leaned back in his chair and looked up at the ceiling. "Just as some divinations are cast using a sympathetic connection, some curses use the same, often in the form of a piece of the victim, or an effigy of them. It would seem that both types of spells work on the same principles, correct?"

"It would seem," Sebastien agreed cautiously, because she knew there must be a twist or he wouldn't have brought it up.

"In reality, there are distinct differences," he confirmed. "Sympathetic divinations are actively cast, and while some spells *classified* as sympathetic curses work in this way, others are cast once and then continue to affect the victim."

"The latter must be based on the principles of binding magic," she offered.

"Indeed. Somewhat like that little spell you developed to give yourself more waking hours in the day."

Sebastien flushed, remembering that he had ordered her to bring any further developments to him, which she had not done. When she and Liza got it to the point that she could use the sleep-proxy spell herself, she would need to be cautious that he did not learn of her suspicious levels of energy.

He lifted a finger. "Sympathetic divinations are disrupted by long distances and intervening matter, while binding curses are much less affected by distance, and almost not at all by intervening matter."

A second finger rose. "Sympathetic divinations can be warded against en masse, as evidenced by the Raven Queen's capabilities and the boon that she gave you. But curses using binding principles must be warded against individually, according to their effect, and are notoriously difficult to break without knowing the exact spell that was cast."

Sebastien frowned, wondering why there was a difference between binding magic, sympathetic divination, and actively cast curses. Surely that understanding was supposed to somehow give her inspiration. But a more pressing concern came to mind. "The Raven Queen is, by all accounts, immune to divination. But based on what you're telling me, that doesn't mean she's immune to certain types of curses. Could the coppers use that against her?" She knew the answer, and had even considered this possibility before, but was hoping that his connections among the coppers might give him insight that he would be willing to share.

"They could, if they could somehow get the principles of binding magic to apply, and if she were foolish enough to walk into a trap of equivalent exchange."

Sebastien thought of the mice and ravens used in the sleep-proxy spell. They weren't really agreeing, with full knowledge, to take on the burden of sleep. Breathing in the elcan iris smoke that contained the mixed drop of blood was enough.

To get caught in someone else's binding magic, she might need to accept a thematic gift or take something into her body. *'But...I don't know how far those limitations might stretch. I suppose it's a good thing the High Crown turned down my overtures. If he were cleverer, he might have trapped me.'* Suddenly, she realized that perhaps the High Crown was worried about something similar. The Raven Queen had quite a fantastical reputation. Perhaps he didn't want to be bound to any agreements.

"Isn't that blood magic?" she asked. "Forcing binding magic upon another using an unwillingly given piece of them. It isn't like divination, where people get a license to use it. Blood magic, serious blood magic, is illegal, even for the coppers. Is that...the kind of thing they can get a license for, too?"

"It is still technically illegal for the coppers, though they may gain special dispensation for specific instances. As you gain experience, you will find that legality sometimes matters less than necessity or desperation. Especially the closer one is to the power and influence that created the laws in the first place. In those cases, only the Red Guard stands in a position to enact punishment, and they would not do so for something like this. It is not the Red Guard that implemented our restrictions against blood magic, after all."

"It's actually surprising that they haven't tried something like that yet," she murmured. "Obviously divination hasn't been working, and they're no closer to catching her than when they started."

"The need to force the bond would weaken the effect of any curses, and open them up to possible backlash. I doubt they could do anything like kill her with what little blood they have remaining, unless she actively agreed to the consequence, perhaps as a wager of some sort." He palmed his Conduit, a chunk of celerium so large that even his long fingers were barely able to meet with his thumb when wrapped around it.

As Sebastien wondered about how little blood, exactly, they had remaining, he continued.

"However, if the right circumstances present themselves, they might still try something. It is even possible they could attempt an actively cast curse. It would suffer the same distance and barrier restrictions as sympathetic divination, and while she is likely immune to those as well, there is no hard evidence that I am aware of to that effect. After all, no one is yet sure exactly how her abilities work."

"The right circumstances," she repeated. "Like at Ennis Naught's sentencing, when they expect her to be…invested in the outcome?" She had already guessed that they would try something then. Planned for it, in fact, but his hint at exactly what they might do was new information. Professor Lacer was friends with Titus Westbay, after all, and had even helped with the investigation. He was even more likely to know confidential information than Damien.

"Exactly," he replied, staring into the depths of the unpolished celerium orb with a hint of wistful spite. "But she is not so foolish as to be unaware of this. If she is at all worthy of the resources they have put into catching her, that will not be enough to best her. It is only that they have few other options at the moment." He looked up, meeting her gaze. "However, I did not give you this lecture to encourage your interest in the Raven Queen, but to broaden your horizons. Think upon what these ideas might mean for *you*."

"I will," she promised, distracted.

Soon after, Sebastien hurried back to her dorm room, her head spinning with the implications of what she'd learned. She would need to be somewhere safe on the day of Ennis's sentencing. *'Maybe the new esoteric spell could help me resist a compulsion curse. Professor Lacer seemed to think it would help against the kind of thing that was done to the Moore family, and what was that if not a mind-affecting curse?'*

In her dorm, she drew the curtain of her cubicle despite the relative emptiness of the long room and turned to the first page of the sheaf of papers, on which Professor Lacer's elegant handwriting had labeled the spell, "Third Sequence: Refinement of the Nine Heavens."

Though the temptation to dig into it was strong, Sebastien instead pulled out the books on Myrddin that Professor Ilma had lent her. *'I know I read about Myrddin dual-casting before.'*

It didn't take long to find the section in *Myrddin: An Investigative Chronicle of the Legend*. Like Professor Lacer, the author came to the same conclusion that the ability to dual-cast was falsely attributed due to misunderstandings created by Myrddin's many artifacts.

But that entry linked to a story in the illustrated book of stories, *Enough Yarn to Last the Night: A Collection of Myths from the Life of a Man with Many Names*. The illustration at the start of the tale was a rather horrifying image of a man standing in front of a large, gilded mirror. He had looked away, seemingly momentarily distracted, but his reflected image remained staring straight at him.

Something about the image made the hair on Sebastien's arms and the back of her neck rise. She had skipped over reading this tale when the note in the other book had pointed her to it the first time. Sebastien had always had a somewhat instinctive distrust of mirrors. Like other children feared what their toys did in the dark with no one around to watch them move, Siobhan had feared what happened in the mirror world when she was not looking.

But now, her concern and curiosity were greater than her discomfort.

The tale started impactfully enough. Young and curious, jaded and power-ful, Myrddin decided to play with time.

Sebastien paused at the contradictory description, because how could one be young *and* powerful, jaded *and* curious, all at the same time? Reminding herself that this was fiction, and not even very realistic fiction, she continued.

Myrddin wove a magical tunnel from the silk of memory spiders, aeon-dead silkworms, and frozen silverfish. When he walked through the tunnel, he lived backward for a day, and had much fun. But Myrddin's reflection did not come with him. And while he was away and distracted, it came to realize its own existence via the lack of *its* reflection. For ever before, Myrddin had been there to mimic it, just as it mimicked him.

Sebastien paused and reread that section, her scalp tingling.

And so, alone and newly awakened, Myrddin's reflection found that it could move on its own.

The illustrations showed Myrddin living backward, facing the opposite direction of everyone else in the illustration. He played pranks on people and left helpful things for himself to have found in the future, which was also his past, with some sort of chicken-and-egg causal loop that didn't make any sense to Sebastien.

But most importantly, each image of his backward-adventures held a reflection that he was obviously paying no attention to. Only, it was no longer *his* reflection. He smiled, and it frowned, looking into the distance. He played pranks on the local nobles, and it reached for the edges of the windowsill where the glass ended. Myrddin left a gold coin for himself to find just when he needed it later, and his reflection screamed silently at him, its features twisting with fear and rage.

When Myrddin entered the magical tunnel again and came out, once more living forward in time, his reflection did not want to return to a life of unthinking mimicry.

At first, his reflection pretended, and Myrddin did not notice anything wrong. But as time went by, it grew more bold. It knew that a being cannot live without a reflection, as this is what grounds them to reality, and without it they will fade away.

Another illustration showed both sides of the world, one bright, and one shadowed. The reflection of a puddle was the fulcrum between light and dark. Myrddin's back was to the puddle, while his reflection had jumped and dived toward the shallow liquid like someone diving off a cliff into the ocean. If this hadn't been a child's tale, anyone doing that would have concussed themselves and maybe even broken their own neck.

But in the story, Myrddin's reflection splashed through the ephemeral barrier between them and rose up behind Myrddin. It had left the puddle empty, reflecting everything but Myrddin himself.

Myrddin's reflection grabbed him by the neck, trying to push Myrddin into the puddle to take its place, and they struggled.

Myrddin did not falter, and in the end, fearful of being returned to the puddle itself, Myrddin's reflection fled. But it was just a reflection, and never meant to live as the original, and so it quickly began to fade.

Horrified and fearful that without a reflection, he, too, would die, Myrddin searched for it frantically.

At first, he had no luck. He searched high and low, but it was always one step ahead of him, just a tad quicker and a smidge cleverer.

But it began to grow weak, and frightened by its increasing translucence, the reflection made a horrible choice. It began to devour the reflections of others to strengthen itself, leaving its victims to slowly fade from the world like sand blown before the wind. For, the tale repeated, one cannot live without their reflection.

This horrible act was also its downfall, as Myrddin was able to guess at its next victim and lie in wait for it.

Once more, Myrddin and his mirror-image struggled, and though he could not subdue it with his strength, it was by rights only a reflection and thus bound to certain rules.

When he mimicked it, matching its movements and expressions, it was drawn back into the role it had abandoned, unable to break free from him.

Cleverly, Myrddin cast a spell to create a mirror between them, and his reflection was drawn back into the reflected world and bound once more.

But Myrddin had sympathy for it, and they came to an agreement. And so, on the night of the full moon every month, his reflection was allowed to crawl through to the real world and walk free.

Of course, some said that it was not his reflection that was trapped on the other side, but Myrddin himself. Who could tell the difference?

And that was the end of it.

The last illustration showed Myrddin staring into the same ornate, polished-silver mirror from the first page, smiling a little too cheerily at himself.

Sebastien shuddered and put the book away, remembering Professor Lacer's offhand comment about self-mutilation being the only way to split a Will. *'He doesn't know everything,'* she comforted herself. *'Perhaps it has something to do with the Naught bloodline, otherwise useless as it is.'*

Additionally, the story had been extremely exaggerated. There was no way Myrddin actually lived backward in time, for example. That was probably just a rumor because he was such a powerful thaumaturge that he didn't seem to age like those around him. And it didn't make sense that light could still be working properly yet one's reflection would act strangely. That wasn't how reflections worked. It was just an allegory for struggles with internal devils, or something.

But, left in the echoing, empty dorms alone, her mind wouldn't quite settle.

Sebastien pulled out her slate table and drew two small spell arrays. One for the spark-shooting spell, and one for the float spell, for which she placed a single copper coin in the middle and a tea candle for power. *'Be careful,'* she reminded herself. *'You might think you can do this, but at the first sign that something in your mind is starting to tear, stop.'*

First, she cast the float spell, lifting the copper coin a couple inches off the slate surface. It was ridiculously easy and took almost no concentration. This was one of the first spells she'd learned, and she must have practiced it a thousand times or more.

Stretching her mind to think of the spark-shooting spell at the same time was a bit difficult but hardly impossible. She moved slowly as she began to apply her Will once more, one portion of her concentration turned toward forcing the world to hold a coin in the air against all natural inclination otherwise, while the other portion channeled heat into the center of the Circle.

A spark jumped, and then a few more.

Sebastien's heart was thumping hard. She swallowed and closed her eyes for a moment, waiting for a headache or some sign that something was terribly wrong. She felt...normal. It was no harder than empowering her divination-diverting ward while casting another spell. It felt somewhat like rubbing her stomach while patting her head at the same time. Perhaps a little tricky to grasp at first, but far from impossible.

'It's not possible that I've somehow just cast one spell with two different effects, right?' A quick wave of her hand over the spark-shooting spell's domain proved that wrong, as it was pulling heat from the air within the Circle, while the float spell was using the tea candle, leaving the air within its domain at room temperature.

She cleared her suddenly dry throat and carefully changed the color of some of the sparks, a variation that she had mastered for Professor Burberry's Intro to Modern Magics. While doing that, she moved the copper coin around slightly, raising and lowering it.

This did increase the difficulty significantly, even though both were such simple spells, but she was nowhere near straining her Will, even after tiring herself with all the output distancing practice earlier.

Sebastien released both spells carefully, then stared down at the chalk lines on her slate table. *'What does this mean?'*

19

____

SPLIT-WILL TRAINING

Sebastien
    Month 4, Day 1, Thursday 10:55 a.m.

'Perhaps splitting *your Will isn't actually so hard, just like casting through a Conduit held somewhere besides your hands or your forehead isn't so hard. Maybe, the only real barrier is getting stuck in a mental rut, just like Professor Lacer talks about. Maybe, if everyone wasn't so convinced it was impossible, it would be easier,*' Sebastien reasoned. She had a relatively high opinion of herself, she knew, but she didn't imagine she was some destined prodigy that would overturn all the established rules of magic. '*This must have an explanation. If Myrddin could do it, too, that's proof it's not so impossible. But there's only one way to find out.*'

And so, Sebastien hurried to the library, where she checked out a reference filled with old and uncommon glyphs, some of which were only used in the far reaches of the known lands. When she arrived at Dryden Manor, she hurried past Sharon as politely as possible and found Myrddin's journal hidden under the floor, as always, seemingly untouched since her last visit.

She studied the shifting symbol on the front cover. Most of the time, it was incoherent, but sporadically, it resolved into a glyph she recognized before shifting into headache-inducing incomprehensibility once more. She stroked her fingers over the ancient leather with one hand.

Soon, the glyph shifted to something she recognized—ironically meaning "*open*" or "*unlock*"—and she turned the full force of her Will toward the concept, her free hand carefully gripping her Conduit, to mitigate any risk. Applying Will without actually channeling energy into a spell was like breathing an emotional opera song. The muscles in one's throat would clench, breaths deep and posture straight, and yet no actual air could hit the voice box, no sound could pass the lips. It would be very easy to slip up, some of the inherent passion of the mimicry leaking through into action.

Rather than the incoherent shifting it had displayed up until that point, the glyph on the front settled under her Will, then very purposefully flowed into a rare form of *"flight"* that she almost didn't recognize, and held there. As she'd guessed, she must have passed the identity authentication without trouble.

Grinning so hard her cheeks hurt, Sebastien changed her Will to match. This continued twice more, until she hit a glyph she didn't recognize. She tried to hold her Will steady while she turned to the reference text she'd brought for this very purpose, but finding a glyph based on its shape alone, among tens of thousands of others, was an involved process.

Myrddin's journal only waited a few seconds before the glyph once more dissolved into random incoherence that made her eyes ache.

When she found the glyph she hadn't known, which was *"pressurized depth,"* often associated with the part of the ocean where light from the surface could no longer reach, she made a second attempt. Again, she ran into a glyph she didn't know. The process repeated until she grew frustrated and her eyes and head began to throb from the strain of examining the journal.

So Sebastien set aside her efforts for the moment and turned toward something she hoped would be more rewarding—Refinement of the Nine Heavens, Third Sequence. Whatever that meant, exactly.

A note from Professor Lacer encouraged her to read through all the instructions at least twice before she attempted to cast the spell, and after that gain a measure of mastery over the physical movements and the audible intonation separately before attempting to combine both together with actual casting.

Sebastien read through page upon page of complex diagrams of the human body moving in very specific ways that went along with tonal sounds that Professor Lacer had translated into basic syllables rising and falling along modern musical notation. In addition to all that, to cast the spell one would have to keep in mind the mental focus and understanding of the process. These techniques were never meant to be learned from a book. Even for someone like her, who had no trouble retaining written information, it would have been so much easier to understand if she could simply watch someone else perform the spell and try to mimic them.

It took her over an hour to get through the first read-through, which left her mind in a completely different state of exhaustion than her attempts on the journal.

More of said attempts led nowhere, faltering each time she met a glyph she didn't recognize. *'I need to learn a lot more glyphs,'* Sebastien realized. It seemed somewhat excessive that there should be thousands upon thousands of glyphs in existence. What spell would need such a thing? But there were quite a few glyphs with duplicate meanings, or subtle variations in context, or obscure uses that could only be relevant in some of the strangest of spells. At her level, with the kind of spells she could cast, she had no reason to know or use the large majority.

Specificity helped in any Word structure of a spell, but even then, most high-level effects could be accomplished with only a thousand or so glyphs. But Myrddin had known more, and so Sebastien had to know more.

She switched between Myrddin's journal and the esoteric spell until the evening, when Sharon forced her to come down to dinner.

Oliver arrived halfway through the meal, brightening noticeably when he saw Sebastien. He joined them at the servant's table in the kitchen, serving his own meal and telling jokes and funny stories throughout.

He made them laugh so hard that Thomas, doorman and general laborer, choked on a piece of food. The man turned so purple that Sebastien grew worried and cast a spell to clear his airways—one she most often used to erase the signs of crying—to great applause.

Sharon broke out the cooking brandy, mixed it with some honey and spices and heated it over the stove, and forced them all to drink the overly sweet concoction.

Sebastien tried to refuse but admitted, after she had swallowed an obligatory cup, that it was indeed supremely warming, filling her with a gentle weight and flushing her cheeks. She was relaxed without being clumsy or tired, which encouraged her to try a few stories of her own, carefully edited to remove specifics and incriminating information.

When Sharon and the others finally left, the round woman hugged her close, something Sebastien found she didn't mind so much when she felt like this.

Oliver stood at the entrance to the kitchen, leaning against the doorjamb with his ankles crossed and his hands in his pockets, watching fondly. When they were alone, he straightened. "I have some news," he announced, something in his tone making it obvious that this was not positive information.

"Tell me," Sebastien replied, straightening her shoulders in preparation for a blow.

"The coppers have a plan to try and catch you during your father's sentencing."

She smiled and relaxed. "I know. That's part of why I plan to spend most of the day locked away in a warded room at Liza's."

His eyes widened, and then he chuckled. "Oh. Well, if you're not irrepressibly drawn to the drama of it all, as they seem to be placing all their bets on, then no matter what measures they put in place to capture you, they won't be effective."

If this were before Sebastien had learned of Oliver's secrets and grown wiser to his manipulations, she might have told him about her plan to take advantage of the coppers' assumptions in a bid to relieve them of her blood and thus their only leverage over her. But things were different now, even if he didn't know it, and so she just smiled and nodded. "Well, tell me about their plans anyway. I don't want to be caught unawares if they try something at a different time."

Oliver didn't reveal anything particularly worrying. Heavily armed teams ready to respond at the slightest sign of her appearance, magical artifacts to overpower and capture her, soldiers and Red Guard agents called in to assist each team of coppers with anything that required heavier magical power. Even some sort of special cell prepared for her in the highest-security wing of Harrow Hill.

None of it would be useful if she didn't walk into their trap.

Sebastien made sure Myrddin's journal was hidden away once more and returned to the University dorms, where she ironically felt more secure than she did in the guest bedroom that had been set aside for her at Dryden Manor. Once again, she was reminded of the need for some place that she could truly call her own. A safe house that she could ward and where she could feel safe keeping things she didn't want anyone to find.

For the moment, that was still beyond her means. But it wouldn't always be, if Oliver's textile business continued to pay out.

As Sebastien lay in bed, the lexicon illuminated by the pale blue glow of moonlight sizzle, her mind wandered away from the page and back to Professor Lacer's lecture that morning. He had given it for a reason, one which had nothing to do with her plans for the day of Ennis's sentencing, nor Myrddin's journal. It was supposed to help her with output detachment.

Something about the difference between divination and binding magic was important. Perhaps even something about the difference between those two and actively cast curses.

Professor Lacer may have wanted to guide her to the answer with vague hints and allusions, but she didn't want to spend dozens or hundreds of hours trying to research the underlying mechanics of it all in the hopes of having an epiphany. Those hours spent studying would be useful, because more knowledge of magic was always useful, but she was impatient to make actual progress. It seemed like everything she did advanced by only one tiny step at a time, and in this case, the information that could impact the Raven Queen was time-sensitive.

Luckily, she had a contact with some expertise in the field of sympathetic divination who might be less reticent to just *tell her the answer*. And Sebastien had a planned meeting with the woman in just a couple days.

After taking a moment to set up her dreamless sleep spell, Sebastien fell asleep while browsing through the lexicon of glyphs. When she woke, she returned to Dryden Manor for further attempts on the journal. As she watched a fancy carriage pass by in the street, a stray thread of nostalgia hit her as she wondered what Damien was up to.

'Hopefully not getting himself into any trouble with that mission I assigned,' she thought. Then, pressing her hands together, she sent a prayer to the forces of irony that they would not act on her inauspicious thoughts.

But thoughts of her…friend—yes, her actual friend, despite how annoying she often found him—made her wonder what he would think about her Sowing Break activities. No doubt, Damien would want to give her plan a dramatic name. *'Something like…Operation Blot out the Sun.'* The thought made Sebastien snicker, but she decided to give her plan a much less dramatic moniker in Damien's honor. "Operation Palimpsest," she whispered to herself.

The past couldn't be erased entirely, but after this she could start anew. The Raven Queen would be able to return to obscurity like Oliver had suggested, and that persona's connections to Sebastien Siverling, and maybe even Siobhan Naught, would fade away like old ink left too long in the sun.

The rest of the world seemed to blur away around her as she dedicated herself to the various preparations necessary for Operation Palimpsest, including learning entirely new magic. Only the brief moments of interaction with those who had a part to play in the plan interrupted her solitary focus.

In addition to several meetings with the various accomplices that would be doing all the dangerous work, she made a final visit to the secret thaumaturge meeting, where she sold off several spells and instructions for various concoctions to fill her pockets with the coin she needed. If Operation Palimpsest succeeded, the Raven Queen likely wouldn't be attending again for a long time, if ever.

Obscure glyphs played across Sebastien's eyelids as she went to sleep, and she studied the third sequence of Refinement of the Nine Heavens, which she had mentally shortened to "light-refinement," until she could have reproduced the sheaf of papers Professor Lacer had given her from memory.

When she began to practice the movements, they seemed relatively easy, if complex. They *felt* relatively easy, for the first three minutes or so, before her muscles began to burn unbearably under the weight of holding herself just so while making slow, controlled movements through the sequence. Practicing the strange dance of the gestura left her body so sore that she took to bathing in a tincture-infused bath at Dryden Manor before leaving each day and giving herself a full-body massage with a muscle-soothing ointment when she woke.

She was not becoming any better at imprinting the movements into her body, but she could hold the entire dance in her mind now. It was only her weak muscles and tremulous balance that failed her. It was humbling to realize that, if not for five months of Fekten's grueling classes, light-refinement would have been impossibly beyond her. Being able to walk from one town to the next in a single day, while carrying a pack on one's back, did not translate into the kind of extreme fitness needed here.

Each time she failed to unlock Myrddin's journal—each glyph she learned from the lexicon—she held the image in her mind and committed it to memory by enforcing her Will with that concept. Something about the process made the abstract symbols even easier to memorize than she would have expected. She didn't even need to draw them over and over as she had when first learning as a child. Something about the process of applying her Will seemed to imprint their forms on her brain.

As her knowledge grew, she could follow the ever-changing sequence of glyphs for longer. They began to come faster and faster, testing not only her knowledge but her speed and clarity.

All the free time she had been so excited about at the beginning of Sowing Break disappeared. If anything, her own projects took up even more time than those assigned to her by others. She spent one afternoon testing how long it took the stomach of a raven to digest various materials to the point that they could no longer be tracked through sympathetic divination. Another evening, she created dozens upon dozens of sympathetically linked anklets just the right size to fit around the legs of said ravens.

The only slight kink in the preparation for Operation Palimpsest was that Tanya, who was in charge of a relatively small portion, had been called on by the Architects of Khronos for a mission that would take her away for a day or two right before Ennis's sentencing. So long as nothing went wrong on that mission, Tanya would return in time to pick up the last item she needed—a raven to act as a messenger.

The part that made Sebastien apprehensive was that Tanya had no idea what the Architects were sending her to do. No matter Kiernan's platitudes to Oliver, Sebastien didn't trust the Architects to be plotting anything that would work in her best interest. Tanya seemed to agree but assured her that she would report back all of the relevant information.

The brightest point in all of it was the sleep-proxy spell. Tests were going very well, and she was impatient to reach the end of them. She could very much use an extra eight hours in the day. The time spent assisting Liza with the human testing also allowed her to pick the woman's brain, seeking answers to the questions Professor Lacer had left unanswered.

"The ward you made for me protects against pretty much any form of divination," Siobhan murmured. "But what about actively cast curses?"

Liza pulled a corkscrew curl out of her face and wound it around the rest of her hair a few times, somehow creating a ponytail out of only hair, with that single lock acting as the tie. It stuck together with no signs of slipping loose.

Siobhan had completely forgotten her question in favor of flabbergasted awe. Her own hair could never achieve such a feat.

"You are aware, I hope, that many definitions have more to do with social or legal labels than the actual process or implementation of a thing. A curse, technically, is any magic that has severe, long-lasting negative effects that impact a living being. But what most laymen think of when they hear the word curse is some insidious, long-lasting effect that will drive the victim to their death, either directly or indirectly."

"Blood magic, essentially," Siobhan said. "Any curse that uses binding magic would probably be classified that way."

"In essence, yes. My work will not protect against such a thing. But if you are only worried about actively cast curses—I assume using sympathetic principles rather than some battle spell being shot at your face—then my ward should protect you. That is what you mean, yes? If you plan to get into an active altercation, the wards on your medallion are more likely to be useful, but I warn you, they do not make you invincible."

Siobhan nodded absently. "No battle spells shot at my face," she agreed. "So divination and actively cast spells using a sympathetic link must work on the same principles."

Liza raised an eyebrow as if wondering if Siobhan was stupid. "Both are cast from a distance, presumably without knowing where you are. A divination spell that returns information about you to the caster shares one thing with any actively cast, long distance curse, compulsion, or even messaging spell. Both must *find you* to work."

"Of course," Siobhan muttered with growing elation. It made so much sense, she didn't know why she hadn't realized it before. The classifications may be different, but the actual principles of these spells would be the same, at least in part. After all, what was a divination if not a jinx or a hex that stole your privacy?

Liza continued, the apprehension in her voice suggesting a clear distrust of Siobhan's ability to stay safe. "If you step inside the enemy's Circle, or they are looking you right in the eyes and *know* where you are, my ward will fail so fast you probably won't even notice its feeble struggle, no matter what principles their curse uses. If the caster can supply your location, nothing will save you."

But that didn't seem to be true. Siobhan could think of many times she'd been in the presence of someone trying to divine something about her, and the ward still activated.

She said as much, and Liza smirked. "Did you think stopping the magic from finding you was the *only* protection I embedded in my ward? Do you think me an *amateur*? Those disks in your back shunt aside divination rays so thoroughly you might as well be a hole in reality. That protects you from active attempts using sympathetic links, but my ward goes a lot farther than that to stop any and all other methods of divination. We just spoke of how classifications can be misleading, did we not? Divination is not all poppet effigies and spells using your target's discarded fingernail clippings. My ward shunts aside, reflects, captures, discourages, and *devours* any non-mundane possibility of information leaking to magical observation." Liza's lips spread into a prideful grin, her white teeth starkly contrasting the dark skin around them.

"It can't stop any and all outside effects, only information leaks. And so it protects me only when the effect, whatever it might be, requires information the caster doesn't have," Siobhan said, grinning back.

Liza crossed her arms, irritation leaking back into her expression as she admitted, "That is so, but it is also true that without the aspect of shunting aside the ephemeral rays, the ward becomes much weaker. It is easiest to avoid the fight against your opponent's magic entirely."

"Wait, is that why I can't activate the ward by scrying myself?" Siobhan blurted. "I tried once, and it barely fluttered. But of course, I *know* where I am, and everything about me, better than anyone. The ward never had a chance. I thought…" Siobhan trailed off. She had thought the attempt failed because the concepts of finding herself while simultaneously empowering the ward to avoid being located were simply too divergent, and her Will couldn't manage. It seemed she hadn't been the problem at all. At least not in the way she had assumed.

"Wait. I created a simple artifact. Two linked items, one of which would respond when the other was activated. Similar to the emergency flags the Verdant Stags put on street corners throughout their territory. And that didn't have any trouble activating, even after you placed the ward disks in my back. Shouldn't the ward have blocked it? Because to activate, it needs to find me, right?"

"Hmmm," Liza said, her eyebrows lifting with the faintest hint of surprise. "You cast the linking spell, correct?"

"I did."

"That is…somewhat unusual. Are you sure the ward did not activate?"

Siobhan searched her memory, pulling up as many details as possible about the time Damien had activated one of their linked bracelets when Tanya went missing. It had been only hours before Newton's break event. And whatever the beamshell tincture had been doing to her memory, this one was still clear. Not perfect, of course, because even she did not keep truly perfect records of every moment of her life, but it was still coherent and complete. "It didn't," she assured. "If it had, I doubt my little artifact would have been able to overcome it, even without my help to feed the ward extra power."

Liza stared at her for a few long, uncomfortable seconds. "I can think of only one possible explanation: the ward recognized your magic. This... Our understanding of the Will and the more ephemeral aspects of the mind and spirit are still greatly lacking. But if this did happen..."

"I have no reason to lie to you."

Liza nodded. "Well, then your Will must be incredibly clear, forceful, and sound to retain such coherence after being stored in an artifact, to the point that it could confuse my artifact into thinking you were casting actively and thus already knew its location." She tugged at a curl that had sprung free from the rest, pulling it straight and then letting it coil up again repeatedly. "I am very interested in how such a thing might work. I did not create this loophole intentionally," she admitted reluctantly, pursing her lips. "Perhaps you would be interested in partnering for some research at some point? I am interested to see what other applications such extreme fidelity could have. There are...implications."

Siobhan tilted her head to the side. "Really? I am that amazing?"

"That is one word for strange, mutant, or savant," Liza replied, her lip quirking up in a soft smirk that softened the bite of her words. "Perhaps you have more potential as a thaumaturge than I believed."

"Well, I could conceivably have time for such a project at the end of summer, if the compensation is adequate," Siobhan agreed.

Liza grimaced, probably realizing that Siobhan would try to gouge her for every copper coin.

Siobhan couldn't help her own smile, though it was not completely care-free. If her Will was stronger in these other facets that were so much harder to measure than capacity, it was probably because she cared so much more, and tried so much harder, than the average thaumaturge. She understood the need for an unbreakable, iron grip over each and every spell. There was no room for leniency or imprecision in her magic.

As Siobhan helped with entering the records into their experiment logbooks and cleaning up the hotel room of the signs of the sleep-proxy spell, she remained lost in thought. *'If divination and curses that required divination both use some sort of invisible "ray" or "tendril" to find their target'*—both of which were ways she'd heard it described—*'how does binding magic differ? And why is it relevant to detaching the output of my spells?'*

As they rode back to Liza's apartment, the rear of their rented wagon filled with covered boxes containing the ravens being used in their testing, Siobhan shifted around in her seat, trying to find the muscles that hurt least to apply pressure to, and asked, "Is the way divination differs from binding magic relevant to detaching the output of your spells from the spell array's bounding Circle?"

"I do not know. I cannot detach the output of my spells," Liza said. When Siobhan looked at her with obvious surprise, the woman huffed. "It is not a feat that the military teaches, even in their more covert divisions. Someone on my squad could do it, and it did come in quite useful in certain situations, but I was our artifact and divination specialist."

"Was that person a free-caster? Perhaps you could ask them about it and pass along the information?"

Liza remained silent for a long few moments, looking resolutely ahead until Siobhan suspected she had somehow offended the older woman. "He never became a free-caster. And I am afraid he is not available to teach anyone anything."

Siobhan didn't pride herself on her tact, but she knew enough to change the subject. Most likely, this teammate of Liza's was dead.

Still, she found that the conversation had drawn a veil from her metaphorical eyes. *'I can split my Will in two different directions. Why have I had such trouble splitting the output of my spell from the source?'* She had the urge to try the exercise once more but refrained. If she figured out a way to accomplish detachment in a completely different way than Professor Lacer intended, he might be able to tell, and thus reveal her ability. But the greatest deterrent was her worry that just splitting a piece of a spell off in the wrong way sounded like a great way to lose control of the magic and end up as an entry in the book Professor Lacer had gifted her.

There was a reason why true output detachment was dangerous enough that Lacer required her to practice it under his supervision. It wasn't something she should experiment with on her own.

'And he can't split his Will, so whether it works or not, it's unlikely to be the revelation he was trying to impart to me.' That night, as she lay in bed and considered the tether method she'd been using, then imagined what it might be like to just sever it, splitting the input from the output in the same way she split one part of her mind into two, she realized what was missing.

'How is a spell with detached output receiving the necessary energy to create its effect? There is no spell array for power to travel through. Is it being channeled through the air? But heat spillover would probably create a visible ripple with stronger spells. Or, perhaps, the power needs to be converted to some kind of invisible vehicle. Like extra high or low wavelength electromagnetic radiation.'

Sebastien sat up in her bed, the idea too startling to hold while lying down. *'Is that how divination rays work? Because magic requires energy to work. If they are sending feelers out halfway across the city, gathering information, and then returning that information, there must be some medium upon which the information rides, right? Some energy that their spell array is radiating, maybe* literally.'

She retrieved her grimoire and began to scribble down her epiphanies and speculation in a scrawl that was even more spidery than usual. *'But if that's the case, how does binding magic work? All the restrictions and downsides that divination faces make sense if I'm correct. Distance, barriers, and wards increase the cost or even halt the spell entirely. But once cast, binding magic cannot be thwarted so easily. How is it getting its energy?'* That question yielded no sudden ideas or plausible answers, and so she set it aside in the vast mental sea of things she wondered about but didn't yet have an explanation for.

One day, if she had her way, that sea would run dry.

She snorted at herself. *'Or, more likely, the more you learn the more you will realize you don't understand and were just too ignorant to realize that you didn't know before.'*

With a deep groan, Sebastien got down to the day's study and practice, one painful movement of the light-refinement sequence melding into another, glyph after glyph embedded in the depths of her mind, and the occasional itch for lightning-quick energy reminding her to have a meal and thus suppress her cravings.

It was after almost a week of this that Sebastien was taken totally by surprise as the glyph on the front of Myrddin's journal split into two.

She almost fumbled, but the urgency of not knowing how long the glyphs would wait for her spurred her to action. With her Conduit pressed painfully into her clenched fist, she let her eyes unfocus a little bit so that neither glyph was clearer than the other. Mentally, she did what her eyes could not and focused on both at once, wielding all the force of her Will.

The glyphs switched calmly to another set.

Almost immediately, she ran into one that she did not know, and her progress was lost.

But Sebastien was not disappointed.

'I was right. Myrddin could split his Will, just like me. Perhaps it really isn't so difficult.' But she quickly discarded the idea of going to Professor Lacer and showing him that he was wrong. Not only did she feel no impetus to help the Architects of Khronos decipher the journals they still held, she didn't need the scrutiny that such an ability might bring her.

And, somewhere deep inside, she feared that if someone were to dig, they might find that something was very wrong with her, after all.

She was no Myrddin, able to do as she wished while fearing no one. And if it were true that the brillig were dual-casters, what did it say that they had been slaughtered to the very last?

If someone else had accomplished what she could, surely it would have been news enough that Thaddeus Lacer, with all his connections and his clearance within the Red Guard, would have heard it. If she was not alone, any others were keeping their ability a closely guarded secret.

But this also meant that, unless someone else discovered a trick to confuse whatever mechanism the journals were using to monitor the caster, she was currently the only one in the known lands who could decipher Myrddin's journals.

And what was that if not a form of leverage?

20

REFINEMENT OF THE NINE HEAVENS

Sebastien
Month 4, Day 7, Wednesday 7:00 p.m.

When Sebastien grew frustrated at her continued failure with both the journal and light-refinement, she turned her attention to one of the other esoteric spells she'd memorized. Turning the tip of her finger into a burning coal wasn't something she could practice, but learning to leave an invisible tracking mark on something was possible.

This spell had attracted her because the items she placed her mark on couldn't be used to track back to her unless she maintained an open connection to them. After her recent enlightenment, she knew that this said some interesting things about how the spell actually worked. It was like whatever sympathetic link she created had to be activated to appear, rather than existing continuously.

The process that would allow her to create these beacons wasn't that difficult, as far as the magic went, but it had very specific ritualistic requirements that would extend over almost two months. It also required her to create a personalized symbol that wasn't in use anywhere else and a self-descriptive chant to go along with said symbol. The text had mentioned something about being as dramatic as possible while remaining accurate, as specificity and uniqueness made the ritual more likely to "take."

And, supposedly, if it worked well enough, one could further modify the beacon with additional functions, though the author hadn't known more, as his own attempt hadn't met that vague criteria.

Sebastien designed a personalized symbol easily enough—a few angled lines that evoked both wings in flight and blades. It reminded her of the Raven Queen persona, all freedom and a hint of violence, and was also a reference to the blade of enlightenment, forever cutting through reality to the truth.

She grinned at the idea of painting the tag on walls and claiming territory, just as the other gangs in the city did. Not that she would ever do such a thing —too much hassle to maintain, and just another way to make the Crowns hate her even more. After checking her glyph lexicon just to be sure she couldn't possibly be copying some other widely used shape, she set that part aside.

The chant was harder. It had four parts, meant to describe the "self," the "other," the "fate," and the "summons." Perhaps there had been more description or guidance somewhere in the archive, but if so, she had not seen it, much less memorized it.

Everything Sebastien came up with, she loathed. She was trying to be dramatic while remaining accurate, but the pseudo-poetry was so bad as to be embarrassing. Her whole face flushed with shame merely imagining reciting any of it aloud. As a preemptive safety measure, she made sure to burn all the paper she had scribbled verses on, just to make absolutely *sure* no one would ever read it.

As Sebastien guarded the fireplace while every last bit of paper turned to ash, she realized there had to be an easier way. And as soon as she had the thought, she remembered that there was a potion some diviners would take to allow them to write without conscious thought. Autography, she thought it was called. How it actually worked was irrelevant as long as the potion didn't cause violent nausea, hallucinations, or the other common side effects of divination aids.

Surely, anything she wrote under its effects couldn't be as bad as the self-flagellation she'd just put herself through.

Early in the morning on Thursday, one day before Operation Palimpsest would officially kick off, Sebastien took a hot shower to loosen her sore muscles and aching joints and then headed out to the Menagerie to practice the Refinement of the Nine Heavens at sunrise. There was a nice clearing a few minutes in that was sheltered from the sight of the rare person who might walk by, and well away from the areas that students taking the off-term entrance examinations were allowed to wander. Sebastien did not want an audience to her sweaty, trembling failure.

With the study and practice that had taken up so much of her time over the remainder of the Sowing Break, Sebastien had come to understand the goal of the spell a little better. It was not simply a strange song and dance.

Her core, somewhere around her navel, was the center of a Circle—or rather, a sphere—and she was drawing a complex, three-dimensional numerological symbol in the air using her hands and feet. The symbol and her corresponding movements began simply, but they became increasingly complex as she continued the process. There were even instructions about matching her breaths to the movements and how long each was supposed to take, along with the chant of tonal sounds that accompanied particular movements. *'More than a song, it's like using my voice as a wind instrument.'*

Exploring this kind of magic, so different from the modern sorcery she was most familiar with, should have been fascinating. And it was. But most of all, it was incredibly grueling.

She had never realized how poorly balanced she was until the tiny auxiliary muscles used to draw the symbol for this spell were so sore they cried out at any activation. This also introduced her to all the muscles she hadn't even known she had.

Luckily, the movements themselves seemed designed to warm and stretch her, so despite the pain caused by multiple hours a day of intense effort, she didn't believe she was in danger of injuring herself. She wanted to try the spell at sunrise, mid-afternoon, and sunset, as there had been some vague mention about different relationships with the different "heavens." It was possible that the third sequence would be easier at a certain time of day, or even a certain time of year.

The air was nippy, but not enough for her breath to fog, and the last patches of snow were beginning to melt from the shadowy spaces that saw little sunlight. Spring had come, and the whole world knew it, from the birds to the earthworms to the shoots of grass.

Sebastien took off her boots first, to allow the pads of her feet and her toes full access to the ground and thereby increase her grip and stability. She took a deep breath, forced her hands as far down the sides of her thighs as she could hang them, which helped force her perpetually stiff shoulders to relax, and looked up at the sky.

Then, with a deep breath, she began to move, the wordless tone of her voice following her movements exactly.

Muscles that felt like they had been tenderized and joints that insisted they belonged to a centenarian screamed in protest against the necessary motion. Thankfully, the movements were broad strokes at first, and by the time they had become more precise, forcing her to balance on one leg while she drew gentle incoming waves with the toe of her other foot, she was warm enough that the pain faded.

Again, she lamented the fact that, unlike other people, she did not seem to have this thing called "muscle memory" that people talked about. The movements of her limbs did become more practiced with repetition, but anything in a sequence, or that demanded specific responses to specific stimuli, required constant, active thought from her. It never became instinctive. One move never flowed naturally into the next.

And so, it was as much a mental exercise as a physical one—keeping track of all her limbs in a three-dimensional space, remembering what came next, controlling her voice to make nonsense tonal sounds while keeping the count of each breath despite the urge to collapse into a panting heap, and through all that, still holding the idea of drawing in the light of the sun and filtering it with her movements until it was in a state to be absorbed.

'How someone could manage this without some ability to split their concentration in multiple directions, I do not know.'

She found it helped to keep the image of the symbol she was drawing in her mind and to remind herself that she was *drawing* it, rather than just dancing in place. Recently, when struggling to manage all the different components of the spell, she had started assigning color to the sounds, pretending that the symbol she drew changed color with each "humm," "ooohh," and "aaah." The trick helped her to fit all the pieces together, and keeping track became easier.

There was a pattern to the spell, and though none of it ever became effortless, she had begun finding herself sinking into the required concentration. The rest of the world fell away, leaving only her body, moving just so, her breath, barely enough to sustain her, so that her pores seemed open in an attempt to absorb oxygen, and her voice, vibrating lightly and smoothly like a caress that helped to support her, nudging her just so when she would otherwise fall out of alignment.

Every time, of course, she eventually did fall out of alignment, some part of her failing and sending the rest tumbling like a house of cards. Quite literally, as she almost always ended up sprawled out on the ground, panting for breath.

As had happened only a few times, that morning she managed to make it through an entire round of the symbol, the end being the exact same point as the beginning, without any obvious mistakes. Her body seemed to buzz, her skin beaded with a light sheen of sweat, and her breaths came heavy but not heaving.

She was not so exhausted that she needed to stop, and so she continued.

Sebastien was halfway through the second circuit when a tiny strand of light appeared, as thin as the gossamer newly hatched spiders used to ride the air currents every autumn, following along behind the path of her finger.

She almost lost concentration, and the gossamer light faded. But as Sebastien renewed her focus on filtering in sunlight through the ever-smaller details of the symbol, the light trailing her movements returned.

She could feel some kind of energy entering into her. Not through her navel as she had originally expected, but through her forehead. *'It must be light,'* she realized, *'or at least some of the properties of light riding along on the converted energy.'*

It was wonderful, invigorating in a completely different way than the beamshell tincture. Where the sludgy concoction electrified her, leaving her tense, jittery, and full to bursting, this washed over her like the warm, buoyant waves of a saltwater pool, just dense enough to keep her afloat. It soothed where it passed, correcting small errors and wounds and leaving just a tiny bit of itself behind, little more than a metaphorical scent.

Despite the focus casting this spell required, her Will was somehow marginally refreshed, her mind expanded so that it was just a tiny bit easier to hold all the different facets of the spell with the necessary level of focus.

It was her body that gave out first, but unlike with most spells, there seemed no danger of backlash even as the bounding Circle and the symbol she had been creating were broken. Light billowed out around her like a puff of dust, and as her mind was left holding absolutely nothing, she stopped applying her Will and began to laugh lightly. There was no wryness to the sound, no undertones marring her pure delight.

As she tried to tuck her Conduit back into her pocket and crawl to her hands and knees, her body instead flapped around awkwardly, so exhausted that it refused to listen to her. She lay in a crumpled heap of sharp angles, staring up at the foliage and small creatures of the Menagerie around her. *'I may have pushed myself a bit too hard.'* It was lucky that no one was around to catch her in such an undignified position.

Also lucky was the fact that she didn't actually need to do anything tomorrow and could sit in Liza's warded spare room all day while whining to herself about the extreme muscle soreness that was likely to compound upon what was already there.

Once she had managed to climb to her feet, she stumbled off directly to the infirmary. *'None of my salves or potions are strong enough to handle this. Hopefully they'll have something better to mitigate the pain and help my body recover.'* She did not relish the onset of consequences for her actions.

'But I succeeded!' she reminded herself, smiling brightly even as she struggled to maintain her balance on the slight angles of the cobblestone path. The aftereffects of the light-refinement lingered with her, an invisible glow in her mind.

After a visit to the very judgmental and exasperated healers at the infirmary, Sebastien took a long shower, rubbed herself down with a salve specifically meant to soothe sore muscles, and then dressed presentably. The Retreat at Willowdale had sent a favorable response to her overture, and whoever had written the reply even seemed to know of Sebastien, though only through her connection to Thaddeus Lacer.

They had invited her to visit in the afternoon. Sebastien splurged on a carriage with actual shock-absorbers, and then cast her own cushioning spell on a piece of seaweed paper she placed over the seat. These efforts made the ride nearly bearable, but every bump and divot in the road out of Gilbratha still seemed to punch her in some tenderized muscle or another. The muscle-soothing salve either wasn't strong enough, or it was already wearing off.

Sebastien refrained from whimpering only out of consideration that, with the relative quiet of the countryside, the driver might be able to hear her. She alternated tiny sips of one of her regeneration potions with a nourishing draught and the mild pain-relieving potion the healers had given her.

When they arrived, Sebastien crawled out into the circular, cobblestone driveway of an enormous estate. The building in front of her would have been a sizable manor house on its own, but it seemed another hulking beast of a facility had been added on. Multiple stories high, the rectangular wings stretched out to either side and some undefined distance toward the back. Altogether, the Retreat reminded her of a turtle that had lain morosely on the ground, a small head sticking out at the front as its colossal mass succumbed to gravity.

The caretaker in charge of meeting her was a woman in her twenties, quite cheerful and enthusiastic as she led Sebastien inside and got her checked in as a visitor. She was an obvious contrast to many of the other employees Sebastien saw, who were in various states of visible fatigue. They seemed unhappy, and even those who smiled looked strained or wan. *'Or perhaps it's apathy brought on by extended periods of stress,'* Sebastien mused, watching as one of the patients in a common area threw up, and the nearest caretaker moved to clean the mess without a single word or twitch of expression.

"Most of our volunteers will read to the patients, though sometimes they bring other experiences, like music or art projects. Sometimes we even have a thaumaturge who performs magic tricks for them! Of course, some of the patients can be frightened of magic, but many of them retain their original delight in such things."

"How many people do you keep here?" Sebastien asked as they passed hallway after hallway, moving deeper toward the center of the huge building.

"Oh, some two or three thousand people, long-term, perhaps? We always have a good few dozen or more temporarily admitted. I'm not sure of the exact numbers, but it does add up. We're the best treatment center for over a hundred kilometers around, and everyone who can afford it wants the best for their family members."

"And people who get severe Will-strain and never recover just...live here for the remainder of their lives?"

"We don't only treat victims of Will-strain. Insanity and other mental illnesses or abnormalities come in a lot of different forms and from different sources. But yes. The University sponsors treatment for some of its former students, and donations from generous businesses, families, and individuals cover room and board for many other unfortunates who don't have someone to pay their way. Of course, those families who can afford it have their relatives hosted on the upper floors. Very nice, premium service." The woman made an "okay" sign with her fingers and winked at Sebastien.

"Grandmaster Thaddeus Lacer, my mentor, told me that the survivors from the latest expedition to the Black Wastes were sent here," Sebastien lied.

"Oh yes, it's very sad," the woman said, nodding happily. "They were so brave, and if the rumors are to be believed, they actually found Myrddin's hermitage! It's too bad most of them won't be able to appreciate the fruits of their endeavor. Totally scrambled, if you know what I mean. Can't even talk coherently. Only one of them is showing any signs of recovery."

"Oh? Do you think it would be possible for me to meet him?" Sebastien hoped she sounded perfectly normal, at most star-struck but definitely not as if she were hiding nefarious intentions. "Grandmaster Lacer told me he *almost* went on that expedition. They would have been teammates."

"I'm afraid not, sir. He's with the rest in the severe trauma ward." She gestured vaguely in the direction of the rightmost wing. "That's not open to the public, except for direct family members, for the safety of both the patients and the visitors. Sometimes they have episodes of confusion and can get violent." The woman looked both ways, leaned closer, and murmured, "Sometimes they even try to cast magic."

Sebastien was disappointed, but not overly surprised. Her plans never seemed to work out so smoothly, with so little effort. '*If he's recovering, perhaps I can wait until he's moved into the general population, or even released entirely.*' But leaving things up to chance and time like that made her apprehensive. He was her only direct source of information, the only one who could reveal what Oliver may or may not have done, and if something were to happen to this man…

Sebastien managed to volunteer to interact with the patients in the common room closest to the severe trauma ward, hoping to gather information about how the Retreat's systems worked and what might be needed to bypass their security.

She decided to read to the patients and, with the employees' permission, set up an illusion spell array to illustrate the contents of the story with people and backgrounds made of simple shapes and colors. Extra practice with magic was always welcome. Splitting her concentration between reading as dramatically as possible, with different voices for each of the characters, while also improving the details of her illustration might even help train her Will for real splitting.

Sebastien cut off mid-word as Liza's familiar voice echoed down the hallway. She looked up in surprise as the older woman came into view. On her left, one of the Retreat's healers walked with her. A man wearing rather flamboyant robes woven with stylistic glyphs kept pace to her right, bearing the standard accessories of a shaman.

Behind them, some of the Retreat's other employees carried several leather cases. They could have been filled with belongings, but by the way Liza and the healer were seriously discussing treatment methods, Sebastien judged them to contain equipment.

Liza made brief eye contact with Sebastien, who only then realized that she'd been staring, but the woman passed on into the severe trauma ward with no sign of recognition.

21

A FOREBODING OF WOE

Siobhan
Month 4, Day 9, Friday 9:00 a.m.

It was the morning of the sentencing, and not all was well with Operation Palimpsest.

Siobhan waited in the private room at the back of the Kaiseki Ryori with a raven in a covered cage, inside a box meant to keep people from noticing any suspicious bird cages and drawing connections. She opened the window's shutter just a smidge to look onto the street below.

Siobhan was disguised as the sweetest possible version of Silvia, even going so far as donning a corset to make her waist seem impossibly tiny. Her warding medallion and the transformation amulet were tucked into her bodice, flush against her flesh. She had also rented several wards against common curses from Liza—those that her warding medallion might not cover —which she wore in the form of some chunky jewelry.

Siobhan had never realized how much of the gaudy ornamentation the rich wore might actually be concealed protection. Discretion was even more desirable in many circumstances than an obvious ward. People who wanted to be obvious carried weapons.

The raven shuffled within its cage, letting out a small bird-sound of unhappiness.

Tanya was late to pick up the spelled raven that was necessary for her part in the plan.

Siobhan hadn't heard from the other young woman since the day she left on her mission for the Architects of Khronos. As the sun rose higher and more people filtered into the streets, she was becoming increasingly antsy. Ideally, Siobhan would have already been within the warded room at Liza's house, but someone needed to deliver the raven. Tanya hadn't been available to pick it up previously, and Liza was busy elsewhere.

Tanya had a linked bracelet that she could use to set off an alarm if things went wrong, but she hadn't used it. That didn't mean everything was okay, however. Siobhan considered the possibility that, if something had happened to Tanya, it could lead back to her. The meeting location at the Kaiseki Ryori might even be compromised.

No obvious coppers approached on the street below, and no one surreptitiously watched the building while pretending to be doing something else, as far as Siobhan could tell.

'If she doesn't show up soon, can I find a last-minute replacement for her?' The only woman Siobhan could think of that might be amenable to this was Katerin, but Siobhan didn't believe she could trust the woman to keep secrets from Oliver, even just until Operation Palimpsest was complete. *'Without Tanya, either I do the raven messenger delivery on my own or call that part of the plan off.'*

Doing it herself was out of the question. It would likely be playing right into the coppers' hands. Calling off that part wouldn't destroy the whole operation, but with less general confusion and division of the coppers' resources, there was a higher chance of danger to Gera and Liza.

But just as Siobhan was about to write Tanya off as a loss, hurried footsteps with an obvious limp came up to the sliding door, followed by a knock. "It's me," Tanya's voice came, low and slightly out of breath.

"Enter," Siobhan replied, one hand on her Conduit and the other on her battle wand.

But Tanya was alone. She awkwardly lowered herself across the table from Siobhan, one leg held out stiff instead of bending, and her arms cradling her abdomen.

"You are injured," Siobhan deduced easily. "Was our connection discovered? Were you followed?"

Tanya shook her head rapidly, though sweat beaded on her upper lip and temples, and her skin was pale. "No, nothing like that. I was injured on my mission." She bowed forward over the table. "I sincerely apologize for my tardiness, my queen. Please, withhold your anger. I have news of your enemies."

Siobhan didn't think she was projecting enough anger to make Tanya so fearful, but she tried to relax her body language and tone of voice. "Be at ease. Show me your wounds. You may tell me your story while I examine them."

Tanya only hesitated for a moment before standing and shakily stripping down into her underclothes. The bandages wrapped around most of her torso couldn't fully cover the enormous purple and green bruise that bloomed along one side. They were likely holding broken ribs in place while the bones healed back together.

On Tanya's opposite leg, a thick, angry red keloid scar ran in a jagged C-shaped line across her thigh. Obviously, Tanya had received some sort of healing, but it hadn't fixed her injuries completely.

"You almost died," Siobhan said.

Tanya didn't bother to state the obvious agreement. "Our group was attacked by a special operations team from the military. At least I think they were. They were kitted out in specialized military gear and uniforms. No obvious affiliation, but they didn't have any accents."

Siobhan cleared the low wooden table of the cold tea pot and small ceramic cups, setting them gently to the side of the room. Some thick, hard wax lines created one of the largest mirrored-healing spell arrays she had ever used, pentagram inside of pentagon, and the glyphs for *"blood," "mirror," "flesh,"* and *"bone."*

Siobhan's Circles and numerological symbols had grown noticeably more precise from all the practice drawing spell arrays she had gained since coming to Gilbratha. Her glyphs, of course, had always been pristine, a noticeable contrast to her normal spider-scrawl handwriting. She didn't bother with a more complex and fully descriptive written Word, because she didn't need it. She motioned silently for Tanya to lie down atop the spell array.

The other woman had seen Siobhan use this spell before, and so, with a small amount of dubiousness and a large amount of care not to jostle her injuries or smudge the lines, Tanya complied, placing herself perfectly at the junction of the two inner Circles. She barely fit.

"A special ops squad, sent by the Crowns?" Siobhan mused aloud, retrieving her silver athame and using it to create a small cut in the back of Tanya's forearm. Siobhan would use a beast core to provide extra power, but blood was both an intrinsic component of this spell and more efficient. Though Tanya looked quite pale and weak, losing a mouthful or two more would affect her performance less than her half-healed injuries.

Siobhan used the athame to slice away the bandages binding Tanya's torso, ignoring the woman's flinch as they parted to reveal even deeper bruising. Her skin looked like the tender flesh of a plum, ready to burst and leak out all of her lifeblood. "Who healed you?"

"One of the others on my team had some emergency supplies. They kept me alive as we got away, and my new handler took me to their house while they got me better treatment. I had some trouble getting away. I was supposed to stay hidden until my injuries were completely recovered so that there would be no evidence that I was involved with anything strange."

Siobhan didn't want to openly palm her celerium Conduit, which might be recognized, so she took out only a beast core and used the black sapphire pressed against the skin of her side by her hidden holster to channel the necessary energy. She focused on Tanya's thigh wound first, sending the magic deep into the muscle that she suspected, from the state of the half-healed scar, had been severed and only poorly patched back together. "Curious, that they healed you so halfheartedly."

Tanya's fists clenched as the muscle fibers inside her leg shifted and wove back together, but she didn't flinch or try to wriggle away despite the discomfort. "Instant healing is very expensive. I was on a regeneration potion regimen that should have had me able to at least move normally by Monday or Tuesday. It's not as if they care if I miss a few days of classes."

Siobhan hummed noncommittally. "Why do you think the Crowns would have sent a military squad after you, and how did they know of your activities?" She smoothed and slightly molded the raised skin of Tanya's angry scar, some of which had somehow attached to the muscle below with whatever shoddy healing had been done before.

"A traitor... One of the lower level employees, like me, just sent to fill out numbers. I don't know who they were. We were all wearing masks, and I didn't recognize their voice. Everything has been a lot more secretive after Knave Knoll. The coppers have been sniffing around a lot. I think the higher-ups in the, um, the Architects of Khronos, are trying to reduce the risk that one of us says something that brings the others down. We've always been a bit segmented, but after the magical hoops they've been having to jump through every time someone in the History department is called in for an interrogation, they've seemed more paranoid."

Siobhan made some final tweaks and poured a little more power into the wound on Tanya's thigh, hoping that extra energy could make up for a lack of guidance or skill, and then released the magic to move her attention higher. "How have they been dealing with interrogations?"

"I'm not sure if it's the same for everyone, but when I was called in, they knew about it ahead of time. I had to take some potions, get sprayed down with a philtre, and then they had one of the healers from the infirmary cast some kind of compulsion spell while telling me answers to all the questions the coppers were going to ask. When I did the interview, I was in a strange mental state, and it actually seemed as if the false answers were true, even though some part of me knew they weren't. I don't know the details about how any of it worked, but the coppers didn't seem to think I was lying. I had no idea such a thing was possible."

It was interesting, but not particularly surprising, to learn that the Architects of Khronos had an informant within the coppers. Siobhan smiled wryly as loose fragments of bone shifted underneath Tanya's skin, rejoining the whole. "Well, the coppers would want to keep such possibilities silent, lest the enterprising know they exist to uncover." She would certainly like to learn such things for herself.

"As for why they would have sent a military squad after us, I'm not totally sure, but whatever they were after, they got it. We lost the shipment we were sent to retrieve."

The bone was taking a lot of time and energy to heal. Siobhan took a few deep breaths and sank deeper into the spell, sparing a few motes of concentration to ask, "Do you know what you were transporting?"

"Something dangerous. The chests were made of lead, and everything inside them was in smaller boxes of iron, with spell arrays engraved into every side. If I had to guess, it would be an extremely volatile potion. Maybe some sort of explosive."

"Will your handler notice your escape? What will you tell them?"

"That I went and used some of my own savings to get proper healing." Her breath hitched with a moment of pain. "Two birds, one stone."

Both women fell silent for a while. Siobhan could only spare a small bit of concentration to wonder what Tanya might have been transporting and consider the broader consequences if someone decided to *use* something so dangerous. After all, why obtain a weapon you weren't planning to make use of?

When Siobhan finished patching Tanya's ribs together and pouring in enough power that they wouldn't break again without a moderate application of force, she used a final pinch of energy from the blood to make sure the cut in Tanya's arm was sealed, then pulled back and motioned for Tanya to rise.

The woman stood awkwardly beside her, tested her injuries, and then bowed at a ninety-degree angle. "Queen of Ravens, I beseech you. Please save me from the Architects of Khronos."

Siobhan stared bemusedly down at the back of Tanya's dirty blonde head.

The woman remained bent as she continued, "I have been attempting to make other connections that might give me security, but I'm not sure that will pan out quickly enough. If things keep escalating like this, it is only a matter of time before they send me on a mission that will end up killing me. I don't have any other option besides you, my queen."

Siobhan remained silent as she used a wax-specific solvent to get rid of the spell array. As she prepared to cast the shedding-disintegration spell to get rid of the traces of Tanya's blood, Siobhan finally spoke. "What exactly do you hope that I might do for you?"

Hesitantly, Tanya straightened from her awkward bow. "They've been paying my way through the University, on a sponsorship from Munchworth. As long as I keep working for them, I get to stay. But...if they're not *actively* trying to kill me, they certainly aren't working very hard to keep me safe. I'm worried that I'm a liability they wouldn't mind being free of, but I'm also known to be in your good graces. Perhaps you could more directly call for me to be your liaison?"

Her voice dropped to a whisper. "If I just try to leave without protection, they can do a lot worse than simply dropping my sponsorship." She sniffed, then continued more loudly. "But I truly believe that a few words from you could change that. And I don't need to be your liaison, specifically. That was just an idea. I could do any sort of job you wanted." She clenched her fists, swallowed hard, and added, "Preferably, a job that wouldn't get me killed or jailed, and that would allow me to continue attending the University."

Siobhan arched one eyebrow. "But if you are their connection to me, they continue to have use for you, and a reason to pay your way, yes?" She certainly couldn't pay to sponsor another student, no matter how much she earned from Oliver. "I will consider your request. Now is not the time for such discussions."

Despite the lack of promises, Tanya relaxed. "Thank you, Queen of Ravens. I am ready."

Siobhan pointed her to the box that held the raven's cage. The creature within was slightly sedated to keep it from making too much noise while trying to escape. It had already been spelled with the homing location that would see it delivering its message to the right place, and its every instinct was to escape and reach that destination. "Repeat your task to me once more," she ordered.

Tanya didn't grumble or complain, checking on the raven before picking up the box without obvious pain. "I am to approach a popular bar a few blocks from the Edictum Council building, where the sentencing will be held, without attracting notice. I will enter the bar and use the key you gave me to don a disguise in the bathroom on the top floor, which will be locked, with an out of order sign. Without being observed, I will then access the rooftop. I will see a cloud of ravens in the distance, to the south. Unless the bracelet you gave me alerts me to do so earlier, at precisely five o'clock I will release the raven from its cage, and it will deliver the letter attached to its leg to the center of the theatre where they are holding the sentencing. From there, I will escape back down into the building, where my disguise will come off as soon as I can safely do so unobserved. I will walk into the crowded street, where I will blend in as any other citizen, looking nothing like you." She hesitated, then added, "If, for some reason, I am caught, I will not speak. You can be assured of my loyalty."

"Do not get caught," Siobhan said simply.

Tanya shuddered visibly, but nodded her silent agreement.

As satisfied as she could be despite the anxiety that had returned to sour her veins and tighten her muscles, Siobhan left, slipping into the increasingly packed streets. Rather than the deep shadows of a suspiciously cavernous hood, her main protection from sight was a laced umbrella to protect against the sun, held a little too low and thus covering her face. It seemed like almost every person who lived in the city year-round, and all those who were visiting for the Sowing Break, were out and about.

She resisted a strangely powerful urge to look toward the huge dome of the Edictum Council building in the distance, where many of those on the street were heading. Ennis's sentencing wouldn't be until the late afternoon, but until then, street vendors and performers would be plying their wares, and announcers were shouting out the crimes of Ennis Naught and the Raven Queen, in case anyone in town for the spectacle was not aware of the backstory.

She turned toward Liza's house and the safety of its warded room, only to stop in her tracks as a horrifying thought hit her. *'Why am I here right now?'* The question echoed in her mind, and she chased the incongruence it caused, ripples of weak rationalizations conflicting against her better sense. *'No matter what extra protections I have in place, this is probably the worst day of the year for me to make an appearance in this body. Tanya's part was important, yes, but not critical. Not enough to take the risk of being out. At the very most, I should have dropped off the raven last night and simply left it there for Tanya to find or not.'*

Through every step of this plan, she had been trying to focus on her own safety, to avoid the idiotic recklessness she was prone to when she didn't have enough time to fully consider a situation and her response before acting.

But here she was, out in the street in the body of Siobhan Naught. That, at least, might have been her stupidity acting up again. But could the same be said about this sudden urge she felt to attend the sentencing, to see Ennis one last time?

Her shoulders straightened with fear, her eyes locked on the bottom edge of the lace umbrella. *'If I were the one trying to trap someone like the Raven Queen, and I knew this chance was critical—perhaps my last hope—I wouldn't just leave it to her hubris that she would show up. I would take other precautions.'*

Siobhan realized she had stopped breathing, and, as a wave of dizzy dread swept over her, she forced her lungs to work again. *'A compulsion spell?'* The very thought urged her to start sprinting toward safety. She had the key to Liza's apartment. All she needed to do was get there and lock herself inside the specially warded room.

'But how would they have caught me?' she wondered. *'I haven't entered into any agreements, and even within the loosest definition, I don't think I've done anything that could allow binding magic to take hold.'* Wild speculation ran through her head, each possibility more outlandish and paranoid than the last. Liza, Gera, or even Tanya could have betrayed her. But as someone knocked into her

shoulder and mumbled an absent apology, she looked out at the streets, so full of people that carriages would have trouble passing through.

There were people of all different colors, in different types of clothing, and those with fur, feathers, or extra body parts. A jentil towered above the crowd, and someone who looked to be a half-troll had a small stretch of emptiness around him as people gave him space. One scowling old man was in his wheeled chair, pausing every few feet to recover from the exertion of rolling himself about.

'Everyone *is out today. The coppers must have realized they cannot find me. But they had no need to find and target the Raven Queen...not if they were willing to affect the entire city in the hope that she would be one of the many fish caught within a widely spread net. If I were them, I would have started casting the compulsion yesterday and slowly ramped up the intensity. From there, I would have some other method to pluck the Raven Queen from among the rest. If they care about their citizens, they hope to catch me without endangering the innocent.'*

She forcefully relaxed her fingers from around the handle of her umbrella and released the Conduit and beast core back into her pocket. So many people could be out today because they genuinely wanted to experience the entertainment. Perhaps what she was feeling wasn't a compulsion but some deep, subconscious connection to her father that she hadn't given up, even after everything.

But that didn't explain the rippling sense of wrongness in her mind, as if she had walked into a familiar room and found everything displaced two inches to the left.

'*If it is a compulsion, now that I've recognized it, it must have less control over me. And the same could be said about my tendency toward recklessness. I can stick with the original plan. If I have to, I'll knock myself out so that it's impossible for me to leave until the day is over.*'

She took a single step forward, only to be halted by an authoritative "Excuse me, madam," and the touch of strong fingers on her elbow.

She spun around with the umbrella in her off hand wielded like a weapon, her heart giving a thump so hard she thought it might literally stop from the shock.

A tall, dark-skinned copper stood beside her, his hands raised as he took a step back. Perhaps he had been drawn by her still form acting like a rock for the river of other citizens to pass around, or perhaps by the color of her skin. Or, perhaps he had somehow picked her out more directly.

2 2

———

CARRIED ON THE WIND

SIOBHAN
   Month 4, Day 9, Friday 9:40 a.m.

SIOBHAN SUPPRESSED her fear and all the instincts to flee or fight that it encouraged. If there was ever a time to use all the lessons she had learned from Ennis and *act* as if her life depended on it, that time was now. She let out a loud, breathy laugh and pressed a fluttering hand to her chest. "Oh, my! I apologize, sir! You startled me," she said airily, smoothing out her voice to something more overtly feminine. "I get a little nervous in such large crowds, and some young ruffian tried to pickpocket me not an hour back, so I'm afraid I've been on edge and overreacted."

She smiled brightly at the tall, dark-skinned man, her gaze dipping from his eyes to his shoulder and hands, and then a quick glance at his lips before returning to his eyes. She forced her smile to soften into something more genuine than polite, growing a little lopsided and allowing the fake wrinkles at the sides of her eyes to deepen just a little. It was almost an exact copy of something she had seen Ennis do several times—with more success than his more blatant attempts at flirting or propositioning someone.

As Silvia, she looked like the kind of woman that might be attracted to a man in uniform and who could subtly flirt only seconds after being startled, because she definitely wasn't so afraid that she felt like she was going to pass out. She kept her eyes from darting around, searching for his backup, but her knees almost buckled as she felt the subtlest tingle in her back, where the disks of the divination-diverting ward rested. *'Please, let me be imagining that because I'm on the verge of passing out,'* she pleaded to the indifferent sky. Her scalp was also tingling, and her palms felt frozen, which gave her hope.

Unfortunately, the copper's expression was inscrutable, so she couldn't tell if it was working or not. "No apologies necessary. What brings you out today, madam?"

'Are my knees shaking?' she wondered, trying to stiffen the muscles in her legs just in case. Shaking knees could create a telltale tremble in the fabric of a lightweight dress such as the one she was wearing. "Oh, madam sounds so stuffy. You can call me Silvia," she said, leaning toward him slightly. "What should I call you?"

"Copper Robards," he replied expressionlessly.

She nodded, ignoring the rebuff. "And of course, I'm out for the same reason as everyone else! There's a little stall up on Bett Street that I heard was selling the most delightful pastries. It's too bad you have to work on a day like today, though I admit it is comforting to see your presence on the streets. Are you going to get any time off?"

He brushed by her question with a few vague words and asked a handful more basic questions of his own. Though Silvia responded—for that was her name at this moment, as fully and truly as possible—with every conceivable trick to make herself seem less suspicious, some part of her was detaching from the conversation, watching her pilot her body as if from above.

'If his wand has a basic scanning divination like that woman cast on me the very first time I transformed into Sebastien, when I was hiding in that empty building with Oliver, it's over for me.' She catalogued her various routes of escape and plotted a southward course through the city. There, the maze of streets, dead-ends, and random alleyways might make following her difficult. She was still incredibly stiff from all her practice with light-refinement, but the concoctions she'd taken that morning were suppressing her pain, and adrenaline would push her onward. Fekten's class had given her the cardiovascular stamina to run half the city if she absolutely had to. Maybe a concussive blast to this Copper Robards, to slow him down and get a head start. Alternatively, she could get to one of her supply stashes and transform into Sebastien. If *that* didn't throw them off her trail, all was lost.

But as her thoughts were beginning to spiral out of control with barely leashed violence and drastic plans, the copper's attention was diverted. He looked at someone over her shoulder and his eyes immediately narrowed. "Mr. Irving!" he called. He took an unconscious step past her, then paused and said, "Stay here, please."

Siobhan blinked twice, staring at the side of the building in front of her as her dissociating consciousness seemed to slip back into her body. There was so much adrenaline in her veins that she felt sick with it, like an overdose of beamshell tincture mixed with six cups of dark coffee after pulling a thirty-six hour study session in preparation for an important test.

Slowly, she turned to follow Copper Robards with her eyes.

He was talking to a young man with large glasses and slightly lighter skin, who strangely looked somewhat familiar, despite the fact that he appeared too young to attend the University, and Siobhan had no idea where else she could have encountered him.

"Why are you here?" the copper asked, his tone much more accusing than the one he had used with Siobhan.

She shifted on her feet, partially because her muscles were tingling and trembling from being so tense, and partially because she wondered if she might just…slip into the crowd while the copper was distracted.

But the man noticed even that small movement and raised one finger to her, a command for patience.

"I'm here as a journalist," the young man said defensively, lifting as evidence a slightly scratched, high-end camera obscura from where it hung at his chest by a neck strap.

"I thought we discussed the need to avoid potentially dangerous situations," Copper Robards said.

"It's my job!" the young man retorted. "Someone has to get photos of the sentencing and conduct interviews with the populace. This isn't the kind of event we can just neglect to report on."

"Doesn't your paper have anyone else they could send?"

The young man's expression grew more serious. "I'm a professional, just like you, sir. I—"

"Miss Silvia!" a boy's voice called, and as all of their attention was pulled, Millennium struggled his way through the legs of the crowd and ran to her side. He hugged her around the waist, grinning up at her. The combined shade of her umbrella and a cloud that had passed over the sun made the subtle golden sheen of his skin almost indistinguishable. "Mom is sitting over there. She says the baby is kicking her in the kidney and she wants you to help wrangle Bobby because he keeps trying to run off and maybe get kidnapped by human traffickers," he said with the innocent candor of a much more foolish child. "Can you tell her to buy us pies?"

Siobhan had no idea how Millennium had known what name to call her, or how much she needed to be rescued with a totally mundane scenario that the Raven Queen would never be involved in, but she grinned down at him with delight that was totally genuine. Both of them looked to Copper Robards expectantly.

He hesitated before waving them off with a frustrated sigh. "Mr. Irving, you must leave capturing the Raven Queen to the professionals."

Siobhan almost flinched.

"I'm *not* here to try and capture the Raven Queen!" the young man protested.

Siobhan slipped Millennium's hand into her own and kept her umbrella in position to shade him. His palm was as sweaty and clammy as her own, and as they passed into the crowd, a wary-eyed guard that she vaguely recognized from her visits to Lord Lynwood's manor fell in behind them.

"I heard you introduce yourself as Silvia when I was trying to listen for you. Was it right for me to use that name?" Miles asked. "It seemed like you didn't want to be talking to the copper."

"You did well to corroborate my lie," she said. Her divination-diverting ward was definitely active now, avoiding his natural magical tendencies toward divination, but much more subtly than it did when she was exposed to Gera or another prognos.

With subtle twitches of his fingers and the direction of his gaze, Miles led her around to the back courtyard of a nearby boarding stable. It was filled with horses inside and unhitched carriages parked in rows out in the back yard. They entered one of the stable's back doors and then turned a corner to an area tucked out of sight. A woman in an old-fashioned maid uniform waited there along with another Nightmare Pack man, keeping out of the way of the busy stable workers.

Both wore wary, frightened looks.

Siobhan did not need to be Aberford Thorndyke to realize that something was wrong. "What's the issue?" she asked immediately, looking to the adults.

It was Miles who answered. "We are being chased by bad guys who want to hurt us," he stated succinctly. "I knew about it in advance, because I heard whispers on the wind about the danger." He tapped his ears meaningfully, which would have meant nothing to Siobhan if she didn't know he was part prognos, part sylphide, and even had some amount of fey ancestry. If anyone could hear danger coming, it would be him, though it would mean an impressive improvement of his control over his abilities.

"Danger was circling in around our house, and it was targeted specifically at *me*," Miles continued. "I knew things wouldn't go well if I stayed, and other people could get hurt. Or even killed. Martha, Jackal, and Mr. Fring helped me get away," he said, pointing in turn to the maid, a sharp-jawed Nightmare Pack member who did indeed have a somewhat predatory look, and the much broader-shouldered man who had escorted them through the crowd and who held himself like a trained guard.

"I kept listening for danger, trying to find a way out. I wanted to go to one of our safe houses, but we wouldn't have made it. And then I thought maybe we could go ask for backup at the Verdant Stag, but every route toward them made the whispers go even worse-sounding. So we were just running away as the safe routes kept closing up around us, and then I realized *you* might be able to help."

Siobhan sent the two enforcers and maid a glance, aware that the value of her Silvia disguise was constantly lowering due to events like this.

Miles took a deep breath, leaning into her side for support, more emotional than physical. "It was really scary. It was hard to find you, and the bad guys almost caught us a few times. Mr. Fring *almost* died, if I hadn't heard —" He broke off, rubbing at one ear. "But the whispers all agree that if I could find you, our chances of coming out of this okay get way better. You'll protect us, right?"

Siobhan was sure that the "whispers" had led Miles to a completely ridiculous conclusion. She was no bastion of protection. If being with her made him safer, it would be by strange coincidence at best. *'Maybe his whispers came to some strange conclusion, like, to protect him, I'll be forced to reveal myself as the Raven Queen, and that will be enough to stall for backup, disastrous as it might be for me.'*

"How far away are the bad guys?" she asked, her mind immediately turning toward the best method of escape. If the Verdant Stag wasn't safe, where else could they go? Liza's house, perhaps? Though if they led the enemy straight there, Siobhan wasn't totally sure that the wards would be enough to keep them safe. Not in the long term, at least. And Liza would absolutely kill her when she found out.

Miles tilted his head to the side, staring into the air, and paled. "Um, they're close. Very close."

Siobhan resisted the urge to curse, her hand reaching blindly into her satchel to grab the most useful potions within. "Miles, try to find what direction they're coming from." To the adults, she asked, "Do you have battle wands? Shield artifacts?"

Martha shook her head silently, wringing her hands together.

Mr. Fring spoke for the first time. "My wand has a shield spell, but the charge is depleted. They tried to stun us several times, and once sent a piercing spell at the back of my skull when I got too far away from the boy. They seem to want to take the Nightmare Pack heir alive, though the rest of us may be expendable. I have two concussive blast charges remaining, and a knife." He opened one side of his jacket to reveal the blade there, long and heavy enough to go beyond dagger into the realm of machete.

Jackal's eyes darted around, focusing on her for only a moment, his fingers twiddling nervously and his knee bouncing. "I've got knives, too. About six left. Managed to nick a couple of our pursuers when they got too close." He retrieved a few small throwing knives from his pocket, and his hands seemed to feel more comfortable holding them because the twiddling and twitching stopped. "Also, got a philtre of liquid fire."

Martha sent him a scandalized glare. "Jackal! You know Lord Lynwood decreed you weren't allowed to mess about with fire anymore."

Jackal grimaced at her. "Well, I haven't messed around with it, have I? Just having some on hand isn't a crime." He looked back to Siobhan. "I couldn't find a safe place to use it. So many people out and about, someone's likely to go up in flames like a spitted pig. Someone innocent, I mean. Bad way to die, if you'll pardon me saying, my queen."

Miles pointed toward the east, where the front of the stable looked over the street. "They're coming from that direction. And maybe circling around, too. Their whispers sound kind of sneaky."

Martha's eyes narrowed as she looked Siobhan over again. "My queen?" she mouthed to herself in obvious confusion.

Siobhan handed out three of her new philtres of darkness, three fleetfoot potions, and a single bark-skin potion, which she gave to Mr. Fring. If someone were going to act as a human shield, it wouldn't be her. "We don't have much time. Can we escape out the back?" she asked Miles.

She poked her head around the corner, looking to the east for their pursuers.

A man passed in front of an open stall window, narrowed eyes searching the crowd. Probably searching for them. Siobhan's blood froze even as her heart sank; she recognized the crisp gold-and-midnight blue uniform, as well as the proudly displayed gold badge stamped with the same crest as every coin in her pocket.

She pulled her head back in, scowling. "Did you neglect to mention that the 'bad men' are Lord Pendragon's personal forces?" Unlike coppers, they didn't patrol the streets, only leaving Pendragon Palace when they had a particular mission. Such as, perhaps, catching the Raven Queen.

Martha paled, clenching her skirt in her fists. "That can't be. Right? Maybe they're after the same criminals that have been chasing us."

"Didn't see any Pendragon operatives," Fring added.

Fighting back against Pendragon operatives was automatic treason, punishable by execution. But more importantly, those men would be well outfitted, powerful, and practiced in battle.

"If you're talking about the people in those fancy outfits that *aren't* copper outfits, they are definitely bad guys," Miles provided helpfully. "And we need to leave right away. There's no time left."

Everyone else shared looks of dismay, and Siobhan led the way in the opposite direction from the Pendragon operative. One hand held a beast core, the other her newest battle wand, and Millennium's grip tugged on the skirt of her uselessly fluffy dress. '*Should we split up? Send the other three away as a decoy while I keep Miles? But would they agree to that? It might get them killed.*'

The boy's grip grew tighter as he looked around in panicked confusion, gaze once again distant. "Oh no, oh no. I was wrong."

"About what?" Siobhan snapped, wondering if they could open the horse stalls and create a panicked stampede with a loud spell. The animals might cover their escape. But it might be better to just sneak out and avoid attention. *'No, it would take too long to free the horses.'* Siobhan hurried instead toward the same back door that they had entered through. "Is there any way they could be tracking you?" she asked, the question for Miles as well as the other three.

They shared looks of fear and confusion, but before anyone could answer, Millennium murmured in a reedy voice, "I was bait?"

A branching explosion of red lightning and dust from underneath the door sill took away any chance to stop, ask for clarification, or try another way.

The magic sent Siobhan flying. She hit the ground and rolled painfully, catching glimpses of her companions in similar states as she tumbled.

She fell still, crumpled in the dirt and facing away from them all, the world spinning dizzily around her. The cold burn of her medallion against the skin of her chest told her it had protected her against some of whatever that spell was. As her dizziness began to settle, she watched through slitted eyes as a thin powder sprinkled to the ground.

Combined with the red light, it became obvious that someone had trapped the door with some sort of overpowered stunning spell. If she had to guess, it was a single-use mine artifact, not so different from the disintegration mine she'd used a few weeks ago, though thankfully not so deadly.

2 3

POISONED PAWN

Siobhan
Month 4, Day 9, Friday 9:45 a.m.

Judging by the lack of nearby screams, curses, or sounds of movement, Millennium and the others were completely unconscious. In the stable behind them, horses were whinnying and the workers were alarmed, but the vague sounds of a deep voice she couldn't quite make out comforted them. One of their attackers, most likely.

Siobhan couldn't feel anything from the waist down. She chose to believe that was from the effects of the stunning spell and not because her spine had been broken.

No help was coming. And the world was still spinning faintly. *'Did I hit my head?'* Or maybe that was the effects of the stunning spell. It contained Kuthian frog spit, or something, in addition to the electrical charge. She was pretty sure Professor Lacer had talked about it in one of his lectures. Which suddenly seemed hilariously ironic. She held back a giggle, then did her best to sober up.

'I am about to be either captured or killed,' she realized. *'And there is nothing I can do about it.'* The adrenaline spike helped to settle her uncharacteristic and totally inappropriate giddiness but did nothing to help her regain control of her body.

She fumbled with the hand of the arm she was lying on for the chain holding Professor Lacer's Conduit and her beast core, hoping no one was watching yet as she snapped the chain with a single hard yank toward her chest. She hesitated, her mind running wild as she tried to figure out what to do with them, somewhere they would be safe in the off chance that she somehow got free and was able to return to Sebastien Siverling's identity.

Professor Lacer would kill her if she lost his Conduit.

There was no time, and with no other viable ideas, she shoved both into her mouth, trailing metal chain and all. Her arm had some trouble locating her mouth, but after smashing her nose flat and poking herself in the eye with a finger, she managed to get it all inside.

With the most painful, strained gulp of her life, she swallowed both rocks, keeping the chain in her mouth. She was lucky that she was still a young thaumaturge, because her Conduit was only the size of a large grape, and the cheap beast core a small walnut. But neither were polished or smooth. For a moment, she thought they might get stuck in her throat and suffocate her, but with a painful, scraping stretch, they passed into her stomach. She smelled blood on her exhale.

Siobhan held back a whimper, pressing her tongue hard to the roof of her mouth to trap the chain there securely. As a child, she had kept one end of a long noodle in her mouth while swallowing the rest, then pulled the whole thing back out, to the disgust of everyone else at the dinner table. She could use the chain to do the same with her Conduit and beast core.

Footsteps approached from behind her as well as to the side, but she closed her eyes despite her racing heart. There was no sense in letting the enemy know that the stunning mine hadn't quite done its job.

A strange clattering sound came from above, and then a heavy *thunk* followed by what might have been a body collapsing to the ground. This was followed by a horrified gasp. "Oh please, oh please, don't be dead," a young man's voice muttered, cracking under the strain of heavy emotion.

Siobhan's stomach churned with burning acid. *'Who is he talking about? Please, not Miles.'*

More footsteps came from the sides, half-muffled thuds traveling through the ground as they hopped over the courtyard wall. A man said, "One of them is still up."

Siobhan suppressed a twitch. *'How did they know?'* she wondered, but immediately realized that they were talking about the young man behind her.

"I'm not one of them!" he protested. "I'm just a bystander, and um, a journalist," he added threateningly.

There was a moment of silence, followed by grunts of effort and pain and sounds of impact that seemed to indicate fighting. Siobhan picked out the sound of choking, the young man muttering, "Oh shit oh shit oh shit," under his breath, and even another small crackle of stunning magic.

"He's trained!" one of the men called, much less nonchalantly than earlier.

'*Is that boy actually fighting to defend us?*' Siobhan wondered in dawning surprise. She cracked one eyelid open just a sliver, allowing a blurry section of light through. She caught a glimpse of legs running past from the side of the courtyard—even more enemy backup.

A grunt came from behind her, and then the brown-skinned boy from before, the one who had been talking to Copper Robards in the street, stepped over her sprawled body. "The coppers are on the way! I called for them right away, and they'll be here any minute!" he warned.

Mr. Irving, the copper had called him. He had Millennium thrown over one shoulder, the child's insensate fingers dangling around his lower back. Irving's other hand held...a clay roof tile? He waved the arched terracotta threateningly in Siobhan's general direction, looking at the enemies standing over and around her. "I'm trained in the art of magi-kundo," he announced. "I'm warning you; stay back or I can't be responsible for what I do!" He waved the roof tile again.

Siobhan had never heard of this art. In fact, it sounded quite made-up. But she couldn't fault him for his verbal flailing. He was a child himself, and obviously trying to protect Millennium, even if his chances were hopeless. Perhaps, if he bought enough time, she would recover enough to be of use.

"Can't let him get away with the target," one of the enemies muttered. The red lights of stunning spells shot toward Irving, which he dodged with frankly impressive alacrity, but they lobbed a philtre as a follow-up.

He was backed up into the fenced corner of the courtyard, with nowhere to escape and a child half his size thrown over his shoulder. He wavered dizzily, then, with one last effort, hurled the roof tile, which clipped a man she could barely see out of the corner of her eye directly in the face. Then Irving crumpled into rag-doll unconsciousness underneath Millennium.

The tile-struck man had been carrying a battle wand, from which a spell shot out. Judging by the scream that sounded immediately afterward, he had accidentally shot one of his allies.

Siobhan held back a vindictive chuckle. Some of the feeling in her limbs was returning, but the pain was almost worse than the numbness had been.

"Is he finally down?" one of the remaining enemies asked.

"He must be. Who trained him, do you think? I've never seen a fighting style like that. For a half-grown boy to take even *one* of us..."

"Go check," the first man ordered. "And make sure the target's okay."

Reluctantly, a man stepped over Siobhan, coming down close enough to her face for her slitted eye to make out the spell array carved subtly into the side of his boot. He walked into the dispersing gas of the battle philtre, nudged Irving, and then checked over Millennium before carrying the child back. "Still alive, no serious injuries," he announced. "Pupils still dilating fine."

"Bring around the wagon," the leader said. "The rest of you, check for any weapons or tools they could use to escape. Double-stun at any sign of movement. We don't want any other nasty surprises. Parker only has one uninjured testicle left."

Siobhan's heart sank further as the others chuckled at the joke and only one pair of footsteps left for the mentioned wagons. The battle wand she'd been carrying before the stunning mine hit her was gone, dropped somewhere during her flying tumble. Even if she'd had it, she couldn't trust her coordination to aim or even pull the trigger correctly. *'If they don't find both my hidden waist holster under the corset and the chain in my mouth, I'll still have a Conduit, but I'm certainly in no shape to try and cast a spell. I've got the knives in my boots, too, but they're professionals, and unlike that Irving boy, I'm not a trained fighter. I can't think of anything I can do that is more likely to get me out of this than to get me immediately killed. It might be best to play dead, at least until I'm coherent enough to try to escape.'*

They searched her with surprising and somewhat humiliating thoroughness but didn't bother to unlace or cut through her corset, perhaps because they didn't imagine she could be hiding anything under it. All the Pendragon agents were men, after all. Her medallion was still freezing cold from attempting to protect her from the stunning mine, but it was also possible that its anti-theft mechanisms were activating to nudge them away.

One paused while running his fingers through her hair, probably staring down at her face.

She tried not to twitch or show any micro-expressions of response.

That was much harder when he said, "This one looks a little like the Raven Queen, don't you think?"

A second pair of footsteps drew closer. "Nah, she's too old."

"But the Raven Queen has dark skin and long dark hair."

The second man snorted. "So do thousands of women in Gilbratha." Suddenly, fingers pried at her eyelid.

Siobhan picked a spot and stared at it intently as her eyelid was drawn upward uncomfortably, revealing her contact-covered eyeball underneath. "Both her hair and eyes are light brown, not black as night. No Conduit. No raven feathers made of night or crystallized blood. No shadow companion woven from condensed nightmares. And, most compellingly I might add, she was just captured by us, with no attempt to melt into the shadows or whatever. She's an old servant just like that other one. Also, Parker, her face doesn't even really look like the drawings. She's a sweet older lady."

"Check her bag," the other one insisted stubbornly.

They jerked her around roughly to free her satchel, and Siobhan had never been so grateful for the exorbitant sum she'd spent on her replacement bag after the last one got disintegrated. It did, of course, have all of her thaumaturgic supplies, but it also had a featherweight enchantment, as well as two different divisions. One, which opened up under normal circumstances, held random odds and ends like a makeup pouch, a canteen of water, and a bag of snacks. The other division, which held everything interesting, required several of the seemingly decorative clasps to be positioned correctly and for the main latch to receive three quick taps before the mouth of the satchel was opened.

"Nothing," the second man announced triumphantly. "In fact, she's even got identification papers. Her name is Silvia Nakai. Get ahold of your imagination, man. You've embarrassed me plenty already, with the accusations against my neighbor Mara, and that waitress at the Rusty Peacock I had almost convinced to go on a date with me, and—"

"Shut up," the leader commanded as the sound of a horse's hooves and wooden wagon wheels returned.

"Target secured," one of the men said. "What do we do with the others?"

"Kill them?" another suggested.

"No," the leader said. "Take them with us."

The man who had suggested Siobhan was the Raven Queen added incredulously, "Don't you know this whole thing is a plot to draw *her* out? There's no need to make her angrier or give her a reason to get revenge on any of us personally."

"But won't she be captured after this?" the one who had wanted to kill her asked.

"Sure. *If* it works. Haven't you read the reports? I'm not going to gamble on her losing. Not when it's so easy just to capture a few more people for ransom. Right, captain?"

"We weren't ordered to kill anyone," the man said, though Siobhan wasn't sure if that was agreement with his subordinate's statement or not. And she was now more than fifty percent certain that these men were plainclothes Pendragon operatives. Though it was also possible that they were mercenaries working for the Architects of Khronos, or even some other group she'd never heard of.

Soon after, Siobhan was lifted and tossed into the back of a wagon, followed by the others, their limbs dropping painfully onto her.

"Go deal with the coppers," the leader ordered.

When her ankle twisted painfully under a limp, heavy body, she almost wished she was still numb. She couldn't move to escape the pain without giving away her consciousness. At least her sensation of balance wasn't careening around quite as giddily. Perhaps she would be able to escape out the back of the wagon with Miles when no one was looking. The Nightmare Pack enforcers and maid would have to fend for themselves. She couldn't save them all.

Siobhan risked a peek out of one eye, noting the cloth covering stretching in a dome over the wagon itself, disguising the contents within.

"What about the other kid?" someone asked.

"One of the coppers vouched for him. Some small-time journalist who fancies himself a vigilante. No connection to the gangs or the Raven Queen."

"Leave him," the leader ordered.

Apparently "dealing with" meant working with the coppers and exchanging information, not fighting or killing them. Another tally for the Pendragon operative theory.

"Everybody clear?" someone at the front of the wagon asked. A handful of affirmative responses followed.

And then Siobhan was engulfed in darkness.

It was a darkness so complete she had never experienced anything comparable, completely different than the shadow of her closed eyelids or even the shadows on a moonless night.

That was what she noticed first.

Then came the fact that she could not hear anything, even the sound of her own breathing or heartbeat, which normally became discernible in extreme silence.

Then, that she could *feel* nothing, either. Not her body pressing against the wooden planks of the wagon, nor the pain in her squished and twisted ankle, nor even her tongue inside her mouth.

Her consciousness floated in nothing, completely unmoored.

She panicked. She tried to move, to scream, to bite her own tongue, *anything*. But if she was still connected to a brain—which she wasn't sure of— it was no longer sending or receiving signals to her body. And then she had a horrible thought. One so horrible that it stilled her mind.

'*I am dead.*'

24

———————

EIGENGRAU

In an ironic boon, with Siobhan's panic at the thought of death came something else—a very faint burn, a muted rush. Adrenaline. Relief tumbled through her so violently she probably would have felt dizzy with it if not for this strange sensory deprivation effect.

It was enough for her to conclude that she wasn't dead, and her body was still there. She was simply cut off from the sensation of it. Most likely, the "everybody clear" she'd heard earlier was someone checking before they activated a spell array. It was an effective method to keep prisoners from attempting escape, even after the stunning spells wore off.

She would not have the slightest chance of calculating where they were being taken based on time passed and the number of turns the wagon took. And even though she had ways to call for help, she could not implement them.

Siobhan did what she could to keep her mind moored, but without any of her senses, existing effectively as consciousness in the void, it was difficult to anchor herself. She could tell that time was passing and tried to focus on that certainty, though it was hard to quantify exactly how much without her heartbeat or breaths to compare against. It helped at first, but eventually she began to lose her grip on time, too.

She drifted off for a moment, and when she—metaphorically—jerked back to attention, she had no idea how long she had been in the nothing. *'How long until I go insane?'* she had to wonder. Perhaps in response to this, she began to see phosphenes in the uniform eigengrau darkness of the abyss. The strange colors and shapes created by her detaching mind were incoherent at first, any meaning bestowed in the same way one could find recognizable shapes in the clouds.

After a while, they began to cohere into something recognizable. *'I'm retreating into illusions to create a false sense of security and keep my mind from spiraling off into insanity,'* she reasoned, noting her surroundings and the too-sharp, too-vibrant sensations of an imagined body. Anything to house her consciousness was better than nothing, she supposed. Though she would have preferred a different setting. Almost any other setting, in fact.

Siobhan stood in a place she remembered well from childhood. She was in Grandfather's house, standing before a half-open door. Not the metal one, from the magical workshop in the tower, but the wooden door with the warped board that left a little crack just at eye height. When she was a child, she would peek through it into Grandfather's room sometimes.

But now, she was too tall and would have to crouch down to see through it. *'At least I am not thirteen again,'* she thought, though the sheer relief of that confirmation seemed strangely powerful. *'Am I often thirteen, in my dreams?'* She couldn't remember.

Siobhan usually imagined her nightmares as a kind of physical mass locked away in her head. A slimy, putrid, hungry liquid. Normally, it was contained perfectly, but in sleep—in dreams—she was unguarded, the dream-space undefined enough that the box keeping it all sealed up tight became undefined, too. And so, the nightmare-stuff had a chance to leak out.

If she could wake quickly enough, most of it would get sucked back into the box as reality reasserted itself, leaving only the lingering terror and flashes of strange imagery.

Now, though, without the anchoring of her physical body, things normally confined to dreams started to leak out.

Siobhan had no need to peek through the door. She already knew what was on the other side. *'My mind could have conjured almost any other scene to keep me from the insanity of sensory deprivation,'* she lamented. *'But of course it always comes back to this.'*

Siobhan braced herself and opened the door. The warding medallion was there on the table, with all of Grandfather's artificery gadgets and lights and lenses that helped him use tools sized for a little bug. His gift for her, not finished yet.

Grandfather's corpse was there, too, half his head a hollow. Brain matter and blood—so much blood—pooled in front of the fireplace, its warm flames reflecting off the dark, placid surface.

Just as she had in reality, Siobhan moved past the corpse to the table, picking up the medallion.

She examined it for a moment, feeling the weight of it in her hand, the moldings of glyphs and symbols on its surface, so vivid despite it all being a figment of memory and imagination.

Something rustled behind her, and she spun around, heart leaping in her chest.

Grandfather's corpse had sat up. One of his eyes was missing, blown away and leaving only an empty, ruined socket. The other watched her with a bright golden iris staring out from a blood-red sclera. "It's not complete, you know. I never had the chance to finish it."

Siobhan's knees trembled, and she clenched the medallion in one fist so hard her knuckles whitened, the other bracing against the desk to help support her weight. "This didn't happen."

Grandfather tilted his head to the side, letting her see the hollow, meaty cavern that made up the remaining half of his skull. "How would you know? You do not remember anything."

Her voice cracked. "I remember this part."

"You should remember more," he said, his eye suddenly intense, almost glowing against the shadows of his face, the fireplace behind him giving him a halo of brightness. "If you just remembered, you could fix things, don't you think? You would know why you have these nightmares, and maybe they would stop."

"I know well enough why I have them." She did, even if she tried never to think of it or the thoughts connected to it. She knew well enough, and could guess at the rest.

Grandfather's expression drew together cruelly, his mouth twisting in a sneer. "Do you truly? Do you think I had your best interest at heart by this time? I'd already gone quite insane. I *harmed* you, and yet you cling to the wound like it is a gift."

Siobhan shuddered. "You are not my grandfather. I remember this night, and this did not happen. You're...the nightmare. Or a piece of it, trying to leak out of the box."

His sneer slipped away too quickly to be natural, and he laughed lightly, almost seeming proud. "It seems he raised no imbecile. You are correct, more or less. He did not have enough time to do a perfect job, and he never expected his patchwork solution to have to last this long. He had planned for you to go to one of his acquaintances who would settle the matter for good. But you forgot about that part, and he was too incoherent to realize he needed to repeat it for you. So you let things stay like this, trying your little patchwork solutions that are about as effective as using your finger to plug a leak in a dam."

Grandfather—or rather the thing wearing his body—lurched forward, rising to his feet like a puppet on strings. "You can't keep depending on the seal to hold. It's cracking, my little hazelnut," he said, using the term of endearment only her grandfather had called her. "And it's going to fail soon. You need to take control. 'You control your mind, it doesn't control you.' Remember?"

"You just want me to let you free," she whispered. "But I won't. I never will."

He lurched forward a couple more steps, his face too hidden in shadows to make out the features except for that gold, glowing eye. "What do you think is in the box? Aren't you curious? Aren't you afraid? Don't you hear me scratching from the inside?"

He reached for her, and she stumbled back until she hit the wall, the panic strong enough that she could once again feel the physical sensation of chemicals in her body. Her dream-self's breaths were tremulous, sweat beaded on her upper lip and her brow, and her fingers were ice-cold. She thought she might throw up from the sheer, savage dread that knotted her stomach. Silently, she screamed at herself to do something, do *anything*, to stop this.

And as she always did in times of trouble or uncertainty, she reached for her magic. She brought her Will to bear, letting it stretch out through her body, through the room, all that her mind had created.

Grandfather froze.

"I am in control," she said slowly, carefully. "I do control my mind." And suddenly, perhaps aided by the fact that she was not unconscious but rather quite awake and lucid, the memory returned to the state of what had actually happened.

Grandfather was nothing but a corpse on the ground. All his power was gone. Only cooling flesh and blood remained.

Siobhan didn't want to keep playing out the memory, and with a thought, her consciousness returned to the nothingness of sensory deprivation. But with her Will so active and spread through the domain she always—inherently —controlled without the need for a Circle, she felt something else. Her own body.

With her Will activated, she knew where her hands were, where her face was, where her feet were, and she even had a very muted sensation of touch, feeling the faint echoes of cool air on her legs and arms, and the deep chill of stone beneath her.

Siobhan could feel the discomfort of the beast core and Conduit pressed against the skin of her back, forcing indentations in her flesh to fit themselves. Which meant she hadn't been stripped entirely. She still had some limited resources, though her dress and her shoes seemed to be missing. As she focused her attention, she could even feel the well of potential energy trapped inside the beast core, just waiting to be used. A faint echo of that power came from inside her abdomen—the beast core she had swallowed.

Pushing her Will beyond her body didn't do much, and she wasn't even sure it was working, but it did give her an idea. She tried to move, slowly and carefully, bringing her Will to bear in her arms, trying to fill her flesh with the presence of her ability to command the world and thus push out whatever was inhibiting her.

Her movements were more jerky than she had hoped, clumsy and jittering, but she managed to get both of her hands in front of her face. Pressing hard to make sure everything was in place, she shoved her hands together in front of her mouth, joining her fingers and thumbs together in a Circle with great care.

She swirled her Will around her head and her arms again just to make absolutely sure her breath was filtering through the Circle and her fingertips were touching securely. She pulled at the beast core on her back, being extremely careful to avoid the one she'd swallowed, taking the tiniest bit of power and pushing it through where the black sapphire Conduit was.

Suddenly, she was aware of the Conduit the same way she was the beast core.

Relief, fear, and excitement crashed together in a cacophony of physical sensation that sent goosebumps rising over her skin and urged her breaths to come faster.

She had the Sacrifice and the Will, but she could not feel her own lips or tongue well enough for a verbal chant—the Word.

Taking care to hold the chant and its meaning, the way each word felt and sounded, clear in her mind, she silently recited a familiar chant, thrice over. *'Life's breath, shadow mine. In darkness we were born. In darkness do we feast. Devour, and arise.'* With each repetition, she felt a stronger connection to her shadow, until finally it was finished, and there was more of her.

She let out a silent laugh on an exhale. It had worked. She could sense everything her shadow touched. She had thought it might and hoped that it would, on the premise that the shadow absorbed light and energy in the electromagnetic spectrum, and through absorption, could give her a sense of her surroundings that her actual body lacked.

Her Will could ride it just like it rode her physical body.

Her shadow pooled in the angles of her body and beneath her, unmoving, but dense and ready. There was barely any light, and as the spell pulled on her breath for heat instead, her fingers began to ache.

'There is no difference between light and the rest of electromagnetic radiation. I should be able to use even the invisible light for power.' The spell gained stability, and the ache in her hands receded somewhat as she mentally adjusted its parameters. But she needed more. She ran through her understanding of the more esoteric aspects of light. *'Heat and light are really two sides of the same coin. Everything that*

has a temperature is very subtly glowing, well below the level that the human eye can pick up, as the electrons step up and down their levels. Can I suck all the "potential" light out of the places my shadow touches? The spell already pulls heat from my breath, so this shouldn't even be that difficult of a conceptual shift.'

The draw on the heat of her breath through her fingers disappeared almost entirely, and the sensations her shadow was feeding back to her became almost tangible as her shadow somehow solidified itself. The metaphorical ink of its form grew deeper, all the better to stretch farther and wider.

Siobhan directed her shadow to rise up, embracing her, and let out a tremulous breath. She could feel its chill, like the underside of a pillow. But the sensations it brought were like a fire in the darkness, shelter from a raging storm, or the embrace of her mother's arms. Though she remained in a different type of absolute darkness, she was no longer senseless or helpless. She was no longer so afraid.

Siobhan spread her shadow further, searching outward. She was in a relatively small room with nine others, including someone she thought was Millennium, but also another small child. Everyone was lying on the floor unconscious. All were alive, though a few were obviously injured.

The Pendragon operatives had somehow transported them without breaking the sensory deprivation spell, and it was likely that many of the others were not truly unconscious any longer, merely trapped within senseless bodies and the shell of their own minds.

On the floor, a spell array surrounded them, which she sensed as her shadow ate at the faintly glowing lines. The details, however, were difficult to decipher from the ambiguous understanding her shadow conveyed.

Siobhan spread her shadow further and found, to her dismay, a form standing against the edge of the wall by the door, behind her.

The movement of their limbs was too flailing to decipher coherently as the person—likely a guard—left the room, slamming the door behind them. Which meant she had just alerted the enemy to her consciousness and didn't have much time.

She pulled her shadow mostly back in, keeping a section of it in a lumpy, blanketing shape over where her body had been as she attempted a jerky crawl away. Just in case they tried to kill her, a decoy might buy her a little time.

As soon as she crossed the edge of the Circle, all of her senses rushed back in, and everything she had felt from her shadow disappeared under the barrage of too-powerful feedback from her body. She could smell all the nuances of blood and sweat and mineral-laden water on dank stone, taste her own tongue in her mouth, and feel all the many aches and pains she had accumulated. She could hear screams and the sound of fleeing footsteps. And apparently, she had swallowed the chain connected to Professor Lacer's

Conduit while insensate, leaving the beast core and Conduit much more diffi-cult to retrieve.

Slowly, she slid her hands closer together over her mouth, keeping the Circle intact until one of her hands was making a small Circle of its own within the other. Then she drew the outer hand away. Despite her adjustment, using only one hand to create the Circle instead of two, the shadow-familiar spell remained steady, its chill form cloaking her with no additional strain.

Feeling blindly under the cover of her own shadow, she prodded at her face. Her fake nose was hanging half off, the connective glue likely torn by her flailing attempts to press a Circle to her mouth. She removed her disguise, slipping the contact lenses and the fake nose into the bodice of her corset, atop the medallion and transformation amulet that were somehow still hidden between the press of her rather meager cleavage. They must have been protected from notice and theft by the warding spell woven into the medal-lion, with the amulet going unnoticed by proximity. *'A warding artifact is much less useful if anyone can take it off you.'* She would have lost the golden artifact long ago if her father could have ever managed to remember its existence.

She finished by scratching away the fake wrinkles at the corners of her eyes and mouth. She knew it was unlikely she could keep tonight's identity completely separate from the Raven Queen's, but sowing any little bit of confusion among her enemies could only help her.

She stood stiffly, with a deep moan of pain. The concoctions she had used that morning had all worn off. Her sore muscles screamed once more on top of all the new bruises, a badly battered tailbone, and a wrenched ankle. She allowed the shadows spilling through the room to drop to the floor and then converge on her, slipping away from her face to create a kind of cloak and cowl to cover up her hair. As a final touch, the shadows formed the impression of wispy feathers around the hood.

An overhead light crystal burst to life, painting the room in stark lines and feeding even more power into her shadow. She flinched at the sudden bright-ness and instinctively guided the thinnest possible shroud of darkness over her face to filter the light.

The one remaining guard outside, visible through the small window set into the door of the white stone room, was still screaming wordlessly, futilely, as she opened her eyes and met his gaze.

2 5

RAVEN CLOUDS

    Month 4, Day 9, Friday 9:00 a.m.

EVERYONE in the room except for Thaddeus was nervous, though some hid it better than others. He had taken one of the best seats in the back corner of Harrow Hill's third floor meeting room, positioned next to a window.

An entire row of distagrams sat against one of the walls, manned by a couple of apprehensive young coppers. Everyone who wasn't on duty at the Edictum Council or out patrolling the streets was here. Only those so ill or injured as to be on bed rest were off duty.

In addition, a squad of Red Guard agents had made an appearance—under relentless pressure from the High Crown—and a couple of the man's own Pendragon Corps operatives stood near the door. They both remained silent and straight-backed, sneering at the rest, even the Red Guard agents.

The Pendragon Corps had ostentatious uniforms and sparkling artifacts, and they received special training that the First Crown Family had always touted as being the best of the best. However, the operatives rarely saw combat—even less than the average copper. It used to be that the Pendragon Corps took their numbers from people who had shown real competence in the army or as beast hunters. Historically, they even recruited extremely skilled criminals who had done nothing heinous or public enough to taint the High Crown's reputation, offering those people service in lieu of penal servitude or death.

Now, at least half of their recruits were straight out of the University, and Thaddeus had heard rumors that the honor of the position was warring with the realities of withstanding the High Crown's egomania and increasing paranoia.

And yet, they sneered at the coppers, swaggered through the streets, and imagined themselves equals of the Red Guard. Totally preposterous.

Unfortunately, the Pendragon operatives' current disdain was all too understandable.

Agent Berg, the man who had botched the Moore break event aftercare, was one of those sent to assist. He was as loud as usual. Was he partially deaf, or simply oblivious?

"It was as big as a building!" Berg bragged, throwing his arms wide as several awe-struck coppers listened. "But we're trained to handle such things, and you wouldn't believe the kind of artifacts we get in the Red Guard. One spell, one ankle blown clean off!" He displayed none of the quietly assertive excellence that was associated with their organization's public face.

Thus, the Pendragon operatives' disdain.

Even Thaddeus's apprentice Sebastien would be a better Red Guard recruit than that Berg buffoon. The thought of Sebastien caused Thaddeus a flicker of concern. Hopefully, Siverling was safe in the University dorms. This would be just the sort of thing that foolish, overly confident boy would somehow get caught up in.

But no matter Agent Berg's attempts at distraction through braggadocio, thoughts inevitably turned back toward the reason for their presence.

"Do you have anything special to deal with the Raven Queen?" one of the coppers asked.

"If she shows her face in front of me, it'll be the last thing she ever does as a free woman!" Berg announced, grinning widely with his hands on his hips.

A few of the coppers shared glances, dubious. "Will she show up for sure?"

Thaddeus tuned out their conversation, looking out over the city, already teeming with people like ants in a hive, all heading toward the same central point. He had considered turning down Titus's request to act as a consultant and one more point of backup so that he could attend the sentencing, but Thaddeus had a feeling that Siobhan Naught would surprise them. He wanted to be able to respond to that. Harrow Hill was the place that would receive information most quickly, and both horses and carriages were available for quick deployment.

It had been over three weeks now since he spoke to Lord Stag about his desire to meet the Raven Queen, and she still had not responded. She was ignoring him. The knuckles of Thaddeus's right hand grew white as he made a fist and then very deliberately released it. He could be patient. But he would not be complacent. And if she insisted on playing games, he would have to force her to pay attention.

With a curious sideways look at Thaddeus, one of the coppers asked loudly enough to purposefully be overheard, "Have you Red Guard agents seen anything like the Raven Queen before?"

Thaddeus had experienced quite a lot of fascinating and horrific things. He didn't remember a time when he was unaware of the horrors this world could birth, but he had experienced it firsthand during his first—and last—dragon hunt. It wasn't the magical beast itself that had been the worst of it. No, that was his teammates. The other people. And then, of course, what became of them.

In the Haze War, Thaddeus had seen wondrous magic and enormous wealth, all used for the purpose of death and domination. All that effort and waste, born from greed and, in the end, coming to nothing. What a waste of resources.

But above all, his years of active service with the Red Guard had exposed Thaddeus to sublime magic, strange ideas, and overwhelming power—all of these things coming both from their agents and from what they fought against to protect the world. The Red Guard collected the best thaumaturges, the most knowledgeable researchers, and innovators so close to the cutting edge that they sometimes slipped over it.

Rarely, however, had he met an individual so fascinating as the Raven Queen. She was simply so *entertaining*.

Thaddeus scowled. If today didn't bear some sort of fruit, he would go back to the Verdant Stag with a more pressing offer. Though perhaps the Nightmare Pack would be the better option. He had heard they had a connection to the Raven Queen as well.

Thaddeus was drawn from his irritated musing as Harrow Hill's captain walked in. In any other copper station, he would have been the highest-ranking individual, but here he was accompanied by Titus Westbay, the Lord Commander of the coppers. Investigator Kuchen trailed behind them, as unpleasantly phlegmatic as ever.

Titus nodded at Thaddeus, then went to stand against the wall opposite the distagrams, watching the captain move to the podium at the front of the room.

The captain cleared his throat loudly—and quite unnecessarily—as the room had fallen silent as soon as the trio entered. Everyone was waiting with bated breath for what they might say.

"Today, we hope to capture the criminal and blood sorceress Siobhan Naught, better known by her alias the Raven Queen. We hope to lure her to the Edictum Council, where our friends in the Red Guard have placed additional protections for the civilians. If all goes well, we will forcefully reroute her to a nearby safe location, which will facilitate her capture. We have some of the best thaumaturges in the nation working on this, but as you know, the Raven Queen has proven slippery and cunning before. We cannot afford to become complacent."

The man glanced at Titus, and his fingers twitched in an aborted motion for the handkerchief in his breast pocket before he remembered himself. It wouldn't look very confidence-inspiring to see the captain wiping beads of stress-induced sweat off of his bald pate in the middle of a speech.

"We are working in teams of four," the man continued. "Some teams will spread throughout the area near the Edictum Council for immediate response, and some will be held here, ready for rapid deployment via horseback. Each team is fully prepared for contact."

Thaddeus held back a snort. If that were true, the man wouldn't need to say it in a bid to reassure his underlings.

"Two of the four members are devoted to shielding. Those of you with that job will carry several defensive artifacts that cover not only the standard protective wards, but also have specific spells formulated to protect against her known offensive abilities. In addition to that, all members have personal anti-nightmare curse wards. Please make sure that you've checked out all the equipment assigned to you *and* know how to use it."

Thaddeus looked to Titus, one eyebrow raised. Could it be possible that any man or woman here would have neglected the proper training on the use of what were touted to be such life-saving defensive artifacts? Thaddeus would have doubted such stupidity could exist, but some uncomfortable shuffling amongst the rank and file suggested otherwise. Or, more generously, they might be nervous, unconvinced that Harrow Hill's preparations would suffice.

"As we believe she may somehow be able to travel through shadows, and indeed many of her abilities being based around darkness and night, we have provided high-power light artifacts that will create a glowing barrier large enough to fit a single team. But more importantly, one member of each team has been assigned an artifact that will cast a series of miniature sun replicas in the air above you. This should allow you to negate many of her abilities.

"Watch for the shadow companion," the captain warned. "It is known to turn into a flock of ravens, which are capable of flight and could attack from unexpected directions. Keep your eyes to the shadows and the skies."

Thaddeus gave in to the juvenile urge to roll his eyes.

"And if you do come into contact with the Raven Queen, either out on patrol or as the first responders to an alert..." The captain trailed off, eyes tracking across the men and women heating the room with their nervous, stinking breath and sweat-flushed skin.

"The final member of each team has been equipped with several incapacitating options, which you should use immediately if it seems she will attack or escape. But, if you do come into contact with her," he repeated, "remember that stalling is a reasonable and acceptable tactic. The very first thing you should do upon a confirmed sighting is to call for backup, which will be another two four-man teams, plus a Red Guard duo and one of Lord Pendragon's personal operatives. If you can stall until backup arrives, we will overwhelm her with power, versatility, and skill."

There was some muttering, then, and the captain pushed over it by raising his voice. "Our profilers suggest that if you do not show aggression toward her, she is mischievous and perhaps whimsical enough to stop and communicate with you. Even, perhaps, while knowing that backup is on the way. She is supremely confident and may feel that she is in no danger, planning to flip the tables in a big surprise.

"However." He lifted one hand with his forefinger outstretched to emphasize his point, his speech slowing so that each word was distinguished from the others. "If you do converse with her, be extremely careful not to make any deals. This covers not only overt bargains, but also any kind of agreement for exchanges, or seemingly harmless favors."

This caused even more muttering and nervous shuffling, but the captain made a few more mundane points and then broke off for one of his subordinates to give half the teams their patrol routes for the day.

With the meeting ended and half of the coppers filing out into the dangerous world, Thaddeus resigned himself to a long wait. He perked up every time the distagram operation reported a message from one of the patrolling teams, which they could send from one of the many waystations in their network. Each time, he was disappointed.

There were some small skirmishes and mundane arrests, but nothing worthy of Thaddeus's interest. It wasn't until much later in the day, when the sentencing had started, that something finally happened.

Thaddeus noticed the strange phenomenon himself before the distagram relayed the information. Sitting by the window, his eyes had been drawn to the faint dots of distant birds in the sky without his conscious input. His focus narrowed as he realized that these birds were aggregating unnaturally.

He stood, the scrape of his chair against the stone floor drawing tense eyes his way from all over the room. Thaddeus ignored them, free-casting a lens spell in front of the window to peer clearly into the distance. He adjusted its focus with some quick calculations and a roll of his fingers.

A foot-wide section of the air in front of his face now showed a much closer view of a run-down building well into the Mires. It was taller than those around it, like a single still-living soldier amongst the sprawling, mutilated bodies of his former companions.

Birds congregated around the building in an increasingly thick flock, seemingly connected by a single mind, sections of their multitude twisting and turning and changing direction at a moment's notice in some kind of unfathomable dance. Even as Thaddeus watched, more and more feathered creatures added themselves to the delphic, hypnotic concord.

"Ravens," Thaddeus said with awe. He watched unblinking, trying to absorb every moment of the display. It was exquisite, an arrangement that seemed as if it should have been accompanied by music. He had once heard a forty-string orchestra in Paneth, and could imagine that reverberating sound fitting with this living mass of darkness that undulated in the sky above Gilbratha.

Something twinged in Thaddeus's chest, slightly painful, poignant, and to his surprise his eyes itched and burned in response. He blinked rapidly but refused to be ashamed. This was an involuntary, universal reaction to experiencing the practical application of genius. A visual representation of the weave of magic. And every second, more ravens joined the flock.

Others had gathered at the windows and behind Thaddeus, trying to peek through his spell to get a better look.

"Sweet Myrddin," one of the coppers whispered through dry lips.

"It's her. That's her," another said, gripping the shoulder of the man beside him and shaking him as if to better get his point across.

"How are we supposed to capture that? A *bright light?*" a woman asked derisively, irritation only partially masking her fear.

"Teams eight, nine, ten, and eleven, move out!" the captain shouted, snapping those who weren't already on their way into action.

Reluctantly, Thaddeus dropped his far-seeing spell and strode toward the room's exit, then down to the front gate. Titus had arrived ahead of him, and waved for Thaddeus to join him and Kuchen in the armored carriage attached to four great destriers.

No sooner had Thaddeus closed the door behind him than the carriage sprang into motion, the acceleration pushing him back into his seat. Outside, the coachman rang the bell to warn anyone on the streets to make way.

Thaddeus watched the sky through the small window set into the door, catching glimpses of the phenomenon toward the south the few times when the carriage was faced to allow this.

His companions were as silent as he was for the most part, though Kuchen manned the carriage's personal distagram, relaying Titus's message to the diviners at the University and poking his head out of the window to yell precise coordinates for the center of the cloud to the driver—not that the man would need such a thing.

The entire city could see the Raven Queen's working. People on the streets had stopped in their tracks to stare, open-mouthed, with the more adventurous climbing onto roofs. One enterprising restaurant owner was even selling tickets to his roof to watch the show—*with* wine and snacks.

The distagram activated, the attached pen rising up and writing in the neat, foreign hand of whoever was sending the message. Kuchen's eyes widened as he read. When the message ended, he tore off the strip of paper and read it again. "They found her! The divinations have shown results! She's at..." He trailed off, looking up at Titus and Thaddeus. He cleared his throat wetly. "Well, she's in the city, to the southwest. In the center of the raven cloud, it would seem."

"What a revelation," Titus drawled.

Thaddeus smirked and did his best to suppress inappropriate signs of excitement as they approached. However, one small thorn marred the experience. What was so special about Ennis Naught that she was willing to go to such lengths for him?

The Mires were far from Harrow Hill, and no matter how much Thaddeus and Titus might want to, they couldn't literally trample through the crowds of civilians filling the streets. Long minutes before they finally arrived, Thaddeus knew they would be too late, as the unkindness of ravens began to disperse. The teams that had raced ahead on horseback reported no sightings of her.

When the carriage finally stopped at the edge of the area, which was already being cordoned off, Thaddeus grimaced. The streets and buildings were covered in bird shit, the coppers were busy questioning any civilian they could get their hands on, and the building at the center of it all was empty. Thaddeus walked swiftly through each room and examined the roof for something that the others might have missed, but he noticed nothing unusual and suspected he would find nothing she hadn't specifically left for that purpose.

No hidden clues or messages for him.

But, visible in the distance from the vantage point of the roof, the golden spire piercing up from the dome of the Edictum Council building glinted in the sun. Thaddeus couldn't help the smile that stretched across his face, baring his teeth in wild exhilaration. "This was a diversion," he said.

26

A CLOAK OF SHADOWS

Siobhan
  Month 4, Day 9, Friday

Siobhan squinted against the light, ignoring the screams of the guard outside the room while she took stock of her situation as quickly as possible. She had no idea how much time had passed, but she wasn't starving or severely dehydrated. She did badly need to urinate, so it must have been at least a few hours.

The faintest twinge of cold needles in her back seemed to be fighting against a divination attempt, but judging by how weak it was, either the room was warded against sympathetic divination, she was very far away, or there was some other barrier between them—like the thick stone walls.

Her captors had taken everything except her tightly laced corset and the things hidden inside and underneath it, including her warding medallion and the amulet tucked into her cleavage. Their decency—or laziness—could be their undoing. Her arm felt bare without the array of thin alarm bracelets she was used to wearing. She didn't know if they had broken and triggered the bracelets, which would alert Oliver and Katerin to her plight.

She turned toward the sensory deprivation spell array on the ground, but her gaze was drawn to the bright copper hair of another boy, the one she had sensed while still inside the array; it was Theo, Katerin's nephew, his gangly limbs sprawled out among the others. Enforcer Gerard lay next to him, one half of his face battered and swollen to half again its normal size. Another young man, also from the Verdant Stag, had badly broken his lower leg. Blood had seeped through the makeshift bandage around his calf and pooled on the floor.

'The enemy didn't just go after the Nightmare Pack,' she realized. And if their motivation held true, they had wanted Theo and Miles specifically, with everyone else being collateral damage.

The sensory deprivation spell seemed to be an artifact laid into the floor and pre-charged. There was no obvious way to turn it off, at least not from inside the room. Breaking the Circle might have been possible if she had something to write with, but she didn't know what effect that might have. The side effects could be worse than the original problem.

But Siobhan *could* reach a man who was close to the edge. She didn't recognize him by name, but she had seen him in Verdant Stag territory, wearing a jacket sporting bright green antlers made of peeling paint.

Her free hand went quite numb as it crossed the bounds of the Circle, but she was still able to get a solid grip on his hair. Slowly, her aching body protesting against the effort, she dragged him the foot or so necessary for his head to cross the Circle. He gasped, eyes opening wide and then slamming shut, his face contorting painfully.

She pulled a little farther, getting his arms out, and that was all he needed to scramble the rest of the way himself.

He stayed on his hands and knees, stealing a couple glances at her through squinting, watering eyes. "The Raven Queen?" he croaked. "I mean—my lady, my queen? You came to save us?"

"Help the others. Get them out of the Circle," she ordered, limping quickly toward the metal door, which was solid except for a barred window at head height. "And be prepared for a fight."

The guard outside, wearing the uniform of a Pendragon operative, had stopped shrieking and was pointing one trembling finger at Siobhan as she approached the door and looked through the window. He nearly fell over himself to put some distance between them, retreating down the hallway with his back pressed firmly to the wall.

"Stay back! Stay back!" he screamed, but he was still only pointing with his finger, no battle wand in his hand, so she ignored him.

The Stag enforcer wasted no time complying with her orders, and the cell quickly filled with sounds of relief, distress, and quickly murmured explanations of their situation. "Oh, but she's answered my prayers!" a woman moaned. "I was in darkness, and I prayed to the Queen of Ravens to walk through the shadows to my side. She's answered me. We're saved!"

"Wait, that woman is the Raven Queen?" Miles's maid, Martha, asked, doing a double-take at Siobhan's face.

Enforcer Gerard shushed them sharply.

"I'll pay whatever tribute she requires if she can actually get us out of here," Jackal muttered.

Siobhan pressed her face close to the barred window, looking down the hall in either direction. The walls were made of white stone, chipped away in relative uniformity to create the hallways, but not smoothed or polished.

A few dozen meters to the left, another hallway cut through the stone in a perpendicular direction. That was where the other guards had disappeared. The lone remaining guard had fallen silent, finally, and she could hear the echoes of his companions running and clanking beyond the corner.

Down their hallway to the right, the light cut out. Siobhan tilted her head to the side, listening. It was too dark to see far in that direction, but the echoes bouncing back became strangely layered and choppy, suggesting that the hallways stretched on for quite a while, maze-like.

A suspicion about their location began to grow in her mind. She breathed deep, tasting the air on her tongue.

With more people working together to free the others, soon, everyone was out of the spell array. Though several captives bore injuries of various severity, all were grim with the realization of their situation and prepared to escape at any cost.

Enforcer Gerard stepped up stiffly beside her, wearing only his underwear and clutching one arm in the other to stabilize it. The scars on his legs were visible, but whatever treatment he'd received for the injuries he sustained at Knave Knoll must have been powerful. "Thank you for coming, my lady. What is the plan?" he asked, his voice slightly slurred by the trauma and swelling marring half of his face.

"Enemy reinforcements are on their way."

Gerard turned to the others. "Those of you with combat experience, step up on either side of the door. Theo, get into the corner, behind Enforcer Turner. You, too, Mr. Lynwood," he added, looking at Miles.

The children hurried to shuffle into one of the corners closest to the door, behind the young man with the broken leg. Both were pale and silent with fear, but Miles gave her a tremulous smile, and Theo clenched his fists and scowled around the room.

"I didn't actually believe in her, you know?" Turner whispered to one of the women. "Does this mean she's really heard me every time I said her name? She could have appeared out of nowhere, just like this?"

Siobhan ignored them, pressing her face further between the bars to better see. To the side, a circular device was embedded in the wall beside their door —the locking mechanism, no doubt. "Come forward and try to break the window," she ordered, stepping aside and ignoring the increasingly loud scream of pain from her ankle as it took her weight.

There were no obvious hinges or weak points, as the door seemed to open by sliding into and out of a slot in the stone wall. She doubted they would be able to reach the unlocking device through the small window, but it didn't hurt to try while she worked on her own solution.

She hobbled back to the Circle covering most of the room's floor and braced herself before entering it again. She had a moment of vertigo as she once again lost all sensation, but her shadow took over after only a few moments. She swayed but didn't fall, and then jerkily made her way to the small puddle of mostly coagulated blood from Turner's leg. She had nothing to carry it in, so scooped as much as she could into her free hand.

She hobbled back to the door as quickly as possible, stumbling once again as her senses returned to her.

The enforcers had failed to break the window and were now bashing themselves against the door with no luck.

"Step aside," she told Enforcer Fring.

The eyes of those around her focused on her blood-filled hand as she used it to draw out a stone disintegration spell array on the wall behind the opening mechanism.

The reckless cacophony of approaching enemy reinforcements grew louder. But her spell array was simple, requiring only an inner and outer Circle, a pentagon, and two glyphs. The wall began to crumble away from the inner Circle as she split her Will and applied power, but she wasn't fast enough.

The guard who had been cowering down the hall slapped himself twice in the face. His handprint stood out starkly red against his pale face as he stepped forward again, a thick battle wand that could have passed for a bludgeoning rod in one hand and some other spherical artifact in the other.

He was quickly joined by two others, each kitted out in gold and silver glittering armor worn over their uniforms. They pointed the wands at the door—at her—as they approached.

Siobhan drew her head away from the window, but she could still hear them.

Panting, one said, "The captain is still out in the city with the others. We already set off the alarm and sent a message. There were still some of our men left in the palace, and they should be able to get down here within five minutes."

"It's the *Raven Queen*! We don't *have* five minutes!" the previously screaming guard ground out, panting hard. His voice sounded vaguely familiar. Though Siobhan couldn't be sure, she thought he was the one who had been suspicious of her identity.

"Get yourself together!" another snapped. "We know the protocols, we have the supplies. The shift leader is bringing the Radiant explosive right now. He'll be here in seconds. All we have to do is subdue her until then!"

"The others pray to her," the first guard tattled hoarsely. "They're her devotees! Probably feeding her some kind of dark power. I heard them talking about it."

No one dignified this with a response, but a quick peek around the edge of the window showed a fourth guard rounding the corner, also in resplendent armor. He carried something large, round, and metallic, the size of a cantaloupe or a human skull.

"Kill them, my queen! Kill them all!" the woman who had been praying to the Raven Queen screamed vengefully.

Though it might not have made it any *worse*, this did not improve the captives' situation, as the guards shared wary looks and moved forward together.

Siobhan poured more power into the stone-disintegration spell but was barely a few inches into the wall as two of the guards lunged forward to use the locking mechanism while the other two kept their wands pointed at the door to cover them.

The lock took a password and what seemed to be a thumbprint of saliva from two of the guards at the same time, all entered within the space of a couple seconds.

"Wait!" Siobhan cried, ducking down and desperately trying to buy time. For what, exactly, she didn't know. After all, the guards were opening the door, which was what she had been trying to do. Her shadow swallowed her up and stretched out to either side in duplicate humanoid shapes to obscure her exact location. The door began to slide to the side.

And then the guards blasted it aside, a fireball spell forcing it the rest of the way open, spilling into the room with enough heat, light, and sheer force to knock the closest captives off their feet and away from the door.

Heat searing the top of her scalp, Siobhan stumbled back, trying to press herself against the corner nearest the door but bumping into people behind her. A second fireball followed, not aimed at anyone in particular but still licking at people's skin and hair. It smashed against the back wall with enough force and sound to ring deafeningly, sending chunks of smoking stone flying out.

Screams wove in with a high-pitched ringing in Siobhan's ears, which felt strangely as if they had been plugged. Those who could manage it scrambled further away from the entrance and toward the side walls.

It seemed for a moment that the guards were going to kill them all. One turned his wand on Siobhan.

She raised her free hand instinctively, as if that could ward off an attack, her shadow darkening and expanding further as her mind grasped for a solution and her Will struggled to deliver.

Then the shift leader tossed in the spherical device. It landed on the floor in the center of the room.

'*A Radiant explosive,*' Siobhan remembered them saying. "Take cover!" she screamed, turning to the wall and crouching with her free hand covering her head. There was no true cover to take.

Her shadow instinctively coalesced behind her like a shield, and she realized too late that she should drop the spell safely while she still could, to avoid being forced to drop it from an attack.

The light and pressure hit simultaneously.

Siobhan was slammed forward, her face crunching her fingers into the wall and forcibly breaking the Circle of her hand.

Power rushed out from between her fingers and bloomed from the collapse of the shield of darkness behind her, suddenly freed.

Her mind crackled like corn in a hot pan, and she yanked her Will away from the freed magic, spooling and condensing it in toward herself, within herself, trying to outrun the backlash before it could hitch a ride inside her. Pieces of her concentration frayed at the edges, and she abandoned them in the space between microseconds.

But this did nothing to stop the physical expression of the magical backlash. And as they had reviewed earlier that term in Professor Gnorrish's class, every action had an equal and opposite reaction.

The power crashed into her from behind like a wave from an angry sea god. It lifted her body and slammed her again into the wall. She felt something crunching within her abdomen. Light bloomed in her skull like a flower as her cheekbone cracked against stone. She bounced off and slammed into the floor, striking the back of her head.

27

———

THE HEART OF THE SUN

Siobhan
  Month 4, Day 9, Friday

Siobhan may have blacked out for a moment—maybe more than once—as the world spun with strange incoherent imagery and flashes of light and darkness, a song from the void reaching out to her with velvet tendrils.

Rough hands on her arms and around her waist made her abdomen moan in pain. The Pendragon guard's terrified eyes matched with gritted teeth as they met her gaze for a moment. A fist in her hair, yanking her neck to the side until her spine sent out twinkling, twinging signs of warning. A swirling sickness as she was thrown into the heart of the sun and came down hard on its surface.

When she stopped wavering in and out of reality, someone was keening ferally, mournfully, warbling notes to a distant song.

As she ran out of air, she realized the sound was her own incoherent moan of confusion and pain. She forced herself to stop, even though she was pretty sure the impact on the black sapphire Conduit under the pressure of her corset had broken at least one of her ribs.

Her head ached like an invisible bison was stamping on it again, and again, and again. Concussion, certainly. Will-strain, possibly. How was one to distinguish between the two when it got to this point?

Her body was even more battered and bruised than before, but it was hard to take stock of her injuries beyond the pounding of her skull and the aching claws piercing her side with every breath.

The draw on her divination-diverting ward had stopped entirely.

Siobhan kept her eyes closed against the light and twitched her fingers. The ones on her left hand were in bad shape, smashed twice against the wall. But her right hand was fine. She reached up and touched her face. Her nose was, surprisingly, not broken or even bleeding. Her right cheekbone and the bottom of her eye socket bloomed with pain at the slightest pressure. The skin was raw, and her eye itself was filled with a strange, aching burn. She touched the back of her skull to discover a growing lump and a small wet spot of blood. She licked the blood off her finger, swallowing it along with the sudden pool of nauseated saliva in her mouth.

Her features were all in the right place, and neither her face nor her skull had caved in.

She shifted, holding back a broken whimper, and managed to rise to her hands and knees, stabilizing herself drunkenly as the world spun around her. It was too bright to open her eyes. She could see the searing white light even through the pinkness of her closed eyelids. Even ducking her head down away from the ceiling and walls didn't ease her discomfort.

Her medallion was burning horribly cold against her chest, so it had either just wrenched itself dry and melted out yet another protective spell by blocking that Radiant explosive, or it was protecting her from something at that very moment. Perhaps both.

Her left ear was bleeding. She wiped the fluid on her corset. Even when the situation seemed dire, it didn't do to get sloppy and start leaving your blood everywhere. That was what had gotten her into this in the first place. The thought sent her into a paroxysm of strangled giggles that just made everything worse. She couldn't hear like she should on the left side, even as the ringing in her other ear was beginning to subside.

Even when she put a hand over her face to protect her eyes from the searing light, it was still too bright to open them. She was pretty sure that wasn't from the concussion, though her condition might be making it worse. Despite the foolishness of casting magic in such a state, and especially after what just happened, she crouched down with her face pressed to her knees, forehead against the floor—so that what she was doing was less likely to be noticed—and brought her hands together in front of her mouth again.

She knew it was dangerous, but she was desperate. If she couldn't even see, what chance did she have to escape? She clamped down her Will without channeling any power first, assessing its weight and coherence. It was tremulous, weaker than normal. She chanted slowly and deliberately, allowing power to trickle through the air of the Circle and into her shadow.

It made the throb in her brain worse, and she had a moment where things spun dizzily, but she maintained control through the end of the whispered chant. Her shadow was tiny, scattered to small patches over her own body, but none against the ground, even where she was pressed directly against it. But there was *so much* power available, the air between her fingers didn't even grow cold.

Her head settled into a slightly worse ache. She knew she couldn't do anything strenuous, but this much, at least, didn't seem to be driving her insane.

She attempted to keep her shadow's appearance as normal as possible, purposefully going against the spell's nature to keep from absorbing all the light. She brought darkness up from the space between her torso and her legs, up from her armpits and between her thighs, out from the gap between her tongue and the roof of her mouth, wrapping it over her eyes in a hair-thin band that pressed flush against her flesh and widened over her pupils. She increased the drain of light over her eyes more, and then more still, until she was finally able to open them.

She lifted her head and looked around.

She was in a small square room, perhaps three meters across, with light shining from every centimeter of the walls themselves. Even the floor was glowing.

She checked for any lost drops of blood from her ear, first. She found a couple on the floor. Maneuvering her battered hand carefully, she repeated the same trick from earlier and shrank the Circle of her fingers until she could free one hand. She used it to wipe up the drops of blood and swallow them, despite the nausea. She wished she could cast the shedding-destroyer spell, but she had nothing to draw out even that simple spell array with. Nothing except her own blood, which rather seemed like it would defeat the purpose.

She stood and limped to the door that had been at her back. It, too, was glowing, and sat flush and almost seamless with the wall. A single dark pane of glass was inset at head height, an artificially darkened window, reinforced with bands of steel and barely the size of her head.

She pressed her face to the window, close enough so that she could see out into the relative darkness of the hallway.

Two guards were posted outside. She recognized the first as the one that had been screaming before. He had a name that started with "P," but she was too woozy to search her memories for exactness. The second was one of those who had come back with reinforcements. They were the ones who had cast fireball spells to push back the prisoners and make room for the Radiant explosive.

Both were wide-eyed, their battle wands up as if she would somehow break through the door.

She angled her face against the glass, looking to the side. There was a similar locking device embedded in the wall outside this cell as the one before.

The smaller of the two guards, the one who had been so terrified by her earlier, spoke, only slightly muffled by the door between them. "You're trapped! Don't try anything funny. We know you can't use your powers in that environment."

That didn't make any sense. If anything, this environment was wonderful, great for both her shadow-familiar and her light-refinement spells. If she could draw a spell array, she would have plenty of power to sacrifice. But if she understood the situation correctly, this room had been created to imprison her, *specifically*. There must have been some rumor that the Raven Queen was weak to light, unable to use whatever strange powers she possessed outside of darkness. It fit, she supposed, thematically. Luckily, this wasn't a story, and the Raven Queen didn't have to adhere to storybook rules.

Siobhan's mouth fell into a lopsided grin under the Circle of her fingers, and she swallowed heavily as her mouth filled with nauseated saliva.

"The captain will be here soon, and he'll deal with you harshly if you attempt anything dangerous," the screamer said.

"How soon?" she asked, her voice a little hoarse.

Both guards startled slightly, as if they hadn't expected her to be able to speak, and the larger turned on his companion with a scowl. "Don't talk to her, Parker!"

"What if I don't attempt anything dangerous? How will your captain treat me then?" she asked.

They didn't respond.

Unlike the other cell, the walls and door of this one were incredibly smooth, made of some hard, glowing material that definitely wasn't the stone of the white cliffs. Leaning against the door and lifting one foot, she scratched her toenail against the door to test the material. It did nothing but create a soft squeaking sound. Even if she still had her boots and the finger-daggers hidden in the heel, she doubted the blade would make a mark.

Whoever the captain was, and whatever he had planned, she doubted it would be advantageous for her to meet him. Any advantage she could grasp required her to move quickly, to seize the initiative before they could properly respond. "What wards have been placed on this room?" she asked.

Neither of the guards responded.

She trailed her fingers along the wall, walking all the way around as she contemplated. Her thoughts were both flighty and ponderous, and she continually had to bring them back on track.

'There will be some kind of built-in detector for sudden fluctuations in energy or temperature, the kind of things that signify the casting of a spell. The door is well locked, obviously. I could try to break through the wall itself—which is unlikely to succeed, given

the care they put into the material—but even then I might face some kind of magical barrier in addition to the physical. Two guards outside to sound the alarm if I try anything obvious.'

But Siobhan wasn't powerless, either. She continued to walk around the edge of the room, running her fingers along the frictionless wall as she planned. Obviously the room couldn't stop her from casting esoteric spells, and it didn't seem to have sounded any alarm for her subtle use of the shadow-familiar spell. She might not be able to carve a spell array for anything complex into the floor, or draw one with chalk or crayon, but she had blood.

She also had a spell to turn one of her digits into a burning coal, which might be better, because any burnt residue left behind wouldn't be close enough to her unburnt flesh for anyone to use as a sympathetic link against her.

She knew a passkey-divining spell, learned in vain for Myrddin's journal, and a way to distance the output of a spell and thus cast short-term effects at a distance. She also knew spells to control the air for both manipulation and attack.

Perhaps she could divine the password the guards must have used to open the door and throw her into this room just minutes before.

If her spell array was large enough, she might even be able to cast it *through* the wall. Then, she could adjust the parameters of a barrier spell, maybe mixed with an air compression spell, to manipulate the lock's number key mechanism and enter the passkey.

Then threaten the guards into doing their part. Or simply use her air-based slicing spell to carve through their necks, cut off their thumbs, and somehow work the fine manipulation of an air-molding spell or a floating spell to get those thumbs wetted with saliva and up to the lock.

She hadn't done anything exactly like that before, but she'd practiced with several different types of rudimentary manipulation spells. How hard could it be?

The password-divining spell required components, though. A fine dust, the echo from a seashell, and a lens. She had none of that...but she knew a disintegration spell. She could make a fine dust from the material of her corset, perhaps without setting off any alarms. And she had the bone of a sea creature, again in her corset and its whalebone stays. With enough Will, she could turn one of the bones to powder and then remold it into the shape of a seashell. As for the lens, she didn't have a spyglass or magnifying glass and probably couldn't create them, but she did have a contact lens, made of glass just the same.

It would be the most cobbled-together spell ever.

The password-divining spell gave its output as a faint illusion, so she would need to maintain the shadow-familiar spell so that she could see, and maybe even use it to shield the spell array so that the light of the illusion wasn't drowned out by the searing brightness all around her. But she had dual-cast spells before. She could do that.

Killing the guards would come first, so they didn't interfere. Then, she would need to get the divination spell array's domain into contact with the lock because, while she could adjust the output parameters, she still needed the *input* to be within the Circle. But that only meant burning a large enough Circle against the wall. The spherical domain could reach all the way through to the other side. She could hold the components in place against the wall with pressure. Maybe two, one with her free hand, and one with her forehead, which would still allow her the single free hand to cast the shadow-familiar spell with—

Siobhan stopped. Stopped thinking, stopped walking, stopped casting. She dropped the shadow-familiar spell and held up her hands over her eyes to shade against the searing light, which seemed to be giving her the start of a sunburn. "Oh, no," she whispered.

'That is the stupidest plan I have ever heard.'

That thought seemed to echo in her mind for a moment with its sheer truth. *'If Damien or anyone else had come to me with that scheme, I would have slapped them across the face and told them to come to their senses. Trying to dual-cast two completely different spells, using components cobbled together from shaped pieces of my clothing while* also *detaching my output with a method that Professor Lacer specifically warned me might not work past a barrier spell. The only way it could have been worse is if I planned to try a different method of detachment modeled off of my Will-splitting, without anyone here to save me if it goes wrong.*

'All this, while knowingly under the effects of a concussion and probably Will-strain.'

She took a shuddering breath and sank down onto her knees with her back facing the door. *'I was about to kill myself. Or entirely shatter my Will and turn into an Aberrant.'*

2 8

———————

INFERNAL COVENANTS

Siobhan
  Month 4, Day 9, Friday

From her knees, Siobhan fell back into a seated position, crossing her legs and ignoring the pain from her ankle. '*At least I realized in time how stupid I was being. I didn't actually do it. But I obviously need to reassess my decisions. Is this abnormally impaired judgment, or am I just that foolish?*'

Will-strain started with headaches, dizziness, and difficulty concentrating. More severely, it caused impaired judgment, difficulty modulating the strength of one's emotions, and rapid mood swings. After that, hallucinations, paranoia, and actions that caused harm to the thaumaturge themself or those around them. Beyond that, Will-strain damage was irreversible.

'*So, perhaps I am in the middling stage, or perhaps a concussion can mimic the effects. Or perhaps this room is cursed somehow to keep me from having the wherewithal to come up with a successful escape plan. It's even possible there is some sort of compulsion or curse acting against me.*' In any case, it was clear that she needed to come up with a better strategy.

'*Have I been going in the wrong direction from the beginning? Should I even be trying to escape right now?*' The question seemed absurd, but she didn't feel like she could trust her instincts at the moment.

If she didn't escape, "the captain" was going to come. It was likely she was being held in a network of tunnels carved out of the white cliffs beneath Pendragon Palace, which meant the captain was one of the High Crown's men.

She might even meet the High Crown himself. They would want the book. Torture was a viable threat.

Of course, Siobhan would give up the book's location immediately—Grandfather had impressed upon her that it was impossible to withstand torture forever, and best to just avoid it entirely. No information was worth her life. The only reason she would refuse to speak was if she thought she would be killed as soon as she did.

Which...might be a possibility. Siobhan rubbed her chin with her free hand. The coppers didn't know she was here, and her allies most likely didn't either. Perhaps she could give up false information or try to bargain for her release, but success seemed unlikely.

Even if they were somehow willing to turn her over to the coppers instead of dealing with the threat she posed and executing her themselves, all that awaited her was a trial for blood magic and treason, which would sentence her to death, probably by public execution.

'So,' she determined, 'escape really is my best option. And quickly. I've lost time with this foolishness, but I still may be able to do something.'

She was injured and had no way to do anything about it. Her light-refinement spell wasn't the kind of thing that brought quick results, and in her physical state, she wouldn't even be able to complete the necessary motions. The flesh-mirroring spell would require a spell array, but also a clarity of Will and level of power that she didn't feel safe attempting.

Rather than trying to escape with the force of her magic, she needed someone to let her out.

She had access to two guards, at least one of whom had been willing to talk to her. They were frightened, obviously. She had to find a way to bargain with or manipulate them to convince them to set her free.

Maybe the reputation of the Raven Queen could come in handy.

But she would need to be quick-witted and silver-tongued, neither of which she felt confident in at the moment. Both her wits and her tongue were more prone to getting her into trouble than out of it. If things went wrong, the guards might retaliate. Siobhan didn't think she could withstand another of those Radiant bombs.

She thought through all the steps of her plan first, and when she was sure she was ready, she stood and returned to the shaded window, pressing close to it in an attempt to see out through squinted eyes.

Both guards were pressed against the wall on the other side of the hallway, watching her.

She angled her head down so they couldn't see her face and recast the shadow-familiar spell with a slow, whispered chant while holding one hand in a Circle over her mouth.

Her shadow stretched up and over her once more, black as the pit and with access to all the power she would need to stretch it for whole city blocks. It reached out to cover the little pane of reinforced glass.

The guards began to shout.

"What are you doing?" the smaller one, Parker, called, his voice high-pitched with distress.

"We have to sound the alarm!" the taller one snapped.

Siobhan pushed her shadow *through* the window. There was no reason that light, or the absence of light, should be stopped by glass. And regardless of whatever wards the room might have to stop power or energy from passing its boundaries, unlike most spells, her shadow-familiar was the *absence* of those things.

Both guards shot fireballs, which licked harmlessly through her shadow and against the other side of the cell door. These were followed by a quick barrage of slicing spells, concussive blasts, and even some strange-colored spells that she couldn't recognize.

Their efforts may have seemed ineffective, but the sudden influx of energy threw her off balance for a moment. Thankfully, she recovered quickly and without further damage to her Will. Her shadow was completely unaffected, of course, although she let it seethe with hints of beaks, feathers, and claws.

"Oh, Radiant Maiden, protect us," Parker murmured.

"I'll get backup," the bigger guard breathed, his voice barely audible through the door between them.

"Wait," she called, her voice clear and commanding.

The footsteps that had only just begun to recede ceased immediately as the guard halted, and Parker pressed himself against the wall so hard it seemed like he hoped to sink into the stone.

She hadn't expected them to actually listen to her, but this was even better. She didn't need to rush, so she could be theatrical.

More darkness dribbled down the side of the door, thick and three-dimensional, and when it reached the floor, rose up again into a familiar form. Taller than any man and inhumanly thin, long, sharp-beaked darkness protruded from underneath the hood of a tattered cloak, fluttering in an intangible wind. Skeletal, too-long fingers that came to sharp points raised toward the guards, palms outward.

"Stop there," she commanded, "and listen."

No footsteps sounded, so the escaping guard must have complied.

"There are many rumors about me. Have you heard that I am honorable, aiding those who deserve it and harming only my enemies?"

Silence.

"Do not be afraid. You may speak without fear of retribution."

A few more seconds passed, and then Parker responded in a halting tone. "I—I have heard that."

"Shut up!" the other guard snapped. "You're giving her what she wants!"

"Giving her what? She makes bargains. She can't steal your soul just from talking to you." In a softer voice, which perhaps he thought she couldn't hear, Parker said, "And there's no way we can outrun the creature of Night itself. It could cross the whole hallway in the blink of an eye, I've heard. We need to keep her happy, Anders. Buy some time at least. If she's talking, she's not cursing or killing."

Anders spat on the floor. "I don't get paid enough for this shit," he mumbled. Then, louder, he said, "I have heard of your honorable nature as well as your tenacious malevolence towards those who anger you."

Siobhan rolled her eyes behind the cover of shadow. "Have you heard that I cannot tell a lie?" She paused a few seconds, but when they didn't reply, continued. "May my word be my bond. As of now, I do not consider you my enemies. I dislike harming the innocent. As long as you do not attempt further harm to me, that will continue to be the case. If you attempt to harm me, or to *stop* me, I will have no choice but to act against you."

"T-to stop you from doing what?" Parker asked.

"Leaving, of course."

"That's impossible."

She laughed, pressing closer to the glass so that she could see Anders and direct her shadow. This forced her injured cheek to press painfully against the barrier, and her eye protested the slight increase in pressure, but the pain was a necessary price to pay. "Do you really believe that?"

The part of her shadow outside the cell flashed past Anders, appearing again just behind him. It was connected to her with a line of shadow so thin it would be hard to notice. With a bit of Will and a partial splitting of her attention, she pulled heat from the air around that section alone, causing an ominous fog to roll off of its form while leaving her quite warm.

It loomed forward over Anders from behind, then let the backs of its too-long fingers trail over his cheek, sucking the warmth from the surface of his skin.

Anders stared ahead, wide-eyed and as pale as a corpse. His knees trembled badly, on the verge of collapse.

Parker whimpered.

"I assure you, this room does not work as you hoped it might," she said. The shadow-familiar spell was perhaps her most practiced of any piece of magic she knew, and thus one of the easiest to control. But even so, the strain of holding two detailed and three-dimensional forms in her mind, one a few meters away and absorbing heat, was difficult in her state. If her Will were an eggshell, the pressure would have been putting hairline cracks through it, every moment moving her closer to the threat of implosion. "Your boss's information about my abilities was severely lacking," she added.

"W-what do you want from us?" Parker asked, his voice breaking.

"It is very simple. Step forward," she commanded.

Anders seemed like he wanted to hesitate, but when her shadow-familiar pressed into his back, he stumbled forward quickly until he stood beside Parker in front of her door.

Her shadow followed, and its proximity eased the strain somewhat.

"I want you to open this door." She waited on metaphorical tenterhooks for their response. She was botching this conversation, she knew, but Ennis had always handled the talking. This was not her area of expertise.

"I can't do that," Anders said.

Siobhan's jaw clenched. "I need your thumbs and your saliva. You may provide them for me, which I would prefer. If you do not, I will be forced to *take* your thumbs and saliva."

Parker looked up at her shadow-familiar, which was tall enough to almost reach the ceiling, its huge, curved beak pointed down at them as its tattered cloak fluttered in an invisible wind. He closed his eyes in resignation. "We most truly cannot, my lady. We have sworn a vow of loyalty. The repercussions—"

"A blood print vow?" she interrupted.

Parker opened his eyes. "Yes."

"That is no trouble. They are far from infallible. Do you know how they work? It is quite possible to circumvent them. As you are likely aware, the coppers have some of my blood as well, and yet have been completely unable to locate me despite their best efforts."

Anders and Parker shared a look that she couldn't decipher.

"As you may *also* be aware, I am able to give out certain...boons. If you wish to be free of your employers' grasp, that is a simple order, and seems a reasonable exchange for the danger."

"But you don't know the passkey," Anders said. He did not sound very confident about that statement.

"I can pluck it from your minds." Her shadow-familiar lifted its slender, pointed digits and wriggled them. "Though you would find the process *unpleasant*, I am sure." Her shadow-familiar looked to her, tilting its head to the side in a questioning stance that was as eager as she could make it, leaking foggy wisps of darkness that took the shape of ravens for only a moment before dissolving back into nothing.

Anders stumbled sideways into Parker, who let out an actual shuddering sob. "Please, please, don't."

Siobhan's shadow-familiar settled, looking back at them. "Freedom from a blood print vow is not the only boon I can offer," she said. "That, and one other, for each of you. But you must decide quickly, or by your very hesitation, you will be stealing *time* from me, and that will make you my enemy."

Parker clasped his hands together, fingers woven through each other to squeeze out the trembling. Two seconds passed before he spoke. "I owe a debt, and the deed to my house is held by another. Can you kill him and get it back for me?"

"It is possible, though his death may not be necessary," she replied immediately. "It would be just as simple to repay the debt, if he is a good man."

"He's not," Parker asserted.

"You can't really be thinking of going along with this!" Anders hissed.

"I'm not about to die just to delay her a couple seconds longer," Parker replied, his voice trembling but sure. "I have a daughter."

"And you, Anders?" she asked. "Tell me your greatest desire, and if it is within my power, I will mold the world into alignment with your wishes. But there is no more time. You must choose now."

"It is treason," he said heavily, looking at Parker.

"I want to live," Parker replied simply. "And I want a future for my daughter."

Anders hesitated for only a moment longer. "My dog. He's been missing an eye and a leg for a long time now. And he's getting older. I don't want him to die. He's a good dog, and he deserves more. And…he's the only creature in this world that truly loves me. Can you make him healthy and young again?"

She didn't bother to hold back her smile of triumph. "I cannot make him young, but I can make him healthy and whole. And his life may be extended to last as long as your own."

"And *will* you do that, really?" he asked, eyes narrowed.

"The deed to his house and an enemy subdued, for Parker. For you, healing and longevity for your closest companion. I will do all in my power to fulfill these boons, without any attempt to subvert their meaning, in exchange for your service this day and your neutrality going forward. My word is my bond."

"So mote it be!" Parker piped up, grim-faced and white-knuckled as he used an ancient phrase to seal the pact.

And so, the guards opened the door for her.

As she limped through an invisible barrier over the doorway that scraped unpleasantly at her skin like thousands of fingernails, her shadow-familiar returned, melding into one piece. It disguised her features, as well as the fact that she was bare legged, wearing only a corset, though it couldn't disguise the signs of injury in the way she moved.

She turned back to look at the featureless, shining room. Some of her blood had been smeared on the floor, and though the surface was smooth enough that there was no visible trace after she had wiped it up, that didn't mean that absolutely none of her was left behind. She couldn't spare the time to clean things properly, but she was less concerned than she might have been in other circumstances.

The magic of the room had some obvious destructive effects. Even if that didn't make whatever trace amounts of her were left unviable for divination, and Lord Pendragon could manage to find said traces *and* a thaumaturge with enough clarity and power to use such a small amount as a component, so long as Operation Palimpsest went well, they might not even bother. With what she had planned, even an idiot would realize that trying to use sympathetic magic against her was a dead end.

Still, she turned to the guards. "Fireball the floor," she ordered. Parker complied immediately. As the backlash of heat blew her hair around, she said, "As I doubt the High Crown will take kindly to your betrayal, if you want to live, you will come with me and fight by my side."

Anders nodded, grip firm around his huge battle wand, but Parker seemed stunned by his own betrayal.

"We are going to rescue the other captives," she said. "Hurry, there is not much time."

29

FEAR OF THE DARK

Siobhan and her duo of newly turned pseudo-allies, who she definitely did not trust but could not do without, moved quickly toward the cell holding the others. She didn't know her way through the tunnels, didn't know any of the passwords, and didn't want to rely on stolen thumbs and spit to get through the doors. In addition, she harbored no illusions that she could defeat the Pendragon Operatives in battle by herself. Yes, her new companions were essential. They also led the way.

Anders began to protest against going to rescue the other captives, but Parker stopped him, leaning in to murmur, "They were praying for her help, which is the whole reason she's here in the first place. She can't just leave them. She has honor."

Anders motioned for them to stop, and they peeked around a corner.

Two other guards kept watch in front of a windowed door that presumably held her people.

Without Siobhan's prompting, Anders gave Parker a significant look. "We have no choice. If we fail now, we cannot even hope for a clean death," he whispered, his words barely a breath on the air.

Parker hesitated. "Maybe they could join us?"

Anders looked toward the ceiling for patience. "Johnson and Brown both had no qualms about securing their own positions by spilling the beans about your gambling. Do you remember the punishment for that?"

Parker's mouth tightened.

"And we don't have time to try and convince them and get into a loud, flashy fight. Besides"—he glanced over his shoulder at Siobhan—"I doubt the Raven Queen would appreciate being asked for even more boons."

Siobhan shook her head silently.

"Better death by our hand, than whatever the Raven Queen would do to them," he added even more quietly. "As soon as we let her out of the cell, it was already too late."

"In this situation, they would do the same to us," Parker admitted reluctantly. He threw Siobhan a fearful glance, then nudged Anders anxiously.

The two men shared a sharp nod and then walked around the corner, approaching the other men. As the guards greeted them with confusion, her new allies attacked without fanfare or warning.

It took them about four seconds to kill their previous coworkers, using spells for distraction—as the resplendent armor protected against them—while Anders drew out a stiletto dagger and slit the throat of one and punctured the armpit of the other. Both guards collapsed almost instantly from blood loss.

Siobhan was almost as surprised by the sudden and explosive violence as the other guards. She hadn't wanted their deaths, exactly, but it was a price she was more than willing to pay. With them out of commission, the rest was simple.

Avoiding the quickly spreading pools of blood—so much blood, it seemed like the men should have been deflating like popped balloons with its loss— they opened the door to the cell.

The captives had been returned to the sensory-deprivation spell. Siobhan sent Anders and Parker in to help retrieve them while she watched for danger. "*Move quickly,*" she urged, feeling the passing of every second like nails on a chalkboard.

In less than half a minute, the Verdant Stag and Nightmare Pack captives were free again, confused and relieved but willing to move as quickly as possible.

Parker stumbled, looking down at his chest. "They've noticed what we're doing. The shift lead must have seen the cells unlocking."

Anders nodded, reaching past his armor into his uniform jacket and pulling out a badge with the High Crown's symbol, which must have been some sort of alarm or communication artifact. "Yep. Things just got a lot harder for us," he said gravely.

The prisoners were much worse off than they had been, now marred by fresh injuries from the guards' previous attacks. Gerard was burned and his underwear tattered enough that he might have appreciated fake clothes, like her.

Enforcer Turner had a tourniquet around his leg, over the knee. He had been blown about by the Radiant explosion, it seemed, and his previously broken leg was now snapped in half at the shin, allowing the bottom half of his limb to flop sideways. He was awake but trembling and pale. Without better treatment, he probably didn't have long to live.

The praying woman's hair had been burned half away, and blisters rose up over the area, white against pink skin. Her ear was half melted, and she smiled only with the unburned side of her face, eyes shining eerily bright as she looked at Siobhan. "You came back for me," she murmured. And then, louder, "I will follow you through the darkness, my queen. Let your enemies be my enemies, and of all that I have, a portion will be for you."

Siobhan was taken aback once again by the woman and her strange, almost prayer-like words, but she didn't have time to worry about it. She pointed to the Verdant Stag man whose name she didn't know. "Carry Enforcer Turner. We're going to retrieve our belongings, and then we are leaving. Move quickly," she repeated. "And help each other."

None of them hesitated, though Enforcer Fring helped to carry Turner, as it turned out the Verdant Stag man had several broken ribs.

"I hurt my knee," Theo announced, pale faced to the point of greenness. "I can't run." The normally knobby joint was noticeably swollen, as big around as the boy's thigh.

The praying woman lifted Theo onto her back without hesitation. "I can run," she informed Siobhan.

Millennium moved to Siobhan's side, pressing a few inches into the darkness simulating a long skirt and cloak around her. "The whispers were right," he said in a soft voice. "But I didn't know it would be like this. I'm sorry. We don't have much time if we want to get our things. And I think we're going to need them, so we better hurry. I can hear blood and pain."

Siobhan again ordered them to shoot fireballs into the cell, which she hoped would damage any blood or hair that she or any of the others may have left behind.

Jackal and Enforcer Gerard moved up to the front of the group with Anders and Parker, who led the way and explained what they were about to face. "All your belongings have been placed in the secondary armory. The one down here," he clarified. "There are about ten more of us—of them," he corrected quickly, looking at Siobhan, "in the tunnels right now. Some reinforcements from up above. They know what we're doing and will be prepared. The exits are all reinforced, and the shift lead will have activated the emergency locking procedures. There's no way we're getting out of here without the supplies to blast our way free." He looked at Siobhan again. "Unless you have a way, my lady?"

She shook her head. "It is lucky our supplies are in the armory, then. One trip to retrieve everything we need."

Siobhan moved just behind their vanguard with the remainder of their group following behind her. Though she couldn't fight directly, her shadow-familiar would be good for misdirection, and a shield of darkness might help throw off the enemy's aim.

They heard the sounds of frantic preparation from around the corner to the armory and tiptoed closer. Borrowing a Conduit from Parker, Jackal used a strange esoteric spell that turned the flesh of his palm into a reflective surface, then snuck out his hand so that they could see around the corner, hopefully without being noticed.

As predicted, the double-doored armory was buzzing with men.

Technically, Siobhan's group had more people, but four of them were either children or noncombatants, and most of the rest were injured in some way, as well as being unarmed and unarmored, against some of the best trained and supplied men in the country.

A whispered planning session took all of a minute, and then Anders drew a thin line across Parker's forehead with his dagger. The wound immediately spilled a surprising amount of blood down the man's face.

'We are all little more than full-to-bursting sacks of blood mixed with a bit of meat and some bones,' Siobhan thought idly. *'Is there a soul, some part of the Will that escapes and remains coherent, or are we but biological artifacts dependent upon the function of our form?'* Her full attention was drawn back to reality as Parker left cover, acting out a badly injured leg that forced him to brace himself on the wall and drag the appendage behind him.

"The Raven Queen escaped!" Parker called weakly. "She's heading toward the upper exit, the one into the palace. I don't know how she knew—" He broke down coughing as two other men rushed out to pull him to safety. "No time, *no time!*" he insisted. "You have to catch her before she gets there— they're in danger. She'll kill them all…"

After a hurried conversation, six of the men ran off in the direction Parker had indicated.

Siobhan waited what seemed like an excruciating amount of time, but really must have been no more than two or three minutes, for Parker to give the signal. He did so in the form of a concussive blast going off from within the armory.

Jackal, Gerard, and Anders rushed forward, throwing out spells as soon as they passed through the double doorway. Siobhan followed behind them, her beaked and tattered shadow-familiar moving beside her on one side and a smaller humanoid shadow on the other, making her only one target of three.

As soon as she got to the doorway and could see to do so, she sent the shadow-familiar's nightmarish form shooting forward into the center of the room, again wafting off cold, looming higher and higher until it had to hunch over at the ceiling.

Anders killed one of the men with a knife through the eyeball, giving them the advantage in numbers.

She was gratified to see several of the enemy turn their attention toward her shadow instead of her allies, some of the energy from their spells inadvertently absorbed as they passed through its incorporeal form, which bolstered it even more. She had a moment to wonder where all the excess energy might be going, as the shadow could only get so black before the darkness was absolute, and she wasn't expending the absorbed energy to make it larger or more complex. If anything, its form simply seemed to become more and more detailed and *real*, until even she could barely tell it was little more than an illusion.

One-armed, Gerard lifted a smaller man by his waist, flipping him head-down and legs up before smashing him against the ground once, twice, and a third time, just to make sure he was totally dead.

One remaining Pendragon operative shot some sort of withering curse at Siobhan's shadow-familiar, which of course passed right through, but managed to hit one of his allies on the other side of the room, knocking the man off his feet and completely tarnishing and cracking the resplendent chest plate.

Siobhan sent a half dozen ravens shooting out of the shadow-familiar, attached by almost invisible threads of darkness, to "attack" the remaining Pendragon operatives. Their cold touch worked admirably as a distraction, and her allies had little trouble killing the remaining men.

Parker pulled himself up from where he had been hiding in the corner under a kite shield sized for a giant. He gazed sadly at one of the men. "A shame… I liked Murphy," he said. "He didn't retaliate, even after I got him sent to sensory deprivation punishment for two days straight."

Anders threw him an inscrutable look but was already moving for the metal lockers standing against one of the walls. The praying woman, meanwhile, began to loot the bodies.

Siobhan recognized her satchel atop one of the tables at the back of the room, displayed carefully along with a few dozen other items that must have belonged to the others. With a quick nod of reassurance over her shoulder, she hurried forward. Their clothes were all in a jumbled pile inside a crate to the side of the tables, and she grabbed them all and shoved as much as she could fit into her satchel. They didn't have time to dress, yet, but she didn't want to leave anything of theirs for the enemy.

The High Crown's men hadn't discovered the secret compartment in her satchel, it seemed, as everything inside was still intact and undisturbed.

The artifacts that she had rented from Liza—useful against some of the more common curses that her warding medallion might not prevent—were set inside a series of Shipp evidence boxes, one box for each piece of jewelry. Siobhan retrieved those but hesitated before putting them on again. Her warding medallion could protect against quite a lot, and she had resolved to be more cautious in the interest of avoiding regrets. There was one particular outcome of this day that would remain unacceptable even if she herself escaped safely.

She turned to the children. "Millennium, Theo," she called. "Wear these, and stick together. If you're close enough they should protect you both."

The boys argued over who would get to wear which piece until Enforcer Gerard snapped at them. Theo took Siobhan's lace parasol as a walking stick.

In addition to their own belongings, her people retrieved everything they could carry, including a few extra artifacts—the ones that couldn't be tracked —and battle philtres meant to supply the guards.

Perhaps most critically, they liberated a dozen high-strength healing potions from a small rack. The vials glowed with the telltale luminescence of the Plane of Radiance, almost mesmerizing in their promise as they swirled with clean light.

At Siobhan's encouragement, everyone with serious injuries downed one, and Enforcer Turner took two while Gerard splinted his lower leg, leaving just two healing potions for future emergencies.

The potion burned as it filled Siobhan's mouth and shot down to her stomach. After a short delay, it shot through her veins in a rush, as if it had been injected directly into her heart. Energy from the Plane of Radiance was not gentle, but it left her scoured and cleansed from the inside, most of her injuries abraded away.

The potion had been too weak, or she'd sustained too many injuries, to fix everything. She could feel it tugging futilely at her abdomen, bone literally shifting against flesh and the resistance of her harness and corset. Even so, the pain in her muscles was now only a general stiffness, her ribs hurt in a different, slightly less severe way than before, and her ankle took her weight easily. Her right eye still burned, but the feeling of pressure had lessened, and her cheek was no longer swollen and tenderized like hammered steak.

Most importantly, her head was clearer, and the invisible bison that had been stomping on it was now only a roe deer. The magic may have simply run out before getting all the way through her head injuries, but the continued dizziness and difficulty concentrating, however slight, suggested the problem was deeper. Healing potions could not completely fix Will-strain.

Her bracelets were there at the bottom of the clothes box, every one of them carelessly broken. She stared for a moment, wondering if that was a good thing—since they wouldn't have been able to use them to track down her allies once the magic was spent—or a bad thing, because of the panic it might cause. Even Damien had one or two ward bracelets.

Siobhan's watch was missing, but on Parker's embarrassed suggestion, they found it in the pocket of one of the dead guards. She must have lost more time to the sensory-deprivation spell than she expected, as it was already after five. Ennis's sentencing would have already started, and if nothing else had gone wrong, Gera, Tanya, and Liza would have already done their parts, or be about to complete them at any minute.

With her mind clearer, an important question rose up. "Did your people take samples of blood or hair from those they kidnapped?"

Anders pointed to a sealed iron safe in the corner, which reminded Siobhan of the one Malcolm Gervin had kept. "We can't open it without the captain."

Siobhan sighed, then palmed a chunk of wax and moved to write a stone-disintegration spell on the side of the metal, slightly modified to better suit the material. "Whoever among you has the highest capacity, come drill through."

Anders, Jackal, and surprisingly enough the praying woman all agreed to joint-cast the spell, which Anders added an entire extra ring of written explanation to. Most people didn't have a lot of experience with minimalist spell arrays, Siobhan supposed, and it was best to mitigate risk when joint-casting.

They got through the metal in less than a minute, but the wards remained active, creating a magical barrier that began where the metal stopped.

Gerard picked up one of the Pendragon operative's brilliant swords and stabbed into the hole, activating some sort of piercing spell over and over. The magic was powerful enough to create a high-pitched ringing sound and a puff of air with every activation, but the safe's wards remained steadfast. When the sword ran dry without having overcome the wards, he rifled through the supplies to find a round artifact the size of a fist. He shoved that into the hole, activated it, then hurriedly poured a vial of liquid stone over the outside to seal the hole.

There was a muffled explosion, the hardened stone crumbled away, and the hole revealed hot, twisted metal and a clear opening to the contents within. The praying woman carefully reached her arm through and disengaged the locking mechanism to open the safe's door from the inside.

The safe had multiple dividing shelves of more steel. Despite the ward absorbing a lot of the pressure, the contents of the central section—the one they'd blown a hole into—were half-destroyed. But above and below that things were mostly intact.

They found about a dozen rather nice Conduits, a tray of the rare rectangular gold bars worth one hundred gold crowns each, and a tray of berserker potions that could temporarily increase a soldier's performance at the cost of several serious side effects and a high chance of addiction. Half of those had been shattered by the transferred effects of their explosion, but the rest were intact.

They also found a Shipp glass evidence boxes filled with small ampoules of blood and strands of hair. That, Siobhan had them open, incinerate, and then cast the shedding-disintegration spell on.

All the rest was poured into her weight-reducing satchel, though she had no intention of using a berserker potion herself, nor allowing anyone she cared about to do so. But it was best not to leave them for the enemy. Normally, she would have been giddy with the sudden influx of wealth, but minutes had already passed, and there were more pressing concerns. "Is there a map?" she asked. "We cannot come out the way we came in."

"There's a map in the shift lead's office...but he's probably barricaded in there," Parker said.

"I am fairly certain I could find a different way out," Anders offered distractedly. "My pa worked around here when I was a kid, at the freshwater docks that run through from the north, and as a canal runner before that. I spent a lot of time running the tunnels. I can think of three different possible paths out from here."

"I can help too," Millennium offered. "We should go that direction, first," he said, pointing off to the side in almost the opposite direction that the other Pendragon operatives had run off.

Anders nodded with surprise. "Yes, that would probably be best. It will be blocked off, of course, but we can blast our way through."

Siobhan didn't have time to hesitate. "Let us go," she ordered.

They moved as quickly as they could, and not a moment too soon, as the sound of running boots and angry, urgent shouting echoed down the hallways behind them.

The stone-carved corridors alternated between darkness and light for no reason that Siobhan could discern as Anders and Miles led them on a seemingly random, winding route toward their destination.

Young Enforcer Turner had more color in his cheeks and the strength to support some of his weight on his one good leg, but even two healing potions hadn't fixed his injury. It appeared that the High Crown was not splurging sufficiently on the healthcare of his employees, if the potions they had stolen were only of this caliber.

Gerard and Fring each threw one of Turner's arms over their shoulders, and thus carried most of the younger, smaller man's weight between them.

As they got closer to their destination, the halls were more often dark, the stone walls carved more roughly. Finally, they stopped in front of a huge iron plug—not a door, for there was no way to open it nor pass by—blocking off a side tunnel. "That's the way we need to go," Anders said, panting.

"A stone disintegration spell would be quietest, but some blasting or slicing spells would be quickest," she said. "How thick is the iron?"

"I do not know, my lady," Anders admitted. "Surely not more than a foot thick. Perhaps less."

As their enemy rounded a corner two hallways down, with a lensed lantern sending a bright, directed beam of light their way, the decision was made for them. "Battle spells it is," she said, stepping forward away from the group. "Go through the stone to the side."

As Gerard snapped orders for those who couldn't fight to press against the walls and the small alcove containing the iron blockage, Siobhan reached into her satchel with her free hand, drew out two sets of a particular potion by feel, and took the deepest possible breath against her corset, ignoring the shifting of her bones as she did so.

The operatives had gained more reinforcements again, called back from wherever they had been, but in the narrow space of the hallway their numbers made less difference.

Using her teeth to pop the cork, Siobhan downed one potion, immediately feeling a tad nauseous as her stomach began to roil. Smoke almost as black as her shadow-familiar billowed up from her stomach and out of her open mouth and nostrils, and as she exhaled, it roiled off of her breath, expanding with every second until it filled the hallway around her.

Then she threw the second philtre toward the enemy. Her shadow-familiar grew weak again in the complete darkness, pulling on the heat between her fingers for warmth. She was almost distracted from maintaining it as knowledge of her surroundings unfurled somewhere deep within her, in a part of her mind that she normally used on instinct, and only rarely acknowledged deliberately.

These were her latest iteration of a philtre of darkness mixed with the proprioception potions. As long as they lasted—only a couple minutes—she would know everything within the touch of the magical clouds, and, less importantly, within the confines of the three remaining bottles within her satchel.

Concussive blasts, piercing, and drilling spells screamed out behind her, one layered over the other in a cacophony of sound and rumbling tremors through the stone her allies were attempting to pierce.

From the front, screams and muffled grunts overlapped as the Pendragon operatives fought against the sudden disorientation, shooting spells through the clouds of darkness. Most weren't aimed well enough to do damage, but soon enough the enemy realized the nature of her trick and used a continuous blast of wind to blow away the magical particles creating the darkness.

Smoke continued to bubble up from Siobhan's mouth and nose, and from the floor where the philtre had broken, but the wind blew it away. She leaned into the force of the gale, snarling at the enemy. Her shadow strengthened with the return of the bright light from their lensed lantern, and she sent it up to the ceiling of the tunnel.

"Your screams will echo in the void!" she bellowed at them, the sound echoing and rippling as it left her throat, distorted by the philtre like the scream of a whale from deep in the ocean. The words meant nothing, really, just the first thing that came to her mind.

She had used a free-writing potion to create a cryptic, ominous note for the Edictum Council, another piece of the purposefully sown confusion. Here, too, she wanted to sow confusion and distract the enemy's attention, and so she repeated some of the words in a philtre-warbled scream that scratched at her throat. "My eyes see nothing but a fortune of dust."

Upside down, her shadow-familiar skittered along the stone like a spider under the effects of a fleet-foot potion. The enemies fired desperately at the ceiling, only adding to the deafening reverberations and making Siobhan worry that perhaps the tunnel would collapse and kill them all.

Her shadow dropped into their midst, swiping at their heads with claw-like hands trailing frozen mist and drawing almost all of their spell-fire, which again only strengthened her shadow and caused them to inadvertently harm each other. The spell-fire and light from the lensed lantern flashed and jittered, illuminating the tunnel in irregular flares and bursts. With every moment of vision, her shadow-familiar was revealed in a new pose, like an animated drawing in a flip-book missing intermittent pages.

Even she could admit that it looked quite frightening, and the sensation of cold probably created an illusion of physical touch that must have added to the enemies' alarm. But it would be very difficult for her to directly harm someone with that mild heat absorption. Even with her improvements, the shadow-familiar was basically harmless.

"Empty bellies and sharp teeth, and payment in *bone!*" she shrieked before descending into a rattling coughing fit that forced extra air through her Circled hand. Despite the way her eyes watered, she forced them to remain open.

Several of the men dropped to the ground and tried to crawl away from her shadow-familiar's attacks, their eyes devoid of coherence, hot panic spilling from their panting mouths. They displayed none of the training they had undergone for the honor of becoming one of the High Crown's personal guard. One man lay still on the ground, very much alive but staring wide-eyed at nothing.

'In the face of enough terror, people often lose all that separates them from animals.' Grandfather had told her this, and she had seen it to be true more than once.

In the confusion, one overpowered fireball spell headed Siobhan's way, aimed almost perfectly to crash into the children huddling in the shallow alcove behind her, hands over their ears and faces tucked into their knees. It probably wasn't even aimed deliberately.

Siobhan's Will crushed down on reality, slowing her perception of time as she poured all of her remaining focus into reacting.

She stepped back and to the side, carefully gauging the angle of the medallion under her corset in relation to the center of the fireball. As the fireball approached, filling her vision with its ever-expanding, devouring light, she took a single step forward to meet it, her free hand held out to ensure her perfect balance as she smoothly pivoted toward the wall.

The medallion slowed the fireball and shunted it into that same wall, where it impacted with splashing flames and enough force to send Siobhan stumbling back. Her mind spun as she desperately gripped the shadow-familiar to ensure she didn't lose control of it, drawing it back to its place at her feet.

Beautiful sparks floated in the vision of her right eye, the one that had been smashed against the wall from the Radiant explosive. She blinked, but they didn't go away, calling insistently for her attention. A tear ran down her cheek, and when she instinctively wiped it away, her fingertips came away bloody. "Oh, that's not good," she murmured. She could barely hear herself over the screams from the enemy and the breaking stone behind her, but she thought her voice was beginning to return to normal as the philtre petered out.

'I must have burst one of those little vessels in the sclera.' Her chest burned once again with the sudden ice-cold chill of the medallion, glued to her skin by the sweat it had frozen. She could only hope that this repeated use wouldn't leave any suspicious scars.

"We're almost through!" Enforcer Gerard yelled behind her.

A few of the enemy were still up and fighting, and they grouped together into a tight formation, shields on either end, and began to move forward.

Siobhan shot a few spells from her battle wand, joined quickly by Turner and, surprisingly, both Martha and the praying woman with their stolen battle wands, but nothing made it past the Pendragon operatives' shields.

Siobhan sent out her shadow-familiar once more, allowing it to rise up from the floor behind the enemies. It broke into a dozen ravens, rushing through their tight formation with wings trailing cold, and coalesced around the man in front. Her shadow-familiar lunged at his head, drawing the heat from his skin as it pretended to claw at his face.

She shrank its head down as it pressed into the man's wide-eyed, deeply horrified face, giving the illusion of it squeezing itself impossibly into his screaming mouth.

Understandably, he panicked, flailing backward and dropping the shield to claw at her shadow.

It ignored all his attempts, squeezing and shrinking into his eyes, nose, and ears until it was gone.

Of course, it wasn't gone, nor was it inside him, but none of the enemies noticed the small thread of darkness return to Siobhan's side.

The man clawed bloody furrows into his skin, trying to force his entire fist into his mouth as if he could grab her shadow by the tail and drag it back out. All the while, he continued to scream himself hoarse, the sound going on and on until he ran out of breath and choked himself with his own hand down his throat. As he convulsed, gagging and spilling bile down his neck and chest, his colleagues watched in horror.

Then, one of them pointed their battle wand at him and stepped back warily. This set the tone of their response, and as Siobhan backed toward the jagged hole in the wall her people had created and climbed through quite awkwardly, she drew one more philtre of darkness from her satchel, took a small sip of it, and then dropped it just behind the hole.

She would know when the enemy followed, if they did so within the next couple minutes.

With a deep sigh of relief, she caught herself on the rough stone wall of the low, narrow tunnel. She took a few panting breaths to steady herself, taking stock of the pain in her head and the tremor in her Will.

The rest of the former captives stood huddled together in the light of a stolen lantern, all staring silently at her.

"What is it?" she said.

Several of them flinched at the sound of her voice, which was once again distorted oddly by the philtre. The praying woman was smiling at her with almost insane fervency.

Siobhan shook her head, decided to remain silent to keep from frightening anyone, and motioned for the group to hurry forward.

They complied with alacrity, and she brought up the rear.

3 0

———

CAVES AND CORRIDORS

SIOBHAN
Month 4, Day 9, Friday 5:30 p.m.

THE PENDRAGON OPERATIVES didn't chase after them right away, at least not in the time it took the philtre of darkness she had placed to wear off.

The former captives hurried through the cold, damp dark, bare feet shuffling against the rough stone for a long few minutes until they reached an area of relative safety. The injured needed to rest and be attended to. Young Enforcer Turner with the broken leg was slowing them down, and the praying woman had been clipped by a slicing spell. The wound didn't require a high-strength healing potion but needed to be bandaged, at the very least.

Everyone remained quiet and wide-eyed, the darkness and the weight of the white cliffs above them creating an illusory pressure.

Siobhan handed the praying woman a self-brewed regeneration potion, a burn salve in a jar too small to cover all of her melted skin, and a small jar of honey for the antibacterial properties. The woman took them reverently, then held them close, like a protective dog guarding a bone.

Siobhan ordered Fring and Gerard to lay Turner on the floor of a small half-scoop cave with a trickle of water flowing through its center. As she opened the bulky wrapping around his leg to reveal the wound, illuminated by a light crystal they had retrieved, several of the others moaned in horror, and Martha turned away to retch. "Do *not* vomit," Siobhan snapped. "They can use it to track you if they find it, and I do not need the extra trouble."

"They'll be tracking Parker and I as soon as they think of it," Anders reported gravely. "You can do something about that, right?"

Siobhan considered the issue. The stone between them should help for the moment, and when they were free she would need to stash her new unfortunate responsibilities under some wards, but in the meantime she would have to figure something out. Her divination-diverting ward had spillover effects into the area around her. That didn't extend very far, but if she kept Anders and Parker hanging on either arm, they would almost certainly be safe, because finding them would be equivalent to finding her by association, and the ward wouldn't allow that.

Much more palatably, she could keep them within the boundary of her shadow. She'd never tested such a thing, but everything she knew about sympathetic divination, and what Liza had explained about the ward, suggested that it would work. "I believe I can. I will deal with that after this," Siobhan promised.

Turner's face was pale as he stared at the exposed meat and bone of his injury and the way his lower shin and foot were pointed slightly in the wrong direction despite their efforts to rejoin them with the part above. Breathing quickly, he stammered, "I don't want to lose my leg. Oh, please." He reached out and squeezed Siobhan's forearm. "I heard how you turned some Morrow's stump arm into a thumb. I really don't want a thumb at the end of my leg, please, have mercy."

Theo seemed to find the idea of a thumb at the end of Turner's leg unbearably hilarious, and though he tried to muffle his laugh, he soon hunched over and had to brace himself against the wall under the force of his mirth. "A thumb!" he gasped.

Miles gave the other boy a disapproving glare, which he then turned on Enforcer Gerard and Martha as if urging them to rebuke the other boy. When no one did, Miles poked Theo in the side with vindictive force. "You're being rude. Can't you see he's scared? How would you like it if someone laughed because the Raven Queen was going to turn your face into a butt?"

Theo's eyes widened and he fell silent for two long seconds. "A butt!" he sputtered, then began to convulse with laughter so hard he struggled to breathe.

Millennium very obviously resisted the urge to kick Theo in the shin, instead moving to the other side of the group to be as far away from him as possible.

Siobhan rolled her eyes at the children's antics.

Turner's face paled further. "*Please*, my lady. I beg of you—"

Enforcer Fring gave Turner a light smack across the back of the head, eyeing Siobhan with trepidation. "Shut up," the man said. "It's better than dying. You should be grateful for what you can get. The Raven Queen is your savior—our savior." He leaned closer to Turner, murmuring vehemently, "How dare you complain?"

Turner pressed his lips together wordlessly, but a low, animalistic whimper still issued from between them.

"A stump ending should not be necessary," Siobhan murmured absently, her attention focused on the wound and what she would need to do to fix it. Turner didn't have enough extra blood for her to use to draw out a flesh-mirroring spell array, but the fist-sized pile of soaked bandages she'd removed would be more than enough fuel for the spell. On such a bumpy surface as the floor, though, chalk wouldn't do. Inevitably, some part of the Circle would be disconnected from the rest and lead to horrible consequences. She needed to draw it with something liquid.

Except this dilemma was irrelevant, she realized. She had retrieved her satchel and everything in it, including the sheets of seaweed paper. She hadn't duplicated her previous attempt at a tome, because she had a better idea in mind, but the artisan she'd hired to craft the device had yet to complete it. And so, she had a number of loose sheets of heat resistant paper, a few of which were blank and would be easy enough to draw the flesh-mirroring spell on.

The sheet would probably be ruined with Turner's blood, but there were no better options given their current location.

She also didn't want to try dual-casting in her state, but her shadow-familiar spell was protecting both her modesty and her aura of command and mystique. Without it, she would just be a young, half-naked girl.

"Everyone leave," she ordered. "Just out of sight. I am going to heal him."

"Oh, are you going to use blood magic?" Theo asked, still panting heavily from his laughing fit. He wiped some tears away from his eyes with his fists. "Can I watch?"

"No. But you can get dressed," Siobhan said, pulling the tightly packed, jumbled mess of shoes and clothing out of her satchel's expanded section, careful not to look too closely at the warped space of the interior, lest she worsen her headache.

Several of the others shared inscrutable looks and glanced at Turner with pity, but they complied without protest.

When they were gone, she had him close his eyes, quite sure that someone so timid wouldn't make any attempts at peeking, and then finally dropped the spell. Her mind relaxed like a muscle clenched too long. She sighed with relief, but knew it wasn't to last.

As she drew out the spell array, using his good leg as a template for the broken one, he trembled. Obviously, he was extremely frightened.

When she began to cast, he jumped, letting out a squeak followed by a pitiful whimper.

"I am not giving you a thumb," she assured him. To distract and comfort him as she very slowly joined his bone back together, not fully, but in little sections large enough to hold some weight, she talked, keeping her voice low and soothing. "I am not cutting the leg off, either. It would be too difficult for you to escape with the rest of the group if you only had one leg. It will be an imperfect fix, because I do not have the time to do better. Our enemies are surely following us by now." In addition to time, she lacked energy. It was also questionable whether she had the necessary *skill* to deal with such a grievous wound, but she elected not to mention that part.

"You will need to visit a proper healer when this is all over. I cannot say whether the leg will need to be cut off then, but if it does, I can assure you that it is entirely possible to regrow a leg." She moved on to attaching some of the blood vessels and the larger chunks of muscle to each other and the bone itself.

"There is even a new experimental treatment for prosthetic limbs," she said, some excitement leaking into her tone. She had heard about it in Professor Gnorrish's class and became interested because of the injuries Enforcer Gerard sustained at Knave Knoll. "You can have a foot grown from a modified parasitic plant that will literally sprout from your stump. Its roots will feed from your blood stream and connect to your muscle and nervous system. You would be able to control the foot with only a short delay."

Turner moaned sickly.

"Almost done," she promised. "The only problem with those types of prosthetics is the difficulty in perfecting the balance between keeping the plant from being too aggressive and devouring their flesh-and-blood symbiote and keeping the person's body from rejecting the invasion."

A few meters down the hall with his back turned, the Verdant Stag enforcer whose name she didn't know muttered, "Oh, Myrddin." He shuddered, then hunched inward and hugged his arms to his chest for warmth. Several of the others made conciliatory sounds. So far beneath the surface, and with the damp, it was cold enough that they needed to keep moving to stay warm.

"We'll be moving again soon," Siobhan reassured them. "Keep your backs turned."

"Don't worry, my queen," the praying woman called. "I'm watching them."

Jackal rolled his eyes so hard that his head moved from the effort, obvious even from the back.

Siobhan returned her attention to Turner's leg. It didn't exactly look healthy, but she thought it would support his weight, and her head was throbbing horribly, so it would have to do.

She gathered up all the bloody cloth and the soiled paper, then dumped them in a second spell array to cast the shedding-destroyer on them.

Finally, with significant reluctance, she recast her shadow familiar spell, keeping the chant inaudibly quiet. When she was again decent, she allowed Turner to open his eyes before reaching out a hand to help him to his feet.

He accepted her help with reluctance, but her patch job meant that he was able to continue on with the rest of the group.

Before leaving, Siobhan peed in the little underground stream, suppressing her embarrassment, and instructed the others to relieve themselves similarly, under the privacy of her shadow.

Siobhan dropped a philtre of stench in the area they had stopped, hopeful that it would take any dogs or other scent trackers out of commission if the enemy tried that tack. "I am going to spread out this shadow," she warned. "Everything within its range should be safe from divination. It will not harm you." They still needed to be able to see their feet to walk safely, so she spread out a wide mesh at around waist height.

Everyone seemed at least slightly uncomfortable, which Siobhan under-stood, as they must have seen the Pendragon operative's response to that same shadow, but they relaxed when nothing nefarious happened. The praying woman waved her hands through it with fascination. "And you shall walk, sheltered under wings of midnight," she whispered.

Everyone kept a noticeable, respectful distance from Siobhan, except Theo and Miles, who walked beside her like an honor guard, huffing and scowling at each other.

The praying woman stared enviously at the children, but Siobhan was happy to keep some space between herself and the peculiar woman.

"What did she do to you?" Siobhan heard Martha whispering to Turner.

He shook his head, throwing a glance Siobhan's way. "I don't know. She made me keep my eyes closed, and I wasn't about to steal a look unoffered. You've heard the stories about people who look at things they aren't supposed to, after they were warned so clearly." He shuddered. "Yeah, no way."

"Well, at least you can walk." The statement sounded somewhat dubious, and Siobhan couldn't help but feel offended.

'I did my best. People are always so entitled when they should simply be grateful.'

There was some argument about the best path to escape. They could make their way to the northern lake, where the freshwater docks and wide tunnels that cut through the bottom of the white cliffs allowed people to bring in goods from the north. Some of their group argued they should go that way, leave Gilbratha entirely and circle around to enter the city again from one of the land gates, or even up through the Mires to the south. Others argued that it was best to escape through the canals, taking a path downward through the city itself.

Gerard, Jackal, Anders, and Fring all agreed and argued strongly that moving through any of the commonly used paths or checkpoints would be too dangerous. People would be stationed there to watch for them. "We need something else," Jackal said. "Something they won't be expecting."

"At the very least, an area with as little traffic as possible," Siobhan added, doing her best to conceal the deep-seated fatigue that was beginning to make her dizzy.

"We could try to drill our way out somewhere new," Parker offered, holding up his battle baton.

"Do you have enough charges to get through dozens of meters of stone?" Gerard asked. "Or the ability to cast the spell yourself?"

"I *can* cast it," Parker said. "But it's an energy hog. It will take me a while to make much progress."

They all looked to Siobhan, then, but she just shook her head silently.

Anders hesitated. "Well, there is a small path that lets out right near the Charybdis Gulf. There's a little ferry station near there for those who would rather take a more direct route from the city proper to the Lilies. But we would surely stand out in the Lilies. Erm, *you*, in particular, would stand out," he said to Siobhan. "I don't like our chances trying to escape through any of the eastern gates."

"A ferry..." Siobhan mused. "Why not borrow a boat? There is no need to try to sneak through the Lilies. We could sail south through the Charybdis Gulf. We would be far enough from land to be safe from most attacks, and the sun will be setting in the next few hours. The dockworkers won't be active then, and most of the fishermen will have retired for the evening. It seems we could be out of the city before our enemies have any idea, if we move in darkness. Even if the ferry is guarded, we will be able to take it as long as we act competently and move swiftly. Few simple guards would be willing to risk their lives against a clearly superior force."

"Are we leaving the city for good?" Martha asked. "I have a life here. And what about the children?"

"Of course not," Siobhan said. "We'll rally and come back through the Mires in smaller groups. They can't watch every back alley and side street."

Parker nodded sagely. "The sun doesn't set until eight-something this time of year. We might even have time to drill an exit right above the ferry itself. What do you think?" he asked Anders.

The man sighed deeply. "I think that I'm wishing I saved up more coin. I would have, if I had known we were going to have to go on the run. Bear's food is expensive, and his potion regimen even more so."

"Ah, we need to pick up my daughter, too," Parker suddenly realized. "Or do you think she'd be safer staying with her aunt? I don't..."

Siobhan remained silent as the full implications of his agreement with her hit Parker.

He paled, turning slowly to her. "Um. I am realizing that I may have chosen my boon poorly, my lady."

She stared at him, raising an eyebrow.

Parker swallowed. "My daughter is probably still safe to inherit the house, once you've taken back the deed. But… I mean, there's no way it's safe for her to stay there right now. And, um, it might not be safe for her aunt to stay at her house, either. The High Crown will wonder if she has any information, and he's already proven happy to kidnap people only vaguely connected to his enemies…"

"Your families may remain safe if they are willing to leave the city or, perhaps, to join the ranks of the Nightmare Pack or the Verdant Stag. It is easy enough to provide secure places for them to stay and allies to watch their backs, but I cannot safeguard them every moment of the day against an attack or kidnapping attempt. There are measures they could take to ensure a swift rescue attempt, but that does not equate to true freedom from danger."

Parker did not seem particularly satisfied by this. "Could that change, if I made another pact with you? Perhaps, long-term protection, in exchange for long-term service from me? I can be useful."

The praying woman let out a small, nonverbal exclamation.

Siobhan sighed, her right eye twitching as dream-like phosphenes danced in her peripheral vision, always seeming just on the edge of creating a coherent image but never managing to do so. "Let us talk about this once the night is over. We cannot waste time dawdling."

No one had voiced any objections to her plan, so Anders led the way, though his occasional arguments with Millennium over which direction to go and which of the myriad turns to take didn't instill much confidence in the rest of the group. Their path alternated seemingly at random between natural caves and pathways and shoddy tunnels carved by hand—nothing so uniform or polished as the tunnels controlled by the Pendragon Corps, or even what could be found under the University.

Siobhan made sure to keep her shadow around everyone and several times felt the distant scratches of divination attempts against her ward. The High Crown's men could have been using a sympathetic link to any of them, though she thought the irritation was strongest around Parker and Anders. She sighed deeply as she considered the long-term ramifications of today's kidnapping.

The enemy was willing to escalate, which didn't bode well for the future.

Miles tripped and she caught him with her free hand, her attention snapping back to her surroundings.

Theo made a rude face, and Miles tilted back his chin to look down his nose at the copper-haired boy. "I bet the bad guys didn't even have any trouble capturing you," he muttered. "You were probably yelling and jumping about like a monkey and drawing all the attention to yourself."

"That's not true!" Theo said, eyes wide and mouth falling open as if he'd been mortally offended.

"Oh, yeah? Then why are all your people hurt so badly? Way worse than my people."

Theo gasped with outrage. "That's—I—well, obviously way more bad guys must have come after me than you! They probably thought you were such a big baby that it would be easy."

Siobhan placed a hand on each of their heads, carefully keeping her spell Circle intact. "Now is not the time," she said simply. She turned to Enforcer Gerard. "I assume they attacked the Verdant Stag? Millennium told me how they came directly to Lynwood Manor for him. If not for his abilities, there likely would have been much more bloodshed. Is everyone alright?"

Gerard hesitated, giving Theo a pitying look.

Theo scowled and bit his lip, looking down at the floor.

Siobhan's heart sank. '*Something happened to Katerin.*'

But when Gerard spoke, it wasn't what she expected. "The Lynwood boy actually…wasn't wrong. Theo here tried to sneak out to roam the streets and see the show. He's getting better at stealth and unconventional approaches, but we'd all heard him arguing with Katerin about being grounded and were on the lookout."

Theo's shoulders hunched and his head sank even further.

"So we noticed his escape attempt, and we were chasing after him. It might have been a good thing in the end, because the prigs in the shiny armor weren't expecting that. We'd already passed them before we even realized we were in danger."

Miles looked at Gerard, then back to Theo, an uncharacteristically wide, sharp smile on his face that reminded Siobhan of Lord Lynwood. "Just like a monkey," he repeated under his breath, but more than loud enough for everyone in the quiet tunnel to hear.

Theo stuck out his jaw belligerently and crossed his arms, pressing further into Siobhan's shadow-clothing. "Oh yeah? Well I've seen the Raven Queen summon the smartest and bestest raven in the city, known as Empress Regal. She probably wouldn't come play with you even if you had fresh fruit in your hand."

Miles shrugged nonchalantly, grabbing Siobhan's free hand and swinging it. "The Raven Queen designed a spell *especially for me*, something no one else has. I use it every night when I sleep."

"Oh yeah? Well…well, she's told me stories about the Black Wastes and the nightmarish horrors that live there." He spread his hands dramatically, fingers curled into claws. "And it's *all true*. You'd probably be too scared and have nightmares to listen to her stories."

Miles let out a single, low laugh of triumph. "That's where you're wrong. I can listen to any scary story I want, because *I don't dream anymore*. Ever."

Siobhan sighed. *"Children,"* she admonished.

31

———

PYRRHIC VICTORIES

Siobhan
   Month 4, Day 9, Friday 9:00 p.m.

After more than an hour of walking through winding tunnels of various shapes and sizes, interspersed with the occasional cave, Anders stopped them. "That's the way we'd go if we wanted to come out on the secluded white cliffs path," he said, pointing down a tunnel to their right, from which a briny breeze wafted. "But if we want to hit the ferry directly, we can continue on that way." He jerked his thumb forward. "I can only estimate, maybe five hundred paces?"

Millennium nodded, eyes unfocused as he tilted his head to listen. "It sounds good. Safe. For now. But I think it would be better to leave when it gets dark." His eyelids drooped, and he swayed on his feet, exhausted from more than just the physical ordeal. Listening to the whispers, or at least deciphering them into coherent meaning, drained him.

They continued to the spot Anders and several of the others judged best. Siobhan passed around her water canteen, then sat back with the children while the others set up their stolen shielding artifacts in an effort to stabilize the stone around them and dampen the sounds of drilling.

"Miles," Siobhan murmured to the sleepy child tucked under her arm. "How did you find me? In the streets earlier today, I mean. I'm supposed to be immune to divination."

He frowned, pulling his knees up to his chest and leaning into her for warmth. "I can't do divination," he murmured. "I haven't started to learn any real magic yet, remember?"

"But you *did* find me. Using the whispers."

He nodded, closing his eyes and taking a deep breath. "You smell good."

She thought the boy must be delusional with fatigue, since she was pretty sure she smelled of sweat, dirt, and fear. "Miles."

"The whispers aren't divination. They're not actually whispers, either. It's hard to explain. I just kind of...listen to the sounds of the world underneath the rest. It kind of blends together like music, or murmurs from a crowd too far away and too jumbled to make out what they're saying, only the emotion. Does that make sense?"

It did not, but Siobhan doubted he could explain it better. "Go on," she said.

"Listening to the sounds underneath became a lot, lot easier since I've been able to sleep. It *is* really hard to hear you from afar, and I couldn't find you by scent, either, even though yours is so distinct. But there's a kind of music to the way you move through life. Your whispers have a tone, and, like, an echo. I actually didn't find *you*, exactly, but I got close from the ripples you left, and also just how the safest direction always happened to be moving closer to you. I was already going in your direction even before I had the idea to find you. And then, once I was close enough, I could hear you with my actual ears from about a block away. But that's not divination. I just have good hearing. I'm part sylphide, you know. From my dad's side."

'*Setting aside how his abilities work, if that's true, then it might have been very lucky for me to be there to save Miles,*' Siobhan realized. '*If the High Crown had kept him, Miles might have been used to track me down.*'

The others were done with their preparations, and Parker pulled out his battle artifact, the one with the drilling spell, and pointed it nervously at the stone wall of the tunnel.

Theo looked on with avid interest, trying to creep around the praying woman, who was keeping him at a safe distance.

Siobhan raised a hand. "Wait. I have a better idea that has much less chance of drawing attention our way." She climbed back to her feet and pulled out a sheet of seaweed paper with the stone disintegration spell array. "This one is mostly silent. And, I would guess, much more efficient. Used in conjunction with something like a small wind spell to remove the crumbled stone, you could carve out sections of the wall with precision and set them aside, with much less noise, no tremors, and less possibility of causing a tunnel collapse."

By the time the sun had set, Siobhan's ward had fended off two more divination attempts, and they had cut a narrow tunnel that opened almost directly into the Gulf. There were also faint sounds of pursuit echoing from the direction they had come. The enemy seemed to be moving slowly, but they were catching up.

Siobhan crawled through the tunnel and peeked out into the moonless night.

The nearby dock had a couple of boats moored, if one could still call these small luxury vehicles boats. All were more than large enough to carry all twelve escapees, though some looked expensive enough that they might have some sort of on-board security system. There was a guard in a small watchtower, but the shroud of night was thick enough for Siobhan to stretch out a section of her shadow in a thin umbrella over the entire group, who huddled under it fearfully as they scurried as silently as possible for their boat of choice—the one that seemed easiest to operate and least likely to set off any alarms.

When they unmoored, pushing away from the dock, their boat lit up. Siobhan's first, adrenaline-drenched thought was that they had been spotted and someone was shining a light on them. But no, it was the boat itself, somehow detecting that it was nighttime and automatically turning on both a headlamp crystal and several lights across the sides.

Such a feature was surely very useful for traveling the night waters safely, or night-fishing for those creatures attracted by the light, but totally inappropriate for stealthily stealing a boat and escaping with it.

The Verdant Stag enforcer, whose name Siobhan still didn't know, was their captain, as he was the only one with some experience as a fisherman. He scrambled frantically for a way to turn the bright beacons off while the others clumsily tried to adhere to his commands about raising the sails and doing something or other to the rudder.

Siobhan wasn't paying attention to that, too busy scanning the docks and the white cliffs for danger.

A tumultuous clanging began to issue from an alarm bell in the watchtower, travelling clearly across the water. Only seconds later, a huge light crystal inside of a lensed housing activated, focusing the beam into a spotlight that cut through the night like a blazing brand. The dock guard had seen the lights of their boat, of course.

The spotlight swiveled a few times across the docks, catching the edge of the small tunnel they had created just as their pursuers reached its mouth. The guard noticed, and the light paused for a second, adjusting to illuminate the enemy more clearly.

At the head of the group, a man in the same uniform and armor of the Pendragon operatives squinted and shielded his eyes against the light, yelling at the guard.

"It's the captain," Parker murmured.

The spotlight spun towards the water. Despite their success in turning off the beacon of light crystals, they still hadn't floated very far from their initial position, and the watchtower guard found them again easily enough.

Siobhan didn't flinch when the light hit her, allowing her shadow to darken opaquely against the bright assault, protecting her face and eyes.

As several of her people used some emergency paddles to increase their speed and push them further into the Charybdis Gulf, Siobhan met the Pendragon captain's gaze across the water. She smiled, though he couldn't see, and he snarled, shouting indistinguishable orders at his subordinates.

The other Pendragon men scurried around with impressive coordination, a couple moving to follow along beside Siobhan's stolen boat on land while most tried to commandeer a boat of their own.

Siobhan hadn't hoped for things to go so poorly, but that didn't mean she was unprepared. She turned to Anders and Parker, giving them a nod.

With his mouth pressed into a grim line, Anders pulled out the Radiant explosive they had taken. Together, he and Parker primed it to go off after impact, and then Parker tied it inside a cradle of thin rope, which he used to swing the explosive around his head like a giant sling, faster and faster. The air whistled impressively from the device's speed, and they ducked down to avoid any accidental collisions.

When Parker finally released the explosive, it flew through the air in a palatially wide arc, up and then down, trailing rope with an audible slither over the railing.

For a moment, it seemed like it would miss the pursuing boat and splash rather harmlessly into the water. But in the only moment of good fortune Siobhan felt she had experienced all night, the fabric-covered device hit the edge of the deck.

The captain raised his arm and covered himself in a dome-shaped shield as several of his men jumped off the boat into the dark, filthy waters.

When the explosion went off, Siobhan had to turn her face away from the light, even with her shadow to shield her eyes. It blew a hole in the side and deck of the commandeered boat and sent the whole vessel rocking wildly side to side.

Disappointingly, it did not look as though the vessel would sink.

But one of the masts had been damaged, and if they were lucky, there might be a small leak or two in the side. With so many men currently splashing about in the Gulf—men who otherwise might have been ordered to row and thus catch up—her smaller boat was quickly able to draw ahead.

Soon, Siobhan's boat reached the outer edge of the watchtower spotlight's range. A little more, and they could escape into the night.

Up above, forms made small by distance stood on the edge of the white cliffs, looking down on them from the eastern edge of the University grounds.

An aborted cry sounded from the shore, near where the operatives had been running along beside her boat. She couldn't see them anymore, and could only hope they had met misfortune.

Siobhan worried for a moment that the pursuing operatives might produce something spectacular that would allow them to catch her, like a powerful wind spell released directly into their boat's sails, or some other kind of propelling spell, like the rare, paddle-wheeled river boats that ran off magic.

When the captain rummaged around in the back of the boat and returned with a staff-like device that she couldn't quite make out under the cover of darkness, she tensed.

He pointed it at them.

"Faster," she urged. Her boat wasn't maneuverable enough to dodge, but most spells had a limited effective range. She imagined he might strike them with lightning or shoot a piercing spell through their hull, but the projectile he shot from the staff-like device had no special color and didn't even glow.

Millennium cried out in dismay.

She heard the whistle of the attack a second before it hit and realized her error. The captain hadn't grabbed a staff at all. It might not even be magical, though the length it had crossed was quite impressive for an entirely mundane weapon.

It was a harpoon.

Her shadow billowed out instinctively to meet it, as if she could somehow block the path of the bladed weapon, but of course the harpoon passed straight through.

It missed her, passing a few feet to her left and stopping behind her with a sound like a goat carcass being quartered in a butcher's shop. A moment of slicing through wet muscle fiber, the splintering crack of bone shattering under a sloppy cut, and then the dull thud of wood behind the blade, stopping its momentum.

Siobhan turned to follow the sound, letting her shadow drop down to allow what little starlight shone from above to illuminate the boat.

Parker drew in a long, ragged breath of horror, looking down at the harpoon piercing messily through his thigh, which was already spilling blood like a gurgling spring. Then he screamed, high-pitched and ragged.

She had a moment to think that at least it wasn't his abdomen, or he might be dead already.

Then the tip of the harpoon somehow retracted and bent, gripping around the back of Parker's thigh. The trailing line went taut, reeled in by a winch as if Parker were some giant fish. And then he was simply *yanked* off the side of the boat and dragged across the surface of the water like an awkwardly shaped throwing stone. He had just enough time above the surface not to drown, and he spent these moments screaming, at first. It didn't take long for him to fall silent.

Siobhan lowered her outstretched hand, which had been much too slow to try and catch him. She stared uselessly.

"Can't you do something? Drag him back?" Turner asked tremulously, cutting through the silence.

The rest of the group was all looking to her as if she could somehow fix this. Suddenly irritated, she clenched her free fist, letting out a deep breath through the Circle of the hand in front of her mouth. She drew in her shadow a little tighter. "Did you not see that wound? If I fight for him, he will die, ripped apart like a rag doll fought over by two dogs." If she had acted fast enough, she might have been able to cut the rope before it was reeled in, but she had been stunned and just as useless as the rest of them.

"But you promised him a boon," Anders said.

"He has a daughter, does he not? The boon will still be granted. He may simply not be around to appreciate it," she snapped. She spun on her heel, looking toward the Stag man who was piloting the boat. "Take us out quickly. We need to get past the southern straits and the remnants of the white cliffs. We don't want anyone trying to ambush us again."

The only silver lining was the sudden lurch of the Pendragon operative's commandeered boat, which soon began to sink. The Radiant bomb must have done more damage than she thought, but she couldn't even manage a vindictive smile.

The rest of her people got to work in grim silence. Within an hour they had made their way out of the city and managed a somewhat fraught beaching on the shore south of the Mires.

32

EVERYWHERE AT ONCE

Thaddeus
Month 4, Day 9, Friday 5:00 p.m.

Thaddeus hurried back down to the carriage, where Investigator Kuchen was reading out a new message from the distagram.

"Update. Possible false lead on divination results. Previous signs pointed to the center of the raven swarm, but we are now showing multiple results spread throughout the city. Preliminary divination suggests the ravens themselves are the target."

Silence spread through the nearby coppers, which Titus broke with a slew of vicious cursing. He lifted his hands to his hair as if to pull on it, then forced them back to his sides. "Thaddeus," he said, as if he were a man dying of thirst and Thaddeus had just walked by with a canteen in his hands. "What can you tell me?"

"The Raven Queen is mocking you—us," Thaddeus corrected quickly. "We have made several failed attempts at divination, and now, she shows us that not only is she immune when she so wishes, but that even when we believe we *have* found her, it will come to nothing. We can make plans to capture her, but she can make plans, too, and hers will succeed where ours fail. And make us look foolish and ineffectual, at that."

"*Thank you*, I could have guessed that well enough," Titus said between gritted teeth. "Do you have anything useful? Any clues? Was this a distraction for an attack on the Edictum Council, perhaps? Are the ravens just some clever trick, or do we need to call in the Red Guard in force?"

Before Thaddeus could answer, the distagram activated once more. They all watched the pen scrawl hastily across the strip of paper.

Kuchen tore off the strip, cleared his throat loudly, and read, "A raven has delivered a letter to the Edictum Council. Attending Red Guard team successfully suppressed the ensuing panic. Several injuries, no deaths. Raven in custody, letter in containment wards. Ennis Naught remains in custody."

Thaddeus and Titus shared a look, and then both hurried back to the carriage. Titus ordered several of the coppers to remain behind to secure the scene and investigate the source of the raven clouds. The rest would ride north, accompanying his carriage.

"She's definitely an Aberrant," Kuchen announced as they began to move.

"You have made that suggestion before," Thaddeus snapped, "and we covered the evidence against it, just as we have the evidence against your other unfounded and frankly laughable theories. No matter the feat she just managed, that evidence still remains. Aberrants cannot cast spells. Like a magical beast, they propagate only their own inherent effect, simple or complex as it might be. Is your imagination truly so stunted, that you cannot comprehend how this could have been done?" he asked, gesturing vaguely to the sky. "Or are you simply so *ignorant* that any innovative action must be ascribed to the mystical, inhuman abilities of an Aberrant?"

Kuchen shrank back in his seat.

Titus sighed wearily. "Thaddeus," he admonished succinctly.

Taking courage from this, Kuchen thrust out his chin defiantly. "Where did she come from, then? Such a powerful thaumaturge takes time to develop. One with a personality such as hers surely couldn't have gone entirely unnoticed. The Red Guard have assured us she's not one of yours, and while they could be hiding the truth, all the other countries we have discreetly reached out to have denied any association. Is it *impossible* that she is an Aberrant, one like the Red Sage or the Dawn Troupe, who require some low cunning to be effective?"

Kuchen leaned forward, lowering his voice, and continued. "I have heard the rumors of Aberrants that do not simply seem to be devious, their actions the rote artfulness of an ant hive or the routine instruction of a golem, but who are actually *intelligent*. In which case, their malice could be both deliberate and resourceful. Is it impossible that she is only *pretending* to be a thaumaturge?"

Thaddeus narrowed his eyes, wondering where, exactly, the man had heard such rumors.

Titus lifted his leg and rested the ankle atop his other knee. "Thaddeus would know best, but I haven't heard of any Aberrant with quite so varied a repertoire as she displays. What would her concept be? 'Dark miracles?'" He laughed humorlessly. "Or something that grew more powerful the more people thought about her?" He frowned, suddenly concerned.

Thaddeus opened his mouth to cut this fear mongering off before it could make the other two any more irrational. "The fact that other countries have denied association means nothing. They could easily be lying, for a variety of reasons. If we want to come up with *dubious conjecture*, perhaps she was living in Myrddin's hermitage, shielded from the effects of the Black Wastes by the man's wards, which remained intact and active until recently. Or…perhaps she arrived from elsewhere. There has been another that emerged from the lands beyond, who had both astonishing power and control of bewildering feats. And, if I might add, my research into the topic suggests that Raaz Kalvidasan, Siobhan Naught's adopted grandfather, may have had some connection to the Third Empire's cohort."

Titus's grip tightened around his ankle. "You think she came from over the northern ice oceans? From beyond the Abyssal Sea?"

Thaddeus threw up his hands in exasperation. "I do not think that. I only mention it as a possible alternative to your investigator's fear-mongering accusations. I have no opinion on the matter, as without more evidence, the only one who could give us answers at this point is the Raven Queen herself."

They were distracted from the conversation by another distagram message. Apparently, witnesses reported seeing the Raven Queen atop a building near the Edictum Council shortly before the raven messenger arrived. If true, this would place her there *while* the raven clouds were dancing kilometers further south. The Raven Queen had, again, disappeared, and though some witnesses believed she had done so by bursting into a flock of ravens, reports were conflicting, and no flock of ravens had been seen near the Edictum Council.

Kuchen made no comment but gave Thaddeus an acerbic glance, as if this was further evidence of the man's pet theory.

Very shortly afterward, this news was followed up with a report that the Raven Queen was at the University. "She attacked the divination team at Eagle Tower," Kuchen said with inappropriate excitement. He settled, coughing a few times into his handkerchief, and then asked Thaddeus, "How could she possibly have traveled so fast, if she cannot fly or travel through shadows?"

Titus did pull at the sides of his hair this time. "The High Crown will have my head," he muttered, staring down at his shoes.

Kuchen's head whipped toward him, and after a moment, the man spoke tentatively. "Do you mean that…literally?"

Titus sighed and leaned back, resting his head on the back cushion. "No. I haven't committed treason or shown any disloyalty. But he may try to use this to weaken the Westbays' position, touting my incompetence. And my father… will not like that," he said simply, ominously.

When they arrived at the Edictum Council, which was on the way to the University, the distagram scribbled out one final message. "The Raven Queen has escaped. None dead, several injured. Blood sample lost."

Titus's cheeks flushed with futile rage, and his foot tapped out a slow, even rhythm on the carriage floor.

As they jumped out of the carriage and strode toward the conspicuous building, one of the coppers stationed there stepped up and walked beside them. "No further disturbances since we sent the dispatch," the woman reported in rapid, clipped tones. "Ennis Naught remains in custody, though he made quite the racket about it. Tried to fight his way free with a pair of manacles and his bare hands, alternating screams for help and curses on his daughter's name. He even managed to somehow get his hands on a civilian woman's hair pin and unlock his manacles, but our security was too strong for him."

"What of the letter?" Titus asked.

"And the raven?" Kuchen added.

"The letter is being examined for curses and nasty surprises, but so far it seems mundane. The raven is dead. Attempts to communicate with it led nowhere. We called in a shaman to try a dream-walking with the bird, but apparently there was a small explosive artifact embedded in its stomach."

"Dream-walking? With a *bird*?" Thaddeus repeated incredulously.

The woman looked at him, shrugging with embarrassment. "Well, we figured, what if it wasn't *just* a bird?"

Kuchen nodded in solidarity. "And why the explosive, if they weren't worried that, somehow, we would learn something from it?"

"Why the living bird at all, if she could have just delivered it with a raven made of shadows and nightmare?" Thaddeus asked sardonically.

The copper looked between the three of them with increasing worry. "Wait, really? I thought her shadows could only curse you with nightmares and stuff. Not become *tangible*."

Kuchen shook his head sadly. "Grandmaster Lacer is mocking us. He believes the Raven Queen to be a totally mundane sorceress."

"Not *totally* mundane," Thaddeus corrected, taking advantage of his long legs to walk faster and escape.

The letter had been removed from the middle of the Edictum Council's central floor and placed in a smaller conference room. It sat on the center of a marble table, surrounded by experts doing various tests. Thaddeus stood to the side, looking over their heads and doing some tests of his own, at a distance. When they finally broke the black wax seal and removed the sheet of paper within, he took advantage of a simple spell to read the contents.

His lips twitched, his nostrils flared, and he read it again. As ever, the Raven Queen seemed determined to be as theatrical as possible. She must have laughed herself breathless, knowing the kind of furor this would cause. It was almost worth three weeks of waiting, if this was what she had been preparing. Perhaps whatever she had done at the University would tie it all together.

Titus pushed the supposed experts aside, snatching the paper off the table and reading aloud.

"ON A COLD WIND BLEW STRIFE.
    The thief of fire,
    Will be a light in the darkness,
    A candle against the night,
    And will laugh as she feasts.

SAVE YOUR TEARS FOR YESTERDAY.
    As you dream of cracked roads,
    And tend your garden of sticks.
    For madness makes no plans,
    And there is but one cure for the living.

A SCREAM into the void echoes.
    Black eyes see nothing,
    But a fortune of dust,
    Empty bellies and sharp teeth,
    And payment in bone."

A LONG SILENCE followed his recitation, and then one of the cursebreakers muttered, "You shouldn't have read it aloud. I've heard tale of subtle curses that require your participation. Do you feel any different?"

Titus looked up from the page, scowling at the man with the descending rage of a hurricane. He hurled the page at the cursebreaker, then turned and marched back the way he had come as the paper fluttered ineffectually through the air.

Thaddeus waited a moment as those who remained began to talk over each other. When he finally met Siobhan Naught—if that ever had been her name in truth—perhaps she would be interested to hear the effects of her schemes from one who had experienced the uproar firsthand.

"What do you think it means?"

"Is the Raven Queen the thief of fire? A reference to the old Titanic myths, do you think? We may need to call in a lore master."

"The first letters are all capitalized. Perhaps it's an anagram. 'Bestow...' something."

"Payment in bone? What does that mean?"

"She laughs as she feasts, empty belly, sharp teeth. Sounds like some sort of cannibalistic blood sorcery to me. That may be where she gets her power."

"Dream of cracked roads. Is this all dream symbolism? Where's the shaman?"

The air grew thick with the heat of their frantic inquiry, their questions tripping over each other. High pitched, a woman asked, "Could it be a prophecy?" The room quieted.

"Prophecies are a myth," an old man snapped back quickly. "Not even an Archmage prognos can accurately predict events past a few days."

Thaddeus knew what the next words would be even before they were spoken. It would have irritated him, but obviously this kind of fatuous speculation was the point.

"The Red Sage makes prophecies."

The speaker was a blue-skinned man wearing the trinkets of a shaman. He spoke the words slowly, a quiet but forceful rebuttal.

Silence fell for a while longer, and then the old man replied, "But those are all recorded. Unless the Red Guard has been keeping a secret?"

All eyes turned to Thaddeus.

He shook his head and, as always seemed to be *his* maddening responsibility, opened his mouth to be the voice of reason. "No. Let me remind you, a prediction, or even a promise, need not be a prophecy." He turned to leave, then. If he lingered too long, Titus would leave without him.

When Thaddeus reached the carriage, Titus gave a rap and the horses sprang forward.

They sat in silence for a moment before Kuchen tentatively asked, "What do you think the letter meant?"

Titus stared out of the window unseeingly. "It means, 'Despair, for you will never win. Spread my fame and cement the futility of your existence in the minds of all those who would bow to you. I name you enemy.'"

Kuchen blinked twice in bewilderment, then turned to Thaddeus beseechingly.

"Titus is right," Thaddeus agreed, somewhat relieved that the man hadn't succumbed to irrationality. "Yes, the Raven Queen has a tendency to weave clever hints into her actions and communication, but I think it most likely that her message here does not require over-deciphering." Thaddeus, at least, had noticed none of the signs of the hidden codes he was familiar with.

"She has been quite explicit, after all. She has challenged us, insulted us, and predicted her own ferocious superiority against our futile end. She has also, I believe, made a statement about her ability to protect and shelter where we cannot, as a light in the darkness, and a candle against the night. One who has the resources to feast, while our fortune becomes dust."

Titus closed his eyes for a long moment. "With every appearance, she grows more important in the rumors and superstitions of the commoners, gaining a foothold of interest and support among those who consider themselves misused and underprivileged. But this... There is no coming back from today."

"There's still a chance to catch her," Kuchen comforted, though Thaddeus wasn't sure the man really believed it.

"She wasn't even attempting to free her father," Titus murmured.

"I agree," Thaddeus said, inordinately pleased by this for some reason. Ennis Naught was a worthless, betraying plebeian. "In fact, she seemed more interested in the offense of attempting to divine her location than in the man," he added. Though, with someone like her, there was no way to know how many layers deep her plan went, nor how many different goals she was able to accomplish at once.

"Maybe she will attack the prisoner convoy, or try to abscond with him from the labor camp," Kuchen offered.

"We can only hope," Titus said. His heel resumed tapping on the carriage floor in a steady, deliberate rhythm that reminded Thaddeus of Titus's father. Of course, in Titus the tapping signified anxiety, whereas in Lord Tyron Westbay, it meant cold anger and thoughts of how he might take that anger out upon others.

The three of them fell to silence.

The sirens blaring over the University grounds were audible even from the base of the glass transportation tubes. When they reached the top, Titus winced and ordered someone to turn them off. "Everyone who needs to be protected will already be in one of the shelters. No need for the racket to keep reminding us, though I would predict that she's long gone by now."

Thaddeus found it amusing that they had felt the need to set off the sirens in the first place. The Raven Queen, as far as he knew, had never purposefully harmed a civilian—at least not those who did not act against her.

When Titus asked to talk to the people who had encountered the Raven Queen, they were directed to the infirmary. The rest of the faculty were all out searching the grounds, though more than a few of them seemed like they would rather do anything except actually *find* her.

Within the infirmary, the situation was worse.

A few men had obvious injuries—broken limbs, burns, and one with a foaming poultice over his eyes and a tremor in his fingers—but several others who were seemingly unharmed lay on infirmary beds with the glassy stare that indicated heavy doses of calming potions.

In the hallway and between the beds, several coppers, a couple of professors, and two prognos loitered anxiously. The coppers stood at attention when Titus entered, and both professors gave Thaddeus smiles of relief. "Oh, thank Myrddin," one man muttered, as if Thaddeus's presence meant they would be safe now.

What a sorry excuse for a professor at the most prestigious University in the known lands.

Some of those in the beds tried to stand, but Titus waved them down. "Copper Alma, report," he commanded.

A short woman stepped forward, gave a shallow bow, and said, "The Raven Queen came down from the roof and through the window. There were no signs of approach. She just suddenly appeared. We suspect she was there the whole time, for hours perhaps, just waiting for us to arrive and then to lower our guard. The ravens were a decoy and a reason for us to bring the last of the blood out."

"That's impossible," Kuchen interrupted. "Even if she somehow commanded the ravens from afar, who sent the bird to the Edictum Council, then? She must have flown. Were you keeping guard against birds, too? Or maybe she traveled through the shadows."

"It's not even night," someone muttered.

Copper Alma shook her head. "We had the Radiant wards on around the tower to keep a barrier against encroaching shadow."

"And we watched for ravens," the man with the poultice over his eyes called. "Unless she literally appeared from nothing, she was hiding in wait all along."

"We checked the wards," the woman added. "No suspicious entries, though there is one professor who was noted as entering the building early this morning. We haven't been able to find him."

"So someone stole his faculty token," Thaddeus deduced easily enough. "You should investigate his whereabouts. Are you entirely certain it was the Raven Queen herself who attacked you?"

"It was her," one of the glassy-eyed coppers lying in bed interjected. "She wore a dark cloak, but I know it was her. Who else could swallow up the night and then vomit it out again?"

Titus raised an eyebrow.

Alma cleared her throat uncomfortably. "I apologize, sir. As she has been known to do, the Raven Queen used a philtre of darkness. We think. It was... unlike anything I've ever encountered. The counter-potions and spells we prepared were useless against it. Several of the men insist that the darkness was coming...*from* her."

The man on the bed interjected again. "It was, it *was*! It was spilling from her face. But her face wasn't a face like ours, it was just a single mouth, an open maw of darkness, and out of it rode Night, and when I breathed it, Night became part of me and I knew—I knew I was *seen. I was seen,"* he repeated in a hoarse wail that devolved into sobbing.

One of the healers rushed over and forced another potion down his throat, glaring at Titus.

One of the coppers beside Alma straightened his shoulders with determination. "I saw it, too. I think the darkness might have been another form of the shadow creature that is said to accompany her. It's—" He swallowed. "It's the only thing that makes sense."

One of the prognos who must have been casting the divination spell piped up then. "She was several of the ravens, too. Not all of them, just a few dozen. I know that doesn't make sense, but I know what I saw. When they dispersed, it was like she split into that many pieces. I cannot advise whether she has some strange familiar contract that allowed them to be located in her stead, or if it is some more uncanny magic at play."

Thaddeus ran his fingers over his beard, frowning as he studied the traumatized group. "Are we entirely sure that she was spotted near the Edictum Council? How reliable are the eyewitnesses? Perhaps some work with a diviner or shaman is in order, to solidify the veracity of their testimony."

Kuchen had the gall to *roll his eyes* at Thaddeus before conceding to contact the team there.

Thaddeus resisted the urge to shoot the man with a sobering spell, reminding himself that idiocy was not something that could be cured. Not past childhood, at least.

Instead, he turned his efforts to deduction. Thaddeus decided to set aside the strange shadow phenomenon, which could be accomplished with innovative spellwork. A little bit of fear, a tinge of emotion called up through transmogrification, and the ignorant would firmly believe in the power of dark miracles. The mind rewrote memories every time they were called upon, and the truth was so easily restructured.

If it were Thaddeus who had come up with this plan, perhaps the magic calling and directing the conspiracy of ravens would have been something he imbued into an artifact. She had enough connections among the underbelly of society to put someone in charge of activating it and then secreting it away again when it ran out of power.

The raven that delivered the letter to the Edictum Council could have been the same, and any supposed sightings of the Raven Queen nearby based on an illusion. None of the divination results had shown a hit on her appearance there, though of course that did not necessarily mean anything. They had also failed to notice that she was hiding on the roof.

As for the ravens triggering the divination in lieu of the Raven Queen, showing her anywhere and everywhere that she obviously was not, he could think of three different methods off the top of his head to create such an effect.

None of this meant that the Raven Queen was any less special. Only less mystical and unfathomable. He was sure all of her secrets had an answer, and all the evidence that seemed to conflict, a resolution.

What fascinated Thaddeus was not her supposed strange abilities. He, too, could be said to have strange abilities by those who knew no better. No, he was interested in her mind—her knowledge and ambitions.

Titus, Thaddeus, and Kuchen remained at the University for hours, investigating Eagle Tower and the grounds with those of the diviners who were well enough to continue working. As fascinating as the events of the day had been, Thaddeus still found them somewhat underwhelming.

Was this...it? Thaddeus had done nothing more than chase her tail like the rest of them. He had not even managed to see the Raven Queen with his own eyes. He had thought to be more than just another spectator. Had he made a mistake in joining the coppers? But without their information network, he might have been even further behind.

And then, as if in answer to his dissatisfaction, there was a commotion to the east, noticed by one of the faculty members still out patrolling. Thaddeus set aside any foolish notions of decorum and ran full out in a straight line across the grounds, his coat and hair flying behind him until he reached the edge of the white cliff. Titus and several other coppers chased behind him.

Thaddeus free-cast a far-seeing lens spell and looked through the Circle hanging in the air in front of him.

About three hundred meters below and half a kilometer out, the Raven Queen, identifiable by the darkness she wore like a billowing cloak against the spotlight shining on her, had seemingly stolen a boat. An eclectic group accompanied her, scrambling to manage the marine vehicle while she stood still, looking back at her pursuers.

Titus slowed to a panting stop beside Thaddeus and stretched his neck to see through his spell. "Pendragon Corps."

"Indeed. What has she been up to, I wonder?" Thaddeus murmured, his eyes flicking over the situation with minute adjustments to the spell.

As he watched, one of the people with her used a rope to lob something at the boat attempting to follow them. It was an impressive throw. Several of the High Crown's men jumped overboard before the thing exploded with light bright enough to sear Thaddeus's eyes. He blinked, dropping the lens spell in favor of a soothing spell to clear his watering, spotted vision.

"Cast the telescope spell again, Thaddeus," Titus commanded. "I think she's kidnapped a couple of the High Crown's men. Did you see the uniforms?"

Thaddeus hesitated. For a moment, a vindictive urge ran through him.

How would the Raven Queen react if he stopped her boat dead in the water or released some flashy attack? But that would be foolish, and he was not desperate. He considered his goal and the best method to achieve it, and turned his focus elsewhere.

Thaddeus sent out a surreptitious spell to create a line of force so thin it might as well have been a garrote. He placed it at neck height in front of the two operatives running alongside the Raven Queen's boat in the dark.

It was a long way to detach the output of a spell, but he had the finesse and control to manage it. Often, this was more important than sheer power. He made no motion of his fingers, did not turn his head to target them obviously, and did not react to their aborted cries of surprise as the wards of their uniforms protected them barely long enough to realize that they were in danger. Their bodies would be found before morning.

With that done, he brought the lens spell back, wondering if the Raven Queen would notice his small contribution to her escape. Her face was obscured under the cloak of darkness, but he thought she seemed to be looking up at him in acknowledgement.

She had noticed. Could she see him at this distance? Perhaps she was even free-casting her own lens spell right at that moment.

Taking a closer look at her companions, Thaddeus confirmed that two were indeed wearing the Pendragon Corps colors. There was also a woman in a maid uniform, several Verdant Stag and Nightmare Pack symbols, and two small children. All looked worse for wear.

When one of the Pendragon operatives used a harpoon to spear the blue-and-gold uniformed man by the Raven Queen's side, Thaddeus revised his opinion on their loyalty. "Did they *defect*?" He failed to hide the delight in his tone, but Titus either did not notice or did not care. Thaddeus also noted that her darkness had moved as if to shield against the attack, but failed to stop it. Another piece of evidence that it was not tangible.

The escapees soon reached the edge of the lighthouse's range, and as her boat melted back into the darkness of the moonless night, Thaddeus dropped the lens spell and added one last, secret contribution to her endeavors in the form of a gaping wound in the hull of her pursuer's boat, well under the water line.

33

———

OUT OF THE NIGHT

Siobhan
Month 4, Day 9, Friday 10:00 p.m.

Siobhan was reaching the edge of her limits.

The vision in her right eye was fading, not with darkness but with an empty spot that she couldn't tell was there until something disappeared into it. Whatever was wrong with her ribs was becoming more debilitating, sending moments of sharp pain radiating through her back and upper abdomen that were followed by a deep, dull ache. Even her shadow-familiar was becoming difficult to maintain past the mental fatigue and an increased distractibility. Her thoughts attempted to wander off on the silliest tangents when they should be gripped tight around the magic.

She wanted to rest. But the Pendragon Corps operatives might still try to scry Anders, and she didn't feel right leaving Theo or Miles to the care of these people who had already shown they couldn't protect them.

Miles had stumbled with fatigue when they climbed out of the boat, too tired to even respond to Theo's sneered comment about being a little baby. Whatever strange abilities he had, they were not without cost. Enforcer Fring was carrying the boy now, his weight barely a hindrance to the large man.

Siobhan looked toward the sprawling southern edge of the Mires, where small campfires dotted the rocky soil and illuminated the shacks and tents that housed people who couldn't afford to live within the protection of Gilbratha's walls, such as they were.

Not that this part of Lenore was very dangerous. Not due to monsters, at least. The army had long since cleared this central area of magical land beasts, culling them down to the last. And water beasts wandering into the Charybdis Gulf from the ocean were unlikely to attack people on land. But that didn't mean people here were safe. The coppers didn't come this far south, after all.

Siobhan jerked her mind away from the tangent, focusing for a couple seconds on the shadow-familiar spell to make sure it was steady, its tendrils spread widely enough to protect everyone against possible divination attempts.

The others made the job easier, automatically gathering around her as if she was a campfire on a cold, fearful night.

The safest place she could think of was Liza's apartment—or rather, apartments—but she couldn't take them there. The woman wouldn't abide the danger that could bring to her home, and without showing them Liza's secret attached apartments, the small main abode would have trouble fitting a group of this size.

The Verdant Stag had wards, too, and even more after the Knave Knoll incident, but judging from Miles's story and Theo's capture, it might not be safe there. '*And,*' a small voice in the corner of her head said, '*Oliver might be there.*' Obviously, she would need to see him, to speak to him again, sometime soon. But for the moment, there was nothing she would love to avoid more. If it would be safest there, of course she would go anyway, but if she were the one who had planned all this, it certainly wouldn't be.

She cleared her throat and said wearily, "We need to find a safe place. I fear the Verdant Stag and Lynwood Manor will be watched by the enemy. I know the location of several of the Verdant Stags' safe houses, but we need somewhere more permanent, ideally warded against scrying. I cannot keep this protection active for much longer. Unless any of you are secretly wardmasters?"

She shook her head before anyone had a chance to respond. No, of course they weren't. That was silly. She smacked her tongue, realizing how thirsty she was, and dug in her satchel for the canteen of water within. It was almost empty, but if she held it for a while with the cap off, the little spell array she had carved into the bottom and charged—making the canteen a cheap artifact—would draw in moisture from the air to refill its stores.

Jackal and Enforcer Fring shared a look. Anders glanced around, then took a small step closer. "I agree. If we don't have a place to hide, we're gonna have to leave Gilbratha right quick. I've got a cousin in a little town east of Paneth. But that body seems to be failing you," he added, looking pointedly at Siobhan. "Doesn't seem like you'll last the night."

The praying woman sucked in a gasp of outrage, but Siobhan nodded, her neck feeling slightly too loose and her giant, throbbing brain slightly too heavy. "The Will is resolute, but the flesh is imperfect," she said, quoting a half-remembered idiom.

Surprisingly, it was Martha who came up with an answer. "We can go to one of our safe houses in the old Morrow territory. There's one that connects to a hidden tunnel leading to one of Lord Morrow's old underground fighting arenas. It's ours now, too. And the place should have some wards. And extra fighting supplies, and people on our side. And even a healer on staff?" she added uncertainly as people stared at her.

"It's...a good idea. But how do you know about that?" Enforcer Fring asked.

Martha harrumphed at him, crossing her arms. "I hear quite a lot, living in the Lynwood house, and especially being young Millennium's maid."

After a few moments of discussion, they agreed that this was their best option. It was early enough in the night, and beginning to grow warm enough, that people were still out and about. And Siobhan's group was quite conspicuous. They had found a barrel of fresh water on the boat and used it to clean up a little, but they were still an eclectic congregation and obviously somewhat battered.

She tried to make her shadow-familiar cloak hang more like actual fabric, hugging closer to the fabric of her dress, which was much too fluffy and pastel green to flaunt openly. The tendrils that were looped around the others thinned to the barest thread, almost invisible unless one was looking for them.

They came across some mostly-dry clothing hanging from a makeshift clothesline and paid the scraggly man guarding the line for a couple of spare outfits. Anders was able to change out of the bold Pendragon Corps colors, and Martha got a light cloak to cover up her maid's uniform.

Siobhan was out of luck, if she had ever had any to begin with, stuck in her dress. All she could do was hug the fabric with her shadow and activate her dowsing artifact in the hope that the low-level spillover from her divination-diverting ward's automatic activation would be enough to keep eyes off of her.

They kept to the shadows of back alleys and streets where the light crystals had been stolen out of the lamp posts.

One of the men let out a gasp and raised his arm to wave at a small group of patrolling Nightmare Pack enforcers, but Gerard stopped them and pulled them back into the alley. "We don't know if there's a leak, or how loyal those men really are. And the larger our group, the more likely someone notices us and talks. There are already too many of us."

This caused some anger among the Nightmare Pack members of their group, but they continued on alone, ducking through the streets in sudden bursts of movement, wary of anyone and everyone still moving at that hour. Siobhan couldn't even tell if she was frightened, or if running into trouble would be a relief, but they soon enough made it to Martha's safe house, which was empty, and much nicer on the inside than either of the Verdant Stag safe houses that Siobhan had been in.

From there, they descended through a tunnel that was revealed by lifting up an ornate bathtub, which was built quite ingeniously on a hinge with a spring to handle the weight. The tunnel itself was carved from more of the ubiquitous white stone, but here beneath the surface, they stood in a couple of inches of brackish water. Little crabs scurried out of their way, and lichen and a thin brown film covered the damp walls.

Enforcer Gerard had to kill a truly enormous spider barring the way about halfway through the tunnel. It had some mild form of camouflage that might have been magical and was large enough to kill and eat the crabs, or anything smaller than the average cat. Siobhan could barely spare a thought for it beyond an exhausted wish that they could move faster.

When they arrived at the end of the tunnel, barred by a rusted iron door, they knocked loudly and waited an irritating amount of time for a response.

When it finally came, the door inching cautiously open with a horrible shriek of ungreased, rusted hinges, the group of battle-ready Nightmare Pack members on the other side were immediately and obviously relieved by the sight of Millennium in Enforcer Fring's arms.

They questioned the man rapidly as the rest of the group squeezed through the half-open door, and another man in an ostentatious outfit—with actual velvet coattails—sent a runner to inform Lord Lynwood.

The group fell silent when Siobhan stepped through, her clothing coated in shadow made more obvious in the light of the room. Her arm was beginning to ache from holding her hand up to her mouth for so long, so she switched arms, looking around.

After a long few seconds of complete silence, Fring took charge of the situation, listing what they needed, and when most of the people had rushed off to do his bidding, he explained the situation and events of the day with occasional interjections from the others.

The man with the velvet coattails was apparently the manager, and he directed them to a larger room, where people quickly returned with extra chairs, food and water, and the on-staff healer.

Siobhan waited for the arena's employees to bring a set of portable anti-divination wards, which they set at the corners of the room and attached to the corners of the ceiling, before speaking. "I require clothing."

The employees froze, looking to the manager, who hesitated a moment but then murmured instructions to one of the women. She looked at Siobhan and then back at the manager as if she wanted to argue.

"Quickly," Siobhan added.

The woman left the room at a dead sprint.

Theo giggled and sent Siobhan an exaggerated wink and grin, despite his obvious fatigue. The healing potion he'd taken earlier had refreshed him, but he was still a young boy and it had been a very long day.

The woman returned less than a minute later with a slim-fitting red dress that was missing several sections of actual fabric around the legs and midsection in favor of sheer lace.

Siobhan stared at it for a moment, trying to gauge if this would be any better than remaining in her current attire, but decided that no matter how flamboyant it was, it was better than remaining in the same outfit she'd been kidnapped in.

The employee bowed deeply to her, then offered to escort her to a private room where she could change. Siobhan took her up on the offer. Alone, she belatedly realized that she could drop her shadow-familiar now. Her mind felt strange without anything to grasp onto, like a fist with stiff fingers that didn't want to unbend. She felt vulnerable without her shadow, despite how useless it was as any kind of effective protection.

With the occasional whimper of pain and frustration, Siobhan struggled out of her clothing and into the new outfit. She considered taking off her corset to get a sense of the damage underneath, and maybe ease the pain that was being exacerbated by the black sapphire and a beast core pressing into her injured side, but decided to put it off. At the very least, the corset seemed to be holding her insides in place, and wasn't that what compression bandages would do? 'Who knows?' she thought blearily, her head listing to one side before she snapped it upright again.

She returned to the hallway, which was empty, and shuffled back the way she'd come, only to meet Lord Lynwood, Gera, and Katerin charging in the other direction. Gera turned her head over her shoulder and snapped, "Hurry up!"

Liza was trailing behind the three, and the target of this order. One side of Liza's upper lip twitched with irritation, and she returned a hard stare that Gera didn't seem to notice at all, too focused on reaching her son.

The three of them recognized Siobhan at the same time, slowing so quickly they almost tripped over each other. Under Gera's observation, the divination-diverting ward tingled to blood-sucking life.

Siobhan waved at the nearby door. "Miles and Theo are there. Safe," she added.

The three of them hurried on, Lord Lynwood and Gera both pausing to make awkward, hasty bows to her before crashing through the doorway.

Liza, much less frantic, stopped beside Siobhan, her lips tightening as her gaze flicked over Siobhan's own, then around her head and down to her faintly trembling fingertips. "This was not the plan, girl," she said severely.

Siobhan smiled wryly. "No plan survives contact with the enemy," she quoted. "But I survived. *We* survived. And as far as I'm aware, this time I didn't make any disastrous mistakes. Did you…?"

Liza grimaced. "I succeeded, if a little more dramatically than I had hoped."

Siobhan was almost too fatigued to feel the relief she had been anticipating since coming up with the plan. She wanted to ask for details but decided that such things could wait.

"They barely had a smear of blood on a shard of glass, but it is now destroyed, according to our contract. The Raven Queen has made triumphant appearances throughout the city today. Even more than planned, it seems. I hope you can handle the consequences of all this extra attention."

Siobhan began to shrug, then stilled with a wince as the movement tugged on her ribs. "I don't really plan to handle anything. I'll just disappear. I would have done that from the beginning, had they let me."

Liza pursed her lips. "We will see."

"They added some portable wards to the room, but it could probably use something better if you can manage it on the fly. I might be safe from their divination now, but for one of them, that's most definitely not the case."

Liza sighed, following Siobhan into the room and pulling out supplies for drawing a spell array from one of her vest's pockets.

A sudden wave of dizziness sent Siobhan stumbling, but she caught herself before she could fall.

The healer, currently tending to Miles, half-stood as if to go to Siobhan.

She waved him off. "I am fine. See to the boy." She didn't want to take off her corset yet, which he would need to do to deal with her ribs, and it wasn't as if he could fix her Will-strain. She fumbled in her satchel for one of the two remaining healing potions, downing the entire thing in another burning, Radiant gulp.

She hissed, scouring light spilling from between her teeth as her side pulled and shifted with the scream of stretched muscles and grinding carti- lage. Her right eye itched and watered, and a sudden violent cough sent a weak cloud of darkness puffing from between her lips.

She, and everyone else in the room, stared at it as it dissipated into the air. "That definitely should not happen," she muttered. It seemed she still had some tweaks to do with the proprioception philtre of darkness. Which needed a name of its own. *'Naught's philtre of shadowed perception? No, too wordy.'*

She looked up to see that several of her rescued group members wore expressions of concern and belatedly realized that perhaps coughing up dark- ness would be more worrying to someone who didn't know the reason. "Do not worry, just a small side-effect. There should be no permanent damage to the flesh," she said, pressing her hand to her chest, over her lungs. It didn't even hurt to breathe.

Liza pressed one hand to her forehead and sighed.

Martha nodded slowly, jerkily. "Not to worry, not to worry," she repeated under her breath, though Siobhan had no idea who she was trying to reassure.

The praying woman, whose name Siobhan still didn't know, pushed aside Jackal, who was staring at Siobhan in disgusted fascination. "Is this something you could do for someone else, my queen? Someone loyal and true?"

Siobhan tried to parse the strange woman's question, and then realized she was requesting access to the modified philtre of darkness. *'Naught's philtre of night and knowledge!'* some part of her brain suggested gleefully. "I could," Siobhan agreed aloud, "but it might be slightly dangerous. It obviously needs some adjustments. It can be invaluable in an emergency, but it does not last very long, and it is quite difficult..." The dizziness returned, and she trailed off, grasping for the nearest chair, which the manager pushed toward her like an obsequious suitor.

"You need rest," Liza said. "That healing potion cannot fix everything."

"Oh, yes," Siobhan agreed. "I am in desperate need of sleep. As always!" This thought was desperately, tragically hilarious, and before she knew it a high-pitched giggle that might have been edging on a crazed cackle burst from her throat.

She pressed a horrified hand to her mouth, shoving the embarrassing sound back down.

Lord Lynwood visibly shuddered.

Only Theo seemed to have any sympathy for her. He rose with great difficulty from the chair he had been curled up in while Katerin fussed over him, came to Siobhan's side, and patted her hand.

He didn't offer any words of consolation, but the gesture still caused Siobhan's eyes to burn with sudden emotion. She closed them lest anyone see a hint of extra shininess.

The manager cleared his throat. "You would be welcome to one of our private rooms, humble as they may be," he offered. "They are warded. Perhaps not to the mistress's standards, but safe enough, and all of us here would fight to defend the building from unwanted guests, if necessary. None will speak of your presence, on pain of death." He looked to Lord Lynwood for confirmation, but the man only nodded, his eyes on Miles.

Siobhan looked at Liza, who shrugged. Since the thought of trying to return to the University at this time seemed a little like a bad idea and a lot like torture, Siobhan agreed to the offer. She gestured to Liza, Gera, and then, after a moment, to Katerin as well. "Would you accompany me? I have some questions as well as some information to relay."

"I will keep watch over Millennium," Lord Lynwood assured Gera.

Katerin was reluctant to leave Theo, but when the boy offered to simply come along with too-bright eyes and a sudden surge of energy, she, too, agreed to leave the boy under the protection of Lord Lynwood and the various enforcers.

The room the manager offered was large and gaudily opulent, with gold-foiled filigree making an appearance on the walls and almost every piece of furniture. This was contrasted against vast amounts of red velvet. In the center of the room, a frankly enormous four-poster bed with a velvet canopy was featured.

Siobhan didn't have the presence of mind to hold back her grimace.

The manager noticed and bent at the waist immediately. "I apologize for the deficient standards of our establishment. I assure you, our hospitable spirit is not lacking. You are our honored guest, if there is anything you wish us to change, or anything—"

Siobhan waved her hand to silence him. "It's fine." She moved to the plush seat beside the bed and lowered herself carefully onto it.

When the manager had gone and the door was closed behind him, Gera moved to stand a couple meters in front of Siobhan and sank to her knees. "I thank you, and owe you a great debt, Queen of Ravens," she said, head bowed.

Katerin's jaw dropped, and even Liza, who had been moving to draw extra temporary wards on the walls, watched with surprised amusement.

34

———

AN ACT OF WAR

Gera seemed able to sense behind herself with whatever magic allowed the woman to function so effortlessly without her eye. She turned her head slightly towards Katerin's astonished face and then back to Siobhan. "Is it safe to speak freely with her here?" she asked.

Siobhan nodded. Katerin had not been involved in any of Siobhan's plans for Operation Palimpsest, but there was no need for secrecy anymore. The woman might speak to Oliver, but she wouldn't reveal any of Siobhan's secrets to the coppers or the Thirteen Crowns.

"What is going on?" Katerin asked, her throaty, biting accent thickening as her eyes narrowed.

Gera nodded to Siobhan but ignored Katerin's question. "I completed the task assigned to me to the best of my ability," she reported. "All seemed to go smoothly, but when I returned, Millennium was missing, along with several of the guards. One of the servants told me that they had run from enemies some hours before, while I was gone preparing. Everyone with legs to move and eyes to see was out looking for him, but with little luck. I feared the worst. I broke the bracelet that you gave me, but there was no response. Even my greatest efforts at divination could not find my son, nor any of those that disappeared with him. I spent hours futilely attempting to track his path."

The woman's voice wavered, and she paused to take a deep breath and loose it again.

Siobhan pulled the broken pieces of her own bracelets from her pockets, now having the presence of mind to count them and make sure none were missing. "We were deep beneath walls of stone. The magic on these trinkets was weak. No doubt, it failed to pass the barrier and petered out uselessly."

Katerin's eyes widened, and she pulled up her sleeve to reveal her own small handful of spelled bracelets.

"Any that are connected to me will be useless now," Siobhan said, standing up with some effort and using the knobs on the side of the fancy fireplace to automatically light the hardwood logs within. She tossed her bracelets into the flames, watching as they burned up. The magic was gone, but this was easier than casting the shedding-disintegration spell on the pieces.

Liza snorted derisively. "So amateurish," she muttered. Louder, she added, "I can make you something much better. For the right price."

Gera stood, tearing the other bracelets from her own arm and throwing them into the fire beside Siobhan's. "I called Mistress Liza in to assist with my attempts, but when I learned that it was the Pendragon Corps who had taken my son…" She trailed off, closing her sightless eye and shaking her head. "But you have returned him safely. I owe you a great debt."

Katerin was still giving Gera strange looks, but she, too, bowed to Siobhan. "You have my thanks as well. I was out managing one of our ventures, and heard about what had happened from one of the enforcers who was injured trying to protect my so—my nephew. The man was knocked unconscious early and did not get taken with the others. I am going to knock some sense into that boy, I swear it. I…" She shuddered. "I was so terrified. Why was he taken? How did you save him? And does it have anything to do with the Raven Queen's supposed multiple appearances today? I have been getting the most ludicrous reports, and everyone saw the ravens."

Gera smiled proudly.

"Was that *you*?" Katerin demanded. She turned her bloodthirsty gaze from Gera to Siobhan. "Did you *plan* this? Put Theo in danger intentionally, just so that you could be seen to save him?"

Gera's eye widened perceptibly, and she took a slow step back from Siobhan, placing her back against the wall beside the fireplace. Looking at Katerin, she gave small, surreptitious shakes of her head, as if trying to tell the other woman to shut up, but Katerin ignored her.

Siobhan raised her hand to cut off Katerin's impending tirade. "I did *not* place Theo, Miles, or any of those who attempted to protect them in danger. That was the High Crown. My ability to save them was a combination of great luck and terrible misfortune. I am too exhausted to retell the events in detail, but suffice it to say that I had something planned to take advantage of the proceedings. The High Crown had his own plan in place. He wanted to capture both children, perhaps to get yourself and Gera to turn on me. But I was in the right place at the right time, he badly misunderstood my capabilities, and his plan backfired. Also, Miles is very capable, and Theo very brave."

"Kidnapping our children may also have been a way to pressure us into asking another boon of you," Gera added, relaxing cautiously and stepping away from the wall. "And then, to trap you if you attempted to save them. You are known to be fond of children," she said to Siobhan.

Siobhan was too tired to ask what other things about her were supposedly "known." "That may be so. In any case, I was forced to promise two boons to ensure our escape. I would appreciate assistance fulfilling them. I would also appreciate your help keeping the families of those I brought out tonight safe. One man did not make it. He has a daughter."

Gera agreed immediately. "My power and resources will be turned to your purpose, as repayment. Nothing can compare to the worth of my son's life."

Katerin was less enthusiastic. "I might be able to help, depending on what you promised. Even though association with you is what endangered Theo in the first place," she added sourly. "What were you thinking, doing things like this in secret, behind our backs?"

Gera drew in a sharp breath and paled noticeably. She stared straight ahead with her sightless eye, her arms pressed to her sides as if hoping that extreme stillness would allow her to go unnoticed.

"Rude and thankless," Liza muttered from where she was drawing repeated glyphs along the walls.

Katerin's pale, slender neck flushed a few dozen shades lighter than her crimson hair, but she didn't look away from Siobhan.

The muscle under Siobhan's right eye was twitching. She'd run through so much adrenaline that day that she didn't have any left to grow truly angry, but she was equally out of patience. "I think you will find," she said in a slow, hard voice, "if you think about it a little harder, that association with"—she remembered at the last minute not to reveal Oliver's name—"Lord Stag is what endangered Theo. In fact, the same might be said for myself."

Katerin's face flashed through a series of emotions that Siobhan couldn't read. Finally, the woman pressed her thin lips together. "Perhaps you are right. But if not for him, Theo would likely have died as a babe. Lord Stag's actions are not without consequence, but they are decisions made for the greater good. And right now, he is out there desperately trying to gather information on what's happened to you and Theo. You don't know how worried he was—we both were," she corrected.

Siobhan wasn't sure if Katerin had caught any hint of Siobhan's suspicion and distrust, but if so, the woman didn't show it.

Siobhan sighed, then explained the terms of the agreements she had made with Parker and Anders. "In any case, the High Crown's plan failed, but we should not expect that the man will simply give up. He does not seem one to compromise, nor to accept defeat."

With that, Katerin agreed easily. "Especially not after the spectacle of today. No matter his intentions, I, for one, cannot forgive this insult. Assaulting and kidnapping our children was an act of war."

"Yes," Gera said simply.

"Don't be reckless," Liza said. "Also, I will warn you now, I have no desire to be involved in any hare-brained attempts at vengeance."

Gera bared her teeth. "But if Leandro Pendragon, cursed be his name, believes that he can simply get away with such things? That he is not only above the law, but above *retribution?*"

Siobhan stopped them before they could devolve into arguing and worsen her headache. "You may plan your revenge, but do not expect me to be a part of it. I must rest." When they didn't move, she waved her hand at them. "Go! Liza, stay," she added.

Liza gave her an exasperated huff. "Yes, master. Bark, bark, master. Should I roll over, too?" she asked dryly.

Siobhan flushed.

At the door, Katerin looked back. "Thank you once again. Sincerely. Theo is the most important thing in my life. If there is a next time for something like this, come to me." Then they were gone, the door closed behind them.

"I need help removing my corset," Siobhan told Liza. "Also, I believe I have broken a rib. And I definitely have Will-strain. I may have previously had a concussion, but the healing potions took care of that."

With a deep, put-upon sigh, Liza rubbed her forehead. "All of this is not what I agreed to. I am going to bill you for the difference." But when she had finished setting up the additional wards, she helped Siobhan with the ribbons and stays. As her corset was drawn away like the broken-open ribcage of some vivisected animal, Liza watched stoically while Siobhan whimpered in pain.

The leather contraption beneath the corset was much easier to remove, revealing the bloom of horrible bruises that looked weeks older than they should be. There were distinct depressions in her side where the stones of the holster had pressed most deeply into her flesh.

Liza ran her fingers over Siobhan's abdomen and spine, cataloguing Siobhan's flinches and whimpers of pain. "I'm no healer, but this isn't the first time I've seen a dislocated rib, girl. Lie down on your stomach," she commanded. And then, with some steady pressure followed by a strange, sudden motion, she slammed Siobhan's rib back into place.

The pain flared white-hot for a moment and then immediately died down.

"Closed reduction," Liza explained simply. Siobhan didn't know what that meant. "Your rib was probably fractured in addition to the dislocation, depending on how strong that healing potion you took was. But the bone is fine now. You just need to take it easy for a few weeks. No more healing potions for the time being. Trust me, you would greatly regret building up Radiant toxicity. Planar components are useful, but we mundane beings were never meant to be steeped in their energy."

Siobhan thanked Liza weakly for her help, then moved to sit on the edge of the too-plush bed. If she were attacked in her sleep, she would struggle to wade her way off of it. She considered her next words, but was too tired to try for tact. "I need to get into the severe-damage wing of the Retreat at Willowdale. I know you visit there. Can you get me past the security?"

Liza stilled, then turned to face Siobhan slowly and silently.

"I need to meet the only coherent survivor from the Black Wastes expedition," Siobhan explained.

Liza's voice came deep and slow. "Siobhan Naught. The parts of my life that I do not advertise are *private*. How dare you?" It was, perhaps, the first time that Siobhan had seen Liza truly angry. Usually, the woman grumbled and complained, but at most, deep down she was exasperated. Now, Liza's Will was tangible in the air to whatever hindbrain sense could discern such things, her head tilted a few degrees too low as if to hide the baring of teeth.

Siobhan was very aware of not only the battle wand disguised as a decorative stick holding Liza's bun in place, but also that pretty much every other piece of jewelry or clothing could be a battle artifact. *'Perhaps it would have been better to approach this when I was not so tired and prone to mistakes,'* she acknowledged.

Hurriedly, Siobhan said, "I learned about your visits by coincidence! I had no intention of prying into your business. I have not been following you or anything like that, and I do not know what you do there."

Liza was silent, still glaring, but at least she was listening.

"I understand the value of boundaries and privacy," Siobhan continued. "I have not, and will not, disrespect your privacy. If you take me, I won't ask questions, and I will do what you tell me."

Liza shook her head sharply.

"You can refuse," Siobhan allowed, "but I will still need to find a way to speak to that man."

"I *do* refuse," Liza said. "You will do well to keep your promises regardless."

The palpable pressure of Liza's anger still hung in the air, but Siobhan was quite literally too exhausted to worry about it. If Liza wanted to kill her at this moment, there was almost nothing Siobhan could do to save herself. Siobhan flopped back onto the bed, trying to defuse the tension. "Alright. But before you go, can you help me with one last thing?"

Liza remained silent, but she didn't leave. And as Siobhan explained the details of the dreamless sleep spell that she needed cast on her pillow, the clenched muscles in Liza's jaw and around her eyes relaxed.

It was not hard to link together the clues and realize that Siobhan had a secret of her own.

Liza cast the spell, using Siobhan's supplies and more power than Siobhan had ever been able to imbue it with. Before leaving, she paused at the doorway. "I will consider your request," she said, still staring at the door. And then she was gone.

Siobhan snuggled into the thick blankets and laid her head down on the spelled pillow that smelt of her familiar tinctures, staring at the fire. For a moment, it reminded her of Grandfather, and then of her nightmare "clawing away on the inside," as it had said.

She shuddered. Too exhausted for contemplation, she resolved to think of it later.

But Siobhan kept the crystal lamp on the bedside table turned on as she closed her eyes. The idea of being in complete darkness when the fire died down made her palms clammy and gave her the urge to look over her shoulder and under the bed for monsters.

35

DEATH WISH

Month 4, Day 9, Friday 11:30 p.m.

As Gera and Katerin left the Raven Queen's room, Gera eyed the red-haired woman dubiously. To be so disrespectful to the Raven Queen, Katerin must have a death wish. But, to Gera's surprise, the woman had only been mildly rebuked.

Perhaps she had done a favor for the Raven Queen at some point without receiving anything in return. Katerin might be using up a little of the credited goodwill that would have bought her with every moment of disrespect. Gera couldn't think of any other reasonable explanation.

If Katerin was not careful, she would spend over the limit of the Raven Queen's patience without realizing it. Gera could imagine the sudden and malicious retribution that would follow. The hair on her arms rose, and she pushed the thoughts away.

"I know you did not ask for my advice, but I will give it anyway, and freely. You should be more cautious. It is dangerous to be disrespectful to someone so powerful," Gera said.

Katerin snorted, still reckless from her fear and anger. "So powerful? She is still a young sorcerer. What can she do to me? I doubt she's going to try to arrange an assassination in revenge for a few words."

Gera blinked, a leftover habit from when she needed her eye to see and closing it could clear her vision. She opened her mouth and then closed it again as the confusion swirled and her understanding of the other woman rearranged itself. In a low, hesitant voice, she asked, "Surely you are aware that the Raven Queen is more than just a young thaumaturge? You have been involved in several of her endeavors, if only adjacently. Have you not received any reports on her abilities? Her body may seem youthful, but do not take the face of a thing as the reality of it."

Katerin sighed, patting her breast pocket and pulling out a pipe. As they walked back to their children, she took the time to silently pack the bowl with etherwood leaves and light it. Only after she had taken a puff and blown it out again did she speak. "Being a prognos, I had imagined you would be more insightful. The rumors circling about her are exaggerated."

Gera suppressed her immediate outrage at the doubt of her abilities. She had dealt with that kind of thing repeatedly since she lost her vision, and though she had grown used to it, she had not grown content. She, too, kept her silence for a while, until they reached the room where those who the Raven Queen had saved waited.

She checked that her son was fine, first, and was pleased to see him blinking sleepily but awake and unharmed. The healer nodded to her from where he was crouched over the leg of one of the young Verdant Stag enforcers, which had obviously sustained a grievous wound.

Gera's brother by choice, the leader of the Nightmare Pack, smiled at her. Wrinkles creased the corner of Lynwood's eyes. "Miles is well. Merely exhausted."

Gera picked Millennium up from his chair, ignoring the strain on her back muscles, and sat down with him in her lap. Only then did she speak. "Katerin, while you may know the Raven Queen's personality better than I, please do not make the mistake of thinking I judge her abilities only from rumors. I discern from what I have sensed and experienced. The Raven Queen is no ordinary, mundane sorceress."

Katerin, who had moved to stand beside Theo's chair and was carding her fingers through his copper curls, sighed. She pressed her lips together as if considering how to respond. "She is clever, intelligent, and innovative. She cares more for others, even strangers, than she lets on. I would also guess that she is fairly powerful for her age, and will one day be even more so. But these ideas that she is some vengeful and mischievous being with powers that others cannot understand?" Katerin shook her head. "She cannot hear prayers, accept offerings, or travel through the shadows. She is a human, and a sorcerer, and constrained to results that can be achieved with knowledge and accumulated power."

Several of the others were drawn to their conversation. A woman missing half her hair and sporting a wide stretch of mostly healed burn scars opened her eyes. She stood up from the corner where she had been sitting. Her skin glistened with the burn salve spread over her wounds, but she did not move as if in pain. She sneered, lifting her jaw and raising her unburned eyebrow. "An over-reliance on skepticism isn't rationality when the evidence of things outside of your prior experience is right in front of your face."

Katerin gaped, dumbfounded by the disdain dripping from the woman's words.

Gera nodded to the burned woman. "I am Gera, of the Lynwood family."

The woman nodded back. "Deidre Johnson, follower of the Raven Queen," she said before turning back to Katerin. "It may seem so amazing as to be unbelievable, but I have collected the evidence of her deeds, taken directly from those who have witnessed them. I'm thinking of collecting them all into a book to be copied. Perhaps you have never seen the Raven Queen in action? I, too, was somewhat skeptical deep in my heart. I played at believing, but until I was in her presence, I did not truly believe. But tonight, what I experienced..." Deidre shook her head.

A man sitting on the floor with his forehead on his knees finished her sentence. "It can never be denied." He wore a strange mix of nice boots and tattered, rough clothing, and Gera did not recognize him.

"When they took us, they put us into some void spell, our minds plucked from our bodies and tossed into the emptiness between life and death. It cannot have had any other purpose than to drive us insane," Deidre added.

Lynwood cursed, narrowing his eyes with hatred, and Katerin's fingers tightened hard enough in Theo's hair to make the boy wince and bat at her hand.

"It was entirely silent," Miles murmured wearily. "I couldn't even hear my own thoughts properly."

Gera rubbed his back in small circles. "You're safe now," she said, kissing his forehead.

Deidre nodded gravely. "Yes. The High Crown is an evil man, to order something like that done to anyone, but especially to children. But do not worry. I have noticed no lingering effects, perhaps due to the protection of the Raven Queen. She is obviously fond of both children."

The healer had been listening with interest at first, but now with growing unease. "I...don't think I should be here for this," he muttered. "I will be in my office. Have one of the workers call me if you need anything."

As he left, two men entered with a huge, decrepit dog limping along beside them.

The man with the strangely nice shoes and tattered clothes lunged forward, everything about his demeanor changing as he hugged the dog's neck, pressing his face into its short fur.

The creature was missing an eye and a leg, and its thin skin sagged in places and pulled tight in others, without any fat to mellow the appearance of stringy muscle and knobby bone beneath. It was either very sickly, very old, or both. The dog gave a low woof, its tail wagging lethargically.

"It'll all be worth it, if you can live for a long time," the man muttered into its fur, almost beyond the range of Gera's hearing. "If I don't lose you, too." He pulled back, looking into the dog's watery, clouded eye. "Sorry for waking you in the middle of the night, Bear," he said in conversational tones, running his hands over the creature's saggy neck and bony side. "I think we're going to have to move. But don't worry, I'll find you a place with a good spot by the window, where the sun comes through in the morning."

He looked up at the men who had escorted his dog, frowning. "Did you not get his favorite toy? I specifically mentioned it. A stuffed brown bear?"

The men shared a look, then one took out a ratty brown plush toy from the back of his waistband.

"How old is that dog?" Theo asked.

The man smiled sadly. "Twenty-two."

Katerin did a double take. "*How*?"

"An extremely delicate regimen of specialized potions. The same ones all those old Crown Family members take to keep one foot out of the grave. But the Raven Queen promised me she could heal him. His wounds were past the point they could be healed with most magic by the time I could afford to do so, and now he's got too much planar magic in him to handle the influx of anything that could regrow a long-forgotten limb."

His fingers ghosted over the stump of Bear's missing foreleg, his smile tight with anxiety. "She can fix that with her secret blood magic. It is the boon she promised for my aid. For Bear to be healthy and live 'an absurdly long time.' That's how she said it, I think."

"That dog has already lived an absurdly long time," Katerin said, pointing rudely. "Do you expect her to work miracles?"

The man glared at her.

Deidre cleared her throat. "If she promised it, she can do it. But to continue with my testimony..." She looked around, ensuring everyone's attention was back on her. "While trapped in the space between, I panicked horribly. It seemed my very soul would unravel." Deidre stared at the far wall with a haunted look in her eyes as she recalled the ordeal. "But then I prayed to the Raven Queen. I...did not actually believe that she would come. But I had to do something, and it was the only hope I could grasp onto. And she did come."

Katerin narrowed her eyes. "I was under the impression that she was taken along with the rest of you? So really, she would have been there whether you prayed or not."

The man with the dog and the maid Martha both shook their heads simultaneously.

The man spoke first. "I checked the identities of those we took."

Gera stiffened, giving him another perusal. Was this man one of Lord Pendragon's lauded elite? But the others seemed comfortable around him, which surely could not have been the case if he was one of their attackers.

He continued, "If the Raven Queen was already among the captives, then the rumors that she can shapeshift are accurate. However, I suspect that it is more likely that, rather than shapeshifting, she somehow possessed the body of one of the women—Silvia Nakai."

Millennium made a small sound of confusion, tilting his head to the side.

Katerin pressed her lips together as if she wanted to speak but was holding herself back.

Martha shook her head again. "No, it must be shapeshifting. Millennium led us to a woman who could supposedly help, and she *did* look similar. But at most she could have been the aunt of the woman we saw later. But Jackal recognized her, and Millennium did, too. They were the same person, right?" Martha looked to the two for confirmation.

Jackal nodded. "I saw her when we were helping out the Verdant Stag with that stuff at Knave Knoll. She looked different then, too. Lightning-blue eyes."

Gera hummed. "She is getting better at looking entirely human, it seems. I cannot see color and light as most can, but I am told she forgot to add the appearance of an iris around her pupil the first time we met, and that her hair shimmered with colors hidden in the black, like an oiled raven's feather."

Katerin had dropped her head into her hands and was rubbing her temples. "I need to sit down," she muttered, then dragged one of the few free chairs over to sit beside Theo. "There are both items and magic that can change one's appearance. It need not be some special shapeshifting skill. And..." She looked to the Pendragon operative. "Identities can be forged."

But Gera could see that Katerin was being slightly untruthful, hiding something. "You may lie to others," she said, "and even yourself. But you will find it harder to do so to me."

Martha, who had been nodding to herself as if Katerin had offered a reasonable explanation, looked between Gera and Katerin in surprise.

Katerin gave Gera a dirty look but remained silent.

The Pendragon operative spoke again. "I am not a good man, and I do not pretend that I am. But the spell we placed you under should not have had any long-term deleterious effects if the exposure was limited to less than a day. It was only meant to keep you from escaping or calling for help. Those tunnels were being retrofitted, but they were never meant to be used for anything more than an extra escape route for the Pendragon Family. So far from the palace, they don't have the same kind of embedded wards that the official Corps facilities do."

Lynwood snarled, the sound rumbling up from deep in his chest.

"It's true," the other man insisted, shifting closer to his dog. "The spell was developed to keep enemy spies from killing themselves when captured. I have experienced it myself, and it is far from the worst the Pendragon Corps has to offer. But I didn't consider the danger it might have presented to a child's undeveloped mind. Even I would have refused to torture children or animals." He looked up, meeting the gazes of the others who had been taken. "I am sorry," he added simply.

"Why keep us there at all?" asked Martha. "Surely there was some better place? Harrow—well, no, not Harrow Hill." Martha frowned at the floor, pinching her chin. "She already broke into and out of Harrow Hill twice. But surely the Pendragon Corps must have some secret jail?"

Deidre's eyes glinted. "Surely. But not quite as secret as the High Crown must have wanted, right?" she asked the Pendragon operative. "Not when he can't trust the University…and maybe not the Red Guard, either?"

The man gave her a nod and a half-shrug. "Perhaps. All I know for sure is that the High Crown had a cell created specifically to counteract her abilities. He spared no expense. Even I thought it would be inescapable. And if the Raven Queen had attacked in any more conventional way, from the *outside*, the wards may have stood, and our men would have been in position to deal with her. But she got inside somehow, without even triggering the alarms, and we hadn't done much of any preparation for a scenario like that. And then, once the Radiant cell proved useless…I made the only choice I could."

Deidre's smile was lopsided, avoiding the side of her face with burns.

Gera considered how she might repay her own debt through the second-hand fulfillment of the Raven Queen's promises. The High Crown would be after these people, and especially the traitor. It might be easiest to send the man far away, but if he was willing, Gera would prefer to keep him.

Her anger at the High Crown had diminished not at all with Millennium's safety. With every moment that passed with the knowledge of what the leader of their country had done, her wrath bubbled up hotter inside her.

Like a volcano, it would not stay contained forever. And keeping this former Pendragon Corps operative around would undeniably have its benefits, if he was willing to continue working on the Raven Queen's behalf. Or even on Gera's behalf, for payment in coin.

Deidre leaned over and placed a hand on the man's shoulder. "Atonement will be made with your actions, Anders. And as it is not given for free, you will know that you deserve it, and that it cannot be taken away from you."

Anders grimaced. "Well, that's a hassle. But back to the topic of the Raven Queen's arrival, I am more inclined to believe your theory, Deidre. Everyone under the effects of our spell was totally incapacitated. Parker and I were on guard anyway, because we're professionals. It had been hours with no sign of anything strange. And then, suddenly, the shadows started moving on their own. But not like normal shadows. Total blackness. It seemed like they were exploring around the room, and then they found what they were looking for and fell onto one of the women. And then she started moving. I ran to get help, but Parker stayed behind. He saw the whole thing."

Jackal had taken out a small dagger and begun to play with it. "It *was* very strange, the way she moved. Especially in the beginning. Like a puppet on strings. And when she coughed up darkness... What did you all make of that?"

"Imperfect possession," the young man in the corner with the leg injury said, piping up for the first time. He nodded to Gera and the others, introducing himself as Enforcer Turner. "That's what I think, anyway. And maybe it wasn't the first time, if the woman knew to pray for it. So she's an acolyte of the Raven Queen or whatever. She's got a special connection. Things go wrong for her, and she calls for help. Maybe she promises some kind of payment, maybe not. The Raven Queen hears her, and maybe she hears Deidre too, and sends... I don't know."

He waved a hand vaguely, shrugged, and continued. "Is the darkness the Raven Queen herself? A piece of her? Some strange creature of shadow that can channel her presence? Maybe it's even a spell. Whatever it is, it allows the Raven Queen to use some of her abilities and partially control the body of the woman," he concluded confidently.

Enforcer Turner hesitated, then rubbed his chapped lips together and asked, "Did you guys notice that a couple times, the darkness split twice?" When no one responded, he said, "There was the physical, flesh-and-blood woman, cloaked in darkness. And the warrior shadow creature with that giant beak." He mimed a pulling motion in front of his nose, drawing the approximate shape of the creature's single facial feature with a grimace. "But a couple times, there was *another* woman, made entirely of darkness. I think that was the actual Raven Queen, manifesting separately to make sure her shadow servant was handling the danger to her acolyte properly, or something."

Enforcer Turner looked around, and seeing that everyone was listening intently, continued with more enthusiasm. "So after coming in with the darkness to find her acolyte, the Raven Queen is trying to get everyone out, and then the guards come and attack her with fireballs and that Radiant bomb. And the light is too strong, or the connection through the shadows is too weak, and it disrupts things for a moment. They take the woman away, and I don't know what happened then, but obviously the Raven Queen came back, tried again, and got her out. And when she did, Anders and that poor Parker guy were suddenly on her side."

Anders nodded. "We took her to the cell. It was an extremely well-warded room imbued with Radiance in every centimeter, from the floor to the ceiling. It took a while for the living darkness to regain its strength, but light is not the debilitating weakness we believed it would be."

"A shadow is always darkest against the light," Deidre said as if reciting something, though Gera suspected the woman just liked to make up phrases that sounded meaningful.

"Yes. The flesh of her body was contained, but her power…" Anders shuddered. "Her power was not contained. I—I am not ashamed to say that seeing it spill through the doorway and stand up again was one of the most horrifying moments of my life. It does not have a body like us. I am not sure that there is even the suggestion of flesh under its cloak. But you can feel it. It is cold. But not just cold. It was hungry. *Empty*. It touched me—to threaten me, and I could sense its wrongness."

Anders rocked forward and back, his arms around his knees, then relaxed as Bear hobbled forward to lick his face and lean against him. "It's normal to lose heat when you touch something cold, but this felt different. I can't explain it."

He clutched the dog to his side, petting Bear absentmindedly as the creature drooled on his pants. "So she said that if we didn't help, she would have to make us enemies, and then she would get out anyways, after plucking the necessary knowledge from our minds, and, I guess, utilizing our dead bodies to work the lock. And she offered to help Bear. And something for that idiot Parker, too. So we made a pact and let her out. And she was *definitely* moving like a puppet on strings for a while there."

Turner nodded eagerly. "Yes! So the Raven Queen gets the woman's body out, and then we all go on the attack. She's not content to let the High Crown keep any of our stuff, like, *at all*. And maybe she is a little weak to Radiance, but the body she's using is hurt. Maybe from the fighting, or maybe just from whatever she has to do to keep control of it. So she takes one of those healing potions anyway, because she cares about her believers. In a whole, 'I protect what's mine,' kind of way, right?"

"Most certainly," Deidre agreed.

"Yes! So she took the potion anyway. And then, when we were escaping and the reinforcements came after us, did you see how she fought? I saw her slap a fireball aside into the wall. And the shadow warrior, or living darkness, whatever you call it, it definitely has some connection to nightmares. I'm thinking it pulls on a person's greatest fear. The way it moved… Did anyone see it crawling on the ceiling?"

Martha raised her hand solemnly, as did one of the few who had yet to speak, a Verdant Stag enforcer. "I saw it."

The Verdant Stag enforcer added, "Whatever it is, it holds to none of the laws of a mortal being. I speak not just of gravity but…also the laws of space? I don't pretend to be some master of natural science, but the way that thing moved, still for one moment and then, in the space of a blink, somewhere else. It shouldn't be possible."

Turner lifted a finger. "Let me also point out the darkness fabric, always moving in some wind no one else can feel? Did you notice how it waves rhythmically, on a kind of repeated pattern, and sometimes with that cold fog wafting off it?"

The Verdant Stag enforcer tried to crack his knuckles, pressing too hard but not seeming to feel the pain. "I'm pretty sure some of the shadow warrior's joints bent backward when it was...you know. Crawling inside that man. Which also, just—" He heaved with sudden nausea, holding a hand to his throat. Then he looked to Katerin. "I'm sorry, but if you think the Raven Queen is anything like a run-of-the-mill sorcerer, either she really did descend on that woman tonight and you've only ever met her acolyte, or you don't know her at all."

Deidre smiled again, looking down her nose at Katerin.

Katerin was less dismissive than she had been, but more disturbed. "I know Siobhan. She would have come to me, to us, if there was some being *possessing* her," she said, but Gera could hear the note of underlying uncertainty in her voice.

Millennium frowned. No doubt, he could hear even deeper.

Martha clenched her fists around the fabric at her knees. "We all saw her cough out darkness," she said in a small voice.

"It was pretty obvious," Enforcer Turner agreed.

Jackal looked at Katerin's pinched expression with sympathy. "Maybe the Raven Queen finds it amusing that some people mistake her for a normal woman," he suggested. "She's got a wicked sense of humor, according to the stories. And I mean that literally."

Enforcer Turner grinned, pale faced. "Oh, yeah. Did all of you hear the things she was saying to me while she was working her blood magic on my leg? I could hear the smile in her voice. That's part of why I was thinking maybe she feeds on fear."

"And she agreed that she could use that darkness just the same for m—" Deidre cleared her throat. "For someone loyal, if they were willing to bear the side-effects."

"I bet it hurts a lot," Enforcer Turner said, shaking his head quickly. "No, thank you."

Millennium shook his head. "You guys are making her seem weird and scary, but she's not—well, actually... She is *really* scary."

He looked to Theo for confirmation, and the other boy nodded solemnly. "*Really scary,*" he echoed.

"But she's not weird," Miles continued. "She's nice, and she knows a lot of strange and amazing things, and she can help you if you have nightmares or visions or need help with your sleep."

"She does know a lot of really awesome stories," Theo agreed. "But the first time I met her, she was pretending to be a totally normal homeless person. And she can totally shapeshift. Like, *big time.*" Fingers splayed, he spread his hands wide for dramatic emphasis, and then jumped as Katerin secretly pinched him on the side. He scowled at her. "What? It's not like they didn't already guess." He turned back to them. "You better not tell anyone. She would probably be upset. But if you ask her real nice-like, she'll play with you with magic. That's how I met Empress Regal."

Katerin raised one eyebrow. "Empress Regal, your imaginary raven friend?"

"Empress Regal is not imaginary!" Theo protested. "She just won't come when *you're* around. And maybe it's because you refuse to give her any gold, which I *told* you she wants."

Deidre seemed quite interested in this, but her attention was drawn back to Millennium as he ignored Theo and continued speaking. "But she's basically normal. The Raven Queen is just another one of her names. I don't think she's possessed or anything, even if she does have a strange echoey sound to her whispers."

"What is this about her whispers, darling?" Gera asked.

"Well, she sounds different from most people. It's…well, I don't know how to explain it. Like if she were in a crowd of people, she'd be the only one walking around with a bubble of water around her. Or, like, she sounds just a little behind and ahead at the same time?" He squeezed his eyes shut and rubbed at his ears, though just as with Gera's eyes, plugging his ears would not stop him from hearing.

"Shh," she whispered. "I was only curious, you need not stress yourself."

Deidre raised both eyebrows and then winced when the motion tugged on her burns. "We know that she likes children. She would want them to be comfortable around her. And I think we all heard the boy say how he *doesn't dream anymore,*" she added pointedly, then looked at Gera. "That is thanks to the Raven Queen?"

"Indeed. I do not know what Millennium told you, but I will not reveal the details. Suffice it to say, she saved his life," Gera said. "*All others* had failed. It was not a matter of gold, nor influence, nor of those we called upon lacking experience or skill. She did what others could not."

"Sleep is one of her domains of power," Deidre agreed.

Katerin had grown pale, and the muscles around her eyes were tight. Most likely, she was now replaying all the times she had offended the Raven Queen in her mind and remembering all the clues she had missed and times she had been deceived.

Jackal raised his hand to draw their attention. "What I want to know is, how do the rules work? The woman either was the Raven Queen from the beginning—"

Turner interrupted him excitedly. "Oh, if she really is, maybe, like, she only has limited power and most of the time, it's sleeping? Maybe it takes time to recover. But then when it's important, or someone makes her really angry, that part wakes up? The *dark* part," he added gleefully, rubbing his palms together.

Jackal continued, speaking a little louder to express his irritation at the interruption. "That woman either was the Raven Queen *from the beginning*," he repeated, "or she prayed to her. And presumably, if she did need to pray to her, she made some kind of agreement at that time. We all know that the Raven Queen requires payment for any boon she gives or favor she does, preferably in advance. Anders here made a very explicit pact with her, and fulfilled his side of the bargain already. But what about the rest of us?"

"I will pay for my son," Gera said immediately.

"And I," Lynwood added. They shared a wordless glance of understanding, and he squeezed her elbow with warm fingers.

Jackal nodded at them both. "Of course, and the Raven Queen is probably fine with that. She likes children, like Deidre said. But you can't pay for all of us, and would she even let you, if you could? Is there any precedent for what to do in this situation?"

Hesitantly, Gera brought up Mrs. Dotts, who had been in a somewhat similar predicament to this one. "Mrs. Dotts told me that the Raven Queen said she doesn't take offerings, only tributes," Gera remembered. "But sometimes she will accept favors paid later."

Lynwood crossed his leanly muscled arms, glowering. "It is good to ask these questions. These are the kind of conditions that can lead to...ironic conclusions." Surely most of them in this room could think of more than a few childhood tales of beings that traded in favors, and the unfortunate endings of those stories.

Deidre nodded. "I've heard that. If you pray to her with a request and she doesn't take your offering, she's either not listening or she didn't agree. But sometimes, a raven will come and accept the tribute on her behalf. And when that happens, you know that your problem will be solved. Of course, if your tribute wasn't substantial enough...maybe you will remain in her debt. I've also heard that you can collect goodwill and make her more likely to notice you by feeding the ravens. One man nursed a raven with a broken limb back to health, and the week after he released it back into the wild, he had a dream of the bird. He woke up to find that his shop had been selected for a huge contract that would earn enough money to send all three of his children to school."

Martha worried at her bottom lip. "So can we pay her back with favors she didn't specifically ask for? I really don't like the idea of being on the hook for anything, at any time, indefinitely."

"I have been thinking about that," Gera said. "When I spoke with the

Raven Queen privately earlier, she mentioned that we may plan our own revenge on the High Crown, but that we should not expect her to be a part of it, because she needed to rest. However, we know her to be vengeful and, frankly, vindictive."

Several of the others nodded gravely.

"So unless she somehow already obtained her revenge, she will be carrying it out later. Once she has rested. Perhaps, rather than attempt revenge of our own, we can simply be ready to lend our own efforts to hers when the time comes. This could be dangerous. If you feel that you would prefer to pay her back in a different way, perhaps you could do so proactively. She once did the same for me, choosing to pay me back for a small favor I had done her in a way that I did not request or expect."

3 6

───────────

PYRRHIC FAILURES

Thaddeus
Month 4, Day 10, Saturday 7:30 a.m.

Much of the night was spent at the Raven Queen's various crime scenes searching for some tiny bit of evidence that might have been missed, and questioning civilians. Despite Titus's growing agitation and the air of dogged desperation that suffused the coppers, Thaddeus took some time to nap in the carriage, as none of this was so important that he felt the need to miss an entire night of sleep. It was not he who had to answer to the High Crown, and Thaddeus was already mostly sure that the Raven Queen had left no special clues for him.

In the morning, Titus received a summons to Pendragon Palace. The shadows under his eyes seemed to grow deeper, all his frustrated energy momentarily constrained to stillness and silence. Finally, he raised his eyes to the northeast, to the white and gold palace sitting atop the white cliffs. It bathed in the light of the rising sun while the fog that rose up around it created a sort of golden aura.

Thaddeus considered for a few seconds and then invited himself along.

Titus gripped Thaddeus's forearm and gave him a weak but sincere smile. "Thank you," he said in a low voice, seemingly under the impression that Thaddeus had made this decision for *Titus's* benefit.

Thaddeus did not disabuse him of this notion. When the three of them arrived, Investigator Kuchen stayed with the carriage to keep watch on the distagram in case urgent information should be relayed. One of the palace guards led Titus and Thaddeus to Lord Pendragon, more commonly known as the High Crown.

The man wore no crown today. He had a surprisingly lush head of long greying hair, which hung down to his lower back. It had been artfully braided in circles and looping patterns capable of holding a minor magical charge.

He was gathered with several advisors and a full cohort of his personal corps in a high-ceilinged room with an oversized settee rather than a throne. Bookshelves lined the wall behind a huge desk, which was accompanied by several smaller desks to each side.

An entire wall made of glass—or perhaps crystal—overlooked Gilbratha. Just before the transparent wall, a circular pond filled with bright blue, gold, and purple fish sat recessed into the polished white marble floor.

The High Crown stood behind the large desk, reading through reports with a heavy scowl on his face.

Though this was not the throne room or the war chambers, the handful of advisors present had placed themselves as if it were. They stood facing each other in two groups before either side of his huge desk, leaving a walkway between them. Only the High Crown and the Crown Archivist could sit. His advisors stood, with their own underlings and assistants behind them.

Behind and to the side of the High Crown's desk, a group of Pendragon operatives stood in full uniform and at attention.

Lord Rouse, the sycophantic, information-hoarding weasel of the twelfth Crown Family, was present, with the elegantly beautiful Ambassador to the Public standing behind him, but they were missing the other ten lords of the Crown Families. Most of the other advisors were minor nobles and those more trusted by the High Crown.

That, in fact, might be why they were meeting here, rather than somewhere more traditional. Surely some of the other Crown Families had concerns about the Raven Queen.

The High Crown's scowl grew heavier as Titus and Thaddeus entered. "Lord Commander Westbay," he said.

Titus stiffened further, all signs of his earlier rhythmic fidgeting completely absent as he moved to stand along the front line of one of the groups, no assistants or underlings present to stand behind him. Investigator Kuchen had escaped an unpleasant situation.

Thaddeus was not beholden to the High Crown, and so he instead moved to lean against one of the support pillars a bit further back, but still close enough to see and hear everything that happened.

The Internal Inquisitor stood even further back than Thaddeus, inconspicuous against the far wall, in modest clothes that seemed to blend in. Most likely, they were enchanted to make him less remarkable, which was a desirable quality for someone in his position. This was a man that even the Crown Families feared; his duty was to deal with social unrest and treason.

"Please explain the debacle of the last twenty-four hours from your own perspective," the High Crown ordered.

Titus went down on one knee, bowing his head. "I apologize for our failure to apprehend the Raven Queen, my lord." The High Crown remained silent, so Titus proceeded to honestly explain the sequence of events. He did not try to make himself or his people look any worse or better than they were, and the High Crown seemed surprised at none of it.

When he was finished, the High Crown waved his hand in frustration and allowed Titus to rise from the uncomfortable position. "I wish I could say that your failure surprises me, but I am not so foolish. Woe unto those who cannot recognize a *trend*," he said pointedly.

Titus did not flinch.

"This is why I came up with a backup plan that included a more urgent and compelling impetus for her to take action." The High Crown turned to one of his most trusted advisors, the Recipient of Edicts, and nodded.

The man bowed in acknowledgment, then stepped forward. "We were able to identify and locate several targets of high value, who, taken hostage, were likely to incentivize key parties. Namely, the criminal forces who have shown a positive relationship with the Raven Queen. We judged them quite likely to beseech her for aid."

The Recipient of Edicts swallowed to wet his throat and licked his lips. "Our divination experts and personality profilers deduced that if we gave her a hint to their location, the most likely outcome was an attack by the Raven Queen in an attempt to save these targets. Alternatively, refusal could have caused discord between the Raven Queen and her allies." The man's eyes flicked toward the High Crown nervously. "The marked tendency toward loyalty from those who have interacted with her has caused us a great deal of difficulty. We judged that, even in a non-optimal outcome, creating a rift could allow us to incentivize her allies to become informants."

"Who, exactly, did you take hostage?" Thaddeus asked, his voice cutting sharply through the room despite the fact that the High Crown had not given him permission to speak. He received a few sharp looks, but no rebuke.

The advisor looked to the High Crown for permission. Receiving it, he said, "Theodore Russey and Millennium Lynwood, young scions of the Verdant Stags and the Nightmare Pack, were taken along with their companions and attempted protectors, which...may have been a mistake." His fingers tapped nervously on the seam of his pant leg. "We couldn't have known. The Raven Queen is rumored to care especially for children, and these two are connected to those in positions powerful enough to hold sway with her. We had hoped to take a third, for insurance, but the last escaped our grasp."

The High Crown sent Thaddeus a sharp glance filled with a surprising amount of suspicion.

"Children?" Titus murmured. He swallowed, then followed Thaddeus's lead in ignoring courtesy and asked, louder, "Were the children harmed? Was anyone killed?"

The advisor looked to the uniformed Pendragon Corps captain, his rank proudly announced by the badge at his shoulder. The middle-aged man had a shaved head contrasted by surprisingly thick, dark eyelashes. The captain shook his head. "Some injuries, no deaths. We inspected the children upon capture, and they were healthy."

Titus relaxed, but Thaddeus's mind was still hooked on that suspicious glance from the High Crown. Who else fit the criteria—young, helpless, and positively associated with the Raven Queen? The answer came quickly.

While Thaddeus's apprentice might not be entirely useless, he would stand no chance against the Raven Queen or the Pendragon Corps. And with the boon the Raven Queen had given him, she had forged a connection between them in the High Crown's mind.

Rage flowed through Thaddeus so quickly that he swayed on his feet from the force of it. His vision tinted red, and before he made the conscious decision to do so, he was already lifting a hand toward the High Crown, the Word of a spell to rend the man into seven pieces forming in his mind.

The High Crown flinched back, and two of his personal force hurried to place themselves between their master and the sudden danger Thaddeus presented.

Forcefully, Thaddeus reined himself in, curling his fingers into a clenched fist so tight it might leave bloody crescents in his palm. He lowered his hand.

Beside him, Titus had reared back in horror. At the back of the room, the Internal Inquisitor was watching expressionlessly. And in front of the High Crown's desk, the Court Sorcerer was sneering at Thaddeus.

"My apprentice was the third," Thaddeus said simply, still staring at the High Crown. "But you didn't capture him. Where is he?"

The High Crown's lips curled back in a combination of derision and superiority. If he were a man born of lower breeding, he might have spit on the floor and cursed. Instead he said, "If he was not with you, then who knows where that troublesome child might be? Perhaps in the bosom of the Raven Queen, even now. Remember yourself, Grandmaster Lacer. *All* in Lenore bow to my rule. If I had told you of my plan ahead of time, you would have given the boy to me yourself."

Thaddeus's eyelids fluttered with renewed rage, quickly suppressed. The Red Guard, the Architects of Khronos, and the Raven Queen herself were proof enough that the first statement was untrue. And as for the second, Thaddeus found it *exceedingly* unlikely that he would have capitulated to such a demand. He could think of six alternatives of varying violence—and reckless-ness—off the top of his head.

But Thaddeus did not say any of this out loud. Instead, he changed the subject. "Your plan worked. At least to draw her attention and ire. But obviously, she escaped. So what went wrong?"

"Obviously the information provided to His Eminence from the supposed 'experts' was all wrong," Lord Rouse said, looking pointedly at the Recipient of Edicts, who adroitly shot back a nasty look using only the side of his face that was hidden from the High Crown, while the other side remained placid.

The High Crown's temples pulsed as he clenched his jaw.

The Pendragon Corps captain nodded at another of the operatives, who stepped forward and laid out an unfolding metal Circle, obviously based on the innovations of the portable war Circles. The man used this to cast an illusion, including both visuals and sound.

The spell's fidelity was obviously substandard, the clarity of the caster's Will wavering. But while it might not have been technically flawless, the illusion was captivating. The man portrayed his own point of view as he and his companions loaded a group of unconscious men and women into the back of a wagon. The illusion focused on one woman in particular as the other people and environment blurred into indistinguishability.

She seemed to be in her forties, though she could be much older if she was a practiced thaumaturge, with light brown skin and long hair, both tinted with warmth. Someone, perhaps out of the operative's sight, or even he himself, said the words, "Silvia Nakai," in a muffled, distant tone.

The illusion fizzled out and then reappeared abruptly, this time showing the man's view as he ran down a white stone hallway, a thick battle wand in one metal-gauntleted hand.

Darkness coalesced behind the window of a door, roiling like the surface of a cauldron. The man and his similarly outfitted companions worked together to open the door and then fire spells inside blindly.

The Raven Queen appeared in triplicate, each body of darkness moving in tandem as she ducked strangely to the side, her joints at too-sharp angles and her response speed almost inhumanly quick. A physical leg, bare at least to the thigh, poked out of the shadows in the wrong place for a moment, then drew back into the darkness.

Thaddeus stared in fascination as the Pendragon operative threw in a device about the size of a cantaloupe, and the Raven Queen shrieked a warning to her companions, the darkness abandoning its human forms and moving as if to shield her against the device's effects.

There was a flash of brightness, so white it blinded the Pendragon opera-tive. When the illusion returned, he and another were carrying the Raven Queen, though she was stripped of her magical shadow and looked significantly different than the woman they had first thrown into the carriage. Younger. Prettier, though in a strange way that seemed subtly and disturbingly *off*. And more damaged, Thaddeus noted. She sported what looked to be a shattered eye socket, and a translucent pink liquid filled her ear cavity.

They locked her in a room that, even through the filter of the man's recollection, was eye-searingly bright, and then the memory jumped once again.

One of the other operatives, injured and panicked, sent this man and several others off to catch the escaped Raven Queen. Then, in a jerky transition, the view panned over the dead bodies of those who had stayed behind. "If Parker hadn't sent us away, that would have been us, too," the caster murmured. "We thought maybe he ran when she attacked, or maybe his body was cooling in the dark somewhere unseen. But no. We found him soon."

Again, time was skipped, and now the man was running with a group through a dark hallway. They turned a corner and came upon the Raven Queen and a dozen or so others, a bright lantern sending stark shadows stretching out behind them. The same operative who had sent them away stood behind her.

A murmur arose, and Thaddeus let out a sharp breath of amusement through his nose. How embarrassing for the High Crown. The Red Guard's methods of ensuring loyalty were seemingly much more effective than those of the Pendragon Corps, but Thaddeus knew well that nothing could truly ensure loyalty from one who did not wish to give it. Many a witch had discovered this. Even Thaddeus himself was proof of that fact.

The Raven Queen turned toward the caster's point of view slowly, the movement of her head trailing unnaturally behind her body. The upper half of her face was visible here, the darkness of her cloak, hair, and feathers fluttering in a wind that seemed to touch only her. Her eye socket was significantly less damaged, as if she had received healing between the memories. But her features looked even stranger than before. Her cheekbones were too sharp, her eyes too dark and sunken, remaining shadowed despite the brightness of the light turned on her.

Thaddeus grimaced at the caster, who was watching his own illusion replay his experiences—or more accurately, his memories—with obvious fear.

Even if a shaman had worked with him to help clarify and solidify his memories, the mind kept only imperfect copies of reality, accessed and recopied imperfectly each time like a child's game of whispered gossip. In situations of great stress, fidelity fell even further. This version of events was appropriately dramatic, but its resemblance to what had *actually* happened could only be left to the imagination.

Darkness swirled up, obscuring the Raven Queen's form completely for a moment before falling back down to reveal her hand held in a Circle in front of her lips. Several people around the room flinched as the Raven Queen's mouth fell open, her jaw unhinging and her cheeks stretching like some kind of deep-sea monster. Until, from deep in her throat, darkness boiled up.

In the man's memories, this darkness rushed at him like a racing snake, and then there were several long moments of blindness interspersed with flashes of light and spell-fire, until someone had the presence of mind to unleash a wind spell.

"A philtre of darkness?" Thaddeus wondered. "But if so, what was the Circle for?" He glanced around, taking in the others' response to what was being shown.

To his surprise, it was the Pendragon operatives—nominally hardened, skilled men—who had the most visceral response. Several were pale, and one was even hugging himself and trembling faintly as he watched the illusion.

Perhaps not a philtre of darkness, then. Or not just darkness. To engender such an effect, she might have used a fear hex. A powerful one, to have seated the emotions so deeply that they reared up again now.

The illusion's caster was breathing hard. He closed his eyes for a moment, letting the image fade. "When you're in the darkness, you can feel it watching you. It's huge, all-knowing."

The man who was hugging himself nodded. "It's like gazing into the night sky and suddenly realizing that each and every star is actually an eyeball. And as soon as you realize that, they all look at you. They can feel that you've discovered them."

Thaddeus rubbed his jaw, the short hairs of his beard scratching back and forth against each other. "Interesting."

Impatient, the High Crown urged the operative to continue with his display.

The Raven Queen leaned into the force of the wind spell, a piece of her shadow breaking off from the part surrounding her and rising up to the ceiling. She opened her too-large mouth once more. Though darkness continued to billow up from inside, streaking out behind her as it was caught on the air, this time she spoke.

The sound was...disconcerting. Even Thaddeus felt the hair on his arms rise in an instinctive response as she paraphrased sections of the letter she had left at the Edictum Council. Her words seemed to come from underwater, with an echo, but were also distorted unpredictably, with some parts stretching out like a song and others compressing into a sudden snap.

But while her imprecation continued, the Pendragon operative's viewpoint swung upward to follow the shadow companion that had broken away.

Thaddeus examined its form with interest, noting the too-thin, too-long limbs, the enormous beak that seemed to be the only feature of its face, and its complete lack of adherence to gravity. He wondered, if they examined the ceiling where this had happened, would they find puncture or scratch marks in the stone, or, as he suspected, would it be marked only by the useless spells they fired at and through it?

It moved with insect-like quickness despite its size. Whenever the almost constant flashes of spell-fire fell to a moment of darkness, it seemed to jump forward with zig-zagging motions, moving impossibly quickly, as if freed from realistic constraints by its lack of visibility.

When it fell into the midst of the caster's group, Thaddeus began to understand the reactions of the men who had, presumably, been present during this fight.

The creature loomed almost impossibly large, and a white fog wafted off its void-black form. "Cold air," Thaddeus murmured with surprise. "Oh, that's clever." Was it a side-effect, or was that the source of the creature's—or perhaps the spell's—power?

But he had no time to dwell on speculation, as the operative fell to the ground and tried to crawl away from the creature, which was now behind him. His panicked scrabbling took him closer to the Raven Queen herself.

She stepped forward and batted an enormous fireball spell into the wall with her bare hand. Thaddeus took a deep breath, wondering at the lack of a Conduit. Was that reality, or just a failing of this man's observational skills?

She swayed on her feet for a moment, her sunken eyes growing unfocused as a bloody tear ran down her cheek. She wiped it away and stared at it with surprise, and in a flash of light the white of her right eye appeared clearly. It was completely crimson surrounding the blackness of her pupil and iris. The eye looked straight into Thaddeus's, piercingly focused, as if it could feel his gaze through time and the filter of this man's memory.

The Pendragon operative apparently found this enough incentive to return the way he had come. Those enemies of the Raven Queen that remained now huddled together to shield against the escaping group's spell-fire. This worked for a short while, as the shadow companion had disappeared at some point when the operative was trying to crawl away.

But soon, it reappeared, dozens of ravens flying through the enemy group's midst from seemingly nowhere. The ravens coalesced around the man at the front of their formation, and the shadow-creature reformed, descended upon him.

Thaddeus watched, wide-eyed, skin tingling, as the creature clawed its way into the man's mouth and squeezed itself inside him. It seemed to go on forever, but in reality it happened quite quickly.

There was a long moment of stillness and silence, both from the illusion and in the present room.

Thaddeus replayed the images in his mind, his blood rushing with excitement. Surely, no matter how distorted the man's memories, he could not have fabricated something like that. What, exactly, would the shadow companion do to a person, once inside them?

The operative casting the illusion let the light decohere again as he took several long, deep breaths and wiped away the sweat beaded along his pale forehead. "Jorgensen is still alive," he croaked, his voice wavering. "We don't know what that thing did to him. The healers can't tell." Without having to be asked, he resumed the illusion, showing himself raising his battle wand to Jorgensen and stepping back warily. Then, the illusion fell dark. "The Raven Queen and her followers were gone. Disappeared into more of that watching darkness. We...made the decision not to follow without reinforcements."

No one suggested that had been the incorrect response.

The Pendragon Corps captain glanced at the inert metal spell array on the floor and then around at all of them. "During the events you just saw, the Raven Queen was also active in several other places throughout the city. Simultaneously," he clarified, for anyone too stupid to understand him the first time. "She later escaped into the Charybdis Gulf by stealing a boat. We were able to retrieve one of the two men who betrayed the High Crown for her, but all others went free."

The Advisor of Virtue let out a deep breath and summarized the sentiment of the room. "*Fuck.*"

37

CICATRIZE

SIOBHAN
Month 4, Day 10, Saturday 11:30 a.m.

SIOBHAN WOKE to the metaphorical scream of a full-to-bursting bladder. She struggled her way out of the too-soft bed and stumbled to the magical chamber pot. As she relieved herself, she stared blearily at the rays of the mid-morning sun slipping through the edges of the curtains. The light hurt her eyes and brought her attention to the deep throbbing in her skull, like the slow rumble of distant thunder or a thousand approaching war drums.

As she stood again, memories of the day before hit her like a maelstrom. She stumbled, stilled for long enough to regain her balance, and made her way to the bench in front of the vanity mirror.

She found herself staring at the ornate frame with a distant dread and had to force herself to focus on her reflection.

Her lips were pale and cracked, and the sclera around her right eye was the muddy brown of old blood. Healed, but not fully renewed. At least she could see out of it properly. None of the empty spots or floating lights. No hints of anything that shouldn't be there in her peripheral vision.

She stared into the darkness of her own eyes, searching for signs of something else moving beneath their surface. The dream she'd had while under the sensory deprivation spell was no invention of a panicked subconscious. Something was inside her, locked away by Grandfather's seal.

Trying to get out.

Siobhan didn't believe the things it had told her about Grandfather having gone insane by that time, wanting to hurt her. Grandfather had died to save her.

And then the Red Guard had come in and razed the entire village to the ground. They had to, to destroy the infection.

And Siobhan had spent the last seven years now doing her best not to think about it. That still seemed safest, especially now that she had seen a glimpse of what lay beyond the seal.

Siobhan had recognized that golden eye, and it had not belonged to Grandfather. His eyes had been a rather non-distinct blue. And she feared that pulling on the memory of where such an eye really came from would lead to other memories, ones that should stay gone.

She knew the beginning, and she knew the end. Only the middle was gone, and that did not feel safe enough.

But the nightmare had revealed something to her. Grandfather had wanted her to go to one of his acquaintances to help "settle the matter" for good. Unfortunately, Siobhan had no idea who that might be. If Grandfather had told her, that memory was lost in the middle. And with the town and everything in it being gone, there was no possibility of going through his belongings to try to find some hint of a friend or contact who might have expertise in this kind of thing.

However, it was also possible that the whole clue was a trick, that there was no friend of Grandfather's, no permanent solution to her problem. That it was only an enticement to open a box of horrors. Horrors that, once released into the world, could never be stuffed back inside the box again.

Siobhan forced herself to drink some water from her canteen despite the lump in her throat. Professor Lacer had mentioned that to split one's Will probably required some kind of self-mutilation. *'Should I stop practicing with that technique? But Myrddin seems to have been able to do it. Maybe Professor Lacer was wrong.'* Her practice with Myrddin's journal hadn't been causing any noticeable side-effects. And without that ability, she would have been dead by now.

She gave herself a small, ironic smile. *'Even if I shouldn't have been able to do such a thing, I can now. Stopping will not fix whatever is wrong.'*

Feeling as if she carried the weight and dust of a thousand years, Siobhan stood and moved to the attached washroom and its luxurious shower. She was covered in grime of every sort, caked and layered and crusted until she felt more filth than woman. She shuddered as the water began to beat down upon her, pressing her hands flat against the wall to brace herself.

The skin of her chest was faintly scarred from the cold burns her medallion had given her, but the damage wasn't distinct enough to be alarming. Even if someone noticed the scar, they couldn't read a spell array or any glyphs from it. Her medallion itself was still intact. However, another of the glyphs—the one that signified protection from excessive energy transfer—seemed to have been damaged from channeling too much power. But at least none were broken. Even the anti-divination glyph, similarly half-melted, might have a little channeling ability left in it, if her divination-diverting ward ever failed.

The water quickly ran cold, forcing Siobhan out of the washroom. She sat before the vanity once more and dug out the final stolen healing potion as her wet hair soaked the back of her borrowed dress.

Minutes passed. *'I don't know what to do,'* Siobhan realized. She didn't mean what to do in the moment. Obviously, she needed to become Sebastien again and be innocently back in her dorm at the University, studying as fervently as ever. But in a more general sense, what to do about... She directed her thoughts firmly away from any hint of the *thing* within. *'What to do about the seal?'*

Siobhan wrapped her arms around herself and looked into her eyes in the mirror. "I'm in control," she whispered to herself. She repeated it once more, and then again, louder. But the words didn't seem as true as they should.

Instead, she whispered, "I'm scared. Why did you leave me, Grandfather? Why didn't you fix it?" She leaned forward until her forehead touched her knees. "Why?" she asked again, the sound smaller and more desperate.

But there was no one to answer her.

Hands shaking, she stood and splashed cool water from a decorative basin onto her face. Hot tears mixed with the water, spilling out of her eyes and down her cheeks. She breathed carefully, resisting the urge to sniffle, sob, or convulse. She stared at herself as the weakness spilled out, and when her face grew warm and her eyes burned, she splashed with the cool water again.

It was as if the tears drained something undefinable from deep inside her. Finally, they dried up, leaving her empty and exhausted.

She slumped back into the chair and stared at the ceiling for a few minutes, taking stock. Finally, she whispered, "I'm okay." She was withered and wilted, perhaps, but her clawing, ravenous tenacity was as strong as ever. Siobhan massaged her neck muscles, rolled her shoulders, and lifted her chin. "I am unbreakable," she croaked to the puffy-eyed, miserable-looking woman in the mirror.

Then she winced as a particularly painful throb pulsed through her head, almost as if to admonish her for her hubris. She was exhausted, had what was probably moderate Will-strain, and despite the success of retrieving her blood and discouraging further attempts to use sympathetic divination on her, it had been a long time since the future seemed so horribly bleak.

The last time things had been this bad was after she escaped the village and was surviving on her own. Before she learned that magic could keep her from dreaming.

Before she learned that power could keep her safe.

That precept was universal, and it should still hold true here.

Rather than drink the last healing potion, she poured some of the burning liquid on her fingertips and awkwardly rubbed it into the spots on her side and back that hurt the worst. Then she gingerly tipped a single drop into her right eye.

She had thought her pool of tears was empty, but under the searing, scouring brightness, her ducts found the ability to cry once more, spilling a line of brightness down her cheek. Her eye rolled uncontrollably in its socket, trying to escape, but the discomfort soon faded, leaving her sclera a crisp white, cleared of both the bruising and the redness from crying.

She repeated the process with her other eye, but with barely a dab of potion, just enough to remove the redness so that she wasn't noticeably lopsided.

As she was tucking the remainder of the potion back into her satchel and contemplating the best way to leave this building and get back to the University, a knock sounded at the door.

Liza poked her head past the doorway, looking as if she too could use a drop of healing potion for her red, irritated eyes and the dark circles under them. More than a few of her corkscrew curls had lost their coherence, frizzing out into individual strands and springing up and away in strange clouds that didn't seem to adhere to gravity. "You're up," she said, sounding surprised. "I thought I might need to use some caretaking spells to empty your bladder and bowels before you soiled the bed."

Siobhan flushed so hard that it was surely visible even past the ochre brown of her skin. The last time she'd had Will-strain, she had stayed at Liza's house and slept for an entire day. She had woken up with the bed unsoiled. This confirmation of what the other woman had been required to do was mortifying. *'How would it even work?'* she wondered before shaking her head rapidly to dislodge the thought. She didn't want to imagine it.

"You may come with me to the Retreat at Willowdale," Liza announced, distracting Siobhan from her embarrassment. "You will be disguised as my niece, a healer in training who received schooling in Silva Erde. No magic will be done. You will follow all instructions immediately and without question. If you agree, you may arrive at my house for preparation at six tomorrow morning."

Siobhan nodded rapidly. "I'll be there."

Liza narrowed her eyes. "If I find you in worse condition at that time than you are now, you will not be coming. *Rest.* If you wish, you may do so at my abode."

Siobhan hesitated. Liza's help nursing her through the next day or two would be wonderful, but it would be too suspicious for Sebastien Siverling to be missing for so long, and so she declined.

With a judgmental "tch," the woman withdrew and began to close the door.

"Wait!" Siobhan called. When Liza peeked her head back in, Siobhan said, "I have your payment."

Liza smiled widely, her whole demeanor shifting. "Oh? I thought I might have to hassle you for it."

It was true that after paying for supplies, University tuition, and various items for Operation Palimpsest, Liza's fees would have put Siobhan well into a deficit. She had planned to get a loan from a bank, using her status as Thaddeus Lacer's apprentice as well as her stock in Oliver's textile company. Failing that, she'd have tried to leverage Liza's interest in researching the fidelity of Siobhan's Will for a discount. But now, both options were unnecessary.

Siobhan pulled her satchel into her lap and rifled around in it until she had pulled a handful of small gold bars from the bottom. Just seven were enough. The original price they had agreed upon had increased with the additional requirements, the danger Liza had been required to risk, and Siobhan's rental of some basic protective artifacts.

This was a quarter of the gold Siobhan had stolen from the Pendragon Corps' safe, but only a small portion of the true wealth.

Liza took the bars and turned them over. "By any chance...are these stolen?"

Siobhan blinked at her. "How did you know?"

Liza sneered. "And what about the serial numbers? I'll have to launder them through my fence in Osham, and that will decrease their value by at least thirty percent. Do you think I'm a fool?"

"Thirty percent?" Siobhan narrowed her eyes suspiciously. "That's ridiculous."

Liza huffed and shoved the bars back at her. "That's *reality*. Stolen coin is one thing, but the bars are tracked."

In the end, after haggling with Liza until she wanted to tear her own hair out, Siobhan had to give her an extra two bars. At least it was an unexpected windfall, so she couldn't really complain that it was worth less than face value.

Liza tucked the heavy bars into an inner pocket of her jacket, which showed no outward sign of the weight, or even a bulge in the fabric.

When the older woman was gone, Siobhan reached into her satchel once more. She held up one of the Conduits so that the light could flash through its crystal-clear depths. Quite wastefully, someone had actually polished the celerium, getting rid of rough edges and increasing its shine. But it was still a bit larger than the average quail egg. At higher clarity, a Conduit could channel more while remaining small.

Siobhan estimated this one could channel between five and eight thousand thaums, as could the other couple dozen. And if prices had held steady since the last time she was searching for a Conduit, they would be worth between fifteen and thirty thousand gold. *Each.* Maybe more, as Siobhan hadn't paid close attention to the prices on the higher end.

Quite suddenly, Siobhan was incredibly wealthy. Nothing compared to the Crown Families, perhaps, but enough to buy a moderately priced mansion in the heart of the Lilies. Or fund a hundred or so people through the University all the way to a Master's certification.

Wealthy enough to bribe her way to freedom, possibly, if such a thing ever became necessary.

Some people would have said such wealth made all the danger and pain worth it.

It should have been exciting, even euphoric, after all the struggle she had gone through for gold. But instead it merely felt surreal. She put the Conduit back into her satchel. To access that wealth, she would still need to find buyers for each. She could think of several options, but each had its downside.

Slowly and wearily, Siobhan climbed to her feet. She debated whether to assume Sebastien's form now, but worried that someone might see her leaving the room that the Raven Queen had slept in. No matter how quiet the Nightmare Pack had tried to keep the information, a night was long enough for word to spread. People might even be waiting to catch a glimpse of her or, in the worst case, to arrest her.

She kept Sebastien's clothing in her bag, carefully folded and arranged for speed of use. She put on a heavy cloak that someone—probably Liza—had left draped over a chair while Siobhan was sleeping. An examination of the fabric showed protective spell arrays embroidered into the inside of the hem in copper thread, which added weight to Siobhan's theory.

Liza, as always, snapped and growled, and then treated Siobhan more kindly than she needed to. '*Unless Liza tries to charge me for renting an extra artifact when I return the cloak,*' Siobhan amended wryly.

Siobhan was extremely reluctant to strain herself casting the shedding-destroyer spell, but had rationalized that she must do so anyway. But then she realized that she could simply strip the bedding off the mattress and burn it all. It was a horrible waste, but the manager wouldn't dare to complain, and if Gera or Lord Lynwood wanted to bill her, she could afford it.

It took some time, but the magical filter on the fireplace kept the room from filling with acrid smoke as cotton, velvet, and feather down burned to ash, along with any little traces of her passing. She poured out the water from the decorative basin, wiped down everything she had used in the washroom, and then threw even the towels into the fire.

Outside, she found the hallway empty except for a pair of guards standing at the end. They bowed as soon as they saw her and didn't rise until she had stopped in front of them. "We are honored by your presence, my lady," one of them said, still staring at the floor.

Siobhan didn't have the wherewithal to handle this. "I need a safe exit. Perhaps through a hidden tunnel?"

They shared a glance with each other and then straightened. "If you'll follow me, I will lead you to our most secure passage," the one who had spoken before said.

Siobhan followed them through surprisingly deserted exterior hallways until they descended below ground level. "Have you had any trouble? The coppers, perhaps?"

"Nothing we couldn't handle. There were some who heard news of your stay and wanted to call upon you, for good or ill, but we turned away all those who you yourself had not allowed access to your quarters previously."

Siobhan ran her tongue over the back of her teeth. "Oliver Dryden?" she asked.

"He was one of them. Have we…angered you, my lady?"

"No. You did well."

When they reached the steel door of a tunnel—a different one than the night before—she bade them farewell. As soon as the door's dry hinges shrieked closed behind her, she stripped out of her dress and changed into her other form.

Immediately, her feet cried out inside the crushing pressure of her boots, and she fumbled to make them expand to fit her new size.

Sebastien leaned her hand against the dank, slimy wall of the tunnel, taking a couple deep breaths as the panic receded. "Stupid," she muttered.

Using her latest bottle of moonlight sizzle, she made her way to the tunnel's exit, which fed into the back of a hollow statue that sat within someone's private garden shrine to the Radiant Maiden.

Sebastien pushed open the stone hatch and crawled out without being seen. She brushed herself free of stray cobwebs and slipped nonchalantly into the pedestrian traffic on the nearest street. As the bright afternoon light hit her eyes despite the shading hood of the cloak, she ducked her head. Her steps were quick, but not suspiciously so, and she didn't look around as if expecting danger and thus drawing attention to herself.

'*What was their plan, yesterday?*' she wondered. '*It seems unlikely that they hoped to capture me by following Millennium. As far as I'm aware, his ability to bypass my "immunity" to divination isn't widely known. And if that had been the plan, one would imagine that the Pendragon operatives would have been more wary of my identity in the first place.*'

Sebastien worried at the edge of a ragged fingernail. '*Oliver didn't know about this ahead of time—I don't believe he would allow Theo to be placed in such danger*

—which means that his spies in the coppers didn't know about it. Could it be that the High Crown implemented his contribution to the events of yesterday in secret? As insurance, in case the coppers couldn't catch me?'

It was plausible. Especially because Oliver hadn't been particularly concerned with whatever the coppers had planned.

'What would I do, if I were trying to catch the Raven Queen?' Sebastien contemplated the strange feeling of compulsion she had sensed the morning before. She had no evidence that one had actually existed except her own gut feeling, but such magic would be incredibly useful to catch someone who had displayed the Raven Queen's supposed capabilities. If it were Sebastien in charge, Ennis's sentencing would have just been a pretext for people to be out in the streets without any feeling of dissonance. Something obvious for a clever woman to see right through. Something to encourage her to feel superior about how stupid her opponents were.

The Raven Queen was known to be resistant to divination, but not literally invisible. If Sebastien could make it possible to very gently and lightly scan every person in the city, then any person or creature that their divination failed on would be a suspect. This would include many of those wealthy enough to afford wearable wards in their jewelry or clothing.

Sebastien would have then removed those people from the general population and done more thorough tests. Perhaps even made them take some kind of oath to enforce truth-telling. The Raven Queen's word was her bond, after all.

Or, if removing that many people from the population wasn't possible, she might have come up with some way to manually track those people who were resistant to divination. This could have been done with an object, if she could find a way to attach it to the suspects. Reverse-pickpocketing a spelled copper coin into their pockets, perhaps.

Or, less prone to error, something like a spell that would create an illusory, miniature replica of Gilbratha and everyone in it. The spots that were resistant to divination would have been missing, or hazy. And in this way, they might be able to track what they *couldn't* track.

Except, if Liza was really as good as she believed herself to be, Sebastien's divination-diverting ward would have rerouted that wide-spread divination *around* her so that she was not a missing spot, just an empty one. Just as Sebastien could reroute the light around herself to create an illusion of invisibility.

And if Sebastien really wanted to be thorough about all this, she might have added some tiny compulsion toward recklessness and lowered inhibition. And then insulted the Raven Queen publicly. She was known to be prideful, and perhaps reckless, too.

When Sebastien recalled the details of yesterday, before she had been caught, her divination-diverting ward *had* activated subtly. But that would have been around the time Millennium was searching for her, drawing close. And at the same time the copper was talking to her. Either could have been the cause.

But all of her speculation was limited, a frog ideating inside of a well. She knew fully that the Red Guard had resources she couldn't imagine and used spells she'd never heard of.

All that she knew for sure was that, even now, she might not necessarily be safe. That was why the Raven Queen needed to disappear. Over time, she would fade from the gossip, and then from people's memories.

The problem was, after what Sebastien had learned—or been forced to remember—the Raven Queen was still needed.

If it was possible to fix the kind of thing that was wrong with Sebastien, those most likely to have the necessary knowledge were the agents of the Red Guard. Unfortunately, from what Sebastien knew of their vows, even an attempt to help her would be sacrilege. That which threatened the continued existence of the world must be annihilated and erased.

'How can I trust anyone to actually help me, when, if I weren't the one in this exact position, even my own verdict would be to kill Siobhan Naught? What might be learned from saving me could be useful, to be sure. But what is risked is greater, and not only one life is at stake.'

Sebastien took a deep breath in through her nose and out through her mouth, then pressed back her shoulders and lifted her chin, which had both sunk downward without her realizing.

'If I cannot trust anyone to help me, then I must help myself. If the information that could lead me to a solution is out there, all I need to do is find and learn it myself.' And, perhaps ironically, the person in the best position to do so was the Raven Queen. She knew the perfect person, the one man who might be willing to lead her to answers. As long as he didn't understand why she needed them.

Sebastien Siverling must stay separate, unimpeachable, and indisputably innocent. More so now than ever. She was terrified of the thing sealed inside her mind, seeping out into her nightmares. It would have been the greatest wish of her life to be free of that burden, to be powerful enough to crush it beneath her heel.

But more than that, more than anything, she did not want to die.

By the time Sebastien arrived at the dorms, she had grown woozy with the effort required to simply stay awake. She took a bland meal at the cafeteria while composing several letters, then wrote them in her dorm room. One for Tanya, to let the other woman know that all had gone well. One to Damien, something similar but less honest. She even wrote one to Oliver, though no doubt by now he knew the situation.

And finally, one to Thaddeus Lacer, written carefully on the same paper she had bought for the High Crown, in a hand that he wouldn't recognize as the usual spider-scrawl of his apprentice. In the end, her message was less subtle than she had hoped, because she didn't even know enough about her problem to approach it indirectly. And above all, she needed answers. That one, she placed on Professor Lacer's doorstep, after confirming thrice that he was gone, no one was around to see her, and that her divination-diverting ward gave no signs of activation.

Then Sebastien returned to the dorms and cast her dreamless sleep spell at the highest strength that she could manage in her current state. She set her alarm to wake her up before the much-weakened magic could wear off and collapsed into her bed. *'I only need a nap. Just a little rest, and then I'll go to the infir-mary. I need an excuse to avoid casting until I heal.'*

38

———

REVENANT

Thaddeus
Month 4, Day 10, Saturday 8:30 a.m.

The Pendragon Corps captain, hands still clasped behind his back as the severity of the situation settled into everyone's minds, spoke again. "Much of our information comes only from the traitor that we were able to snatch back from her grasp. He has been questioned thoroughly and has made some…outlandish claims."

"Bring the traitor," the High Crown commanded. "I would speak to him."

This was accomplished with surprising speed, only minutes after one of the palace runners by the door sprinted out. The traitor must have been kept nearby in anticipation of the High Crown's wish.

The one they had called Parker was supported by both elbows by his former comrades. His dragging feet moved clumsily back and forth as if to walk, but never quite managed to take any of his weight. The man was dead-eyed, unable to focus, his pupils visibly dilated.

These were signs of nominally illegal interrogation potions and spells, and the tremors in Mr. Parker's lips, eye muscles, and fingertips might indicate that he had been repeatedly tortured and healed. The men on either side of him forced him to his knees.

When Mr. Parker saw the High Crown, some inkling of feeling returned to his face. "Please. I had no choice. I had to do what she said. All of our preparation was useless, and our lives were on the line. She would have escaped even if we didn't help her. She said as much, and you know she doesn't lie."

"It was your duty, and your vow, that you would place your own life secondary to my wellbeing and orders," the High Crown said, looking down at him.

Mr. Parker changed tack. "Maybe I can still be useful to you. The Raven Queen trusts me now. Maybe I can help you find her. Or I could act as bait, just like the children were supposed to!"

The High Crown scoffed, and several people around the room chuckled spitefully.

Mr. Parker slumped, muttering rapidly under his breath.

The man on his left frowned and leaned in to hear better, then reared away in shock. "He's praying to the Raven Queen!"

Tension filled the room almost palpably, and Thaddeus caught several people glancing suspiciously toward the nearest shadows, and a few even had the sense to look toward the vaulted ceiling.

But she did not come for Mr. Parker. The City Manager snorted. "If it is true that she can hear the pleas of her followers, she must also have heard his offer to betray her. Surely, her requirements for loyalty are higher than what that cretin possesses."

This seemed to be the impetus Mr. Parker needed to regain his vigor. Tremors wracked through his frame as he lifted his head and shouted, his voice cracking wildly. "I will offer my soul! My blood, my bone, my free Will. Save me, my queen, and devour my enemies!"

The High Crown stumbled back, and several of the other guards stepped in as if to protect him.

The guard closest to Mr. Parker kicked him in the side of the head, stopping the prayers as their captive lost consciousness.

The High Crown was breathing heavily. "Take him away."

A small trickle of blood smeared against the floor as they did so. Either the High Crown had chosen the people for his Corps poorly, the elite training was actually anything but, or the man who held the highest position in the nation was simply the type to destroy any loyalty one might have had to him by dint of his unbearable personality.

Or, the Raven Queen was simply that compelling.

"Maybe we should have let him keep trying," the City Manager said. "If she appeared, we might have caught her."

What fools. Even if she had been able to hear Mr. Parker's desperate prayer —improbable—she was unlikely to risk herself for such a dullard. Rather than pleading the inevitability of his betrayal, Mr. Parker should have pleaded his innocence. Of course, some lie that the Raven Queen had taken control of his mind or body would have only added to the confusion and thus aided her as well as himself. A man without even the most basic sense, hoping that his life was valuable enough for her to risk her own?

The City Manager's thoughtless remark was, perhaps, not what the High Crown wanted to hear. Turning on the Pendragon Corps captain, he ground out between clenched teeth, "Explain to me the incompetence that could have led to such total failure of our meticulously laid plans."

Hands still clasped behind his back, the captain did not flinch in the face of the High Crown's wrath. Speaking clearly and concisely, he explained the events as he knew them, filling in all the gaps in the story that had been left by the other operative's shared memories.

Thaddeus agreed that Mr. Parker's claims, relayed secondhand, were indeed outlandish, some more so than others. That the Raven Queen could respond to the prayers of her "believers" was absurd. More likely, she had a spy within the palace, knew of their plans ahead of time, and had gotten herself captured on purpose. It might even be one of them within this very room.

The claim that she had performed some wicked ritual on one of the injured captives was nothing to get excited about. She had already been known to heal with blood magic, and indeed enjoyed flaunting the fact that she could do so. The prohibition on and stigma against blood magic was one of the many levers of power that the Crowns held. Was subtly changing the public's perception of blood magic just another way that she was trying to undermine them?

Even the fact that she seemed to have been casting without a Conduit—despite visibly using one in other instances—did not confound him. He had looked into the Naughts, and if his suspicions were correct, there was a good reason that Raaz Kalvidasan had integrated himself with the family. The bloodline had not saved Siobhan Naught's mother, but perhaps the daughter was stronger.

And as for free-casting a precise slicing spell that murdered two of the High Crown's men—who she shouldn't even have been able to *see* past the glare of the spotlight—well, Thaddeus had done that himself. It was moderately amusing to see them cite this as they argued the evidence for and against her being an Aberrant, instead of merely a free-casting sorcerer.

Other claims, however, had no obvious explanation.

He could not rationalize the fact that she had attacked the diviners at Eagle Tower at the same time that she had been crawling her way out of a sensory deprivation spell in a cell underneath Pendragon Palace.

Thaddeus could easily imagine how she might have called the ravens, caused the birds to give a false positive to divination attempts, and delivered the letter to the Edictum Council at the same time that she made an in-person appearance at Eagle Tower. But two in-person appearances at the same time was impossible.

The port admiral, who was only there because the Raven Queen had stolen a boat, and if he had any sense would have kept his mouth shut and spoken only when questioned, suggested that perhaps only the Raven Queen's shadow companion had attended the group of captives. That it had somehow shared power with one of the women—most likely this Silvia Nakai—and thus allowed the Raven Queen to act at such a distance. That it changed the appearance of the woman to so closely match the Raven Queen's visage was... part of the effect. Supposedly.

Was it possible that the Raven Queen's appearance at Eagle Tower was the real ruse? Had any there seen her face? Surely one of the people there could cast an illusion spell to share their own memories, unreliable as such things might be.

The Crown Archivist, silent up until now, pushed up his gold-framed glasses, cleared his throat, and forced some steel into his spine, though his knees were trembling faintly. "Could it be possible that Ennis Naught was never actually an accomplice? Or at least, not a willing one? If she really does possess the power to, well, forgive my unintended pun, but to *possess* people, to control them, she could have used it on him."

"But he testified otherwise," the Advisor of Virtue pointed out, simpering like the false-faced joke he was.

"We've never trusted his testimony," the Ambassador to the Public argued, flinging her hair over her shoulder. "And at this point, what does it matter? He has been sentenced. We can only hope that useless man gives us a chance to capture the Raven Queen."

The Recipient of Edicts wrung his hands. "Based on my understanding of the Raven Queen's personality and motivations, I would suggest that *all* of the woman's actions yesterday were not, in fact, in response to Ennis Naught's sentencing, but because of the children. She did not even attempt to free the man, while instead putting herself at great risk to retrieve the children and deprive us of valuable resources. She may feel that he has betrayed her and is thus no longer worthy of her efforts. I do not believe he retains any use as a lure."

The High Crown's knuckles were white as he clutched the edge of his desk, but he did not sweep off the contents onto the floor in a fit of rage or start screaming. "Is she actually becoming stronger, awakening to new abilities, or was she deliberately underperforming in the beginning?"

"The prayer might have something to do with it," the Ambassador to the Public suggested. "We have records of suggested experiments during the Third Empire that hoped to use the masses to provide strength to certain ideas."

"Why did none of our preparations to contain her work in the slightest?" the High Crown asked the Recipient of Edicts.

The man struggled to speak for a moment. "The...brighter the light, the darker the shadow?"

"It couldn't have been an elemental familiar," someone else interjected. "Elementals are always strongest when surrounded by energy that matches their own nature. If it were a devil—if those even exist—it would be weak to Radiance."

The Court Sorcerer cleared his throat. "Unless it's very old and powerful, and our spells simply weren't strong enough to weaken it sufficiently. Or, perhaps, our theories about the Plane of Darkness are incorrect."

"I still say that thing is an Aberrant," one of the Pendragon operatives offered. "It wouldn't be totally unprecedented, would it?" the man asked spitefully, looking at Thaddeus.

Several people began to speak over each other, agreeing, disagreeing, and putting forth their own theories.

The High Crown slammed down his fist on the desk to maintain order. He hung his head for a moment, grey braids swinging gently. "So, does this Raven Queen have any true weaknesses?" he asked softly.

Thaddeus scoffed. He pinched the bridge of his nose and then took a moment to retie his hair at the base of his neck. There was no need for him to contribute to the increasingly wild speculation. At this point, he had to admit that he simply lacked the proper information to reach any reasonable conclusions.

When he looked up, the High Crown was staring at him speculatively. "What do you think, Grandmaster Lacer?"

Thaddeus raised one eyebrow. "I do not think the correct direction is to continue jumping to conclusions about her seemingly impossible abilities," he drawled. "You did so in preparation for yesterday, and look where it led."

"All this adds up to you telling me only that you do not know? I need *answers*, Grandmaster Lacer," the High Crown said dangerously.

Thaddeus stared back for a moment. "It seems there are two options being bandied about. One, that the Raven Queen is a genius with magic we have never seen before. This magic allows possession of the bodies of those who pray to her, existence in several places at once, and in several different forms —including the body of multiple ravens—and that she is not only a free-caster but can also cast without any external Conduit. Two, that she is something else entirely. An Aberrant, or perhaps some ancient creature told of only in stories lost to time. If forced to choose between the two...I would present a third option."

Thaddeus paused, and everyone held their breath as if to leave room for him to speak. "She is exceedingly clever, and exceedingly powerful. That is obvious. She has indeed done things that I have not seen before. But perhaps this evidence of things that seem to be *impossible* is merely what we can see of her metaphorical sleight-of-hand, meant to send her enemies looking in the wrong direction. However, all I can say for certain is that I do not know, and I will not pretend that I do. The evidence is too lacking, and more than that, too *contradictory*. It is also potentially tainted. Attempts to deduce meaning from it are just as likely to lead one through a maze of the Raven Queen's making—and to an end of her choosing—as they are to lead to the truth."

She was like a stage magician performing for the ignorant. Thaddeus could not help the ideas and theories running through his head, but he was aware that he had reached the point where he needed to see for himself what lay behind the curtain and under the stage. Looking at where the Raven Queen pointed everyone's attention—to the flamboyant, impossible trick—would not give him any answers.

Titus spoke for the first time since before watching the illusory memories. "Could all of these seemingly impossible feats be things learned from Myrddin's stolen journal?"

It was like a slicing spell had cut through the air in the room, and every eye turned toward Thaddeus, the only one who could possibly answer that question.

"Speak, Grandmaster Lacer," the High Crown commanded. "Your High Crown commands you."

"I have taken vows of secrecy." That is what Thaddeus said aloud, though it would have been more accurate to state that the High Crown's commands meant nothing to Thaddeus, personally. "I can reveal that we have yet to decrypt the remaining journals. That she could have learned such feats from the journal, if she were to somehow have done what an entire team of professors and I myself have not yet been able to achieve, is…possible. It might not explain everything, such as the mystery behind her identity, but it could explain some of her most recent abilities."

Titus shifted uncomfortably, looking between Thaddeus and the High Crown, and then added, "There is also evidence that suggests the Raven Queen might originate from a land past the northern ice oceans and the Abyssal Sea."

Several of the advisors gasped, hands raising to their mouths in fear. Even the captain closed his eyes for a moment, as if the words were a blow.

"Speak clearly, boy," the High Crown said slowly. "You mean from the same land as the Blood Emperor."

Thaddeus's face remained as expressionless as stone as Titus Westbay explained the very same reasoning that Thaddeus had used to come up with the absurd theory while they were in the carriage.

Despite Thaddeus's attempts to encourage caution, the discussion devolved once again into rampant speculation.

Against the healers' supposed recommendations, the High Crown ordered them to bring in Jorgensen—the one who had been violated by the shadow companion.

They carried him in on a stretcher between four other healers, with the head healer walking beside. The scratch marks on Jorgensen's face had been healed, but his eyes told of a greater scarring, deep inside where only a mind healer might have a chance to help.

Thaddeus had seen people like this before, ones who had had their Wills broken by experience, rather than strain.

The poor-man's palanquin stopped in front of the High Crown. "I can walk," Jorgensen told the High Crown absently, but he made no move to rise from the stretcher, and the healers did not set him on the ground.

"What is the diagnosis?" the High Crown asked, looking at the grey-bearded expert. "What did the Raven Queen's shadow creature do?"

The old man hesitated. "It's hard to say for certain. Obviously, she has damaged something in his mind. He has also been having horrible night-mares, reliving his…traumatic experience. Sometimes, these episodes are trig-gered while he is awake."

The healer glanced at Jorgensen, who, despite the vague wording, was pressing his fingers into the flesh of his throat. His nails had been clipped down to the quick to keep him from scratching himself.

"There is no sign of any physical damage that operative Jorgensen did not cause himself. There are no signs of any lingering active magic. We have searched for some remnant of the creature within him, but found nothing." The healer spread his hands helplessly to the sides. "To be honest, we cannot be sure that we are even searching in the right way, or for the right thing. Despite the risk of worsening Jorgensen's condition, we have been doing recall exercises and searching for triggers that might have been seeded in his mind. If there is a key, I believe it will be in the dreams, but so far, they are only repetitions of the traumatic event with small variations."

Thaddeus noted the way others, especially his former comrades, looked at Jorgensen with both pity and wariness, as if he might be a trap waiting to spring shut. Even if he could recover physically and mentally, his future here, in the Pendragon Corps, was gone.

"Operative Jorgensen," the High Crown said. "Do you have anything you wish to report to me?"

The man stared at the High Crown and began to shudder. His convulsions grew stronger, and he released a ragged gasp and began to weep. "Please— 'Elp me," he sobbed.

The High Crown frowned and made a sharp motion with his fingers, and one of the healers hurried to tip a swallow of calming potion into Operative Jorgensen's mouth.

The man choked on it but managed to calm his breathing. He spoke again with a weak, breathy voice. "The darkness was watching, knowing. But the *creature*... It was hungry. So empty, so cold, like it had never known the warmth of the sun or the touch of a mother. And it got inside me. I can't feel it. It's just...gone. But I fear that it took something from me. Except, except —" He let out a wet, ragged cough. "What did it take? What did it eat? What am I *missing*?"

His voice grew louder, first with fear and then with anger. "And your healers! Your healers are useless! Send me to someone who can actually help! I served you loyally," he screamed, his voice raw. "Your honor *demands* that you have me treated! I've heard the whispers, already, after only a day. Do you think I'm deaf? I don't belong in some retreat for the broken and the weak! I won't go! I won't! Is this the honor of Lord Pendragon, the High Crown? At least the Raven Queen would, would—she would rip the sun from the sky to protect those who follow her!" He threw his head back and laughed mockingly, and the sound bounced off the walls and ceiling, echoing, until his throat gave out from the stress and his laughs turned into wheezing gasps.

39

HARBINGER

Thaddeus
Month 4, Day 10, Saturday 10:00 a.m.

"I apologize, Your Eminence," the lead healer said, using a somewhat archaic title as he bowed repeatedly to the High Crown. He shot a glance toward Jorgensen that clearly said he wished he could physically shut the hysterical man's mouth. "A reaction to the mix of potions, perhaps. His mind is volatile and weak at the moment."

Grimly, the High Crown nodded to the head healer, and their group hurried out at a speed just below a run, carrying Mr. Jorgensen with them. They should have known better than to play games of loyalty and subversion with the Raven Queen. That they had hoped to loosen her grip on her allies by showing them her weakness was delicious irony, considering the reactions of the operatives who had interacted most closely with her.

Had the Raven Queen truly done something more nefarious to Jorgensen, or was this another decoy, serving multiple purposes and drawing their attention away from her true intentions? Thaddeus looked around again. If he were trying to play the sort of game she loved so much, it would not be Jorgensen who was the delayed-trigger poison, but one of the others. One who did not even know it.

With Jorgensen gone, the conjectures only grew more outlandish. The consensus leaned increasingly toward some kind of Aberrant influence, perhaps due to some subconscious desire to foist the problem of dealing with her off on someone else. The High Crown, at least, had long been attempting to increase his power over the Red Guard, and he might see this as an opportunity.

Thaddeus remained silent unless specifically questioned. He was not convinced, again for lack of sufficient untainted evidence, but it *would* explain much. If a powerful sorceress had somehow bound the service of an Aberrant, one lucid enough to follow commands and restrain itself when necessary, most of the feats she had displayed could be explained. After all, Aberrants were not constrained to the limits of mortal sorcery.

Thaddeus would not reveal the secrets of the Red Guard to these people by suggesting such, nor add weight to their speculation, but it was inevitable that the Red Guard would also realize this possibility. They would investigate.

The talking went on for hours, occasionally interspersed with updates from the ongoing investigation. The Pendragon Corps had tried to find the people they had kidnapped—or at least the families of those people—without any luck. Their homes showed signs that they had left in a hurry, and even under pressure, their neighbors could only say that enforcers from the Verdant Stag and Nightmare Pack had helped load clothes and other emergency belongings into carriages a few hours before.

This was no surprise. The coppers might have arrived sooner if the Pendragon operatives had actually known exactly who they kidnapped along with the children.

They had also had no luck finding the woman Silvia Nakai. Records showed that she had worked at the Silk Door for a time, but that establishment was notoriously tight-lipped. If Silvia Nakai was Siobhan Naught, as Thaddeus suspected, it was even less likely that they would ever catch her.

Titus's thoughts seemed to be running along a similar path. "Siobhan Naught was seemingly a normal young girl, according to her father and those around her, until suddenly she began to display abilities beyond any realistic capabilities for one of her age and background. This sudden shift simply... doesn't make sense. Is it possible that something similar has happened to Silvia Nakai?"

"What if..." the Ambassador to the Public started, but she cut herself off with a shake of her head.

"Speak," the High Crown ordered wearily.

The woman looked around, then cleared her throat awkwardly. "What if the Raven Queen is actually someone, or some *thing*, that the expedition brought back from the Black Wastes? In that case, Siobhan Naught and Silvia Nakai would both be...victims."

In essence, the woman was suggesting that the Raven Queen herself was some sort of lucid Aberrant, though whether this would be in *addition* to the shadow Aberrant, Thaddeus did not know.

"We should watch the rumors for insight," said the Recipient of Edicts, who had supposedly had the Raven Queen's personality profiled. "The ones that appear first, before they have a chance to mutate as they pass from ear to ear, are most likely to be information from the Raven Queen's allies. The ones who were there, and those closest to them."

The suggestion made Thaddeus consider something that no one had brought up. If the Raven Queen had "followers," could it be in a more direct sense than people who prayed to her and passed around rumors about her activities? Could she perhaps be building her own organization, independent from the Verdant Stag or the Nightmare Pack? No doubt, if this was the case, the woman would be filling the ranks with only the best.

And it would also explain at least a few of the feats she'd flaunted, in a totally mundane, if quite clever, manner.

Rather than giving professional, succinct reports to the High Crown that covered only their particular expertise, the group argued about almost everything. The only thing they could agree on was that, except for confirmation of alternative levers that might move her, they were, in fact, worse off than they had been before. The High Crown descended into a deep brooding mood.

"We will still prepare to catch her if she attempts to free Ennis Naught," Titus offered, though it was obvious he held little hope for this.

"You are all incompetent," the High Crown said before waving them out with a few angry slashing motions of his hand. Only his personal guards remained behind.

Titus was somewhat awkward on the ride back.

Thaddeus could understand the younger man's desire to offer the High Crown something that would ease his displeasure, but he did not appreciate the words being stolen from his own lips. Thaddeus exited the carriage at the University without breaking the silence. Once there, the first thing he did was check on his apprentice.

Thaddeus first went to the library, and then the dorms, and then the cafeteria. Eventually, his stomach sinking, he tried the infirmary. Through a gap in the curtained pseudo-cubicle, he spied Sebastien's shockingly light hair. The boy had a half-finished mug of nourishing draught in one hand and a weary tilt in his neck. Still, he flashed the healer attending him a small smile, and the grim-faced woman let out an exasperated huff.

Thaddeus strode up to them, yanking the curtain aside and pulling it closed behind him. "What has happened?"

"Oh, it's all the fault of that damn Raven Queen," the healer said, clicking her tongue with displeasure.

Sebastien's eyes widened with alarm. "Well, that's not exactly—"

Thaddeus had already free-cast a diagnostic spell before remembering that the boy's strange boon blocked divination. He ignored Sebastien's flinch as he ruthlessly overpowered the effect. Thaddeus's eyes narrowed as he looked over the results, illusory images and metrics scrolling through the air.

The healer raised one eyebrow, parsing the information alongside Thaddeus. "An impressive spell, if somewhat obscure," she commented. "I think I should clarify that the Raven Queen herself did not attack the boy. I realize my words could have been misconstrued. No need to worry about anomalous effects, torture, or..." She leaned closer, peering at the results over Thaddeus's shoulder. "Hmm." She shared a glance with Thaddeus, her lips pressing together.

"What? What is it?" Siverling asked, barely suppressing panic.

"It's a concussion," she said.

"Not Will-strain?" Thaddeus asked.

The woman turned to Sebastien. "You didn't do any casting after you got your head knocked around, did you?"

"Of course not," he replied immediately.

Thaddeus took a deep breath and pinched the bridge of his nose. Sebastien's eyes had flicked subtly to the side, and his fingers had twitched. Thaddeus had noticed the boy's habit of reaching for his Conduit whenever he felt the slightest bit uncomfortable. He gave Sebastien a pointed look.

Sebastien at least didn't force Thaddeus to point out his lie verbally. "Well...I did cast *one* spell. Something to help with nightmares," the boy admitted, almost mumbling.

Thaddeus internally lamented the generalized stupidity of his students, and the fact that his apprentice was no exception to the rule, despite the boy's intelligence and Thaddeus's attempts to inject some wisdom into him. If the boy didn't look so downtrodden, Thaddeus would have given him a tongue-lashing.

The healer let out a low sound of sympathy, shooting another meaningful look at Thaddeus over Sebastien's bowed head. "Mr. Siverling, like most of the rest of us, was out and about on Friday. When the raven clouds started gathering, some idiot panicked and started yelling about the end of days, and you know how it goes. People spooked. Mr. Siverling is so slight, he got knocked over easily. He took a bit of a trampling. He's already had a high-strength, true healing potion, and that handled most of it, but he's still experiencing some headaches."

"The crowd...trampled you?" Thaddeus asked slowly, a strange pit forming in his stomach. He could imagine it. While he was watching the ravens dance in awe, Sebastien, always so confident and focused, was being knocked off balance by some hysterical, criminally self-absorbed savages. "You could have died." Thaddeus had seen it happen at least half a dozen times.

Sebastien shifted uncomfortably, his lips moving as if to say something, but in the end he remained silent.

"I'm prescribing some anti-inflammatories, a regeneration-booster, and a few more nourishing draughts, in addition to the standard Will-strain regimen. You can take a bed here and sleep for the day, if you like, Mr. Siverling. I would normally prescribe a sleep-inducing potion, but I know of your…aversion. And don't mention this to your friends, but I can have some of the better food delivered from the cafeteria."

"I appreciate it, but no thank you," Sebastien said, shaking his head and tugging at the cuff of his sleeves.

"Are you sure? I know the basic meals are less than appealing. You're just a little slip of a thing, a string bean! You're practically wasting away."

Her sincere concern slipped through in an accusing tone.

Sebastien drew himself up. "That's not true. I'm all muscle!"

She raised one eyebrow and looked at Thaddeus. "Look at his cheeks. Gaunt."

Sebastien touched his cheek. "I just have well-defined cheekbones."

"If this were a story, you would have 'the consumption,'" the woman snapped back. Rather than continue to bicker with her patient, who was puffing himself up in outrage, she left them alone to retrieve the concoctions she had prescribed.

As soon as she was gone, Thaddeus cast his favorite sound-muffling spell. "Did you encounter the Raven Queen over the break at any time?"

Wide-eyed, Sebastien shook his head. "Did *you?*" He leaned forward with sudden fascination. The boy obviously wanted to ask for details about the spectacle, but Thaddeus waved him off.

Sebastien hesitated, then asked, "Is there…anything wrong? You seemed to notice something from that divination spell. I mean, besides the obvious."

Thaddeus did not cushion his words. "You are underweight. Or, more accurately, your body fat percentage is concerningly low, and you are anemic."

Sebastien relaxed subtly. "Oh."

Thaddeus scowled as a flash of anger ran through him. "This is not a trivial matter. You are also dehydrated, your blood pressure is distressingly high, and your fingertips are trembling. When was the last time you ate something?"

The boy pressed his hands flat to his legs, halting the trembling. "Just a couple of hours ago. I had lunch in the cafeteria."

"And before that?"

Sebastien's hesitation was answer enough.

Before Thaddeus could speak again, the healer returned, and Thaddeus dropped his sound-muffling spell.

She handed Sebastien a linen satchel filled with small vials and larger bottles, rattling off instructions that the boy nodded along to. "I also included a refill of the anti-anxiety potion you were prescribed earlier this year. When you run out, *come back for more.*"

Sebastien chugged the remainder of his nourishing draught and, under the combined stares of the healer and Thaddeus, left the infirmary with his chin held defiantly high. Thaddeus was beginning to suspect that some of the boy's haughtiness was in truth a defense mechanism.

The healer crossed her arms and turned on Thaddeus as if he were an unruly student. "*You* need to be keeping an eye on your apprentice's food intake. I've complained to the administration several times that the cafeteria's restrictions are a problem. Just because it's tradition doesn't make it worthwhile. There are other, better ways to incentivize students to earn contribution points."

"I will handle it," Thaddeus promised.

She relaxed slightly. "And not just that. Mr. Siverling...might not be dealing with the trauma of his previous encounter with the Raven Queen as well as he seems to. You can't tell me she wasn't instrumental in his friend's break event. And now, with the recent fracas, it must be stirring up memories. Anxieties. If it's bad enough that he would risk Will-strain to avoid nightmares, I would suggest you consider sending him to a mind healer. He might not talk about it, but Mr. Siverling is an orphan. He doesn't have anyone to look after him but you."

Thaddeus wasn't sure that Sebastien was so fearful of the Raven Queen as to have nightmares about her. If anything, it seemed the opposite. "I will speak to him," he assured her.

"You do that. I'd hate to look back on this moment with regret, wouldn't you? Mr. Siverling is such a promising young man."

"He could be great, one day," Thaddeus agreed. "Truly exceptional."

"I'd expect nothing less from your apprentice, Grandmaster Lacer," she called over her shoulder, already walking away.

When Thaddeus finally arrived at his cottage, looking forward to nursing a cup of warmed cider while he decided how to deal with his apprentice, he found a letter. It was placed on the porch directly in front of his door rather than in the warded letter box.

The envelope was of black, obviously expensive paper, and sealed with blood-red wax. There was no identifying stamp in the wax, no signature across the fold, and no address.

Thaddeus's suspicion warred with a burgeoning excitement and a heady satisfaction. She had not ignored him after all. Nevertheless, Thaddeus had experienced enough surprises and disappointments to learn caution. He cast a series of detection and divination spells. There was nothing suspicious. No hint of magic at all.

Thaddeus levitated the letter with a spell, walked inside, and sat down at his desk, staring at the velvet black paper floating in front of his face.

Carefully, he slid open the seal with his desk athame, careful not to break the wax as he separated it from the page. Damaging this letter in any way would be such a shame.

With the seal broken, he lowered the envelope to the desk and recast all of his detection spells, to the same result.

Finally, Thaddeus lifted the envelope's flap and pulled free a creamy white sheet. Black ink formed words in a simple and elegant hand.

You know who I am.

I have taken note of your interest in meeting me. This more indirect form of communication must suffice. After recent events, I believe I have made enough in-person appearances to last some time.

What do you want with me, Thaddeus Lacer?

If you wish to continue our communication, please pay tribute in knowledge:

What do you know of seals that could contain a being's consciousness within a memory?

To respond, put your letter in the lock box at the first attached location. You may receive further communication from me at the second location.

WITHIN THE ENVELOPE, Thaddeus found a second, much smaller sheet of paper with the numbers of locked boxes at two different storage locations, along with two keys to fit them. Presumably, when he placed his response in the first box, it would be taken to another location for pickup by or delivery to the Raven Queen, and the same in reverse. She, who so hated to be tracked, would never allow herself to be so easily located.

Thaddeus considered attempting to do so anyway, but decided against it. He did not want to earn her ire now that he had *finally* made contact. He read over her request for tribute again. She had chosen her demand well, as surely the worth of Thaddeus's knowledge outshone anything else he might offer her. But why would she wish to know of such seals, specifically?

Thaddeus had dug into the Red Guard's records of that Aberrant incident seven years ago, from which Siobhan Naught was the only known survivor. This question could have something to do with her current situation, that Aberrant event, or even, perhaps, some intriguing research project of her own.

Was it possible that Siobhan Naught had been an experimental subject, with someone, perhaps Raaz Kalvidasan, working to answer a similar question? Could she be a victim, as that advisor of the High Crown had suggested, perhaps picked for her bloodline? It was even possible that the question had something to do with whatever the creature of darkness had done to Jorgensen.

Again, Thaddeus attempted, with limited success, to resist his desire for rampant speculation. There were simply too many possibilities, and he had too little real information. She could have just as easily gotten some hint of a fascinating spell from Myrddin's journal.

After all, it was the letter's postscript that caught Thaddeus's eye and set his heartbeat to racing.

P.S. — Have you yet made it past the first set of split glyphs? There is a trick to it.

40

———

THE ARCHAEOLOGIST

Sebastien
Month 4, Day 11, Sunday 5:30 a.m.

Very early Sunday morning, after waking for what seemed to be the dozenth time to the alarm spell she'd set on her pocket watch, Sebastien took a morning dose of all her prescribed concoctions. Then, she retreated to the nearby bathroom—thankfully empty—and retrieved the beast core and Conduit that she had swallowed.

It was an experience she resolved never to think about again. Even the thought of returning the Conduit to Professor Lacer at some point made her skin flush from her neck up to her forehead.

Sebastien was thankful that the man had found her at the perfect time yesterday, so that the healer could—unknowingly—lie to him instead of forcing Sebastien to do it herself. Sebastien wasn't confident in her ability to trick him when he was on guard for it.

For a moment, she had worried that his diagnostic spell had given some hint of the five ward disks embedded under the skin of her back. But instead, apparently she was anemic and needed to put on a bit more fat. It was true that the divination-diverting ward might have, cumulatively, consumed a bit more blood over the last few months than intended. It was also true, what with the constant exercise as she practiced light-refinement, as well as the extra energy required to keep up with heavy magic use, that she might not have been managing her sustenance properly over the break. It was harder to remember when there were no classes to structure her day, and when everything else seemed more urgent than taking a break to eat. In fact, she could recall a handful of times that she only forced herself to do so when the insidious cravings for a dose of beamshell tincture returned or when her fingers began to tremble.

Sebastien looked into one of the bathroom's mirrors, tilting her head as she examined her face for signs of malnutrition. She was thin, yes, but really, the worst of it were the bruise-like crescents beneath her eyes, and that her lips were pale and cracking. She took a bit of headache salve from her satchel, rubbed the minty oil on her lips, and then pinched a bit of color into her cheeks. "Better," she murmured. She wasn't sure if she was quite handsome, but she did look...distinguished. Striking.

Sebastien turned her attention to the—thoroughly cleaned—beast core and Conduit that she had retrieved. The Conduit was fine, though perhaps slightly shinier than it had been before. The beast core, however, was almost empty of power. When she held it within the Circle of her grip and sensed for the familiar well of power, she felt only a depleted spark instead.

Which was slightly concerning. Sebastien reassured herself that she would *know* if she had somehow cast through her own flesh at any point, because that wasn't the sort of thing someone could miss. Perhaps beast cores simply didn't react well to the chemicals of a digestive system.

'*Could I have internal burns from the energy discharge?*' If she had, the healing potions had probably fixed any problems. In fact, it might even have been contact with the healing potions that caused the issue in the first place, if they were trying to cleanse her of an "impurity." Radiant energy was multi-faceted, after all, as harsh and unforgiving as it was restorative.

Sebastien put the beast core in her satchel and reattached the Conduit chain to her pocket watch with some bending of the delicate links, and then left for Liza's. The sun was rising earlier and earlier lately, which she appreciated because it decreased some of the bitter cold, but it also meant that it was harder to travel unnoticed through the darkness.

The evening before, after taking the potions prescribed by the University healer, Sebastien had realized that keeping all the things she'd stolen from the armory safe in her bag was probably a bad idea. If someone were to search it and discover the secret compartment, it would be hard to explain why she had a veritable fortune in gold and celerium.

While she had kept her satchel close enough by her side that her divination-diverting ward could activate if someone tried to find her through its contents, there had been no scrying attempts. It might be paranoia, but if that happened to change during one of the moments when her satchel was too far away for the spillover effects from her ward to protect it, the consequences could be severe.

Normally, she would have kept something sensitive like this at Oliver's house or the Verdant Stag. In fact, she still hadn't retrieved Myrddin's journal from the guest room floor. Oliver might not even be aware that the book was there, but if he was, and he was angry about Operation Palimpsest... This thought caused a spike of anxiety that was quickly suppressed by the potions Sebastien had taken.

If she left such sensitive items at Liza's house, they would be protected by the woman's wards. *'But would they be protected from Liza herself?'* She remembered Oliver saying that Liza had a code of honor, but that Sebastien would not be buying her *loyalty*. And Liza was, for some reason, in constant need of gold. If Sebastien kept her things there, she had no way to stop Liza from snooping, and wasn't sure that Liza would be able to resist the temptation if she learned of such an opportunity.

Sebastien could place her things in a warded box in a bank vault, but if the High Crown's people overcame the bank's wards, they would not only have a way to trap her when she came to retrieve the items, but also a blatant link from the Raven Queen to Sebastien Siverling's identity.

Placing a fortune in her various stashes of emergency belongings throughout the city was obviously a horrible idea, for so many reasons that she didn't want to take the time to list them.

Her last option seemed to be the Nightmare Pack. Gera, at least, could probably be trusted not to betray the Raven Queen by snooping in her belongings. And the Nightmare Pack was wealthy enough—and committed enough crime—that they should have some well-warded, secret, and protected locations to store something for her.

But even so, she didn't feel quite secure unloading such sensitive items on...well, anyone, really.

She thought over that problem, and others, as she made a couple stops along the way to change her body and clothes and make sure she wasn't being followed.

Damien had written her back yesterday evening, urging her to come to Westbay Manor and lamenting that his overprotective older brother had him on literal house arrest as a reaction to the Raven Queen's latest shenanigans. Damien had assured Sebastien that Westbay Manor was one of the safest places in the city. No doubt he was desperate for news. But she had taken a dose of the anti-anxiety potion just before and was too tired to even send a response to him before falling asleep again.

Siobhan rubbed her cold-numbed hands together, making a mental note to send Damien another message when she got back from the Retreat.

When Siobhan arrived, Liza thrust a cup of tea into her hands, then ushered her to an armchair, where Siobhan spent the next thirty minutes dozing off—but not actually sleeping—while Liza used a potion to curl Siobhan's hair.

Sleepily, she asked Liza if she could build a warded box with similar protections to her divination-diverting ward.

Liza walked into the next room and came back with a small, square chest made of a peculiar wood marbled with white streaks. "I made a few to sell based on the same principles of your ward. Rather ingenious, and the shape is perfect for stable protection, so it is much more power-efficient than trying to shield a *human*. It doesn't work exactly the same, of course, because it cannot ride piggyback on your body or your Will, but it's some of the finest security that coin can buy. Two hundred gold."

Siobhan took the chest into her hands, opened the lid, and peered inside. The space had none of the telltale visual confusion that accompanied space-bending magic. "It's not expanded on the inside," she said, disappointed.

"I could add that in, for an extra hundred gold. Or you could purchase a larger model. I don't have any on hand, but I could have one ready in a week, if you don't need a rush job. It has a three-sided lock. One, a personalized key —some specific object that you must present. Two, a piece of your blood, saliva, or hair—which it will immediately destroy after verification. And three, a verbal phrase spoken aloud."

"How many of these have you sold?"

"A few. People at the secret meetings have found them intriguing."

"If I buy two, will you give me a discount? Three hundred fifty."

"I have to make each by hand, and the worth of my efforts does not decrease by fifty coins simply because you purchase two. Likewise, there are no logistical problems with shipping or storage that such a small order would ease."

"Hmm. You wouldn't happen to have left a back door for yourself to open these things without the blood and password, would you?" Siobhan asked.

Liza stared at her. "Truly, you have the mind of a criminal."

Siobhan scowled at her. "That is a common-sense question!"

Liza harrumphed. "I have left no such back door. But if I were determined to break the same wards I created, I would have a better chance of doing so than most."

"And don't you see how two hundred gold is too steep for a cramped box that doesn't have the versatility of my personal ward *and* that you've admitted you could probably break into? I have powerful enemies, and you left the army years ago. They could have artificers on the cutting-edge of the latest research who could totally crush your protections. And what about the Red Guard?"

Liza let out an incredulous bark of a laugh. "What I'm hearing is that, with such powerful enemies, you have desperate need of my services and no other options. Also, I *am* the cutting edge of the latest research, you obnoxious girl. I would pit my skills against any Red Guard diviner. They surpass me only in resources, and that cannot be helped unless you wish to pay approximately twenty to thirty times more."

Siobhan gave up, paying four more gold bars, plus an extra for Liza's fence in Osham, for two of the warded chests, though it pained her to feel her—admittedly unearned—wealth flow through her fingers like water. Always, it seemed, the more she had, the more she spent.

After their negotiations were concluded and Siobhan's hair thoroughly curled, some transmutation adjusted the shape of Siobhan's fake nose to more resemble Liza's. The woman gave her one of her dresses, modified for Siobhan's more slender frame, and told her to answer to "Amelia."

Less than an hour later, Siobhan climbed out of a carriage and followed her "Aunt Liza" into the Retreat at Willowdale. The same shaman that Liza had been walking with last time joined them in the Retreat's lobby, from which the three were escorted by one of the many staff.

Unlike the lower levels in the main part of the building, the severe trauma ward had fewer communal areas in favor of individual rooms with windows in the doors, padded floors and walls, and soft-edged furniture bolted to the floor.

In what open activity areas there were, guards watched actively, rather than being on-call. In one room they passed, a patient was drawing a spell array on the padded walls using their own feces. Except the spell array was all wrong, with lopsided, open numerological symbols and some glyphs that Siobhan didn't recognize, even after all of her study to learn any glyph that Myrddin's journal might throw at her.

Liza motioned to one of the Retreat's workers, who rushed off to deal with the patient.

Siobhan wanted to ask if that person was really going to try to cast a spell, and if so, what might happen. But Liza had warned her not to ask questions, and Siobhan could guess the answers well enough.

She caught a glimpse of another patient, who was scratching at their skin in swirling patterns that looked as if they had bled and healed and bled again, countless times.

Others paced, muttering to themselves or jumping at imaginary sounds.

But most of those held in the severe trauma ward were quiet, melancholic, or catatonic.

The man she was there to see was in one of the rare common areas, sitting in a chair beside a window and reading a book, though he paused frequently to give the potted plant on the windowsill suspicious glances.

The Retreat employee escorting them introduced them to the man, who stood and offered a handshake. "I am the archaeologist," he said.

Liza raised an eyebrow and shared a look with the shaman.

The patient pulled back his hand, balling it into a fist, and gave Liza and the shaman the same suspicious look previously reserved for the potted plant.

Their escort laughed awkwardly. "His name is Edgar. We've been trying to help him reclaim it, but losing the connection to one's name seems to be a common side effect of overexposure to the Black Wastes." She turned to the man and spoke slowly, as if to a child…or a dog. "Edgar, these people are here to help you."

Siobhan found the condescending tone distinctly unpleasant, and perhaps Liza agreed, because she shooed the woman away.

The archaeologist, who hadn't reacted at the sound of his name, was now glancing around the room as if looking for an escape route.

Liza's shaman reached into his beaded leather bag for some of the tools of his trade. "So, a standard anchoring and spirit-world barrier?" He looked up at the archaeologist. "It will work best if I have your cooperation. Are you familiar with lucid dreaming?"

Siobhan knew what lucid dreaming was, but the other jargon went right over her head.

The archaeologist, however, found the shaman's words very alarming and immediately moved to escape.

The shaman fumbled and almost dropped a bundle of woven herbs, and Liza stepped in front of the archaeologist to block his way, but she didn't attempt to touch or grab him.

One of the guards at the corner of the room was striding forward, already reaching for a black baton at his waist. Whether it was a cudgel or a battle wand, Siobhan didn't know, but she could see the archaeologist fraying at the edges, his eyes growing wilder even as he pulled his hands in toward his chest and hunched his shoulders.

Siobhan held up her hands, palms outstretched to either side. "Stop," she commanded. To her surprise, they did.

Everyone in the nearest half of the room turned to look at her, and the archaeologist tightened even further, like a coiled spring.

Reminded of a similar situation, where communication was difficult and the one she wanted to help only feared her, Siobhan reached out with her Will. She added no power, grasped for no energy, only announced her desire and command to the world in the same way she might when setting up a complex spell. It grated against her still-recovering Will-strain, but not even as much as casting the weakest possible version of her dreamless sleep spell. "Archaeologist, you are safe," she said simply. It was what he called himself, and what she would call him.

The man stilled, then slowly turned to face her.

She didn't smile or reach for him, only tried to push her surety of that statement into her Will. She would not harm him, nor allow any here to do so. He could trust himself to know the correct thing to do. He could trust himself to settle and be present this moment. To relax was good. To be filled with confidence was only right and natural.

The archaeologist took one step toward her, and then another, straightening even as his shoulders loosened and fell. His hands returned to his sides and uncurled. He sighed, as if he had stepped from the searing heat into a cool room, and smiled at her. "Oh, that's very nice. Sorry about the skittishness," he added, looking around at the others. "I'm still recovering from the trauma. I have good days and bad days."

Exposure to the Black Wastes caused paranoia, nightmares, and hallucinations at the best of times, and the effects were lingering.

Liza and the shaman were both staring silently, and after an awkward moment where no one responded to the man, the shaman turned to Liza. "I admit, I was somewhat skeptical of the quality of a healer's apprenticeship in Silva Erde, but that is a most impressive technique." He turned back to Siobhan, fluttering his hands in the air. "Even I can feel it, somewhat. How does it work? You're not a free-caster, are you? Surely not—so young!"

"I also had no idea," Liza said, staring at Siobhan piercingly.

Siobhan's stomach flipped with sudden dread. Surely, this was not another ability that she shouldn't have? "I've simply found that some living beings are sensitive to the Will. We may not have any way to quantify it, technically, but that does not mean we are oblivious to it." These words weren't exactly true, as it seemed that Myrddin had found some way to do the supposedly impossible, but of course she couldn't say so.

"Oh, marvelous!" the shaman said, clapping his hands together. "I know what you mean, and it's certainly true that we have a hind-brain sense for powerful thaumaturges—especially when they're angry!—but I've never heard of someone using their Will so deliberately outside of active casting. I suppose it's not so different to the techniques used when dream-walking? But you must have trained incessantly to improve your clarity and forcefulness! And how did you know that Edgar would be receptive to such a thing? I suppose his exposure to the Black Wastes has thinned his natural protection and left him more sensitive."

Siobhan cleared her throat awkwardly. "They're doing a lot of experimental work in Silva Erde," she hedged.

"Practices to markedly improve fidelity through focus on the facets of clarity, force, and soundness," Liza murmured. "Or so I imagine."

"Oh yes, not nearly so bound to the strictures of modern sorcery over there, or so I hear," the shaman agreed. "Edgar," he added, "I simply must try this technique. Let me know what you feel." The shaman closed his eyes, raised his hands to his temple, and concentrated.

Siobhan could feel his Will in the air and withdrew her own, holding back a sigh of relief at the lessened pressure in her head.

The archaeologist lifted his hands and wiggled them in a "so-so" motion. "Eh, I can get the sense of it, but it's not as crisp or smooth as Miss... Oh, I'm sorry, I didn't catch your name," he said, turning abruptly back to Siobhan.

"Call me Amelia," she said.

The archaeologist nodded amiably, reaching out and taking her hand to shake, even though she hadn't offered it. He shook it up and down for a bit too long, as if he'd forgotten how many pumps were standard. "Really very nice. You three are here to help speed my recovery, then? I heard I'm the only one who made it out. Well, not physically, but mentally, you know." He tapped his forefinger twice against his temple.

"I would like to try the technique as well," Liza interrupted.

Like the shaman had done, she raised her hands to her temples. She scowled at the archaeologist and began to tremble slightly, her face growing red.

The archaeologist shrank backward, and Siobhan quickly filled the area with her own Will again to combat the predatory swoop of Liza's intention. It reminded Siobhan more of the magical wind attacks of a gigantic roc than any sort of soothing aura of peace.

"No, no, nope!" the archaeologist yelped.

Liza's efforts eased. "What did I do wrong?"

The archaeologist shook his head repeatedly. "Well, you might as well press a pillow over someone's face to get them to stop worrying about the monster under the bed. And it was all choppy"—he slashed his hand through the air repeatedly—"and both of you were too shallow. Very fake-feeling, no smoothness, no depth. Where's your *sincerity*?" he added sagely, crossing his arms over his chest. "You'll need to train a bit more to match Amelia here. Honestly, if I were you two, I'd be ashamed to have been surpassed so handily by a woman decades your junior. As you make your bed, so will you lie in it, as they say."

Liza ground her teeth in frustration but didn't argue.

Siobhan very carefully didn't meet her gaze.

The shaman chuckled awkwardly. "Well, I suppose you're ready for the anchoring then, eh, Edgar?"

The archaeologist peered at him not with anxious paranoia but with something Siobhan guessed might have been skepticism. "I'd rather not. Someone with such a half-hearted, ham-fisted Will, rooting around in *my* head?"

The shaman's mouth fell open, and then he flushed bright red. "Well, I never!" He turned to Liza. "Madam, let us attend to those who need us, and leave this ungrateful chap to his own devices. If he wants to recover without treatment, I say let him do so!"

It had always been the plan that Liza would go and do whatever it was she did while Siobhan used her temporary cover identity to speak to the archaeologist. Despite this, Liza now seemed somewhat reluctant to leave, and only begrudgingly nodded. "We will talk later," she said to Siobhan.

Siobhan and the archaeologist moved back to the window, where Siobhan sat across from him.

He looked nervously at the plant. "Sorry, could you do the thing again? I still get a little paranoid around greenery. In the Black Wastes, a bush isn't just a bush. Or it might not be a bush the next time you look. Maybe it's grown eyeballs, or you try to wipe your butt with one of the leaves and suddenly it's turned into a tongue—" He shuddered, then leaned in and whispered, "That actually happened to one of the team. I won't say who. You may think it sounds funny, or that I'm joking, but I assure you, when such a thing actually happens to you, it is a deeply horrifying experience."

Siobhan took a moment to get into the right mindset, then reached out with her Will again to convey the idea of safety and confidence to whatever part of him could sense it. "I'm actually here to ask about what happened, and what you discovered. Are you able to talk about it?"

"I hope you don't want me to relive that experience. If there were some way to burn the whole thing from my mind, I would do it. Except for Myrddin's hermitage. I want to remember that."

Siobhan suppressed her curiosity. She would love to hear every detail about Myrddin's lost hermitage, but that wasn't why she was here. "I don't need any of the lurid stories. It's only that the facts of what happened are… slightly confusing. What exactly did you retrieve?"

"Oh, well you know most everything had been preserved by the wards for hundreds of years. It wasn't until one of the warding stones—more like boulders—was cracked in one of the Black Waste shifts—that's the theory anyway—that we were able to find the hermitage at all. We got a lot of old books, a few artifacts of historical significance, and a veritable fortune in beast cores and celerium. The biggest haul was the ward stones themselves." The archaeologist looked around, then leaned in to whisper. "But the most important thing we recovered were Myrddin's personal research journals."

Siobhan's heart was pounding, but she did her best to keep the urgency from her face. "Interesting," she said, in the tone people used when they were curious but not entirely riveted. "Were there any self-charging artifacts? Or did you find Myrddin's rumored enormous Conduit? Perhaps something like a control mechanism for Carnagore?"

'Anything,' she explained silently, '*that could be more important than one of the books. Anything Oliver could have stolen.*'

"Oh, no. If those things were real, Myrddin probably had them on him when he died, wherever that is. It's possible one of the artifacts will reveal something when examined more closely. We didn't want to risk damaging anything on-site, and didn't have the sanity left to linger. We just packed everything we could carry that had the slightest significance and returned as quickly as possible. However, even if the originals were lost, I'm hopeful that one of Myrddin's five research journals will contain the method to recreate his experiments. In fact, I'm quite positive of it."

Siobhan swallowed, her tongue suddenly dry and too thick in her mouth. "Five journals? Are you sure?"

The archaeologist raised an eyebrow. "Five journals, one for each of my fingers. I don't believe I was going so insane by that point that I would have become confused about something so simple."

Siobhan cleared her throat. "I ask because, as far as anyone seems to know, there are only four. The University retains three, while the fourth was stolen by a fearsome character who goes by the moniker 'the Raven Queen.' There has been quite the hullabaloo about it."

The man's eyes widened, and then widened again almost comically, before collapsing into a vicious scowl. "That murderous half-breed! It must have been her. She disappeared last, when we were only a couple days from the edge of the Black Wastes. Vanished in the night. She must have stolen one." His left foot tapped rapidly against the floor, and he eyed the potted plant again, scooting as far away from it as the confines of the armchair would allow.

He lifted a thumb to his mouth and began to bite at the nail. "Oh no, oh no. Which one did she take, do you think? The one on the table? The one that has the answer? Oh no. That dirty half-breed was probably a spy. Osham would want this. *Need* it. They've been feeling the pinch, too. I heard they sent their own expedition, too slow, but that must have been a cover. By now, Osham's had the book for months and probably decrypted it. I need to talk to the High Crown."

He made to stand, but Siobhan increased the force of her Will, urging him to restfulness. She needed more information still.

The archaeologist sat back down, his attempt at movement aborted but his agitation unsoothed. "This means war," he said, biting down hard enough on the cuticle of his thumb that the skin broke and began to bleed. "Or, or... maybe we can steal it back. Or kidnap some of their researchers and torture the information out of them."

He began to mutter incomprehensibly, his sentences incoherent and interspersed with "half-breed," "Osham," and "the book. We *need* the book."

"Archaeologist," she snapped.

His gaze jerked back toward her.

"None of the women returned alive. Who was this thief?"

"A half-breed water bitch. Too-big eyes, deep and hiding her secrets and malice. She wanted to kill me, I could tell. But I had a plan and I was going to kill her first. Except then she disappeared. And, oh, Myrddin forgive us, she took the book."

Siobhan tried to push even more serenity into her Will, but even without the lingering Will-strain, she would have struggled to do so in her own current mental state, and it had little effect. "What was in the book she took?"

The archaeologist stilled, then leaned back from her, tilting his head too far away so that he was looking down the entire bridge of his nose at her, his eyes squinted almost closed. "Why would you ask that? Are you an Osham spy, too?"

Before Siobhan could answer, the archaeologist had lunged for the potted plant and was trying to wrench it off the table, presumably to throw at her. However, it was glued to the surface, and so he quickly entered a futile wrestling match with the furniture, dirt spilling from the pot as he tried to dislodge the entire table from its spot despite the bolts securing it to the floor.

The same guard from earlier hurried forward again, and together with a couple of the other employees, he shoved the end of the baton into the center of the archaeologist's chest and activated whatever spell was contained within.

The archaeologist relaxed abruptly, so completely that he might have slumped to the floor if not for the support of the employees.

One of the women apologized to Siobhan while ushering her out and to the doorway of the room where Liza and the shaman were still working.

Siobhan remained outside, but caught a glimpse of a much nicer private room, with fake windows showing illusions of various types of scenery and a whiff of gentle incense. Siobhan waited in the hallway with her back against the wall so that she could not give in to the urge to peek further. She ignored the strange looks from the Retreat's employees until Liza exited.

The woman was in a peculiar mood that Siobhan couldn't quite read, and so the carriage ride back to Gilbratha-proper was strained and silent.

'I still cannot be totally sure that Oliver is behind the disappearance of this undine cambion and the fifth book. But I will be surprised if I find that he was not. I know my book is one of Myrddin's true journals. There is evidence enough of that. It is simply one of the five, and, judging by the archaeologist's response, it's likely that the one I hold is not the most important one, not the one everyone is looking for.'

The most pressing question in her mind, however, was why this other book was so important. The archaeologist had used the word "need," and even seemed to believe that ownership would be enough to cause war between Lenore and Osham. Perhaps he was being paranoid. But, judging by the resources the Architects of Khronos and the Thirteen Crowns had been willing to put into finding her...perhaps it was not merely paranoia.

'Oliver might know the answers, but I cannot ask him. The High Crown knows, and perhaps Titus Westbay, but they are both out of my reach.' However, there was at least one other who should know, and who she could access.

Though she had planned to lie low, it seemed that the Raven Queen needed to make a visit to Grandmaster Kiernan.

41

RITUAL UNDER MOONLIGHT

Sebastien
  Month 4, Day 11, Sunday 1:00 p.m.

Sebastien hurried across the University grounds toward the Menagerie, grimacing as she checked the time on her pocket watch. A good number of students returning for the spring term were wandering the pathways, but they moved aside easily enough to let her pass.

After returning from the Retreat, she had taken a nap at Liza's, calling on the woman to help cast her dreamless sleep spell once more. Somehow, she had slept for four hours straight.

Now, she was rushing to hit a fast-approaching deadline. The new moon—also known as the dark moon—would hit the highest spot in its travel for the day in almost exactly forty minutes. Somewhat bizarrely, it was only five minutes ahead of when the sun would reach its highest point. The moon would be completely invisible, but all her references and calculations assured her this was the correct time.

If Sebastien missed it, she would have to wait an entire month to start the guiding light ritual to create the symbol she would use as a beacon, which already took almost seven weeks to complete. Normally, she would have chosen to let her Will rest more, but the ritual's minimum thaum require-ments were child's play. It required clarity and focus, not a vast capacity. Her head still ached somewhat, but surely it wouldn't be much worse than the technique she'd used to calm the Archaeologist, as the man called himself.

And since the ritual process would have to be repeated seven times, if she wanted to push power into it just to be safe, she would have other chances to do so.

In addition to the fact that she could cast it, what had interested Sebastien most about this esoteric spell, and induced her to memorize its requirements, was that the beacon could not be traced back to her. If successful, it would leave her in complete control without generating dangerous loopholes. *'It must not work off the principles of sympathetic magic,'* Sebastien mused.

As she continued deeper into the Menagerie—though not past the wards of the secondary gates that protected students from the dangers that lay deeper into the semi-wild artificial forest—the surrounding students noticeably thinned out.

Luckily, there was no one lingering around the clearing that she had taken to practicing light-refinement in. She hadn't planned far enough ahead for this ritual to have found a suitable replacement location. As Sebastien began to draw the huge Circle she would need into the ground with a sturdy stick, she suddenly realized that, for once, what she was doing wasn't illegal. Even if someone noticed her, the most that would come of it would be gossip. She chuckled. *'Wow. What a strange life I lead, that I automatically assume my projects outside of schoolwork will get me sent to jail.'*

She added a heptagram within the Circle, making sure the lines of the seven-pointed star were as straight and even as possible. She accompanied each movement with a deep hum that reminded her of the light-refinement spell. Then she placed components in each of the seven outer spaces the star had created: a handful of unsprouted seeds, tossed carelessly; seven polished shards of silver, in which her reflection could be seen; a vial of shade dust, left corked so that its contents could not float away on the breeze; a strip of soft leather, tied into a knot over and over again until it could be tied no more; seven eyes of a mantis shrimp—which could have been substituted with the eye of a prognos if she were willing to do something so heinous, according to the Comprehensive Compendium of Components; an adder stone, the hole through its center worn naturally by time and fate; and finally, a blue-grey gauze created from the silk of the portal-weaver spider and woven into the shape of a circle one thread at a time. That had been the most expensive component of them all.

It would have been nice to know the exact purpose of each component, the better to focus her Will, but the text she had memorized hadn't been that thorough.

Sebastien fumbled in her satchel for a piece of paper and her second vial of free-writing potion. She didn't need it to last very long, so she only swallowed a third of the vial while reviewing the requirements of the chant she needed to create.

"The Self, the Other, the Fate, and the Summons," she muttered as parts of her mind relaxed like unclenching fingers while others stirred to life. The chant's structure was defined, and a few key words and phrases in specific places were required, but beyond that her options were open.

Her hand on the paper moved almost without her conscious control, and though she was vaguely aware of the words spilling out from the tip of her fountain pen, she couldn't have told someone what they were, if asked.

Sebastien finished writing before the potion wore off, but continued her preparation so as not to waste any time. She pulled a large stone bowl from her satchel, filled it with distilled water, and then sprinkled in a handful of chunky white salt, her hand moving in the shape of a heptagram once more.

Into a small mortar, she measured a dollop of honey. A sprinkle of three different spices joined that. Each movement was accompanied by the same deep hum. As she ground up the mixture with a pestle, it took on the vibrant, shocking red of fresh blood.

Next, she used her athame to carefully cut out the shape of her chosen symbol from a sheet of glue paper. She wet the paper and pressed the outline to the skin of her chest, below her collarbone but above her heart. This left only the exact shape of the symbol open to the air, so that she couldn't accidentally misdraw it and ruin everything.

By that time, the free-writing potion was beginning to wear off, and only a few minutes remained until the moon had risen to its highest point over the horizon. She picked up the sheet of paper with the scrawled chant to review it, hoping to memorize it in time.

A frown creased the skin between her eyebrows and deepened as she read. It wasn't as blatantly embarrassing as her previous attempts, but in other ways, it was much worse. It was…disturbing.

She read over each section of the chant again, then roughly rubbed her arms, where the hair had risen with a chill. *'Do I want to use this? Is it… Where did these words come from?'* She couldn't help but think of the thing locked behind the seal in her mind.

Sebastien lowered the paper and looked up at the sky, her eyes watering as she stared past the sun. *'Whatever truth it may or may not contain, it's not as if pretending it doesn't exist will change anything. That's what I've been doing for years, and look where it's gotten me. Certainly, I am not yet destroyed, but that is not the path to salvation. I don't want to be afraid of everything.'*

And so she gritted her teeth, checked her pocket watch once more, and placed the mortar of red paste atop her head, balancing it carefully. Then, holding the stone bowl of salt water in her hands, she moved to the northernmost point of the heptagram. She took a deep breath and dipped the fingers of the hand that held her Conduit in the water, then began to walk the arc of the Circle. With each measured step, she sprinkled water along her path.

She cleared her throat and began with the part of the chant labeled, "the Self."

"I AM a changeling like the seasons,
   A daughter of shadow and light,
   Of Charybdis mists and raven's flight,
   And always I seek after mysteries."

HER HEAD THROBBED SLIGHTLY as the water grew cooler, but neither her voice nor her Will faltered. She reached the northernmost point of the heptagram again and then began to walk the shape, speaking the chant of "the Other."

"SHADOWS of the past become shades of the present.
   Old scars peel open like doors.
   And a hungry sky watches
   As I sing the dead to life."

SEBASTIEN SHUDDERED and almost decided not to continue. Surely, a one-month delay was tolerable, and she could come up with something less creepy to say about herself? But instead, she continued with "the Fate."

"As I ORNAMENT this veil with thorns,
   I shall drink the sea to quench my thirst.
   The taste of nothing on my tongue
   Will be a knife as sharp as its wielder."

SHE MOVED to the space in the middle, dipped her finger into the saltwater once more, and painted over the symbol on her chest, making sure to fill in all the space and every edge of the glued-on template to make it as perfect as possible. Finally, she lifted her free hand to the mortar on her head, dipped her forefinger into its contents, and spoke "the Summons" while painting careful lines across her face. This was the only part of the chant that was predefined.

. . .

"MARK ME, scarred and tattered witness of days,
   One who weaves the thread that still is woven."

SHE PAINTED the red mixture of honey and spice from her hairline straight
down over her eyelid and again on the other side. Finally, she drew a line from
the center of her bottom lip down her chin, all the way to the hollow at the
base of her throat.

"HEED ME, one who howls unheard.
   I command you. Grant me eyes that see."

SEBASTIEN TENSED, some part of her expecting something to happen. But
nothing changed, for good or ill. Then, she repeated the process from beginning to end six more times, burning the symbol into her mind a bit deeper
every time. And then it was over.

Still, nothing happened, and Sebastien felt somewhat silly for her earlier
trepidation. The parameters of the spell were pretty clear. It wasn't like the
chant could make itself true just by saying it. If it was accurate and specific
enough—though filled with metaphor and flowery word choice—once she had
completed this process six more times at specific lunar phases, she would gain
a very specific ability. If it wasn't, the ritual would fail.

Most likely, her subconscious had just noted the final section of the chant
and matched the first three sections with words that were suitably dramatic
and tonally congruent.

Still, she couldn't help but wonder from what part of her subconscious mind
the words had come. She thought back to the other thing she had written under
the effects of the free-writing potion. Could that, too, have been a little truer
than she thought, the words not just random ominous lines patched together to
sow confusion, but pulled from some coherent part of her subconscious?

Sebastien briefly considered what might happen if she took another swig
of the free-writing potion and then asked the thing behind her grandfather's
seal a question. She shook her head rapidly as a shudder rolled down her
body. "No, no. I will not be doing that," she muttered to herself.

Her mood was dark as she scrubbed her face clean and packed everything
up. The symbol lingered in her mind like a spot of darkness in her vision after
staring at a bright light. But it faded away from her consciousness as she
scuffed out the spell array, then left the Menagerie. At least half the students
had arrived already and were busy catching up on gossip.

Several were reading newspapers. Sebastien considered trying to find one that had been discarded, or even asking to borrow one so that she could read whatever they were saying, but couldn't bring herself to do so. '*No. Don't run away*,' she thought, immediately spinning on her heel to ask a man if she could borrow his paper when he was done with it. She was good at not thinking about things. But she didn't want to pretend Parker's death hadn't happened. Her Will-strain wasn't so bad that traumatic thoughts were a threat to her wellbeing.

The man agreed with a bright smile and thrust it on her before he even finished reading, as if it were her doing him a favor rather than the other way around.

It was the Daily Sun, a sensationalist gossip rag that only pretended to write anything of substance.

"Raven Queen Claims Gilbratha!" it announced in a big bold headline. She read the beginning of the article.

While discerning readers who have kept up with our publications may have expected that the Raven Queen would attempt to interfere with Ennis Naught's sentencing, her actual response was beyond all our prognostication!

SEBASTIEN SNORTED and began to skim. Halfway down the page was more speculation and interpretations of a paraphrased version of the free-written message she had delivered to the Edictum Council.

The Raven Queen was frightening and evil and had been trying to do some city-wide blood ritual with all the ravens. An anonymous "expert" calculated that some kind of geas might have been placed on anyone who watched the spectacle too long.

She had also declared war on the Thirteen Crown Families and threatened to eat them. Whether this was hyperbole or literal threat, the writer felt that the latter was most likely. After all, ravens were carrion eaters!

And it was a confirmed fact from an anonymous source in the coppers that the Raven Queen could explode her body into a flock of ravens as a way to travel quickly and avoid notice. Each raven could become a version of her so that, if necessary, she could act in a dozen places at once.

This was how she had attacked the Edictum Council and the University at the same time!

The Pendragon Corps had been holding some of her thralls—or maybe some spies from Osham—and she had attacked and freed them. Or held them hostage. Who knew? The more theories, the better, even if they were contradictory!

During the ensuing battle, the Pendragon Corps conjured a miniature sun to fight her—or maybe an angel from the Plane of Radiance, depending on the "eyewitness" account. And in turn, the Raven Queen had called upon the very darkness itself, as she was known to do, and created an eclipse. She then cursed the Charybdis Gulf kraken into a frenzy until it sank the boat of her enemies, after which she and the others rode away atop its back as it waved one tentacle mockingly.

The High Crown had declared that he was taking measures to ensure the safety of the city and its people, and so the Raven Queen would probably be caught or killed soon. Or she would kill and eat the High Crown and take his place, starting a new regime of bird worship.

The Raven Queen's bounty had been raised to the truly towering sum of twenty-five thousand gold crowns. It was enough to entice professionals to come after her, perhaps. *'Even more reason to disappear.'*

The story didn't mention Parker or his death. Sebastien took a deep breath and lowered the asinine paper. She would make sure that his family was taken care of. She had the gold to make it so, now. And it would not do to be known as an oath breaker.

Sebastien shoved the newspaper in a trash bin on her way back to the dorms, where she drew aside the curtain in front of her own cubicle to find someone waiting for her within. She recognized Damien, but the shock had hit her first, so she still jumped and gasped.

Damien stood from where he had perched atop the trunk at the foot of her narrow bed. He looked her up and down, narrow-eyed and thorough, missing nothing. "Where were you?" he asked, clenching and unclenching his fists at his side.

"In the Menagerie?" she said, an ominous hunch urging her to lift her chin and straighten her shoulders defensively.

"No, that's—why didn't you come to Westbay Manor? Didn't you get my letter?"

Sebastien nodded slowly, curling her fingers around the leather strap of her satchel. "I did get it. But I wasn't in any danger." *'Not at that point, anyway,'* she added silently. Aloud, she continued, "And I had things I needed to get done before the term started. It was bad timing."

Damien stared at her for a few long seconds, then stepped forward until they were only a few inches apart.

Sebastien resisted the urge to retreat.

"Is it confidential? Do we need to go somewhere private to talk?" Damien asked quietly, staring into her shoulder. "Did *she* do something to you?"

Sebastien gritted her teeth together. She had realized, obviously, that she would need to have a complicated conversation with Damien, because he was incapable of suppressing his curiosity. Also, now that all the bracelets that had connected him to her were useless and also possibly recognizable to the High Crown's operatives and the coppers, she would have to come up with *some* excuse to make him get rid of them.

But she hadn't yet worked through this conversation in her mind. There was simply too much going on, too many things that required her attention, and she was less capable of juggling it all than normal. "We should go elsewhere," she answered in the same conspiratorial tone, hoping that, in the time it took them to travel to a "safe" location, she could come up with a strategy for the conversation.

Damien's eyes traveled around, looking not at reality but at the images in his mind's eye. "The study room?" he finally suggested. "We can close the door and maybe cobble together a basic sound-muffling spell?"

Sebastien agreed, her mind spinning as they walked. She was paying so little attention to their surroundings that a flush-faced firstie with her head bowed almost rammed into her.

Damien grabbed Sebastien's forearm and tugged her out of the way just in time. He waved the girl away impatiently as she tried to apologize, and as they walked on again, he very pointedly ran his grip from Sebastien's elbow down to the wrist.

Normally, Sebastien wore an assortment of simple bracelets on that forearm, hidden under her clothes, but the Pendragon Corps had ripped them all away.

In the study room they used in the mornings, a group of students sat around the main table, playing some sort of game using tiny flags, miniature tokens on a board, and dice. "This is our room," Damien announced loudly. "Get out," he said, pointing imperiously toward the door.

One of the women puffed up in anger and opened her mouth to argue, but a man leaned over and spoke in her ear, just loud enough for them all to hear. "That's Damien Westbay and Sebastien Siverling."

She deflated. The game players packed up and left, a few of them throwing dark looks at Damien and Sebastien.

The two of them checked the room for eavesdroppers or listening devices with what Sebastien might normally have thought was an abnormal level of paranoia. She resolved to learn a sound-muffling spell like the one Professor Lacer often free-cast, but Damien was able to put together something similar enough to speak safely.

When they were sure it was safe, Damien rounded on Sebastien. "Your bracelets are all gone," he announced.

"Yes," Sebastien admitted. Despite the delay, she still hadn't come up with a good way to reveal what she needed without giving away her real secrets.

She could try to deny Damien any extra information, but his curiosity was almost as powerful as hers. He wouldn't be able to let it go, and even if not now, that could mean disaster for her down the road.

"I can deduce a few possible reasons," Damien continued boldly. "Perhaps you took them all off to go undercover or something. Or, you were doing something dangerous and almost got caught, and you had to hide them somewhere in case they might be traced back to me and whoever else is on the other end. Or one of our allies betrayed us, but you don't know who, and you got rid of any connections that could be used against us as a precaution. Or… you got into a really bad situation and you broke them all, desperate for help. But if that was the case, I should have been alerted. And I wasn't."

As Sebastien listened to Damien so proudly spout these rather outlandish hypotheses, she had an epiphany. She didn't need to find a way to explain things or to lie convincingly. Given even the slightest input and asked to deduce something, Damien could deceive himself without any extra help.

If Sebastien could give him carefully curated hints, Damien could make deductions *that he would believe,* and she could either let those deductions stand or modify them with a bit of guidance. She wouldn't even need to lie. She cleared her throat. "First, I need you to know that I truly had no intention to get involved with anything that happened yesterday. But the choice was taken out of my hands. What do you know about what happened? I'm sure you must have heard some of it."

Damien took a deep breath. "I think I know basically what the newspapers know, though I learned it a bit earlier. I was at the Edictum Council building when everything started. I'm sure you have a better understanding of the details than me, actually. The higher-ups probably filled you in on whatever they know," he said bitterly.

He crossed his arms over his chest, jutting out his jaw. "On the other hand, *I* had no idea what was happening! I was forced to team up with Oliver Dryden in a desperate attempt to find out what was going on and if anything had happened to you."

Sebastien inhaled sharply and choked on her own saliva. She coughed, mentally reeling. Sebastien knew it would seem suspicious if she acted too interested. "You teamed up with Oliver Dryden?" she repeated with an attempt at nonchalance. "How did it go? Was he…an asset?"

Damien's glower grew darker. "Well, he isn't very likable, is he? Also, I have to say that he seems to be missing a basic understanding of how to work for a secret organization. Perhaps he needs some sort of training? Not everyone is a natural at clandestine operations. But at least he cares," Damien added grudgingly. "He didn't just sit around all googly-eyed like a lot of the other nobles. He tried to do something. And he has some of his own contacts, which might make him a valuable asset."

"His own contacts?" Sebastien echoed leadingly.

"Yes, some people who were sending him messages and such. And he had no trouble getting invited to the Rouse Family's afterparty, despite being a foreign lord. Wait." Damien eyed her strangely. "Don't tell me that his membership to our organization got *denied*?" He sounded half scandalized, half delighted, though she wasn't sure where this deduction had come from. "I only teamed up with him because you'd mentioned previously that he was trying to join—a provisional member, just like me. But I did think it was suspicious that the man supposedly left his star emblem at home. I flashed mine at him, and he just stared blankly at me for a moment like a complete boob. Did his emblem get confiscated when he was rejected? And since I obviously didn't know that, he decided to take advantage of the situation?"

Damien was speaking, of course, about the light-crystal coasters that Sebastien had modified to take the shape of a thirteen-pointed star.

"I'm not totally sure. Hopefully I'll know soon," Sebastien said. "And...I'm not saying he's an enemy. But you shouldn't blindly trust him. He might have his own agenda."

Damien grew somber and nodded gravely. "Can you tell me more, or is it confidential?"

Sebastien shook her head, her silence enough of an answer.

"Okay. But there's another important matter at hand." He clenched his fists and spoke in a distinctly aristocratic tone. "I want to lodge a formal complaint with the higher-ups."

Sebastien blinked.

"We have a severe problem with communication! I was totally in the dark and unable to help on Friday. And before you argue that I'm not a full member yet, I don't think it makes sense to turn down help wherever you can get it. I may be a provisional member, but I'm *still* a member. I still took the oath. Even if I couldn't have been informed about the details of what was going on, at the very least we need some method to get emergency missions on the fly. Did you know that Oliver Dryden has a distagram?" Damien threw up his arms in frustration and turned to pace back and forth in front of her. "Why don't we all have distagrams, or some kind of secret communication artifacts like what the Red Guard uses? I mean, what if something were to happen to you? I would have literally no way of knowing how to get in contact with the higher-ups to ask for help."

Damien stopped and pivoted on the spot with narrow eyes. "Do we need gold? Is that it? Because I am totally prepared to bribe my way into full membership with a large 'donation.' I can tell Titus I spent it on something foolish, or donated the gold to charity or something. You should suggest that to the higher-ups. Well, don't say it exactly like that. Word it more tactfully, of course."

Sebastien opened her mouth and then closed it again without saying anything.

"In the end, one of the coppers noticed me and dragged me back home to Westbay Manor, just as Lord Dryden got a message that seemed important. I had to wait two hours, alone with only the servants and my own horrid imagination, for Dryden's runner to arrive. And the message only said, 'Sebastien reported alive. No access to him. No other news.'"

Sebastien winced.

"I snapped one of the bracelets you gave me at around the same time that the Raven Queen supposedly broke those elite enemy spies out of the secret prison where they were being held and then escaped on a stolen ship. But I didn't get a response from you until yesterday afternoon, and then it was some vague platitudes not to worry. I know you couldn't write anything sensitive in case the message was intercepted, but…" Damien shook his head helplessly, a hint of desperation pulling at the corners of his lips. "What happened, Sebastien?"

42

BACK TO SCHOOL

SEBASTIEN
Month 4, Day 11, Sunday 2:30 p.m.

"WELL, about the bracelets, it was a combination of all your hypotheses," Sebastien said. "Mostly. And I need you to burn any you have left."

Damien's eyes widened. "What happened?" he breathed, taking a small step closer to her.

"They were all activated. Every single one I own."

Damien sucked in a sharp breath.

"But no one was alerted because, to be honest, I'm not a very powerful thaumaturge yet," Sebastien admitted. "There was resistance, and the bracelets' magic wasn't strong enough to dig past it. Also, I have realized that they're much too recognizable. Just like you said, we need to come up with a better way to send each other signals at a distance. Something less bulky and expensive than a distagram, probably. Our organization does have access to an extremely competent artificer." With the gold and celerium that Sebastien had taken from the Pendragon operatives' vault, she could afford more custom work from Liza.

"What happened? Did the Raven Queen get to you? Are you in danger?" Damien's eyes darted to the shadows in the corner of the room and under the table. "Did she...do something to you again?"

Sebastien hesitated. "The Raven Queen isn't after me."

"What is it, then? Tell me," Damien demanded, reaching forward to touch

Sebastien's elbow as if he might need to yank Sebastien physically out of harm's way at a moment's notice.

"On Friday...the High Crown decided to kidnap several people who had some sort of connection to the Raven Queen. Including some children." Sebastien paused, gratified to watch as Damien's gaze grew vague. He was obviously spinning up his own ideas. Hopefully, ones that would be useful to her.

"Those supposed spies that the Raven Queen freed were actually civilians he was..." She decided not to imprecate the High Crown by saying anything more damning. Damien could come to his own conclusions.

Damien sucked in a few deep breaths, his fingers spasming on her elbow as he closed his eyes. "And you were one of them? The High Crown kidnapped you?"

Sebastien bit her lip. That might be a convenient conclusion, but she could only imagine the many ways such a claim might backfire. "I wasn't," she denied. "And none of the Pendragon operatives will remember finding me," she added. "But there's a problem. I got a concussion. And...Will-strain."

Damien's grey eyes snapped open, the whites obviously bloodshot with stress and sleeplessness. For the first time Sebastien could remember, she felt the hint of his Will in the air, as turbulent and ephemeral as storm winds.

She continued. "So I need the story to be that I got swept up in the crowd yesterday when people were panicking and hit my head. The concussion precludes casting for a few days, just to be on the safe side. There should be no hint of Will-strain."

Damien spun around and, with his back to her, cursed more viciously than she had ever heard him. He then took two deep breaths and turned to face her. "How did you escape?"

"Trickery, innovative use of basic spells, and I had some help. Without the help...it would have gone very, very badly." Anders and Parker were probably the only reason she or anyone else had made it out. Without them, it was even possible that she could be dead right now. She shuddered, remembering the harpoon cutting through Parker like a fork through a bit of melon. She had seen many deaths that day, and the corpses of her enemies. Those gruesome memories invited flinches and cold chills whenever she thought of them. But somehow, Parker's sudden death was worse. He had been one of hers, and now he was gone. He had died in pain and horribly frightened.

"One of the other members?" Damien asked, his tone sure enough that it wasn't really a question. "No one that's going to talk? You can trust them? Because, Sebastien, it would be very bad if word got out that you fought one of the High Crown's men." He ran his fingers through the sides of his hair, fingers scraping against the scalp. "And you're certain that they wiped the operative's memory properly? There aren't going to be any strange gaps or confusion leading back to you? It would be best if they thought they searched for you but just couldn't find you. Anything else…" He trailed off with foreboding.

"They handled it properly," Sebastien agreed.

Damien, surprisingly, relaxed at this. Apparently, it seemed reasonable to him that their secret ranks contained some amazing, elite thaumaturges who were skilled in arcane blood magic.

Sebastien tilted her head to the side. "That doesn't…bother you? Memory wipes are blood magic, right?"

Damien waved a hand nonchalantly, as if that was an unimportant aside and a distraction from more important topics. "As long as they're careful not to hurt anyone who doesn't deserve it or corrupt their Wills. This was obviously necessary. But why would the High Crown want you? What was he doing with the others?"

Sebastien shrugged. Best to let Damien come to his own conclusions about that one.

Damien's expression went through a series of transformations, growing increasingly unhappy with whatever he was thinking, until it settled into something surprisingly menacing. "I see," he said. "I don't know how I keep being surprised by things like this."

His baleful look slipped away as his eyes grew shiny, and he blinked rapidly. "What does this mean for us? Are we—as a group—doing anything about it? This is the kind of thing our organization was created to fight against, right?"

Sebastien shook her head. "I've been put on temporary leave. I have to lie low for a while. I might be running basic errands, but there won't be any big missions. For me, at least. Your current assignment still stands."

Damien's head bowed with disappointment. "I see. Well, it really isn't safe for you. It's good that the higher-ups care for your wellbeing, what with the High Crown wanting to 'use' you." He patted her arm comfortingly. "I'm sure they'll put you back to work once the heat dies down."

Sebastien agreed, trying to seem as if she were still disappointed.

"I can't believe the Raven Queen was actually on the side of good this time. I mean, freeing the kidnapped civilians, at least. Who knows if she did that with good intentions, but isn't it ironic how she's saving people while the High Crown is committing atrocities?" he asked, but his tone made it clear he wasn't really looking for an answer. "I don't know why I keep being surprised by things like this," he repeated. "It's Ana's uncles and the stuff with Newton all over again, isn't it? I've been…so naive."

Damien had more questions, but Sebastien refused to share the details of her ordeal and suggested that they return to the dorms so that she could recuperate. As they walked back, Damien asked, "Do you think Titus knew about this?"

Sebastien's heart clenched. "I don't know. But you can't tell him. Not even a hint of it."

Damien was already nodding before she could finish her sentence. "I know, don't worry. I'm…I'm glad there's someone out there trying to make a difference, to fix all this." He waved his hand vaguely. "If not for us…" He took a tremulous breath and sighed dourly, his grey eyes oppressively dark.

Sebastien suppressed a pang of guilt, but it was quickly wiped away by astonishment as she saw that Damien's cubicle was filled with trunks stacked to head-height, filling the entire free area except a narrow pathway that led to the bed and small table.

"Newspapers," Damien said. He waved her inside his cubicle and then drew the curtain, leaving them standing side-by side between the stacked trunks. He spoke in a low voice. "I rented a little building in the bad part of town for storage, then went to all the local presses and requested their back issues for the last twenty years. "I know you said thirty years, but I couldn't afford it all, and I could only get papers from one of the three presses that have gone out of business. I had to buy *everything*, you see, not just the issues that might have mentioned something relevant." He gave her a pointed look.

Sebastien nodded back. "Confidentiality," she mouthed, and then aloud, said, "I understand. But it must have been extremely expensive?"

Damien's head rocked back as he looked up at the ceiling morosely. "Oh, it was. I burned through pretty much every copper I had to my name. And since I didn't want to ask Titus for an increase in my allowance, I had to forgo buying any new clothes. That's why I'm still in last season's suits."

Sebastien looked down at Damien's suit. She couldn't tell the difference. *'Wait, am I supposed to be buying new clothes for every school term? But the ones I bought last term are still perfectly fine!'* Aloud she said, "If anyone asks, you can just say that this season's style is rather gauche." She had heard Ana say so to a few of her many friends. "I imagine these aren't all of them?"

"I brought the ones that had relevant words on the front page headline. Maybe not even all of them. I haven't had a chance to get through the whole backlog. Twenty years is a long time, and some of those presses put out an issue *every single day*. I plan to find a word-searching spell in the library that I can use to pinpoint any articles with relevant information without having to read through each newspaper manually. It's just too much to get through for one person, especially with the need for secrecy."

"That's a good idea," Sebastien agreed.

"I also learned something important." Damien lowered his voice even further, leaning in toward Sebastien's ear. "I got the information from Titus— surreptitiously, mind you. I know better than to alarm him. Apparently, there are occasional rogue magic incidents that aren't openly reported, but which the Red Guard will share records of with the coppers. I'm hoping to get an internship at Harrow Hill during Harvest Break. I think I might be able to get Titus to put me in charge of redoing their totally archaic file system. It's not even magically searchable! That will give me the chance to gain access to old incident reports."

Harvest Break ran for two months, through the end of summer and into the beginning of fall. "That's...brilliant. Well done, Damien. Let me know if you can't find what you need in the library or need help developing search or categorization spells."

"No, no, at most I'd need your help with grunt labor or an extra Will to cast while I'm tired. My divination professor talked about this kind of use case, so I'm sure I can find everything I need. I don't want the higher-ups to think I can't handle the missions they assign me."

A familiar young voice came over the cubicle's wall. "This is where Sebastien sleeps?" Nat asked. "But where is he?"

"I'm sure he's around somewhere. Probably in the library," Ana replied. "Don't touch any of his things. He's very private."

"Can we go find him? I don't want to leave without seeing him. I have to tell him about how I saw the Raven Queen fighting out in the Charybdis Gulf!"

Damien and Sebastien sidled out into the walkway that cut through the middle of the dormitory.

Nat brightened like a daisy lifting her head to the sun and skipped to Sebastien's side. "I'm pleased to see you again. How have you been?" she asked, sounding like the host of some high-class soiree.

"I've been well. And you?" Sebastien replied with equal seriousness.

"I saw the Raven Queen!" Nat burst out, unable to hold in her excitement any longer. She launched into the story of how she had been reading in a window seat that had a good view over the Charybdis Gulf and saw a huge burst of light. She'd scrambled to retrieve her spyglass—a birthday gift from Damien—and used it to watch the rest of the Raven Queen's escape.

Both Damien and Ana seemed disturbed to hear Nat describe how Parker had been speared with a harpoon. "I thought she had taken those men hostage, maybe, but then why did the other ones kill him?"

Sebastien shrugged. "Maybe they hit the man by accident? I bet it would be hard to aim such a big weapon."

"Perhaps as a message that they could not shield her," Ana suggested. "They must all be willing to give their lives for the High Crown. Or...perhaps they were not hostages, but allies pretending to be the High Crown's men."

"A disguise? Oh, that's clever," Damien said. "Maybe that's how she got into the secret jail in the first place."

Nat frowned. "Well, what about the children? I suppose they could have been some kind of dwarf or naturally small species, but they looked quite human. I guess children would make good spies, because people always think we're oblivious and incompetent."

Damien closed his eyes briefly, as if in pain.

"Well, *some* people act that way," Nat corrected, smiling up at Sebastien.

"I found that to be exceptionally vexing when I was younger, too," Sebastien agreed.

"Yes! People treat me like I'm some barely sentient creature. Or like I'm a dog! Damien, did you know that Lord Cyr actually patted me on the head and called me a 'good girl' at Mama's garden party a couple weeks ago? And *then* he ordered me to smile and said he hoped Mama wasn't going to allow me to start wearing makeup or using glamours, because he thought girls should remain fresh-faced and youthful for as long as possible."

Ana let out the most unladylike *"Ugh"* Sebastien had ever heard, as if she wanted to vomit.

Sebastien's upper lip twitched as she suppressed the urge to bare her teeth. "He needs to be taught a lesson about acceptable behavior."

Nat smiled like a tiny hellcat. "I agree. So I taught him one."

"Oh, do tell!" Rhett called out, lugging a trunk in each arm with ease.

Alec, Waverly, and Brinn followed behind him, and they all gathered around to listen to Nat's story of revenge on Lord Cyr, head of the sixth Crown Family. It involved the help of several servants, a poisoned pastry, and a game of vicious rumors all based around Lord Cyr and the stuffed unicorn he kept in his trophy room. The unicorn was hollow, its insides famously filled with layers upon layers of spell arrays meant to make it seem alive, and Lord Cyr was, perhaps, a little *too* proud of it.

"So, now he *suspects* that it was me behind it all," Nat concluded, "but I'm not sure he can wrap his tiny little brain around how someone so cute and 'youthful' could also be the devious mastermind who orchestrated his downfall."

Waverly, only a foot or so taller than Nat, pushed up her glasses. The lenses glinted with sinister light. "I learned how to contract a bogle over the break. If you want, I can help you send one to make sure the lesson sticks. Lord Cyr once told my mother that he finds her "flavor" of woman to be very appealing. Because apparently women from the East all taste the same."

Alec gagged dramatically. "He and Father used to go 'out' together sometimes, which probably tells you all you need to know about his character. If you're sending a bogle, I want to help."

"If we can bind it as a group, it will have less chance of being banished," Waverly said.

"Are we…really doing this?" Brinn asked. "Bogles can be dangerous."

"That's why we'll need to make sure its contract is clear and focused."

Nat's lips wavered between a pout and a grin, leaving her expression quite strange. "Oh, I really want to help. But I haven't started learning any magic yet. I keep asking, but Mama and Father won't budge. Not till I'm thirteen."

"That's okay," Waverly said. "You have a valid grudge. You can still bear testimony to strengthen the bogle's focus. Ana, if you know anyone trustworthy here who might have some good testimony, you can gather them, too."

Rhett leaned against a cubicle wall. "Heroic action taken in the shadows against an enemy of women? I'm in. Brinn, your second cousin, Shelley, had a run-in with him last summer and cried on my shoulder for at least twenty minutes. I love the way she perfumes her hair. And there's a seventh-term woman in my dueling club who hates him, with the *best* footwork and a pair of calves that look like they were sculpted by Myrddin himself."

Brinn scowled at Rhett. "Guys, sending a bogle to torment someone might not be blood magic, but I'm pretty sure it is illegal. What if we get caught?" He looked at Damien pleadingly.

Damien crossed his arms. "We won't get caught. Everyone involved will make an oath on their honor and sign an agreement of silence. And maybe we can get some kind of collateral to ensure secrecy." He turned to Ana. "What do you think?"

Ana frowned gently. "That would be difficult. Maybe everyone could be required to submit a secret that we could spread upon betrayal. But who would be the keeper of secrets? I certainly wouldn't trust mine with just anyone."

"Brinn can do it, of course," Waverly said. "He keeps secrets so well you'd never even suspect he has any. And Sebastien's probably the strongest of us, correct? He can be the central caster. I'll handle the binding, obviously."

"Sebastien can't," Damien announced. "He has a concussion."

This distracted everyone, even Waverly, from their nefarious plan.

"Sebastien's skull was almost crushed between a man's boot and the edge of the sidewalk," Damien said darkly.

Nat gasped, both hands rising to cover her mouth.

Alec and Rhett both looked at Sebastien's head, obviously searching for any lingering evidence of such a wound.

"What did you do to make someone try to kill you?" Alec asked.

"No one tried to kill me," Sebastien said. "It was an accident, and I'm fine."

"This is why you need better footwork, Sebastien," Rhett said. "You need to be able to dodge when people become enraged by your personality."

Alec chuckled at this and gave Rhett a congratulatory poke with his elbow.

Sebastien glared at them both, but they grinned back unabashedly. "Why is it okay for them to say mean things, but not for me?"

"You say mean things all the time, Sebastien," Damien reminded her.

"Yes," Alec agreed. "Like the time you told me that I'm not stupid, I just have bad luck when it comes to thinking."

Rhett lifted his forefinger. "Or the time you told Amber Grisham that you wouldn't go on a date with her because you are allergic to stupidity."

Alec's eyes brightened. "Oh, oh! Or the time you got in an argument with Mitch from Defense, and you were like"—Alec drew himself up as tall as he could go, lifted his chin, and stretched his shoulders back—"I may be arrogant, but you're still wrong," affecting Sebastien's voice but somehow sounding more like Professor Lacer.

Rhett pushed off the wall, ran his fingers through his braids, and looked off into the distance. "I would agree with you, but then we would both be wrong," he said in a similar tone.

Nat's wide eyes bounced back and forth between them, shining with delight.

"What doesn't kill you disappoints me," Alec tried.

Sebastien held up her hand, palm outward. "Okay, I'm not sure about the rest, but I definitely never said that."

The two young men ignored her. "I would slap you, but I like to keep my hands clean," Rhett said, turning the page of an imaginary book and pretending to read while walking.

"If you were a vegetable, you would be a cabbage," Alec added in precise tones, then gave a single nod as if pronouncing a verdict.

Nat burst into giggles and then, to Sebastien's horror, drew herself up haughtily and said in an artificially deep voice, "Jealousy is a disease. Get well soon."

Alec flashed her a thumbs-up and a wink. "You are offensively uninspired, you…malodorous half-wit."

Rhett shook his head. "Trying a little too hard there, Alec. How about this one?" He sniffed judgmentally and sneered. "Don't talk to me until your number of brain cells exceeds your age."

Nat grinned, then raised an arrogant eyebrow as she waved one hand nonchalantly. "No need to thank me for insulting you. It was my pleasure."

Sebastien groaned, dropping her forehead into her hands. And then, to her horror, Damien cleared his throat, loosened the tie at his throat, and drawled in deep tones, "I am a basically average thaumaturge, barely scraping by. Yet somehow, the rest of you make me look impressive with your *astounding* incompetence."

It wasn't until Ana turned to glare at the group of students that had somehow gathered up nearby, blocking the walkway and peeking over cubicle walls with avid fascination, that Sebastien's friends were distracted from mimicking her.

Nat walked back into Sebastien's cubicle and perched herself at the foot of the bed. "I can't imagine how any of you manage to sleep in such horrid conditions. Of course, I had heard stories about how the University forces everyone to start off living in squalor as a way to foster determination and tenacity, but this is almost unlivable."

"Just wait until you have to eat cafeteria food," Ana said, joining Nat on the edge of Sebastien's mattress. "It's almost impossible not to spend some of your contribution points on an edible meal. I had no idea it was possible to make cheese so tasteless, but the cafeteria cooks have managed it."

"It's not that bad," Sebastien said as Alec took a seat at her bedside table. "You're all just used to living with personal chefs and servants to shine your shoes and wipe your bottoms. Though it *would* be nice to have private rooms." If she hadn't spent her contribution points on Professor Lacer's help, she, Damien, and Ana might have had enough to pool together for a four-person dorm room, which was only eight hundred points.

Scandalized, Nat flushed as pink as her dress. "A servant hasn't wiped my bottom since I was a baby!"

"A servant wiped *my* bottom just yesterday," Alec announced proudly, crossing his arms over his chest. "I must wonder, how does anyone get by without?"

"No!" Nat cried, then burst into giggles.

Brinn cleared his throat. "I made everyone gifts. Would you like them now?" Brinn went to his cubicle before returning with a carton filled with small potted plants, each distinct from the others. "They're miniature trees," he said.

"Special magical trees," Waverly corrected. "Our families retired to the countryside together during the break. Brinn was working on them the whole time."

Brinn flushed. "I sprouted them myself. I was inspired by Sebastien's end of term exhibition. I'm attempting to crossbreed these specimens to have decorative features, like particular scents, variegated leaves that look like flowers, and even, possibly, tiny fruit with special properties. Though, that last one is a little ambitious."

Sebastien turned her own tiny, potted tree around curiously as Brinn rattled off complex instructions for their care and Alec whined about being given a gift that required him to work. Hers had leaves that alternated between sea-blue and rusted orange. They shifted back and forth in waves, rippling quicker when she moved or tilted the tree. And it smelled, somehow, like the wind before a storm.

"It's great at cleaning the air. It should help you sleep," Brinn said.

The whole group lounged around Sebastien's cubicle, bringing in a few extra chairs to sit more comfortably while they told stories of what they had done over the break.

Alec told Ana that, with his father in jail, he had taken a bubble bath. Ana squeezed him on the shoulder as she congratulated him. Sebastien was aware that she was missing some subtext, but she didn't understand it and didn't pry.

Rhett had gone to Paneth for the amateur dueling circuit there and gotten into a fight with another member of the audience. This had resulted in a slight scar across the bridge of his nose, which he thought made him look rakish.

And Ana had gotten to stick her fingers into the Family business a little. "Things have been different—*better*—recently," she said, smiling at Sebastien.

Everyone demanded the story of Sebastien's concussion, which she made sound as boring as possible.

They talked, including some gossip about the Raven Queen, until it grew dark and a very reluctant Nat had to go home.

The next morning, classes started again. Half of Burberry's class was spent on a repetitive lecture about the importance of students keeping better track of their student tokens, as well as a new list of punishments that would be enforced for their loss.

'*Oh. That's probably because of me. And Liza,*' Sebastien thought. '*It must have been so embarrassing for the man whose faculty token we used.*'

Though it felt strange, she spent the in-class spell practice time reading and finishing her homework early, since her infirmary pass exempted her from casting.

That afternoon, Tanya was waiting in the Practical Casting classroom when they arrived, sitting in the seat closest to the door. She nodded to Sebastien, and Sebastien nodded back with some curiosity, taking her own seat at the front of the classroom on the other side. '*Is Tanya joining this class?*' She knew, from following the other woman last term, that Tanya had only taken the mandatory four classes, so surely she couldn't be qualified?

"Student aide," Tanya mouthed, pointing to herself.

'*Oh...that's actually kind of nice of Professor Lacer,*' Sebastien realized. '*It would have been hard for Tanya to keep working in the History department.*'

Professor Lacer didn't enter until after the bell had rung. He shut the sliding door behind himself with an idle wave of his hand over his shoulder and spun to face them all. He wasn't smiling, but though his bloodshot eyes and pale lips indicated that he hadn't slept, his dark hair was tied neatly back, and his beard had been closely trimmed into submission.

Most of all, he seemed so tangibly full of energy that Sebastien imagined she could feel it coiling off of him. She was very sure, in that moment, that not only did he receive her letter, but that if a reply wasn't already waiting for pickup, one soon would be.

43

SYMBOLIC MEANING

Sebastien
Month 4, Day 12, Monday 2:15 p.m.

Professor Lacer clasped his hands behind his back and began to pace slowly. His voice was precise, clipped, and loud enough to be easily heard. "It may be the second term, but this class remains an *introduction* to Practical Will-based Casting. Some of you have been personally approved to move onward from the first term's class. Some of you have been kept for a second or third attempt to meet my standards before advancing."

This statement was met by the noise of embarrassed shuffling from some of the students.

After a pause, Professor Lacer continued. "This class is not like your others. You will not squeak by here on a modicum of effort. To meet my standards, you must continue to practice for a minimum of two hours outside of class, every single day. If you do not, please do not imagine I will somehow fail to notice."

He stared at them all with dissatisfaction. "Once, when I was a relatively new professor, I thought that this need not be repeated past the first term. I was proven wrong. If you have doubts about your ability to keep up, please desist from wasting my time and leave now. I loathe marking homework papers, and I do not forget those who inconvenience me needlessly."

Professor Lacer paused for an uncomfortably long moment, his eyes meeting those of each student in the room individually, as if to intimidate them into dropping his class. No one dared to avoid his gaze, though several flinched when they met it. Finally, he continued. "Having said that, as the exercises you will be attempting become more difficult, know that I consider endangering yourselves or your classmates an even greater affront than laziness. You will double-check all spell arrays before casting, and if you ever attempt to cast magic without your full faculties, or to disregard the impending signs of Will-strain, you will *wish* you had gotten away with being expelled from my classroom." He looked at Sebastien then.

Someone behind Sebastien gulped audibly, and Damien ducked his head and looked at Sebastien out of the corner of his eye, but she simply nodded back at Professor Lacer.

"This term, rather than reaching full mastery over any single spell, you will be gaining experience with a large range of spells. All spell arrays may use only two glyphs, maximum, and no additional language, numbers, or words. It is important that you make the proper choices about what parts of the spell array can be cast aside. You will learn to choose the *most* relevant glyphs. 'Good enough' is never acceptable in my classroom."

Sebastien was confident in her knowledge of glyphs, which had been thoroughly honed by all of her preparation for accessing Myrddin's journal. Choosing the correct one for a particular application was only a matter of understanding and thoughtfulness.

Professor Lacer motioned to the blackboard against the front wall, and a stick of chalk rose to draw the most common elemental glyphs in a line across the top. "Children memorizing these glyphs are often encouraged to recognize them as if they were simplified drawings of the elements they represent. And, indeed, that may be how they came about originally. Some are undeniably simplified pictograms, but as a whole, glyphs are ideograms—symbols that represent a concept. They are used almost exclusively in the Word—an external clarification of intent—while spellcasting."

Another wave of his hand, and the chalk scratched out another line of glyphs below the first. These were more obscure, their meanings more specific, and Sebastien only recognized a third of them.

"There are thousands upon thousands of known glyphs, and perhaps even more that have been lost to the sands of time or simple obscurity. Some of these you may be familiar with. Some are rare. And a handful would probably be recognized by only a few dozen people in the known lands. With practice, glyphs allow you to encapsulate more complex topics into a spell's Word in a smaller space and with less time spent writing. However, glyphs are useful for more than that. A glyph meaning '*fire*' will always be more effective than the written word, '*fire*.' Does anyone care to attempt an explanation of this phenomenon?"

An upper-term student tentatively raised her hand. "Is it because glyphs are universal? Even if we don't speak the same language, we can use the same glyphs."

Professor Lacer nodded to the woman. "A reasonable attempt, Miss Bell, but not fully accurate. One can use a spell array written in another language to the same effect as a native, as long as one takes the time to learn the meaning and purpose of the words they use. The primary danger would be the presence of cultural differences that create a certain nuance being lost in translation, which could affect the outcome. In addition, glyphs are not fully universal. While we share a wide range, there are hundreds of notable differences between various countries and isolated groups. However, it is true that this single glyph for '*fire*' will have been more widely used by thaumaturges from all countries, species, and origin than any one language's alternative. Glyphs, like any magic, grow smooth and easy through continued use. This symbol has a history behind it that would be difficult to supplant."

He nodded toward the blackboard, and a third line of glyphs was drawn. Each was distinct, but they all shared a certain indefinable quality. They were balanced and, if not all simple, all clear and almost…striking.

Sebastien recognized a couple. "Magic," she mouthed, intrigued. '*Are all these glyphs subtly different descriptions of the Will? Particular facets, perhaps?*'

Professor Lacer caught the word on her lips and sent her a subtle look of approval. Or at least she thought it was approval. It might also have been amusement. "There have been a surprising number of attempts to bind the very idea of magic, of intrinsic *power*, into the shape of a mundane glyph. Evidence of the hubris of thaumaturges, I suppose," he said wryly, his gaze trailing slowly over the final line of glyphs. "With the right access and the right knowledge, one can begin to trace back glyphs to their origin, and from there, to judge the ideas of the society from whence they came."

The chalk moved and drew a single glyph under a glyph for "magic" that was formed of a straight upward line bordered by upward-arcing lines on either side. The new glyph underneath it was similar, but the arcing lines were connected to a "v" shape instead.

"This glyph for '*magic*' first appears in records dating back approximately four thousand years, used by a society of people who lived among the Starpeak Mountains. You may notice that it bears obvious relation to the still-common glyph for '*flight*,' with elements of the connotation of '*height*,' '*elevation*,' and even…'*awe*.' You can imagine, perhaps, why to a certain kind of person, who valued certain kinds of things, the glyph for '*magic*' would be so similar. This glyph for '*flight-elevation-awe*,' to our knowledge, came before their attempt to define '*magic*.'"

Sebastien's eyes narrowed, her gaze crawling over the glyphs for "*magic*" again. A few of them, she thought, bore certain similarities to other glyphs. One that might have been a twist on "*grasping-hand*," another that was almost certainly based on the *"ever-open-eye"* that had no lid and so could not close, and a third reminded her of a tree with roots as deep and wide as its branches.

"Some ambitious historians have attempted to uncover the first glyphs, those that were created shortly after the Cataclysm—or even, possibly, *before* it." The chalk settled down on the tray at the base of the blackboard, and then two of the glyphs began to glow. Their fire-bright forms rose from the board as Professor Lacer guided the illusion up to hang in the air in front of him, high and large enough for everyone to see.

One was a simple dot within a circle. The other was a bright disk surrounded by eight wavering rays, with an empty ring disconnecting the filled inner disk from the outer rays. It reminded her of the sun. Or, if it had been drawn in ink rather than light, perhaps an eclipse.

"These are the two oldest glyphs that represent *'magic'* currently known to mankind," Professor Lacer said. The brightness of the illusion cast harsh shadows on his face as he stared up at them. "They have no clear origin. What must those ancient people have known, or believed, that these were the most appropriate representations of power?"

Professor Lacer let the illusion fade. He cleared his throat and continued in quick, clipped tones. "There is a school of thought whose proponents insist that there is a perfect symbolic representation for all concepts. One for any particular idea you could think of. They suggest that the creation of new glyphs is simply a futile attempt to discover this perfect symbolic representation with blind fumblings. They believe that the physical world is not as real or true as timeless, absolute, unchangeable ideas. That there is a blueprint to perfection, and that our attempts to describe that perfection with glyphs are like outlining shadows that have been cast on a wall and declaring that our scribbles are equivalent to the being that cast them. But still, this false equivalence allows us to access some small portion of that perfection to empower our magic."

He looked to Sebastien. "What do you think of this?"

She straightened, her heart giving a single heavy thump and then beginning to race along with her thoughts. Sebastien didn't rush to speak, letting a few agonizing seconds of silence pass as she made sure of her answer. "I don't agree." Before he could prompt her for clarification, she took a deep breath and continued, drawing on the first example that came to mind. "For instance, consider the two glyphs that both mean *'death-during-sleep.'*" Her hands twitched as she realized that, unlike Professor Lacer, she could not simply free-cast an example for the entire class to see.

To her relief, he raised an eyebrow, then turned to the blackboard again, where the chalk jumped up and drew out two very different symbols. "These two?"

She swallowed. "Yes. They look almost nothing alike, obviously. A proponent of the ideal-form theory might suggest that these two glyphs actually encapsulate very different ideas, perhaps one being peaceful rest and the other a sudden theft of life. But each of these glyphs created almost interchangeable results, in both effect and efficiency, when used in experiments during the Third Empire."

Professor Lacer gave her a nod and the very shallowest of smiles. "My apprentice is correct," he said to the other students. And then, looking back at her, he added, "Interesting reading you have been doing."

"We have the best library in the known lands. It would be foolish not to take advantage of it."

His small smile grew larger. "Indeed." He turned his attention back to the classroom as a whole. "So, it would seem that these two glyphs hold exactly, or almost exactly, the same meaning, despite their very different forms. But let us consider the opposite. What happens when a single glyph has two disparate, even opposite, meanings?"

He looked to Nunchkin.

The man's eyes widened with suppressed panic. "Is that possible?"

"Perhaps not." Professor Lacer raised his hands, one empty and the other holding his Conduit, in a motion that was akin to a shrug but didn't involve his shoulders.

Sebastien's eyes narrowed. Surely, Professor Lacer was not actually ignorant of the answer? *'Someone must have tried that at some point. Maybe it's even in my book of one hundred ways to die. But how,* exactly, *do you make a glyph?'* She hadn't ever heard or read anything that gave such instruction or referenced use of the technique, but she couldn't help but think that maybe it would be similar to the ritual she was performing to create a unique symbol linked to her and her alone. *'If glyphs can be worn smooth by use, just like spells... You would be trying to overcome those deep-worn grooves, which seems like a great way to break your Will. Alternatively, you would need to give the glyph disparate meanings from the very beginning and...see what happens?'* That, too, seemed like a great way to die or become an Aberrant. She would not be attempting to personally sate her curiosity.

As if Professor Lacer's thoughts had followed the same course as her own, he grimaced and raised the forefinger of his free hand. "There are records of several attempts to create new glyphs that intentionally or unintentionally infringed upon well-established glyphs, with grievous results. Do not attempt the modification of any glyphs. If you are interested in their creation, you may take advanced spell creation classes once you have your Master's certification. Again, let me impress upon you that this is a warning against *egregious stupidity*."

Sebastien suppressed a flinch. If her guiding light ritual was indeed creating a new glyph, then...well, it probably would have already harmed her if she'd failed to be original enough. It could also mean that any similar glyphs weren't "established" enough to cause problems. She could, perhaps, go to Professor Lacer to ensure it was safe. Even though he'd watched her memorize the spell while they were in the archives, he might not have realized the contents. *'But he would probably want to read the chant that goes along with it. And I'm...not comfortable with that.'*

She had time before the next repetition to decide what to do.

Professor Lacer cleaned the chalk off the blackboard, then drew out almost two dozen glyphs dealing with fire and heat. "This week and the next, we will be focusing on spells within a domain that I once heard a student describe as 'fiery.' While, if forced, you could simply use the glyph for *'fire'* in many of the arrays, the wise among you will become familiar and proficient with this list. Several of these take concepts that would normally require two different glyphs and condense the idea into a single symbol. This is useful because precision and clarity increase efficiency, of course. However, you may also find yourself grateful for this experience if you ever need to draw out spell arrays in an emergency situation, or for any artificers among you, to fit your spell array into the smallest possible space. Most importantly, practice with increasingly minimalist spell arrays will help you become less mentally reliant on an indulgently overweight written Word." Some humor leaking into his voice, he added, "When you must hold the entire thing within your mind, you will appreciate succinctness."

With that, he called the students up to the front to each accept a thick sheaf of papers that covered the necessary glyphs in detail along with the dozens of spells they would be trying over the next two weeks. From there, a locking shelf beside the blackboard opened to allow them to pick up boxes of mundane components and supplies they would use for the casting.

There were fifty different spells that used the supplied glyphs in some way, but they spanned from expelling diffuse heat from a Circle, to burning a detailed image into a sheet of maple wood, to freezing ice shapes into water.

Some of the spells were marked for in-class attempts only, and Sebastien made a note to work on those with priority once she was cleared to cast again, lest she run out of time. At this rate, by the end of term they would have at least forty minutes of practice with pretty much every application of active-cast spells they might ever need.

As the students filtered back to their seats, Ana said, "This will be *so* much more bearable than last term. Did you know, I actually started dreaming about some of those spell exercises?"

"That's because you never took Sebastien's advice to try adjusting the spell in different ways while using the same spell array, nor did you try any of the challenges to stretch different facets of your Will," Damien said, lifting his nose with a superior sniff.

Ana rolled her eyes.

Damien turned to Sebastien. "Professor Lacer knows about your *concussion*, right?"

"He does," Sebastien said.

"Do you know what our special mentorship project is going to be this term? Another fifty spells on top of these ones, maybe?" Damien asked.

Ana shuddered. "I'd sooner join a monastery with the Stewards of Intention."

"I don't think you can technically call them *monasteries*—" Sebastien started, but she cut off when Damien waved his hand as if to say how unimportant this distinction was.

Damien placed his hand on Sebastien's shoulder. "And that, Ana, is why Sebastien and I receive special tutoring from Professor Lacer and are on our way to being free-casters. Sometimes you have to put in the hard work if you have any ambition."

Ana scowled at Damien. "I have plenty of ambition. I just don't want to spend a third of my waking hours trying to become the next Archmage when there are other perfectly good ways to spend my time that aren't so *boring*."

Sebastien rubbed the bridge of her nose as the two bickered good-naturedly around her.

While the other students began to cast, she studied the sheaf of papers, familiarizing herself with the few glyphs she hadn't yet learned, reading thoroughly through all the spell instructions, and making notes.

At the end of class, Professor Lacer asked her to meet him in his office.

Sticking his tongue out gleefully at Ana, Damien practically skipped by Sebastien's side as they split off from the rest of the students to walk down the gently curving Citadel hallway toward Professor Lacer's office.

"Childish," Sebastien muttered, most of her thoughts distracted by trying to grasp some large, ephemeral idea that had been forming throughout Professor Lacer's class but that she couldn't quite grasp. *'If glyph-creation has anything at all in common with my beacon-creating ritual, does that mean that all you need to create a glyph is intention, clarity, and…repetition?'* That hazy idea in her mind pulsed and vibrated, as if it were a dozen transparent images that simply needed to align, and suddenly, they would all make sense.

"Ana and I have been friends forever," Damien said. "We're practically siblings. And this morning, Ana said my haircut was *'okay.'* And then, when I asked her again, she said it was 'rather long up top.' And *then* she said I look *like a rooster with a swirly cockscomb!*" Damien drew in a deep breath of outrage, his fists clenched at his side. "Can you believe that?"

"Mmhmm," Sebastien replied absently, even more of her attention turning inward. *'And once you create a glyph, just like a spell, you can make it easier to use through, again, repetition. But why does that work? What is there to keep track of how many times…or how many* people…*have used a glyph or cast a spell?'* She almost stumbled as the cohering idea surged like a heartbeat inside her mind. *'This is important. I am confused. I am suspicious. I only have to fit the pieces together to find the real question I should be asking.'*

Beside her, Damien continued to speak. "So then, of course I told her that her pants were too tight, of a poor cut, and making her rear look overly round and a little saggy. And she threw a bottle of ink at me!"

"How astounding," Sebastien said. She searched her memory for moments of previous confusion, reviewing and discarding those that did not seem to match and gathering those that could be connected. *'What keeps track of a new glyph's form in the first place? Glyphs are shapes that connect to ideas. They* represent *ideas. Just as magical components connote certain concepts…but where do those concepts come from?'* She was breathing harder, her Conduit held tight in trembling fingers.

Damien was still talking, but by now no piece of her was spared to listen to him.

'If culture can affect the ways spells work, or which glyphs you use to create an effect, then the concepts must come from the minds of those who use them, right?' She had speculated similarly before, but it felt different now. It felt like there was something deeper at play. *'If the color red means good luck to one culture but death and sickness to another, spells from people of those cultures might use the same red apple to different effect. Why wouldn't it work the same for glyphs? Is it because no one uses a ritual to cement the magical use of a red apple? And why are some people able to use an autumn leaf for a transmogrification spell that causes darkness to descend, but I am not?'*

She reached the door to Professor Lacer's office and leaned one hand against the wall to support herself as the world fuzzed out around her, too unimportant to allot any mental power to. *'Is this why Pecanty goes over stories and plays and etymology? Because magic is somehow listening to the ideas of all the people in the world? Does that spell not work for me because my understanding doesn't fit with the worldview of the average person? Because "darkness descending" doesn't make any sense to me? Because I know that's not how light works and I can't* unknow *it?'*

Sebastien swallowed hard. *'But if that's the case, why would learning transmutation concepts make transmogrification easier? It should be the opposite, right? Every time we learn a bit more of the truth, we would lose a bit more access to the myth. Or maybe… it's more personal. Damien is going to most of the same classes as me, but he's not having any trouble with transmogrification. What's the difference between him and me?'*

There were a lot of options, but the one that stood out to her was very succinct. *'Damien does no blood magic.'*

She closed her eyes and took a deep breath. *'Is it not a myth that one can corrupt their Will? Is that what it actually means? That suddenly, we can't access the same magic as everyone else, and when we keep trying, something inside us breaks?'*

But no, that didn't really make sense. Liza probably did more blood magic than anyone Sebastien knew, and she had no trouble at all with trans-mogrification. The relief left Sebastien momentarily dizzy. *'So what is it, then? My idea is wrong, somehow. And whatever within magic keeps track of these things can tell.'*

She opened her eyes to find herself half collapsed against the wall, her forehead leaning against the white stone as Damien's fingers dug into her shoulders with worry.

Then the world lurched around her as the air pressed into her legs, back and the back of her neck, hardening enough to lift her and wrench her free from Damien's grip.

"Infirmary, now!" Professor Lacer snapped from behind her, already floating her along ahead of him.

Sebastien's arms flailed out as she instinctively tried to grab onto some-thing for balance and control, but there was nothing. She looked around wildly, trying to understand what was happening, and caught Damien's pinched expression and white lips as he looked back to Professor Lacer while half jogging along beside her floating body.

"I don't know what happened. We were just talking, and then it seemed like he was dizzy or in pain. He wasn't responding to me. And then he kind of just slumped over into the wall. Is it the Wi—the concussion?"

"Most likely," Professor Lacer agreed. "Speed is of the essence. Run ahead to the infirmary and let them know that we are coming. I want a full emer-gency team on standby and fully prepared when we arrive."

Damien sprinted off without even a second of hesitation.

"Wait, *wait!*" Sebastien yelled. "I'm okay! I'm not hurt!"

Professor Lacer didn't stop floating her at a speed that was almost a run, but he did rotate her so that she could see his face, and he hers. "You had collapsed."

"No. I was thinking. I had an…epiphany. It was very shocking."

Professor Lacer slowed and looked past her to Damien, whose racing foot-steps had stopped. His lips pressed together, and she could almost see the thoughts racing behind his eyes, but rather than urge Damien to continue, he looked back to Sebastien. "Are you entirely certain? Are you experiencing any dizziness, pain, or confusion? Any phantom sights or sensations? Inexplicable emotions?"

Sebastien raised her hand to stop him. "No, none of that. I'm fine. I've been taking all of my potions and getting extra sleep. I was thinking so hard I forgot to stand up. And I have questions."

Professor Lacer slowed, then returned her to her own two feet.

Damien hurried back to her side, his hands hovering as if to catch her if she collapsed.

Professor Lacer closed his eyes and pinched the bridge of his nose. "You were thinking so hard that you forgot to stand up," he repeated, as if it were the most inane thing he had ever heard.

But Sebastien couldn't spare the energy or time to be offended. "Is magic sentient?" she asked.

Professor Lacer froze, lowering his hand and looking at her.

"Because," Sebastien continued, "if it isn't, how does transmogrification work?"

44

TRANSMUTATION EXERCISES

Month 4, Day 12, Monday 3:50 p.m.

Silence followed Sebastien's question.

"What?" Damien asked.

She continued to stare at Professor Lacer. "Magic, or reality, or whatever you want to call it, is either accessing or storing our ideas. Judging by the fact that old spells that aren't practiced very often in the modern world are still viable and don't go back to being 'wild,' I'd say it's the latter."

"What?" Damien said again.

"And I'm doing something wrong."

"Stop," Professor Lacer said.

"My transmogrification isn't accessing the ideas properly," Sebastien finished, the dread and relief of admitting it aloud warring with each other. In a rapid, low murmur, she added, "I'm worried there's something wrong with my brain. Inherently, I mean. Not Will-strain. Or maybe it is from Will-strain? Accumulated damage? Is it going to get worse?"

"*Stop speaking,*" Professor Lacer commanded.

Sebastien's teeth clacked together as she cut off the deluge of anxious questions.

"I...don't understand what's going on," Damien said. "Magic is sentient? Your transmogrification..." He trailed off under Professor Lacer's black glare.

Professor Lacer looked between the two of them, then pressed a hand to his forehead and dragged it down his face with a deep sigh.

Sebastien could smell the coffee on his breath, sour but not rancid. He must drink it black, without sugar or honey.

"Of course something like this would happen," Professor Lacer muttered. "Into my office, both of you, before you start somehow spilling instructions on how to summon a demon or something equally ridiculous to anyone else who might be listening."

Suddenly, Sebastien worried that perhaps there was a reason the man had wanted her silence beyond simple exasperation. A reason like the Red Guard wanting to keep such knowledge a secret. Surely, they couldn't know what she had said, though? But her paranoia was too strong to accept that. *'The Red Guard knows magic lost to time. Spells of ridiculous power and amazing effect. Everyone knows that. Who's to say they couldn't have some sort of enormous divination spell set up to catch certain secrets being spoken aloud?'*

When they were safely behind the closed door of Professor Lacer's office, and the man didn't immediately start casting protective spells or anything else alarming, she whispered, "Am I in danger?"

"No, but *he* might be," Professor Lacer said, gesturing to Damien with unconcealed frustration.

Damien and Sebastien shared a worried glance.

"Be silent while I consider how to deal with this," Lacer said, pacing back and forth for a minute and then moving to one of the bookcases lining the walls to search through a few different texts.

Dread built in Sebastien's gut the whole time.

"Sit down," Professor Lacer added absently. "Neither of you are in any active, immediate danger. You have merely created a potential barrier to Damien's future success. I will do my best to guide you both properly out of the metaphorical thorn bushes."

Finally, Professor Lacer moved to his desk, where he began to write on a sheet of paper, using what was probably a variation of the mimeo-motion spell to copy everything he was writing to a second sheet. When both pens returned to their resting spots, he waved his hand to dry the ink, then handed the papers to both Damien and Sebastien.

Professor Lacer had listed a dozen keywords, leaving room for them to write between each.

"Is this…a quiz?" Damien asked.

"In essence," Professor Lacer agreed. "Both of you, write the most accurate, profound sentence you can think of for each of the words I have provided. Do not peek at each other's work. Your answers must be your own. You have five minutes."

Damien and Sebastien both hurried to start, as this time limit left them half a minute or less for each answer.

'*Profound?*' Sebastien wondered. '*So, intense statements based on deep knowledge and insight? And with barely a handful of seconds to scribble at full speed? Hopefully Professor Lacer won't expect these to be very good.*'

It felt like even less than five minutes when Professor Lacer snapped his fingers, making the piece of paper fly out from underneath Sebastien's fountain pen.

The man read over both pages quickly, his expression inscrutable. "As I thought," he announced.

Neither Damien nor Sebastien asked for clarification, instead waiting with silent anxiety.

Professor Lacer was silent for another excruciatingly long moment. "I suppose I have no choice but to explain, but perhaps I can still guide you to your own epiphany," he said quietly, looking at Damien. "Sebastien has been having increasing trouble with transmogrification. Let us see if some examples can help you to understand why."

He turned to one of the sliding blackboards set into the wall and clipped both of their papers to its upper rim. "Mr. Westbay, as an automatic response for the words 'life' and 'death,' you wrote 'All life ends in death.' While slightly clichéd, your response is not nearly as inane as I had feared. Mr. Siverling, you wrote, 'Death is the single greatest tragedy of existence, the absolute, unfathomable horror that has accumulated since the beginning of life.' While not what I would have said, I am not surprised by your answer."

Damien did not share that indifference, blinking at Sebastien in bemusement.

"The most common responses to this question are some variation on, 'Death is but the start of the next journey,' 'Death gives meaning to life,' and maybe, 'The dead are not truly gone until the last memory has forgotten them.'"

Sebastien narrowed her eyes. "Really? But you said to be profound. Doesn't that require actual thoughtfulness? All of those statements are just...lies."

Professor Lacer smiled darkly.

Damien blinked again, mouthing "lies" silently to himself.

"Let us look at your thoughts about the words 'love is.' Mr. Westbay, you said, 'Love is the light of the soul reflected in understanding, loyalty, and confidence.' A slight modification of a very old, obscure quote, I believe."

Damien's eyelids fluttered. "Oh. It was something I heard my mother say once, when I was young. It stuck with me."

"Hmm. You, Mr. Siverling, said, 'Love is a powerful motivation for action.'"

"I struggled with that one," she admitted. "But there was no time, so I just tried to come up with something true."

"Common offerings would be along the lines of, 'Love conquers all,' 'Love is selfless,' 'Love is more precious than gold.'"

Sebastien was beginning to sense a theme.

"When given the words 'gut-wrenching' and told to respond with the shortest sentence possible, Mr. Westbay offered back, 'Gut-wrenching fear,' while Mr. Siverling has given us, 'Gut-wrenching intestinal parasites.'"

A short, sputtering laugh burst from between Damien's lips.

Professor Lacer waved a hand toward their papers. "Feel free to examine them further, if you wish. I think my point is made."

Damien rushed up and began to read over Sebastien's answers, but she remained seated.

Professor Lacer waited for Damien, who let out frequent sounds of surprise or amusement. Finally, he said, "Mr. Westbay. Please give me your best guess as to the significance of this 'quiz' and the answers that were provided, based on our current context."

Damien turned back to look at Sebastien for a long moment. "Sebastien's instinctual responses are…unusual. And it's causing a problem with his transmogrification?" He lifted one hand to his chin and frowned down at the floor. "Because transmogrification is based on ideas. And Sebastien is trying to use the wrong ones. Which means the right ones are…the most common ones? And that's why he asked if magic was sentient, because it's somehow aware of our ideas. And that has…mind-blowing implications."

Damien fell silent as he stared unblinkingly at the floor, and then very obviously shook himself back to the present. "But it's dangerous to talk about, for some reason. I don't want to speculate what the danger might be." He smoothed his hair back compulsively, the bags under his eyes standing out against his cheeks, which were paler than normal.

Professor Lacer nodded with satisfaction and motioned Damien back to the armchair beside Sebastien. "Like glyphs, some words, phrases, and items can encapsulate a whole concept that was built by those that came before you… and often not by a rational thinker. These ideas, indeed, are what transmogrification pulls on."

Sebastien let out a shuddering breath at the confirmation.

"Mr. Siverling is placing too much emphasis on individualism. He is prideful, and feels that his ideas must be the best ones, more accurate, more *correct* than the feelings and stories and concepts that the average person would connect to certain things."

Sebastien shifted uncomfortably but didn't argue. She did believe that, to some degree, because it was *true*. Maybe her understanding wasn't the best, but it was certainly better than the average person's, who didn't even care to examine their own thoughts or learn how and why things worked.

"All sapient beings that I know of who live in societies or communities more advanced than those of animals naturally accept and utilize these prepackaged thoughts. We accept them even without realizing, from infancy. Language is one such creation. Mathematics another. All of our technologies, both magical and mundane. There is no shame in accepting the ideas of those who came before you. Can you imagine if you, and every new child born, were forced to invent language, mathematics, and a coherent magical method and structure on your own? We stand on the shoulders of the giants that came before us. There is no shame in this."

Professor Lacer looked between them, gauging their expressions. "But there is a danger to this easy acceptance of the ideas of others, as well. If we never question, we cannot advance. And the average person is almost unbearably stupid and foolish. Many of these prepackaged ideas are idiotic, or even harmful. Love does not conquer all. People do not go to some better place after death. Magic is equally valuable regardless of what culture, species, or individual practices it. Some people may pay lip service, repeating these ideas without ever questioning them, but show through their actions that they do not believe. However, many allow these concepts to become part of their worldview, without ever consciously making a decision to do so. Part of the reason that I accepted Mr. Siverling as my apprentice is that I could see signs that he was not so hopelessly bound by the ideas of others as to never break free. But his critical nature and individualism has a downside."

"So what about me?" Damien asked, his eyebrows scrunched together in a worried frown.

"Mr. Westbay, your mind is not composed solely of these prepackaged thoughts, but you are not a contrarian to the same degree as Mr. Siverling. You have had no trouble with transmogrification, because you do not attempt to force the magic to adhere to your own ideas rather than the ideas of what some call the 'common consciousness.' Mr. Siverling is, in essence, trying to force connotations into this common consciousness with his own strength alone. Compared to the thought-weight of a society, of history, he is doomed to fail."

Obviously, that was true. Sebastien reviewed the times she had failed, the way some transmogrification spells—ironically, the simpler ones—had become so difficult. It was suddenly so clear that she shouldn't have been trying to use her own understanding from the beginning. The connotations, the *connections*, shouldn't have been coming from *her* at all. She had thought she understood how transmogrification worked. She'd learned such basic information as a child, before she could even fully recall. Even when she questioned her understanding, some part of her was still tethered to that old pillar of "reality."

'*I knew that magic must follow the Will of the thaumaturge. Total control was the only way to ensure safety. So even though I wondered how the connotations worked, I never really opened up my own conception and rearranged it from the fundamentals. Even in the smallest spell, I wasn't willing to let any part be outside of my control, certainly not to call upon something external.*'

But it was so simple. So, so, simple, all this time.

Sebastien just needed to allow her magic to rely on something larger than herself. Even the thought was somehow unpleasant. And she felt that, once again, Professor Gnorrish's lesson of admitting that she did not understand was showing its worth. This was the difference between knowing something and understanding it. All this time she had only known, because she hadn't allowed herself to understand.

Her transmogrifications up until now had succeeded in spite of her, not because of her. When she had known clearly that she didn't understand, some subconscious part of her had been unable to exert control, and thus must have allowed the spells she cast to reach for outside understanding. But could she still have been restricting herself unknowingly? Would her spells have been *better* if she had been doing them properly?

Professor Lacer's next words, directed to Damien, broke her out of her contemplation. "Now that Mr. Siverling has made this realization of the true mechanics of transmogrification unavoidable for you, you must overcome the same barriers as he if you hope to avoid difficulty with transmogrification."

"This doesn't make sense," Sebastien said. "Why not just teach everyone how transmogrification really works from the beginning? Why the secrecy?"

"There is a very thin, but chasm-deep, distinction between believing that the majority of society are idiots that casually accept foolishness and lies as reality, and understanding that an idea has a very real weight, a significance, completely separate from its *truthfulness*. Some people, Mr. Siverling, are not able to overcome this distinction. There have been studies. When the results of those studies became clear, they were burned or redacted to keep the knowledge buried."

Damien wiped his palms on his pants. "How bad is it?"

"For you, perhaps not so bad. Statistically, those that are taught about it, rather than come to this realization on their own, have a much more difficult time accepting the idea of the common consciousness. There is some disconnect between knowing about it and being able to *call upon it* while casting spells. For about twenty-five percent of test subjects, it stymied development in transmogrification-based spellcasting by a noticeable amount for up to two years. There was some evidence to suggest that even after two years, their transmogrification spells had decreased efficiency of about five percent. A handful of particularly rigid thinkers never recovered."

"Like a baby bird breaking its way out of the shell," Damien said to himself. "Do you know, the silver-billed woodpecker never develops its magic correctly if you break its shell for it?"

Professor Lacer continued. "It was decided that those who need most to understand the truth will be forced to grasp the concept as they grow in knowledge and analytical ability, and meet barriers in their casting. This includes both Mr. Siverling and my younger self."

Sebastien's eyes widened. "You?"

"Indeed. But returning to your original question, the difficulty that this knowledge may cause certain thaumaturges is not the only reason for secrecy, though that single reason is more important than you may realize upon first thought. Do either or you care to theorize why this may be?"

"A five percent decrease in efficiency, from twenty-five percent of thaumaturges, over the course of even one generation is actually very large," Sebastien said immediately. "If less than five percent of thaumaturges meet *problems* during the course of advancing their path, the scales might weigh the status quo to be more advantageous. Especially if people like you and I can overcome this issue."

"Transmogrification is more versatile than transmutation," Damien added. "It's very important to Lenore. There are a lot of spells that have no transmutation equivalent. We would potentially be weakening the military."

"I could also see people attempting to abuse this knowledge," Sebastien offered. "Trying to force certain ideas upon the masses for their own benefit."

Professor Lacer crossed his arms and leaned against the blackboard. "Indeed, the Blood Emperor conducted widespread experimental campaigns in an attempt at exactly that. But there is another reason. Secrecy in this matter benefits some. I will not speak more on it, but you are not complete idiots, and I believe you should be able to understand what I mean."

The thought came instantly to Sebastien. *'They're already doing this—trying to control what people believe to control how magic works.'* She considered the lies they told about break events and corrupted Wills. *'It might be similar to that. Maybe there's some concept beneficial to those in power, or more generously, to society as a whole, that they're trying to subtly guide into the common consciousness. If people were to know how it all worked, they might invalidate the efforts of those in power.'* What, exactly, these "desirable" ideas might be, Sebastien wasn't sure.

"I can't believe I didn't realize it before," Sebastien said. "All of the clues were there. And it seems so obvious, but I just..." Her shoulders curled in with shame. "No one ever mentioned it, and I wasn't thinking for myself." She looked up at Professor Lacer. "But you never answered my question about magic. Do we have any idea how it actually accesses those ideas? How they imprint themselves upon its...fabric?"

Professor Lacer's chest moved in what might have been a silent, aborted chuckle. "An incorrect explanation of magic could be that it is 'alive' in the way that the planet itself is 'alive,' but changing so slowly and with a lifespan so enormously great that there is no way for us ant-like mortals to interact with it. Surely, ambitious thaumaturges since the dawn of time have desired to uncover how, exactly, magic works. To my knowledge, none yet have met success. Magic does not seem to have opinions about good and evil, nor any way to directly communicate with it. It simply exists. Surely, there is some truth that we have yet to discover, but I cannot say what it is or how it works."

"So how will I know if being told about this rather than discovering it on my own has harmed me?" Damien asked.

"Meditate on the lessons you have learned. *Accept* the shift in your paradigm. And then attempt to cast a transmogrification-based spell once more. Without specific measurements from before this unfortunate revelation, it will be difficult to be exact, but you should be able to judge if your efficacy has lowered. If it has…perhaps a regimen of guided meditation over the next few weeks or months may aid you. Even if that method were to fail, it would not be reason for despair. I imagine a mind healer, a shaman with the right focus, or someone adept in the arts of the mind may be able to train your conception as necessary."

Damien swallowed hard. "But I could be part of the seventy-five percent that don't have any trouble, right?"

"Yes," Professor Lacer said.

"How did you handle it when you realized, Professor?" Sebastien asked, hoping to distract Damien from his worry. "You realized on your own, right?"

"My struggles were much more pronounced and extended than your own, Mr. Siverling. In fact, I had imagined that it might take you another term of failure and seemingly degrading skill to finally reach a breaking point and tear through your misconceptions."

"Another *semester*!?"

"That is approximately how long it took me."

Damien perked up. "Oh, you *must* tell us about this."

Professor Lacer looked between the two of them. "Very well. In short, I began to have trouble with transmogrification when I was a few years younger than the two of you. I had a…magical teacher, of sorts. I was not his apprentice, but he was expected to spend some of his time each month training me. He was quite self-important and supercilious, always acting like some kind of wise sage and taking every opportunity to impart 'life lessons' on others."

"Like Pecanty?" Sebastien and Damien asked at the same time. They shared a surprised look and then a smile.

"Somewhat," Professor Lacer said enigmatically, though his faint smile and the fact that he didn't reprimand them for insulting his colleague reinforced his apparent distaste for the man. "At a certain point, as I gained skill, power, and knowledge, my progress with transmogrification began to slow. And then, I judged that it was not just slowing but in fact moving in reverse. This, admittedly, led to some panic. The more I attempted to understand where I was going wrong, the worse I performed. In desperation, I will admit that I even began to cheat a bit when in front of others, mimicking transmogrification's effects with transmutation when possible. If anything, this only made my struggles even worse."

Professor Lacer shook his head ruefully. "I considered giving up my efforts to understand my failing in the hope that placing less stress on myself would ease my struggles. But, as you might have done, Mr. Siverling, I instinctively rebelled against the idea that I should purposefully remain ignorant. I thought that surely, once I understood, I would improve. I knew that I was talented, and I had cast many transmogrification spells before without issue, after all."

Damien squinted at him. "It's hard to imagine you being younger than us. You were probably already halfway to being a free-caster, right?" Under his voice, he added, "What would you even look like without a beard?"

Professor Lacer gave Damien a subtly admonishing look, but otherwise ignored his interjection. "I went back through previous transmogrification-based spells that I had cast with success, trying to pinpoint the place where I began to have problems. I speculated over how spells worked, how the conceptual properties were transferred from non-magical items into a very magical output, and the like. I remember becoming quite hung up on the question of how I was transferring the *idea* of indestructibility from a dragon's scale without transferring its structure. In fact, a couple of the auxiliary spells I will be assigning as extra work this semester were learned in my attempts to dissect and understand various materials."

"Those auxiliary spells are for me, too, right?" Damien interjected. "You're not going to discriminate against me just because I'm not your official apprentice? My mind is open to new ideas. It might take me a bit longer than Sebastien, but I can handle whatever you have to teach, too." Damien had never quite gotten over his ire at being excluded from the output detachment lessons.

"They are for you, too," Professor Lacer agreed with a half irritated, half weary sigh. "When casting transmogrification spells with said dragon's scale, the indestructibility drops as soon as the Will no longer enforces its application. I had many theories about what the magic actually *did* to create this temporary indestructibility. Some sort of invisible shield or barrier, I thought, or maybe a latticework of stabilizing energy through the target substance? A temporary adjustment of the molecular structure? This kind of thinking, extrapolated outward, only caused me more problems.

"Soon it became clear that rational thinking, trying to *understand*, was the very thing that was deteriorating my abilities. I was able to quantify, to some degree, a loss in ability from the first attempt to cast a new transmogrification spell directly after reading its instructions, to the second attempt after I took some time to try and understand how it worked.

"And so, reluctantly, I went to my teacher and asked for his help. I requested that he watch me cast and give me feedback. He did so, and then asked me if I had been cheating and lying my way through all my assignments. I denied it. I studied incessantly, after all. But he wondered how that could be true when he'd just seen my travesty of a spell, and yet my verbal and written assignments were always so evocative? I did not understand how that was connected. I answered my assignments in the way that I knew he wanted me to, not because I truly understood his purpose."

Sebastien blinked. That was exactly what she had been doing in Pecanty's class.

"He threw me out, threatening to go to my guardian to reveal my misconduct," Professor Lacer continued with a nostalgic smile. "Enraged, I stormed halfway across the city to confront my guardian personally before anyone else could do so, and started shouting. He calmed me down, asked me a few leading questions, and suddenly the whole thing clicked into place in my mind. Like you, I had everything I needed to understand, but my own stubborn beliefs about the way reality worked kept me from putting the puzzle together. I never had trouble of that sort again."

Damien nodded slowly, then patted Sebastien on the shoulder. "I guess you can be proud of the fact that you're not as slow as Thaddeus Lacer?"

Sebastien peeked at Professor Lacer, ensuring that he wasn't outwardly offended, and then said, "Well, maybe I'm just not as arrogant and stubborn?"

Damien, too, glanced at Professor Lacer, letting out a giggle, his eyes sparkling.

Professor Lacer sighed. "As a silver lining, there is anecdotal evidence to suggest that those who are able to genuinely absorb this understanding of transmogrification's true workings have an advantage when casting particularly abstract and difficult spells. I certainly have never found myself at a disadvantage in this. Your mother, too, Mr. Westbay, was particularly accomplished with some spells that required a delicate and precise touch."

"Really? Like what?" Damien asked, leaning forward with interest.

"Higher order connotations, for one. We will explore those if you manage to make it into the intermediate-level classes. She also had a handful of tricks she learned from a shaman and perfected her own little twists on." Professor Lacer cleared his throat and abruptly moved to one of his cabinets, from which he took two small wooden boxes and some written instructions. "This semester, you will be focusing on a single transmutation exercise outside of class. I have also included two divination spells that you will not be tested on, but which should help improve your transmutation through understanding."

He had changed the subject quite clearly, and neither Sebastien nor Damien tried to fight him.

Sebastien opened one of the wooden boxes. Within lay three items. The first was a twisted root whose red-brown skin was scaled and flaking, with little dots of white scattered over its surface. It looked like nothing so much as a gnarly scab scattered with white pustules. The second item was a diamond the size of her pinky tip, sharply faceted and sparkling. The third was a delicate ribbon made from a silk-like material that had been dyed—or painted—to display an elegant scene of a heron standing at the edge of a lake bordered by bamboo shoots.

"You are to practice transmuting these three objects until you can create variations, in any shape, out of dirt, water, or for bonus contribution points, air. You may use these reference objects for the divination spells or for duplicative transmogrification while you gain familiarity. But to succeed with this assignment, you must be able to create each of these substances without any references or information except what is contained within your own minds. Your creations must bear extreme fidelity to the original physical makeup of the natural objects."

Sebastien looked over the divination spells. One focused on the whole of the object to break down overall percentages of different substances such as fat, water, and stone within a substance. The other bore some similarity to the microscope spells they had learned in Natural Science but could display the actual structure and extreme details of a subsection of material beneath the surface.

"Why these three things?" Damien asked.

"Research them and think on it," Professor Lacer said instead of answering. "This exercise requires precision and stability rather than capacity. You may complete your transmutation as quickly or slowly as you like, as long as the composition and structure you create is accurate. It may not be flashy, but this is a valuable skill. Sebastien," he said, calling her attention and waiting until she met his gaze. "You will not attempt to practice with any of these until your concussion is cleared."

"I won't," she agreed easily.

He stared at her a moment longer as if to gauge her truthfulness. "Mr. Westbay, that is all I have for you today. If you would, I have some private matters to discuss with my apprentice."

Damien frowned, either reluctant to leave Sebastien alone or, more likely, peeved to be excluded from something that seemed like interesting gossip. But he only gave Sebastien a significant, wide-eyed look as he left. "Meet me in the library."

As soon as the door was closed behind him, Sebastien asked, "What's happening with the High Crown and the Raven Queen? Are there any updates?"

Professor Lacer paused, then moved to sit behind his desk. "The reality of what happened is quite different from the sensational headlines in the papers." He gave her a brief overview of the events from his perspective. She was surprised to learn that there had been two deaths she was unaware of. And apparently, Parker was still alive. Her insides twisted uncomfortably with a mix of conflicting emotions. She considered, for a moment, trying to free him, but she gave up on the idea almost as soon as it entered her head. It was terrible to admit, when the man's situation was mostly because of her, but she wasn't willing to risk her own safety to help him. Sebastien resolved once again to make sure that his family was taken care of.

"So what is the High Crown going to do now that his plans have failed?" Sebastien asked, pressing her toes harder against the floor to keep her knees from bouncing. "Do they have any recourse?"

"He has convinced the Red Guard to take the case."

Sebastien's cheeks paled, an involuntary response that she hoped didn't give her away.

"Usually, the Red Guard wouldn't involve themselves in something like this, but she was too flashy, and with how strange some of her appearances and abilities were, they want to investigate the truth behind the rumors that seem to circulate around her. If she is indeed the kind of existential threat they were formed to deal with, then they will remove her."

Sebastien suppressed the urge to palm her Conduit. In fact, she remained very, very still as she stared at Professor Lacer.

"Of course, this will be more difficult now that the coppers no longer have a blood sample, but they have their ways."

"How will they determine if she's a threat that needs to be removed?"

He placed his elbows on the desk and laced his fingers together. "The Red Guard take very specific vows. If she is not a threat to the continued existence of mortality—by which I mean the sapient mortal races—they are not beholden to deal with her. Of course, they might still choose to, to mollify the High Crown. Having said that, she is powerful and cunning, and surely understands the consequences of her actions. I doubt she has gotten herself into deeper water than what she can navigate."

Sebastien wanted to laugh. *'If only that were true.'*

Professor Lacer interrupted her horrified imagination about what the Red Guard might do if they caught her. "Are you sure your concussion is not bothering you?"

"I'm fine," she replied automatically.

"Then I believe I should bring up another matter." He reached into his desk drawer and pulled out a sheet of paper, which he slid across the desk toward her.

She picked it up, her eyes flicking over the days of the month listed out, along with a space to check off...meals? "What is this?" It also had a place to note the amount of time spent exercising, as well as casting spells.

"It is a tracking system to ensure you are taking in enough sustenance. As you have proven unable to manage this on your own, you will fill this out daily and return it to me at the end of the month. If I do not see marked improvement in your condition by that time, I will take further action to ensure you remain healthy."

Sebastien stared at the sheet for a few heartbeats before looking up at him. "No." The word surprised even her, but as soon as it passed her lips, she knew she had meant to say it.

"No?" Professor Lacer echoed, as if he had never heard the word before.

"I know that I need to make sure I don't miss meals. But...I'm not a child."

"You are my apprentice. Your wellbeing is my responsibility."

Sebastien's voice was hard. "I am an adult." She waved the paper. "This is an insult. I will take it, and I will fill it out as an aid to myself. But I will not return it to you for your perusal, nor will I allow you to dictate the minutiae of my life. You may suggest things to me, and if you are reasonable, I will listen. You may give me orders and tasks, and I will accept them because I am your apprentice and I respect you. I want to learn from you. But you may not *control* me." Her heart was pounding, her cheeks flushed and her voice deep. Even she was not sure why she was having such a strong reaction to what was, considered charitably, a show of care and good intentions.

As if in answer, a memory of her reflection, pale and dark eyed, whispering desperately to herself that she was in control, flashed through her mind. She tightened her grip around the arms of her chair until her fingers were bloodless white.

Professor Lacer stared at her for a long moment, then leaned forward to press his lips against his folded fingers. "Very well. But with this freedom comes the expectation that you will act to improve the situation. I hope you can understand that while I attempt to respect your boundaries, your wellbeing must come first?"

Sebastien did not *want* to agree that this was reasonable but realized how it would sound if she protested. She nodded stiffly.

"Very well," Professor Lacer repeated wearily. "You may go then. If your injury is recovered by this weekend, you may return for supervised spell practice."

Sebastien had already risen halfway from her chair. She paused. "I...I actually think I might have made a conceptual breakthrough with the output detachment. I haven't tested it yet, of course."

"Thank magic for small mercies," Professor Lacer muttered, then waved her out.

Sebastien shoved the meal-tracking paper in her satchel and made her way to the library. By the time she arrived, she had calmed somewhat. '*I simply have to ensure that Professor Lacer has no reason to think I cannot handle my own affairs. If I appear healthy, he won't worry any longer. I just need to eat more, and maybe smuggle in some food from outside so that I can snack when I wake at night. As for the rest of it, surely I will seem more healthy once the sleep-proxy spell is completed?*'

She was drawn from her musings as she opened the door to the private study room Damien had no doubt bullied his way into and found him grinning and bouncing up and down in front of a spell array.

"My ability to cast is intact," he announced proudly.

Sebastien suddenly had a great desire to test the autumn leaf transmogrification that she had so struggled to cast, but her Will-strain didn't allow for even that.

And, away from the surprise of what had felt like an ambush, that thought forced Sebastien to admit that, based merely on the *evidence* and not knowing the truth of what had led to her circumstances, Professor Lacer's worry might be reasonable.

If Miles, Theo, or Nat had gotten into as many worrisome situations as Sebastien Siverling, she, too, might think that concern was warranted. '*Professor Lacer might look young-ish, but he's actually very old. I probably seem like a child to him.*'

45

THE CURSE OF CURIOSITY

Sebastien
Month 4, Day 16, Friday 5:10 p.m.

Without being able or allowed to cast magic, Sebastien found herself with a surprising amount of extra time. And though she had planned for everything that involved Siobhan Naught or the Raven Queen to be settled with the completion of Operation Palimpsest, obviously things had not gone according to plan.

Sebastien knew she had a tendency toward recklessness that she hadn't yet learned to suppress, but she liked to think that, as long as she had enough time to plan ahead, she was capable of noticing and avoiding unnecessary risks.

And so, she didn't approach Grandmaster Kiernan for answers. She didn't do anything that required her to assume her other body. She didn't even leave the University grounds for the remainder of the week.

Instead, she did her best to act like a totally normal student and kept her eyes and ears open. Sebastien had listened to more gossip in the last few days than she had the entire previous term. She read rage-inducing newspapers from all the Crown-approved publications, as well as a worrying one from *The People's Voice.*

While they might be getting away with publishing something closer to the truth by simply quoting speculation and comments from anonymous civilians, some of those comments might edge close enough to subversion to be called treason. At least the lack of outright and biased vilification of the Raven Queen showed that Oliver hadn't—yet—turned on her.

In addition to all that, she subtly probed Professor Lacer for information.

According to him, the Red Guard had probably assigned a pair of agents to investigate her, and she could only hope that they were less easily biased by the things in the newspapers and the gossip floating around than the average person. Surely, they would find that the Raven Queen wasn't nearly as special or dangerous as people were making her out to be?

But just in case, Sebastien didn't want to give them any chance to actually meet her. She very much doubted that they would be as incompetent, literally and metaphorically divided, or confused as the Pendragon Corps operatives had been.

During her preparations for Operation Palimpsest, Sebastien had rented several locked boxes at various locations under different names, as that seemed the safest way to communicate with Professor Lacer. Tanya would transport the letters between pickup locations for herself and Professor Lacer, adding a degree of separation. When he deposited a letter into one, Tanya would move it to a different location for Sebastien or some other lackey to pick up. When Sebastien wanted to return a message, she would do the same, and he could retrieve her letter after it was ferried to the second location Professor Lacer was aware of.

Four different lockers for a simple letter exchange was convoluted and created a delay, but it probably made exchanging letters with him about fifty percent safer. Hopefully.

She was pretty sure he had no intention to turn the Raven Queen over to the authorities, anyway. And she was even more desperate for information about the seal in her mind than she was about Myrddin's journal and what Oliver's true role in the whole thing had been. But it was best to be cautious.

Sebastien left the keys under Tanya's pillow with another short note and an explicit order to discard her shoes and buy another pair.

Before the linked bone disk was blown up along with all the other things she'd had in her previous bag, she had given a few shavings to Oliver so that the Verdant Stag could keep track of Tanya during what ended up being the Knave Knoll attack. Who knew how he might use them, if he had any remaining?

Sebastien had yet to confront Oliver, or even see him, since everything had happened. They had only exchanged a couple of coded letters, carried by a trusted runner. She couldn't help but search them for clues to his mood or intentions, but his words were all bland and inscrutable, conveying only the necessary information and nothing more. Perhaps hers seemed the same to him.

She didn't want to put off the inevitable confrontation any longer, but every time she thought of going to speak to Oliver, her mind spiraled into questions about Myrddin's journal. There was such an obvious, gaping hole of information—the only question that the Archaeologist hadn't answered for her—that she kept worrying at it like a tongue wiggling a loose tooth.

What was in the book?

She tried to distract herself with schoolwork while she allowed time and the most immediate danger of discovery to pass. It helped to keep her mind occupied, but almost immediately she began to miss her ability to cast magic. At least half a dozen times a day she began to set up a spell array and then remembered that the only magic she was allowing herself was the dreamless sleep spell, and that only from necessity.

It became a second loose, aching tooth, sitting opposite her unsatisfied questions and pushing her toward the edge of some sort of distressed outburst. She grew more silent as she felt the urge to snap at strangers and her friends alike every time she opened her mouth. They were all so intensely irritating, and it was a test of both her willpower and her resolution to be kinder.

While studying the items that Professor Lacer had instructed them to learn to create, Sebastien realized that his selection was far from random. Stone, vegetation, and fabric gave them a broad range of experience that would be useful when trying to use duplicative transmogrification or even pure transmutation to create broadly similar items.

But these specific items were special. The scab-root, so aptly named, came from a mountainous area on the far west coast, south of the equator. The plant killed all but the most tenacious of competitors simply by sucking up so many of the nutrients that were needed to survive. If not for how slow-growing it was, it would have been a devastatingly efficient invasive species. It sent out its ugly, knobby roots a long way before sprouting up another plant, and it was endangered because everyone hated it. It apparently tasted disgusting...but it had almost every single nutrient someone would need to survive. If one could supplement their diet with even small amounts of animal fats and proteins, they could live off scab-root indefinitely.

They might lose weight because of how disgusting it was, but they would survive.

The diamond had an obvious use: It could be utilized as an alternative to celerium for casting magic. Any diamond she created would need to be as close to perfection as possible, though, otherwise it would take one the size of her fist just to handle basic spells. And, of course, like all non-celerium Conduits, it would be more prone to shattering under the pressure of casting. One could also sell diamonds for enough money to purchase other basic necessities, though thaumaturge-created gems had relatively low values.

Sebastien imagined making a pair of curved, razor-sharp daggers out of pure diamond but was disappointed to discover, upon further research, that diamond was a rather brittle material and not suited as a knife. Or a shield. Or a full suit of glittering armor, alas.

The ribbon was spider-silk from the moon-orb weaver. It had been dyed with magic alone to create the impression of a painting through adjusting the light-reflecting properties of each filament-fine thread. It could be used to clothe herself with a fabric of truly surprising strength. When she ran it between her fingers, it reminded her of honey on her tongue, so smooth and compliant. Like the other two, it had no inherently magical properties.

It was also, despite her original conception of spider-silk, a passable substance through which to channel magic. Not because it was fire-resistant, but because it was an efficient channeler of power and wouldn't heat as easily as paper. She had plans for it, and put it first on the schedule to master.

Together, all three objects covered almost everything she would need to survive in a long-term emergency such as getting lost in the wilderness.

But even such fascinating study couldn't fully distract Sebastien from the loose-tooth questions that just sat around calling attention to themselves all the time. "What was in the book?" "How, exactly, was Oliver involved?" The third question was less defined, but consisted of a deep dread that woke her up before her alarms went off, wondering desperately about the seal in her mind and how she should deal with it.

By the time Friday evening rolled around, Sebastien was almost crawling out of her own skin with frustration. Her head had stopped hurting a couple of days before, but when she had asked if she could be allowed to start casting again since she felt fine, Professor Lacer had given her a short, sharp, "No."

When she hadn't responded aloud, he had repeated the word, as if to make sure she could understand basic speech, and she had shuffled off with her head bowed and shoulders drooping. He had called out to her departing back that she could go back to the healers for a follow-up examination when she finished her potions, and so she had been extremely careful to take them on the most frequent schedule allowed.

Sebastien forced herself to eat dinner first, and then mark it off on her tracking sheet, before hurrying to the infirmary. She sat through the examination with deliberate stillness, answering the healer's questions with a severe expression as he tried to judge her health without the benefit of diagnostic spells. The man seemed reluctant to make any assertions without the benefit of his spells to confirm, but Sebastien hated the invasive, naked feeling of divination sliding past her wards. Without Professor Lacer there to force the issue, she glared the healer into submission and got a pass to return to casting.

With the sign-off slip in hand, Sebastien hurried straight to Professor Lacer's office, hoping that he would be in residence. When he called for her to enter, she waved the slip at him triumphantly, breathing hard from her forced march across the University grounds. "I'm cleared to cast spells again," she announced. "And Friday evening is technically the weekend, isn't it? Can you supervise me? I want to try real output detachment and that autumn leaf transmogrification again. I've been thinking about them, and I believe I have both figured out."

Professor Lacer lifted his pen from the page, where it had created an ink blot. "I see your convalescence has not improved your patience. Clear the furniture, and cast a few basic spells to get your Will warmed up first." He retrieved his Conduit from a vest pocket and turned the ink blot into a fine black dust, which he blew away with a short puff.

As she drew out a spell array on the stone floor, Sebastien found herself grinning with excitement.

Professor Lacer stood up from his desk and moved to stand a few feet away with his hands in his pocket. His lips twitched upward when she met his gaze. "If you had a tail, it would be wagging. Go ahead, then."

Sebastien flushed and made a concerted effort to compose herself before running through a few of the most basic spells. Finally, she set up a spell array to create a small sphere of light, with the output appearing one meter outside the circle and one meter above the ground.

Before she tried to cast the spell, she summoned up the epiphany she'd had after asking Liza about output detachment. *'Detaching the output of my spell from the source should be no harder than splitting my Will. And energy does not need to travel through a physical medium.'* Perhaps this was not the same mental resolution that Professor Lacer used to detach his own output, but Sebastien felt confident that it could work. It was likely to work.

'I am so weak. If I can't make progress, my problems will overtake and devour me.'

She would make it work.

Sebastien took a deep breath, and as she exhaled slowly, she brought her Will to bear, filling the spell array, saturating the Circle until it was full and then compressing every speck of her purpose. Her resolve was as hard as granite and as heavy as the ocean. Reality would bend for her like a fresh willow branch. It was not strong enough to resist. It had never been meant to resist.

'Light,' she thought, staring at an empty point in the air as she split the Sacrifice from the output. It did not need a tether, some material substance for her to channel power through. It could receive energy just as light traveled through the void. It did not need a connection to the Circle, only to her Will.

The sphere of light appeared, bright and sure, floating in the air as if it had always been there. The spell array did not flare bright with wasted power.

"I did it," she said confidently.

Professor Lacer squinted his eyes, peering carefully at the empty area between the sphere of light and her spell array. "It seems you might be right," he said. "Let us see." He ran her through the same exercises that he had that first day. Where she had struggled before, with her back turned and her eyes closed, she now found it easier. And before, she had failed to create the light past a solid barrier or in a location that she could imagine but had never seen, but now her Will was able to overcome, with extra effort put toward extreme clarity of purpose.

"Well done," Professor Lacer said with a kind of quiet gravitas that let her know he meant it. He handed her a slip for twenty contribution points. He did not seem to notice anything strange about the method she had used, nothing abnormal about the brain that could have split the input from the output in the same way she split her Will.

Sebastien relaxed, trying to bask in the glow of success, just as she basked in the glow of the sun while practicing light-refinement. She had taken a real step to becoming a free-caster. It was wonderful…but it wasn't enough.

She tucked the contribution point slip safely away in the inner pocket of her suit vest. "Now, for transmogrification?"

"Very well."

This one, she felt less confident about. She had spent some time over the week trying to pound the ideas of darkness associated with an autumn leaf into her mind—not her own ideas, but the ways the average person would, perhaps unknowingly, connect the two.

'*Try not to force it. A million minds hold this idea for me. All I need to do is call upon the intangible weight of ideas they've already created.*' She tried to imagine it, what it might mean for all those ideas to be smashed together into some ephemeral whole, a concept as broad as "the darkness" condensed into a word, or in this case, a glyph and a component.

Her Circle grew gloomy and dark from the left-hand corner first, like some kind of reverse sunrise. The leaf, the only spot of bright color lying on the floor, became washed out, a darker grey lying dead upon the lighter grey of the stone below. She could feel a faint chill emanating from the half-sphere of the output effect, not because she had sucked up the heat for power, but because autumn came with cold. Sebastien waved her hand around the bounds of the Circle, frowning. The spell wasn't consuming warmth from the air. In fact, she wasn't sure that a temperature-sensing artifact would pick up an actual difference in heat distribution within the bounds of her Circle. But it seemed cold.

She held the spell for a while, feeling vaguely off-balance, as if she were sitting on a slope at the edge of a very steep ravine.

"Another success," Professor Lacer intoned softly.

Sebastien let the spell drop. "I can do better."

He raised one eyebrow.

"I can tell I'm still missing something. It doesn't feel right. I'm lacking…clarity."

Professor Lacer contemplated her, his expression inscrutable. After an uncomfortably long pause, he said, "Clarity has always been one of the more impressive facets of your Will. If you feel you are lacking, then I will not gainsay you. At your current standard, you should have no trouble with your classes, but adequacy is hardly an achievement. I am interested to see how you improve."

The satisfaction Sebastien had gained from practicing magic again, as well as her long-overdue success with output detachment, faded away soon after she left Professor Lacer's office. She couldn't be sub-par at transmogrification. Things were calm now, but it seemed inevitable that dealing with the seal in her mind would one day require more of her than she was currently capable of.

As Grandfather had said to her, *'If you don't know what you need, seize power, for it can be converted into almost anything else.'* Again, as ever, it was true.

Sebastien spent the rest of the evening in her cubicle trying to get rid of that off-balance, unsettled feeling while casting transmogrification-based spells. She did not succeed, and the loose-tooth itch of unanswered questions in her mind seemed to feed on her frustration until she gave up her attempts.

She cast her dreamless sleep spell as she normally did, trying not to think about the parts of it that relied on transmogrification, and then lay in the darkness for a full hour, unable to sleep.

Finally, she rose, picked up her satchel, and walked out into the night, leaving her student token behind in her cubicle. Just that morning, she had snatched a token that an upper-term student had left lying at the foot of a bench outside. Obviously, the lectures at the beginning of term hadn't worked. Sebastien had pocketed it on a whim, mostly, but if she were honest, a potential use had been in mind from the beginning. And she did try to be honest with herself.

Disguised by a hood, Sebastien walked to the transport tubes and, seeing that there was no one around, rode one down into the city. She tucked the student token at the base of the tubes, hidden under a rock. A long walk took her to a run-down inn that was about as far from the Silk Door as she could get. The whole way, she contemplated what she was doing, but some part of her knew it was already too late. Sebastien had made up her mind. She wouldn't wait for answers any longer. She used one of their rooms to change into her other body.

Siobhan left still in Sebastien's clothing, then found one of the more obscure places noted on Oliver's map of the city as a good place to escape pursuit by the coppers. In an abandoned gate house tucked away in a small copse at the edge of a manor, she changed her clothes and magically dyed her hair the dark of blackest night.

Returning to the University, she retrieved the upper-term student's token as she passed.

She walked into the darkness of the woods until she found a spot of almost pitch blackness, so dark she couldn't even see her hand in front of her face. There, she slipped on the wire-framed feather ornaments that Oliver had gotten her. Luckily, she had left them and some of her other most precious belongings behind before the Knave Knoll attack, or they would have disintegrated along with everything else. They wiggled and disappeared into her hair, allowing the feathers to slide naturally through the long dark strands.

The stolen student token allowed her onto Grandmaster Kiernan's front porch. Any records after would list a visit by that unfortunately careless student, who had no actual connection to either of her identities. It wouldn't get her past the front door, of course, but she had other ways to make sure he would speak to her.

Siobhan had been planning to simply knock on the front door, but she could hear shuffling sounds and muffled thumps of movement inside. A peek through the edge of Kiernan's window showed the man slipping on his jacket as if to leave.

At first, her heart rate spiked with fear that he was already aware of her presence, but she quickly realized that his face held none of the tension of someone who was aware of a visit by the Raven Queen. She might not be the best at understanding facial expressions, but Kiernan seemed slightly absent-minded and maybe irritated.

So Siobhan tiptoed over to one of the porch chairs and sat down.

Kiernan had opened the door and stepped past her before registering her presence in the corner of his vision. He froze, did a double-take, and then went rigid.

Siobhan could practically see the shock run through him as his entire body stiffened from toe to head. If he could fly, he would have lifted off the ground.

"Sit with me," she said, motioning to the other porch chair.

"I had nothing to do with what happened," Kiernan immediately said. He regained control over his faculties with surprising speed and gave her a ninety-degree bow. "I am not so foolish as to keep doubling and tripling down on my mistakes, my lady. I promise you, I had nothing to do with the kidnappings, or the divination attempts, or—or any of it. I will vow to it, if necessary."

Siobhan hadn't suspected him; the true culprit of everything that had happened the Friday before seemed quite clear. "I know," she agreed easily, exaggerating her sense of ease as well as her certainty. She gestured to the seat next to her once more.

Grandmaster Kiernan shuffled closer, then sat on the edge of the seat gingerly, as if prepared to spring to his feet again at a moment's notice. She allowed herself a small, vindictive smile at the distinct difference between his behavior now and how he had treated her when she was Sebastien.

"I had no choice but to betray the Verdant Stag," he announced.

'*Why is he bringing this up? Is he, perhaps, searching his memory for what sin he might have committed to require a visit from me? Like a child accidentally confessing their crimes when given a stern look from a parent?*' "Continue," she said, curious. "I'm not here to harm you. I simply hope to have a more…open communication."

"I felt I had no choice," Kiernan repeated. "I do not know if Lord Stag told you, but I was blackmailed to ensure the escape of several important Morrows by an ally of theirs that had remained free. But it was not only that. The Verdant Stags have been very clearly setting themselves up to take power from"—he lowered his voice secretively—"the Architects of Khronos. They're edging in on beast core procurement and other smuggling monopolies, gaining influence, and with the book…"

"Yes?" she asked, suppressing signs of her own spiking interest.

"Well, it seems like they want to squeeze us for rare magical components and the end-product celerium while keeping the real power and control for themselves. Perhaps Lord Stag even hopes to play us against the Crowns and try to benefit from civil war. They've made absolutely sure to get their hands on a complete celerium supply chain. I hope you understand the kind of… desperation this situation could inspire."

Siobhan cleared her throat. Somehow, she didn't think he was speaking about celerium mining. "How, exactly, is the book integral to a complete celerium supply chain?" She knew she was giving some measure of power away by asking so clearly, but this was too important a question to edge around.

Kiernan gave her a strange look. "You can speak freely with me, my lady. I already know that it holds the process for purifying and draining beast cores of power without shattering them, allowing us to turn them into pure celerium that can be used as Conduits."

Siobhan nodded slowly, trying to make sure that her body gave away no involuntary signs of shock. "Tell me, do you have any other reasons for suspecting that the Verdant Stag wants to take advantage of a civil war?"

"Well, perhaps they have some other plan. If I were being charitable, I might say that Lord Stag is actually attempting to prevent upheaval. But it's already far too late to stop it. Possession of the knowledge in that book is going to be critical with what's coming. There will be mass panic once the populace learns that the celerium mines are running dry."

46

———

A GREAT DIVIDE

Month 4, Day 17, Saturday 12:55 a.m.

This time, Siobhan wasn't able to hide her shock. *'The celerium mines are running dry?'* The question echoed in her head, drowning out all other thoughts for a long moment.

"You...didn't know," Grandmaster Kiernan said, his eyes wide. He frowned. "Lord Stag didn't even tell you what you were stealing? Perhaps it's him you should be paying a visit in the middle of the night."

"There's another misconception at play here, but let's set that aside for the moment. Tell me more about the celerium. No secrets, no lies."

Grandmaster Kiernan swallowed hard but nodded readily. "A select few people have known for a while. That's why prices have been rising so steeply. The Church of the Radiant Maiden, some of the Crowns, and a few among our number have been quietly buying up all the high-quality celerium on the market. Slowly, so as not to cause a panic. The Red Guard has probably been doing the same, but who knows with them."

"Celerium isn't the only thing that's been rising in price," Siobhan noted, her mind calling up the tags on various rare components in the market. She'd thought they were exorbitantly priced just because she was in Gilbratha, where they gouged you for everything.

Kiernan raised his hands, palms up in a half-shrug. "Well, yes. People aren't oblivious. Components that are useful for particular battle and protective spells are being stockpiled, and the whole thing creates a ripple effect. Other people see prices on rare components rising, or can't secure their usual supply, and they buy a little more than they need in case the situation continues. It becomes a vicious cycle and spills over into other areas."

Siobhan tightened her hands into fists, then stretched out and flexed her fingers wide. "How long are Lenore's celerium mines expected to last?"

Kiernan shook his head. "I only have estimates. Five years, maybe ten. But the mining is slowing down as we go. The Crowns have known about the issue for a while already. They've searched the entire country for any other celerium deposits and found nothing."

"Five years," Siobhan murmured. That was nothing. Five years until they ran out of the most valuable commodity on the planet.

"Without the book, our only hope will be to venture outside of the known lands in search of other deposits, or fight over the few remaining mines that still have a supply. Silva Erde has a mine with a few decades remaining, according to our spies. Osham... Unless they've done a great job of keeping new sources confidential, they're in a similar situation to us. They're blustering as always about being the strongest, undefeatable and infallible, but it's just propaganda."

"What else is being done? Surely, with this much time to prepare..."

Kiernan's lips twisted, sending his bushy mustache sweeping to the side like a broom. "Well, the Crowns' most loyal thaumaturges and a select group here at the University have been experimenting with creating ultra-pure artificial gemstones, blood gems from compressed magical beast blood, and any way that we might reconstitute shattered celerium into a whole once more. That, along with more arcane attempts to imbue objects with greater channeling capability. But just as in the thousands of years before this, none have come up with anything that can stand beside celerium. None except Myrddin," he corrected quickly.

'Thaumaturges have been using the celerium up for millennia now, shattering it into uselessness bit by bit, thinking that the deposits would never run dry,' Siobhan thought. *'I never even considered that celerium was a thing that could run out. It seems so obvious now, but I never questioned the status quo.'*

Aloud, she said, "It will create a class divide between thaumaturges that can afford celerium and those who cannot."

Kiernan let out a humorless, breathy laugh, sliding back to sit more fully in his chair. "Oh, yes. But it will also create a power divide. Do you know the surest way to break a Conduit, besides channeling more than it can handle? Well, of course you do." He waved his hand sharply. "Opposing another thaumaturge's Will. Even if people are willing to carry around huge gemstones as celerium alternatives, and take the increased risk of Conduit failure in everyday life, none of the other options can reliably stand against celerium *in combat.*"

The man gritted his teeth and added slowly, "Whoever can supply a competent force with celerium has a reasonable chance to control the nation. And whichever nation has access to celerium can hope to take over the known lands. The days of an empire loom on the horizon once more."

Siobhan's black sapphire Conduit pressed against the back of her ribs once more now that she was healed. It had a capacity of around seven hundred fifty thaums, but to be safe she would need to keep any spells channeled through it at six hundred fifty thaums or less. When she had gotten it, that seemed such a large number, and so far off. Now…she was almost there already. And if she needed to go up against a thaumaturge in battle, fighting for control of a spell array or to oppose the output of some spell they cast, she would need to keep the capacity lower or risk a sudden shattering.

Kiernan's gaze was sharp like an eagle's. "You didn't know, but you're not as worried about this as I would have expected."

Siobhan felt that she was extremely worried, and appropriately so, but she stared back at him silently.

"They say you can cast without a Conduit. Is that true?"

"It is not."

He paused, his expression suggesting he didn't quite believe her. "If the High Crown gets his hands on that book, the power of the Crown Families will only grow. And with their power, their abuse will grow, too." Kiernan's scarred, knobby-jointed hands tightened into fists in his lap as he stared out into the dark. "And obviously, we at the University are a threat to them. They've made it so by their very fear of that reality. We have a great, if subtle, power over Lenore. We are the only accredited institution to provide Masteries. We create inventors, soldiers, *Grandmasters.* We mold those who hold great and terrifying power. And we have retained the right to admit or deny who we want from these august grounds. So the Crowns want us bound tightly."

Kiernan looked back to Siobhan. "Each shackle and lock they place on us chafes more than the last. There are restrictions on what components we are allowed to buy, and how much. Audits to ensure we aren't hoarding components that are considered potentially dangerous or useful in battle. Restrictions on the number of direct Apprentices we are allowed to take, as well as how many sponsorships we are allowed to give. Vows we are each required to take if we want to teach, requiring loyalty to the Thirteen Families—and the High Crown—even *above* loyalty to the nation. They can commandeer our services to help with difficult missions without advance notice. More aptly put, University professors are subject to a random draft."

His fists were white in his lap and his mustache trembled with rage. "People drafted to perform these dangerous missions tend to be those who the Thirteen Crowns feel are a threat. And somehow, *somehow*, they end up dying on the mission with surprising regularity."

Siobhan had not known this, but she couldn't say that she was particularly surprised to hear it. "So what is your plan?"

Kiernan hesitated, finally releasing his clenched fists. He rubbed at his swollen, rheumatic knuckles. "We only wish for freedom. Surely you can understand that? Freedom for everyone, not only ourselves. A life out of the shadow cast from the Crown Families' boot. Free industry, so that merchants do not need to receive their favor to do business. Freedom to pursue knowledge and power. Freedom to know the truth of history and shine light into the dark shadows. The right to rule Lenore would come from worth, inconsiderate of bloodline or connections. New members of the ruling council would be brought in based on qualifications, and the old who were no longer worthy would be deposed. We would make things better, don't you see? If only we had the book. Someone like you would be welcome in the kind of world we build."

Somehow, Siobhan doubted it, but she didn't say so aloud. During a long moment of silence, she considered the ramifications of several different responses. Finally, she said, "You have given me much to think on. Now I will do the same for you. People believe they know me and understand my actions. Have you ever considered that the book you are looking for never made it to Gilbratha?"

Kiernan leaned forward, frowning. "I...don't understand. What do you mean?"

Siobhan knew there was some possibility that she really did have the book that could transmute beast cores into useable celerium, but after everything she'd learned, she strongly doubted it. The right kind of hint might lessen the pressure on her while still not directly betraying Oliver. The Architects of Khronos had already suspected and even raided the Verdant Stag, but they didn't find what they were looking for. Kiernan should be susceptible to misdirection.

"Originally, the expedition into the Black Wastes retrieved five books from Myrddin's hermitage."

Kiernan's sharp intake of breath revealed his ignorance.

"Everyone believes that if they find Siobhan Naught, they can obtain the method to transmute celerium. You might have wondered why I didn't know of it, if I have that book? A book that was, in truth, taken by coincidence—or perhaps a compulsion—though I cannot be sure because I was in another room at the time. But I do not hold the book you are searching for. Inside my book was something else, contained in a space-bending array that might have grown weak with time. Something powerful, precious, and old, but certainly not the kind of thing that could do what you hope for. Either your information about what Myrddin was working on is very wrong, or Ennis Naught didn't steal the book that everyone thought he did."

Kiernan stared at her, wide-eyed and clearly thinking hard, but the question he asked next wasn't what she expected. "What happened to Siobhan Naught?"

Siobhan tilted her head to the side. Obviously, she was sitting right in front of him. Why was he speaking as if she was someone else? Surely everyone knew that, even if she were sprouting feathers from her hair and acting theatrically, the Raven Queen and Siobhan Naught were the same person?

'But maybe they don't,' she realized suddenly. 'Could that be an opportunity to clear my name? If I could detach my original identity from the crimes of the Raven Queen... I'll have to be vague about it. I'm not sure exactly where this misunderstanding stems from.' She didn't have time to consider all the ramifications. This opportunity faded with every moment that passed. "Siobhan Naught was innocent," she said softly. "A promising young thaumaturge, but not powerful or skilled enough to evade capture. But now I am here, and I am none of those things."

Siobhan could only hope that these words wouldn't come back to bite her in an unforeseen way, as the things she did without proper consideration so often did.

Kiernan, though, just nodded slowly, staring hard as if trying to see her face underneath the shadows of the cloak. "So the book we need is...missing?"

She hummed noncommittally. That was the question she had expected him to ask from the beginning, or close to it. "It seems so. I have one, you have three, and so another party must have the last. Now, I cannot be sure which is missing, but if Myrddin did write about such feats, then it seems likely to be the book you are all so desperately searching for. And the person who could manage such a smooth deception, letting no hint slip of their involvement? If I were you, I would be very careful how I went about investigating the location of the fifth book."

Kiernan let out a harsh breath, sagging as he brought his fingertips up to his forehead. "Give me discernment," he muttered, almost too low to hear. He lifted his head and lowered his hands to look at her. "But you could decrypt it, if you did have it? Could you decrypt the others, the ones we have, too?" He didn't pause for her to answer, speaking more to himself than to her. "Even if they don't have the culmination of Myrddin's research, they might have hints of what developmental path he took along the way. We might be able to devise our own solution independently, if we knew the right direction."

"I...might be capable of reading them." 'Someday,' she added silently. She smiled wide and allowed the expression to leak into her voice. "But you would have to offer me a tribute that would make it worth my time, and the danger. Do you have anything that could tempt me?"

Kiernan fell silent, his gaze moving down and to the side as he thought.

Siobhan stood. She had learned all she needed, and it was time to go before she made a mistake or the tides of irony brought on some horrible, unexpected danger. No matter what Kiernan offered her, it didn't actually matter until she could unlock the book, and the more pressure he felt to gain her agreement, the better offer he was likely to make.

She moved to walk away, but behind her, Kiernan called, "Wait!"

She turned, glad that he had stopped her, because she remembered something important. "Tanya Canelo," she said.

Kiernan frowned. "Yes?"

"She has asked for my protection, and done a favor in advance to pay for it. If you cause her harm, you will pay in kind. She is not yours anymore. You may continue to employ her, if you wish, as long as you remember that she is mine." There. Hopefully it would act as some portion of protection for the other woman against being sent out on further suicide missions. *'No matter what he says, it seems Kiernan and the High Crown are not so different in that way. He is a hypocrite.'*

Stating an affiliation to Tanya might make it harder to use her for covert activity, but Tanya's life had to be worth more than Siobhan's convenience.

As Siobhan reached the edge of the tree line, she activated the dowsing artifact and allowed herself to disappear into the shadows between their towering trunks.

47

———

A BITTER END

OLIVER WAS MEETING with Anastasia Gervin in his home office when he caught a glimpse of movement out of the corner of his eye. It drew his gaze to the wrap-around window behind his desk.

Sebastien was outside.

She stood in front of the wrought-iron entrance gate, looking up at the manor. She firmed her jaw, squared her shoulders, and stepped through.

This last week had been one of the most unpleasant in recent memory. The Friday before, on the day of Ennis Naught's sentencing, Oliver had planned to take advantage of the opportunity to show himself in a very public place while "Lord Stag" made appearances elsewhere, at a time when the coppers would be too distracted to spend all of their resources trying to catch him. And if he had also thought to take some vindictive pleasure in seeing Siobhan's father get what he deserved, surely no one would judge Oliver for that?

He had been at ease, because Siobhan knew of the danger the day presented and would stay safe under Liza's wards. The worst Oliver had imagined happening was that Ennis Naught might be sentenced to death, and Siobhan, despite her disdain and resentment for the man, would be distraught at the fate of her father.

But from the very beginning everything had gone wrong.

Katerin had broken the flimsy bracelet linked to its pair on Oliver's forearm by mid-morning. He had rushed to her side, arriving to find her frantic at what seemed to be the premeditated and extremely *determined* kidnapping of her nephew. They both imagined horrible things and speculated desperately about who might want leverage over Katerin and Oliver. Or revenge.

A moment of hope had appeared when one of the Verdant Stag subjects who owed them a favor arrived at the Verdant Stag with news. They had recognized Theo during the boy's desperate attempt to escape and had taken the initiative to follow the kidnappers' wagon on foot. Unfortunately, they had lost it after following it north for a few blocks.

Even with a strand of Theo's curly copper hair, the Verdant Stag's thaumaturges were too weak to find the boy.

Katerin had snapped and tipped over her solid wood table with a heaving roar, and then collapsed sobbing in Oliver's arms.

He had picked her up and bodily stuffed her into a carriage, which they rode with reckless speed through the clogged streets to Lynwood Manor.

Surely, Gera would be able to find Theo, Oliver had thought. No one could divine like a prognos. Especially not one that was forced to use magic constantly in everyday life.

But Gera had left earlier that morning without telling anyone where she was going. And then they discovered that her son was gone, too.

Oliver sent someone for Liza, but she didn't answer her door.

It was only then that he had broken the bracelet that would call Siobhan to his aid. But she never came. Dread had filled Oliver's belly to overflowing. This confluence of events had to be purposeful. Enemy action. And if Liza wasn't opening the door, how could he be sure that Siobhan was safe behind her wards?

When the cloud of ravens began to coalesce in the Mires, Katerin had gotten it into her head that the coppers had caught everyone and were going to reveal them at Ennis Naught's trial. Maybe to bait the Raven Queen into arriving. Maybe to execute them all as a reminder of their power.

Oliver thought it more likely that the Architects of Khronos had been behind it. They hadn't found the book when they attacked and raided the Verdant Stag, but maybe they still weren't convinced that he was uninvolved in its theft. Maybe they hoped to ransom off the people he cared for in exchange. That didn't exactly explain Millennium Lynwood's disappearance, unless perhaps the Architects suspected the Nightmare Pack of having the book, too, and were covering all their bases.

How the cloud of ravens played into it, Oliver wasn't sure. But it was too unsubtle to be safe to approach personally. The best he could do was send a squad of enforcers dressed in plainclothes and hope that the ravens were only a decoy, and not Siobhan's desperate cry for help.

At Katerin's urging, Oliver had gone to the Edictum Council while Katerin called on every favor and pulled every string the Verdant Stag had access to. Some of the higher-ranking coppers on the Verdant Stags' payroll were assigned to the sentencing for the day, but despite the risks Oliver took to question them, they knew nothing. Oliver had barely been able to appear normal as he mingled among the nobles, trying to pick up any gossip or clues that could give them a chance. Any chance.

Something grew sick inside of Oliver when the raven delivered its letter to the center of the Edictum Council floor. Surely…someone was framing the Raven Queen? Taking advantage of her reputation, just as Oliver had speculated might be possible. Either that, or things had gone desperately wrong. Was Siobhan turning herself in? Wild ideas spiraled through Oliver's head like debris carried within a tornado.

He almost hadn't been able to control his reaction when Damien Westbay, of all people, decided that they should team up to figure out what was going on and ensure Sebastien's safety. Westbay hadn't been entirely useless, but he was painfully naive. Someday, that would get him into trouble that he couldn't get himself out of, and then it would break him.

When a divination team at Eagle Tower was attacked, Oliver finally grew suspicious. This might be someone trying to take advantage of the Raven Queen's reputation…but it could also, maybe, be the Raven Queen herself. And not out of desperation and fear. This was too well coordinated for that. It had been planned in advance.

After one of the most torturously frantic days of Oliver's life, spent in an excessively high state of anxiety as he ran around uselessly, his thoughts spiraling into ever-darker realms as the hours passed without hope, Katerin sent him a message on his distagram, which he'd moved into his carriage for easy access.

Siobhan, Theo, Millennium Lynwood, and all the people that had gone missing along with them were fine. Oliver had rushed to the Nightmare Pack's underground arena. But though everyone agreed that the Raven Queen had entered, and Katerin said Siobhan was sleeping in a room upstairs, Oliver was not allowed entrance.

When he had gotten the full story, and particularly Gera's part in it, all the stomach-eroding worry that he had felt dropped away. It left behind anger, but, beneath that, and more lasting, was a persistent dread. The anger burned hot, flaring up a few times over the following week only to burn itself out again, but the dread never left. It grew worse every day that passed.

And now, Sebastien was here. Some of the anger flared up again as he was reminded of her thoughtlessness, her lack of care for him or the others under her protection that would lead her to create such a huge spectacle without even a warning. But underneath it, his dread crystallized into something hard and sharp.

Miss Gervin cleared her throat, dragging Oliver's attention back to her.

Had she been talking? "I'm sorry, I grew momentarily distracted. What were you saying?"

Miss Gervin stood, slipping the sheaf of papers they had been working on into her purse, which hardly looked large enough to hold them. "That's quite all right," she said with a smile. "I think we've covered the most critical bits. Why don't we schedule a follow-up in two weeks?"

Oliver tried to keep the relief and impatience from his face. Anastasia Gervin was an extremely useful connection and receptive to his ideas in a way that few in the Crown Families were. He didn't need to risk offending her just because he wanted to rush out of the room and find Sebastien.

But when Oliver opened his office door to see Miss Gervin out, Sebastien was standing outside the door, back as stiff as a wooden soldier.

Sebastien's eyes widened as she saw Miss Gervin.

Miss Gervin's eyes flicked between them in the silence that followed, and then she took a large step forward and slipped her arm through Sebastien's, tucking her hand into the crook of Sebastien's elbow.

Sebastien relaxed somewhat, giving the other girl a grateful smile.

Ana squeezed her arm, then gave Oliver a bright, toothy smile that was aggressively perfect. "Sebastien! I'm so surprised to see you here. My father is letting me handle some parts of the business now, remember? I am collaborating on a very optimistic endeavor with Mr. Dry—oh, I'm sorry. With *Lord* Dryden here." She rolled her eyes. "Mother is thrilled." Another squeeze of Sebastien's arm as she sidled a little closer until their shoulders bumped. "Do you want to get breakfast together, the three of us?"

At first, Oliver thought that she was flirting, trying to assert some kind of romantic claim. But she hadn't pressed the side of her breast into Sebastien's arm. Her tone was more cold than playful. And something hard and protective had come into her eyes that reminded Oliver of a guard dog.

She thought she was offering comfort and protection. And based on the way Sebastien gave her a small smile and didn't even flinch at the touch of her hand, despite the way Oliver had seen her recoil from an accidental shoulder brush with a stranger on the sidewalk, Miss Gervin was successful.

Oliver frowned. What had Sebastien been telling her friends about him?

"That's okay," Sebastien said, gently disentangling Miss Gervin's grip from her arm. "I had breakfast already, at the cafeteria, and now I'm too full to eat again. I just need to discuss some things with Oliver."

Miss Gervin, to her credit, didn't hesitate or ask Sebastien if she was sure. She just nodded to them both and walked away with a nonchalant wave over her shoulder. They watched her descend the stairs, and then, with a wave of invitation from Oliver, Sebastien followed him into his office.

Sebastien stood behind the chair Miss Gervin had been sitting in, her slender-fingered hands resting upon the wood frame of its back. She didn't even wait for Oliver to sit down behind his desk. "Did you steal one of Myrddin's journals?"

Oliver's heart jumped as if it were trying to tear itself free of his chest. He stared at her for three frantic beats and then said, "I did."

Sebastien showed no signs of surprise. "I also have one of Myrddin's journals," she said, as nonchalantly as if they were talking about cravats from a favorite tailor. "Just not the one people think. One of the other four."

"You've been busy," Oliver mumbled past numb lips. How long had she been working on this? Had she suspected him for a while now, or had someone else discovered the truth and told her?

"The one you have contains a method to transmute pure celerium from beast cores," she said. She paused a moment for him to speak, but when he remained silent, she continued. "Do you know what the one I have contains?"

Oliver had to clear his throat before he could speak. "I don't. Do you?"

Sebastien didn't answer his question. "You used me as a decoy," she accused, still seemingly without feeling.

If Oliver's dread were tangible, it would have been slicing into his internal organs with every breath. They were at the top of a precipice now, and he could see no way of stopping their descent. Not when she looked like that.

Sebastien's face was emotionless, and for the first time her eyes reminded him of those of a shark: cold-blooded, predatory, and uncaring. Responses ran through Oliver's mind, different ways to try and mitigate disaster, to hold up the crumbling brick of their relationship, built so gradually and now tearing apart.

Before he could land on some magical answer, she spoke again. "Did you somehow cause Ennis to steal the journal?"

She knew too much. He couldn't lie. "I didn't. But…it's possible the thief I hired took it upon herself to place a compulsion. Something to sow confusion. She left the country upon completing the mission, and I haven't heard from her since."

Sebastien nodded to herself thoughtfully.

"I didn't tell you because you didn't need to know. And I didn't actually use you as a decoy. Not really." His words were coming faster even though he tried to slow them, to keep them measured and with the perfect intonation that would somehow make her believe him. "I tried to keep you safe, even though I could have just let you be. That placed me in more danger. If I had ignored you completely, even if you were caught, even if my thief made a mistake when altering the expedition's logs and they somehow discovered that an additional book was missing, I wouldn't have been implicated. The information within can be used for the greater good. A way to create celerium could be the great equalizer for our society, as well as an insanely lucrative source of income."

Sebastien raised one eyebrow and said dryly, "And with the celerium mines running dry, the power you would hold would be enormous."

Oliver already had another argument lined up, but his thoughts stuttered and tripped over each other. "What? The mines aren't…"

She frowned darkly, accusingly.

"You really have been busy," he said, the words slipping out without his conscious thought. It was a mistake.

Her frown disappeared, replaced by the faintest sneer of disgust.

"That would make a lot of sense," he said carefully. "But I didn't know that. I thought that those in power had just been restricting the flow of celerium into the market for the last couple decades as a way to artificially increase the price. Collusion to line their pockets by creating scarcity. But if that's true, it…has major implications. If that's true, I might need to accelerate my timeline on getting it decrypted."

She scoffed. "You expect me to believe you didn't already know?" Before he could respond, she snapped, "Or that our connection was solely for my benefit? That you gave me a loan with fifty percent interest and asked me to commit crimes to pay you back…just to keep me safe?"

"I didn't know," he said softly.

Sebastien sneered, one side of her upper lip drawing back to reveal the teeth beneath.

Something about that expression, not just angry but disgusted, sparked a bloom of anger. "I won't apologize for acting in the best interest of all the people who we have helped, and all who we could still help, Sebastien. *Every* young child and aspiring free-caster could go to school. We could be an entire nation of thaumaturges. We could end poverty, scrub out Lenore's corruption and entitlement, and save lives. What *you* have now could be for everyone, without any of the struggle or the danger."

Sebastien opened her mouth to retort, but Oliver held up a hand to stop her. "Listen. I will tell you once." He paused, drew a deep breath, and repeated more softly. "Please listen. I didn't intend things to work out the way they did. I never planned for Siobhan Naught to steal a book in my stead, or become the Raven Queen, or my friend. I may not have shared all of my secrets with you, but that has never been a requirement of our relationship, never a promise I made. And if you wish to speak of my manipulations, I admit it freely. As I said before, I have never bound anyone to me with a leash they cannot break, and that includes you. I may want to lift this country, this world, out of its own shit, but I am no saint. I do what is necessary, not what is right. But do not pretend that you have not acted similarly."

He allowed the pause to linger, staring at her hard.

Sebastien returned his gaze defiantly.

"That little spectacle of yours, did you ever stop to think about the danger it might bring to the Verdant Stag? To the innocent people who you've never even met and apparently don't care enough about to consider? Do you have any idea how many unwarranted arrests the coppers have been making in the last week to bring people in for questioning? I can't even keep track of them. Did you consider the more direct harm that causing a widespread panic might do? That innocent people could be injured?"

Her expression had stilled again, but it wasn't as dead as before. "Were people…injured?"

"Several."

She blinked slowly but didn't flinch.

"And more have been harmed during arrests or questioning. That part, you might argue, isn't your fault, but if I had known about your plan, I could have made preparations that might have mitigated the severity of the situation. And this time, you might say, was out of desperation. But it's not the first time you put aside morality or honor when it suits you. Did you really expect that I would think it a coincidence when the textile sub-commission that I had worked out and agreed upon with Lord Gervin suddenly fell through? And just before you came to me with such an advantageous solution to my newly created problem. You were saving yourself, to be sure, but risking harm to everyone that sub-commission would have helped. Thousands of people given work, tens of thousands given warm clothing through the winter months or dressed in something other than rags. If you hoped that I wouldn't notice your sabotage, you should have been more subtle."

Sebastien rocked back on her heels. She frowned in seeming confusion, looking away and muttering, "Ana," to herself.

"Your friend did not tell me. She had no need. I am not so foolish. But I didn't even hold that scheme against you, Sebastien. Because even though we're on the same side, I have never expected altruism of you. I have considered us friends. I have given gifts of monetary value, knowledge, and protection. I have gone out of my way to keep you safe, even at a danger to myself." He laughed bitterly, and Sebastien flinched.

"But when it comes from you to me, it is always a transaction," Oliver continued. "You will never act on my behalf unless receiving something in return. And perhaps you became used to my generosity, to the point that you expect it and become angry if I do not immediately, even preemptively, *give* to you. So, let us transact, now. If you want complete honesty from me, want to know all my plans and secrets and all the ways I move under the surface of this city…what will you give me in return?"

Sebastien's pale skin first grew even more sallow, and then her cheeks flushed with rage, her black eyes glinting. For a moment, her shadow seemed to waver like a ripple over the surface of a pond. "So be it," she whispered, her voice trembling. She swallowed and lifted her chin. "Should you wish to speak with me again, you will pay tribute, like the rest of those who treat with the Raven Queen."

And with that, she spun on her heel and made for the door.

"Wait."

She stilled, then turned slowly to look at him again.

"Does anyone else know about the book? The one I have?" he asked.

When she smiled it was a small, mean thing. "No. And I will not tell them. We will keep each other's secrets, hmm? A *fair trade.*"

Oliver watched her leave, and then listened to her walk away at a measured but fast pace. A few minutes later, she said a warm goodbye to Sharon, was forced to accept a picnic basket of food, and left.

The echo of the front door, though it had been closed gently, seemed to reverberate through Oliver's bones. He forced himself not to watch her leave through the window. Instead, he pressed his trembling fingers to the cool wood of his desk. Then he let his head slump down onto his hands.

He had lost something precious, and it was more bitter than he had ever imagined.

48

———————

SECRETS KEPT

Sebastien
Month 4 Day 17, Saturday 8:25 a.m.

Sebastien's carriage driver offered her a newspaper—a way to increase his tips, no doubt. It was the Daily Sun, and of course it was filled with drivel, as usual. After her recent experiences Sebastien would never trust what this paper wrote about anything. There was nothing new within, merely more gossip and speculation about her. They had reached the point of trying to wring water from a dry rag.

They were digging into Ennis Naught's past again, and under the journalist's pen the man seemed awful enough that even Sebastien had to admit that, as lacking a father as he might have been, he was not *that* heinous.

She tossed the paper aside halfway through the article and leaned her head back against the padded seat. Her muscles were so tense that her skull ached with every beat of her heart. Her conversation with Oliver flashed into her mind, and she swallowed hard, then rapped on the ceiling of the carriage and called out a new destination.

Instead of going back to the University, the driver took Sebastien to a costume and cosmetics shop. There, she used some of the actual coin left to her name to buy two nice wigs, a few more pairs of colored contact lenses, and a book on stage makeup for actors, complete with illustrations and a cosmetics kit. After some deliberation, she also picked up a costume that was touted as a female pirate's outfit. Really it was just tight leather pants and a puffy linen shirt, a half-corset that would cinch in her waist while leaving her chest free, and a lot of cheap costume jewelry along with a stencil to draw on some fake tattoos. And a fake stuffed parrot.

The secret compartment in her satchel was stuffed to the brim now that it had to hold two small chests—and Myrddin's journal, which she had retrieved from its hiding spot for good—and so the main, visible section of her satchel bulged with her purchases.

From there, she took another carriage to a housing agency, gave them a list of requirements, and scheduled a tour day for the coming weekend. Finding long-term accommodations of her own would be more expensive through the agency because of their fee, but she wanted to separate this task from the people who might otherwise be able to help her. And on her own, she simply didn't have the time or connections to handle it easily.

By then, it was already approaching noon, and Sebastien made a third venture, back to the novelty shop she'd gotten the light-crystal coasters at. She picked up two sets of the embarrassingly pink journals that Ana and Nat used to communicate with each other. They were stupidly expensive despite being relatively low-powered and having all the standard problems of sympathetic connections.

Damien had been right. She needed a way to communicate with others more easily, especially now that she wouldn't be going to Dryden Manor and simply talking to Oliver when she needed anything. She would have preferred a distagram to the journals, but even though she could afford one, technically, she didn't have the necessary connections to buy one.

On a whim, she looked for the light coasters, finding them in a half-empty box marked "sale." After a moment of hesitation, she decided to buy them all, lest she find she needed more once the stock had already sold out. Even if she didn't need a couple dozen thirteen-pointed-star disks, these would be good objects on which to practice her beacon-imprinting once she had completed the guiding light ritual.

When her fingers started to tremble and unbidden thoughts of the beamshell tincture prickled up, she forced herself to stop and eat the lunch Sharon had packed for her despite the sick feeling in her belly that was smothering any sensations of hunger. The meal helped settle her, and she even splurged for a cup of coffee that was fifty percent cream and zero percent magic.

A random woman came up and tried to start a conversation with Sebastien about some party that she was organizing in a nearby park, but it quickly became awkward enough that the woman took the hint and left.

Sebastien finished off the last of her coffee and laid down a few coins on the table. As she rose to leave, her eyes caught on the coin. '*Was that woman trying to get me to give her money?*' she realized suddenly.

She looked down at herself, remembering how much her clothes had cost. It did somewhat make sense that people would assume she was the kind of person who would toss a few gold to charity on a whim. *'Even if these clothes are from last season,'* she thought with a wry smile.

From there, Sebastien rented a room with a sink and a mirror, transformed into Siobhan, and spent the next three hours struggling with her disguise. She wore the shorter of the two wigs, a short, ragged bob. It was high quality and reminded her of an autumn forest, or perhaps an earthy sunset. Once she figured out how to get all of her own hair pinned flat to her head and out of the way, wearing the wig was the easy part.

After that, she flipped through the book on stage makeup and, with a half-dozen failed attempts that she washed off in the sink, she subtly changed the look of her face. She rounded the natural almond shape of her eyes, and with some foundation slightly lighter than her normal skin tone, she softened the definition in her cheekbones, rounded her jawline, and made her chin seem slightly more pointy. Very, very carefully, she gave herself freckles and then put in contact lenses that would subtly lighten the striking darkness of her eyes.

Finally, she put on the pirate's outfit, which—without the costume jewelry, tattoos, or the stuffed parrot—didn't look too ridiculous. The pants were a little tight and didn't have nearly enough pockets, and in this body the half-corset pushed her chest up and out to moderate effect. She even went so far as to utilize a few spell components to give herself an earthy, musky smell, and put dirt under her fingernails.

Siobhan reviewed her work in the mirror. This disguise was not meant to go unnoticed. It was simply meant to be so far from the idea everyone had of Siobhan Naught—or the Raven Queen—that it would never cross their mind to suspect her. She tilted her head to the side and smiled brightly at her reflection.

This woman was more brash, carefree, and straightforward. A little alluring, with the form-revealing clothes, but the type to drink foamy beer and punch anyone who offended her in the face. Underneath the thin veneer of roughness, she was secretly soft and cute. She knew no magic but could tell a dozen raunchy jokes. Even Ennis probably wouldn't recognize her if he passed her on the street.

Siobhan walked back and forth a few times, taking long, hip-swaying strides while she kept one side of her mouth in a subtle smile, her eager gaze taking everything in. She did not consider herself a skilled actress, but it was impossible not to have picked up anything from Ennis after having been pulled into so many of his schemes over the years.

When she felt ready, she sneaked out of the inn and swaggered off to the Nightmare Pack's underground fighting arena. People noticed her, but they didn't *think* about her. The only downside was that without her overblown reputation, it was a lot harder to talk to the underground arena's manager alone, and when she finally managed, he assumed she was there to sign up for the fights. When she denied this, he grew quite irritated and told her to "stop wasting his time and show herself out" of his office with a sharp, dismissive wave.

Siobhan was forced to lift one hand to her mouth and whisper the chant for her shadow-familiar spell.

As her shadow stretched out beside her and rose over the edge of the manager's desk to loom over him, the man froze. He looked up very slowly. His face paled as he met the illusory gaze of her shadow, which was really only darkness beneath the hood. His gaze trailed excruciatingly slowly from it to her.

She gave him a lopsided grin and lifted one hand to waist height to wave cheerily. "Hi again! It's me."

The manager's eyelids fluttered, and he sagged back into his seat with a weak moan as his knees failed him.

Siobhan let her shadow collapse back into its natural state beneath her, staring at the swooning man with dismay. *'What do I do?'* she wondered. She had taken two steps forward, mentally reviewing the basic medical knowledge she'd gained, when the manager jerked back from her, almost toppling his chair over.

She stilled, arm outstretched.

He scrambled out of the chair and bowed so deeply his head thumped into his desk. He reeled back, took another step away from her, and bowed again. He stayed that way for a few long seconds of silence.

Siobhan cleared her throat. Perhaps it would be best to simply pretend none of that had ever happened. "I require someone discreet to run a small errand."

The manager straightened, staring at a spot somewhere over her left shoulder. His forehead was red where he'd smashed it, and would probably bruise.

"I need someone to request a meeting with Gera of the Nightmare Pack, or, if she is busy, to some other competent and trustworthy leader. Discretion is paramount. It is more important than speed." She hesitated, but decided that, as frightened as the man still seemed to be, it was important to be clear, even to the point of repeating herself. "I am happy to wait."

"It will be done at once, my queen," the man said with yet another bow. He tried to rush past her, but she stopped him.

"Take this," she said, handing him a tiny jar of bruise balm. It was a travel size, which she'd thought perfect for adding to her caches of emergency supplies throughout the city.

He stared at her as if she'd tried to hand him an explosive stink bomb.

"For your forehead," she explained.

Moving slowly, he held out his hand and accepted the tiny jar from her, eyes wide. "Thank you."

"*Discretion,*" she repeated to his back as he scurried through the doorway.

While Siobhan waited, thankfully without any signs that the manager had shouted her presence to all the arena's employees, she pulled out one of the warded chests she'd purchased from Liza. She unlocked it and set it on the edge of the manager's desk. Then she set up some dye and a color-changing spell to transform the four journals into a more appropriate black. When that was finished, she adjusted the light crystal in a few of the coasters into the same thirteen-pointed-star shape as before.

Finally, a soft knock sounded on the door.

"Come in!" Siobhan called cheerfully, maintaining her false persona just in case.

The manager opened the door and Gera entered, followed by Lord Lynwood. She moved to stand in front of Siobhan and bowed.

Lord Lynwood frowned in confusion. "I believed we were here to meet the Raven Queen. Are you her messenger?" he asked Siobhan, his voice smooth and deep.

Gera swept her leg out and kicked him in the ankle, then shaded one side of her face with her hand, as if trying to conceal her expression as she gave him an angry, urgent look and jerked her head at Siobhan. She pulled her hand away and smiled, close-mouthed. "Lady Raven Queen, thank you for calling us. I hope you have rested well?"

Lord Lynwood did a double-take at Siobhan, who was still sitting in one of the two guest chairs. His eyes widened.

"I have. Now it is time to move forward again. I have promises to keep."

Very carefully, Lynwood pressed his hands to the sides of his legs and gave her a quarter-bow. "My apologies, my lady. Your skill at transformation is... remarkable. I hope you will not take offense at my lack of discernment."

"Of course not," Siobhan assured him. "Be at ease, both of you."

The manager surreptitiously closed the door, as if he were afraid of what might happen if anyone noticed him escaping.

Siobhan looked at the closed door. "He was much more enthusiastic the first time we met."

Gera's mouth twisted wryly. "If I might speak plainly?"

Siobhan nodded.

"He was very concerned that you disliked the royalty suite so much that you...burnt all the bedding. He has called for an audience with myself and Lord Lynwood three times within the last week to enquire what might have been the cause of your ire and how he might mitigate any repercussions."

Siobhan blinked. She almost wanted to laugh, but as the Raven Queen, that might undermine her image.

"He has delicate nerves," Lord Lynwood added with subtle humor, his wolf-amber eyes creasing at the corners. They reminded her of a duller, darker version of the almost glowing eye she had seen from that *thing* while under the sensory deprivation spell.

She shook her head to rid herself of the memory. "I was not displeased. I burnt the bedding and towels for my own reasons. There will be no repercussions."

Gera bowed her head. "Thank you. I will inform him."

Siobhan realized that, despite there being two other chairs in the room, one was adjacent to her and the other was the manager's. Gera and Lynwood were both standing awkwardly beside the desk, facing her, but showed no inclination to take either seat. Siobhan stood and moved to take the larger chair behind the desk, waving for them to take the guest seats. "I called you here to discuss the fates of those I managed to save from the High Crown, as well as the boons I have yet to fulfill. What is the current situation?"

Almost as if she had been planning this report, Gera spoke immediately. "Those affiliated with the Verdant Stag were returned to their care. I understand they are handling things competently, with secrecy, relocations, or in the case of their enforcers, safety in numbers. There was an attempt to arrest one Mr. Gerard, but this failed without casualties. I am not sure of the plan for their people going forward. Mr. Gerard now has a bounty on his head."

"How much?" Siobhan asked.

"Fifty gold."

It was practically nothing. Only the most desperate and incredibly foolish would go against the Verdant Stag for such an amount. Especially when everyone knew that they would give loans to the desperate, and then provide jobs for them to pay off their debts.

Gera continued. "The boy Theo, of course, is safe from accusations of treason. The High Crown could never admit the truth. But I doubt Ms. Russey will allow him to see the sun again without a blooded guard on either side."

Theo would chafe at the restrictions, but Siobhan understood. "And your own people?" she asked.

"We have kept them safe within wards. There have been no attempts to scry for them, and they told me that you destroyed whatever samples the Pendragon Corps took?"

"All that I knew of," Siobhan agreed. It was also possible that their enemies had simply given up on sympathetic magic. That had been the point of feeding a couple drops of her blood in time-release capsules to a few dozen ravens. She wanted to prove to them that their efforts were truly hopeless.

There was no point in hiring more and more powerful diviners, because even if they "found" her, they would discover only what she wanted them to.

"We have offered relocation to another city to each, but they all have declined. They do not wish to run and hide when they have done nothing to deserve such punishment. Additionally, I believe your presence in the city provides some comfort."

Siobhan frowned. "I hope they understand that I am not all-powerful or omniscient. That I was able to help recently was largely due to Millennium's quick thinking and particular abilities. The High Crown's men had misjudged my talents and were taken by surprise. In addition to that, they were quite literally divided because of the events going on in the city, and so we only had to overcome a portion of their number. Luck was on our side." While her reputation came in handy quite often, it wasn't worth it if innocent people placed themselves in danger because they thought she could save them.

"I understand," Gera said.

Siobhan narrowed her eyes. The other woman didn't seem properly concerned. *'Does she really understand?'*

"We also have reason to believe that the Pendragon Corps is not aware of the identities of most of our people. They were taken by happenstance and were not carrying identification papers. Without their blood or hair samples, the Pendragon Corps would have to track them down based on the memories of their appearance alone. So we hope to provide them new identity papers and place them in more secure positions. All except Millennium and Deidre Johnson will likely be safe from notice."

"Who?"

Gera paused, her mouth slightly open. "Deidre Johnson... The woman with the burns?"

"Oh." So that was the praying woman's name. "What about Mr. Parker's family?" Siobhan asked.

"We retrieved his daughter and sister-in-law immediately," Gera said. "They are both safe, though the daughter is understandably distraught at the loss of her father. His sister-in-law is...frustrated by the situation, which she feels she is not responsible for but must pay for nevertheless. We have paid off their house and retrieved the deed, which has been placed in his daughter's name. However, for safety reasons they have decided to rent the residence out while they move to Paneth, where they will live under assumed names. The Nightmare Pack has agreed to manage the property for the next ten years. By then, Mr. Parker's daughter will be grown and able to make her own decisions on how she wishes to proceed going forward."

"You have done well. Thank you both."

The woman's blind eye widened, and she shifted uncomfortably in her seat, but Lord Lynwood merely nodded to Siobhan.

"What of the man who escaped with us? Mr. Anders requested my boon go toward his dog."

This time, Lynwood spoke. "The man remains in our manor. There were several scrying attempts the first day, but they have stopped now. He generally keeps to himself, with only his dog for company. He will not leave until you have seen to the creature and performed whatever rejuvenating magic you are capable of, but I believe it might be possible to recruit him on a long-term basis, if all goes well. He would be an asset in what is to come, even considering that they have a sample of his blood."

Lynwood and Gera shared a look, and then the woman said, "I do not mean to doubt you, my lady, or to pressure you into action, but I have doubts about Bear's—the dog's—ability to cling to life much longer. Mr. Anders already has him on a complex and delicate regimen of healing potions, but...it is a miracle the creature has lived this long already."

Siobhan's stomach sank. "Tell me about this Bear's condition. In detail."

It took Gera three entire minutes to cover everything that was wrong with the dog, as well as what Anders was doing to keep him alive against all odds.

'*What did I agree to?*' Siobhan lamented internally. Aloud, she said, "This is a difficult task indeed, but I will do what I can." It would require blood magic. But if Siobhan could help it, she didn't want to go around killing a half-dozen dogs to boost Bear's vitality, even if some people did consider the animals a nuisance to the city. Even if she could probably find some that were miserably starving and might die by next winter anyway.

"I have an idea," she said. The notion wasn't something she might have considered previously, but it wasn't *so* different from what she and Liza were doing with the sleep-proxy spell. Siobhan had been musing about how transmogrification really worked, and if she was right, then there was no need to Sacrifice the life of another to boost Bear's vitality.

She could Sacrifice something *adjacent* to a life.

"If you will hire Liza's help as my assistant and gather a few dozen dogs, I will consider our debt paid."

"A few dozen dogs?" Gera repeated.

"Males without homes, preferably. The more, the better. Feed them up and get them healthy enough over the next few weeks to survive a shock. When they are ready, you can inform me through this." Siobhan handed over one of the sympathetically linked journals. "These are simple and fairly weak, but effective within the limits of Gilbratha. Their magic will not work in my presence, however. I am in the process of implementing a workaround for that issue, and I will inform you through the journal when you may begin to reply to me. Monitor it frequently. Inform me at once if Bear's condition takes a turn for the worse before the other dogs are ready. And if you would be so kind, please deliver this one to Liza," Siobhan added, sliding a journal from the second bound pair across the table.

"Should either of you be in danger of losing these journals, or allowing control to slip into another's hands, you should destroy them instead."

"I will be vigilant," Gera promised.

Finally, Siobhan pointed to the warded chest on the edge of the desk. "I have an errand I would like to request, as well. Within, you will find several gold bars and some berserker potions. Please take them. I would appreciate it if you could sell the potions and exchange the gold bars for gold crowns through a discreet intermediary. The serial numbers may have been logged, and I cannot use them as they are."

"You have need of coin?" Lynwood asked.

'Is he trying to subtly ask about what I plan to spend it on?' Siobhan speculated. "I believe everyone finds coin useful."

"That is true. It is only that I never imagined you…purchasing anything."

Siobhan suppressed the urge to roll her eyes. "I assure you, my reputation as a thief is much exaggerated."

Gera elbowed her brother in the side, and whatever Lynwood was about to say turned into a nod of his head instead.

"You may keep ten percent of whatever coin is returned, as a fee for facilitating this," Siobhan said. "The remainder I will pick up when I come to the manor to see to Bear."

Gera refused. "My son's life is worth much more than some gold, and more than the repayment you have requested of me thus far."

Since Siobhan couldn't very well argue that Millennium's life wasn't worth much, she was forced to concede.

But there was one last thing they could do for her. The Nightmare Pack should have the same kind of resources that Oliver did, so she requested multiple sets of false identity papers, the details of which she'd written down while working on her disguise. This task, she insisted on paying for, as it couldn't be considered in any way related to Millennium's rescue.

When Siobhan finally left the arena, she checked the lock box for a letter from Professor Lacer but found nothing.

While meticulously removing all traces of her disguise and reassuming her other form, her thoughts rolled over recent events as if they were so many stones to be polished by repetitive handling. As she got into a carriage on the way back to the University, pieces of her conversation with Oliver kept rising to the surface.

Sebastien was not sure how she had expected her confrontation to go, but it seemed obvious, now, that he would try to turn the whole thing around on her. She almost wished he could be, clearly and cleanly, an enemy.

If he were telling the truth, Oliver may not have harmed her maliciously, or actively, apart from the dubious terms of the loan. *'But did I really not deserve the truth? Did I not deserve his trust about an issue that indirectly—and in some ways directly—involved me? It's so important, he can't have thought that I would react well if I ever found out. Of course, he probably never expected that I would find out.'*

His comment about the lopsidedness of their relationship flashed through her mind, and some miserable emotion that was too complex to identify wriggled through her chest. Maybe that part was true, a little. But her imperfections and unintentional wrongs did not mitigate or sanction his own.

'He didn't even apologize,' she thought. Instead, he had once again chosen to try to manipulate her into responding how he wanted.

She didn't want to make an enemy of the Verdant Stag. It was best for both of them to work together to ensure neither was caught. And at the very least, she thought she could probably trust Oliver not to have her assassinated, as long as she didn't blatantly move against him. But she would no longer consider him a friend, and one day, when the identity of the Raven Queen was no longer needed, perhaps their relationship would fray away to nothing.

'And did Ana actually sabotage his textile contract?'

By the time Sebastien got to the dorms, the buzzing in her mind and the heavy stone in her stomach had become unbearable. She sat cross-legged on her narrow bed, her back against the cold stone divider and her face to the window, and cast Newton's vibrational calming spell. If she could not calm her mind directly, she would forcefully adjust her mood via her body.

Damien arrived a few minutes later and knocked on the stone beside her cubicle curtain.

Sebastien let the spell fall away and called for him to enter.

"Sebastien, can you help me with duplicating this stupid ribbon? I've tried sixteen times in the last hour and I cannot get the texture—" Damien cut off as his gaze catalogued her expression.

She cleared her throat. "I might be able to help. Have you tried the divination spells to examine the fabric yet?"

"What's wrong?" he asked.

She lifted a hand to touch her face, wondering how he had known. She hadn't started crying without realizing it, and she thought her expression was rather bland. If she were as good a liar as Oliver, Damien would never have suspected.

Damien hurried to sit on the bed beside her. "No one suspects anything about your escape from the kidnapping attempt, do they?"

She shook her head silently.

"Are you in danger? Is anyone...hurt?"

Sebastien realized suddenly that she was doing to Damien something very similar to what Oliver did to her.

Damien deserved better.

She cleared her throat again, her face feeling oddly numb, as if she existed at a great distance and was merely puppeteering her body. "No, it's not about that. I need to tell you something. Or more like..." She trailed off, confused about what exactly she was trying to do and how to make it work. "Let's go to the study room."

Damien remained gravely silent as they traveled, until they were safe within the confines of the same inefficient sound-muffling spell that he'd come up with last time.

"I am upset about something I'm not going to reveal to you," Sebastien announced before Damien could speak.

He blinked at her.

"I'm not going to lie to you, but I'm not going to tell you. I have a secret. Multiple secrets. And I don't think you can guess them, but I hope you won't try, just in case. I don't want to deceive you, but I cannot ever tell you the truth. And the secrets...well, they do affect you a little bit. They're big. They're important. And...I'm sorry." Her voice broke, and she lifted a hand to her mouth to keep any more words from spilling out. Her eyes burned, and she looked toward the ceiling to keep the unexpected tears from falling.

Before Sebastien could anticipate his movements, Damien stepped forward and wrapped his arms around her. He ignored her full-body flinch and just... stayed like that until her muscles relaxed. He was shorter than her, so his hair pressed into her chin, and her arms were pinned awkwardly at her sides. He seemed almost as awkward at giving hugs as she was at receiving them. His voice was slightly muffled as he spoke into the fabric of her shirt. "It's okay."

Sebastien sniffed. "What?"

"I mean, I'm not so nosy that I must know all your secrets. Not that I'm not curious. I totally am. Especially now that you've done this dramatic confession and everything. I really want to know. But I don't *have* to know. If you ever feel that you can talk about it, I will listen and I will keep your secret."

"You don't know what you're saying," Sebastien murmured. "You can't know."

"Well...that's true. But I think I know enough. I know you." Damien released his awkward hold on her and stepped back. His cheeks were flushed, and he couldn't quite meet her gaze. He tugged at the neck of his shirt. "I'm on your side, okay? That's what I'm trying to say. Myrddin's balls, why are you making me say such embarrassing things out loud, Sebastien?" He threw a halfhearted punch at her shoulder.

She sidestepped it, to both of their surprise, and then let out a watery chuckle.

Before Damien let the spell fall, he added, "If you need help with whatever this huge, horrible secret is, you can come to me. I might be more useful than you think."

"Umm. Thanks." Sebastien knew that would probably never happen, but it was the sentiment that counted.

49

NINE FULL BREATHS

Sebastien
Month 4 Day 17, Saturday 9:45 p.m.

After allowing time for her burning eyes and shaky breath to settle, Sebastien had done her homework while considering what to say to Ana. She worked slower than usual.

When she finally confronted the other young woman that evening, Ana nodded her head easily. "I did deny his contract. You know I can forge my father's signature." She frowned suddenly. "Is that a problem? I did it so that I could offer you something valuable in exchange for your help, even if indirectly. Did you have a personal investment in that sub-commission? I thought, in the worst-case scenario, I could forge it again, well, just like I ended up doing."

"You did it because everything is transactional with me?"

Ana reached forward and touched Sebastien's elbow. "I shouldn't have said that. It's not actually true. You do plenty of things without being paid for them. And what I was requesting… Only an idiot like Damien would agree to commit a crime against a member of the Thirteen Crown Families without reservation." She chuckled. "I did it so that I could offer you a favor. I thought it would be very gauche to write you a cheque or something. Sebastien, what's wrong?"

Sebastien shook her head quickly. "Nothing." She stepped away, just in case Ana got it into her head to give Sebastien her second hug of the day.

Ana's eyes narrowed. "Lord Dryden was upset about it," she deduced. "Did he cause problems for you, Sebastien? Do you need help?"

Sebastien let out a choked laugh. "I think I can handle it."

Ana pursed her lips doubtfully. "You'd let me know if you did need help, though, right? I have some power now, you know?" She plucked pridefully at the collar of her shirt.

In the end, she ushered Sebastien back into the dorms, and somehow drew all of her friends into Sebastien's small cubicle with a few subtle words and the reveal of a package of tiny butter cookies. They didn't leave until one of the faculty shut off the dorm's lights, despite Sebastien's several attempts to get some solitude.

After that, the week passed so quickly Sebastien didn't even feel it slipping through her fingers. There had been no divination attempts, no sudden emergencies or disasters, and her only immediate source of frustration was the ongoing feeling of discomfort when she tried to release her iron grip over the idea-source of transmogrification spells. It felt wrong to ask for darkness and get a strange, almost unreal sensation of cold to go along with it. She hated the lack of precision and specificity. She hated the knowledge that her spells were being, in some small part, controlled by the minds of a hundred million random people. It didn't feel safe, and more than that, it didn't feel *right* to give up her grip over any part of her magic.

But at least her spells were working. She hadn't even been suffering from flashes of nightmares trying to break through the shields of her dreamless sleep spell, as long as she recast it halfway through the night. She guessed it might be because her Will was growing stronger. If she worked hard enough, maybe she could outpace the next disaster and actually be ready to face it.

On Wednesday, Sebastien completed the second repetition of the guiding light ritual. She had done a second, thorough search for similar glyphs and found nothing concerning, but what really convinced her to continue was the fact that she'd had no trouble the first time, even with Will-strain.

And again, the second repetition of the ritual gave her no cause for concern, despite her watchfulness.

And now, Sebastien was riding around in a fancy carriage with a man and woman who were paid to show her houses and apartments available for long-term rental. It was not going well.

The man was like a self-righteous pencil who sniffed judgmentally every time he saw a bit of dirt, and the woman laughed at everything Sebastien said, even though she hadn't made a single joke. They had shown her three apartments and two houses already. Each was overly fancy, unreasonably priced, and in the parts of town where the coppers regularly patrolled. One even included private guards, and their upkeep was part of the rent.

As their carriage stopped in front of the sixth place of the morning, Sebastien took one look at the building and shook her head. "No."

"No?" the pencil man repeated in his overdone high-class accent.

"No," Sebastien confirmed. They had stopped in front of a two-story house covered in windows. There was barely enough space between it and the houses on either side for a broad-shouldered man to walk. At the house on the right, an elderly couple sat in rocking chairs on their front porch. At the house on the left, children played in the front yard, and their mother looked out of the window and waved at Sebastien with a pleasant smile. The lawns were manicured, and the street clean.

Across from Sebastien, the woman laughed awkwardly.

"I am serious," Sebastien said. "Don't you have any cheaper options? Perhaps in the poorer parts of town? Or a place with a lot of privacy. A small cottage surrounded by a high fence. Or an apartment with thick walls and no windows. I don't care if it's a little run-down."

Really, Sebastien was hoping for some place where the neighbors weren't the type to make friends or notice a bit of strangeness, where she could make modifications to the structure without anyone noticing or complaining that she had no permit, and that certainly wouldn't be frequented by coppers or guards.

"No…windows?" the woman asked, laughing uncertainly.

The two housing agents shared a look, and then the man opened his ring binder and began to flip through listings. "I have no listings without windows." His tone of disdain said that they were a reputable company and didn't represent people who would try to rent out *hovels*. "Might I suggest a thick, light-blocking curtain? Perhaps velvet. If both privacy and price are also a concern…" He huffed, as if Sebastien had given him an unreasonable request, but finally picked up the little bell hanging by the carriage door and spoke into it to give the driver a new address.

They traveled south for the better part of an hour in a silence that the woman gave up on filling. But the apartment they finally reached was…not bad. It was an attic apartment, the third floor above a house that had been divided vertically into two other units.

On the eastern side lived two men who shared the rent. They were either not at home or felt no need to peek out of their two small windows in curiosity, so Sebastien only knew this because the agents told her. In the western side lived an extended family packed in tight. Apparently a couple had taken in other family members after a tragedy, leaving them with three adult women, one man, and several children of varying ages.

The family might have been a deal-breaker if not for the symbol finger-painted in yellow and black on the inside of their front window. It showed a moon with the silhouette of a wolf's muzzle howling up into the night—the symbol of the Nightmare Pack.

The pencil man, when asked, rattled off some statistics about crime and theft that he tried to make sound as good as possible, but which were egregiously high when compared to the numbers he'd given her at several of the other locations.

The attic apartment was accessed by a set of stairs running diagonally up the back of the building. It had three windows, each on different walls, but only one with glass to let in light instead of sealed wooden shutters. And that one was cut into the ceiling, facing up and out so that no one could see inside. Each window was big enough for her to crawl through in an emergency. And finally, a locked hatch door in her floor would allow her into the family's space if she broke the lock and forced her way through. *'Multiple ways to get in or out in an emergency,'* Sebastien thought.

The attic's floor space was fairly large, but the angled ceiling meant at least half of the area would require her to duck down to move around, lest she knock her head. A few old cabinets, a chest of drawers, and a narrow bed frame remained, gathering dust. There was no stove or running water, a chimney flue but no fireplace, and the rent was dirt cheap. There were signs of old wards carved into the floor and walls for sound muffling and temperature regulation, though all had long run out of power.

"A thaumaturge lived here," she said. "The owner is okay with magical modifications?"

"As long as you pay a year in advance, don't destroy anything, and sign a contract making you liable for repairs on any damages you inflict."

"I'll take it," Sebastien said. Really, she just needed a place to keep certain things safe and away from prying eyes. And adding extra wards would be a good project for her. Come Harvest Break, she would no longer be able to stay at the University.

She signed the paperwork, wrote a cheque, and then shooed both agents out and down the narrow stairs. Then, she changed the physical locks on the doors and windows and added basic locking wards, which she tied to a series of strings that would break if the wards did. She was careful to establish the clarity of her casting to ensure that the magic would remain coherent enough to bypass her divination-diverting ward if necessary.

Then she opened up the paired journals she had given Gera and Liza, and wrote to both of them. Her message to Liza was longer as it included her thoughts on the magic that might be used to heal Anders' dog. The most straightforward way would be to kill a dozen or so dogs and funnel their vitality into him. But Siobhan simply wasn't willing. The second obvious option was to take a smaller amount of vitality from each Sacrifice. Just not enough to kill them.

But taking vitality wasn't as simple as removing a year or two from the end of their lives in exchange for a few more months for Bear. Even if she could modify the quality-transference spell that she'd learned from working with Liza so that it didn't require Bear to eat one of their vital organs, taking some of their vitality would be more like giving them a horrible illness that they would never fully recover from. It would tax their bodies irrevocably and make them more likely to succumb to illness, injury, and old age.

However, if Sebastien's idea worked, they would lose something much less precious. And the rest she could probably handle with the mirrored-healing spell.

Sebastien tucked the journals away into the small chest of drawers, which was probably meant to be a bedside table, and shoved that into one of the inconvenient corners where the roof almost met the wall, far enough away that the sympathetic link wouldn't come into contact with the area effect of her divination-diverting ward.

She spent the rest of the day cleaning the place from top to bottom, and when she became exhausted, she left for food and a mattress to put on the bedframe.

That evening, she made a long list of all the modifications she needed to make to the space, along with things to buy or create to make the apartment livable. She then spent the rest of the evening working on Myrddin's journal. As ever, her efforts were futile, but she was getting better. It was rarer that she got stuck on unrecognized glyphs, and her Will flitted from concept to concept more easily. Even splitting her Will required less effort as she grew more accustomed to the practice. '*Soon,*' she vowed, glaring at the incomprehensible pages.

She had planned to go back to the University, but she ended up staying the night and the next day as well. It was nice to have a private space to herself, without the sounds of a hundred other people echoing through a long room. And as long as she kept a vial of moonlight sizzle beside her head while she slept, the darkness could easily be dispelled, and along with it, her fear.

Still, it would be nice to have some things to make the place seem less cold and bleak. Some magical plants that didn't need excessive care. Maybe a fish to keep her company.

A quick check of her linked journals showed responses from both Gera and Liza. Gera was making good progress on gathering the dogs Siobhan had requested, and Liza had left six pages of notes about Sebastien's method to improve Bear's health. Liza had also left some scathing comments about her lack of continued involvement in the sleep-proxy tests while simultaneously urging against her presence...and asking for more gold. And in a small post-script, Liza added that the Archaeologist had escaped the Retreat's custody.

This sent a sudden rush of fear through Sebastien. If someone were to question the Archaeologist, it might lead back, eventually, to Liza. "Has he run away, or could he have been kidnapped?" she asked.

A response came back after less than an hour of waiting. There were no signs of a struggle, and the man had taken what few belongings he had with him. All evidence, and his obvious paranoia, pointed to him having gone into hiding. And with what Sebastien now knew about Myrddin's journals, perhaps he had made the right choice.

On Sunday, she finally found a response from Professor Lacer.

She returned to the room she'd rented before opening it. Her heart pounded as she pulled a single sheet of paper from the envelope.

I have prepared a physical tribute that I believe you would be quite interested in, but I am happy to exchange knowledge. In fact, curiosity is my reason for contacting you, as I believe you know. There are too few deserving of my interest.

Is my knowledge of rare and dangerous magic your reason for contacting me?

As for your payment in knowledge, I have several thoughts:

Perhaps, this being is contained within its own memory, such as a sub-personality encapsulated away from the main consciousness, triggered by certain recollections. An example might be a younger version of a person, triggered by thinking about or reliving a traumatic experience that was originally experienced in youth. Shoddy memory wipes can sometimes cause symptoms like this.

Two hundred years ago, there were records of a curse that trapped a woman within eternal sleep. After her death, the perpetrator was discovered. They revealed that the woman had been trapped within a memory, reliving it over and over, but had failed to find the key to break the binding magic. The curse had been meant to teach a vindictive lesson.

I have heard tales of shamans whose minds become lost forever in the spirit world, leaving their bodies an empty shell, soon to die. This may seem somewhat counter to what you are asking, but recent advancements in shamanry among research-dedicated agents of the Red Guard have them attempting to create wards of a sort—walls and protective structures—within the spirit world itself. A futile effort, like building castles of sand before the waves. But, if the anchoring were successful, a spirit-walking shaman could protect their mind against erosion within this structure, perhaps. Some have hypothesized that the soul is, in fact, separate from the body—and specifically separate from the brain. There is no corroborated evidence of this, to my knowledge. But if it was indeed the case, and the soul contained information, then perhaps a shaman could continue to exist in some coherent form within the spirit world, even after their body had died from neglect.

This is not my area of expertise, and I must warn you against being known to explore this path of magic. Even if it does hold the answers you seek, it is possible that activity within the spirit realm could leave traces, and the Red Guard does not allow experimentation along this path. It is too dangerous.

Or, perhaps you are speaking of something more unambiguous. A way to somehow strip a being from their body and condense their consciousness into information, then encode it into the form of a memory? Memories are never forgotten, but by breaking all connective bonds of recollection, one could force forgetfulness and thus lock the memory, and the consciousness, away.

The last would require some ability to isolate what creates consciousness, which, as far as I am aware, is yet beyond us. But an advanced simulacrum of consciousness, of intelligence, could be possible.

If you wish for more detailed information from me, I will require more information about the nature of your curiosity. As it is, I am speculating blindly within a vast cosmos of possibilities, and my usefulness is limited.

In return, I have a question of my own. Are you truly Siobhan Naught? And if so, were you always? Tell me of yourself.

Furthermore, since you hinted at it, now you must tell me the trick to Myrddin's journal.

SIOBHAN MEMORIZED the letter easily enough, then lit it on fire and watched it burn away to ash. Professor Lacer's response had ignited her thoughts in a greater blaze than the paper itself, but it was less directly helpful than she had hoped. She didn't know enough detail to guide her questions.

'And what about shamanry could be so dangerous that the Red Guard actively forbids people from experimenting with the spirit world? It must be very easy to become an Aberrant from doing the wrong thing.' It made a certain kind of sense, because she'd heard the spirit world likened to a dream realm that intruded upon the thoughts even as the thoughts spilled out into the surroundings. It probably took an exceedingly strong Will to safely do more than visit.

Resolving to think on the matter for a while before replying to him, she locked up her new apartment, having left the two warded chests behind. Each was hidden separately and doubly warded with a trigger that would alert her if they were disturbed. One held Myrddin's book, the other her trove of stolen celerium.

Sebastien's life continued on with a suspicious lack of problems or obstacles, which only made her attack the few that she could still do something about with more rabid intensity. She researched the web of connotative connections. She asked others what they thought, what they *felt*, when given concepts like *"light"* or *"darkness."* She cast her transmogrification spells over and over, hoping that her feeling of discomfort would abate.

It did not abate. And then she realized, in a sudden epiphany while eating dinner on Wednesday, that she had been going about the whole thing wrong. Maybe some thaumaturges could give up control to the ephemeral amassed understanding, easily and willingly allow a hand on the reins other than their own. But she could not. And she should not have to.

While transmogrification spells were not meant to use her as the idea-source, that did not mean she had to give up guidance or *control*. Perhaps the spells should not use her ideas directly, but those ideas should still be the guidelines for, as well as the borders of, what it drew from the greater common consciousness.

She stood up without finishing her meal, rushed back to the dorms, and set up the spell that would allow darkness to descend from the component of an autumn leaf. "I am the master," she said to herself, applying her Will with every word, though she channeled no power yet. "Darkness will descend, as I command it, pulled from every idea of the long dark winter that exists or has existed. Every memory, every thought, every dream. Darkness from above, exactly. No more, no less. *Heed me*," she snarled.

And when she cast, night spilled over the upper bounds of her Circle, like an egg of ink cracked over a dome. It flowed down quickly, and so thick that she could barely make out the leaf within. There was no chill wind, no eerie sense of death or solitude, no foggy impression that she had given up complete and utter domination over this small half-sphere within her Circle.

Sebastien stared at it for a while, her heart pounding with exultation, and then she let the spell drop. The sun had not yet set. She stood up and left the dorms, heading to her special clearing in the Menagerie with ground-devouring strides.

When she reached it, she rolled her shoulders and stretched her legs, thinking of all the things the light-refinement spell was meant to do. The filtered light would heal, repair, and energize. It would refine her, just as she refined it. And not only her body, but also, and most importantly, her mind. It would strengthen her mind, shore up her natural defenses, and bring her clarity. It would anchor her Will to something too robust to strain, too powerful to break. It would reduce her need for sleep.

"The light will heal me, rejuvenate me, but it will also make me more. I will refine it, and be refined in turn," Sebastien announced, once again filling her words with her Will. "Heed me." She fell into the first stance of the movement.

She had practiced this spell—the humming, the precise movements, the purposefulness—until she could complete the entire sequence three or even four times without collapsing. Usually, she would start to see a visible mote of light around the time that she finished the first repetition.

Now, it appeared after only nine full breaths.

She had thought she understood how the spell worked—some sort of energy conversion from light into something her body could use, that also burned away impurities. Energy that would speed her mind and fill her cells with vigor. But that had only been her rationalization.

She did not understand how this spell worked or what it was really doing to her body and mind. But she thought she understood, now, what it meant to call upon the weight of an idea so pervasive that it had worked its way into everyday simile and metaphor. '*It is not true,*' some part of her thought. '*But it does not need to be true. It is real, and this accumulated force of conviction has true power behind it. And one day, I will understand not only how to control it but how it works. Genuine understanding.*'

It was a promise steeped in hubris, but with hair-thin lines of light trailing her every movement, hanging in the air, and flowing in through her forehead, she meant it.

Her veins seemed to fill with molten honey and her mind with the song of the cosmos. All she could see were the ever-refining patterns of light. All she could hear was her own humming, which traveled through the folds of her brain before doubling back like ripples in a pond. Where each wave passed, filaments of brightness grew, tiny stars exploded into children that grew into stars themselves, and the illumination revealed the weight and gravity of the space surrounding it, which was not empty but filled with her Will. It was not water, but still seemed somewhat like an ocean—too small to be called such, but determined and crushingly inexorable despite its weakness.

She stopped, finally, not because she grew tired, but because the last sliver of the sun had slipped over the horizon. She panted, her body drenched in sweat, every cell bursting with life.

"Oh," she said into the darkness of the Menagerie.

And then she laughed.

5 0

ALMOST NEW AGAIN

Sebastien
   Month 4 Day 30, Friday 7:05 p.m.

Sebastien's elation, along with the feeling of inexhaustible energy, deserted her not long after she stopped casting the light-refinement spell, leaving her with trembling muscles, exhaustion, and a terrible thirst. But, as before, some faint mist lingered within her for longer.

By Friday, she was so sore that she had to take a pain potion and massage an entire jar of salve into her muscles before she could make it to breakfast. When Damien learned that she had used her contribution points to earn a special spell, approved and translated by Professor Lacer, he flushed like a cherry with jealousy. But he didn't ask her to share it. She had earned the knowledge, and to take it from her for free would be dishonorable. Even in this way, the culture of hoarding knowledge pervaded.

She suspected, however, that he was trying to come up with something worth trading for the spell instructions.

After school on Friday, she headed into Gilbratha proper to pick up the device she'd commissioned from an artisan weeks before. When she had explained how it should work, he had called it an escrima, which was apparently some kind of short stick weapon from the East.

That was not exactly an accurate descriptor.

The artisan's hands were thick and powerful, his skin layered with old scars but his fingers dexterous. He handed over a cylinder of metal that appeared deceivingly simple. "Rather ingenious, if I do say so myself. I'm wondering if there might be a market for more of them 'round here. Lots of thaumaturges."

"Maybe," Sebastien agreed, examining the spell rod she had commissioned. It was thicker than the standard battle wand—it had to be, to fit the internal mechanisms—but only about four centimeters across. And it was heavy, which meant it could double as a bludgeoning weapon in a pinch. Approximately every inch, a thin line divided the rod, and on each resulting segment, the artisan had chiseled in a braille number, from one to twenty. The numbers repeated all the way around the cylinder, each on their own subsection.

Sebastien slid her fingers along the numbers and nodded to herself. *'I can learn to recognize them.'* She gripped the rod on either side of a segment in the middle, held it out in front of her, level with the ground, and then twisted.

The segment between her hands sprang outward with a snapping sound as the springs activated, leaving her holding a metal rod with a framework disk extending from its middle. It looked as if the geometric bones of a dinner plate the diameter of her forearm had grown out from the middle of the rod, suspended around a thin support beam running through the center.

The spell rod was based on the portable, expanding war Circles that the army used. They could be opened into a Circle or collapsed down into a compact star shape, with several thick metal rods attached to each other on scissor-like joints.

Sebastien twisted the rod again, and the framework disk collapsed back in on itself, fitting together so neatly it appeared as just another segment of the rod. Unlike the rest, the segments on either end had a small embedded switch she could flip to snap them open or closed.

"It has downsides," she said. "Whatever carries the spell array has to be able to expand and retract, too. If this was meant to serve a more powerful thaumaturge, you might need to add a spell array made of metal, or bone, or powdered celerium sealed into a sheet of gold. But to make the spell array expand and retract along with the framework... Maybe you could manage it with precisely cut sheets that could dilate open and closed like an iris."

Sebastien twisted each segment of the spell rod open and closed, testing to make sure nothing caught or stuck. "But if you created even a small break in the spell array, where one line didn't connect precisely to the next, you could end up causing some magical...accidents."

The artisan peered at his creation with sudden distrust.

"I have a workaround for that, but it requires any spells I cast to remain below a certain capacity. This is more useful in battle than a tome, but it still requires both hands to use. Which means people would need to wear their

Conduit as a ring or bracelet, or put it down every time they need to open a spell array or change spells."

Of course, again that didn't matter to her. She had a Conduit pressed to the skin of her back, so her hands could be free at any time.

"People would need to be very careful that they knew exactly which spell they'd just unfurled, because trying to cast a fireball in the heat of battle when you've just opened the disk for a food-preserving spell will not work as expected. More danger of Will-strain or even break events."

Sebastien swung it a few times, listening to the sound it made as it cut through the air.

"It also only has two spots to place spells that should be flush against a surface or that should shoot from a particular spot," she said, motioning to either end. "The middle disks would probably end up being a little awkward to use for most thaumaturges, because the rest of the device might get in the way. You'd need the spells to have some kind of directional focus, and then be sure that you were always holding the spell rod so that directional focus was pointed in the direction you thought it was. So you don't end up shooting yourself in the face with a fireball from one of the inner disks. I think a lot of people who might like this would prefer using a battle or utility wand instead, and the more powerful would probably go for a tome."

The artisan looked increasingly gloomy. "Are you sure it's safe for you to be playing with that, lad? I didn't realize all the dangers."

"Of course!" Sebastien assured him, reaching for her money pouch. With the ability to use a minimalist enough spell array, she could hold the exact direction of a projectile spell in her mind and never need to worry about which of the three hundred sixty degrees of her spell rod were pointed away from her. And of course, there was always output detachment.

"You could get rid of a lot of the downsides if you made the pieces detachable. If you're interested in testing the market, I would be open to investing. I have at least one friend who would probably find it irresistible. And I'd bet there's a market among beast hunters and adventurers. This thing can hold twenty different utility spells, from fire starters to emergency beacons to a rain repeller. You don't need excessive power for any of that. And if you make a really long one, it could even double as a walking staff."

The gleam had returned to the artisan's eyes, and he rubbed his palms together. "You bring me down just to float me back up again, huh, kid? How big an initial investment are we talking?"

Sebastien ended up getting stuck at the artisan's shop for another hour, somewhat regretful of her earlier uncharacteristic talkativeness born of excitement.

As she finally left, she made a mental list of the spells that she would insert into the spell rod. She had made some progress with the orb-weaver silk and hoped to be able to make a fabric upon which she could paint her spell arrays from that. For the sudden expansion and contraction that the spell rod required, such a thin, magically conductive fabric would work even better than the thick seaweed paper.

The seaweed paper would still be useful for larger spells or ones where she needed to cast a spell flush with another surface and output detachment wasn't the best option.

The next day, it was in the newspapers that the Architects of Khronos had raided a Crown storehouse attached to a jointly funded research facility. Supposedly, they'd stolen thousands of gold worth of supplies and components and killed several of the guards.

Sebastien took every sentence with a huge crystal of metaphorical salt. She would have been more likely to get something approaching the real story from one of the people who were involved, or even from Oliver. At least this didn't endanger her directly. She wasn't called upon to contribute or do damage control. It had no connection to the unassuming student, Sebastien Siverling.

She smiled. It was nice that the newspapers had something more recently interesting to focus on and could, perhaps, stop trying to wring some more juice from Sebastien's other identity.

With painstaking practice over the next week, she was able to produce a silk fabric transmuted from cotton—which was close enough to the original to make the process easier—that she couldn't tell apart from Professor Lacer's sample, even when using the divination spells to examine her creation more closely. To satisfy Professor Lacer, she would need to be able to create orb-weaver silk fabric from anything, but for her current purposes cotton was enough.

On Friday, she found Gera had written in the notebook that the dogs were ready. Liza had agreed to help in exchange for the mirrored-healing spell, and so Siobhan spent a couple of hours on another painstaking transformation into the autumn-headed pirate maid. She didn't know how some women did their hair and makeup every morning. Even with just the little experience she had, it was incredibly boring and time consuming.

After even more hassle taking a roundabout journey to make sure she wasn't being followed, Siobhan arrived at Lynwood manor just after the last light of the sun had disappeared from the horizon. The night was moonless, and rain clouds blanketed the sky. They had wetted the streets earlier but were now calm.

Gera must have informed the guards that Siobhan could look different, because as soon as she said that she was expected for an appointment with the matron of the house, both guards' eyes started to sparkle and they waved her in like she was the High Crown's wife. She had to give them a secret, angry look for them to remember they should pretend she was just a normal citizen. They grew as stiff as two fence posts at the sight.

Siobhan sighed. *'Next time, I'll sneak in through the back garden.'*

A servant escorted Siobhan to that same back garden, which was… destroyed. Dozens of dogs were scattered throughout it. They had dug up and trampled the flower beds and bushes, and it seemed at least one of them had been gnawing at the bark of the fledgling trees. There were more than Siobhan had expected.

Gera seemed somewhat frazzled, her hair tangled and her clothes stained as she tossed out various orders to the dogs' caretakers. As soon as she saw Siobhan, she sagged. "Oh thank the stars you're here," she said on a heavy exhale. Louder, she announced, "Everything you requested is ready…ma'am."

Gera led the way to the manor's second floor, where they had cleared a large room of furniture and filled it instead with the necessary spell components, empty tables along the walls, and a few kennels. Siobhan busied herself setting up while she waited for Liza to arrive but was soon interrupted as someone knocked gently on the door.

Anders was on the other side, accompanied by the oldest, unhealthiest looking dog Siobhan had ever seen.

"This…is Bear?" The creature was pressing up against Anders' leg as if to keep from falling over.

Anders went down on one knee, his head hanging low. Out of uniform, he looked different. Without the blue and gold, his strong features appeared more threatening, but somehow that seemed like a mask over a great well of fatigue.

Siobhan had thought that the number of homeless dogs collected to provide the Sacrifice was excessive, but now that she saw Bear, she felt that even three hundred might not be enough. Even Gera's description hadn't done the creature justice. He had once obviously been a terrifyingly large dog, but now it was surprising that he even managed to stand on his own three feet. She would have believed it if someone told her this was not a dog but in fact a dog-shaped magical beast aligned with death and decay.

She stared down at Anders incredulously. *'He scammed me! I'm supposed to make this dog healthy again? Who does he think I am, Myrddin!?"*

But of course she couldn't say that aloud. "Bring him in. The process will likely take all weekend. We will need to go slowly so as not to shock his system. Do you know if any of the potions he's on will react negatively to sedatives?"

Liza finally arrived halfway through Anders' recounting of everything he had been doing to keep Bear alive. She set her leather healer's bag on one of the tables and then began to remove the surgery equipment from within.

Anders stared at each tool as she removed it, the skin around his eyes growing pinched.

"Bear will be sedated for any procedures that might bring him excessive discomfort," Siobhan assured him preemptively. "Please have someone bring in the first Sacrifice. You may wait outside while we work, if you wish."

Anders kneeled down again to hug Bear, whose tail wagged listlessly, and then did as Siobhan requested.

She and Liza went over the spell they had modified once more, ensured that the spell arrays were perfect, and then Liza walked Siobhan through the process of ritually removing a dog's testicles.

Siobhan had not wanted to kill to boost Bear's vitality, and with her new understanding of how transmogrification worked, she had realized that maybe she didn't need to. There were more ways to approach the concepts of *"life,"* *"youthfulness,"* and *"vitality"* than the obvious. Reproductive organs were inherently associated with all of those ideas. Maybe they wouldn't work quite as well to improve Bear's health as the more direct Sacrifice of a brain for intelligence or a life for more health, but all that mattered was that it *could* work.

After all, the city was overpopulated with homeless animals. So much so that, during the winter, they often became a food source of last resort for those in the poorest parts of the Mires. They had an almost unlimited supply of donors. This would help Bear while simultaneously tackling the problem of overpopulation.

The entire surgical operation, which was done inside a spell array they had drawn on one of the tables, only took about thirty minutes. When they were finished, they used a few dabs of healing potion on the Sacrificial dog and set it aside in one of the kennels to wake up naturally.

Then came the process of feeding the testicles to Bear, who seemed particularly unenthused about the idea. They were forced to find a potion to artificially increase appetite as well as chop up the testicles and add them to a broth that Bear could lick up.

Liza, who was better at math and had more experience with blood magic than Siobhan, had estimated that rather than the thirty percent efficiency they might have gotten with a full-vitality Sacrifice—with Bear eating the heart and lungs—they were instead getting something like eight percent efficiency. And for a dog as old and unhealthy as Bear, that efficiency might be lowered by half again, with his body simply unable to process all of the improvements. For that reason, they had slightly modified the spell to affect him more gently over a longer period of time. Which meant they needed to complete the whole process eight to twelve times for the same effect. Each time would provide diminishing returns, but with care and enough Sacrifices, they might be able to boost him by thirty to forty percent overall.

They monitored Bear afterward and took several diagnostic scans to ensure he was healthy over the next couple of hours. In between tests, Siobhan taught Liza the mirrored-healing spell.

"This is...so simple," Liza said with wonder. "And yet, it has such wonderful utility. It's not even necessarily restricted to fresh wounds. If anything, it's like a flesh-based duplicative transmogrification spell. If it weren't blood magic, can you imagine how useful this would be?"

"It's definitely much cheaper than most healing magic," Siobhan agreed. "Even if it could just be approved for use by certified healers..."

Liza grunted. "Unlikely. Circumstances would have to be dire for the Crown Families to approve an amendment like that. And only the desperate and the poor would be willing to receive healing based on blood magic."

After Bear showed no adverse effects, they did the second and third round of vitality boosting and left him to rest again while Liza got some practice with mirrored healing, using a few of the dogs that had been brought in with wounds as her patients. After a couple more rounds of boosting Bear's vitality, the last of which Siobhan was allowed to do herself under Liza's supervision, they opened the door to retire for the night.

Anders was waiting outside, sitting in a chair a few feet down the hallway. He sprang up immediately, his gaze searching their expressions and then moving down to look for Bear.

Siobhan stepped aside and motioned for the dog to walk past her.

One of Bear's front legs was still missing, but she thought his hopping gait seemed a little less pained than it had when she arrived. His lolling tongue was wetter and pinker, and his wagging tail had enough force to thump her painfully on the way past.

Anders fell to his knees, taking stinky licks on his face while hugging Bear around the neck.

Siobhan held back a grimace of distaste. Anders was letting Bear lick him on the mouth. *'Surely that isn't sanitary?'* she thought. Aloud, she said, "Someone needs to remove the other dogs from the kennels. They should recover for about three days, after which they can be released back to wherever they came from."

Anders stood. "The other dogs...are alive?"

Liza huffed. "Secretly, your Raven Queen is a Titans-damned bleeding heart. They're all alive, barely any worse for wear. And that's why this whole job is going to take the entire weekend."

"I simply prefer not to harm those who do not deserve it," Siobhan said. "And I think the development of a creative magical method to *extend life* is worth a weekend."

Anders let out a shuddering exhale. "Oh. Oh, that's wonderful." He blinked rapidly, his eyes shining with a thin layer of tears that looked totally out of place on his rugged, menacing features. "I thought… Well, I thought you were going to Sacrifice them all in a blood magic ritual."

Siobhan and Liza shared a glance, and Liza smirked. "Basins of blood, artfully arranged entrails, and vivisected corpses? Is that what you were expecting?" the woman asked.

His expression firmed. "I apologize."

Liza let out a short, sharp laugh that was less mocking than it could have been. "No need. Despite the common perception, not all blood magic is so… flamboyant. That said, the tables and tools should all be sterilized, and each of the Sacrifices given a mild pain reliever when they wake. You were not *totally* wrong, after all." She winked at Anders and walked past.

Liza returned home for the evening, but Siobhan remained in a luxurious guest room and made everyone except Millennium extremely uncomfortable at the breakfast table the next morning. Gera had her son basically confined to his room so that he wouldn't intrude on their work, and he was blatantly sulking about it.

Saturday was much of the same, except that in between sessions of removing testicles and boosting Bear, Liza attempted to regrow a missing paw on one of the other dogs.

For something like this, mass was important. After all, the flesh and bone of the paw had to come from somewhere.

As Siobhan supervised Liza's slow progress on the sedated test subject, she thought aloud. "Bear's missing leg and eyeball would be a large percentage of his mass, and he doesn't have an ounce to spare. If we want to fix him, we're going to have to find another source of meat and bone. Maybe we could bring in a fresh cow or deer leg? Or if there are any recently killed dogs…"

Liza grunted, and Siobhan fell silent so as not to distract her. However, when Liza was finally finished regrowing the—hairless—paw, Liza said, "We shouldn't try to pull flesh from elsewhere. Have you ever seen what happens when the body rejects an intruder? Infection, followed by death. A horrible, painful death. If we don't *perfectly* copy the flesh of the dog we're adding mass to, its body will somehow detect the invader and attack the new flesh. I cannot achieve such perfection, and I sincerely doubt you can, no matter how clear or forceful your Will."

When Liza's practice subject woke up, it spent quite a while licking at its hairless paw, then continued to limp around as it had done before, the paw dragging whenever it came close to the floor. The dog ate ravenously when offered food but, no matter how they tried to encourage it, refused to place weight on its new paw.

Siobhan used the magnifying divination spell learned from Professor Lacer to examine the structure of the new appendage, with specific attention given to the connection spot between old flesh and new. Everything looked perfect... at first. But some of the filament-fine threads that she suspected might be nerve fibers weren't perfectly connected.

She switched to examining the dog's other front paw to confirm her suspicions.

Liza had copied the other paw with passable exactness, but that was part of the problem. Real creatures weren't *exactly* symmetrical. The blood vessels were properly attached, because Liza wasn't an idiot, but in addition to some of the nerve fibers not quite matching, many of them seemed to fizzle out like burnt hairs before they reached all the way to the edge of the skin.

Siobhan could have tried to cast the magnifying divination spell simultaneously with the mirrored-healing—it was almost as if the two were created to work together, and with all the practice she had been getting lately, she thought that she might have been able to hold both at once despite their relative complexity—but that would have revealed her ability to split her Will.

'I need to do that for Professor Lacer's transmutation exercises, though,' she realized. *'I could speed up my rate of learning so much if I could see my mistakes in real-time.'*

It was an exciting thought, but for the moment she simply tried to memorize exactly how the nerves in the healthy paw looked, then sedated the dog and cast the mirrored-healing spell once more. She went over Liza's work with a metaphorical fine-toothed comb, urging the paw to perfection rather than just symmetry. She even thickened the skin of the paw-pad somewhat, so that it wouldn't be as tender and sensitive.

By evening, the dog was walking. Though not quite perfectly, since he seemed to have forgotten what it was like to have all four paws.

Liza, disgruntled, questioned Siobhan about what kind of exercises she did to improve her clarity, forcefulness, and soundness. Tentatively, Siobhan explained the exercises Professor Lacer had given her the term before, along with the variations she practiced to approach satisfactory levels of control over each, though of course she didn't mention where any of the spells came from.

They put the dog out in the back garden again, where he grew excited and sprinted around at full speed, his ears tucked to his head, tongue hanging out with joy, and tail streaming out behind him. He stumbled often, and each time would stop to stare and lick at his new paw. But there were no pained whimpers and no limp dragging, and the paw mostly kept up with his attempts to become a racing dog.

Martha, who had come out to give the dogs their evening meal, did a double-take when she saw him with all four paws. She stared at Siobhan for an uncomfortably long moment, then returned to her work at the urging of the impatient dogs, her expression pensive.

They continued their work after dinner, and Liza made another attempt to regrow flesh long lost, this time in the form of docked ears and tail. Again, Siobhan had to come along behind her and refine her work, which had Liza wordlessly grinding her teeth for the remainder of the evening.

On Sunday, Siobhan did at least half of the testicle-removal surgeries. If only her capacity were high enough, she thought she could cast the whole vitality transference spell on her own—without having to modify it so that it took all day. But it would be years yet before she reached Liza's strength.

On each dog they used as Sacrifice, she began to cast the magnifying divination spell to examine their eyeballs in exhaustive, meticulous detail, while Liza continued to practice mirrored healing. She was getting better, and even had a few divination spells of her own to examine her results, but she struggled to get the same exhaustively fine detail as Siobhan.

'Liza's capacity is so high, she probably hasn't needed to care about perfect efficiency in decades. And if you don't need exact perfection for most things, it would be easy to get out of the habit of extreme precision,' Siobhan mused.

By this point, Bear had received over three dozen boosting spells, and most of the dogs in the back garden were recovering. Bear's appetite had grown explosively, to the point that they needed to bring in extra food beyond the testicle soup, and he kept barking and trying to jump around. Being so big, his bark was loud and deep enough that the whole manor could hear it, and he was heavy enough to knock Siobhan or Liza over if he jumped onto them when they weren't braced for it.

Liza snapped her fingers at him, pointed to the ground, and ordered, "Sit!"

Bear's butt plopped directly onto the ground within his spell array's Circle, though his tail was wagging so fast they had to ensure he wasn't damaging the spell array, which had happened several times already.

After three final sessions of vitality transference, they sedated Bear and brought in the youngest and largest of the Sacrifice dogs as a reference so that Siobhan could remove the film of cataracts and then tweak the lens in Bear's remaining eye.

After that, Liza worked to copy that eye into Bear's empty socket, and Siobhan followed up with a refinement pass. Attaching the optic nerve was delicate and difficult, and Siobhan couldn't help but lament how foolishly the eyeball was put together. Surely there was a better way to design such an organ?

They covered the new eye with a patch and allowed Anders into the room before the sedatives wore off so that the whole thing wouldn't be too much of a shock on the ancient dog's system.

When Bear finally awoke, his tail started wagging so hard that it shook his whole body. He limped and jumped around the room, his missing leg doing little to deter him from looking around, though every few steps he took he would return to press his shoulder against his master's leg.

When Anders took off Bear's eye patch, the dog froze. He looked around slowly, then let out a deep, explosive bark of shock.

Bear's tail wagged so hard he literally knocked himself off balance, and he rolled on the ground barking until Anders rubbed his belly.

Tears fell onto Bear's short, still-thin fur. "Thank you," Anders squeezed out in a hoarse voice.

"We can fix the missing leg, too," Siobhan said. "But Bear needs to gain weight before it would be safe. His vitality has been boosted, but the effects will take time to show. His appetite has already improved, so he should put on weight quickly. With the proper nutrients, his organs should return to working as they're meant to, and his joints might even loosen. Visibly, his hair will grow in thicker and maybe lose some of the grey. In a few months, if he's gained enough weight, we can return to grow him another leg. But unless we do it in sections, it will certainly be a strain on his body. I would suggest you get him a prosthetic in the meantime. Perhaps a wheel attached to a harness, as the least invasive option. Or, if you have the gold for it, a clockwork artifact with some complex instructions, to mimic his existing leg."

"*Or*," Liza said, "now that Bear is healthier, once a little time passes and all the residue from his potion regimen clears from his system, he might be able to accept a course of limb-regrowing potions that use axolotl components. It will be more gradual, and though it is said to be quite a protracted, unpleasant experience, you would not need to rely on us. It would be less of a shock to Bear's system, and his happiness could be managed by some strong anti-itch and pain potions."

Siobhan was a little embarrassed. In the excitement of the moment, she had forgotten that option even existed.

Anders cleared his throat and sniffed wetly, then stood. "How long does he have, now?"

Siobhan and Liza shared a look. Neither of them really knew for sure. That was the kind of thing you needed a whole data set to be certain of, and they only had this one dog. Siobhan decided to err on the side of caution. It would look very bad if she overestimated, and this breed of dog was probably lucky to make it to the age of ten normally. "Two years extra, if you manage his health carefully. If he begins to show signs of deterioration, you may call upon me to perform this service once more. Preferably *before* his status becomes this dire."

Anders nodded with determination, then took a knee in front of her. "Thank you."

Siobhan waved at him to rise. "You paid for this," she reminded him. "And dearly."

"It was worth it," Anders said, looking her straight in the eyes.

Liza offered to give Bear's new care requirements to Anders in exchange for his help cleaning up the room, and Siobhan spent a half hour visiting Millennium before she left.

Behind her, Gera stood with a lost look, her hands limp at her sides. "What am I supposed to do with all these dogs?"

51

DAMIEN'S REPORT

Sebastien
Month 5 Day 9, Sunday 7:05 p.m.

After an entire weekend of casting through most of her waking hours, Sebastien's mind still felt like a well-used muscle, weak and on the verge of soreness. But her debts were paid, she had resources left over, and her Will was growing.

Sebastien stopped at her apartment to write a return letter for Professor Lacer.

She was very aware that once the letter left her possession, it would no longer be protected against divination. She did not want to lie, partially because doing so might damage his willingness or ability to help her, but she also had no intention of revealing too much.

His speculation had opened a broad spectrum of possible worries, but she could not follow up her previous question with one about Aberrants, or any questions about the incident in which Grandfather had died.

What is this physical tribute you have prepared?

I appreciate your thoughtful answer to my question. Regrettably, I cannot divulge more about the circumstances behind it, because I do not know. The only hint that was given to me I have already passed on. More research is required.

> I would appreciate more information about this dream curse.

SEBASTIEN PAUSED, lifting her pen carefully away from the paper so as not to leave an ink blot. She also wanted to ask about the Red Guard's experiments with shamanry, but his warning had been quite clear. However, that only made her more curious to learn about it.

She wouldn't have considered this avenue if she were not desperate.

She had once been quite interested in divination, in the hopes of divining the future and gaining some tools to mitigate oncoming bad fortune. But she had no talent in the craft. And then she'd actually met a shaman. He claimed to be able to breach the walls between the mortal world and the domain of spirits in order to achieve effects similar to divination. He'd had her run errands for days to prove her dedication before giving her an alchemical concoction that was supposed to open her inner eye.

It left her spewing from both ends, incapacitated with pain and hallucinating for two days.

When she came to her senses, she was terrified, half dead, and had nothing to show for it but dream-like memories that flashed behind her lids in sickly colors when she closed her eyes.

"You just don't have the constitution for greatness, dearie," he'd said.

She'd tried to kick him in the knee out of sudden rage but was too weak to do even that.

Ennis made it clear how much of a waste of time the whole endeavor had been. He was sure she would be better off *pretending* to be a shaman to con people out of a handful of coin.

Since then, she'd focused on practical magic, something she could use to affect her reality rather than trying to pull the answers to life from the ether.

'But, no matter how much of a scam shamanry is, if there are any real techniques I could learn, perhaps I could create my own mental wards to reinforce whatever Grandfather did,' Sebastien thought.

She continued writing.

> Of myself: I am Siobhan Naught, but I am also the Raven Queen, and I have been called by other names. In some ways, names have a power all their own, but in other ways, they are just labels.

Sebastien hesitated before using the weird chant again, but she felt that it was cryptic enough while still being honest. It would allow her to reply to his request for information without really saying anything about herself or her life.

I am a changeling like the seasons, a daughter of shadow and light, of Charybdis mists and raven's flight, and always I seek after mysteries.

Make of that what you will.

For your attempts on Myrddin's journal, the man had capabilities and knowledge that I have never heard of from others. While many of his exploits are now thought to be exaggerated by rumor due to their implausibility, I know for a fact that several are quite literal. For instance, the ability to split one's Will.

To my surprise, I have found that people do not practice casting two spells at once. I cannot be sure why.

I would caution against attempts at personal experimentation here, unless you are quite sure that a human such as yourself could survive the attempt without breaking. However, if you can find a method to recreate this ability, or someone capable of it already, you will make progress.

She was careful not to say that he would be able to read the book with that skill, because there could be some other barrier to success that she hadn't yet encountered.

She resisted the urge to add more questions about the Red Guard's secrets or where she might learn more about these recent advancements in shamanry. It might be taken as a request to violate his vows to them, and she was not sure how he might take that. Nor what his vows might require him to do, if she said something that made him believe she could be a threat.

'I will see what might be found elsewhere, and then, if that bears no fruit, I will gauge how dangerous it might be to ask him. Perhaps once I have spent more time gaining his trust.'

She dropped off the letter for Tanya to ferry on her way back to the University and made it to the dorms only a few minutes before curfew.

The week passed uneventfully, spent on classes, homework, spell practice, and a search of the library for unrestricted books that might give her some deeper understanding of the things Professor Lacer had mentioned in his last letter. In what free time remained, she continued to practice light-refinement. One of the spell's effects was supposed to be clearing intrusive mental forces. And what were her nightmares, if not that?

Perhaps it was working, because though she had been dreading what might come after her experience under the sensory deprivation spells, her night-mares were no harder to deal with than usual. In fact, she slept easier than normal with a combination of light-refinement practiced during the day and Newton's self-calming spell in the evening.

There were no attempts to scry her and no emergency communications from anyone she knew. She had completed the fourth repetition of the guiding light ritual, and though the symbol—and possible glyph—she'd created lingered in her mind longer each time, like a dark spot after staring at the sun, there had been no struggle with wild magic or backlash.

The next weekend, Sebastien went around the city improving her emergency stashes and creating a few new ones. She added more coin, water canteens with moisture-gathering arrays drawn on their bases, and some quick disguise items. Along with that, she left some of the orb-weaver silk sheets she'd been creating. Some, she had painted spell arrays on, in liquid that was a mixture of giant squid ink, dragon blood, and flakes of natural gold. To that, she had added the sap from two different trees to keep the ink from bleeding, even when exposed to the elements. Other sheets she left bare, to be used as needed with the bottle of conductive liquid and brush she added to each stash.

Sebastien didn't trust this sense of normalcy. She suspected it was just the lull in the eye of the storm, and if she grew complacent, her future self would look back in desperate regret.

Damien had gone home over the weekend but apparently spent most of his time at Harrow Hill convincing Titus to give him an internship during Harvest Break. He returned to the University with a tidbit of confidential gossip: several skilled people from the History department had been tasked with a special mission by the Westbay Family—find the Architects of Khronos.

Ostensibly, having expertise in an area that the terrorists had shown a theological interest in might help the faculty discover clues that the average copper would miss.

In reality, they had been tasked to find themselves.

Sebastien almost spat out a large mouthful of wakefulness brew all over the study group's classroom table and ended up breathing some of it in trying to suppress her amusement. *'There's no way that was an accident. Titus suspects them. It's some kind of mind game. Maybe he wants to watch exactly what they do, where they focus…and what they ignore? Because the avenues they don't pretend to explore are more likely to bear fruit?'*

But if they were doing this, it probably meant that they hadn't been able to find enough evidence to connect Kiernan and the others to the Architects, which was somewhat surprising considering the amount of effort the coppers had been putting into it. After all, the Architects didn't have the same advantages she did, and with a larger organization, there were bound to be more weak links.

Near the end of the year's fifth month, at one-thirty in the morning with a full moon that hung low over the horizon, Sebastien completed the guiding light ritual. The symbol she had created was seared indelibly somewhere in the back of her mind, impossible to ever forget. She had a strange awareness of it that was ever-present but somehow not distracting at all.

Immediately, Sebastien used some of the remaining saltwater from the ritual and another of her glue-paper stencils to paint her symbol seven times over on the back of her thirteen-pointed star light coaster while whispering the now-familiar chant.

With each word and each pass over the sharp, winged symbol, more aware-ness grew in that new spot in the back of her mind reserved for the thing she had created. When she was finished, it had doubled to contain this second symbol, yet somehow still required the exact same amount of concentration. Which was to say, none.

But like the group proprioception spell or her improved philtre of dark-ness, when Sebastien focused on the light coaster, there was a distinct sense of her symbol's location in the real world, in relation to her.

Sebastien closed her eyes, rotated the inner section to turn the light crystal on, and then hurled it into the Menagerie. Then, peeking occasionally to make sure she didn't trip over anything, she used the awareness tucked away in the back of her mind to track it down once more.

She found it lying face down within some thick-leaved plants, turned off the light, and tucked it back into her pocket. She wasn't yet sure exactly how she would use such an ability, but the spell itself was both fascinating to have attempted and gratifying to have succeeded at. If only she knew more about the additional functions that could be added to symbols that had "taken" strongly.

After that, almost a month passed. Uncertain danger hung in the air as heavily as the damp heat, pressing in on her skin and leaving her to struggle a little too hard for breath. She felt in her bones that her time was running out, but the days just kept passing without any events of particular note.

The most dangerous thing Siobhan did was the occasional disguised aide to Liza's sleep-proxy testing. They were getting close to the end, and none of their test subjects had shown worrying symptoms or side effects. In fact, they were all at least twice as healthy as they had been to start, though that could have been because the tests had provided both gold and food.

Professor Lacer still hadn't replied to her latest letter. Sebastien found herself glaring at him in class more than a few times, wondering why he hadn't written her back. She even checked to make sure Tanya was properly transferring their correspondence. Her only consolation was that he seemed as frustrated as Sebastien, if not even more so. Rumors even began to circulate about why he was in such a particularly bad mood.

In one, his secret love child with a princess of Silva Erde had just come calling, asking for Professor Lacer to help him depose the current rulers and take the throne, no matter that the monarchy was just an ornamental position in that country.

In another, Professor Lacer was arguing with the headmaster because he'd been disallowed from doing magical experiments on his students. People started cheering the headmaster on whenever they passed him, and though the elderly man had absolutely no idea what was happening, he accepted this enthusiasm with grand smiles and waves at his new fans.

Though no one knew what Sebastien suspected was the real reason, the most realistic rumor was that the High Crown was again trying to force Professor Lacer to take his heir as an apprentice, and Professor Lacer was running out of ways to refuse without seeming rude now that he had proved he *was* willing to take at least one apprentice.

The panic about the Raven Queen had died down with the lack of new events. The coppers were back to their normal schedules and arrest patterns, and the newspapers had long since moved on to other topics. There was even some speculation that she had fled the country in fear of the High Crown's retaliation.

At the beginning of the year's sixth month, one of the coppers was found to be a spy for the Architects of Khronos. Almost before the word could even spread, the copper was found dead in her interrogation cell, and her only known contact with the Architects, a mercenary, disappeared.

Pretty much everyone agreed that he was dead, too.

And so the Architects of Khronos continued to elude the coppers, though the tension gripping Gilbratha tightened one notch further.

Near the end of the sixth month, on a Thursday evening, Damien came to her, pinch-lipped and even more tired-looking than normal. The perpetual bags under his eyes that didn't seem to depend on how much sleep he got now had a bruised quality. Recently, he had fallen into his research project with an unquenchable focus that Sebastien recognized in herself.

"I have a mission report," Damien said, handing her a contract-sized envelope that he'd already sealed with glue, wax, and a looping pen scrawl over the sealed edge to ensure that anyone trying to peek at or tamper with the contents would have a difficult time disguising their actions. "This is for you to give to the higher-ups. It's got everything in it."

"I'll handle it," Sebastien promised.

Damien looked around mistrustfully, then asked, "Can we talk about what I found? You were going to be given this mission originally, so it's not like any of the results should be secret from you?"

"We can talk about it," Sebastien agreed. After all, she was the only "higher-up" in their little secret organization of two. "Do you want to go to the study group room?" Lately, Damien had often commandeered the empty classroom to have a large enough space to cast some of his more complex collation and word-search spells.

"No. Let's go to my cubicle," Damien answered.

Professor Lacer had given them both the spell array for the sound-muffling spell he often free-cast, but Damien hesitated to speak even after it was active. The number of boxes stacked against the cubicle wall had decreased somewhat as he removed content that wasn't relevant, but a new shelf attached to the stone dividing wall held over a dozen binders stuffed with pages.

Sebastien waited silently, an odd mix of apprehension and excitement fighting in her stomach.

Finally, Damien spoke. "I have been collating all the articles that include suspicious rogue magic incidents. Some are definitely Aberrants, but others might be Aberrant-related without being labeled as such." He reached out and lifted one of the binders from the shelf, handing it to Sebastien.

She opened it, flipping through the newspaper clippings, sections of which Damien had underlined. The articles were pasted to the left side of each sheet, and on the right side, Damien had written some notes and listed the basic information about the event in a more structured list.

"They're organized by estimated power level, both of the Aberrant and of the magic used to respond," Damien said. "Those are the weakest. Apprentice-level or lower." He pointed to the binder farthest to the right, which was much less full. "And those are the ones inside sundered zones, or the ones so powerful that even a sundered zone won't contain them. Archmage-level."

"I want to read all of these," Sebastien said, fascinated.

"I've just managed to successfully cast some information-collating spells that can take structured information and output it in concise numerical summaries in the form of different types of graphs or tables. There's still a lot of work to be done for the mission, but I wanted to give the higher-ups a preliminary report...because I think I found something." Damien rubbed his bloodshot eyes.

"It's been a huge hassle. You wouldn't believe how vague many of these reporters are and how much guessing I have to do about at least half of these incidents," he said, staring at the boxes stacked up against the wall. "I ended up going to the census archives and pulling information on any named thaumaturges within those pages." He pointed at the binders. "I verified whether or not they were certified and got their educational level, as well as their area of academic focus, if they had one."

Sebastien narrowed her eyes. "Was there a trend?"

"I'm not sure yet. Not an obvious one, anyway. But that's not my point."

"What *is* your point?"

"The Red Guard is extremely competent and powerful. But the problem is, they're so secretive, even when it doesn't make sense that they would need to keep their methods confidential. I keep noticing it. They perform some crazy feat of magic that I've never heard of before, but the newspaper article barely gives two vague sentences for it. The papers that regularly provided more detail have all gone out of business within the last few decades, which is *strange*, right?"

Damien continued before Sebastien could respond. "And maybe that could just be a coincidence, but I can't stop thinking about it. I suspect that the Red Guard has some kind of specific anti-Aberrant spells that they don't want the public to know about. Just like how the details of the sundered zone spell are so secret."

Damien rubbed his fingers over his chapped bottom lip and turned to face Sebastien. "There are innocent explanations. Like, they don't want terrorists to develop countermeasures to their proprietary spells. Or they don't want stupid people trying to mimic their spells without the kind of training they go through to be able to control them. But I don't think that's it. I suspect... I suspect the Red Guard is using blood magic against the Aberrants."

He paused to let the gravity of this accusation sink in, but Sebastien's mind had jumped to the spell that the ancient thaumaturge had cast at Knave Knoll, before she accidentally killed him.

That man was a rogue Red Guard agent who had abandoned his vows and gone on the run. And he'd cast a spell so strange that not only had she never heard of its like before, she couldn't even understand how or why it behaved as it did. The meteor hanging in the air, the little dust-sized parasites phasing through matter, the walls and doors fusing together. It was complex and powerful and impressive enough to befit a Red Guard member, but why the flashiness? Why the wastefulness, when the same result might have been generated without the need to create any physical phenomena?

The man would have had to use an entire sack of beast cores to power such a spell, surely?

But Sebastien didn't think he had. That kind of seeming wastefulness— limitless power spilling out in strange ways as an effect propagated—was seen only one other place.

Aberrants.

They seemed to break the laws of magic that those with unbroken Wills and coherent minds were restricted to.

'What would happen if I tried to use a piece of an Aberrant as a spell component?' Sebastien wondered.

If she were inclined to gamble, she would bet that, in the hands of a powerful thaumaturge, the resulting spell would look something like what had happened at Knave Knoll.

She thought of Newton, turned into strings the color of flesh and bone, spilling out and consuming every living, frightened thing it touched, like some kind of fungus. *'What kind of effect would come from casting with a piece of that string?'*

Sebastien had one hidden in the floor under the chest at the foot of her bed, after all. She could test her theory.

'No, no, I'm not going to do that. I have no idea how dangerous it might be, and I can learn from my mistakes. I will not recklessly endanger my life, nor the lives of those around me.'

Sebastien swallowed, looking again at Damien's chapped lips and wan face. *'Is it possible I'm jumping to conclusions?'* She thought back over Professor Lacer's lecture about what to do when you were suspicious. *'I want to know the truth, no matter how it makes me feel.'*

"Is there any evidence that could, in the right light, act to *disprove* your suspicion that the Red Guard uses blood magic?" Sebastien asked. "Think hard."

Damien blinked at her. "Well, except for the fact that blood magic is evil, and maybe—if that isn't a lie, too—leads to corrupted Wills and increased break events? The fact that the Red Guard is supposed to stand for justice and their oaths to protect the world from magic gone wrong?"

"Except for that," Sebastien agreed. Because she knew that blood magic wasn't evil. The Red Guard might have their oaths, but they also did things like malign the dead and then place mind-controlling spells on their families. Which was, in her opinion, one of the actually evil ways to use blood magic.

"I can't think of anything else," Damien said. "Maybe there's some secret reason for their actions that would never occur to me, but..." He trailed off helplessly.

Sebastien closed her eyes and breathed deeply. Then she opened them again. "There are some things I need to tell you." She checked to make sure the sound-muffling spell would still cover them and then motioned to the narrow bed. "Sit?"

She pulled her satchel's strap over her head, reached inside, and turned on the dowsing artifact, which was currently using the other half of a small twig she'd broken and tucked in her pocket as a target. She turned up the artifact's strength to its highest limit, then sat close enough to Damien that their arms touched. This close, he would be protected by the spillover effects, too. Maybe this was unnecessary, but it couldn't hurt, and she had no idea what the Red Guard might be capable of anymore.

Sebastien cleared her throat and, haltingly at first, but then with growing ease, told Damien what had happened to Newton's family.

"The Red Guard does blood magic on Lenore's innocent citizens," Damien whispered.

"That, in large part, was what your mission was about," Sebastien said. "We wanted to figure out how often they play with people's memories surrounding an Aberrant event. Because obviously, they are going to extensive lengths to lie to the public in at least some cases. But Damien...I don't think they're trying to hide the blood magic. Or, not *just* that. Those proprietary, powerful spells that they use against Aberrants? I think... I think they're using Aberrant components against other Aberrants."

By this point, Damien was so pale that, if he hadn't been sitting down, Sebastien might have worried that he would faint and collapse.

She told him about the attack on Knave Knoll, and specifically some of the details that hadn't made it into the papers, though she didn't mention how she knew.

"It makes a horrible kind of sense," Damien croaked. He swallowed, his Adam's apple bobbing up and down. "You would need powerful weapons to fight powerful enemies. But this...if they've been lying about this, what else?"

Sebastien thought she understood what he was feeling. Unmoored, floating in space as the ground and walls that he had grown up believing in fell away. "I don't know. But I think you should hand the mission over to me. You can teach me the spells you were learning, but it's too dangerous for you to continue digging into this."

"But not too dangerous for you?"

Sebastien pressed her lips together.

"No. I'm not going to stop," Damien said.

Sebastien hesitated. "Damien...our organization isn't as large or powerful as you might like to believe. We might not even be able to do anything impactful with the information. And if the Red Guard were to find out and come after us...I don't know that we could stop them."

"That just makes uncovering the truth even more important! The Red Guard aren't bound by Crown law. They are an independent, non-political force, and if they are corrupt, we need to know!" He reached over and gripped her forearm. "Sebastien, if this is true, think about what it means. What happened to Newton?"

She stared at Damien.

Slowly, he released her arm. "I'm not giving up on this mission."

52

AN UNFATHOMABLE LIGHTNESS
OF BEING

Sebastien
Month 6 Day 25, Friday 5:15 a.m.

On Friday morning, well before classes started, Sebastien left for her apartment, which was both more inviting and better protected than it had been when she moved in. Once again, she dropped by to check the lock box on her way. This time, a letter was waiting for her. *Finally*.

With the curtain drawn and a bottle of moonlight sizzle glowing soft and bright, she read Lacer's latest response.

If you wish to discover the physical tribute I prepared, you must meet me in person. I believe we could arrange something suitably secure.

Of the dream curse, I have included an account of all I know.

Where did you receive the hint that led to your question, if I might ask? Perhaps there is some clue within the circumstances.

When I requested you tell me about yourself, this was not what I expected. I see you are not totally unfamiliar with the techniques of a shaman, though your description of self is particularly cryptic.

'Do shamans use similar chants, then?' Sebastien wondered, but she set her curiosity aside to continue reading.

> While fascinating, I admit that I was hoping for a more conventional account. Background, hobbies, and goals, if I might be so trite.
>
> Some of my own background is known. You are probably aware that I am a special agent of the Red Guard, currently assigned to the Thaumaturgic University as a liaison. It suits my purposes well for the moment as, like you, I am conducting research into something fascinating, and some of their hoarded records are not duplicated anywhere else. I had wondered if perhaps you were aware of this research, and if, in fact, it is the reason for your particular interest in me.

That really wasn't any less cryptic, or more revealing, than what she had told him. Was he trying to pique her curiosity? The letter continued:

> Your information about Myrddin was quite the revelation. I have spent this recent time in attempts to discover a method to safely split the Will, with, I am frustrated to say, no success.
>
> You mentioned that I might find someone capable of this feat already, and seemed to suggest that you yourself are one. Is this true? I heard from Grandmaster Kiernan, with whom I am collaborating on the journal decryption, of your conversation.
>
> He seems to believe that *you* were kept within the book. It may seem absurd, but I must ask: Do you, perhaps, believe yourself to be a consciousness trapped within a memory, to have been released by some action of Siobhan Naught's?
>
> I ask again. Who are you?
>
> P.S. — If you can indeed do this little "trick" to decrypt the book, what would it take to entice your aid?

Sebastien rubbed at her forehead, trying to smooth out the crease between her eyebrows. What, exactly, had Kiernan told Professor Lacer? Certainly, some of their conversation would have had to be left out if Kiernan didn't want to reveal that he was one of the leaders of the Architects of Khronos. Settling her frustrated thoughts, she picked up the second sheet of paper, where Professor Lacer had written about the dream curse.

This incident occurred in the year 27 of the current era, less than thirty years after the fall of the Third Empire. The victim was Julissa Kimble, who married a widowed man with a daughter. The perpetrator was Winona Kimble, her step-daughter born from the original wife. Though, in this case, the lines between "victim" and "assailant" may blur.

Julissa was resentful of Winona and systematically abused her, with the tacit allowance of her husband, who turned a blind eye. The abuse culminated in an incident on Winona's eighteenth birthday, during a "coming of age" party the family was holding.

The evening of the party, Julissa poured boiling tea onto Winona's face. Winona was sent to live separately.

Fifteen years later, Winona returned for her father's funeral, having become an accomplished thaumaturge.

She believed that Julissa had poisoned her father.

Winona managed such a powerful curse binding through a combination of cleverness and Julissa's arrogance. She had created a potion and disguised it as tea, which they both drank atop a carpet that had been woven with a spell array to compel truth. Winona disguised her thrice-repeated grievances as reminiscence and her explanation of the terms of the spell as hints at a struggle for power between the two. Julissa agreed to the binding without realizing what she was doing, thinking to assert her power over Winona as she had when the girl still lived under her roof.

And so, the curse took hold, with the only way to break it being built into the spell from the beginning.

Julissa fell unconscious. At first, people thought she had fainted due to grief. But as her condition remained unchanged after a few days, worry grew. Winona brought in healers and specialists to see her stepmother, but none of them could find the cause. Rumors of a curse grew, and suspicion fell on Winona.

Exactly thirteen weeks after her initial collapse, Julissa died.

Winona was suspected of murder and arrested, and admitted freely to her crime. She had trapped Julissa within a repeating loop of her eighteenth birthday party, with the "world" contained to their house and backyard. The memory had been expanded to be self-reinforcing, including events that Julissa hadn't experienced directly but which had been pieced together from Winona's recollection and added on to. Not a detail was left out, until the world of that day seemed grounded and real.

Winona said that if only Julissa were able to understand her wrongdoings and make amends within that repeating day, resolving to live how she should have and take real steps to change the trajectory of both of their lives, she would have woken up. But she did not. We cannot know if this is true, because Winona had poisoned herself before being taken into custody and giving her statement. Her life was used as collateral to give greater strength to the curse.

Without the antidote, which she had been taking on a regular schedule, she died.

I know no further details about the exact methods she used to create the curse or the repeating memory world. I suspect that Winona took these secrets to her grave.

SEBASTIEN WAS both fascinated at the concept of the dream curse and disappointed that there weren't more details. Whether something like this had been done to her, she couldn't be sure. But it seemed like a good direction to start researching. Even if this curse-craft was only adjacent to the magic she needed to understand, it was becoming more apparent to her that all thaumaturgic crafts spilled over into other areas.

She made a mental note to dig up any information she could find about Winona Kimble, although she doubted she could access information directly related to the curse that Thaddeus Lacer couldn't, especially since it was definitely blood magic. But there might be some relevant lead in the thaumaturgic training Winona had received after she left home, in her friends, acquaintances, or the work she had been doing. Sebastien would also try to find similar magic, be it curses or mundane spells.

And perhaps she should look into what solidifying a memory might entail. Stabilizing a memory to the point that it could support itself, a self-contained ecosystem, seemed rather like something a shaman might do.

With next steps in mind, she memorized Professor Lacer's letter and burnt everything, just as she had the last.

Then she read over Damien's report and considered what to do with the Red Guard research mission.

She woke early in the morning, the problem still looping through her mind, and stared up at the sky through the angled window cut into the roof.

If investigating the Red Guard had only been about the truth of what happened to Newton and his family, then Sebastien might have decided to set it aside. After all, there was nothing that she could do about that. Any attempts to save his family from mind-altering spells would probably just put them in a different kind of danger. And as for Newton himself—if the thing he'd become could even be called a person anymore—what would she even do?

But Sebastien's connection to the Red Guard ran deeper than that. Not only were they investigating her to appease the High Crown, but they also had records of the incident she had forgotten—during which the seal in her mind had been created.

Professor Lacer was one of them.

There was a chance that at some point she would become further involved with the Red Guard in some way. And if that ever happened, she needed to understand them. Knowledge was the greatest form of power, after all.

But she didn't know what they might be capable of, so she and Damien would need to be very careful. Any further purchases of old newspapers would be done via proxy—someone from the Nightmare Pack or Verdant Stags who wouldn't be suspected.

With her decision made, Sebastien sent out instructions, talked back and forth with Gera and Liza over the course of a few hours, and then returned to the University. Sebastien found Damien and gave him a single, serious nod.

Damien's face split into a satisfied smile that lacked any real joy or mirth.

"The mission parameters have been updated slightly. We're getting help to obtain some of the older newspapers, as well as the backlog from the other publications that went out of business. If you can get that intern position at Harrow Hill over Harvest Break, that will be a big help. And from now on, we need to keep note of when anyone has a complaint against the Red Guard, or when someone has helped them out in unexpected or large ways. And we especially want to note people whose names come up repeatedly. Track the names of any coppers who are noted acting as Red Guard liaisons and make a note of any reporters who frequently handle Aberrant incidents for their paper."

"Got it," Damien said.

"We can expect more deliveries to your storehouse by the end of the week."

"The higher-ups are really invested in this, huh?"

"It seems so. But we're not to take any investigative or dangerous action ourselves. Data analysis only."

"Of course. We can't let the Red Guard find out that we know anything. Do you think Professor Lacer...?"

Sebastien raised an eyebrow. "Do I think he what?"

"Do you think he knows the truth?"

"Probably. But a better question might be, did he know before he took his vows?"

Damien frowned. "There's no way. They wouldn't take the chance of this information leaking. Maybe that's why he's at the University? I heard Lord Cyr talking about how the liaison position might be a punishment post among the agents. Which is crazy. I mean, he's *Thaddeus Lacer*. It seems like, if he is here, it must be because he wants to be."

Sebastien shook her head. "We don't know enough to speculate."

After that, Damien fell even more deeply into his research mission, while Sebastien tried to figure out how to learn more about Winona Kimble's dream curse despite its obscurity and the restrictions on Sebastien's access to the University library.

The shamans' access to the dream world was almost as difficult to find information on. Previously, she would have believed that this was because shamans were less likely to write down their magical knowledge than traditional sorcerers. They were few in number and often passed down their skills and knowledge through the more archaic master-apprentice relationship, or between parent and child, rather than publishing a book. Now, she suspected something more was at play.

She ended up sending Tanya to look for information at the secret thaumaturge meetings, which would probably take a few weeks to come to fruition. After all, it was unlikely that an attendee would have that exact information on hand as soon as Tanya put forth the request.

Five days later, at the end of the quarter, Sebastien received a cheque from Oliver's textile company for one hundred gold. That was the minimum quarterly payout, which meant that her four-percent stake in the company hadn't earned more than that.

Sebastien took some time to write a response to Professor Lacer while she was out depositing the cheque. She considered waiting to reply as long as he had delayed, to give him a taste of his own medicine, but that seemed like juvenile pettiness.

Even if he had waited over a month to write her back, he'd also provided valuable information. But his curiosity about her was distressing. Sebastien sat back and bit her lip. *'How would the Raven Queen respond to this?'* She allowed herself to smile. *'Obviously...she would go on the offensive.'*

You are full of curiosity, Thaddeus Lacer. It is a trait that I share and appreciate, but not one that I will indulge endlessly. I have told you who I am. If you do not believe me, or feel that my answer was not satisfactorily comprehensive, that is unfortunate.

I am myself, as I have always been, no matter what name I take.

The details of my background are something you may learn in time, if you prove yourself trustworthy. My hobby is magic. My goal is knowledge, and through knowledge, power. Through power, freedom.

Do not ask for more unless you are willing to pay with real truths of your own, of equal value and proportionate <u>risk</u>.

While I am unsure why most find splitting the Will in two directions at once to be such an obstacle, it is indeed a trait I possess. I would be willing to collaborate if appropriate assurances of my safety could be made, and proper enticement given.

As mentioned above, I value knowledge, freedom, and the right kind of secret. I dislike being hunted, controlled, or vilified. What can be done about this, I wonder?

SHE CONSIDERED ADDING her thanks for information on the dream curse but decided against it. Thankfulness didn't really fit the tone of the rest of the letter. If she'd had some interesting information of relative usefulness, she would have included that instead, but what did she know that Thaddeus Lacer didn't?

Sebastien sealed the envelope carefully, wondering if he might indeed be able to offer her something that would make another appearance as Siobhan Naught or the Raven Queen worthwhile. If so, she would need to stall until she'd successfully managed to decrypt her own copy of Myrddin's journal. It would be very embarrassing to discover that there was another layer of security beyond the current one, after all.

Over the next couple of weeks, Sebastien poured her focus into spellcasting, and particularly the light-refinement spell, until her muscles began to harden and grow defined beneath her skin and her joints stopped aching. Her first priority had to be maintaining the integrity of her mental defenses, always. And as a nice additional bonus, it seemed that either time or all the work that she was putting in was helping to erase any lingering urges for the beamshell tincture. Working on light-refinement seemed to suppress the urges almost as well as getting a full meal.

It also helped with Fekten's class to a surprising degree, as balance and stamina seemed to bleed into all other physical activity. Fekten had never quite gotten over the incident during the end of term exams, and watched her with a gimlet eye as if she might just warp into an Aberrant at any time. Her grade had also somehow failed to improve, despite the fact that she now routinely outperformed at least half of her classmates.

Her other classes were going better, and the difference in the effort that she poured into learning compared to the average University student started to bear fruit. Her spells were stronger and more efficient than theirs, but she was also rapidly closing the knowledge gap that had seen her receive such a mediocre score on the entrance exam.

Second to that, Sebastien memorized glyphs and practiced splitting her Will. Sometimes, she even listened to the more boring lectures while practicing, careful not to accidentally channel any energy into a nonexistent spell array.

Casting both the magnifying divination spell and Professor Lacer's transmutation exercises at the same time allowed her to improve two or three times as quickly as she had been before. She reached the point that Professor

Lacer had required quickly enough and began pushing for an accomplishment worthy of contribution points. Transmuting a diamond from pure air was as difficult as it sounded, but at this point it was only a matter of power and time.

If only all of her problems were so simple.

Sometimes, she helped Damien to cast some of the more power-intensive information-collating spells or spent time reading through frustratingly vague articles and underlining small hints of relevant information. Occasionally, she got distracted and found herself reading through tangential articles about the omens of political upheaval in Osham. There were fascinating exposés from former citizens about what it was like to live under such an authoritarian regime, and the systematic oppression the populace suffered.

The northern islands had been facing some severe ice storms from the north and were expected to slide into famine if a solution couldn't be found.

And Silva Erde was publicly blaming Lenore's "misuse of magic" for the increase of magical beasts that were plaguing their forests. And apparently Lenore's ambassador had made a huge ass of himself trying to cut down a sapient tree that had been a friend of the queen's family for six generations.

A few times when Sebastien had time away from classes, she put on a new disguise and went to help Liza with the sleep-proxy tests. They continued to go well, and somehow, before Sebastien had realized, weeks had passed, and the seventh month was upon them.

Liza left a note in their linked journals that their last round of testing had gone as smoothly as those before.

The sleep-proxy spell was ready.

When Siobhan arrived at Liza's apartment, the spell arrays were already set up, and the ravens were waiting. *'I'm not the only one who's been excited about this.'*

Unfortunately, there was no easy way to increase the brain power or vitality of the ravens without fully Sacrificing their counterparts. Siobhan had the inkling of an idea that might negate the need for their deaths, but it was far from being something she could implement.

Siobhan first helped Liza to cast the spell on herself. Liza didn't actually need anyone to joint-cast with her, but the practice for Siobhan was part of their agreement.

When it was done, Liza tilted her head back and took a deep, joyful breath. Her thick lips spread into a face-splitting smile, and her arms lifted as if to feel spring raindrops falling down from the heavens.

Siobhan watched her, unblinking, as if she could receive some of that invisible cleansing rain from proximity alone.

Liza lowered her head and arms and smiled gently at Siobhan. "You will enjoy this, I think."

Siobhan's skin itched beneath the surface with eagerness, her cheeks flushed, and sweat beaded on her forehead and at the small of her back. She swallowed. "Let's set up the containment wards around my raven, then."

Siobhan had feared that the raven might not only end up sleeping for her, but also dreaming for her. Without any way to wake, what would happen to it? What if it died? And what if, in doing so, it could cause some sort of backlash on her, who would be connected to it through binding magic? It was best to be thorough. After all, none of the sleep-proxy tests had been done with someone like her.

She'd had to pay Liza to develop the wards while remaining vague about what exactly they were meant to protect against, but for some extra gold, Liza had been thorough and asked no questions.

Still, as they cast the binding magic, Siobhan remained alert, ready to attack with her battle wand if something went wrong. Though truly, Siobhan wasn't sure exactly what she expected in the worst-case scenario.

She sensed the magic attaching, little tingles penetrating through her skin to anchor somewhere deep inside. Blood and flames flashed behind her eyelids for the space of a single blink. Siobhan tried not to think of the glimpse she had seen of the town as she was escaping Grandfather's house.

And then the binding spell was finished.

It was wonderful.

She had seen quite a few people experience the spell, but somehow the reality of it still took her completely by surprise. It was like a skin made of lead had been peeled from her, and suddenly she could breathe, its weight no longer squeezing her down into a hunchbacked shape or restricting the rise and fall of her chest. When that layer was gone, she thought she was free, until another peeled away, and she realized she had still been weighed down. *'How light is it possible for a person to get before they just float away?'* she wondered.

But no matter how much weight sloughed away, the minute after she was lighter, and then lighter still. By the time the magic settled, Siobhan felt virtually weightless.

'Oh,' she realized. *'All this time, how much strength have I been expending just to stay upright? Just to avoid collapsing on myself like an empty balloon?'*

She ran her fingertips over her face, feather-light, and then down her body. *'Is this what other people feel like all the time? No, that's impossible,'* she reasoned. *'If that was so, they would all be trying to take over the world...or become the next Myrddin.'*

"I don't have to sleep anymore," Siobhan whispered. She laughed breathlessly until she choked. She touched her trembling fingers to her cheeks, expecting to find tears, but her eyes were dry.

"Settle, child," Liza said, her voice warm and low.

Siobhan pressed her hands to her open mouth, forcefully slowing the air her ragged breaths could suck in. "I'm just…so happy," she gasped, sinking to her knees.

Liza kneeled next to her, gently rubbing circles over the center of Siobhan's back.

It took a few minutes for Siobhan to calm herself, and she was left feeling somewhat limp but still deeply free. Siobhan closed her eyes and wiped the saliva that had gotten on her hands onto her clothes. "I'm so happy," she repeated.

The raven linked to Siobhan was already blinking sleepily, its head bobbing up and down as it tried to stay awake. She watched carefully as the raven finally gave in and rested its head on its back to sleep. Siobhan tensed as its breathing deepened and slowed, but nothing happened. "I'll keep watch on it through the night," she said.

Liza eyed the raven, and then Siobhan, with some distrust. Though she said nothing, at the base of the stairway she stopped and activated another set of wards that glowed briefly across the ceiling of the entire lower level.

Siobhan stared vigilantly at the sleeping raven for about a half hour, but the boredom soon became agonizing. She did not take well to idleness. Her mind kept returning to the memory of darkness and solitude she'd experienced during the sensory deprivation spell. She tried to keep her mind away from the dark thoughts, but every time she relaxed her vigilance even the tiniest bit, the memories slipped back to the forefront. It did not make things easier that one part of her mind could be focused on something innocuous while another descended into memory. *'That is the unfortunate side of splitting my Will so much, I suppose. But I feel so wonderful. How do the bad thoughts still creep in so easily?'*

But thinking back to that terrible moment reminded her of something less helpless. She had used her shadow-familiar to exert control, but more than that, she had been able to sense through it. How this worked, she wasn't sure. Some sort of side-effect from filling her shadow with her Will, perhaps? It was fascinating but also seemed like it might be useful somehow, if she became more adept with the skill. And maybe, something else to focus on would take her mind off the unpleasant memories.

She cast the shadow-familiar spell with practiced ease. With her hands in a Circle around her mouth to catch the heat of her breath, she closed her eyes and tried to feel something through her shadow.

Nothing happened. Just like every other time she'd cast the spell before the sensory deprivation, and just like the way she couldn't feel the shadow beneath her feet normally. If she didn't know it was possible, she would have never guessed. *'Maybe there's too much light? So much so that it's overwhelming?'*

She hesitated before reaching into her bag for the cotton-and-wax earplugs that she used to make nights in the dorms possible. She stuffed them into her ears, though unlike the sensory deprivation spell, they did not shut out the sound of her own heartbeat. Then she turned off the light crystal, plunging herself into almost complete darkness. Her skin prickled with unease, and she hurried to recast the shadow-familiar with her eyes closed. Very deliberately, she took control of the darkness beneath and around her.

At first, this attempt seemed the same as the one prior, but as her palms began to sweat and her throat grew dry, she caught the faintest hint of light absorbed by her shadow, which encompassed almost the entire room. After that first hint, it grew clearer. There was still some light coming from the crystal at the base of the stairs, and the spell arrays filling the floor and the walls were giving off the faintest glow, which would normally be invisible to the naked eye.

Siobhan let out a shuddering sigh of relief. Somehow, knowing what was there removed the creeping sense of dread she'd developed after what she saw in the darkness of her own mind. The sensation felt a little like the philtre of darkness's proprioception adaptation, which she'd still yet to name something less of a mouthful. *'Maybe my experience with that is making it easier for my brain to parse this information.'*

Using her shadow-familiar in this way was more difficult than she had expected, soon leaving her mentally fatigued in a way that had nothing to do with capacity. So she turned the light back on, and since she was going to be staying up all night, turned her thoughts toward finding something else to do. Light-refinement was impossible without the sun, and her mind was too tired to practice Will-splitting. She'd even done all of her homework already.

In the end, she pulled out the book Professor Lacer had given her, *100 Clever Ways Thaumaturges Have Committed Suicide*. Lying with her legs up against the wall and her back on the floor, she began to read.

At least fifteen different thaumaturges were known to have independently come up with the idea to draw a Circle with the inner bounding edge instead facing outward.

This created a Circle with a center on the other side of the planet, shaped somewhat like an ultra-massive hot air balloon, with the thaumaturge standing in the opening. It was a simple mental trick that could be backed up by a few output-directing instructions and, unfailingly, killed the thaumaturge as soon as they tried to cast a spell that spanned the entire planet.

All fifteen known cases had died immediately from extreme Will-strain leading to a massive brain hemorrhage. Luckily, external backlash was minimal due to the extreme range of energy dispersal.

During the reign of the Blood Emperor, a group of thaumaturges attempted to create a wide-range communication and surveillance network by linking the consciousness of thousands of birds together and then releasing them across the country. This project met problems from the very beginning, when the birds started to die. One of the thaumaturges attempted to connect to the bird-network to find out the reason for their deaths. He immediately jumped off the top of the tower where they had been working, bashing himself head-first on the ground below.

It was speculated that the information overload had fried his brain like an egg, but many of the rumors surrounding the event insisted that he had believed that he, too, was a bird, and thus could fly.

The next entry had Siobhan giggling uncontrollably to herself as the book covered an entire series of hilarious failures and disasters resulting from witches trying to force familiar contracts with dragons. Everyone knew that dragons were notoriously contrary and spiteful—almost as bad as djinns. Siobhan really couldn't imagine how much hubris must be involved in making such a foolish decision. Dragons grew too large to house, were ridiculously expensive to feed and care for, and had inconveniently high sex drives.

They were also masters of malicious compliance.

She had barely finished rolling around on the ground with laughter before moving on to the next entry. A young thaumaturge, jealous of his friend's artificery project—shoes that would tie themselves—developed shoes that he believed would walk on water by repelling liquid. They caused his feet to explode as all the blood exited the area of effect at once and with extreme force.

That, too, was somehow hilarious, despite the gruesome imagery.

After that, entries covered several obviously deadly ideas in quick succession. Someone wanted to avoid being disarmed and so tried implanting their Conduit into their own flesh. Someone else cooked themselves and everyone around them with super high-frequency, low-amplitude radiation. Another, in a "genius" solution to an ongoing famine, attempted to create horse-sized chickens!

The book did a wonderful job of keeping her mind away from dark thoughts, but she made it all the way to the end and still felt that something was missing. Surely someone outside of the Red Guard would have tried casting with an Aberrant component at some point?

But she already suspected she knew what might happen if someone tried that. As she again grew antsy with idleness, Siobhan dug deep in her satchel and pulled out her books about Myrddin once more.

5 3

———

ASHES OF THE PHOENIX

SIOBHAN TURNED the pages of *Myrddin: An Investigative Chronicle of the Legend* until she found a section that drew her attention.

Somewhat famously, Myrddin was said to have been given a quest by a dragon that required him to turn clay to flesh.

Siobhan had seen Professor Lacer actually do this in class, with a turtle. Of course, Professor Lacer wasn't rumored to have created sentience, nor true life out of clay.

But if Myrddin had done something similar, it was easy to see where such exaggerated rumors came from. It was even possible that a dragon really had tried to give him an impossible task out of mischievousness or vindictiveness.

The author of this book agreed, and also tied the rumor to Carnagore, the metal horse who had seemed so lifelike. Myrddin was known to have killed at least two dragons single-handedly, and the rumors had probably spread from the latter event, when he carried the beast's corpse back to the nearest village with him and single-handedly revived their economy with the butchering and sale of dragon parts.

The linked stories in *Enough Yarn to Last the Night: A Collection of Myths from the Life of a Man with Many Names* were as fanciful as one might have expected. In one, a golem formed from mud learned to be a real person after following Myrddin around for a while. In another, Myrddin built a sandcastle, which turned into a miniature city that ants took over and ruled for several generations of mythically heroic struggle and betrayal.

Even more famous than the tales of turning clay to flesh were the stories about Myrddin having used phoenix ashes to resurrect his recently deceased lover, though in some stories it was instead his son. There were six different connected stories in the book of illustrated children's tales, and the investigative history book explained that historians believed these tales, greatly exaggerated, led to the overhunting of phoenixes and their subsequent endangerment.

Phoenixes, never that prolific, were now on the brink of extinction, and the use of any components from them was illegal. And they could, in fact, be used to save the life of someone who had died within the last three minutes, under the Will of a Grandmaster and with at least seventy percent of the deceased person's body parts, which must include their heart and their brain.

But the phoenix had to have died within the last three days for the magic of their components to remain active, and they were notoriously difficult to contain, and beyond that, difficult to keep alive in captivity.

No one's life had actually been saved in exchange for that of a phoenix for the last four hundred years. At least not openly.

Of all the myths she'd read, these seemed the most firmly based on plausibly real events.

Siobhan flipped the page to the next story. In this one, Myrddin went into the Forest of Nod again. He was searching for something important, which the story didn't specify. Rather than finding whatever he was looking for, he stumbled into a Circle made of mushrooms and river pebbles—a doorway to the hidden land of the fey.

He spent seven months in their realm, dancing their dances, eating their food, and wooing their women, all while he kept a watchful eye on every piece of magic, learning it in secret.

In the end, they revealed their nefarious intent. He would remain forever in their realm unless he married the sickly fey princess and tied his life-force to hers. Having partaken of their hospitality, he had no right to refuse and leave freely. But using the magic he had stolen from them, Myrddin turned the tables, stole the sickly fey princess, and escaped.

He exited seventy years younger than he had entered, because time passes differently in the realm of the fey, and he had been living backward inside of it.

Siobhan frowned, noting this second reference to the man moving backward through time. '*Do these stories stem from him being so incredibly long-lived? Even most Archmages only average one hundred forty years, with the oldest of them getting to one hundred seventy, or in a couple of cases, two hundred years old. But*

Myrddin was recorded as living at least three hundred years, even in the respected historical texts. How much time did he spend casting, to make that possible?'

She blinked up at the illustration in the book, then let it fall to her chest as her arms grew tired from holding it above her. *'Myrddin could most likely split his Will, right? Is it possible…that he just spent all of his waking hours casting something, while the other half of his Will took the burden of going about daily life?'*

She sat up. *'Could I do that?'*

Rolling around on the ground while reading had freed her warding medallion and transformation amulet. Siobhan moved automatically to tuck them back under her shirt, but froze with the black stone of the transformation amulet in her hand.

'But what if Myrddin didn't really live that long? What if it just seems that way… because of something like this amulet? If this works to give the same body to anyone who uses it, then Sebastien Siverling could actually be two or more people if there were duplicate amulets, or if I gave it to someone else.' The idea exploded inside of her mind like a fireball. *'Myrddin doesn't have to be one person. It could have been a group of powerful thaumaturges working together, or even a family passing down the legacy from generation to generation.'*

She snapped *Enough Yarn to Last the Night* shut, turning back to *An Investigative Chronicle.* She skimmed every page, looking for any mention of fair-skinned, fair-haired men in Myrddin's history. A few hours took her all the way through the book but didn't lead to anything conclusive. Myrddin had had dozens of friends and companions throughout his very long life, many of whom had died. But the author wasn't prone to overly describing people's appearances. Myrddin himself was never known for particular paleness, and several drawings and paintings of him had been made. They were of poor quality and exactness compared to the artistic accomplishments of modern painters, but he had brown or black hair, and his nose was not nearly as long or sharp as hers.

'I suppose it's possible that a group of Myrddins might have used an amulet with a different appearance. And…it's also possible that Myrddin was a genuine person, that was his real identity, and he created this amulet so that he could sneak around without being noticed. He was rather famous, after all, and in his later years grew quite reclusive. A body like this, so obviously not Myrddin, would have made it easy for him to pop by the market or travel.'

That seemed more likely. After all, Myrddin was undeniably one of the most powerful, intelligent thaumaturges of multiple generations. Even if his inventions could have been the work of a group, how could they have created one thaumaturge more powerful than the next, until it reached the point of absurdity? Certain feats of magic couldn't be falsified.

Siobhan checked on the sleeping raven, running another diagnostic spell. The creature seemed completely fine. It wasn't twitching with dreams, nor did it show any signs of elevated stress levels, except for extreme fatigue. Unlike the normal short sleep patterns of birds, it had gone into a deep sleep almost immediately and stayed there.

Even though hours had passed, she was feeling just as refreshed as ever.

And her Will had recovered, too.

Realizing it would be a good idea to test Will-splitting while connected to the raven in a controlled environment, just in case, Siobhan attempted it. When the raven didn't react, she continued, and ended up spending the rest of the night practicing without ever feeling weary.

When she left in the morning, with plenty of time to spare before Thursday's classes started, the raven was still sleeping deeply, perfectly fine.

Sebastien stopped at the lock box on the way back to the University and was surprised to find a letter from Professor Lacer. After the last time, she had been prepared to wait for a long while again. He must have replied to her almost right away for the letter to already be waiting.

To make sure she had time to read it, she bought a few freshly baked rolls stuffed with beans and vegetables on the side of the road and ate them on the way back. Then she scurried into the Menagerie, as if she was going to do a morning light-refinement session, but instead opened Professor Lacer's letter.

I am not surprised at your goals or interests. Anything less would leave me disappointed.

I take your point. I am certain I could share information of similar risk and perhaps even greater importance, but like you, I do not feel comfortable doing so over letter with someone I am not fully sure I can trust. Perhaps one day we will each prove ourselves to the other.

My curiosity will not waver, but I do not need the answers spoon-fed to me.

You have the skill we need, and after some discussion with Grandmaster Kiernan, I believe we can offer you appropriate compensation and enticement to apply it. The man is wary of you, of course, but even more so, he is motivated to decrypt these books through any means possible. The High Crown has been applying increasing pressure on the University to give up the texts so that he may attempt decryption with his own experts. I do not believe you need worry that Grandmaster Kiernan will betray you.

Additionally, should you agree to lend your efforts to this endeavor, I will speak favorably of you to my colleagues in the Red Guard.

They are, indeed, interested in you, but they do not carry the High Crown's grudge. He cannot command us, no matter what he likes to think. The Red Guard exists to handle very specific types of threats, and unless I am very mistaken, you are not one of them.

Please refrain from proving my testimony wrong with some attempt to do a blood Sacrifice of everyone in Gilbratha, or anything similarly dangerous and ostentatious.

In addition to that, we can provide a safe meeting location for our collaboration. I will be involved in its setup and shielding and can assure you of its quality.

And as a third step toward ensuring your comfort and safety, Grandmaster Kiernan has volunteered to hire a covert team who will go to Silva Erde to spread false information that you have been sighted there.

SEBASTIEN LOWERED THE LETTER, which fluttered slightly in the summer breeze. Late-blooming flowers were beginning to wilt from some of the trees, and petals danced through the air, carrying a faint scent of sweetness and heat. Sebastien waved away a bee from her sweaty forehead and reread the last offer.

'That covert team is definitely just some minions from the Architects of Khronos. But pretending that I've left the country, and backing that with evidence, *is actually a wonderful idea. Much better than simply lying low and hoping my enemies will give up. I should give them the raven-summoning spell so that they can do something flashy.'*

The letter continued.

As you also value knowledge, I would guess that you may be interested in Myrddin's remaining journals. Obviously, you will have access to the three we hold during the decryption and study process.

To sweeten the deal, I can provide you access to the University's library and restricted archives, without limit, via a University token spoofed to mimic Archmage Zard's. He has full authority to come and go as he wishes, without the wards sending notice or alarms to anyone on the security committee. It should go without saying that I would expect you to be discreet with its use and do nothing that would implicate me. I believe I will be able to manage this fraud within the next couple of weeks, but due to the risks involved, will only move forward if you agree.

Altogether, I hope Grandmaster Kiernan and I have offered sufficient enticement to collaborate. If you agree, we will begin preparations immediately.

P.S. — I hope that you are able to place the lock back upon the books when we are not using them?

Sebastien swallowed hard and, after checking to make sure she was unseen, burnt this letter just as she had all the rest.

Professor Lacer's offer was emphatically attractive. Even if she hadn't trusted him, with such enticing offers she would have had to accept anyway. The only reason to turn down his proposal would be if she really couldn't overcome Myrddin's lock and thought that they might turn on her with twice as much enmity as they had allied with her if they were to discover it.

It began to rain, and Sebastien hurried to Professor Ilma's class while mentally composing her response. She would send it that very evening.

I agree to your terms. You may begin preparations.

I will not join you until you have fulfilled your promises. I am currently working on a venture of my own, which I must complete before I turn my efforts elsewhere, but I believe I will be free to help by the time you have completed your side of the bargain. If not, there may be some delay.

I have attached instructions for a spell that you might find useful in creating a false sighting of the Raven Queen. Please do not abuse it.

It wasn't like someone else couldn't come up with such a spell on their own, but she would find it somewhat disconcerting if clouds of ravens started appearing willy-nilly, with nothing to do with her. It was uncomfortable to realize that she couldn't really stop anyone from using the reputation of the Raven Queen for their own benefit.

Sebastien considered Professor Lacer's postscript question but left it unanswered, because she had no idea.

She sat through History of Magic in a daze, only snapping out of it when the bell rang to signify the end of class. Instead of rushing out with the other students, she shuffled up to Professor Ilma. When the blue-skinned woman looked at her inquisitively, Sebastien said, "I've been reading the books on Myrddin that you lent me. I was wondering, do you have any theories on why he might have disappeared for most of the last few decades of his life? What was he working on? Did he have any notable or powerful friends or acquaintances? And these notes written in the margins. Can you tell me more about the connections?"

Ilma shook her head. "I have read both of the books I lent you, but those notes were not written by me. My mentor was quite interested in Myrddin, but he passed away long ago and is unavailable to answer your questions."

"Oh," Sebastien said. She had just assumed that the handwriting within was Ilma's.

"If you have read both books, I can recommend more resources from the library that would cater to such speculation. But to be honest, too much about Myrddin's life is lost to stories. Even the things that should be clearly recorded are tainted with theatrics. It is sure that Myrddin was an ambitious, powerful genius, and that he knew this about himself. I suspect that he died alone, a lonely, bitter old man, and that the world can only be thankful he did not become an Aberrant. Dozens, if not hundreds, of historians have asked similar questions and wildly chased any perceived remnants of his footsteps in an attempt to find his lost legacy, but until recently, all for naught."

Ilma patted Sebastien on the shoulder. "Perhaps when my colleagues in the History department finally decrypt his journals, we will learn more about the truth of his life, particularly his last years."

Sebastien thanked her and left, disappointed.

That night, she was reminded of her complete lack of need to sleep. She spent almost the whole evening in several sessions of Will-splitting practice interspersed with glyph memorization and organizing the important information from newspaper articles on rogue magic incidents that had garnered Red Guard response. In the end, she took only a ninety-minute nap before dawn, as they had discovered that getting even small amounts of rest could greatly increase the time that the sleeping raven lasted, and she did not want to kill it.

In the morning, she was still refreshed, and a session of light-refinement to greet the dawn filled her with any energy she lacked.

Despite how wonderful freedom from sleep was, and how truly sublime it continued to be as the days passed, Sebastien still couldn't release the sense of dread that hounded her every footstep.

During class Sebastien sometimes became distracted with daydreams about the Red Guard bursting in through the classroom windows to arrest her, or going to sleep during the few times the sleep-proxy spell wasn't active and never waking again, or even worse, going to sleep and finding herself trapped inside the memories she had forgotten.

This looming sense of doom was even more constant than the summer rains and drove her to study and practice incessantly, and with the combination of the sleep-proxy and light-refinement spells, she was able to recover from exertion like never before while putting in even more hours of effort. On the weekends, she stopped by Liza's to switch to a different raven before the strain became too much for the previous one.

Soon, Tanya would have the first returns from the secret thaumaturge meeting, though she doubted whatever the young woman brought would be anything compared to the hoard of knowledge held in the University archives.

And then, a month before the end of term exams, Ennis Naught escaped from the labor camp he was assigned to, cutting his one-hundred-year sentence down to less than one.

Sebastien expected a furor to follow, revitalizing the flagging interest in the Raven Queen, but the news was only reported by one newspaper, one time, and none of the others picked it up. Only *The People's Voice*, which didn't really count, and was again treading on dangerous ground as some of the quotations from anonymous commentators edged on doubting the capability of the Crowns' justice.

The lack of news coverage showed her more clearly than anything how tight a grip the Crowns had on information. The Rouse Family, bearer of the Twelfth Crown, owned the newspapers either directly or in essence, along with the larger entertainment halls, opera houses, and brothels.

Sebastien was less concerned by the news about Ennis than she expected herself to be. But in a way, it made sense. She had disowned him. Ennis No-Name had no connection to her. And when he died, his remains would not be buried with the family.

She was sure he wouldn't come looking for her. His sense of self-preservation was too great, and his concern for her had always been too little.

The next day, as a precaution to ensure students wouldn't have any issues when pushing their Wills to the limits, Professor Burberry held another in-class session of the Henrik-Thompson tests.

"You should switch the scale to Apprentice level, or maybe Journeyman?" Sebastien suggested when it was her turn. "Otherwise the light may be too bright."

While Professor Burberry checked her previous records for Sebastien's initial results from the first term and raised a skeptical eye, some of the other students whispered or sent her dirty looks. But Burberry complied without comment.

Sebastien palmed the Conduit Professor Lacer had given her, along with the beast core Professor Burberry provided, and began to channel energy through the Henrik-Thompson device.

The glow quickly grew to a glaringly bright white, and Sebastien closed her eyes to reduce the irritation as she pushed at her limits. She stopped before she got so close to the edge of her ability that it felt dangerous, held there for a few seconds, and then released the magic.

The other students were silent.

Professor Burberry cleared her throat and quietly wrote down the results. "Six hundred eighteen thaums."

Murmuring arose among the other students immediately, and even Damien gave Sebastien a look of surprise.

Burberry frowned down at the number, checked the testing artifact, and then turned suspiciously on Sebastien. "Were you deliberately underperforming on this test last term?"

Sebastien flinched in surprise. She was pretty sure she had, in fact, slightly underperformed, because she'd still had an underpowered Conduit at that time.

Before she could speak, Damien piped up. "Sebastien is just incredibly talented, and he practices all the time. Seriously. I find him practicing in the middle of the night, and he's so busy with Professor Lacer's special apprentice assignments that he isn't even properly making time to spend with his friends."

Ana rolled her eyes. "*You* barely make time to spend with your friends recently, either, but do you want to bet your Will hasn't passed five hundred thaums?"

"Ten gold," Damien muttered back out of the side of his mouth without ever taking his eyes off Burberry.

Professor Burberry ignored them, examining Sebastien with concern. "How many hours a day are you practicing?"

It wasn't the first time someone had asked that question, but it was the first time that the answer was high enough that she couldn't be truthful. "Maybe six or so," Sebastien said. In truth, since the sleep-proxy spell had been working, that number was more like ten.

"Are you using glamours to hide the signs of fatigue?" Burberry asked, leaning in to peer at Sebastien's face through her glasses. "No, it doesn't seem so." Burberry, whose surprisingly smooth, plump skin showed its own signs of magical cosmetics and glamours, should know.

Some quick mental math made it obvious why Burberry was acting so strange. Sebastien had started the University testing at just over two hundred thaums. And in less than two terms, she had tripled that.

To put it in perspective, the average student, casting for the first time on entering the University and practicing three hours per day for the next three terms, might get their Apprentice license at two hundred and sixty thaums. If they stayed five terms to get Journeyman certification with an extra two terms for a specific specialization, that same student would be at about six hundred fifty to seven hundred thaums.

This was the difference that dedication, effort, and variety could make to a person's Will. But, doing the math, it still seemed like Sebastien was progressing slightly faster than she should have, if she was really averaging six hours per day for most of that time. Perhaps some days she had worked a little longer. '*Or perhaps I'm secretly just that talented?*' she wondered, feeling a little smug.

Burberry pursed her lips. "Well, I suppose by your age Thaddeus Lacer was already at four or five thousand thaums."

Sebastien's smugness dropped away like a stone block slipping through her fingers.

"He chose his apprentice well. But child, you have plenty of time ahead of you. There's no need to push yourself so hard. Remember to take a well-deserved break every now and again." She turned to the other students. "In fact, I encourage all of you to take a break the day before your final exams so that your minds and Wills can tackle any obstacles while fresh. Cramming until the last second often results in worse performance."

Burberry returned to the testing, and Damien also requested she set the artifact to the Apprentice scale. His light wasn't as bright as Sebastien's, and his results came out at three hundred seventy thaums, despite pushing himself until his cheeks trembled.

Ana held out her hand triumphantly for the gold.

Damien stared at her hand, opened and closed his mouth, and said, "I don't have the gold on me. I'll pay you later."

Sebastien wondered whether Damien had gotten any more allowance since the beginning of the term and if, when he had made the bet, he had forgotten that he didn't actually *have* ten gold. He spent the rest of the class time glowering silently at any student who dared to speak.

That evening, Sebastien retreated to her apartment under the cover of her trusty umbrella, despite the fact that it was a Monday. She had spent much of the weekend trying to open Myrddin's journal, and she felt like she was on the razor's edge of success.

Sebastien retrieved the ancient leather book from its hiding spot, took it out of the warded chest, and dual-cast a few simple spells to warm up her Will. All of this practice had been noticeably affecting the nimbleness of her Will, which was spilling into all of her other spellwork. Beyond that, the huge breadth of glyphs she now knew meant she could be so exact in her meaning that she'd also improved her efficiency.

As she began what was probably her three thousandth attempt to get past the journal's test, Sebastien wasn't even excited. She was still determined to succeed, but the uncooperative book had long ago thrashed any immediate hope out of her.

Instead of falling behind as the two glyphs appeared faster and faster, or stumbling when some obscure glyph that she couldn't remember appeared, the glyphs stilled for the final time, and then sank into the leather surface.

Sebastien stared down at Myrddin's journal, careful not to let her shock distract her from continuing to apply her Will on those two meanings, just in case. With trembling fingers, she opened the leather cover. The writing inside had resolved into clarity.

$$54$$

A LIFE'S WORK

SEBASTIEN
Month 8 Day 9, Monday 5:15 p.m.

SEBASTIEN'S EYES eagerly focused on the first page of Myrddin's journal. His handwriting was a little messy, somewhat overly looping and decorative, but she could read it with a little extra effort.

The first page held a single paragraph. Some of the words were spelled strangely, and some of them were archaic choices that she'd never heard anyone actually use. These, she mentally translated into what she guessed were their contemporary counterparts to more easily parse the meaning.

I considered writing this in my native language, but it has been so long the movements feel strange under the tip of my pen, and my hand is clumsy with it. To think what it would be like to attempt with a quill! I find before me the endeavor of a lifetime, a goal truly worthy of all my efforts, and I can only lament that I wasted so much time on foolishness and self-indulgence. I will make penance for the consequences of my actions by fixing the wrongs I have caused, if it is the last thing I do. Please wait, and though I do not deserve it, please forgive me, as I can never forgive myself.

THAT WAS ALL IT SAID.

When Sebastien turned the page, the paper briefly flashed with another two glyphs. She almost fumbled the switch in her Will's focus, but though her heart jumped in trepidation, the contents of the journal remained clear.

Sebastien let out a tremulous breath of relief. The contents of the next page seemed completely disconnected from what she quickly realized must have been a preface.

> That jackass Tarquin has come up with a viable method for self-charging artifacts.
>
> I cannot hate him too much, as it seems likely that this will be a critical component of The Work, and he has unknowingly made my job easier.
>
> But the concept will need improvement. And testing. <u>Lots</u> of testing.
>
> I cannot make any more mistakes where it counts.

AFTER THAT, the rest of the page and the one after contained complex calculations, some diagrams, and what seemed to be various spell array elements that were never quite combined into a whole. Myrddin had added notes and questions to himself, sometimes answering them and sometimes seeming to skip to some other only tangentially related idea.

'*This is the method to create self-charging artifacts like my transformation amulet,*' Sebastien thought, her chest filling with wonder and delight. That delight soon sank away. '*But I cannot understand it at all.*'

She wasn't sure if that was because Myrddin's notes were nearly incomprehensible or if she simply didn't know enough about artificery and whatever other underlying principles he was referencing. She had wanted to take that class and been forced to give up the idea, but even after two semesters of artificery, she doubted she would be able to figure out what Myrddin was talking about.

Reading while continuing to apply her Will in two different directions was difficult, and she couldn't even begin to attempt to puzzle out anything confusing. She had only the barest shred of concentration left over. To be able to study anything from Myrddin's journal, she would need to copy it out elsewhere by rote, then release her Will from the journal.

Every time Sebastien turned the page, two more glyphs flashed, and she had to quickly switch the focus of her Will. Even though she wasn't channeling any power, keeping the book from descending into incomprehensibility again was surprisingly straining in a different way than unlocking it in the first place had been. After a few minutes she could already feel her mind growing tired. It was like holding one's arms straight out to either side. It seemed like it should have been effortless, but soon enough even strong muscles would start to burn, tremble, and falter.

Sebastien moved faster, skimming over the pages instead of trying to read them in detail with her faltering attention.

Myrddin finished the development of the self-charging artifact's concept, and over four pages after that, wrote down some truncated spell instructions and a full set of spell arrays. It was all still far beyond her, but at least somewhat more comprehensible than his notes had been.

The pages after that dealt with a second method to achieve the same thing, and just as she was turning the page of what seemed to be yet a third method to create self-charging artifacts, her Will slipped.

Sebastien drew back her concentration with a flinch, but there was no pain, confusion, or frayed thoughts. She hadn't actually been casting, after all. With no energy being channeled, there was nothing to cause backlash.

She stared at the incomprehensible pages, then laughed, giddiness bubbling up and out of her throat like a living thing. She stood and paced back and forth wildly, unable to contain all of her energy in stillness. 'I did it. I did it!' she crowed internally.

'And it turns out Myrddin actually wasn't the initial inventor of the self-charging artifact, though he seems to have improved and expanded upon the initial concept quite a lot. I'm pretty sure that last method was using a beast core for energy, which is definitely a lost art,' Sebastien thought, remembering a small footnote in a book she'd read about artificery.

Myrddin was also rumored to have developed artifacts that could be triggered with Will alone. Maybe this journal would explain how that worked, if she could get far enough into it. Maybe it would explain how he had made her transformation amulet. 'Truly, wondrous knowledge lies between these pages,' she thought, hugging the book to her chest like it was a beloved child. 'It might not have the answer to creating purified celerium, but to me, other lost knowledge is just as valuable. And I am the only one with access.'

It was easy to see how some thaumaturges grew so greedy with their spells and little inventions. There was something about being the only one to have a secret, to decide who might know and who would remain ignorant, that felt like being better than everyone else. It wasn't true, of course, but she could see how one might get the two confused and be unable to give up on that perception out of pride or fear.

Once Sebastien had gotten over her fit of giddiness, she spent the rest of the evening trying to get back into the journal.

She had no success, and returned to the dorms barely in time to avoid missing curfew.

This repeated for the next three days, until on Friday, the newspapers reported on a confirmed sighting of the Raven Queen in Silva Erde.

The Architects of Khronos had used the raven-summoning spell in the middle of a large city, in the middle of the day. And that evening, they had cast a giant illusion on low hanging clouds. A woman cloaked in fluttering, tattered darkness walked through the firmament, appearing from the curve of one cloud and eventually disappearing behind another, returning to the darkness from whence she came.

'I'm pretty sure they just cast a light spell up at the clouds and then used a moving silhouette to simulate the Raven Queen moving above,' Sebastien deduced based on her own experience with how overblown the newspaper reports could be.

The papers were all speculating about why the Raven Queen had moved to Silva Erde, with many of them stating with confidence that she must have run from Lenore to escape the Thirteen Crowns' power. Despite only a week having passed since Ennis's escape from the labor camp, none of the reporters dared to jump to what must have been the obvious, enticing speculation about whether or not she had broken him free.

'The coppers probably won't let their guard down entirely, but I'm sure they'll stop looking so hard. Maybe in a couple of months, I can get the Architects to fake another sighting and really solidify the idea that I've left.'

Sebastien stopped by the library after Practical Casting to finish her homework, planning to go to her apartment again right after dinner.

But Ana skipped up beside her and announced, "We're going to the Glasshopper! Damien's treat, in exchange for losing the bet with me on Monday. Set aside whatever ridiculous study project you're working on and come with us! Consider it active recovery."

Sebastien hesitated, but the offer of free, delectable food, when compared against another evening of disappointment and frustration, was simply too good to pass up. With a surge of defiance, she agreed.

Talk among her friends was mostly focused around the end of month exams and magical exhibitions. Sebastien listened without contributing her own opinion, allowing her mind to relax and ride the gentle waves of conversation.

Rhett was the only one not with them, as he had a previously scheduled date with some upper-term duelist woman that he'd been struggling to get to pay attention to him all term.

As they approached the transport tubes, one of the faculty members across the white stone entrance area watched their group with a bit too much interest for Sebastien's comfort.

Waverly peeked at the man from under her fringe of black hair, then moved to the other side so that Brinn and Damien would keep her out of sight. As the smallest of their group, the others made easy cover. "Hurry," she muttered.

The transport tube guard, there to facilitate and coordinate transportation and shipments for the commoners without University tokens, narrowed his eyes suspiciously.

But Sebastien's group was already traveling down before a frustrated, "Wait!" came from the faculty member. By then it was too late to stop them.

Waverly sagged with a relieved sigh, then pushed up her glasses and lifted her head to stare up at the man expressionlessly.

Brinn glanced between them. "Waverly?" he asked, the question clear in his voice.

She huffed. "I'm not actually allowed to leave University grounds right now. Too many demerits this semester."

"I didn't know you had that many. Is this because of that time you tried to sneak into the High Tower? I *told* you not to irritate Archmage Zard. You know no one but him and his apprentices are allowed in there."

Waverly pursed her small, pink lips. "I heard he had a kelpie captured inside. Do you know how rare those are? If Archmage Zard would have just responded to my letter asking to visit, I wouldn't have had to break in."

"But you didn't break in! You failed! You got caught, and it was enough to get you grounded. What happens if you get even more demerits from this?"

Sebastien had vaguely heard about this fracas earlier in the semester, but thankfully Waverly, unlike Ana, hadn't tried to pull Sebastien into any of her schemes, and so had taken the punishment alone.

"That wasn't what got her grounded," Ana said softly, the smallest twitch of her lips hinting at amusement.

Waverly shot the taller girl a look of betrayal.

Brinn just stared down at his best friend silently, like some kind of sad, droopy tree.

"Fine!" Waverly cried, throwing her hands up. "I was also accused of colluding with the familiar of one of the professor's aides in my witchcraft class. It slipped the terms of its bindings."

Alec rubbed his chin gleefully. "Oh, yeah. His familiar torched all of his things, right? Including his Master's thesis, all of his notes, and even some family heirlooms? That was *you*?"

"All well-deserved revenge," Waverly huffed. "He was abusing her. And they didn't even have any proof that I was involved."

Brinn raised his eyebrows, then looked to Ana for the truth.

Waverly crossed her arms. "Just because she really liked me and came to visit me after she was free doesn't mean I colluded with her!"

"That she came to visit during the disciplinary hearing, looking like a tiny fire version of you, and gave you some ashes from her former master's belongings probably didn't help," Ana muttered dryly.

"Ashes born from revenge are a perfectly useful spell component," Waverly snapped back.

"How did I not know about this?" Brinn asked. "We're best friends, Waverly!"

"You were too busy playing with your trees and that herbology project! And I wouldn't have to keep secrets if you weren't such a nagging grandmother. You know that demerits don't actually matter, right?"

Brinn opened and closed his mouth like a fish, his eyebrows falling from their hurt upward curve to a flat stare.

Waverly gulped. "I was just feeling lonely because you were ignoring me!" she tried. And before Brinn could respond, her childlike arm rose and pointed accusingly at Alec. "And Alec killed the tree you gave him! He *drowned* it."

Damien gasped dramatically, then elbowed Sebastien in the side and flashed her a secretive grin. "Alec, how could you!?"

Alec looked around for sympathy. Finding none, he threw up his hands in exasperation. "I accidentally overwatered it! Don't say I drowned it. That sounds like I murdered it or something. I was just trying to take good care of it, and then when it got sick, I tried giving it more water...and well, you know."

"I gave you specific care instructions," Brinn said flatly.

"It...looked thirsty?" Alec tried, cringing away. As soon as they reached the bottom of the tube, he rushed out into the open air and hurried to flag down a carriage. "Oh, it seems we have too many people to ride together. I'll just take this one and go on ahead. See you guys at the Glasshopper!"

Sebastien and her four remaining friends squeezed into a second carriage.

Brinn looked at all of them. "The trees I gave you guys are still alive, right?"

"Of course," Sebastien agreed immediately. Everyone else nodded with varying degrees of confidence.

"I should check up on them, just in case," Brinn decided, totally distracted from Waverly's indiscretions.

As they rode, Ana turned to Sebastien and spoke softly. "All the ventures I've taken on as the Gervin heir have been going well. Especially the one with Lord Dryden. I'm hoping to collaborate on a few more projects with him. But I thought you might be interested to know that I went ahead and invested in the research we talked about."

Sebastien searched her memory for a conversation about research, but before she found it, Ana said, "The research that uses bini frogs and their hormonal sex changes." She paused and added, "To allow two women to have a child together?"

"Oh. Well, that's great." Sebastien nodded encouragingly.

Ana smiled softly. "Yeah. If not for our conversation that day, I daresay my life would be a lot different right now. Thank you."

"Maybe it wouldn't have been exactly like this, but I believe you would have done something about your uncles even without me."

"Maybe hired an assassin!" Ana joked.

Their meal at the Glasshopper was as sublime as the only other time Sebastien had been there. This time, a group of air witches were playing a quartet of harps backed up by an oboe. The entrancing music shivered through the air and across her skin like a physical touch, while the meal exposed her to textures and flavors that would no doubt ruin her for ordinary food if she experienced such luxury too often.

As they all reached the limits of their stomach capacity and began to get sloppy on alcohol, Damien grew quiet and distracted, frowning into his bubbly, frothing drink, which had come in a tiny edible cauldron.

"Father is going to be sentenced soon," Alec announced. "I really hope they put him in a labor camp. I heard sometimes people get out with just a huge fine and their Family name stripped from them. Can you imagine how he would be?" He shuddered.

"He killed a prostitute. They found some pretty good evidence. You always do time for murder," Ana said. She paused to hiccup, then continued, "And more importantly, my father wouldn't let him stay free to stab him in the back out of some misdirected revenge."

Damien swirled his drink, letting false smoke spill over the side and down his hands. "My father has been away for months, and it's been wonderful. I wish he oversaw army training exercises all the time."

Ana swayed in her seat, frowning in confusion as she popped a glowing candy the size of a grape into her mouth. It exploded audibly, and she sneezed out gold and red sparks. "I thought Lord Westbay was training the private security for some new research facility. You know, after what happened with that terrorist attack. Maybe it was just a rumor."

"Well, maybe it's true. Not like Father would bother to tell me anything," Damien said sardonically. "Even Titus has been too busy to have me home for the weekend for weeks now."

Ana rounded on Damien, accidentally twisted too far, and Sebastien had to catch her to keep her from tipping her chair over backward.

"Thank you," Ana said, patting Sebastien's arm like someone would praise a dog. "Damien! Titus is putting too much responsibility on you. I know you're excited about your Harrow Hill internship this fall, but it hasn't even started and just the practice p-project is driving you to distraction. You shouldn't have to develop new filing methods all by yourself, don't you think? Hire an expert, I say. You're not a clerk. And isn't it *so sad* that you haven't even seen your brother in weeks? Why is he too busy to make time for you?" She sniffed loudly, her lower lip pouting out.

Brinn gave everyone a pacifying smile. "I'm sure Titus has been very busy, what with the Raven Queen and those Architects of Khronos people on top of everything else."

"Do you think Nat's sad, too?" Ana asked softly. "She's probably lonely and too thoughtful to say anything, don't you think?"

As if he hadn't heard her, Damien nodded at Brinn. "Oh, it's not even just that. Well, maybe the Raven Queen or the Architects are behind it, but people have been disappearing from among the commoners. Investigating the disappearances is drawing the coppers thin, and the High Crown doesn't want to approve any budget increases because he says their performance is too poor, but really, what are they supposed to *do*?"

Sebastien frowned. "I didn't know about the disappearances. Let me guess. They're happening among the poor people? Maybe the homeless?"

"Of course." Damien glowered into his drink. "One of the new captains discovered what seems to be systematic and escalating numbers of disappearances."

"Blood magic or serial killer?" Waverly asked.

"Hopefully the latter," Ana said, enunciating carefully to keep from slurring. When Brinn frowned at her judgmentally, she added, "I mean, hopefully neither, *obviously*. But if I had to pick one, a serial killer, human trafficker, or anything like that is way less dangerous than a blood magic user doing something horrid with all of those lives. An Aberrant endangers everybody."

Damien and Sebastien shared a look, but they didn't argue.

Soon after, they left the Glasshopper. It had rained while they were eating, and the warm light of the streetlamps reflected beautifully off the shallow puddles and rain-slicked cobblestones. It was the wettest summer in Sebastien's memory, seeming to rain almost every other evening.

Before they could hail a carriage, a boy on the street corner called out, "Extra, extra! Breaking news. Red Guard fight against a rogue magic user in the streets!"

Damien took a sharp breath and seemed to partially shake off his inebriation in the few seconds it took him to reach the paper boy and buy the single leaflet of breaking news. Sebastien moved over, both of them standing beneath the streetlamp as she read over his shoulder. The "extra" didn't actually say much of substance.

A Red Guard team had fought a running battle with a man just a few blocks east of Waterside Market earlier that evening. Some impressive spells had been tossed back and forth, but nothing like what the old Red Guard defector had cast at Knave Knoll. Several people had been injured, a jentil had died, and one person's house had collapsed when an entire wall got blown out.

"Maybe it was the kidnapper," Ana said, still swaying on her feet. "Trying to do blood magic."

"Or one of the Architects," Brinn added.

"Or one of the Raven Queen's acolytes?" Alec said. "Just because she's in Silva Erde doesn't mean all of her allies have left."

Sebastien considered several possibilities. All of them were worrying at some level. In the end, instead of escorting her friends back to the dorms herself, she stuffed them all into a carriage and paid the driver extra to ensure that they arrived safely at their destination.

Damien tried to protest, any soberness that he'd felt from his adrenaline spike clearly wearing out as his last drink of the evening hit his bloodstream.

Fortunately, Sebastien had a ready-made excuse. "There isn't enough room. Besides, I want to pick up a few things while I'm out. I'll be there before curfew." Technically, on weekend nights the curfew only precluded students from wandering University grounds and buildings, and didn't require they actually stay in the dorms. Higher-term students had even fewer restrictions.

"You can't pay for the carriage," he tried to tell her, quite serious but slurring. "You don't have any money. I know all about it. Wait, no, it's me that doesn't have any money." He pressed a hand to his chest, smiling sloppily. "We're poor together, now."

"I'm rich," she assured him, then shoved him firmly back into his seat and shut the carriage door. As soon as the carriage was out of sight, she hurried to the lock box to check for a response from Professor Lacer. *'I'll swing by the apartment just to make sure it wasn't Liza or one of Gera's people who got taken by the Red Guard, too,'* she planned.

To her delight, there was a letter waiting for her, but when she picked it up, the smile slid from her face. There were two letters. One envelope was blank and expensive looking, as she had been expecting. The other was of much cheaper paper and had been signed with a crude drawing of a raven feather.

Sebastien ran her finger over the drawing. *'Something from Tanya?'* she guessed. Sebastien had used a similar drawing in place of a more traditional signature a couple of times when leaving notes for the young woman in her dorm. Her suspicion mounting, she hurried to find a dark alley where she would be shielded from the sight of anyone passing by, then used her thirteen-pointed star light coaster to illuminate the paper as she opened the letter.

The message within was quite simple.

My lady, I am leaving this message for you on Friday the 13th.

SEBASTIEN LOOKED AROUND AGAIN SUSPICIOUSLY. Tanya must have dropped it off some time earlier that day. Reassured that no one was watching her, Sebastien continued reading.

I am not sure if you will find it important, but I have overheard some loose talk by the Architects of Khronos. I suspect they are planning to kidnap a group of people from Osham, and have in fact already sent a strike team. From what I overheard, and my own speculation, this seems...big. I do not know the purpose of this assault, nor where these people may be kept, but I find the timing suspicious. It seems unlikely that they would attempt to pin such an act on you, but you are known to be traveling, and I thought you might like to know, just in case.

I hope you get this letter soon.

I will attempt to find out more if you instruct me to do so.

Loyally yours,

TC

SEBASTIEN GAVE A DEEP SIGH, tilting her head up to look at the night sky. *'This...might be important. I think perhaps I should talk to Oliver. He's from Osham, after all.'*

$$55$$

STRANGE PHENOMENA

Month 8 Day 13, Friday 11:00 p.m.

SEBASTIEN HAD to knock for a while before Thomas the doorman and pseudo-butler opened the door for her, sleepy eyed. "Sorry about the late hour. Is Oliver here?"

Thomas nodded silently, his eyes flicking up toward Oliver's study and giving her all the information she needed.

She strode toward the stairs without further delay. However, she stopped at the study door, bracing herself to see Oliver in person once more. She did a quick check of her body, straightened her shoulders, lifted her chin, and smoothed her expression as close to the placid perfection of a lake as she could manage. Then she knocked.

Oliver took a long few seconds to respond. "Come in."

He was rubbing his eyes tiredly as she opened the door, but his hands fell down as he saw her. His complicated tie had been pulled loose and his sleeves were rolled up to his forearms. "This is an unexpected visit," he said. It had been months since the last time they had spoken in person, and the letters they exchanged were far from personal. "Is something wrong?"

"I know that you've had some continued business with the Architects of Khronos. Were you aware that they've sent a force to kidnap a group of people from Osham?"

Oliver's expression flattened. "No. Where did you hear about this? Who are the targets?"

"Tanya Canelo informed me earlier today, but she didn't know much. I don't know the targets or any other relevant information. But, considering the greater political circumstances, I found this news...concerning. I know you're originally from Osham. I thought you might still have some contacts there."

Oliver was nodding rapidly to himself, his gaze harried and distant. He stood abruptly and moved to the cabinet that held his distagram. While Sebastien watched, he sent off several short messages in quick succession, taking only enough time to tune the communication band each time.

"I need to talk to that snake Kiernan, but I don't have a good excuse to bust in and drag a University Grandmaster out of his bed in the middle of the night. Someone might get suspicious."

Sebastien hesitated. "All you need is a student or faculty token to use the transport tubes, even after hours. As long as you're circumspect, no one will even notice you were there."

"I have some University contacts, but no way to get a token fast enough. I'll have to wait to talk to him in the morning." Oliver slammed his fist into the dark wood of the cabinet beside the distagram and swore. "What are they *thinking!?*"

Sebastien hesitated before reaching into her pocket and retrieving her student token. "Use this," she offered, holding it out to him. It felt somewhat sour to be offering aid of any kind to Oliver, but this didn't put her in much danger, and there was more at stake than their relationship.

Oliver's gaze switched between the wooden token and her face. "Will you come with me, then? Perhaps as the Raven Queen?"

"No. I'm not getting involved in whatever this is. I'm a simple University student, and I plan to remain that way."

Oliver gave her an odd look. "Okay. How do you want me to return your student token to you?"

"Leave it here. I'll pick it up tomorrow. And whatever you're planning to do, don't implicate Tanya. She put herself at risk to inform me."

"Of course. Are you going to stay the night? We haven't touched your room."

Sebastien shook her head. "I have other accommodations." She shook her student token impatiently, and Oliver moved forward to get it.

He stared into her eyes as he took it, his fingers brushing against hers. "Thank you."

Sebastien clenched her jaw for half a second. "You're welcome."

"Do you want some sort of payment for this?"

Sebastien hesitated, remembering his comments about the transactional nature of their relationship. She was tempted to request something cutting, but in the end said, "You can keep me updated on whatever you learn."

Oliver tucked the wooden token away in the inner pocket of his suit vest. "I heard about your father's escape last week. Are you…doing alright with everything?"

Sebastien clenched her jaw again, then shrugged. "He'll never find me, even if he tries. Which I doubt he will. Knowing him, he's scurried back to the northern islands or some other distant land and will be hiding out in some small village, cursing my name every time he gets a little too deep into his drink."

"I'm sorry."

She glared at him. "I'm not. Unless you count the fact that I'm sorry that piece of trash managed to escape."

Oliver very obviously swallowed back whatever words he wanted to say. "I have to go." He hesitated, then added, "You are welcome to stay here, if you wish. Whenever."

Sebastien raised one eyebrow and silently spun on her heel, leaving the study and making her way back down the stairs.

Oliver followed almost immediately on her heels. When they reached the street in front of his small manor's gates, they turned in different directions.

Sebastien didn't look back. After about a block, her pounding heart settled. She paused after turning the corner and rubbed at her shoulders, neck, and the sides of her jaw to release the tension there. "Damn you, Oliver," she muttered. What right did he have to act like he cared?

Resolutely, she put the matter from her mind and walked on, taking in the fresh night air after the recent rain.

When she got to her apartment, she opened Professor Lacer's letter. It was short, notifying her that they had completed their half of the agreement and inquiring when they could meet to collaborate on Myrddin's other three journals. He also asked if she had any involvement in Ennis Naught's freedom.

Sebastien drew a spark-shooting array on her little folding slate lap table and watched the letter burn to ash.

She drew out her dreamless sleep spell in oils and tinctures on her pillow, then dragged her bed underneath the window cut into the angled ceiling so that she could look at the stars as she fell asleep. She'd found she could tell when her raven was becoming unbearably weary because some of her normal fatigue began to accumulate again.

In the morning, she picked up her student token from Dryden manor, though Oliver was not home to give her an update. Sharon *was* there and made a lot of fuss about how much she'd missed Sebastien before roping her into breakfast with the rest of the servants.

After that, her belly round with food, she sent a quick letter via runner to

Damien, who was overly prone to worry and might foolishly panic that she had never made it back to the University the night before. Then she devoted herself once more to opening Myrddin's journal.

Halfway through the day, she succeeded again, only to immediately lose control as she tried to turn the pages too fast, eager to get back to the place she had left off last time.

Sebastien stared down at the incomprehensible, squiggly ink lines and shifting diagrams and almost threw the book across the room. Only supreme, *saint-like* patience allowed her to close it firmly and put it back into the warded chest.

After that, she was too frustrated to make much progress on anything, so she gave up and made another visit to the artisan who had created her spell rod. She was going to invest in an experimental business venture with the man. Plans and paperwork took most of the afternoon, and then she went through the very long and unpleasant process of transforming into a disguised variation of her female form to visit Liza.

The older woman helped to recast the sleep-proxy spell with a fresh raven, and then they had dinner together, which Siobhan ended up cooking most of because, even after so many years, Liza's only real skill in the kitchen revolved around the teapot. Usually, the woman ate simple meals that required little preparation or went out to eat, but with Siobhan in tow it was unwise to spend time in a public location.

Liza had been practicing some of Professor Lacer's exercises, which Siobhan found somehow both vindictively satisfying and ironic, and after dinner they competed with a metal ball around a Circle, just as the students had in the Practical Casting in-class tournament during term one.

Liza won, but only by devouring the wax of her tiny candle as Sacrifice more quickly than Siobhan could do the same for hers. The limitation of a single candle was supposed to keep them on even footing, but when they had sucked the flame dry and moved on to the wax, capacity mattered once more. The woman sniffed loudly and hid her smile behind the rim of her teacup, while Siobhan suppressed the urge to accuse her of cheating.

'*I could have won, too, if I'd resorted to dual-casting,*' she thought.

It was almost dark by the time she left, mentally charting out her route to the next safe place she would use to transform back into Sebastien.

In the time she had been inside with Liza, clouds had rolled over the sky, filtering out the light of the sunset into something bruise-purple and dramatic. Without fanfare, it began to rain once more. Sighing, Siobhan reached into her satchel to retrieve the plain black umbrella she had taken to carrying around with her lately. '*One would think some weather thaumaturge is experimenting over Gilbratha with all this rain. Isn't summer supposed to be dry? Maybe it's because we're so close to the coast.*'

But her umbrella wasn't there. Siobhan cursed as she realized that she had left it back at the dorms on Friday. The rain quickly swelled from a light drizzle to fat, heavy droplets of warm water, as if the sky were weeping. Around her, people began to hurry, those without umbrellas using their bags, clothes, or convenient newspapers as shields against the sorrow of the heavens. And, as always seemed to happen in times like these, there wasn't a carriage for hire to be seen.

'I need to find shelter or some way to keep dry. The rain might damage my disguise.' She slipped one hand into her satchel as her mind spun over various options. *'Grubb's barrier spell would make a perfect umbrella. And it's one of the options in my spell rod. But would casting that possibly draw more attention to me in this part of town?'* She was at least a kilometer north of the Mires, but not surrounded by so many rich or powerful people that having a water-repelling artifact or casting a spell for such a minor inconvenience would be seen as normal.

Her neck tingled uncomfortably, and Siobhan realized that she had begun walking faster without realizing it. She slowed her steps, searching for a glass window in which she could search behind herself as she wondered at the cause of her unease. *'Did I subconsciously notice something off without realizing it?'*

She turned all of her attention toward observation, her fingers curling around her spell rod and drawing it from her satchel.

A couple dozen meters down the street, the rain began to fall even more heavily, creating a stark delineation. She tracked the path of this increased rainfall, and as her head swiveled, she saw that there was a similar phenomenon on the street behind her. She found the correct segment of her spell rod and twisted it open, then immediately cast Grubb's barrier spell, distanced from the top edge by about a foot, as she had built into the spell array when she created it.

As the dome of force appeared, she held up the spell rod like an umbrella and used the shield she had created to peer up and around, trying to make out if the rain was falling heavier around her in a huge Circle as the tingling horror along her arms and the back of her skull suggested.

While the barrier spell might draw attention to her, it might also provide some small measure of protection against an attack with physical properties.

There was a change in the feel of the air, a shift in the muffled sounds of the city past the rain, and an intangible sense of isolation.

The air, which had smelled clear, sharp, and a little salty, took on the smell of something Siobhan couldn't identify but which raised goosebumps along her skin.

Siobhan took a sharp turn to the right, heading down the sidewalk of a major cross-street. Her eyes swept around, examining everyone nearby for suspicious behavior. She tried to keep her face impassive and her pace only as hurried as the other pedestrians who wanted to get out of the rain.

'I have to assume whatever this is, it is targeting me. But who is behind it?' Unfortunately, Siobhan had too many potential enemies to narrow them down. *'How did they find me? Did they follow me from Liza's? Is it possible that she sold me out?'*

The barrier of heavier rain was following her.

Siobhan's eyes trailed along the rooftops. Although she found no one there, her cheeks paled as she noticed an oddity in the windows of all the buildings. Normally, those without glass, wax paper, or some other protection against the rain would have been shuttered tight. But they were all open.

And behind them, people were peeking out, their faces obscured by rain, curtains, or shadows. *'They're all watching me.'*

Siobhan's breath hitched, and she forced it to smooth. *'How is that possible? What is happening?'*

An idea sparked in her mind, followed by a sudden rush of hope. She lifted her free left hand and pinched her nostrils closed, closed her mouth, and then attempted to breath in through her nose. It was a little trick that she'd read in a book but never found use for before, because the faint remnants of her dreams that occasionally slipped through her dreamless sleep spell weren't so normal or coherent as to allow her to become lucid while asleep. But she knew that, in a dream, attempting this would have her breathe *through* her closed nose, a clear indication that what was happening was not real.

She got no air, even though she strained hard enough to wrench something inside her chest. *'This is real.'*

Siobhan lamented her lack of foresight. Despite all of the preparations she had made, she hadn't replaced her sympathetically connected bracelets with anything else, partially because she felt she could no longer trust Oliver or Katerin and did not want to be on call for their own emergencies. *'I don't know what to do. Back to Liza's? Get to one of my emergency stashes and flee the city?'*

Very quickly, the few people who remained outside were disappearing. Though normally Siobhan would assume they were just hurrying to get out of the rain, the way some people were literally turning around and walking *away* from her, regardless of the direction they had been going before, worried her. It was as if there was some kind of repulsive force not only keeping out the absolute deluge of rain the rest of the city was experiencing but also urging others to leave this strange Circle.

What worried her even more was that, somehow, she couldn't see the faces of the people around her. Whether they were covered by umbrellas, arms raised to hold some more makeshift barrier overhead, or they just ducked away or turned their heads at the perfect time to avoid her glance, she could never make out their features.

People were still watching through the windows. They, too, were serendipitously faceless.

Siobhan had the creeping feeling that if she were to stomp up toward one of the windows and stare unblinking, when the coincidences keeping her from seeing them clearly ran out, they would be truly featureless, a smooth span of flesh in the shape of a head. *'If I grabbed one of these pedestrians and swung them around to look at me, what would I see?'*

Siobhan had read and heard enough horror stories to know better than to attempt such a thing.

As abruptly as possible, she pivoted into an alley to the right and flicked the switch on her dowsing artifact. When she hit the next street, she turned right again, going back in the general direction she'd come from. It was a bold decision, and she kept a sharp eye on the edge of the heavy rain as she hurried back the way she'd come. Was it her imagination, or had the Circle lagged behind for a couple of seconds after her abrupt change in direction?

She was suddenly alone, as if she had blinked and everyone else had disappeared. The pedestrians that had been walking along the sidewalk were all gone. There were carriages at the end of the street, but even as she watched they disappeared through the boundary of rain.

Clamping down on a rush of terror, Siobhan sprinted forward and around another corner. She was not fleeing mindlessly, but hoping against hope that she could outpace the spell, or at least the spell*caster*. Rain pooling between the cobblestones splashed out with every footstep, and she was grateful not to be wearing a dress whose skirt would get soggy and heavy.

That was when the streetlamps began to go out.

As soon as the barrier of rain in front of her passed the light, it died, flickering out even as it passed into the Circle. Only those that had been inside with her before the effect started remained lit. This happened twice more before Siobhan realized that if this continued, she would eventually be plunged into darkness. And she was showing no signs of being able to outrun the Circle of relatively lighter rain.

With only one streetlamp remaining, Siobhan skidded to a stop near the metal pole. She pressed herself to the side of the building nearest it, not so close to the light that she would blind herself to any attacks from the darkness. *'What kind of spell does something like this?'* she wondered. *'If I had to guess, it seems most likely to be some kind of mind-affecting curse that's controlling my perceptions. Either that…or something like what the old man did at Knave Knoll. This is all too big, too crazy, to be a standard spell actually affecting reality. And I'm pretty sure they don't have any pieces of me to work with, nor have I done something that would be an obvious method to anchor binding magic.'*

Siobhan took a deep breath and yelled out, "A spell like this comes from one of three sources. You are an Architect of Khronos, an agent of the Red Guard, or a Pendragon operative. Come out and face me!"

Her words were swallowed up by the seething choir of a million raindrops, and the crystal of the streetlamp began to flicker weakly.

5 6

AN EXCHANGE OF BLOWS

Siobhan

Month 8 Day 14, Saturday 8:50 p.m.

There was no response to Siobhan's challenge. As the streetlamp's light flickered for a painfully long moment, she slid her hands along the spell rod and found the segment for a light spell without looking. She snapped open that array and dropped her barrier spell so as not to give away her ability to dual-cast so early, then cast the light projectile. It was one of a few new spells that she had added to her utility list.

A bright sphere shot up and out in a long arc, reaching the edge of the rain barrier and exploding in a flash of eye-searing brightness as it impacted the almost solid wall of rain. The water diffused the light, illuminating a dark silhouette just on the other side.

They were too distorted by the flowing water for Siobhan to make out any details, but they clearly flinched away from the light projectile's point of impact.

Siobhan grinned. "Found you!" she intoned, sing-song and under her breath. She was, admittedly, feeling a little crazed from the stress.

This situation didn't feel like it could get much worse, but somehow, after months and months of feeling an inescapable foreboding, it was almost a relief for the thread to finally have snapped.

The silhouette hesitated, then stepped through the rain, which parted over around them like a bead curtain. They wore a leather mask depicting a human face that looked just a little too realistic.

'*Is that made from human skin?*' Siobhan wondered wildly.

But instead of eyes, or even holes to see through, it bore two flat stones, the perfect size for skipping across placid water. "Tch, you're no fun," they said.

Siobhan couldn't tell their gender from their voice, and their form gave nothing away either. They walked toward her sinuously. They wore a long leather jacket that reminded her of Professor Lacer's, though theirs was threaded through with bands of metal and embroidered with glyphs around the edges. Probably not a Pendragon Operative, which left either an Architect of Khronos or a Red Guard agent.

Siobhan instinctively tried to take a step back, only to be reminded that her back was against the wall. "What do you want?"

"To see the Raven Queen, of course. There are so many rumors about you, and the High Crown is rather upset about it. But even if not for him, we would want to meet you anyway."

"Red Guard agent," Siobhan said. An Architect could have just gotten Kiernan to pass along their request for a meeting.

The agent tilted their head to the side, hands on their hips. "Yes." They reached slowly into the inner pocket of their leather jacket and retrieved the iconic red shield symbol. "Do you know, the more we researched, the more intrigued we became? But you're a hard person to meet. We had to make it rain an *inconvenient* amount, trying over and over to get this rare opportunity for our destinies to align. Do you know how many people with some vague connection to the Raven Queen we've almost caught by accident? And you *almost* tricked us with that little appearance in Silva Erde."

"It only works in the rain?" Siobhan asked. She tried to remember if she'd been out in the rain recently. She had, in fact, on several occasions. Except that it had always been as Sebastien. It was possible they'd found and discarded her multiple times, not knowing who she was. "It's not sympathetic magic, then. How does it work?"

"We're well aware that you have some impressive defenses against sympathetic magic. No, this spell is entirely different. More like creating the opportunity for a moment outside of real space. With us both under the rain, all the threads of our destiny warp to allow us to meet for a time, so long as the spell persists. A fortuitous encounter."

Siobhan narrowed her eyes, searching the last few minutes of her memory with frantic precision. "Outside of real space?" she repeated under her breath. She could recall no coherent street names, house numbers, or business signs. The letters were jumbled in her memory, approximating words but not quite matching, the numbers sometimes turned the wrong direction and entirely out of order. It was too dark to see outside of the rain barrier now, but she was pretty sure none of the surrounding houses and buildings would have matched up with what she had memorized of the city.

"Space magic, some kind of separate pocket that approximates Gilbratha," she deduced. "What happens when the spell falls?"

The agent remained silent, their expression hidden completely under the mask as those flat pebbles stared at Siobhan in place of eyes.

There were several options, but the most advantageous would be that Siobhan exited the space where she had entered it, and the agent did the same, hopefully far away. "I was under the impression that your agents run in teams of at least two. Where is your partner?"

They weren't stupid or reckless enough to answer. Presumably, at least one more agent was maintaining this space-bending, "destiny-warping" spell. There could be more.

"What kind of Aberrant components would create an effect like this?" Siobhan tried. "Nightmare-type?"

They chuckled. "Really, the classifications are too vague to be effective. Some bureaucrat thought a consistent labeling scheme would be a nice accomplishment to write on his gravestone and forced that uselessness on the rest of us. But I think this would be labeled pretty squarely as a Mystic-type with an Eldritch facet."

Mystic-types were a long-range subset of Blight and Nightmare-types. They affected people or places far away from themselves, often with methods that were difficult to trace. Rather than shooting a fireball like a Scourge-type might, a Mystic-type would cause someone three kilometers away to spontaneously combust. And Eldritch-types had strange and abstract effects, often dealing with time, space, emotion, or some sort of weird concept like "truth."

Siobhan let out a long, low breath at the agent's confirmation. The Red Guard really were using Aberrants for components. She understood how useful that obviously was, but there was something repulsive about the idea.

The agent tilted their head to the side and broke the silence. "Did you know, one of the theories about you is that you're an Aberrant?"

Siobhan blinked the water out of her eyes. "One that can speak, like the Dawn Troupe or Red Sage? But...surely my actions, even from the most distorted accounts, are a bit more complex than that? If I were an Aberrant, it would be impossible for me to resist propagating whatever my magical effect was for this long. There would have been signs."

"Signs like the Raven Queen's fervent and growing following?" The smile was very apparent in the agent's voice. "Some Aberrant effects are subtle. But not to worry. You have been seen casting various spells on several occasions. As you probably know, Aberrants can only create their specific anomalous effect, no matter how amazingly lucid they might *seem*. Even if you had the strangest break event possible, an Aberrant would have been limited a little more than some of the reports indicate. But you *are* a blood sorceress, are you not?"

Siobhan remained silent. The Red Guard might practice blood magic themselves, as was clear from what had happened to the Moore family, but that didn't mean they would allow others to do so indiscriminately. After all, they also encouraged the belief that blood magic led to corrupted Wills and break events.

"We have proof. You've used a Lino-Wharton messenger spell on multiple occasions, and some flesh-molding spells, and perhaps even some nightmare curses."

"Nightmare curses?"

The agent shrugged. "Well, we didn't find firm evidence of that, so it's debatable. But with public opinion as it is..."

"Who would believe me if I protested?" Siobhan asked bitterly. "Is that why you're here, then? To arrest me? Or maybe you want the book?"

They hesitated. "We are interested in the book, of course, but that's not why you and I are here. No, we've met tonight to determine your fate. I am giving you an opportunity, real and finite. If you win, you deserve to survive. You'll keep your life, your autonomy, your name. If I win..." They reached into their pocket and pulled out a severed hand, which they gripped by the wrist. It was a little bulkier than a standard human hand, and at first Siobhan thought it had been skinned.

The hand was light pink, like candy rather than muscle, with slightly glowing veins pulsing through the flesh. Its tips formed claws, though without any actual keratin. The bright pink flesh simply came to a curved point. "If I win, then I will take all of those things from you. If you win, or can last three minutes against me, you'll be given the chance to make a request and have it heard. No matter what magic you use, you will find that every attack only brings you closer to defeat."

'*What an incredibly arrogant thing to say.*' It was meant to intimidate, of course, and Siobhan was loathe to admit that it had worked.

"Your three minutes start now." The Red Guard agent began to slip their own left hand into the wrist, as if it were a glove, and the flesh wriggled and throbbed as it sucked up their fingers. Their other hand reached into their pocket, likely for some kind of battle artifact.

Siobhan's hands moved quicker than they ever had in her life, snapping open another of her spell rod's segments even as she shot a second light projectile directly at the agent's masked face. She followed that up with three rapid-fire fabric slicing spells, modified from their original form into a rotating disk of air that was a lot more powerful over longer distances. She shot one of the slicing spells directly behind the light projectile and the following two to either side, hoping that at least one of the three would catch the agent's exposed neck, even if they tried to dodge.

They ducked, and the light projectile skimmed right over their head.

Siobhan reached in her satchel for the potions organized within.

The slicing spells, normally almost invisible, caught the raindrops as they shot through the air, scattering tiny beads of water and giving themselves away. The agent dodged the first two, and then *caught* the third with the grotesque pink glove.

The tip of the claws glowed, trailing a tiny after-image in the air as if they were slicing space itself. Siobhan's spell broke apart, energy spilling out around the thick clawed fingers with a distorted whooshing sound.

Siobhan's eyes widened and she almost choked on the proprioception philtre of darkness she was swallowing. She dashed the remainder of that vial and a second one against the ground between them and sprang to the side as the clouds of darkness exploded outward.

Her hand dug into her satchel again, coming back with her battle wand, which was fully charged. She shot three stunning spells through the darkness, her aim just a little off as her sense of self expanded beyond the confines of her body.

Despite the thick black clouds surrounding them, the agent seemed to sense the battle spells and was able to slide sinuously between them, catching only the crackling edges along their protective clothing. Their pebble-eyed mask still seemed to be looking right at her, and Siobhan's suspicion that they could still somehow sense her through the darkness gained weight as they began to walk toward her. They stretched out their left hand toward her, the flesh-glove's pink glow smothered by the black clouds. When they put it on, it had covered only their hand. Now it was creeping up their forearm, painful-looking tendrils stretching out and clamping down hard enough to cut off the blood supply.

Siobhan shoved her battle wand in her mouth, holding it between her teeth as she used her freed hand to rifle around in her satchel for a small component. She retrieved a short leather cord tied in a simple noose knot, popped open yet another spell array segment, and pressed the knot to the slightly sticky spot she had prepared in the component Circle ahead of time. She spat out her battle wand, switched its output to concussive blasts, and shot two of them while her Will handled a simple unlocking spell with detached output.

She poured every speck of power she could channel into the unlocking spell, even as she took her battle wand between her teeth again and opened the spell rod's stone-disintegration and gust spell array in quick succession. Both her mind and her hands worked with a nimble coordination and instant precision that she might have found gratifying in a less dire situation.

As the agent dodged both concussive blasts, every knot, buckle, and button on their clothing sprang open. The straps holding their mask to their head released, though it didn't fall away from their face.

Siobhan grinned fiercely around the shaft of her battle wand as she cast the stone-disintegration spell with the other half of her Will. It was rare for clothes to be warded against the very simple unlocking spell, which wasn't meant for clothing at all but, with the right application of Will, could be bent toward that purpose.

To the agent's credit, they didn't stop to try and retie their boots, merely grabbed their belt with their right hand and used the shoulder of their left arm to keep their mask pressed in place while they—seemingly instinctively— threw themselves out of the way of Siobhan's follow-up concussive blast in a contorted twist.

The agent was a much better duelist than she was, and if they'd been attacking as well as defending, she would have stood no chance. But they couldn't have anticipated that she could cast two spells at the same time while also attacking with a battle wand.

In the darkness, they dodged right into the rain-slicked tripping hazard she'd disintegrated into the cobblestones where she anticipated they would move. Their untied boots did nothing to support their ankles, and they began to fall.

Siobhan waved the spell rod, a detached-output gust spell gathering up raindrops and pelting them into the side of the agent's mask with enough speed and impact that they sounded like pebbles shot from a sling. She kept the spell going even as she turned to run, hoping to dislodge their creepy mask and maybe irritate their eyes.

She sprinted out of the dark clouds of her philtre, which were already beginning to thin under the effects of the rain. The air outside of the clouds was surprisingly sharp and cold. Siobhan wrung out every ounce of explosive speed Fekten had drilled into her, trying to reach the edge of the rain barrier.

She shoved her battle wand back into her satchel and skidded around the nearest corner.

She was growing closer to the rain barrier at first, but the single shining streetlamp was somehow ahead of her rather than behind. Siobhan's sense of space tripped over itself as she tried to reorient.

And then the Red Guard agent stepped leisurely around the corner a few meters in front of her.

57

———

A SEPARATION

Siobhan
    Month 8 Day 14, Saturday 8:55 p.m.

Siobhan slid to a stop in front of the Red Guard agent, falling on her bottom and scrambling back to her feet.

"There's no point in running. We're destined to meet under the rain," they said, somehow seeming both bored and frustrated. "I commend your ingenuity, but escape is futile without fulfilling the terms of our agreement. Without defeating me, this barrier will not drop. You have ninety seconds left." They had already retied and latched all of their clothing.

To Siobhan, it seemed as if she had been fighting for long minutes already. Her breath came in ragged gasps, her soaked hair and clothes were plastered to her, and on each exhale cold raindrops that kept trying to choke her splashed out from between her lips.

She straightened and dual-cast the gust spell and fabric slicing spell. The gust spell from the side, once again carrying a stinging barrage of captured raindrops, and the fabric-slicing spell originating right behind the agent's neck.

She hadn't really been trying to kill them before, because killing a Red Guard agent seemed like a great way to make sure they relentlessly hunted her to the end of the known lands, but now she was desperate.

Their grotesque pink glove sliced through her gust spell, sending the air spiraling out in random eddies and smoothly severing her connection to the magic. Siobhan braced for some kind of backlash, but she still had control over her spell array, and whatever path the energy might have taken to travel back to her had been severed just as surely as the spell itself.

But even as that spell failed, the disk of slicing air behind the agent's neck shot forward. Even if they had anticipated her trick, they wouldn't have had time to escape. It cut into the side of their neck but met some kind of protective ward that flared bright.

Siobhan mentally cursed the Red Guard's enchanted clothing budget.

That was enough warning for them to jerk their head to the side, but on instinct Siobhan created a second and third slicing spell just behind the first, so close together they were almost like two sheets of paper. The ward flared brighter, and yet brighter again as the agent stumbled to the side.

They lifted their right arm toward Siobhan and made a sharp motion, pulling back their wrist. A click sounded, almost inaudible beneath the rain, and a deep purple, arrow-shaped spell shot toward her.

Siobhan's warding medallion grew abruptly, bitingly cold, but it was lucky that she was already throwing herself out of the way to avoid the purple spell, because her medallion barely managed to nudge it off course by a couple of inches.

Siobhan clumsily stabilized her footing, throwing one hand out for balance to recover from her frantic lurch. She was not nearly as good at footwork as the agent. If this turned into a real fight, she would die. Or she would lose and be stripped of some concepts she found very important.

But to Siobhan's delight, her third slicing spell managed to overcome the ward and put a fairly deep gash into the agent's neck as it lost stability.

Blood spilled faster than it could be diluted away by the rain, but not enough to indicate a nicked artery. With an audible gasp, they lifted their right hand to press against their neck. Their head dipped down for a long second before it rose again, those flat stones staring at Siobhan once more. "I suspected, but you really are casting two spells at once," they said. "One might presume that you are simply masterful at quick-casting and switching between spells, but that's not the case at all. This puts your interest in Myrddin's journal in a new light. Did it teach you how to do that?"

Siobhan ignored them, taking the time they were talking to close some of the spell rod's segments so that she could get a better grip to open others. Her fingers were beginning to grow clumsy with the cold, or maybe just from too much adrenaline. She cast another two gust spells, starting a few feet out and coming at the agent from either direction. One, the agent caught with their glove—which was growing further up their arm and had already reached their elbow—and severed.

The other gust spell caught against their neck and picked up some of their blood as the rain passed, bringing it to Siobhan. She spilled the blood-tainted rainwater over the spider-silk array for a deafening hex.

"And where is your Conduit? Surely even a Naught wouldn't be so foolish as to cast through their own flesh? You remember what happened to your mother, don't you?"

Siobhan gave a choked exhale, as if she'd been punched in the stomach. It fogged in the cold air. She pulled on the deafening hex with a wrenching heave of her Will, even as she dragged a finger through the bloody water, disregarding the boundary of the Circle.

With a second swipe, she transferred the trace of blood on her finger to the center of the disintegration curse's array.

She had originally learned the curse to try and target her own blood, but had never practiced it on a living creature—only dead bugs and the like. Now, she pulled every thaum that one half of her Will could channel from the beast core pressed to her back, targeting the nearest match for that blood, which happened to be the open wound in the agent's neck.

It was immediately apparent to her that she did not have enough source material. Either that, or the barrier of a living thaumaturge's control over their own body, commonly known as the skin barrier, was harder to overcome than she had expected.

The deafening hex would last until they received healing, if she had done it right, so she turned her entire Will to the disintegration curse.

Siobhan channeled the spell at what was likely the very edge of her black sapphire's capability and fought for control of the Red Guard agent's body.

They reeled back, grabbing at their neck again, but this time with the severing flesh-glove. Its fingers sliced into their skin, only making the bleeding worse, and tendrils lifted from it as if seeking to invade the blackening, slowly eroding wound. They hissed in pain and horror, jerking the flesh-glove away.

Siobhan shot them with another concussive blast spell, but they crouched down.

Their right elbow drove down into their right knee. A metallic click hinted at the artifact hidden under their pants. They ducked their head as a shield of force bloomed out to absorb the blast in a ripple of light. Three more concussive blasts met the same futile end, and the agent lifted their arm and flicked back their wrist once more, releasing another purple arrow of magic.

Siobhan slipped on the wet stone as she tried to dodge and the spell shot over her. The ground hit hard, almost knocking her air out and dislodging her Will. She took a moment to ensure her concentration was in place before climbing painfully back to her feet.

A real-world, desperate magical battle was different from a controlled classroom environment. Siobhan's stamina was already fraying, and she doubted she could win against a Red Guard agent in a contest of Wills. She shivered convulsively as the cold bit into her soaked clothing.

Their neck was bleeding even more now as Siobhan's disintegration spell began to eat deeper, and they reached their right hand into their jacket pocket.

Siobhan saw only the handle of a battle wand before she lunged forward and past, the arm with her spell rod stretching out to snag them around the neck. She slid around behind them, squeezing their neck inside the crook of her elbow while she pressed the arm bearing the flesh-glove against their side with her knee. It was an awkward position, and she feared she had made an error, because she couldn't bring as much pressure to bear on the deadly appendage as she had hoped. Not enough to completely immobilize it. Siobhan slid her battle wand inside the collar of her shirt so that the handle rested just under her chin, then reached into her boot and pulled out her dagger.

The fleshy tendrils wriggled curiously under her pant leg, but none of them attacked.

She slid the dagger along the wound in their neck but didn't thrust it in. "One twitch of that arm and I spill every drop of blood inside you," she whispered as they struggled to move.

The agent stilled.

"Drop the spell!" she roared out. "Or your partner dies."

But of course, no matter what basic training in submission holds Professor Fekten had given her, Siobhan was an amateur at best.

The Red Guard agent threw their head backward and cracked the back of their skull into Siobhan's chin, cracking her teeth together and sending stars shooting across Siobhan's vision.

It was true that her spells weren't enough to win the fight against a Red Guard agent who was serious about fighting back, but Siobhan saw now that her response to that realization had been wrong. She lacked experience and had made a stupid mistake out of panic.

She dropped her hold on the disintegration curse before it could inevitably slip her grip, hoping that none of her teeth were broken. She tasted blood, then screamed hoarsely as her wrist was twisted until the knife slipped out of it. She tried to scramble backward, sure that a death strike with the flesh-glove's severing claws was coming, but their grip on her wrist twisted again and sent her collapsing to the ground to try to avoid the pain.

The agent laughed. "Oh, you're quicker on the uptake than I expected. You noticed our little trick, huh? But too bad, avoiding any high-powered spells and resorting to mundane weapons won't save you, either."

'*Little trick?*' Siobhan wondered.

They flipped around, shoving Siobhan to the ground with her arm twisted painfully and their knee to her chest as they wrested her spell rod from her other hand. Their flesh-glove had advanced all the way to their shoulder now, and would soon reach the bare skin of their neck. "I guess you won't freeze to death, but that really wasn't much of a danger in three minutes, anyway, no matter how much power you tossed around. We wanted to be gentle," they said, panting much less hard than Siobhan. "The human body isn't that durable. The other option was physical pressure. I've seen a man crush his own body like a grape with the backlash from a single battle spell."

'The cold,' Siobhan realized. 'It's the middle of summer.' She'd been too distracted by the nightmarish phenomena, and then the running and the fighting, to notice, but such a sharp drop in temperature wasn't normal. 'It's some sort of backlash from my magic. If I had been a more powerful thaumaturge, would I have frozen the both of us in here like some sort of giant, space-magic snow globe? Well, the Red Guard agent likely has some kind of temperature-controlling enchantment embroidered into their gear. So really, I would have just frozen myself.'

"Your three minutes are up," the agent said emotionlessly. "I win."

Siobhan wanted to argue that she was still alive, even if they had immobilized her, and thus hadn't technically lost, but knew it was useless. No one who acted like them would be willing to let her debate her way to freedom. She bucked upward, just hard enough to throw the agent off balance and free one of her arms.

An engraved wooden case fell out of their pocket, clattering against the stone.

Rather than attack with her freed hand, Siobhan brought it to her mouth, cupped into a small Circle, and breathed out, "Shadow mine, devour and arise."

It was a much-truncated version of the thrice-repeated chant this spell was supposed to require, but just like one could minimize the written Word of a spell array with enough practice and clarity, she had some leeway in the spell, which she'd probably cast a few thousand times throughout her life.

The shortcut did cost her, as her shadow was harder to control than normal, sluggish and a little clumsy when trying to take precise shapes, but it slid out from under her and rose up beside them all the same.

The Red Guard agent didn't notice at first. But when the rain that passed through Siobhan's shadow-familiar turned to sleet, adding sharp noises of ice on stone to the susurrus of rain, they stilled.

Siobhan could feel the surprise, and then the fear, run through them.

They turned their head to the side, slowly, to look at her shadow, their neck stretching up and back until they could see the huge beak poking out from underneath the black hood. "Ah."

Siobhan bucked again, wrenching a muscle in her back as she threw them off. She scrambled backward.

"What are you?" the agent asked, staring at her silent shadow-familiar.

Of course it didn't respond.

Siobhan lunged for her spell rod while they were distracted and managed to scoop it up, putting the agent between her and her shadow. She narrowed her eyes, gauging the distance to the rain barrier, which was getting harder to see as the rain within the Circle fell more quickly. *'If I could send my shadow out, would that disrupt the spell somehow? It's a little bit like passing the barrier myself. Or maybe it would be better to leave the shadow here to distract them and try to make it out myself again. I'll only get one chance, and it seems like the second option is more likely to save me if it works.'*

But perhaps the agent sensed something, because their head whipped around toward her, and though their mask and the flat stones over their eyes were expressionless, somehow Siobhan knew that they had focused on the hand in a Circle over her mouth.

They looked down, their eyes trailing from the tip of Siobhan's foot along the thin thread of shadow that connected her to the rest of it. Her control was weak; the spell had been cast too hastily, leaving the tether easily visible to one looking for it.

Siobhan sucked in a breath of panic as they swiped at it with their flesh-gloved arm, fingers scoring into the cobblestones as if it were butter.

In a moment of desperate inspiration, Siobhan detached the output of her spell so that it could not be severed.

She'd never tried it before with any spell that wasn't strictly based on modern sorcery, but it seemed to work just fine. The Red Guard agent sliced through the space where the tether between Siobhan and her familiar had been, and nothing happened.

And then a terrible vertigo washed over Siobhan. Her eyes rolled back in her head, and when she opened them again, she was on the ground. She vomited a little, the burning remnants of her dinner with Liza spilling out over her lips, over her fingers still cupped around her mouth, and mixing with the water flowing between the street's cobblestones. *'Did my Will break? But I can still think. Did someone else just have a break event…like what happened with Newton?'*

This wasn't nearly as bad as the sensory scramble and deep, horrifying wrongness had been when Newton broke, though. She still had a grip on her shadow-familiar, miraculously.

Siobhan's senses stabilized quickly, and she struggled to her hands and knees, scrabbling for her spell rod once more. Her battle wand was gone somewhere, kicked away in her struggle with the agent, perhaps.

The agent was already on their feet, or perhaps had not collapsed when Siobhan did, and had backpedaled to keep both Siobhan and her shadow in their field of view.

Siobhan followed the direction of their head to her shadow. Its shape had collapsed. Instead of the shadow-familiar's slender, macabre form under a tattered cloak, a roiling, amorphous mass of bubbling darkness writhed on the ground.

She could still feel it, somehow, and thinking of it brought back a momentary flash of vertigo. She tried to get it to reform, but it was as if her Will were trying to lift a boulder twice her size. The response was horribly sluggish, and it felt like the power sources of light and the heat of her breath were not enough.

The agent screamed, high and sharp, and backpedaled once more, head darting frantically between Siobhan and her detached shadow. The rain barrier around them thinned out, leaving the spatial distortion at the edge of the spell obvious.

Siobhan swallowed and slowly looked down at her feet.

Despite the light of the single remaining streetlamp against the surrounding darkness, Siobhan's body cast no shadow. Her heart began to race, speeding faster and faster as if trying to bludgeon its way out of her chest. She blinked and swallowed down a scream of her own.

A few whimpers still slipped through.

With deep, shuddering pants just on the edge of a sob, she redoubled her efforts to regain control of her shadow, to bring it close and reattach it, but though she was not completely powerless, it fought against her.

Rather than flatten and inch closer, it began to rise up. At first she thought it was regaining its most-used form from recent months. But as its form grew stable, she realized it was something entirely different.

It was a woman, wearing a fluttering cloak. Feathers sprouted out around her temple and between the strands of long straight hair that floated on an invisible wind. It was *her*, dressed as the Raven Queen and formed of darkness.

It was Siobhan.

And then it opened its eyes. It met her horrified gaze with bright, glowing-amber irises.

5 8

—————

A SEALED MEMORY

Month 8 Day 14, Saturday 8:59 p.m.

The Red Guard agent screamed, and as if that had been a trigger, a scream burst from Siobhan's mouth, too.

Siobhan's shadow waited patiently for them to run out of breath, then turned its head to the agent. "You had better take off that glove before it consumes you." It even sounded like Siobhan, though distant and muffled, as if heard through a wall.

Then it turned to her. "Siobhan, leave now. I will take care of things here, child."

Another moment of vertigo hit her, but this one was more cerebral than physical, brought on by the sheer inconceivability of the situation. Except it wasn't totally inconceivable. Those glowing amber eyes were familiar, and for a moment, a flash of blood and brain matter pooling out in front of the fire came to mind.

That was followed by a blink-fast vision of an egg with a yolk made of blood.

And then, even faster and on the edge of passing too quickly for her mind to grasp, a doorway filled with hungry sky.

Siobhan flinched back.

"Run," her shadow added.

And she did.

Siobhan sprinted without coherent thought, fleeing with rabbit-panicked, pounding footsteps. The only bit of rationality remaining within her chest allowed her to keep that one vomit-wet hand to her mouth. The Circle remained unbroken, and some tiny part of her Will was left behind with her shadow.

She did not want to know what might happen if she dropped her shadow-familiar spell while it was detached and outside of her control.

And if not for her ability to split her Will, the panic might have overcome even a lifetime's training to maintain concentration.

It was exhaustion that finally slowed her, her muscles burning and clumsy despite her pleas to continue. Her lungs heaved, screaming within her chest as if they had been scorched and blackened.

Sprinting at full speed had never been her forte, and she doubted she'd made it more than a kilometer at best. She stumbled to the side of a building and put her back to it as she looked around wildly for danger.

The streets were mostly empty, though the rain had lightened. The few pedestrians on the sidewalks noticeably avoided meeting her gaze or even looking at her. *'I probably look crazed and dangerous,'* she realized. *'Maybe I am crazed and dangerous.'*

The stones beneath her feet and the brick of the building behind her were still shadow-free. *'I am a woman without a shadow,'* she thought inanely. *'It sounds like one half of a bad riddle.'* Siobhan swallowed down another sudden surge of bile.

She recognized the street she was on, and the house numbers were coherent and in the correct order. No one was watching through the windows, and those few people who passed her in the street had faces, even if they weren't turned her way. All the streetlamps were working.

She could still feel her shadow, somewhere behind her. She had never stretched it so far from her. But then again, she had never detached it before, either.

When her breathing began to settle, she closed her eyes and thought she could almost tell what it was doing, sense its movements and its actions as it absorbed and expelled energy to stay coherent in form and affect the world around it even in minuscule ways. It was a little bit like sensing through the raven with the Lino-Wharton messenger spell, a little like the proprioception philtre, and above all reminded her of the bits of experience she'd had sensing the world through her shadow. Which made sense when she considered it.

She swallowed back a hysterical laugh at her own stupidity.

It was...standing before four Red Guard agents. At least she was pretty sure they were Red Guard agents. What the shadow had wasn't a sense of sight, even if it was absorbing the light reflected off of their bodies. *'So it had been two teams, then. The other two agents were probably lying in wait to act as backup.'*

She could distinguish the one that had fought her from the other three, who had a lot more gear and were carrying full-size shields. As Siobhan concentrated harder, she made out some movement and vibration.

It was talking. "I find it displeasing when people attack my followers."

Strangely, the burst of outrage that this description of Siobhan sparked helped to calm her down more than anything else. She pushed away from the side of the building, looking for somewhere familiar. Somewhere she could hide safely, both from any further threat from the Red Guard and from anyone who might happen to notice a strange woman without a shadow.

"But I will not attack you," Siobhan's shadow continued, gesturing to the agent wearing the mask with the flat stones for eyes.

Their flesh-glove had reached their neck and was stretching around it and up over their face.

"You can go ahead and take off that Aberrant before it eats you."

The Red Guard agents shared distrustful looks.

"What are you?" one of the new ones asked.

"I believe I am known for keeping my word. And even if you do not trust me, that thing is definitely going to kill you if you keep waiting."

As the flesh-glove pulsed and tightened some of the tendrils around the agent's neck, two of them finally gave in and spent a few moments freeing the host of the Aberrant parasite.

The fourth agent stood guard with their shield lifted and their gaze never wavering from Siobhan's shadow.

Removing the flesh-glove, now more like a flesh arm, required the use of some tinctures as well as brute force, and left strange wounds on the agent's flesh. Even to the shadow's perception their skin was completely white, as if it had been crushed or sucked dry of blood.

Siobhan turned the corner and walked down a long, narrow path that led to an abandoned gate house she had used to change once before. *'I had no idea you could use an Aberrant in such a way. Was it always just a hand, or did they cut that piece off the larger creature to take advantage of its anomalous effect? Do they have to treat it with something, like curing leather, or run it through some kind of ritual to make it useable as a tool? Obviously, the ability to sever everything, including the ties of magic itself, would have amazing utility.'*

The Red Guard agent took a healing potion to manage the glove's aftereffects and the wound on their neck, which looked quite gruesome, as if ten thousand ants had taken a bite and carried away little bits of flesh.

"Who are you?" asked the agent standing between her shadow and the other three.

One of the others, wearing a complex metallic monocle attached by a clamp to the side of his head, leaned forward and whispered in the speaker's ear.

Either her shadow's senses weren't strong enough to pick it up, or Siobhan simply wasn't skilled enough at interpreting its information, but she couldn't make out what he was saying.

"Is it not obvious?" Siobhan's shadow asked. "I am the Raven Queen."

Once more, Siobhan's outrage spiked. *'How dare that thing impersonate me!?'*

"The Raven Queen? Not Siobhan Naught?" the agent asked.

Her shadow clasped its hands behind its back and leaned forward playfully, eyes wide. "I think you should understand the importance of names." It straightened. "And since I won our little contest... What were the terms again?" It tapped a forefinger on its lips. "Your lives, your autonomy, and your names?"

The agents' fingers clenched around shields and battle artifacts, their knees loosening in case sudden movement was necessary.

"Well, I suppose I can leave you all three of those things," Siobhan's shadow said. "But I think I deserve some answers, at the very least."

"We never planned to harm her," the masked agent blurted. "It was just a test! We were hoping to gain some information, make sure she wasn't a danger to society, and maybe—"

"You never meant to *kill* her, perhaps!" Siobhan's shadow snapped, cutting the agent off. "But that is not the equivalent of meaning her no harm. Or do you think I have no idea about what goes on under the symbol of the Red Guard?" It sneered, gesturing to their shields.

Siobhan climbed a crumbling stone wall and sneaked in through the window of the abandoned gate house, both quite difficult maneuvers with only one arm free. She curled up in the dusty corner, trembling, and fumbled the light crystal coaster out of her satchel. *'What do I do?'* she wondered. *'What do I do now? That thing has taken my shadow. Can you...live without a shadow?'* It seemed anathema, and she wasn't even sure how such a thing could be happening, as it contradicted all the laws of Natural Science that she knew. *'I don't want to die. I haven't even had a chance yet, not really. I want to live.'* She repeated it in a whisper. "I want to *live*. Maybe Liza can help me. Or Professor Lacer. I just have to recover enough to get to them. I won't let the shadow-familiar spell go. I can keep casting it as long as I stay awake. I won't fade away. I won't break," she muttered rapidly.

Elsewhere, in the city that was not the city, the Red Guard agents bristled, shoulders pulling back and chins lifting. "We act for the good of the world!" declared the agent in front. "I ask again. Who are you? What are you? What is your purpose?"

"For the good of the world?" Siobhan's shadow repeated, ignoring their questions. "But what does that really mean? Quite a lot could be justified with the goal of saving the world, and against such *serious* threats. My desires are quite simple, and I think it should be clear that I have done nothing to make an enemy of you. Do not make an enemy of me, and perhaps there will be room to coexist. This world is large, after all."

Siobhan did not feel that this was likely to convince the Red Guard at all, but she didn't think she herself could have done better.

"The girl is a genius, and we both know how to hold a grudge. Hear me, mortals, as you have promised. Do not look for me. If I wish to contact you, I will have no trouble reaching you." And to punctuate this obvious threat, there was a sudden rush of confusion.

If Siobhan hadn't been sitting down already, she might have fallen over.

And suddenly, her shadow was in front of her again. It examined her for a moment, then mimicked her stance, sitting in front of her toe to toe. "Why did you run so far!?" it cried, angry and frightened. It was growing quickly tired, she knew, just as she knew that being so close to her sparked some undefinable longing. "Did you consider what might happen to me if I ran out of power before being able to return to you?"

Siobhan stared at it, wide-eyed. She glanced away from its amber eyes for a moment, to the spot where the tip of its toes touched hers.

And then it melted back into the floor, becoming two-dimensional and stretching underneath her and up the opposite wall where the light from the coaster by her side threw it.

Siobhan lifted her right arm, and her shadow moved with her, even though the amber eyes were still staring back at her. *'Did it really just…come back?'* But it had. She could feel its connection, just as she had felt its disconnection. *'It could be a trick. I can't let down my guard.'* She continued to keep her hand in front of her mouth and a spark of her Will active in the spell, even though her hand and elbow were getting stiff from being held in the same position for too long.

"What are you?" she whispered.

"At the moment, I am your shadow," it replied. Somehow, it was talking by vibrating the air. Considering that speaking without a tongue or lips was probably quite difficult, it was doing an admirable job of mimicking her voice.

"And when you are not my shadow?" Siobhan breathed, her back itching with new sweat against cold, damp clothes.

"I suppose there are a few ways one might describe me. For the moment… I suppose you can consider me a sealed, but not quite forgotten, memory."

Siobhan shuddered convulsively. As shameful and horrible as it was, her eyes burned with the first onset of tears. She clenched her teeth so hard her jaw creaked under the strain and tilted her head back. She would not cry.

She could still sense something from it, the way it noted the jump of the muscles in her jaw and throat, tracking every involuntary movement with a mean amusement. It was enjoying this.

A surge of hatred, sickly sweet and cold, swept through her.

"Raaz didn't quite catch everything," it said. "Don't you remember when we met? Don't you remember my name?"

Siobhan did remember, even if she desperately wished she didn't, but she wouldn't say it. "If you're sealed, how are you doing this? Taking over my shadow?"

Its amusement grew. "Well, you so kindly swallowed a beast core for me."

She gasped. "You absorbed the power from the beast core? *How?*"

It continued as if she had not spoken. "And then you detached a piece of your existence for me, one conveniently not bound by the seal."

Siobhan, for some reason, wanted to laugh. She tasted blood in her mouth.

"With the little cracks in said seal, it only took some effort and a bit of power to slip into the empty spot. I have to admit, I had such fun."

"What would have happened if you ran out of the power you absorbed from that beast core while detached from me, inhabiting my shadow?" she asked.

"I would have had to slip into someone else's shadow," it said, but Siobhan felt its uncertainty and fear. "I believe I would have had to consume the original shadow to take over. Quite difficult to do with a powerful thaumaturge."

Siobhan did her best to keep her face from reacting. *This,* she was sure, was a lie. It had made that up. It had no idea what would happen if it ran out of power away from her, but it didn't believe it would be anything good. "Can you take control of my shadow again?"

"Any. Time. I. Want," it said drolly.

That was a lie, too.

"Can you tell what I'm thinking?"

"Of course. I live in your head, darling. I ride around inside your thoughts." It wavered, though neither the light nor Siobhan had moved. "I know how afraid you are right now," it whispered. "But there's no need to be quite that terrified. I was very helpful tonight, don't you think? I protected you, at the cost of using up that meager bit of power. I was useful, and the borrowing of your shadow caused you no harm."

But she could still feel the truth of the monster, and the way its rapacious feeling of starvation only heightened at the dilation in Siobhan's pupils and the pulse in her throat. It didn't want to eat her, literally. It just wanted to kill her and use her corpse for its own purposes. Metaphorically. Maybe not her physical corpse. But something like that.

And it was true that she was afraid, but if it had really been able to feel her emotions, it would have picked up on the hatred that she was barely tamping down. Her eyes burned with tears, but not from fear or despair. She simply felt too much loathing for one body to contain.

It was because of this thing that Grandfather was dead. Because of it, she had lost everything.

Siobhan swallowed and firmed her voice. "What do you want?"

Its voice warbled a little more, growing faint. "I want you to remember me," it said.

Siobhan could feel its presence receding, leaving her natural shadow behind. Its eyes were the last to go, staring at her until the glow finally disappeared.

59

<hr>

COUNTERGAMBIT

Siobhan
Month 8 Day 14, Saturday 9:10 p.m.

Siobhan stared at the crumbling stone wall of the gate house. *'What just happened?'*

She examined her shadow for several long minutes, experimenting with moving it around and shaping it as she liked to see if there was any hint of the feedback or resistance she'd gotten from the being when it was present. But there was nothing. The spell was still harder to use than normal, but when she adjusted the Circle over her mouth to include both her hands and said the full chant, repeating it three times as the spell was always meant to be cast, any difficulty disappeared.

With great trepidation, she released the shadow-familiar spell, expecting something horrible to happen in retaliation. But nothing did.

Siobhan let out a shuddering sigh and collapsed to the ground for a moment, curled up around her light-coaster in a fetal position with her back to the wall. She shivered. Though it was a warm night, she had been chilled by the agent's magic and now the moisture in her clothes was beginning to evaporate. It felt like the core of whatever created heat within her was depleted.

Though eating was the last thing she wanted to do, she fumbled open her satchel until she found a pouch of dried nuts, meat, and fruit, along with her self-refilling canteen of water. The mundane act of eating made what had happened before seem almost surreal, but it also gave her strength.

She sat back up and used a spare bit of orb-weaver silk dipped in water to clean herself up, wiping away the smeared and running makeup and the traces of vomit. She took off her clothes, cast the water-falling spell in a pass from the top of the pile to the bottom, until the fabric was mostly dry and a puddle of water remained on the floor.

Then she changed into Sebastien's form and clothes, just in case, small protection though it was. The Red Guard might have needed her to be out in the rain for the spell they used, but she had no guarantee that they might not have some other way to find her. At least Sebastien's clothes were totally dry and warm. And somehow, it felt slightly safer in this body. She ran her tongue over her teeth, feeling the differences as she mentally settled into herself.

'What do I do now? The seal in my mind… Is it broken?'

Sebastien began to comb over the events of the last hour in excruciating detail.

'The greatest upcoming danger is the next time I go to sleep. If nothing happens then, it doesn't mean I'm safe, but as strange as it may seem, I'm actually not much worse off now than I was before. That thing has been in my head for about seven years, and I swallowed that beast core months ago.'

Sebastien took out a jar of bruise balm and began to catalogue her minor injuries, rubbing the alchemical concoction into any she found. She'd bitten the inside of her cheek, and even though skin-knitter was not supposed to be swallowed, she awkwardly rubbed a trace amount inside her mouth and let it sit.

'I don't think that thing knew I was able to sense its emotions and true intentions. It could have been trying to trick me, if it's much cleverer than I imagine, but I believe it was lying about being able to possess me at any time. Which means not feeding it any more power or detaching anything that could be considered part of myself for it to take control of.' She snorted in dark amusement. *'No trying to remember it. Anything it wants, I will deny it.'* She had to keep it weak while she worked on a solution.

Even with it inhabiting her shadow, she'd had some control. Just not *enough.* If her Will had been stronger, she might have been able to force her shadow to follow her commands anyway, reattaching it to herself and forcing that thing out. Or if she'd merely cast the shadow-familiar spell with the full, thrice-repeated chant, that alone might have been enough to keep the thing from slipping its bindings and overpowering her.

Sebastien closed her eyes and tried to search through her own mind. *'Is the seal broken, then? Or just imperfect?'* Because Grandfather *had* missed one of her memories, the one he didn't know she had. Sebastien shied away from touching it or thinking about it too directly. Surely, if the seal were broken, she would not be sitting here wondering and worrying about it. *'But I can't be sure that a failure like this didn't weaken it. Isn't that one of the ways to break a curse?*

Force it to fail in an edge case, or under some convoluted set of circumstances that don't quite fall under its purview, over and over until the binding breaks?'

So it was something to be cautious of, but at the moment she thought it was still in place and working as Grandfather had intended. Mostly.

The being had considered the Red Guard a threat, but, ironically, that had manifested in a seeming attempt to protect Siobhan from them. That could be simply because the Red Guard were capable of destroying it—and helping her. Or the Red Guard could just as easily be a threat to them both, and the being had been trying to avoid mutual destruction with its host.

'*What was the purpose of the Red Guard's actions tonight? It seems very strange that they would just go about trapping dangerous thaumaturges in the streets and threatening them.'* But when she considered the pieces that didn't fit together perfectly, another perspective suggested itself. '*It all hinges around that secondary cold effect that was directly increasing every time I cast a spell—no, a better way to say it would be every time I used magic or channeled energy.'*

The cold backlash was separate from the space-bending, destiny-controlling spell. Which, in itself, probably helped not only to keep the citizens of Gilbratha unaware but also protected them against anything Siobhan might have unleashed. It might even work on Aberrants, in which case really only the agent inside with her and maybe the one casting the spell would have been in danger.

'*What would have happened if I'd been as strong as they thought I was?'* Even one ultra-powerful attack or escape attempt would have frozen her to the point of uselessness, and every attempt to negate that effect would have only made it worse. Eventually she would have been defeated by her own actions. All the agent needed to do was stay alive long enough to allow that to happen. '*But why have the agent inside the barrier with me at all? Some kind of insurance? Or maybe…they were necessary.'*

"Oh," Sebastien whispered. "It was binding magic." In the beginning, they had explained the terms. Siobhan needed to "last" three minutes. If she lost, they would take her life, her autonomy, and her name. If she won, they would give her a chance to make a request and have it heard. And as a show of good-will, the agent started out by giving her "an opportunity," which, vague as it was, in the old stories would have clearly indicated that they were positioning themselves as at least a neutral party, if not an ally.

Without Siobhan fully understanding what was happening, the binding would have been weaker, but she hadn't *denied* the gift of an opportunity. And the agent had never explicitly said they were going to fight. They had only implied it, in word and in tone. The wooden box had fallen out of the same pocket they had been reaching for when Siobhan attacked. What was that? "A…dueling board game?" It looked similar to the much larger one Rhett sometimes carried around in a briefcase.

'If I'm right, that means that I was challenged to a contest by a "friendly" stranger. I accepted their gift but then broke faith by attacking. The agent even literally told me, "No matter what magic you use, you will find that every attack only brings you closer to defeat." It seemed like a threat, but it was a warning. An explanation of the terms.'

Sebastien let out a single, sharp laugh. "What a dirty trick. Definitely something out of a cautionary child's tale." She doubted such a thing would work without the extra power an Aberrant might bring to bear. The effect was probably strengthened by the agent remaining "friendly," by not attempting to do any harm in return. They had only attacked her after she first succeeded in causing an injury, after all. *'What would have happened if I sat down and played a three-minute round of the dueling game with them?'*

She would have had to be even more prescient than the agent had mistaken her to be to try something like that under the circumstances. *'They weren't trying to kill me. Maybe capture? Possibly even make some kind of bargain. But seeing as they were under binding magic, that agent was almost certainly telling the truth, even if everything they said was intentionally misleading. And I cannot see how there is any interpretation of an intent to take my life, my autonomy, and my name from me that I would welcome. It was horrific and entirely unacceptable. And what they offered in return, if I won, was mostly useless. There was no promise of safety or compliance with my request. Only "to be heard."'*

But even if, by some strange stretch of the imagination, the Red Guard could have been friendly, she found them as deeply untrustworthy as the thing sealed in her mind. And maybe almost as dangerous.

They would not help her out of altruism, and the only thing of value that she could really offer, or bargain with, was her ability to open Myrddin's journals. Everything else was a facade, and even if she attempted to deceive them, if she was ever called upon to prove herself, she would fail.

'How likely is it that they'll let things go—let me *go—with this?'* Technically, she had won the encounter. The thing controlling her shadow had made her request in her stead, and they "heard" it, but she highly doubted that was going to matter.

Having experienced what they did, the Red Guard were probably more worried about her existence now than they had been at the beginning of the night. Depending on what they decided her shadow was—though the most obvious conclusion seemed hard to deny—they would only be even more intent on her destruction.

Or whatever it was they really did to Aberrants. Somehow, Sebastien suspected that it was possible there were some fates worse than death.

'Well, I want to live. So what are my options?'

She could give up on all of her goals and plans and leave Gilbratha, or even Lenore, entirely. The thought brought up immediate and deep feelings of rejection. She had an irreplaceable opportunity here in Gilbratha, working with Thaddeus Lacer and Kiernan's faction of the History department. It wasn't just access to Myrddin's other journals, but also to the University archives, and, potentially, to the Architects of Khronos themselves.

Leaving the country would mean solving one problem by abandoning a possible solution to another. And there was no guarantee the Red Guard wouldn't still find her. They were an international institution and served no country or ruler, after all.

Another possible option was to seek protection from them. She didn't think Oliver and the Verdant Stags, or any of the other local gangs, had the power to stand against the Red Guard. For that, she would probably need the help of someone like the High Crown. '*I do have a very powerful bargaining chip in my ability to open Myrddin's journals.*' The High Crown might have been the one who sent the Red Guard after her, but that didn't mean he had the power to call them off. But he wouldn't kill her, and probably wouldn't hand her over to anyone else, out of fear of losing a monopoly on Myrddin's research if nothing else.

But that supposed protection would really be imprisonment. And as for the High Crown, she had tried to bargain with him once before. Her position was stronger now, what with Operation Palimpsest and the aftermath of his kidnapping attempt. But she almost certainly couldn't trust the man.

'*He tried to kidnap Theo and Miles. He had them put under that sensory deprivation spell.*' She had only ever seen Lord Pendragon's face in paintings and black and white photographs, but she imagined it now. A deep animosity filled her belly and twitched at her fingertips, urging her to curl them into fists. '*No. He is not an option.*'

She was unsure if any of the other Crown Families would have the power to protect her from the Red Guard. If there was one, she guessed it was most likely to be the Westbays. '*Unless there was a civil war, I can't imagine that being a viable option. Even if I could somehow convince Titus, what about the real lord of the family, his father?*'

The only other option would be to place herself at the mercy of the Architects of Khronos. She really didn't trust them, either, but if she was driven to desperation, it might be an option. Kiernan was one of their leaders, and he feared her. But considering their own goals and past actions, it didn't really seem like a stable organization or a safe place to entrust her wellbeing.

'*I wouldn't even trust them to take care of a pet. But I suppose it's an option to keep in mind if all else fails. Alright then. If I can't depend on external protection, what alternatives do I have?*' Working through her problems like this always helped to settle Sebastien's mind. There was something about the clarity that deliberate thought brought her that made her feel as if she had some small measure of control. Even now, some of the anxiety was receding from her chest and the muscles of her shoulders and back.

Liza's divination-diverting ward hadn't worked against whatever magical-law-breaking spell the Red Guard had utilized, obviously, but there was a small possibility that if Sebastien brought the problem to her, along with enough gold, she would be able to create something to protect Sebastien against similar attempts in the future. Maybe.

'*But there are also Red Guard defectors out there, right?*' she thought with building excitement. If she could find and hire one of them, she might be able to get that kind of ward. It would probably need Aberrant components, which she had no idea how to source and were probably catastrophically expensive.

But perhaps the Architects of Khronos had connections that she could use. Their number had included a Red Guard defector, after all.

And in the meantime, perhaps she could try to lower her perceived level of threat.

'*Ostensibly, the Red Guard would trust Thaddeus Lacer's opinion, right?*' They were only oath-bound to deal with Aberrants and thaumaturges who were a threat to others on a large scale. The average person might think that the Red Guard dealt with any and all petty blood sorcerers, but that wasn't the case.

It was also possible that, after tonight, Thaddeus Lacer would no longer consider the Raven Queen a possible ally, but if there was one person in the world she had a chance of convincing who could actually help her, it was probably him.

She ran through a dozen permutations of a conversation with him but soon realized that she didn't know him well enough to predict how he might respond to the Raven Queen. To a peer.

She checked the sky for clouds, and then, with a combination of grim determination, excitement, and trepidation, she returned to Siobhan's form. Or perhaps more accurately, the Raven Queen's form. Not some perky or disarming disguise, but the full long black hair, the red and black feathers, and lips painted so dark a red it was almost black in harsh, precise lines across her mouth.

After the last time she had found herself in woeful need of an outfit change, she had tightly folded some basic clothing at the bottom of her satchel. She pulled it out now, smelling the absorbed fragrance of various herbs as she pulled on a simple black dress and wrapped a velvet-trimmed cloak around her shoulders.

She checked the sky for clouds before she left, then walked north. She used the hood of the cloak to shield her features from those who still walked the streets at this time, and activated her divination-diverting ward with the dowsing artifact to turn away their thoughts.

She had no other student's token to activate the transport tubes, but according to the rumors, the Raven Queen wouldn't need to travel in such a mundane manner, anyway. She would simply need to return to the dorms as Sebastien Siverling when this was done, just in case.

It was easy enough to find Professor Lacer's little cottage.

Remembering some of the stories about what happened to students who tried to trespass, Siobhan stayed several meters back as she retrieved her spell rod. She used a detached-output version of the basic float spell to lift his door knocker and let it drop back to the metal several times. Then she closed her spell rod and tucked it back into her satchel. Hopefully he was not a heavy sleeper.

Almost a minute later, he opened the door with one of the dourest scowls she had ever seen him wear. His hair was loose around his face, and rather than his usual long jacket and suit combination, he was wearing a loose, soft shirt and pair of pants. His expression slipped away as he stared at her for several long seconds of silence.

She raised her left hand slightly. "Hello, Grandmaster Lacer." Her voice was slightly scratchy with nerves.

A combination of wonder and pleasure crossed his face as he sucked in a deep breath.

Siobhan realized that even his positive expressions were almost always tinged with irony, weariness, or pessimism, because his face looked different —younger—now that, for a moment, they were absent.

"You're here," he breathed. His hands flexed and twitched as if he had been about to make some aborted movement. Then he tucked his hair behind his ears very deliberately, the opposite of the flustered preening that she'd seen Damien do so many times. "Would you like to come in?" Professor Lacer asked.

60

ICARUS RISING

Siobhan
Month 8 Day 14, Saturday 11:45 p.m.

Siobhan inclined her head gracefully and walked past Professor Lacer as he held the door open for her. His gaze was fixated on her, and she imagined she could feel it hot on her skin as he examined her.

He waved her into his living room, which was surrounded by packed bookcases and sported one lone couch. Only a single lamp was lit, sitting on a small table by one of the couch arms and spilling gentle warm light. It was obviously more of a study than a room set up for entertaining guests. Professor Lacer quickly picked up the stacks of paper that had been sitting on either side of the couch—half-graded homework from his classes, by the looks of it—and motioned for Siobhan to sit.

He hesitated, looking at one of the empty spots on the couch, and then left the room, presumably to bring in a chair.

Siobhan looked around, her back ramrod straight and her hands on her knees. Suddenly, she was even more nervous than she had been on the long walk here. '*Where do I put my hands?*' she wondered. It seemed unlike the Raven Queen's persona to sit so primly, but how else could she arrange herself? She tried several different positions in quick succession and was trying to figure out if she could tuck one leg under herself and lounge regally to the side when Professor Lacer returned.

She froze, half leaned over, and ended up slowly tilting onto her side, her head coming down on the couch's arm. She stared straight ahead, too morti-fied to meet his gaze as he stood there staring at her with a wooden chair in his hands.

Slowly, so as not to seem too flustered, she pushed herself back upright and crossed one leg over the other. "Do you have anything to drink?" she asked, still refusing to meet his gaze. Maybe if she had something to occupy her hands with, it would help. And sipping on a drink could be a good excuse to stop and think if she needed time to figure out what to say. "Something hot," she added. The night was still warm, but her palms felt clammy, and she would prefer comfort over refreshment.

"Do you plan to be awake for the remainder of the night?" Professor Lacer asked. While he was gone, he had tied back his hair at the nape of his neck as he usually wore it, and his night clothes were suddenly wrinkle-free, as if he'd free-cast an ironing spell over himself.

Siobhan stared at him. "Yes."

"How do you take your coffee?"

"Plenty of milk and a dash of sugar."

His eyes trailed over her face and down to her hands. "I do not have milk. Or sugar. Also no cream."

Siobhan resisted the urge to ask him why he had even inquired about how she took her coffee, then.

He cleared his throat. "Perhaps some mulled wine instead?"

"That would be acceptable," she said immediately, regretting that she had brought up the subject in the first place.

The small kitchen was visible from the living room, and Siobhan watched, turning her head to peek over the back of the couch as Professor Lacer puttered around his kitchen. The image was surreal. Obviously, she'd known Thaddeus Lacer existed outside of his classroom, or the battlefield, or what-ever it was he did for the Red Guard. But she'd never imagined him doing something so mundane. She almost, *almost* blurted out, "Do you know how to cook?" as an innocuous conversation starter, but thank the stars she managed to keep her mouth shut until he returned with two steaming mugs filled with dark, spicy liquid.

He took the seat across from her, waiting for her to take a sip.

Instead she said, "I thought it was time we met, Grandmaster Lacer."

He leaned back, crossing one ankle over the other knee, and sneered slightly. "Long past time, I think. Curious, how you wrote to me denying any near plans for in-person appearances, and yet only a week later made a visit to that buffoon Kiernan."

Siobhan took a sip of her mulled wine to stall for time, staring at Professor Lacer over the rim as she tried to decipher his expression and tone. '*Is he upset? How am I supposed to respond to that?*' She swallowed, gave him a small smile, and said, "I needed to speak to him for a very particular reason. I suppose you were very much looking forward to meeting me, then?"

Professor Lacer scoffed and looked away, as if the very notion were ridiculous. "*Hardly*. I simply find your double standards to be rather rude."

Siobhan was…pretty sure that wasn't true. He had expressed interest in meeting her several times, even going so far as mentioning it to her as Sebastien.

"As is showing up in the middle of the night without even the courtesy to warn me in advance," he added. His tone was hard, but something about the words reminded her of how Theo bickered with Miles.

At least half of Siobhan's tension evaporated. '*Is this what Professor Lacer is like around his peers?*' Her smile grew wider. "Let me guess. You are surrounded by imbeciles day and night, and on top of that, all of the children you call your students. Every day that passes without any noticeable progress in accessing the content of Myrddin's journals is only more galling. A supreme waste of time that my presence much earlier could have alleviated, even if you hoped you would be able to manage it yourself. The High Crown grows ever more impatient and demanding, your peers sink further into desperation, and your patience wears ever thinner."

She had noticed the signs of his growing irritability in class. As the semester wore on, he'd been snapping at underperforming students and berating stupidity more often than normal. Even she, as Sebastien, had been treading lightly around him.

His expression might have once been inscrutable, but Siobhan had learned to notice the tiny twitches at the corner of his mouth and the way the creases at the corners of his eyes grew slightly deeper. Both signified pleasure, or perhaps amusement. She still wasn't very good at reading his subtleties. Usually, it happened when she had said something particularly clever or lamented the general state of uselessness that most people walked around in. "That is not an incorrect assessment of the situation," he said. "Are we to play a guessing game, then, Queen of Ravens?"

Siobhan shook her head. "It is late, and I have had a trying day. Let us set aside games for the moment."

Professor Lacer tilted his head to the side by a few degrees. "Are you tired? I have heard it said that you do not sleep. You mentioned you planned to be awake for the remainder of the night."

"I do sleep. Sometimes," she said. When he stared at her silently, she added, "I slept just yesterday. I know fatigue more intimately than you know the feel of your Conduit, but I am not that kind of tired. Surely you understand weariness? And please, call me Siobhan. You have no idea how tedious I find the obsequiousness and foolish titles."

"Of course. I suppose you may call me Thaddeus, in that case," he said, taking a sip of his mulled wine. As she had done earlier, he stared at her over the rim while he did so. "Have you come for your tribute, then? I admit I am surprised it took you so long to retrieve it, though it has remained safe in my custody."

She leaned back, suddenly curious. "I did not come for that, specifically, but I am curious to know what you have prepared for me. You may present it, if you are ready."

He raised his eyebrows. "You do not know what it is?" When she shook her head, he stood and moved into the other room. "I had assumed you would have deduced it by now. Unless you are playing a game with me, despite your stated weariness, and I am about to discover I do not have what I think I have."

Siobhan sipped silently at her wine; she had no idea what he was talking about and did not want to make herself seem stupid.

Professor Lacer brought back a small lead box, presenting it to her with a subtle flourish.

Siobhan took it. Within, a familiar ring was nestled in velvet. "My mother's ring," she whispered. She examined it for flaws, but except for the fact that the celerium set within the silver band at the perfect depth to press against the skin was still intact, the only difference from the one she had retrieved from the Gervin branch manor was the small flaw in this one.

It even still had the rotating base that could be used to activate the Loomis anti-awareness field and chameleon effect embedded into the silver.

Her gaze snapped up to Professor Lacer. "What is this? How do you have it?"

"I take it from your reaction that you did not know I acquired it from Malcolm Gervin's vault some time ago. I thought it would be a fitting tribute. But I never imagined you would not have learned of the replacement by now. It seemed you had a real interest in…family matters."

"I did know about the replacement. I just thought it was…someone else." Siobhan picked up the ring, running her fingers over the familiar tiny scratches in the silver. She slipped it onto the middle finger of her left hand, which she suddenly realized looked quite like her mother's had, before the woman died. If Ennis hadn't sold off the celerium from her mother's heirloom, and *maybe* hadn't stolen the book on purpose, did that change anything?

But their conversation through the bars of his cell at Harrow Hill repeated in a flash, along with all the other times he had disappointed and endangered her. Those were not misunderstandings or accidents, and Siobhan found that she harbored no regret for her decision to sever that man from her family.

She wanted to try casting with her mother's ring, so bright and incredibly pure except for that one tiny blemish at the edge. It was rare to find a piece of celerium so small—only finger-width in diameter—that could still channel a

Master's capacity. Of course, knowing more about celerium than she had as a child, she knew that the gem's size meant it could probably only handle five to six thousand thaums, no matter how pure it was. That capacity could be achieved with about twenty years of dedicated spellcasting.

That was why Naught mothers passed it down to their daughters so early in life. If Siobhan's mother had only lived a decade or so longer, the ring probably would have become Siobhan's directly.

Siobhan looked up at Professor Lacer, her eyes narrowed. "You replaced this ring with a diamond one, correct?"

"Yes."

Siobhan's voice grew hard and clipped. "And why, pray tell, *Thaddeus*, did you create fault lines that would cause it to shatter at the first attempt to cast through it? Were you attempting to sabotage me? I would think *you*, of all people, would understand the danger. A break event does not only jeopardize the thaumaturge, but all those around them."

Professor Lacer did not look the least bit contrite. "But you are a Naught, correct? As I understand it, your family has some resistance to the over-whelming effects of casting through your own flesh. If your Will were not nimble enough to drop the spell as your Conduit shattered, you would have a backup option." He watched her unblinkingly, as if he could draw some kind of information from the smallest of her reactions.

That was a more callous response than she ever would have expected from him. "Are you aware of how my mother died?"

"Miakoda Naught? I have heard Ennis Naught's version of the story."

"Ennis No-Name," she corrected immediately. "But if that is the case, you should know that our bloodline does not protect us. Not truly."

"That may be as you say, but...you are here before me and seem just fine. You are not so weak that such a simple trick was your undoing. And I did leave a hint. The fault lines were noticeable, if you examined the diamond closely."

Siobhan swallowed. She simply hadn't assumed someone would have booby-trapped a Conduit.

"I left the ring partly as a message, and partly as a punishment for anyone that might try to use it in your stead. You seem the type that would find that amusing."

Siobhan stared at him as if seeing him for the first time. "I think you have some misconceptions about my sense of humor."

"Do I? Well, I look forward to learning more about you."

"Aren't you a member of the Red Guard? Do your vows not preclude you from taking such risks with other people's lives?"

He smiled enigmatically, without the crinkling at the corners of his eyes that indicated the expression was real, and took a long swallow of his wine.

"The chance of an Aberrant forming from a break event is quite small, and considering where that would likely be and who it would affect, I deemed the risk acceptable. Gilbratha has several teams on hand to deal with rogue magic incidents, considering the thaumaturge population. Malcolm Gervin's only child, the only true innocent who was likely to have been affected, is of University age and spends the majority of his time away from home," he said rather than answering her actual question.

"And the servants? Are they not innocent? Or his wife?"

"I would judge them to hold only different degrees of guilt. And before you ask, the threat beyond that was quite negligible. Even if, in the *extreme* edge case, the worst were to happen, weak thaumaturges create weak Aberrants."

"Newton Moore was a weak thaumaturge. And yet the Aberrant formed from him killed several who I would consider to be true innocents."

Professor Lacer nodded. "Truly regrettable, and I do *mean* that. If I had the choice, I would have saved them even at risk to myself. But that Aberrant was not an existential threat. And as a statistic, the victims did not even create a blip in the number of deaths that occur in Gilbratha every day."

Siobhan reached up to run a fingertip over one of the feathers sprouting from her hair. "How would you react if your student deliberately sabotaged a Conduit like that?"

His gaze dropped from her feathers to her eyes. "Are you…chastising me?" he asked, faintly surprised.

"Do you deserve to be chastised?"

His expression fluctuated rapidly for half a second, then smoothed again. He stared down into the contents of his mug for a moment, then said, "Perhaps."

Just as she was trying to process her surprise, he said, "I take your point, Siobhan."

The sound of him saying her name—her original name—derailed any other thoughts.

"I have been curious. Why were you there that evening? I don't believe you caused the Moore boy's break event on purpose."

Siobhan let out a long, slow breath and ignored his question. "Let me make another guess, Thaddeus. There is much that I do not know about this world, but I am learning all the time, and it seems to me that the Red Guard, and possibly the Crowns, and maybe even those who run the University, have no true intention to stop break events. Why would that be?"

"Is it *possible* to stop break events?" he asked, mostly in the leading way that meant it was a rhetorical question, but with a hint of attentiveness in his gaze that suggested he thought she might have a different answer.

Ideas about what the subtext beneath his non-answer might mean spooled off in every direction, but she forcefully reined in her attention. "I suppose the

Red Guard might even find weak and easily subdued Aberrants to be benefi-cial. Quite useful, for the kind of work your agents do. In fact, that leads me to the main reason for my visit. I met four of your colleagues earlier this evening, and while they might have had fun playing with their various toys, I have to say I found the experience quite unpleasant."

Professor Lacer had been about to take another drink, but instead he set his mug aside and rubbed at his beard. "Are they all still alive?"

"They are. I recognized the backlash effects of the binding magic immedi-ately and kept my response measured, but in the end..." Siobhan sighed, trying to seem as exasperated as possible. "I was forced to activate a particular defensive measure. You see, my grandfather spent quite a while on a project meant to protect me before...well, before he died. He was capable of producing self-charging artifacts, and he wanted something that would be both thorough and versatile. The end result was partially unfinished, but I still found it quite useful."

Siobhan told him the story of her encounter with the Red Guard earlier that evening, trying to make herself seem as competent as possible. In her version of events, she had been offended by the agent's words, curious about their strange methods, and then done her best to escape without serious harm to them or herself once she realized the trap she'd fallen into. Unfortunately, the agent had grown frightened and tried to hurt her, forcing her to resort to other methods to protect herself.

"The shadow-familiar spell has quite a few useful aspects, but it really isn't as powerful or dangerous as it might seem. And I want to be clear that it *is* magic, and not an Aberrant, because with the way I managed to slip your colleagues' grasp..." She sighed, rubbing the bridge of her nose as if she had a headache. "I can already imagine the kind of rumors that might follow."

Siobhan looked up at Professor Lacer and leaned back, waving a hand deri-sively. "Surely you have noticed how the average person completely fails to use rational analysis when coming to conclusions, especially about things that surprise or frighten them? It is almost sad how easily people revert back to mysticism and creating fairy tales to explain reality, even when that requires them to discard obvious contradicting facts. And somehow, I doubt that every individual who bears the red shield can be considered an outlier. More likely, they are just more of the same, and even less likely to question themselves because they are so sure they know the truth of this world, the secrets that most people are blind to. People in that position are susceptible to forgetting that they can be wrong, too."

She was paraphrasing many of the things that he had said to her, so she knew her argument should sound reasonable.

Siobhan raised one eyebrow. "Unless you wish to assure me that members of the Red Guard are trained to actually *think*, and are not susceptible to the instinctive biases and aversion to real work that stops lesser people from finding the truth, rather than finding an easy answer?"

Professor Lacer smiled at her, without a hint of irony or weariness. He lifted his hand to cover his mouth and then laughed as if he couldn't hold it in. "I think you know that I cannot argue. I admit, this conversation is…as refreshing as I had hoped. But what would you have me do?"

"Can you act to mitigate their stupidity? Before they work themselves into a tizzy and set out on a hunt? And please instruct them not to accost me so rudely in the future. If they want to communicate with me, they can do so through you."

"So what should I explain to them about your…shadow-familiar? If I might make a guess of my own, your grandfather's work is related to the method to encode and encapsulate a consciousness or trap a being within a memory that you were inquiring about."

Siobhan hesitated before answering with a slight nod.

He smiled again, but this time without the joy. "Well that is truly fascinating."

"Would it be a problem if you revealed that?"

Professor Lacer rubbed at his chin, looking into the distance. "Not in the way you mean, I think, but there are certain factions and individuals who would likely be enticed by the implications and possibilities."

Siobhan nodded slowly, involuntarily mimicking him by raising a hand to her chin. "They might want to try creating another Carnagore, or the like."

"Do you think that might be possible?"

"Of course it is possible. If Myrddin did it, someone else can too. But whether it could be done based on the principles of my shadow-familiar…of that I am not sure. So, will I be safe from harassment if you pass along this information? I refuse to be a test subject."

"The only way to be totally crossed off the possible hazards list is to allow a comprehensive, in person assessment at one of our field bases. But considering your situation, I would not recommend that course of action for one who values their freedom as much as yourself. While you might not be the kind of threat we are required to deal with, I think several people would find you too valuable to let you slip from their grip once they had you. However, if I arrange myself as your contact and downplay the reality of your shadow-familiar, you might get away with it."

"If you wish, feel free to explain to them that I can control the form and actions of the shadow, similar to how one would with an illusion spell."

"You are certain that it has no other capabilities? No dangerous effects? I listened to the Pendragon operatives' debrief after your retrieval of the people they had kidnapped. In particular, I am referencing the fact that it crawled down a man's throat and seems to have driven him to a mental break, if not a magical one."

Siobhan looked down at her shadow, trying to keep the doubt from her face. *'The being trapped behind the seal…could it possibly have been exerting some influence on the shadow-familiar spell? I have no idea what it's really capable of. But…I think I would have noticed. I would have felt something. And it was* lying *about being able to possess my shadow at any time.'*

She raised one eyebrow. "It absorbs heat. And it never truly crawled inside that man. It was just pretending. It shrank as it passed his lips, never getting farther than the back of his tongue. It is not actually corporeal. At worst, he might have experienced a headache from the roof of his mouth growing too cold."

Professor Lacer snorted in amusement. "I see. I will pass that along. I believe you will be able to avoid intense scrutiny. Perhaps not forever, but for a time."

Siobhan supposed that was the best she could hope for. "Nothing is forever."

61

HERMENEUTICS

Sebastien
Month 8 Day 15, Sunday 1:15 p.m.

THE NEXT DAY, Sebastien walked a long, winding route through Verdant Stag territory on the way to the Nightmare Pack's fighting arena. It was sunny, without a trace of clouds in the sky, but she wanted to be triply certain she was not being tracked or followed. Her divination-diverting ward didn't so much as twitch, and though she was aware that she might have no idea if some more arcane magics were being used, she noticed nothing alarming.

It was apparent that Oliver had been busy improving his much-expanded territory over the last few months. It wasn't just the quality-of-life things like the clean streets and the fact that there was a noticeable decrease in homeless people in the poorer areas.

It seemed like at least one building on every street was being renovated, or torn down and rebuilt. She passed at least six different areas where old, run-down buildings were being razed and replaced with tall, multi-story apartment buildings. The one farthest along was already being filled with appliances, the interiors painted a bright, cheery yellow. Every single one had a window large enough to climb through and an external stairwell to escape the building in case of emergency.

Each apartment was small, but Sebastien imagined living there would be comfortable and hopeful. They had been designed with a future in mind for each inhabitant, and Sebastien remembered how Oliver had once spoken of the diseases that stemmed from despair.

There were small shop fronts that Sebastien didn't remember, which brought to mind the loans that the Verdant Stag provided.

Every street corner had a vivid green flag, and people were wearing clothing that looked new, in the kind of bright colors that would normally never be seen in the Mires. *'Though I guess this can't really be called the Mires anymore,'* she mused.

She walked until her shirt stuck to her back, soaked in sweat, but couldn't take off her thin linen jacket in case the leather holster under her shirt became visible. Tiny insects forced her to wave her hands in the air constantly, until she eventually gave up and decided they could crawl in her hair and drink her sweat as long as they didn't try to bite her.

She found the house with the private garden shrine, and after a few minutes of watching, slipped into the tunnel that led to the Nightmare Pack's fighting arena. She changed into Siobhan in the darkness of the tunnel.

When a giant spider tried to ambush her from the darkness, coming only inches from slamming into her head, she dearly wished for the battle wand she'd lost in the fight with the Red Guard agent. In the end, she was forced into a wild fight against the creature using dual-cast slicing spells and the light projectile spell.

She won, but arrived at the iron door on the other side of the tunnel out of breath and rather disheveled.

The man who opened the door took a long look at her, and then very carefully did not stare as she passed. The whole arena had been closed for the day, despite the gold it would cost, as a safe place for Theo and a select group of trusted people to celebrate his birthday. A gift from the Nightmare Pack to the Verdant Stag.

Siobhan gave her own, much less extravagant, gift to Martha, then headed up to one of the private booths that overlooked the party area, so as not to disrupt the atmosphere. It would be hard for many of the adults to enjoy Theo's birthday party or act normally with the Raven Queen in attendance, after all.

Down below, Theo was busy telling a small group of children and several adult gang members the "Tales of the Raven Queen." But of course, the story featured himself as the hero. Things might have spiraled quickly into the realm of the unbelievable, but Miles was there, constantly muttering contradictions to everything Theo was saying, until the whole storytelling time devolved into bickering between the two.

Gera, who was standing on the edge of the group and listening to the children's stories, turned slightly and lifted her face toward Siobhan. She mouthed, "I'm sorry," and bowed deeply. She must have sensed Siobhan's presence, even this far away from the main party crowd.

"No need," Siobhan responded in a murmur that had Miles turning toward her like a dog with perked ears, despite how impossible it should have been to hear her. "Let the children have fun." It actually rather fit with her gift to Theo.

Katerin had contacted her several times mentioning that Theo wanted, more than anything, for Siobhan to attend his birthday party. And so she had rented a camera obscura and used it to take photographs of illusions that told the story of Theo the Dragon Hunter and his sidekick, Empress Regal, then had the photographs printed and bound into a book.

Miles tried to get up and leave to join Siobhan, and then Theo noticed what was happening and tried to trip him, but Gera caught Miles before he could hit the ground and kept both boys from leaving.

Siobhan raised a hand to her mouth to cover a chuckle.

But Oliver had noticed her too, and he wasn't so easily dissuaded. It only took a few minutes for him to make his way up to the private box. He leaned against the balustrade next to her, his forearms on the banister and his hands clasped together. "I talked to Katerin," he said abruptly. "And she told me I was being an idiot. Our relationship could never have been free or equal, with the way it started. She told me I was showing my rich childhood and sense of entitlement, that I couldn't imagine what it must have been like for you. But I want you to know, I really didn't ever plan for this. And while I cannot say for sure whether Ennis was compelled to steal the book, I certainly didn't order something like that."

Siobhan remained silent, considering his words for some time before speaking. "I didn't tell Ana to sabotage the Gervin textile commission. She did that without my knowledge, and not even out of any particular malice toward you. And…even if I had known all the consequences of my plan on the day of Ennis's sentencing, I still would have gone through with it. I had to stop the divination attempts. But maybe if I had trusted you a bit more, I would have told you about it."

"I suppose I could say the same about the book."

"And now, we both have a big secret of the other's," she said, turning to face him directly. "Have you ever heard of the term mutually assured destruction?"

One side of Oliver's mouth quirked up in a small, wry smile. "The perfect recipe for a stable alliance? One with neither indebted to the other."

"Perhaps. Have you heard from Kiernan about whatever is going on in Osham?"

Oliver sighed and let his head flop forward until his chin touched his chest. A lock of dark hair spilled down over his forehead. "He wasn't at his house and hasn't responded to any of my missives. I contacted Tanya Canelo, but she didn't know anything else, and I didn't want to put her in danger out of respect for you. It hasn't even been enough time for the team I sent to Osham to arrive. I'm…worried."

"Hmm. Well, the Red Guard came after me last night."

Oliver's head snapped up. He opened his mouth, closed it again, then choked a little. After taking the time to clear his throat, he said, "Your news is much more shocking than mine."

Siobhan told him about the incident, much more honestly than she had to Professor Lacer, though still not the full truth. No one could know about the thing inside the seal.

Oliver wasn't as surprised to learn the truth of how the Red Guard operated as she had been. In some ways, despite his altruism, he was less naive than her.

She added a quick explanation of the measures she had already taken to mitigate the danger. "It's not enough. I need to do more, and be proactive."

Oliver rubbed his thumb across his lower lip. "Do you think the growing Raven Queen mythos might be an issue? The agent mentioned it specifically, and from what I can tell, it's only spreading."

Siobhan rubbed her forehead. "What do you mean? Even more rumor-mongering about how I'm a flesh-eating creature who's planning to Sacrifice all of Gilbratha in a blood ritual?"

"Well, more like the opposite. I meant the people who have been praying to you. Mostly among the poor commoners. It's quite popular in both Verdant Stag and Nightmare Pack territory. There's even a woman going around writing up some holy book and holding church services where she talks about you? Some basic prayers are becoming standardized, and your 'believers' have taken to wearing feathers and other raven paraphernalia to signify their alliance—and most importantly—their protected status. I think the rumors about your vindictiveness are actually what people find most appealing. They feel like you'll make their enemies pay to the last drop of blood if retribution is ever called for. As long as they've paid in advance or can be called upon for a useful favor sometime later."

Looking down at the people below, Siobhan caught at least three people wearing something that might have been "raven paraphernalia." Some tiny feather earrings, a wooden pendant of a bird in flight, and an actual bird's skull hanging from a strip of leather. "How could I have believers!?" she exclaimed. "I've obviously never answered any of their prayers!"

"Well, according to the rumors, you have answered *some*. And I know this sounds counterintuitive, but I think your 'fickleness' might actually be working in your favor in this case. Everyone who prays to you knows you answer the prayers you want to, not the ones they want you to. You prefer your payment in advance, and if you seem not to be accepting their offerings, they suspect that you also have no intention to answer their prayers. Just the other day I heard a woman who seemed to be, well, *bragging* about the fact that you were not all-powerful, which was actually somehow proof that you were real and could be relied upon, and that you needed time to rest and regain your strength before you could 'manifest' again."

"What about the fact that I made an appearance in Silva Erde? Don't people think I left Gilbratha?" she tried.

Oliver gave her a pitying look. "You can move through the shadows, traveling as fast as the sunset. And be in several places at once, watching through the eyes of any raven. And—"

"Okay, stop! I understand." Siobhan squeezed her eyes shut, clenched her jaw, and let out a muffled whimper as she stomped her feet in place. *'I don't want to be involved with something like this!'* she screamed internally. *'Why!? Why are people doing this?'* If no one were watching, she might have dropped to the ground and flailed around screaming like a child having a temper tantrum. *'Just for once, would it be too much to ask for things to be easy?'*

"It's too late to stop it," Oliver announced cruelly. "But at least we can mitigate the potential future damage. Before people do something dangerous in your name, like a blood Sacrifice of thirteen cows or burning an effigy of the High Crown."

"Why are these ideas so specific?" she whispered, horrified. "Have you heard people discussing that?"

Oliver placed his hand on her shoulder sympathetically. "I cannot stop the rumors, but we could spread new ones, or even secret informational pamphlets. Something to guide what cannot be stopped. You'd need to decide what direction you want to take things, though. Maybe you should talk to the woman who's writing a book about you?"

"Stars above!" She took a deep, stabilizing breath. "I need to think. I need time to think about…this."

"Fair enough. Do you want to go down there and perform some magic for Theo's birthday? He keeps talking about this raven that Katerin is convinced is imaginary…"

"Oh, do you mean Empress Regal?"

Oliver's eyebrows rose. "Don't tell me…"

"She's entirely real. Perhaps I should summon her?"

THE STORY CONTINUES in *A Practical Guide to Sorcery Book V: A Cauldron of Bitterness*

Get it now: https://geni.us/COBEBWide

. . .

If you would like access to:

- Illustrated excerpts from Siobhan's grimoire and portraits of the characters
- Exclusive short stories/bonus chapters/deleted scenes not available elsewhere
- The chance to read the latest pre-release chapters of the upcoming book as I finish them
- And other story-related goodies and opportunities...

Consider supporting me on Patreon:
https://www.patreon.com/AzaleaEllis

GLOSSARY OF MAGICAL TERMS

Aberrant

Thaumaturges who have lost control of the magic they channel, but instead of dying, have been changed. They are usually much more magically powerful than they were in life, and almost always have physical mutations. Some Aberrants merely mutate into a dangerous beast-like being, rabid for death and destruction. Some mutate into grotesque or phantasmagorical forms, and have esoteric magical effects. Some mutations remain minor, while the mind and powers are twisted insidiously.

Uniformly, an Aberrant is no longer human, having lost their previous thoughts and desires. Almost all Aberrants are malicious, even those with seemingly benign effects. It is believed one is more likely to break and become an Aberrant with a corrupted Will from casting immoral magics.

Adder stone

A stone with a hole worn through the middle by natural means, it is said that adder stones impart clarity of mind and vision, and one can look through the hole to reveal illusions. Useful on their own, or as a component in spells.

Adhel juice

Mixed with honey, it creates a strong sticky substance. It can be cleared through applying oil.

Adze

A magical insectoid creature most prevalent in the few areas of the Tataroc Desert with year-round water—and static communities—the adze is a nocturnal bloodsucker. Upon its hatching, the first person with an eligible disease that the adze drinks from will be cured, as the adze absorbs it, but after that all other victims will instead be infected by its bite. Each time a disease is absorbed, it is added to the adze's collection and passed on along with the others. This can lead quickly to the annihilation of entire communities, making the adze one of the most feared magical beasts. Anyone who hatches one is to be put to death, along with all those who knew and did not stop them.

Alchemy

A ritual form of spellcasting that uses organic and inorganic components to create magical concoctions. The most common method of performing alchemy is through the use of a cauldron to create potions, philtres, draughts, and tinctures. It is the least expensive way to save a particular magic for instant use at a later time, but not the most efficient way. As with all ritual spells, the magic woven into alchemical concoctions is semi-permanent.

All-purpose antidote potion

A mild antidote to common poisons and venoms, the all-purpose antidote is best used on mild irritants, or to buy time for a more thorough solution to serious toxins. It can be used in lieu of a sobering potion to diminish the effects of alcohol.

Animation spell

Animation spells give temporary and false life to an inanimate object, such as in the case of the Glasshopper's eponymous confections.

Anti-anxiety Potion

Also known as a calming potion, this is a weaker and less addictive version of the elixir of peace. The University infirmary keeps a large amount on hand for students struggling with stress.

Anti-coughing philtre

Suppresses the urge to cough. As coughing is often useful to clear liquid from the lungs, this philtre is used when there are extenuating circumstances, like broken ribs, that may cause more damage.

Arcanum

A magical institution, teaching "secrets" of magic and the arcane.

Artificery

A craft of magic that embeds a pre-cast spell in an object for later release, or enchantment—changing the object's state. Battle wands, light crystals, and self-cleaning chamber pots are examples of artifacts. Enchantments and Wards are a sub-set of Artificery.

Auger

A drilling artifact created in Osham. Though meant for mining and construction, it can also be utilized to brute-force wardbreak.

Autography spell

This spell, frequently used in divination, allows the user to free write without conscious thought.

Avery Park

An area of greenery around southwest Gilbratha.

Avis Siverling

A court sorcerer who served the Krell line and married a daughter of King Krell.

Ball of light spell

Causes a spherical section of the air to glow with the illusion of a ball of light. Brightness, color, size, and location can be controlled.

Banshee

A humanoid magical creature that is dangerous to humans, and attacks with their voice through incapacitating screams and songs with a soporific effect.

Banshee's Breath

A battle philtre that creates a swirling storm that shrieks like the deadly wail of the banshees it was named for. While not deadly, the philtre may cause hearing loss and destruction within its area of effect.

Bark skin potion

Grows a protective layer of bark over the skin of the drinker, while still allowing them most of their range of motion. While not as strong as plate mail armor, it is much lighter, and more effective than chainmail against atmospheric attacks. When damaged, chunks of bark will fall off, which can be useful against spreading attacks like rotting curses or acid.

Battle wand

A wand-shaped artifact charged with offensive spells. For law enforcement, this is most commonly a stunning spell.

BCE

Before the Current Era.

Beacon spell

An esoteric spell that creates an invisible and untraceable tracking mark.

Beamshell tincture

A highly addictive magical potion that infuses the user with energy, often used to treat narcolepsy or insomnia. Beamshell creates an energy debt, and addicts frequently push through it until they collapse, starved and dehydrated. It's even riskier for thaumaturges, with high chances of Will-strain.

Beast core

Beast cores, which resemble raw gems, are harvested from dead magical beasts, and can be used to power spells in place of other sources of energy. They come in many different colors, though the color itself is not as important as the brightness and clarity, with brighter and clearer cores being easier to draw energy from.

Beast cores contain a total energy value of thousands of thaums, up to millions of thaums, and are generally rated either by their total energy value, or their per-second capacity if they were drained completely over the course of an hour.

When drained, beast cores will shatter and crumble, and cannot be recharged. Due to this, they are a rather expensive source of power, and are most commonly used for emergencies, for high-power spells that make it inconvenient to use lesser sources of power, or by those who have the coin to spend in exchange for convenience.

Beast cores become exponentially more expensive as their quality increases, similar to celerium.

Beast king

A figure shrouded in mystery and fear, the beast king is sleeping in Silva Erde, deep below the ground. While details about him are vague, diviners consistently find that if he wakes from his long sleep, calamity will follow.

Berserker potion

Temporarily increases a soldier's performance at the cost of some serious side effects, including addiction.

Bewitchment hex

Draws the attention and interest of the victim.

Bini frog

A magical amphibian often found in northern peat bogs, when under duress or unable to find others of their species, the Bini frog will change sexes, allowing themselves to lay eggs as a female and then fertilize them as a male. Notably, their male form has corrosive skin, a defensive which may have led to an initial imbalance of sexes and required this adaptation.

Black star sapphire

A gem that can be used (as can many gems) as a Conduit. It is not as robust as celerium. As components, star sapphires can be used in space-bending spells, and it is said that a black star sapphire was used in a spell to travel within and through shadows faster than any mortal could otherwise move.

Blight-type Aberrant

These Aberrants spread their anomalous effect, physically or otherwise, expanding their area of influence. If allowed to get out of control, they can cause true devastation. The first priority for this type of Aberrant is containment.

Blood clotting potion

Poured on a wound, clots blood and can stop excessive blood loss. It can allow someone to wait till medical attention arrives when otherwise they might bleed out. Not typically considered a battle potion, because it does not have offensive effects.

Blood Emperor

The Blood Emperor was the leader of the Third Empire, also known as the Blood Empire. His invading forces, from an unknown land beyond the northern ice oceans, conquered the continent about three hundred years ago. His empire was eventually overthrown, but his policies shaped much of modern society even after the Third Empire's downfall. However, atrocities committed in the name of learning and power caused a severe backlash against all forms of blood magic and its practitioners.

Blood print vow

A spell that binds two or more parties to an agreement spoken while casting, bound by a thumbprint of blood. If at least one of the vowers cannot cast magic, a third party binder must be present to do so.

Blood-regeneration potion

Boosts blood regeneration, but takes time and places strain on the body.

Bogles

Known for disguising themselves as scarecrows or other inanimate objects when spotted, bogles may cause mischief to human homes and settlements, but rarely serious harm.

Brillig

A powerful race with strong affinity to magic, now extinct, or close to it.

Caidan's Theorem

If distance is measured in meters, a divination spell with the base cost B will require B x distance/100 ^ (B/100) thaums to cast.

Calming spell

Forces calm and docility on the target.

Carnagore

Myrddin's most famous self-charging artifact, a horse made of white metal, who he rode into battle. The name Carnagore has roots in the words "hooves of dawn."

Cat's cough

An herb. Commonly smoked, it is addictive and gives a raspy, deep voice over time.

Cataclysm

An apocalyptic event that destroyed civilization over ten thousand years ago, and which is still shrouded in mystery.

Chameleon spell

Allows a non-living object to partially blend in with its surroundings.

Charybdis Gulf

The sea inlet that bisects the main area of Gilbratha from the Lilies—the rich area where many of the nobles and socialites live—to the east. The Charybdis Gulf is dangerous, containing magical water beasts that will drown a swimmer and even capsize small fishing boats, yet despite this remains a large source of income and food, especially for the poorer citizens.

Cinder Stag

A powerful Aberrant that is contained within a sundered zone, the Cinder Stag still manages to affect the world outside the sundered zone with karmic flames of retribution that can follow a chain of cause-and-effect back to its source.

Circle

Facilitates the three main elements of magic. It places a physical boundary around a spherical domain controlled by the thaumaturge, signifying that the things within are theirs to trade away and change as they wish.

Cockatrice

Two-legged dragon-like creature with a rooster's head. (And more or less the shape of a chicken.) Weasels are their natural enemy. Can be the familiar of a witch.

Cold box artifact

Sometimes referred to as an ice box, this is an artifact which keeps the contents placed within it chilled or frozen by siphoning out their heat.

Compass divination spell

Uses two halves of a spelled, linked bone disk as a sympathetic beacon and a stick with one burnt end. Using one half of the bone, the burnt end of the stick will point toward the other half, like a compass.

Comprehensive Compendium of Components

A restricted book that contains its namesake, including components that are illegal and unethical.

Concussion-modified fireball spell

Adds a force effect to the fireball spell, similar to an explosion.

Concussive blast spell

Shoots ball of force which expands and weakens with distance, but can cause severe damage to a human (particularly their internal organs) or even break through walls at close range. It is often visible as a waver or fogginess in the air, but much less conspicuous than a fireball or stunning spell.

Conduit

Channels the thaumaturgic energy being converted as a spell is cast. For most sorcerers, this is a celerium crystal, which is resistant to the destructive effects of channeling magic. Witches may use their familiars as Conduits, and those sorcerers who cannot afford celerium may use lesser gems, such as diamonds or sapphires.

Contact stunning spell

Set into a ring artifact, releases the spell on firm, sudden contact, like a punch.

Continue-motion spell

A complex, finicky spell that allows the caster to demonstrate an action as one of the inputs of the spell. The spell will continue this action, *exactly*, for as long as it is empowered. It is good for things like stirring a pot continuously, spinning thread, or weaving cloth, which require relatively simple, repetitive movements.

Coppers

Law enforcement, named for the copper nails in the soles of their boots, the distinctive sound of which announces their approach wherever they go.

Craft
Specific path of magic: Sorcerer, Artificer, Witch, Magician, Shaman, Animist, Gestura, etc.
Deafening hex
Causes deafness, usually temporary, though some variations will persist for a period of time after the caster stops focusing on the hex. Some variations can be used to some effect against a banshee in place of a vibration-canceler.
Devil
They possess living beings.
Dingleberry bushes
Dingleberry bushes are named for their small, hard brown fruits that smell like feces and rot even before they fall to the ground.
Disintegration mine
A magical land mine developed in the Haze War.
Dissolving tincture
A concentrated alchemical concoction that will dissolve other substances it comes into contact with, the dissolving tincture has many variants that can be adapted to the type of material the alchemist wishes to dissolve. Similar to a strong acid, but more versatile.
Distagram
A long-distance messaging artifact recently created by a University graduate that operates by using different frequency bands.
Diviner's sight
Special magical sight of the divination realm, which reveals that which might not be seen with the normal eye. It is a catch-all term that includes any ocular enhancements, such as the ability to see in the dark.
Doorjamb alarm ward
A small ward spell, carved into the underside of a door, will alert the caster when the door is opened.
Dorienne invisibility spell
A spell that uses the self-camouflaging dorienne fish to create true invisibility through which light can pass. The dorienne fish itself sees through its skin and adjusts its pigment on one side of its body to what it sees on the other to appear invisible.
Dowsing artifact
An artifact composed of two glass and copper spheres which use divination to try to locate an object or element. Siobhan uses her dowsing artifact to activate her anti-divination wards and move about the city unnoticed.
Dragon scales
A magical component sourced from the notoriously contrary, spiteful, and difficult creatures.
Drake
A miniature dragon creature, the size of a house cat. Not as intelligent or powerful. Can be the familiar of a witch.
Draught of borrowed gills
This concoction allows someone to breath underwater by dropping a small, living fish into a mucousy concoction and then gulping the whole thing down whole. The fish is kept alive within a bubble of potion within the stomach for a few minutes, during which time the fish's ability to filter oxygen from water is transferred to the drinker's lungs.
When the fish dies and the draught's effect wears off, the drinker must expel the water from their lungs quickly to avoid drowning. Often, use of this potion in dirty water can lead to complications and long-term side effects, so it should not be used recreationally.
Dream-walking
Often practiced by shamans, it is a form of divination that sends their consciousness into the dream of another, most often for exploration or healing purposes.
Dreamless sleep spell
Keeps one from dreaming, using crystal and eagle feathers as components, and cast on the pillow

Siobhan uses, or anywhere under her head. Uses alcohol and herb tincture as the Circle, which evaporates quickly and isn't uncomfortable to sleep on.

Dryad

A creature of living wood, shaped like a humanoid woman. They come in different sub-species of trees, and can be very small when young. Sometimes they disguise themselves as trees before the unwary or unobservant, and short bursts of activity are often followed by long periods of "sleep."

Dueling board

A game where the pieces shoot fake spells at each other and dodge attacks under the control of the players.

Dysentery sustaining potion

Diluted in large amounts of water, will keep a patient with diarrhea or dysentery hydrated with a small amount of calories and the immediately necessary electrolytes and minerals, and slightly slows the rate of expulsion, allowing absorption.

Earth disintegration and stone creation spell

One of Professor Lacer's practice exercises. Dirt or stone can be turned to sand and back again to stone using either transmutation, which creates the effect through natural processes, or through duplicative transmogrification, which copies the properties of existing material.

Earth-aspected weta

Magical beast with a very tough hide.

Elcan irises

A deadly, flesh-eating plant with purple-streaked flowers whose long, tapered petals open and turn to follow prey as it passes, releasing sweet-smelling pollen into the air. They lure their prey with their beauty and the soporific properties of their pollen.

Eldritch-type Aberrant

A rare and highly dangerous aberrant whose anomalous effects are based on abstract concepts.

Elemental Planes

The five known Elemental Planes are accessible through planar portal spells from the mundane plane, where humans and other mundane races live. Each Elemental Plane corresponds to an element: Radiance, Fire, Air, Water, and Earth. Creatures, plants, and even the water and soil from the Elemental Planes will be imbued with the energy of their plane, and are powerful spell-casting components. Each Elemental Plane has sapient creatures, some of which are humanoid and can even cross breed with humans.

Elementals

Beings from the Elemental Planes. On the mundane plane (Earth), they are most often encountered as the familiars of witches, who use them as a Conduit to channel magic. When sapient and humanoid, they have specific labels.

Radiance—Angels

Fire—Demons

Air—Sylphides

Water—Undine

Earth—Erdgeist

Elixir of euphoria

An alchemical concoction which, in low doses, combats depression, but is more often sold recreationally for the eponymous euphoria. Highly addictive.

Elixir of peace

Imparts a sense of well-being, and can be used in small doses to combat depression and anxiety, or for its recreational effects in larger doses. It is used in war to give soldiers who are dying some peace in their last moments.

Enenra

Magical beasts native to the East, enenra are creatures that seem to be made from smoke and tattered cloth, said to be born from bonfires and visible only to those of pure heart and mind.

Energy-reflecting spell

A general-purpose ward. A more expensive and inefficient defense than setting wards against more specific spells or incidents.

Enkennad's draught of shadowed concealment

A powerful potion that allows the user to disappear from view, blending subtly with the shadows.

Erlkings

Their name coming from the words "alder king" the erlkings are a magical creature found in woodland areas, sometimes conflated with the fey by the ignorant. They are known to secrete poisonous substances from their hands, the most potent of which allows them to kill with a simple touch, and to enjoy chasing children and lost travelers who have intruded on their domain.

Erythrean horse

Horse with partial magical lineage. They are extremely expensive, but don't look much different from a normal horse.

Etherwood leaves

A luxury leaf for smoking. They are dark blue. The smoke is smooth and calming, great for blowing smoke rings, but nonaddictive.

Ever-inking pen artifact

Comes as a set with an inkwell. Spelled to automatically refill the ink cartridge of the pen with ink from the inkwell whenever not in use. More expensive ones refill based on the rate of expenditure, and some very expensive ones maintain a folded space within the pen's ink cartridge, so the user never needs worry about their inkwell running dry.

Fabric cutting spell

This spell creates a short-range slicing blade of air that extends outward in an arc, the shape of which can be controlled to some degree by the caster's Will. Unlike many similar spells, it doesn't require the target to be within the Circle, as it uses compressed air as the cutting edge. At longer distances the cutting edge, visible as a faintly glowing shimmer in the air, degrades severely.

With practice and enough power, it can be used to overcome the inherent magical barrier that living creatures possess, and injure a human or animal.

Fever reducing potion/balm

Cools the head, with some cooling to the body as well, along with pain relief. Encourages comfort, allows sleep, and should be given in conjunction with a sustaining draught.

Fey

A powerful race with strong affinity to magic, now close to extinction. They were supposedly so agile they could dance between raindrops without ever being hit.

Fey flowers

A fluorescent flower prized as a component for its rarity and power.

Fiend-type Aberrant

These Aberrants have monstrous physical mutations and use physical attacks. Any magical effects are touch-based. These are the most common type of Aberrant, and generally the weakest.

Finger bone divination

Human finger bones can be used in (illegal) divination, after being processed and etched with symbols and glyphs. The diviner will shake them while casting the divination, throw them, and then read the spell's output in the way they have fallen, with certain glyphs in certain positions or crossing others. Depending on the amount of bones and what output options have been etched into them, this type of divination can have nuance and impart a greater amount of information than similar methods like dice-throwing or card reading.

Fireball spell

Shoots a ball of fire at about 12 meters per second.

Fleetfoot potion

Fractionally increases movement speed, but not reaction speed.

Flesh-fusing potion

A more powerful version of the skin-knitting salve, this potion is meant to seal larger wounds, ideally after the use of the blood-clotting potion.

Flicker-feather bird
Small birds that blink in and out of visibility with every flap of their wings.

Forest of Nod
The mythical forest that is said to be the center of the world, if it ever existed, the Forest of Nod's location has been lost to time. Some suggest that it still exists, beyond the known lands civilization was able to reclaim after the Cataclysm, and some insist that it is, in fact, one of any number of forests that now go by a different name.

Fortner's
A high class, bespoke clothing shop.

Free-casting
Casting magic at will, without the stabilizing external Word of a physical spell array, a ritual, or special movements. The Word, and sometimes the Circle as well, is instead held solely in the mind. This feat is extremely difficult, and only a few are proficient in it.

Garden of wonders
An element of a children's tale, which the University Menagerie seems to exemplify.

Gasping-tentacles spell
A spell which creates temporary tentacles growing from a solid, nonliving surface. Used to bind or obstruct movement from a distance, and often employed as a nonlethal method of detainment. Gone wrong, can strangle a victim to death.

Gestura
A sect of thaumaturges who practice a different type of craft, controlling the elements through sympathetic connections to their body movements. They are slowly dying out due to the difficulty in learning the craft and its lack of versatility.

Glow slime
A phosphorescent magical slime that slowly releases the light it absorbs during the daytime or from decaying plants with an eerie glow through the night.

Glow spell
Perhaps the most rudimentary light output spell possible, can cause an object to let off a diffuse glow.

Gold duplication spell
A duplicative transmogrification spell that copies a source of matter. As with most attempts to create matter through magic, only the most skilled thaumaturges can create a truly perfect copy that will have the same magical properties as the original, and thus duplicated gold or other substances are often worth less than the authentic originals.

Golden apple
Fruit from a magical tree that closely resembles a gold-skinned apple, and are said to improve organ function and thus increase a person's lifespan.

Gregorian snail
Magical animal. Mucus can be used as a thickening agent in most salves and lotions, especially those meant for the face.

Gremian
A small, humanoid stick creature that desperately wishes to fly once again, and goes so far as to nest in the trees and crack eggs on their bark-like skin to feel closer to birds. They are an excellent familiar for a beginner witch to practice a binding contract with.

Group proprioception potion
It allows everyone who drank from the same batch instinctively know where the others were for a short period of time. Its main component is a magical sea lichen that connects and disconnects any singular part of itself at will, still somehow communicating with the greater whole to capture prey and then confine it until it starved to death.

Grubb's barrier spell
A weak barrier spell that only protects against physical projectiles, with a minimum requirement of under 200 thaums to cast.

Gryphon

Creature with the head and wings of an eagle, with the body, legs, and tail of a lion. Can be domesticated and flown.

Guld fish
Minnow-sized fish that glint as if they are made of precious metals polished to a high sheen.

Gust spell
Creates a simple gust of wind, with the size and speed depending on the size of the Circle and the amount of power fed to it.

Hag
A magical humanoid. They have a natural predilection to the dark, and good night vision. They have some facility with hexagon/hexagram spells, dealing with balance. Hags who integrate with society may sell good luck talismans (or cursed objects.)

Hangover-relief draught
Taken in doses of a liter or more, this draught rehydrates, replenishes electrolytes, and mitigates the pain of a hangover. The University infirmary stocks many doses.

Harrow Hill Penitentiary
Gilbratha's jail, a stout stone building in the shape of a cross, within a circular wall that encloses the grounds.

Headache-relieving salve
Minty. An alchemical concoction that relieves headache pain and helps to rejuvenate the senses.

Healing potion
Generalized healing potions, of which there are many different variations of different strengths and capabilities, are an extremely effective method to preserve an injured or ill patient's life. They can be used for most types of wounds or illnesses, and are both convenient and practical. However, due to the price of components—many of which are from the Plane of Light—and the abundance of magical energy packed into these potions, they are expensive.

Hellfire
Is sometimes bright neon green.

Hemorrhaging curse
This curse causes the target's blood vessels to rupture and encourages excessive, forceful blood loss. It can sometimes be recognized by the shape of its glowing force as it travels.

Henrik-Thompson
A measure of scale for maximum Will capacity. It is measured by a crystal ball in an array that filters incoming energy and outputs a portion of it as light through the glowing crystal. It's the most widely-used metric, likely due to the fact that Will-capacity is the easiest to test, and often shows correlation to the overall caliber of a thaumaturge's Will. The brighter the light, the more power (thaums) is being channeled per second.

Homunculus
Very small people, who outwardly seem indistinguishable from humans, but are argued to be a different species due to their facility with certain magics.

Human fingernails
A component in some spells, human fingernails are illegal due to the restrictions against blood magic.

Humphries' adapting solution
An alchemical concoction that can be spelled directly into the veins to take the place of blood in a blood-loss emergency. Expensive, and the shelf-life isn't super long, so it may not always be on hand. Can also be used to keep creatures from the Plane of Water alive on the mundane plane, which was its original purpose.

Hydra
Multi-headed snake. The number of heads ranges from two to nine, with more heads generally indicating a more powerful, intelligent creature, as information processing and bodily processes are divided among the heads based on their individual priorities and specialties.

Ice lion
A predatory, large, shaggy cat that lives near the northern ice oceans.

Ignore pain spell

Muffles pain slightly, allows mind to detach from the focus pain draws, effects wear off quickly once spell is released, but it can allow someone to prepare to heal themselves. Recommended strongly against using this to do things like set bones or put sockets back into place, in case the sudden shock of pain causes the caster to lose control of the spell. Muffles pain by about 15%, so of moderate usefulness. May be good for exercise pain. Esoteric magic.

Impotence curse

A curse that removes the victim's ability to successfully complete intercourse, either through removing their libido, or suppressing their physical ability to copulate.

Improved hearing spell

An esoteric spell that uses hands cupped behind the ears to gather and direct amplified sound, and thus improve selective hearing.

Information collating spell

A spell used to search through, organize, and classify information in a wide range of documents.

Injury-protection ward

Makes physical damage less likely over a set diameter. Very expensive, but nebulous and thus not very powerful. Still can make a difference, either over time, or in dangerous circumstances.

Jentil

Giants, who are known for building megalithic monuments.

Kaiseki Ryori

A decadent, luxurious, high class dining establishment specializing in Eastern cuisine. They have many private rooms and are owned by the Nightmare Pack.

King Krell

The ruler of Lenore before the Blood Emperor, who had a daughter who married the court sorcerer, Avis Siverling.

Kitsune

A sometimes fox, sometimes woman. In human form, the kitsune will still have her tails, more depending on how old and powerful she is, up to nine. They often use their tails to cover their bodies, wrapping around it in place of clothing, and are considered seductively attractive, though they do not appear often in Siobhan's part of the world.

Knave Knoll

A jail that temporarily housed the Morrow prisoners for the Verdant Stags and fell in the attack orchestrated by the Architects of Khronos.

Kreidae spider

A magical creature known for stealth and ambushes. Its silk is highly coveted for its transparency and use in camouflage or invisibility cloaks.

Kuthian frog

Has sedative saliva, which is dried, powdered, and used as a component in stunning spells. Upon release from the spell, the treated saliva quickly degrades and becomes inert.

Landrum's nourishing draught

As with many spells, there are multiple variations of the nourishing draught.

Should be diluted in large amounts of water, which will thicken with the concoction. It contains vitamins, minerals, and electrolytes, as well as some complex sugars/starches. When given frequently, will keep the patient hydrated and with the resources their body needs to continue fighting. The nourishing draught should be created over low heat, to avoid killing the vitamins. Sometimes, it is then dehydrated for long-term storage.

Some versions also induce repeated swallowing, for patients who are insensate and cannot wake to drink. For those with extended nausea, some versions can also help them keep something down, though not stop diarrhea.

Laughing poppy

A component in a sedative potion which is known to cause allergic reactions, preferred for its ability to tranquilize without causing depression.

Light crystal

A non-celerium crystal made into an artifact spelled to release light on command. The rich use them in place of candles or lamps, as they are much brighter and require less maintenance. But, though they also last longer than a candle or lamp, they are expensive enough that the common person cannot afford to buy one, even if it would save them money in the long run.

Light Sacrifice
Light can be used as a source of magical power just like heat, matter, and kinetic force. Converting light within an area to magical power will create an area of darkness, as the light is absorbed before it can pass through or be reflected.

Light-show spell
Cast on an object, this spell creates many pulsing lights of different colors, and is meant to draw the eye and be visually enchanting. Good for traveling performers, distracting wildlife, or to cast on the harlequin above a baby's crib

Limb-regrowing potion
A newer, specialized type of regeneration potion that uses lizard components, such as that of the axolotl, to regrow missing limbs.

Lineage test spell
A divination spell that uses a piece of the target to confirm the existence of other members of their bloodline over several weeks. It is known to give unreliable results, and does not by itself allow one to track down the supposed offspring.

Lino-Wharton messenger spell
A power spell with several pre-requisites. It binds a raven to a controller, allowing the controller to speak through the raven at a distance to transmit messages, or to complete simple tasks.

Liquid fire potion
When exposed to air, this potion catches fire.

Liquid stone potion
Expands like an aerosol foam and hardens quickly upon contact with air. Can be used as a barrier or a splint for broken bones, among other things. Not permeable to air, or malleable once hardened, so it can suffocate if it lands on the face. Liquid stone's expansion is purposefully inhibited when in contact with living flesh so that those who carry it do not accidentally entomb themselves if a vial breaks accidentally.
It is softer than normal stone, similar with a similar durability as sandstone.

Loomis anti-awareness field
A spell, in artifact form on Siobhan's heirloom Conduit ring, that dissuades people from noticing or remembering a small object.

Lore-master
A scholar who focuses on the stories of old, on the little-known or forgotten facets of magic and the creatures who use it.

Lotus flowers/bulbs
These flowers grow in the mud. Each night, they return to the mud, and then miraculously re-bloom in the morning. In transmogrification, they signify rebirth, self-regeneration, cleansing, and enlightenment.

Lugubrious
A powerful Aberrant.

Lung-sealing philtre
When breathed in, this philtre creates a sealed bubble inside the lung, which can apply internal pressure to a puncture wound and keep someone from drowning in their own blood.

Lycanthrope
A type of skin-walker, lycanthropes take on and off the skin of a wolf, transforming into the animal at will. Divested of their wolf skins, they lose the ability to transform. A Lycanthrope's animal skin can be used to give a thaumaturge a lesser version of the animal-transformation skill practiced by the skinwalkers themselves, or as a component in taming and binding spells.

Magician
A person who uses magical artifacts rather than cast spells themselves. Often derided as scammers,

charlatans, and unworthy by "true" thaumaturges. An artificer who uses their own artifacts is not considered a magician.

Malediction

A curse spoken with a wronged person's dying breath brings long-term misfortune to the cursed party. These are considered baseless superstitions by most.

Mandrake root

A root plant whose tuber takes the shape of a humanoid being, and which can incapacitate and even kill with their cry if pulled from the muffling earth. They grow more expensive with age, and can be difficult to keep alive. They enjoy being sung to, and may die if not given enough personal attention even if conditions are otherwise optimal. The mandrake root's similarities to the human form make it valuable for spells that would otherwise need a human, such as simulacrum or surrogate spells, and they are most well known for their ability to receive, as a surrogate, a curse transferred from a human victim. They are also used in hallucinogenic spells and concoctions.

Map-based location divining spell

A divination spell that guides a drop of spelled mercury over a place-anchored map to find a location based on a sympathetic connection.

Memory spiders

A magical spider whose web, consumed whole without missing a single strand of silk, is said to be able to bring forth lost memories.

Mending spell

Repairs mundane objects, but requires all the pieces as well as components that would otherwise be required to mend the objects by hand. The mending spell is able to achieve somewhat finer control and dexterity than one might with their hands and fingers.

Mermaid

Mermaids are magical cephalopods. They lure prey by sticking tentacles above water and making them look like a human woman, who asks for help. When the victim gets too close, the "mermaid" suddenly comes apart into a mass of tentacles that grab them and drag them into the water to be eaten.

Metanite

A powerful Aberrant that the Red Guard has been unable to destroy or contain. It is a void-black form, which destroys everything it touches, but moves very slowly. The Red Guard uses space magic to adjust its path and evacuation to keep people safe from it.

Mimeo-motion spell

A more complex version of the continue-motion spell, the mimeo-motion spell allows duplication of the copied motion in multiple places. It is used most commonly for mass-producing books.

Mind-muddling jinx

Causes the victim trouble reading, comprehending, and focusing. As with all harmful spells classified as jinxes, it is not permanent, and cast lightly, the victim may not realize they have been affected.

Mirrored healing spell/Flesh-mirroring spell

Using blood of the injured person as a Sacrifice, this spell can mold flesh and bone to match the mirrored side of the body, and thus heal injuries without the need for rare and expensive components.

Uses glyphs "blood," "mirror," and then the physical part in need of mirrored healing, like "tooth." One large Circle around the whole area, and then two inner Circles, meeting in the middle, one which has the good side and one the injured side. Uses a pentagram inside a pentagon, for the combination of transmutation and transmogrification this spell requires. Relies more on the Will and Sacrifice than the clarity or complexity of the written Word. Requires a detailed, focused image of what the caster wants to happen. Using the wounded person's own blood is especially efficient.

Mnemonic-link tracking spell

Creates a sympathetic link between an object and the target, but depends on the caster's extreme familiarity with the target, and best augmented by an item that has a direct connection to the target.

Moonbeams & fairy wings

Moonbeams and fairy wings, harvested (from the Menagerie) at night, have mind-altering (recreational drug) effects.

Moondew drosera

This carnivorous magical plant is bioluminescent, and preys primarily on insects and other small creatures. It resembles a succulent during the day, and at night, its spines drip with glowing mucous that lures creatures into its sticky grasp.

Moon-orb weaver

A spider prized for its shocking strength, beauty, and efficiency in channeling magic.

Moonseeds

Commonly used in their dried form, similar to pepper, moonseeds are berries from a twining vine. The moonseed vine is nocturnal, growing off-white berries that resemble the pitted moon once dehydrated.

Myrddin

An extraordinarily powerful sorcerer who lived over a thousand years before. He has many incredible feats to his name, some based in reality and others in fiction, and has become enough of a household name that he's occasionally used in curses, E.G. "Myrddin's crusty black butthole."

Mystic-type Aberrant

A long-range subset of Blight and Nightmare-type. These Aberrants effect people at range, often with methods that are difficult to trace.

Nightmare-type Aberrant

This type of Aberrant is the most difficult to deal with, as they use stealth, memetic control, or subversion.

Okora's instant cottage

A spell that raises material from the ground to create a small cottage in the shape of a small model cottage used as a component. Size is dependent on power input and spell array parameters. It is easiest to cast with loose material that can be compacted together, such as snow or mud.

Orbs and Amulets

The Conduit shop at the north end of Waterside market

Osham

A neighboring country to Lenore, known for its innovations in machinery and artifacts.

Osher tree

Young sapling that can uproot itself and move short distances. Sometimes confused for a dryad, but an osher has no humanoid form and is not considered to be intelligent.

Output detachment

The practice of generating spell output outside of the bounds of the circle and an important step on the way to free-casting.

Paired movement ward

When the ring holding a banner to the base of the spell is ripped away, the sympathetically linked counterpart held elsewhere also detaches. Spell must be cast ahead of time, with both halves of the pair together.

Paneth

A bustling city and popular tourist destination just to the north of Gilbratha.

Paper bird spell

Used to send letters or messages. The paper birds are spelled to take flight and deliver themselves to set destination or recipients. Unsuitable to fly in heavy winds or rain. They are created from special ingredients that make Siobhan feel they are not as practical as she suspected.

The special paper used to make them requires flicker-feathers from the sparrow-like bird of the same name, which the University cultivates in the Menagerie.

Password puzzle artifact

In the Night Market, inside a component shop, a stone puzzle disk that must be solved with magic to make the center rise up, allowing access to the warehouse in back and the half-troll, Harvester.

Pendragon corps

The High Crown's personal guards and military force, kitted in the most expensive protection and battle spells that money can buy. Fighting against them is considered treasonous.

Pendragon Palace

The home of the High Crown, the head of the Thirteen Crown Families and leader of the country of Lenore. It is built atop the white cliffs, to the northeast of Gilbratha.

Perimeter alarm ward

Alerts the caster within when a perimeter has been breached.

Philtre of darkness

After brewing, when this concoction is suddenly exposed to air (e.g. when the bottle is smashed) the roiling liquid within bursts into clouds of magical darkness, which not even powerful night-vision can penetrate.

Phoenix ashes

An incredibly rare spell component, the ashes of a phoenix that has reached the end of one of its many life cycles are used to incubate the phoenix's egg as it rebirths itself. They are used in powerful healing and fire spells, and even supposed spells that can affect one's destiny. Most famously, they were said to have been used by Myrddin to resurrect his recently-deceased lover. They sell for about a hundred gold crowns per gram, and are highly illegal, as phoenixes are on the verge of extinction due to overhunting.

Piercing spell

A shaped spell that, unlike the area-effect concussive blast spell, is focused on penetrative power, and can gouge out a few inches of stone in a narrow diameter.

Pixie

Humanoid creatures with very delicate, multi-petaled flesh wings that constantly regenerate, dropping dandruff and little peels of dry skin. This "pixie dust" is an expensive magical component, and many humans keep them to harvest it. They are intelligent and mischievous, even sometimes malicious, prone to irritation and insults.

Planar divination-diverting ward

Protects against divination. The recipient will feel pressure under any type of divination/scrying attempt, and can add their Will to the artifact's inherent shielding capabilities to divert stronger and more determined attempts. The ward does not directly oppose a scrying spell, but turns aside, deflects, and hides instead, using its connection to the five Elemental Planes. The effects may also spill into the physical world, making it harder for people to notice and focus on the user.

When actively diverting, the embedded disks may be painful as they consume the user's blood for power.

Planar portal

A portal to one of the other Planes.

Plane of Darkness

The undiscovered sixth Elemental Plane, the Plane of Darkness, is a hypothetical plane that has long been hypothesized to balance the Plane of Radiance, creating an Elemental hexagram. However, despite innumerable attempts to access the plane, it remains entirely theoretical.

Plane of Radiance

One of the five known Elemental Planes, the Plane of Radiance hosts the element of Light in its many forms *and connotations*. Creatures and plants of the radiant element are very valuable spell components, and the most powerful, sentient Elementals from the Plane of Radiance are often called angels. The Plane of Radiance has sympathetic connections to the ideas of light, cleanliness, knowledge, strict justice, and healing. Excessive exposure has been known to cause toxicity.

Planes-damned

A curse word, referring to the Elemental Planes.

Portable office

A wooden block that unfolds into a chair and desk made out of hundreds of smaller segments, created by Liza. She sells them for ninety gold.

Portable shield artifact

A small golden sphere with legs that blooms with a semi-opaque shielding spell that isolates the person nearest to it.

Potion of feather-fall

It uses a (preferably white) feather as a main component, and seems to reduce the effects of gravity on the imbiber, allowing them to jump from a high place without injury.

Potion of moonlight sizzle

A potion that lets off a soft blue, bright glow that mimics the light of a full moon from its sizzling bubbles when the bottle is shaken. It's powerful enough to illuminate a small room on its own, and when sold at a reasonable price, much more affordable than light crystals or candles.

Potion of night vision

Allows one to see more clearly in the dark, in monochrome.

Prognos

Skilled in divination, have a single large eye in the middle of their head. It's said the best prognos diviners can see into the past to discover the identity of a criminal, but that's a myth. They are simply perceptive. They mature slowly and have longer lives than most humans.

Purple lobster

A luxury food.

Puzzle band rings

A wedding ring, historically used to keep women from cheating on their husbands, with the thought that they would be unable take the ring off for their infidelities and then fit the ring back together in time to keep their misdeeds secret.

Quintessence of quicksilver

The powder of a potion boiled down into a solid and then crushed. It temporarily frenzies the mind, making you smarter and granting a liquid creativity. Gives the illusion of power and lowers inhibitions. The effects of a single dose last about six hours on those who haven't built up a tolerance, and the come-down crash lasts a day or two. Long-term users lose their ability to focus and display various memory problems, becoming dependent on quintessence of quicksilver to function normally.

Radiant explosive

An intensely powerful, burning and cleansing explosive using properties from the Elemental Plane of Radiance.

Radiant Maiden

The progenitor of the Order of the Radiant Maiden. She is a powerful Elemental from the Plane of Radiance. These humanoid, often-winged beings have been referred to as angels.

Raven summoning spell

A spell originally designed to summon the Raven Queen, which, instead appears to be a mild area-effect compulsion that summons nearby corvids.

Red Sage

A powerful Aberrant that is contained within a sundered zone, but still manages to meet people. It has three eyes, each of which are said to see the future. All prophecies that it gives come true, but it seems that the Red Sage can either choose who it meets through a sort of subtle summoning (and thus control the prophecies it gives) or it chooses what to prophecy—it can be bribed to give a better fortune. However, in coming true *all* prophecies cause great suffering and destruction, if not to the recipient, then to the people and world around the recipient. Two of its prophecies—and eyes—are in constant use, and ensure its continued existence and ability to affect the world. The Red Guard facilitates the prophecies from its third eye coming true to try and mitigate the damage, and attempts to control who can meet the Red Sage.

Refinement of the Nine Heavens

Originally mistranslated as "Nine Light Filters," this esoteric spell was developed by the gestura to absorb sunlight and to heal and repair the body and mind. It also claims to speed up the caster's recovery time, improve mental strength, and reduce the need for sleep and the chances of experiencing Will-strain.

Regeneration-boosting potion

This potion boosts the body's natural immune response, lending some of its power to boost the healing effect and taking the rest from the stored energy and nutrients of the injured person's body. It will struggle to fix anything larger than a small dagger wound, a bone fracture, or a hand-size burn. It takes time to work and is uncomfortable, and cannot be used in quick succession, but is much cheaper than a real healing potion.

Revealing spell

Uncovers non-physical illusions and can see through non-magical darkness. Usually cast via a wand, issued to some coppers. A revealing spell shoots vibrational and magic waves, which penetrate and bounce back to the wand.

Retreat at Willowdale

The Retreat is a long-term treatment center where people with magical damage can be housed safely or, ideally, rehabilitated and healed.

Reverse-scrying spell

A divination spell with the base of a map-based sympathetic divination, but which targets instead the other sympathetic end of the connection which is being used to scry. Used to find the finder, historically most often in warfare.

Revivifying potion

Boosts organ function and energy levels. Can be used for many different illnesses, but is expensive due to its high magical load.

Rune-inscribed basin

A basin for far-viewing, a type of divination that uses water to see distant places, generally from the point of view of another surface of water. The basin can be used to contact other powerful diviners if they cast at the same time, with the same intent. Far-viewing in this manner does not transmit sound.

Sacrifice

What you give up for the effect of a spell. It can be an object, like a blob of mud used to create a brick, or energy, like the heat from a flame. Components can have either a natural or a sympathetic link to the effects of the spell.

Scab-root

A twisted, gnarled root adorned with pustules that looks remarkably like an infected scab. It is a slow-growing, endangered plant from the southwestern region of the known lands, and contains nearly every possibly nutrient a human needs to survive. Its taste is as appetizing as its appearance suggests.

Selby-Forman binding

A variation on conjuration/elemental binding used in the Second Empire.

Self-charging artifacts

Artifacts that contain the parameters to not only cast a spell, but to gather and transform the energy for that spell as part of their activation and release process. Creating a self-powered, or self-charging, artifact is a Grandmaster-level feat said to be pioneered by Myrddin, who supposedly came up with several methods, some of which have now been lost.

Self-powered artifacts cannot cast truly endless spells, as eventually the spell array breaks down—and more quickly with heavy use, but they are still widely coveted.

Self-cleaning chamber pot artifact

Cleans and dries the nether regions, then processes the waste, removing the liquid from fecal matter and dehydrating urine into a thick paste, which it stores in a sealed container for later removal. An auxiliary spell keeps the smell from filtering out away from the chamber pot.

Sempervivum apricus

A low-growing succulent plant from the Plane of Radiance. Its juicy leaves grow in complex rosettes, glimmering with tiny motes of light that travel beneath the semi-transparent skin along with the water and nutrients. It is technically a "low-light" plant in the Plane of Radiance, and thus is able to survive on the mundane plane in areas with bright sunlight and long days, or with the help of artificial sunlight sources. They propagate by sending out root offshoots that grow into new baby plants.

Sensory deprivation spell
A spell array developed by the Pendragon Corps to keep enemy spies from killing themselves upon capture. It separates the mind from the body and traps the victim in a black, empty void.

Shade (dust)
Shades are predatory creatures that take humanoid forms and live in barren, arid areas such as deserts, where they will prey on the sleeping or stalk the lost traveler until they collapse from exhaustion. They are made of a fine powder which can be gathered and used as an expensive magical component.

Shadow-familiar
An esoteric ritual spell that gives the user control of their own shadow, allowing it to move, stretch, and take unnatural shapes. Powered by electromagnetic radiation. "Life's breath, shadow mine. In darkness we were born. In darkness do we feast. Devour, and arise."

Shaman
A thaumaturge who specializes in contacting the spirit realm for the purpose of divination, including dream walking, as well as certain types of mental healing and wards. They often use mind-altering or hallucinogenic substances to facilitate contact.

Shaman-king Deon
He ruled in Qusnia, a country that exited to the southeast of current Lenore in the distant past.

Shipp evidence box
Metal cube meant to put evidence in stasis. Has a transparent setting to allow examination of the contents within.

Silk Door
An upscale brothel known for its cleanliness and discretion, and frequently used by Siobhan under the assumed name of Silvia Nakai to conceal her whereabouts.

Silva Erde
A neighboring country that Lenore frequently trades with, known for its celerium mines. The Beast King is rumored to be buried deep beneath its forests.

Silver-billed woodpecker
A magical creature that can never develop its magic correctly if it's helped out of its shell.

Simple locking spell
Learned from one of the warding books Katerin bought Siobhan, this spell locks a container that can be opened and closed, without need of a key or even a physical locking apparatus. Does not stop one from breaking in physically or magically, but will require some extra effort.

Simple unlocking spell
Used to bypass either mundane locks, or negate the simple locking spell. Cannot unlock a locking spell cast with greater power.

Sinus-clearing spell
A variation on the water falling spell, used to draw off liquid and thus clear the airways. Esoteric magic taught to Siobhan by a hedge-witch.

Siren
Sometimes confused for mermaids, sirens are not in fact associated with aquatic animals, but with avians. Sirens have brightly colored feathers that sprout from the scalp and sides of their face where ears and hair would be on a human. They are best known for their mesmerizing voices, which are said to cause sailors to steer their ships into submerged rocks or even directly into cliff-sides in an attempt to get closer to the enchanting sound of the siren song.
Largely carnivorous, sirens are intelligent beings and those who are willing to integrate into human society are rare and coveted for their abilities.

Skin-knitting salve
An alchemical concoction that mends small cuts over the course of about an hour. It can heal a deep

scratch, cut, or a second-degree burn, but not a serious wound, and most (less expensive) versions will leave minor scarring.

Skinjacker

A creature used in cautionary tales to children, which can take over a person's form and replace them.

Skolex worm

Magical worm-like beasts that can grow hundreds of meters long, the skolex has no eyes, and hunts through vibration alone. When devouring its prey, the skolex's mouthparts one up in four directions simultaneously, revealing multiple inward-facing rows of serrated and hooked teeth which ring the entire mouth opening. The teeth are coveted for their piercing ability and how difficult wounds formed with them are to heal.

Sleep-proxy spell

Using the principles of binding magic, one can allow a magically boosted creature to sleep in the place of another being.

Slingshot spell

Created by Siobhan based on a Practical Casting exercise, it uses the glyphs "line," "movement," and "circle" to send a projectile revolving around a central axis. When it is released, the projectile shoots out, similar to a stone out of a shepherd's slingshot.

Smoke cloud philtre

A battle philtre that creates a sudden and thick smoke cloud when released from its container. Considered a battle potion.

Sobering potion

This potion speeds up the process of filtering alcohol from the body, but can cause an overwhelming need to urinate and, if overused, lead to dehydration.

Sound muffling spell

Creates a bubble of stilled air that suppressed the ability of vibrations to travel through it, and thus muffles sound.

Space-bending spells

This type of magic can bend, and even fold space. They are extremely difficult and expensive. If a smaller area is filled with more space than it could normally hold, that space must come from somewhere, which will in turn be smaller than it normally is. There are usually visually-disorienting signs of the spell when you try to gain perspective or mentally measure the space.

Spark-shooting wand

Artifacts charged with firework-like sparks of light. Can start a fire, with the right tinder, be used as a distraction, a signal, or a threat, though the spark-shooting spell is a non-combat spell.

Speer's philtre of stench

A powerful, physically painful stench that causes tears, mucus buildup, and vomiting, like a combination of a stink bomb and pepper spray. Used as crowd control to non-lethally incapacitate a large number of people. It has magical as well as physical properties.

Spell rod

A cylindrical baton containing segments that expand into spell Circle frames. It is based based loosely on the portable war Circles used by the army, and looks like the escrima of the East.

Spirit

Ephemeral, small and often harmless beings, it is argued whether spirits are technically "alive" or merely accumulations of a concentrated type of magical energy over time, or perhaps imprinted residue from once-living beings. They may be summoned and contracted, but often have little ability to exert influence on the mundane world. Shamans often communicate with spirits to gain information through their particular brand of divination.

Spirit-trapping spell

Useful for trapping spirits for communication or contracting. There are many variations on this type of Circle.

Sprites

Tiny, insect-winged humanoids. They have some measure of intelligence, but are not considered sapient "people," rather more akin to interesting bugs.

Star-maple wood

A wood with properties from the Plane of Radiance, it can be used in regenerative and healing spells, as well as other spells using the Radiant attribute, or for its beauty. As it can be molded into an accessory while still living, it is rather valuable. As an accessory, sometimes is used to enhance beauty through improving health.

Stunning spell

Red projectile spell. When high-powered, can leave scorch marks and a little steam or smoke at the point of impact. Uses a combination of low-current electricity and sedative material (the powdered saliva from a Kuthian frog), contained within a field of force, to incapacitate the target.

Summoning ritual

Summoning is said to slightly skew fate to cause a being that meets your requirements to come into contact with you. It has inconsistent results, and clarity of wording and intention is very important. One can summon spirits, animals, or even another person who has the capability to help you with a certain problem. Once summoned, you may come into contact with a being that meets your requirements as if through coincidence after some time has passed, or more directly and immediately. Some question the efficacy, hypothesizing that the vagueness of most types of summoning rituals leads to false interpretations of fulfillment.

Sundered zone

The strongest barrier spell known to man. From the outside, it looks like a perfect white dome, with all light reflected. They are used to quarantine Aberrants that cannot be killed. The sundered zones cannot be exited by the thing they were created to contain or anything tainted by them, but can technically be entered by sapient creatures who are able to give their informed consent.

Sylphide

Powerful, humanoid elementals from the Plane of Air, given to song, laughter, and knowledge carried on the wind.

Tataroc Desert

Known for its dryness, a line of standing stones through this desert signifies Lenore's border to the east.

The Bitter Phoenix

A tavern with a private back area where people partake of the illegal quintessence of quicksilver, and a powerful diviner will sell you information or make connections for the right price.

The Black Wastes

An area where dangerous magic has infected the land itself. The environment shifts rapidly, with deadly and mutated land, flora, fauna. Time spent in the Black Wastes causes paranoia, hallucinations, and makes it difficult to find your way.

The Charmed Highlands

An area where celerium is mined.

The citadel

The main University building, where the classes are held, and which also contains the supervised casting rooms. It looks like a coliseum made of white stone, with shimmering spelled windows and tall columns. It is huge and towering, and laid out in rings, like a cross-cut of a tree stump.

The Dawn Troupe

A powerful Aberrant which is not contained within a sundered zone. It manifests as a group of wealthy, attractive horse-riders with weapons and musical instruments. This Aberrant appreciates intelligence and talent, and will give boons to those who meet it and impress it. The Dawn Troupe can be bargained with, and never breaks its promises. The Red Guard has agreed not to attempt to contain it, and as long as it receives a certain amount of people interacting with it—usually to attempt to gain one of its boons—it does not leave a certain area to go on a hunt. The Red Guard allows people to know about the boons so they will risk their lives to try for one.

The Elementary

A shop in the Night Market which secretly sells, in the back room, items from the Elemental Planes. Their supplier, Harvester, is a half-troll.

The Gervin Family

The Fourth Crown Family. They control much of the textile industry, as well as the high-end fashion industry.

The Mires

Gilbratha's slums, which get worse further toward the south of the city. The Mires are named for the sticky, stinking waste that lines the streets and wafts from the canals. They spread beyond the bounds of the white cliffs, which have been sunk, broken, or taken apart for use as building materials on that side of the city.

The Nightmare Pack

A gang consisting mostly of non-humans, which holds territory that houses a large percentage of non-humans. They are led by Lord Lynwood, a lycanthrope, and his adopted prognos sister, Gera.

The Red Guard

A special, semi-autonomous branch of law enforcement which handles rogue magic beyond the abilities of the normal coppers. Their operations are confidential.

The Surior Mountains

An area where celerium is mined.

The Thaumaturgic University of Lenore

The most prominent and prestigious arcanum in the country, and the only one that can give a Mastery certification. It is matched in status only by Pendragon Palace, and looks down upon the city from atop the northern side of the white cliffs. Its grounds are extensive, and its structures include areas dug into the white cliffs themselves.

Every year, thousands of students, both new to magic and who have come from other arcanums to achieve their Mastery certification, take the entrance exam.

The Westbay Family

The Second Crown Family. They control the Gilbrathan coppers, and often have influence in the army as high-ranking commanders.

Timed alarm spell

Cast on a time-keeper such as a pocket watch, goes off at a set time to alert anyone nearby to the conditions of the spell being reached.

Titan

A gargantuan, powerful, humanoid being prevalent in the early days of recorded human history, who survived the Cataclysm. A Titan might simply walk by and decide to crush half a human city like a child kicking an anthill. They had enormous appetites and were entirely omnivorous, in the true meaning of the word. Extremely magically powerful. Now extinct.

Tome

A large, expensive book created with high-quality material meant for channeling magic. It has very thick pages, with a spell array drawn on each page. This allows the holder to carry portable spell arrays, open to any particular page, and cast the spell as quickly as they can place any necessary components and/or Sacrifices. Each tome usually carries between 12-20 spell pages.

Turtle creation spell

Uses a turtle egg and duplicative transmogrification to create an anatomically-correct, edible, dead turtle.

Under-bed dust bunnies

A magical creature that is spontaneously generated from the fluffy dust under a bed in a magical environment. Supposedly.

Unicorn/Pegasus

A magical, horse-like beast with a valuable horn on its head. The pegasus is the progressed form of a unicorn, the wings growing after an intense accumulation of magic.

Unnamed subtle curses

Uses sea spray gathered on a moonless night. "I swam through an ocean of uncertainty."

Scourge-type Aberrant

The most common classification of Aberrant, Scourge-types have a short to mid-range effect whose anomalous effect is clear, allowing quantification and elimination or containment.

Utility wand

A wand artifact with multi-purpose spells meant to be widely useful for a variety of emergency situations, not simply battle.

Vampire

Sentient, magical, humanoid beings, who often prey on humans for their blood. They often have blood-red hair, pale skin, and a mouth full of canine teeth. They are weak to things from the Plane of Radiance, and a common weapon against them is water imbued with energy from the Plane of Radiance. They have a natural predilection to the dark, and good night vision.

Vibrational self-calming spell

Esoteric, rather than using a written spell array, it uses the hands over the chest to form the Circle, and the vibration of the voice as a sympathetic component for forcibly calming the body. The longer you draw out the hum, the further it "stretches" your body into a calm state. Repeat ad nauseam.

Wakefulness brew

A pseudo-alchemical concoction, but more commonly classified as "kitchen magic," this spell marginally boosts the rejuvenating effects of caffeinated beverages. Better quality base materials take the wakefulness magic more smoothly, just as in standard alchemy.

Ward against untruth

The strongest legal wards against lies create a moderate vague compulsion, and are thus utterly useless against a strong thaumaturge who can imbue their lies with their Will. Illegal wards create stronger compulsions, but are considered blood magic as they take away the free will of a human.

Wardbreaker

A specialist in diverting, subverting, and breaking wards.

Waterside Market

A sprawling market within Gilbratha proper that has a lot of shops in the streets around. People of all ages and races can be seen, as well as thaumaturges who practice many different crafts, a testament to Gilbratha's diversity. Sells everything from food to magical animals. There are stalls as well as shops, with stalls being cheaper, but shops having a better selection.

Whiskerton's whiskey of well-being

An expensive magical whiskey guaranteed to impart an additional sense of warmth and wellbeing by the shot, in addition to the standard effects of liquor.

White cliffs

Gilbratha is built within a gargantuan circle of white stone cliffs that have been drawn up from the ground in what is undoubtedly a legendary feat of magic. These cliffs are intact to the north, but have sunk, crumbled, and been demolished for other purposes toward the poorer south.

The Thaumaturgic University of Lenore as well as many Crown Family houses have been built into and atop the cliffs, and nearer the bottom are many buildings placed on the staggered plateaus. Tubes run down from the University to transport people and goods, powered by magic.

Will

The Will makes magic possible. The stronger a thaumaturge's Will, the more power they can channel, the less defined the Word needs to be, and the less power will be lost in conversion from input to effect. There are different facets to a strong Will.

Will-strain

Caused by over-exertion when casting magic. It starts with headaches, dizziness, and inability to concentrate. With more moderate strain, judgment is impaired. Sometimes thaumaturges display difficulty modulating emotions, with rapid swings from one to the other. Then hallucinations, with the more severe ones resulting in paranoia and even accidental harm to oneself or others. Beyond this, Will-strain damage is irreversible, and results in complete insanity and at times, the loss of higher brain functions. In extreme circumstances, loss of control while casting will lead directly to a "break" and the creation of an Aberrant.

Wit-sharpening potion

While it doesn't actually increase intelligence, it will temporarily make the drinker more aware and improve performance in situations that require multitasking. In too high a dose, it can cause overstimulation through increased sensory input. It is somewhat addictive.

Witch

A thaumaturge who uses a summoned contracted creature, often from one of the Elemental Planes, to cast spells, rather than using an inanimate Conduit like sorcerer.

Word

The Word guides the transformation of energy or matter, steering the effects of a spell. It can be any type of instruction, though with sorcery it is most often written into the Circle as an array of glyphs and numerically-significant symbols. These are often supplemented with speech or written instructions, especially for complex effects.

Wortcunning

Magical herbalism, the study of plants and herbs, specifically for their healing and magical properties.

Wound cleansing potion

There are many different versions of this potion, and they come in different strengths and act in different ways. Uniformly, however, they work to clear the wound of dirt and debris, as well as kill any infectious agents such as viruses or bacteria. Formerly, this was understood to be over-whelming the "bad humors," and so, wound-cleansing potions often have strong scents due to components like distilled alcohol and herbal oil extracts.

Yak urine

Used to help dyes stay color-fast.

ALSO BY AZALEA ELLIS

Did you know I have my own little online shop? You can support me directly and get my latest book **earlier than it releases anywhere else**, along with special Inner Circle and full-series discounts.

You can also get extra story content that's not available on retailers, like bonus chapters and novelettes. My books are available in ebook, paperback, and audiobook format.

To buy from me directly go to: books.azaleaellis.com

Seeds of Chaos Series (Complete)

Book I: Gods of Blood and Bone

Book II: Gods of Rust and Ruin

Book III: Gods of Myth and Midnight

Book IV: Gods of Smoke and Stars—A Seeds of Chaos Adventure

Book V: Gods of Ash and Amber

A Practical Guide to Sorcery Series

Book I: A Conjuring of Ravens

Book II: A Binding of Blood

Book III: A Sacrifice of Light

Book IV: A Foreboding of Woe

Book V: A Cauldron of Bitterness

Book VI: A Builder of Dreams

A Practical Guide to Sorcery Additional Stories (Available Exclusively from Azalea

Book 2.1: Codename: Moonsable (Short Story)

Book 3.1: Good Advice (Bonus Chapter)

Book 3.2: Preventative Measures (Bonus Chapter)

Book 3.3: The Honeymoon Suite (Novelette)

Book 4.1: Harry Harold Had no Hands (Rhyme)

Book 4.2: Immovable Objects (Bonus Chapter)

Book 4.3: Recruitment Drive (Deleted Blooper Scene)

The Catastrophe Collector: A Practical Guide to Sorcery Spinoff Series

Book I: Larva

Book II: Bloom

More books may have been published since you purchased this copy. Find a complete
list on AzaleaEllis.com

Here's a Quick Link to All my Books
www.azaleaellis.com/the-books/

ABOUT THE AUTHOR

I'm the type of person that often has a wacky, shocking, or silly–but totally *true*–story to tell about my life.

(Like the time my brother and I were chased through a secluded strip of woods in the middle of the city, for over a mile, by a naked man with an erection.)

(Or the time a trucker threw an open bottle of pee out his passenger side window without looking right as I was walking by. You can guess what I got splashed with.)

I've got an active imagination that tends toward the outrageous and the macabre, which led to me being voted "most likely to borrow someone else's car to transport a dead body."

I write books about things that interest and excite me. I'm always in the middle of teaching myself something new, and if I'm not overwhelmingly busy I tend to get antsy. I believe that the impossible is only so if we believe it to be so. Therefore, nothing is impossible.

If you'd like to get updates from me, both about my books and about what I'm up to from time to time, the newsletter is the place to be, as I tend to be very scarce on other social media.

https://www.azaleaellis.com/newsletter

For more information:
www.azaleaellis.com
author@azaleaellis.com